THE SCRIBNER ANTHOLOGY OF CONTEMPORARY SHORT FICTION

Fifty North American Stories Since 1970

Lex Williford and
Michael Martone, Editors

SCRIBNER PAPERBACK FICTION
PUBLISHED BY SIMON & SCHUSTER

SCRIBNER PAPERBACK FICTION
Simon & Schuster, Inc.
Rockefeller Center
1230 Avenue of the Americas
New York, NY 10020

This book is a work of fiction. Names, characters, places, and incidents either are products of the author's imagination or are used fictitiously. Any resemblance to actual events or locales or persons, living or dead, is entirely coincidental.

DESIGNED BY ERICH HOBBING

Manufactured in the United States of America

1 3 5 7 9 10 8 6 4 2

Library of Congress Cataloging-in-Publication Data

The Scribner anthology of contemporary short fiction : fifty North American stories since 1970 / Lex Williford and Michael Martone, editors.
p. cm.
1. Short stories, American. 2. Short stories, Canadian. 3. American fiction—20th century. 4. Canadian fiction—20th century. 5. United States—Social life and customs—20th century Fiction. 6. Canada—Social life and customs—20th century Fiction. I. Williford, Lex, 1954– . II. Martone, Michael.
PS648.S5S425 1999
813'.0108054—dc21 99-39518
CIP

ISBN 0-684-85796-0

Please see page 669 for continuation of copyright page.

ACKNOWLEDGMENTS

A special thanks to Rosellen Brown for her wonderful introduction. We also would like to thank Cherise Grant, Trish Todd, and Penny Kaganoff for their help and encouragement at different stages of this anthology's development; Auburn University Professor Bert Hitchcock, who helped with the original book proposal; Scribner Best of the Writing Programs series editor John Kulka, who helped refine the original proposal; Jeff Wilson in Contracts; the Doe Coover agency and Witherspoon Associates agency; Angela Fountas, who painstakingly tallied the survey results, copied stories, and helped with editorial suggestions; Will Belford, who spent late nights copying stories; the University of Alabama Department of English for funding the survey's postage and graduate research assistants; John and Claire Keeble for their many kindnesses; and the following writers and teaching writers who thoughtfully filled out our surveys: Lee K. Abbott, Gail Galloway Adams, Jonis Agee, Margaret Baughman, Jonathan Baumbach, Joe David Bellamy, Joan Connor, Jeff Elzinga, Raymond Federman, Lucy Ferriss, Robert Flynn, Gloria Frym, Catherine Gammon, Greg Garrett, Molly Giles, Eric Goodman, Anthony Grooms, Barbara Haas, Alyson Hagy, Elizabeth Harris, William Harrison, Tom Hazuka, Patricia Henley, Michelle Herman, Susan Kenny, Beth Lordan, Erin McGraw, Ian MacMillan, Lee Martin, Wendell Mayo, Bill Meissner, Valerie Miner, Lorrie Moore, Cornelia Nixon, David Romtvedt, Sheila Schwartz, Maya Sonenberg, Marly Swick, Jean Thompson, Melanie Rae Thon, Judy Troy, David Foster Wallace, and Will Weaver. Responding generously to our attempt to keep this anthology as democratic and affordable as possible, authors represented in this anthology have all agreed to equal compensation for permissions to reprint their stories. We thank them all.

ACKNOWLEDGMENTS

Special thanks to Rawley Grove for her wonderful introduction. We would like to thank [illegible] [illegible] [illegible]

CONTENTS

FOREWORD

In *Writing in General and the Short Story in Particular* (Houghton Mifflin, 1987), Rust Hills, former *Esquire* editor, writes of the "growing role in all the processes of contemporary literature of the colleges and universities of America":

> If one but stands back a bit and looks, one sees that it is no longer the book publishers and magazines, but rather the colleges and universities, that support the entire structure of the American literary establishment—and, moreover, essentially determine the nature and shape of that structure. (184)

The current listings in the ninth *Associated Writing Programs Guide to Writing Programs* confirm this observation: There are now almost eight hundred English departments across North America that offer undergraduate fiction-writing minors and majors, half of these programs including curricula for the study of fiction writing at the graduate level, and these numbers continue to grow. Justifiably, critics balk at the elitist idea of any literary establishment, academic or otherwise. Others argue that the quantitative rise of academic writing programs over the last three decades has led to a corresponding qualitative decline in short fiction, generations of student writers cranking out a kind of uniform workshop "McStory" on an assembly line of increasing literary mediocrity. Our experience has been different.

Mentored by teaching writers in writing programs, then becoming teaching writers in writing programs ourselves, we've come to recognize that these programs feed gifted writers who might not otherwise be fed. Just as important, we've come to believe that teaching writers are perhaps one of the most qualified sources of opinion about the remarkable diversity of the contemporary short-story form. After all, other than writing-program students, editors, the comparatively few readers who buy literary short fiction, and the even smaller group of writers who make their living writing fiction, they are perhaps the most widely and deeply read audience of the medium—*and* often its principal practitioners.

The original premise of *The Scribner Anthology of Contemporary Short Fic-*

tion was that many teaching writers across the country—one of the largest pools of people qualified to select stories for publication—historically have had little or no say about the work that appears in the contemporary anthologies they read and use to teach writing. Wanting as much as possible to democratize the process of story selection, we created a database of more than 200 teaching writers from the eighth edition of the *Associated Writing Programs Guide to Writing Programs* during the fall of 1997. Our extensive four-page survey asked writers and writing teachers to identify the five examples of contemporary short fiction published since 1970 they most often returned to as readers, writers, and teachers, identifying for us their level of satisfaction with the current offerings of short-fiction anthologies on the market.

To our surprise, we received about fifty responses, a greater number than we expected. Many of the respondents wrote at great length not only about the stories they most admire, teach, and return to, but also about the principal reasons why they bring these stories to their classes again and again—their discussions covering everything from thematic to technical concerns. Sixty percent of the respondents acknowledged that they are dissatisfied with the current offerings of contemporary short-story anthologies for their own reading and for their literature and writing classes. Some wrote that the most representative stories are never in one volume and that many stories go to waste because teachers use so few. Others complained that too many of the same mainstream authors select the same mainstream stories, that too few anthologies highlight the contemporary and too many lack an aesthetically diverse mix of traditional stories and experimental stories that push the boundaries of the short-story form. Some respondents also noted that current anthologies either do not have enough gender, cultural, ethnic, and racial diversity or their selections are too tokenized, and that many anthologies emphasize theme over fiction-writing technique. A large number of our respondents wrote that short-fiction anthologies are often either too general in focus or too long in their time spans or too specific in their focus or too short in their time spans. Many, too, stated that these anthologies are often too expensive or that the less expensive annuals (*The Pushcart Prizes, The Best American Short Stories,* and *The O. Henry Awards*) are often wildly uneven from year to year. The results of our survey seem to indicate that teachers are always looking for something new, the perfect anthology, yet the current offerings satisfy no one.

As the editors of this anthology, we've tried as much as possible to select stories based upon the comments and results of our survey, using our own very different but complementary aesthetics. And we've included all but a few of the stories that received the most nominations.

The most nominated story in our survey, Tim O'Brien's "The Things They Carried," is included here. The other most nominated stories were (in approximate ranking): Cynthia Ozick's "The Shawl," Raymond Carver's "Cathedral," Richard Ford's "Rock Springs," Charles Baxter's "Gryphon," Denis Johnson's "Emergency," and Lorrie Moore's "You're Ugly, Too." All of these but one are represented in this anthology. (Because the nominations for Carver's work were spread fairly evenly over many of his stories and because several respondents suggested we choose a less widely anthologized story than "Cathedral," we selected Carver's "Errand," one of his last stories—based upon the last hours of Anton Chekhov's life—since it represents both the work of an author at the peak of his creative powers and the additional irony that infuses that work when the writer's life is cut short at so young an age.) Our other selections were more difficult than we expected because a tremendous variety of stories were nominated at nearly equivalent rankings.

Our primary aim then was to choose stories representative of diverse aesthetics, voices, and geographies, including contemporary "classics" as well as new discoveries and lesser-known stories and writers. And, yes, we've left out a few of everyone's favorites. While there's always the danger that in trying to please everyone we've pleased no one, we believe that this anthology represents the largest, most comprehensive selection of contemporary North American short fiction published in one volume. That Scribner—perhaps the most respected publisher of fiction since the last renaissance of the short story in the 1920s—should publish this anthology is, we hope, further evidence of our belief.

We appreciate any suggestions on ways in which we might improve this anthology in future editions and any commentary and story suggestions by writers and teaching writers wishing to participate in future surveys.

—Lex Williford and Michael Martone

INTRODUCTION

Rosellen Brown

Fiction writers who meet their public are routinely subjected to a few of the most famous *Paris Review* interview questions re-tooled for the technological generation: "Do you write with a pencil?" has become "Do you write on the computer?" (the answer to which seems to me about as revealing as "Do you drink coffee or tea?" but which, perhaps, offers an unthreateningly familiar entry to the life of the imagination for an audience who finds it too mysterious to approach head-on). "How (or when) did you decide to become a writer?" is frequently replaced not even by "Did you get an MFA?" but, on the assumption that of course you must possess that license-to-operate, "*Where* did you get your MFA?" (second only to "How do I get an agent?").

And then, for those of us who teach, what follows is often the skeptical question, a challenge, really, which many who ask it have already firmly decided in the negative: "Is it really possible to *teach* writing?"

I admit I am bewildered by the almost hostile resistance implied by the question. Does anyone suspect the actor who has studied with Uta Hagen or Lee Strasberg or at the Royal Academy of Dramatic Arts or who has, at a simpler level of technique, learned to fence or stage-fight? Is there something deluded about the painter with an art school degree, the violinist who sits at the feet of a Dorothy Delay or the pianist who works, to endlessly acknowledged effect, with a Rosina Lhevine, alone or in a master class?

What is there about writing that, to the general public, seems to exempt it from "learnability"? Is it that language is available, free, to anyone—hence the patronizing, self-aggrandizing boast no writer has failed to hear, which reduces our work to weekend tinkering: "If only I had time I'd write a book!" Is it that "natural story tellers" seem to be born, not made? Every family has one, after all, if only in the form of the habitual retailer of jokes, clean or dirty.

Any honest writer, I think, will answer—leaving aside the complexities of institutional ratification or the issue of sending graduates forth with a costly degree into a sea of vocational uncertainties—"Let's divide the question. Can you make a writer out of anyone? No." (Though you might help some hobbyists and create a good many more discerning readers.) Can you give guidance based on taste and experience, and speed up the process of the learning of a craft to someone with talent and will? Of course. Are you responsible for the alleged mediocrity, the short reach, of the "workshop story"? Every generation produces merely competent practitioners of every art—music, painting, ceramics, basketball (yes, that's an art if there ever was one)—and then throws up a few Horowitzes or Michael Jordans to come closer to the ideal than we dare imagine. If most of us are earthbound, why should we blame our teachers?

Patiently I explain to the skeptical that a writing instructor—a coach, if you will—teaches first by enthusiasm, singling out the best that's already been accomplished, and provides a receptive ear and some lucid methods of analysis. Mundane strategies, clichés all. Very disappointing, especially if one is looking for magic, the raising of the dead. If there's mystery in the process—genius in the writer or genius in the teacher—it will issue from daring, need, personal idiosyncrasy and obsession, none of them teachable. But if brilliance, like luck, favors a prepared mind, then it will be nurtured by a familiarity with what has gone before and an attention to pesky issues of technique best studied not in the abstract but on the page, in the most stirring examples.

And what a fortunate course of study and apprenticeship, which does not demand that we learn the names of bones—femur, fibula, tibia—or the various ways of computing interest or the precedents concerning divestiture, but rather the means by which Cheever covertly studs a paragraph with intimate information or Woolf takes us into the tunnels of consciousness by a control of syntax that seems to parallel the intricate grammar of our own thinking. Compared to the mastery of those other "terms of art," this hardly seems like work. And so, to those skeptics who say, "You can teach this stuff?" it seems as if writers have nothing to learn.

Here, now, comes this compendium of what Carol Bly has elsewhere called "The Passionate, Accurate Story," not exactly a How-to book but a set of dazzling opportunities for admiration and analysis that a few dozen writer/teachers have found valuable to the point of indispensability. I will assign this collection to my students gratefully, though by containing so many of my favorite, most finger-smudged stories, it will rob me of credit for thinking up a fabulous reading list of my own. Of course every teacher will supplement the anthology with other new discoveries, not to mention the necessaries of a time earlier than 1970. (Chekhov! Both O'Connors, Flannery and Frank! Delmore Schwartz's "In Dreams Begin Responsibilities"! Guimaraes Rosa's "The Third Bank of the River"! D. H. Lawrence's "The Blind Man" to accompany Raymond Carver's "Cathedral," compare and contrast; Grace Paley's "Wants" and Tillie Olsen's "Tell Me a Riddle" and Elizabeth Bishop's "In the Village"! I cannot teach without them.)

But look what lessons are to be learned here, in the stories at hand. Some of this may sound a shade too absolute (like Donald Barthelme's famous dictum that no one in his classes could write about weather). Still, let us consider the evidence before us:

That not one of these writers begins a story in a car en route to the action, or in bed with the ringing of an alarm to signal the arrival of a Big Day. Instead each plunges headlong into the deep waters of character or situation, sink or swim, but always, always in a sharply defined voice. ("'Jesus, this is hard on me,' says Floyd Dey." "Cherry Oxendine is dying now, and everybody knows it." "The pump repairman was cautious." "You had to get out of them occasionally, those Illinois towns with the funny names: Paris, Oblong, Normal." "My sister's voice was like mountain water in a silver pitcher; the clear, blue beauty of it cools you and lifts you up beyond your heat, beyond your body.") An acting or a basketball coach, a painter leaning toward the canvas, all would say, and be satisfied with those examples, "What I want to see is a vivid attack. A sense of urgency. Where is the force of personality in this? Do you convince us that this is the way it *must* be?" Fiction is not for the faint of heart.

Which does not mean that it is, instead, for the sensation-seeker. It is not to be assumed that every story must contain a bona fide tragedy (murder, suicide), nor its polar opposite, that quiet epiphanic moment when a character looks off into the trees or closes the door with a discreet click and understands everything, but gently and perhaps only metaphorically.

Nor do these writers confuse journalism with fiction, serviceable fact-mongering language with eloquence, linearity with clarity. Writing is performance. Indecisiveness stifles. Modesty of conception and of style is not the default setting; it must be chosen. What I want to say to my students, which these stories demonstrate as a matter of course, is: You are an actor now. Inhabit your role.

What a reader needs to learn is how to ask questions of the story without the voice of that coach over his or her shoulder, without the questions at the bottom of the page. A "non-professional" reader might enjoy Richard Ford's "Rock Springs," for example, as a provocative glimpse at a man who doesn't see himself very clearly, a petty crook, self-serving lover, abstracted father, fairly far down a path toward self-destruction—but *how* does he show us this? What does the narrator say and what does he not say that we pick up his signals so clearly? (But wait: Doesn't most of this story take place in a car, which three paragraphs ago was held up for mockery? It does, but not as a stalling device to prepare us for the action. The journey, in this case, *is* the action.) For a writer open to instruction, the "unreliable narrator" is more than an interesting perspective; it's a set of decisions the author has made, a technique borrowed from what we'd call "real life"—people unintentionally show their self-deceptions and unsanctioned intentions all the time—revealed subtly, sentence by incriminating sentence, in a carefully constructed mock-world that gives the illusion of reality and completeness. I remember a very inexperienced reader of "Rock Springs" saying to me once, "I didn't know you could *do* that. It's like he's telling on himself but he doesn't know what he sounds like!" The next step, of course, is for the student writer to try that technique exactly as if it were a run on the piano in which the thumb needs to be passed under the third finger, or the hands have to cross at middle C. An exercise, not to be confused with inspiration but instructive to otherwise inert muscles.

Because it's the vivid individuality of these voices that cannot be borrowed, however much they may teach us after the fact. Borrowed, they are copies, not originals. What they model for us, beyond technique, is daring. These conceptions, no two alike, achieve what Clark Blaise, in a perpetually useful essay, "To Begin, To Begin," calls the breaking of a silence—the genius is in the first sentence, that moment when all the strangeness happens, when the Ancient Mariner clutches you by the arm like a sharp-taloned bird closing its feet around a perch, and demands that you listen.

The best of these stories will never happen again; they exist as challenging one-of-a-kinds, tributes to focus, passion and expertise. But the spirit that insists they can instruct another generation exists in hundreds of classrooms these days: master classes, taught jointly by creators and their interpreters. The Horowitzes and Rubinsteins, pouring out a thousand beautifully shaded notes a minute, and the Jordans hovering in the air like unlikely hummingbirds though no one can claim credit for teaching them to do that, are most likely students in those seats listening hard, taking coaching and eventually, we hope, moving beyond it on their own. They are learning to dissect without murdering. Watching, or rather, hearing them find their unique voices is the reward we are granted as teachers. As artists, payment has been tendered and received the moment the ball or the note or the monologue has gone out into the air and been caught and held tight against someone's body and cherished there.

ROSELLEN BROWN (1939–) is the author of four novels (*Before and After*; *Civil Wars*; *Tender Mercies*; and *The Autobiography of My Mother*), three collections of poetry (*Some Deaths in the Delta; Cora Fry* and its sequel, *Cora Fry's Pillow Book*), a collection of stories (*Street Games*), and a miscellany containing essays, stories, and poetry (*A Rosellen Brown Reader*).

She has published widely in magazines and her stories have appeared in *Prize Stories: The O. Henry Awards, The Best American Short Stories,* and *Pushcart Prize* series anthologies—and most recently *The Best American Stories of the Century,* edited by John Updike. She has been the recipient of an award in literature from the American Academy and Institute of Arts and Letters and fellowships from the Guggenheim Foundation, the Ingram Merrill Foundation, the Bunting Institute, the Howard Foundation, and twice from the National Endowment for the Arts. She was also selected one of *Ms.* magazine's twelve "Women of the Year" in 1984. *Civil Wars* won the Janet Kafka Prize for the best novel by an American woman in 1984. She teaches in the Graduate Creative Writing Program at the school of the Art Institute of Chicago.

THE SCRIBNER ANTHOLOGY OF CONTEMPORARY SHORT FICTION

SHERMAN ALEXIE

This Is What It Means to Say Phoenix, Arizona

SHERMAN ALEXIE (1966–) is a Spokane/Coeur d'Alene Indian from the Spokane Indian reservation in Wellpinit, Washington. Alexie's several books of poetry include *The Business of Fancydancing, Old Shirts & New Skins, First Indian on the Moon,* and *The Summer of Black Widows.* Alexie's novels include *Indian Killer* and *Reservation Blues,* which won him the Before Columbus Foundation's American Book Award. He earned a 1994 Lila Wallace–Reader's Digest Writers' Award, was a citation winner for the PEN/Hemingway Award for the Best First Book of Fiction, and was named one of *Granta*'s Best of the Young American Novelists. His collection of short stories, *The Lone Ranger and Tonto Fistfight in Heaven,* served as the basis for the film *Smoke Signals,* which premiered at the 1988 Sundance Film Festival, where it won the Audience Award and Filmmakers Trophy.

Just after Victor lost his job at the Bureau of Indian Affairs, he also found out that his father had died of a heart attack in Phoenix, Arizona. Victor hadn't seen his father in a few years, had only talked to him on the telephone once or twice, but there still was a genetic pain, which was as real and immediate as a broken bone. Victor didn't have any money. Who does have money on a reservation, except the cigarette and fireworks salespeople? His father had a savings account waiting to be claimed, but Victor needed to find a way to get from Spokane to Phoenix. Victor's mother was just as poor as he was, and the rest of his family didn't have any use at all for him. So Victor called the tribal council.

"Listen," Victor said. "My father just died. I need some money to get to Phoenix to make arrangements."

"Now, Victor," the council said, "you know we're having a difficult time financially."

"But I thought the council had special funds set aside for stuff like this."

"Now, Victor, we do have some money available for the proper return of tribal members' bodies. But I don't think we have enough to bring your father all the way back from Phoenix."

"Well," Victor said. "It ain't going to cost all that much. He had to be cremated. Things were kind of ugly. He died of a heart attack in his trailer and nobody found him for a week. It was really hot, too. You get the picture."

"Now, Victor, we're sorry for your loss and the circumstances. But we can really only afford to give you one hundred dollars."

"That's not even enough for a plane ticket."

"Well, you might consider driving down to Phoenix."

"I don't have a car. Besides, I was going to drive my father's pickup back up here."

"Now, Victor," the council said, "we're sure there is somebody who could drive you to Phoenix. Or could anybody lend you the rest of the money?"

"You know there ain't nobody around with that kind of money."

"Well, we're sorry, Victor, but that's the best we can do."

Victor accepted the tribal council's offer. What else could he do? So he signed the proper papers, picked up his check, and walked over to the Trading Post to cash it.

While Victor stood in line, he watched Thomas Builds-the-Fire standing near the magazine rack talking to himself. Like he always did. Thomas was a storyteller whom nobody wanted to listen to. That's like being a dentist in a town where everybody has false teeth.

Victor and Thomas Builds-the-Fire were the same age, had grown up and played in the dirt together. Ever since Victor could remember, it was Thomas who had always had something to say.

Once, when they were seven years old, when Victor's father still lived with the family, Thomas closed his eyes and told Victor this story: "Your father's heart is weak. He is afraid of his own family. He is afraid of you. Late at night, he sits in the dark. Watches the television until there's nothing but that white noise. Sometimes he feels like he wants to buy a motorcycle and ride away. He wants to run and hide. He doesn't want to be found."

Thomas Builds-the-Fire had known that Victor's father was going to leave, known it before anyone. Now Victor stood in the Trading Post with a one-hundred-dollar check in his hand, wondering if Thomas knew that Victor's father was dead, if he knew what was going to happen next.

Just then, Thomas looked at Victor, smiled, and walked over to him.

"Victor, I'm sorry about your father," Thomas said.

"How did you know about it?" Victor asked.

"I heard it on the wind. I heard it from the birds. I felt it in the sunlight. Also, your mother was just in here crying."

"Oh," Victor said and looked around the Trading Post. All the other Indians stared, surprised that Victor was even talking to Thomas. Nobody talked to Thomas anymore because he told the same damn stories over and over again. Victor was embarrassed, but he thought that Thomas might be able to help him. Victor felt a sudden need for tradition.

"I can lend you the money you need," Thomas said suddenly. "But you have to take me with you."

"I can't take your money," Victor said. "I mean, I haven't hardly talked to you in years. We're not really friends anymore."

"I didn't say we were friends. I said you had to take me with you."

"Let me think about it."

Victor went home with his one hundred dollars and sat at the kitchen table. He held his head in his hands and thought about Thomas Builds-the-Fire, remembered little details, tears and scars, the bicycle they shared for a summer, so many stories.

Thomas Builds-the-Fire sat on the bicycle, waiting in Victor's yard. He was ten years old and skinny. His hair was dirty because it was the Fourth of July.

"Victor," Thomas yelled. "Hurry up. We're going to miss the fireworks."

After a few minutes, Victor ran out of his family's house, vaulted over the porch railing, and landed gracefully on the sidewalk.

Thomas gave him the bike and they headed for the fireworks. It was nearly dark and the fireworks were about to start.

"You know," Thomas said, "it's strange how us Indians celebrate the Fourth of July. It ain't like it was our independence everybody was fighting for."

"You think about things too much," Victor said. "It's just supposed to be fun. Maybe Junior will be there."

"Which Junior? Everybody on this reservation is named Junior."

The fireworks were small, hardly more than a few bottle rockets and a fountain. But it was enough for two Indian boys. Years later, they would need much more.

Afterward, sitting in the dark, fighting off mosquitoes, Victor turned to Thomas Builds-the-Fire.

"Hey," Victor said. "Tell me a story."

Thomas closed his eyes and told this story: "There were these two Indian boys who wanted to be warriors. But it was too late to be warriors in the old way. All the horses were gone. So the two Indian boys stole a car and drove to the city. They parked the stolen car in the front of the police station and then hitchhiked back home to the reservation. When they got back, all their friends cheered and their parents' eyes shone with pride. 'You were very brave,' everybody said to the two Indian boys. 'Very brave.' "

"Ya-hey," Victor said. "That's a good one. I wish I could be a warrior."

"Me too," Thomas said.

Victor sat at his kitchen table. He counted his one hundred dollars again and again. He knew he needed more to make it to Phoenix and back. He knew he needed Thomas Builds-the-Fire. So he put his money in his wallet and opened the front door to find Thomas on the porch.

"Ya-hey, Victor," Thomas said. "I knew you'd call me."

Thomas walked into the living room and sat down in Victor's favorite chair.

"I've got some money saved up," Thomas said. "It's enough to get us down there, but you have to get us back."

"I've got this hundred dollars," Victor said. "And my dad had a savings account I'm going to claim."

"How much in your dad's account?"

"Enough. A few hundred."

"Sounds good. When we leaving?"

When they were fifteen and had long since stopped being friends, Victor and Thomas got into a fistfight. That is, Victor was really drunk and beat Thomas up for no reason at all. All the other Indian boys stood around and watched it happen. Junior was there and so were Lester, Seymour, and a lot of others.

The beating might have gone on until Thomas was dead if Norma Many Horses hadn't come along and stopped it.

"Hey, you boys," Norma yelled and jumped out of her car. "Leave him alone."

If it had been someone else, even another man, the Indian boys would've just ignored the warnings. But Norma was a warrior. She was powerful. She could have picked up any two of the boys and smashed their skulls together. But worse than that, she would have dragged them all over to some tepee and made them listen to some elder tell a dusty old story.

The Indian boys scattered, and Norma walked over to Thomas and picked him up.

"Hey, little man, are you O.K.?" she asked.

Thomas gave her a thumbs-up.

"Why they always picking on you?"

Thomas shook his head, closed his eyes, but no stories came to him, no words or music. He just wanted to go home, to lie in his bed and let his dreams tell the stories for him.

* * *

Thomas Builds-the-Fire and Victor sat next to each other in the airplane, coach section. A tiny white woman had the window seat. She was busy twisting her body into pretzels. She was flexible.

"I have to ask," Thomas said, and Victor closed his eyes in embarrassment.

"Don't," Victor said.

"Excuse me, miss," Thomas asked. "Are you a gymnast or something?"

"There's no something about it," she said. "I was first alternate on the 1980 Olympic team."

"Really?" Thomas asked.

"Really."

"I mean, you used to be a world-class athlete?" Thomas asked.

"My husband thinks I still am."

Thomas Builds-the-Fire smiled. She was a mental gymnast too. She pulled her leg straight up against her body so that she could've kissed her kneecap.

"I wish I could do that," Thomas said.

Victor was ready to jump out of the plane. Thomas, that crazy Indian storyteller with ratty old braids and broken teeth, was flirting with a beautiful Olympic gymnast. Nobody back home on the reservation would ever believe it.

"Well," the gymnast said. "It's easy. Try it."

Thomas grabbed at his leg and tried to pull it up into the same position as the gymnast's. He couldn't even come close, which made Victor and the gymnast laugh.

"Hey," she asked. "You two are Indian, right?"

"Full-blood," Victor said.

"Not me," Thomas said. "I'm half magician on my mother's side and half clown on my father's."

They all laughed.

"What are your names?" she asked.

"Victor and Thomas."

"Mine is Cathy. Pleased to meet you all."

The three of them talked for the duration of the flight. Cathy the gymnast complained about the government, how they screwed the 1980 Olympic team by boycotting the games.

"Sounds like you all got a lot in common with Indians," Thomas said.

Nobody laughed.

After the plane landed in Phoenix and they had all found their way to the terminal, Cathy the gymnast smiled and waved goodbye.

"She was really nice," Thomas said.

"Yeah, but everybody talks to everybody on airplanes," Victor said.

"You always used to tell me I think too much," Thomas said. "Now it sounds like you do."

"Maybe I caught it from you."

"Yeah."

Thomas and Victor rode in a taxi to the trailer where Victor's father had died.

"Listen," Victor said as they stopped in front of the trailer. "I never told you I was sorry for beating you up that time."

"Oh, it was nothing. We were just kids and you were drunk."

"Yeah, but I'm still sorry."

"That's all right."

Victor paid for the taxi, and the two of them stood in the hot Phoenix summer. They could smell the trailer.

"This ain't going to be nice," Victor said. "You don't have to go in."

"You're going to need help."

Victor walked to the front door and opened it. The stink rolled out and made them both gag. Victor's father had lain in that trailer for a week in hundred-degree temperatures before anyone had found him. And the only reason anyone found him was the smell. They needed dental records to identify him. That's exactly what the coroner said. They needed dental records.

"Oh, man," Victor said. "I don't know if I can do this."

"Well, then don't."

"But there might be something valuable in there."

"I thought his money was in the bank."

"It is. I was talking about pictures and letters and stuff like that."

"Oh," Thomas said as he held his breath and followed Victor into the trailer.

When Victor was twelve, he stepped into an underground wasps' nest. His foot was caught in the hole and no matter how hard he struggled, Victor couldn't pull free. He might have died there, stung a thousand times, if Thomas Builds-the-Fire had not come by.

"Run," Thomas yelled and pulled Victor's foot from the hole. They ran then, hard as they ever had, faster than Billy Mills, faster than Jim Thorpe, faster than the wasps could fly.

Victor and Thomas ran until they couldn't breathe, ran until it was cold and dark outside, ran until they were lost and it took hours to find their way home. All the way back, Victor counted his stings.

"Seven," Victor said. "My lucky number."

* * *

Victor didn't find much to keep in the trailer. Only a photo album and a stereo. Everything else had that smell stuck in it or was useless anyway. "I guess this is all," Victor said. "It ain't much."

"Better than nothing," Thomas said.

"Yeah, and I do have the pickup."

"Yeah," Thomas said. "It's in good shape."

"Dad was good about that stuff."

"Yeah, I remember your dad."

"Really?" Victor asked. "What do you remember?"

Thomas Builds-the-Fire closed his eyes and told this story: "I remember when I had this dream that told me to go to Spokane, to stand by the falls in the middle of the city and wait for a sign. I knew I had to go there but I didn't have a car. Didn't have a license. I was only thirteen. So I walked all the way, took me all day, and I finally made it to the falls. I stood there for an hour waiting. Then your dad came walking up. 'What the hell are you doing here?' he asked me. I said, 'Waiting for a vision.' Then your father said, 'All you're going to get here is mugged.' So he drove me over to Denny's, bought me dinner, and then drove me home to the reservation. For a long time, I was mad because I thought my dreams had lied to me. But they hadn't. Your dad was my vision. *Take care of each other* is what my dreams were saying. *Take care of each other.*"

Victor was quiet for a long time. He searched his mind for memories of his father, found the good ones, found a few bad ones, added it all up, and smiled.

"My father never told me about finding you in Spokane," Victor said.

"He said he wouldn't tell anybody. Didn't want me to get in trouble. But he said I had to watch out for you as part of the deal."

"Really?"

"Really. Your father said you would need the help. He was right."

"That's why you came down here with me, isn't it?" Victor asked.

"I came because of your father."

Victor and Thomas climbed into the pickup, drove over to the bank, and claimed the three hundred dollars in the savings account.

Thomas Builds-the-Fire could fly.

Once, he jumped off the roof of the tribal school and flapped his arms like a crazy eagle. And he flew. For a second he hovered, suspended above all the other Indian boys, who were too smart or too scared to jump too.

"He's flying," Junior yelled, and Seymour was busy looking for the trick wires or mirrors. But it was real. As real as the dirt when Thomas lost altitude and crashed to the ground.

He broke his arm in two places.

"He broke his wing, he broke his wing, he broke his wing," all the Indian boys chanted as they ran off, flapping their wings, wishing they could fly too. They hated Thomas for his courage, his brief moment as a bird. Everybody has dreams about flying. Thomas flew.

One of his dreams came true for just a second, just enough to make it real.

Victor's father, his ashes, fit in one wooden box with enough left over to fill a cardboard box.

"He always was a big man," Thomas said.

Victor carried part of his father out to the pickup, and Thomas carried the rest. They set him down carefully behind the seats, put a cowboy hat on the wooden box and a Dodgers cap on the cardboard box. That was the way it was supposed to be.

"Ready to head back home?" Victor asked.

"It's going to be a long drive."

"Yeah, take a couple days, maybe."

"We can take turns," Thomas said.

"O.K.," Victor said, but they didn't take turns. Victor drove for sixteen hours straight north, made it halfway up Nevada toward home before he finally pulled over.

"Hey, Thomas," Victor said. "You got to drive for a while."

"O.K."

Thomas Builds-the-Fire slid behind the wheel and started off down the road. All through Nevada, Thomas and Victor had been amazed at the lack of animal life, at the absence of water, of movement.

"Where is everything?" Victor had asked more than once.

Now, when Thomas was finally driving, they saw the first animal, maybe the only animal in Nevada. It was a long-eared jackrabbit.

"Look," Victor yelled. "It's alive."

Thomas and Victor were busy congratulating themselves on their discovery when the jackrabbit darted out into the road and under the wheels of the pickup.

"Stop the goddamn car," Victor yelled, and Thomas did stop and backed the pickup to the dead jackrabbit.

"Oh, man, he's dead," Victor said as he looked at the squashed animal.

"Really dead."

"The only thing alive in this whole state and we just killed it."

"I don't know," Thomas said. "I think it was suicide."

Victor looked around the desert, sniffed the air, felt the emptiness and loneliness, and nodded his head.

"Yeah," Victor said. "It had to be suicide."

"I can't believe this," Thomas said. "You drive for a thousand miles and there ain't even any bugs smashed on the windshield. I drive for ten seconds and kill the only living thing in Nevada."

"Yeah," Victor said. "Maybe I should drive."

"Maybe you should."

Thomas Builds-the-Fire walked through the corridors of the tribal school by himself. Nobody wanted to be anywhere near him because of all those stories. Story after story.

Thomas closed his eyes and this story came to him: "We are all given one thing by which our lives are measured, one determination. Mine are the stories that can change or not change the world. It doesn't matter which, as long as I continue to tell the stories. My father, he died on Okinawa in World War II, died fighting for this country, which had tried to kill him for years. My mother, she died giving birth to me, died while I was still inside her. She pushed me out into the world with her last breath. I have no brothers or sisters. I have only my stories, which came to me before I even had the words to speak. I learned a thousand stories before I took my first thousand steps. They are all I have. It's all I can do."

Thomas Builds-the-Fire told his stories to all those who would stop and listen. He kept telling them long after people had stopped listening.

Victor and Thomas made it back to the reservation just as the sun was rising. It was the beginning of a new day on earth, but the same old shit on the reservation.

"Good morning," Thomas said.

"Good morning."

The tribe was waking up, ready for work, eating breakfast, reading the newspaper, just like everybody else does. Willene LeBret was out in her garden, wearing a bathrobe. She waved when Thomas and Victor drove by.

"Crazy Indians made it," she said to herself and went back to her roses.

Victor stopped the pickup in front of Thomas Builds-the-Fire's HUD house. They both yawned, stretched a little, shook dust from their bodies.

"I'm tired," Victor said.

"Of everything," Thomas added.

They both searched for words to end the journey. Victor needed to thank Thomas for his help and for the money, and to make the promise to pay it all back.

"Don't worry about the money," Thomas said. "It don't make any difference anyhow."

"Probably not, enit?"

"Nope."

Victor knew that Thomas would remain the crazy storyteller who talked to dogs and cars, who listened to the wind and pine trees. Victor knew that he couldn't really be friends with Thomas, even after all that had happened. It was cruel but it was real. As real as the ash, as Victor's father, sitting behind the seats.

"I know how it is," Thomas said. "I know you ain't going to treat me any better than you did before. I know your friends would give you too much shit about it."

Victor was ashamed of himself. Whatever happened to the tribal ties, the sense of community? The only real thing he shared with anybody was a bottle and broken dreams. He owed Thomas something, anything.

"Listen," Victor said and handed Thomas the cardboard box that contained half of his father. "I want you to have this."

Thomas took the ashes and smiled, closed his eyes, and told this story: "I'm going to travel to Spokane Falls one last time and toss these ashes into the water. And your father will rise like a salmon, leap over the bridge, over me, and find his way home. It will be beautiful. His teeth will shine like silver, like a rainbow. He will rise, Victor, he will rise."

Victor smiled.

"I was planning on doing the same thing with my half," Victor said. "But I didn't imagine my father looking anything like a salmon. I thought it'd be like cleaning the attic or something. Like letting things go after they've stopped having any use."

"Nothing stops, cousin," Thomas said. "Nothing stops."

Thomas Builds-the-Fire got out of the pickup and walked up his driveway. Victor started the pickup and began the drive home.

"Wait," Thomas yelled suddenly from his porch. "I just got to ask one favor."

Victor stopped the pickup, leaned out the window, and shouted back.

"What do you want?" he asked.

"Just one time when I'm telling a story somewhere, why don't you stop and listen?" Thomas asked.

"Just once?"

"Just once."

Victor waved his arms to let Thomas know that the deal was good. It was a fair trade. That's all Thomas had ever wanted from his whole life. So Victor drove his father's pickup toward home while Thomas went into his house, closed the door behind him, and heard a new story come to him in the silence afterward.

MARGARET ATWOOD

Death by Landscape

MARGARET ATWOOD (1939–) was born in Ottawa and grew up in northern Quebec and Ontario, and later in Toronto. She is the author of more than twenty-five books—novels, short stories, poetry, literary criticism, social history, and books for children. She has won many awards, including the Governor General's Award, the Trillium Book Award, the City of Toronto Book Award, and the Canadian Authors Association Award. Her novel *Alias Grace* won the Giller Prize in Canada and the Premio Mondello in Italy. She is the recipient of numerous honors, including *The Sunday Times* Award for Literary Excellence in the United Kingdom, the National Arts Club Medal of Honor for Literature in the United States, and La Chevalier dans l'Ordre des Arts et des Lettres in France. She lives in Toronto with novelist Graeme Gibson.

Now that the boys are grown up and Rob is dead, Lois has moved to a condominium apartment in one of the newer waterfront developments. She is relieved not to have to worry about the lawn, or about the ivy pushing its muscular little suckers into the brickwork, or the squirrels gnawing their way into the attic and eating the insulation off the wiring, or about strange noises. This building has a security system, and the only plant life is in pots in the solarium.

Lois is glad she's been able to find an apartment big enough for her pictures. They are more crowded together than they were in the house, but this arrangement gives the walls a European look: blocks of pictures, above and beside one another, rather than one over the chesterfield, one over the fireplace, one in the front hall, in the old acceptable manner of sprinkling art around so it does not get too intrusive. This way has more of an impact. You know it's not supposed to be furniture.

None of the pictures is very large, which doesn't mean they aren't valuable.

They are paintings, or sketches and drawings, by artists who were not nearly as well known when Lois began to buy them as they are now. Their work later turned up on stamps, or as silk-screen reproductions hung in the principals' offices of high schools, or as jigsaw puzzles, or on beautifully printed calendars sent out by corporations as Christmas gifts, to their less important clients. These artists painted mostly in the twenties and thirties and forties; they painted landscapes. Lois has two Tom Thomsons, three A. Y. Jacksons, a Lawren Harris. She has an Arthur Lismer, she has a J. E. H. MacDonald. She has a David Milne. They are pictures of convoluted tree trunks on an island of pink wave-smoothed stone, with more islands behind; of a lake with rough, bright, sparsely wooded cliffs; of a vivid river shore with a tangle of bush and two beached canoes, one red, one gray; of a yellow autumn woods with the ice-blue gleam of a pond half-seen through the interlaced branches.

It was Lois who'd chosen them. Rob had no interest in art, although he could see the necessity of having something on the walls. He left all the decorating decisions to her, while providing the money, of course. Because of this collection of hers, Lois's friends—especially the men—have given her the reputation of having a good nose for art investments.

But this is not why she bought the pictures, way back then. She bought them because she wanted them. She wanted something that was in them, although she could not have said at the time what it was. It was not peace: she does not find them peaceful in the least. Looking at them fills her with a wordless unease. Despite the fact that there are no people in them or even animals, it's as if there is something, or someone, looking back out.

When she was thirteen, Lois went on a canoe trip. She'd only been on overnights before. This was to be a long one, into the trackless wilderness, as Cappie put it. It was Lois's first canoe trip, and her last.

Cappie was the head of the summer camp to which Lois had been sent ever since she was nine. Camp Manitou, it was called; it was one of the better ones, for girls, though not the best. Girls of her age whose parents could afford it were routinely packed off to such camps, which bore a generic resemblance to one another. They favored Indian names and had hearty, energetic leaders, who were called Cappie or Skip or Scottie. At these camps you learned to swim well and sail, and paddle a canoe, and perhaps ride a horse or play tennis. When you weren't doing these things you could do Arts and Crafts and turn out dingy, lumpish clay ashtrays for your mother—mothers smoked more, then—or bracelets made of colored braided string.

Cheerfulness was required at all times, even at breakfast. Loud shouting and the banging of spoons on the tables were allowed, and even encouraged, at ritual intervals. Chocolate bars were rationed, to control tooth decay and pimples. At night, after supper, in the dining hall or outside around a mosquito-infested campfire ring for special treats, there were singsongs. Lois can still remember all the words to "My Darling Clementine," and to "My Bonnie Lies over the Ocean," with acting-out gestures: a rippling of the hands for "the ocean," two hands together under the cheek for "lies." She will never be able to forget them, which is a sad thought.

Lois thinks she can recognize women who went to these camps, and were good at it. They have a hardness to their handshakes, even now; a way of standing, legs planted firmly and farther apart than usual; a way of sizing you up, to see if you'd be any good in a canoe—the front, not the back. They themselves would be in the back. They would call it the stern.

She knows that such camps still exist, although Camp Manitou does not. They are one of the few things that haven't changed much. They now offer copper enameling, and functionless pieces of stained glass baked in electric ovens, though judging from the productions of her friends' grandchildren the artistic standards have not improved.

To Lois, encountering it in the first year after the war, Camp Manitou seemed ancient. Its log-sided buildings with the white cement in between the half-logs, its flagpole ringed with whitewashed stones, its weathered gray dock jutting out into Lake Prospect, with its woven rope bumpers and its rusty rings for tying up, its prim round flowerbed of petunias near the office door, must surely have been there always. In truth it dated only from the first decade of the century; it had been founded by Cappie's parents, who'd thought of camping as bracing to the character, like cold showers, and had been passed along to her as an inheritance, and an obligation.

Lois realized, later, that it must have been a struggle for Cappie to keep Camp Manitou going, during the Depression and then the war, when money did not flow freely. If it had been a camp for the very rich, instead of the merely well off, there would have been fewer problems. But there must have been enough Old Girls, ones with daughters, to keep the thing in operation, though not entirely shipshape: furniture was battered, painted trim was peeling, roofs leaked. There were dim photographs of these Old Girls dotted around the dining hall, wearing ample woolen bathing suits and showing their fat, dimpled legs, or standing, arms twined, in odd tennis outfits with baggy skirts.

In the dining hall, over the stone fireplace that was never used, there was a huge molting stuffed moose head, which looked somehow carnivorous. It was a sort of mascot; its name was Monty Manitou. The older campers spread the story that it was haunted, and came to life in the dark, when the feeble and undependable lights had been turned off or, due to yet another generator failure, had gone out. Lois was afraid of it at first, but not after she got used to it.

Cappie was the same: you had to get used to her. Possibly she was forty, or thirty-five, or fifty. She had fawn-colored hair that looked as if it was cut with a bowl. Her head jutted forward, jigging like a chicken's as she strode around the camp, clutching notebooks and checking things off in them. She was like their minister in church: both of them smiled a lot and were anxious because they wanted things to go well; they both had the same overwashed skins and stringy necks. But all this disappeared when Cappie was leading a singsong, or otherwise leading. Then she was happy, sure of herself, her plain face almost luminous. She wanted to cause joy. At these times she was loved, at others merely trusted.

There were many things Lois didn't like about Camp Manitou, at first. She hated the noisy chaos and spoon-banging of the dining hall, the rowdy singsongs at which you were expected to yell in order to show that you were enjoying yourself. Hers was not a household that encouraged yelling. She hated the necessity of having to write dutiful letters to her parents claiming she was having fun. She could not complain, because camp cost so much money.

She didn't much like having to undress in a roomful of other girls, even in the dim light, although nobody paid any attention, or sleeping in a cabin with seven other girls, some of whom snored because they had adenoids or colds, some of whom had nightmares, or wet their beds and cried about it. Bottom bunks made her feel closed in, and she was afraid of falling out of top ones; she was afraid of heights. She got homesick, and suspected her parents of having a better time when she wasn't there than when she was, although her mother wrote to her every week saying how much they missed her. All this was when she was nine. By the time she was thirteen she liked it. She was an old hand by then.

Lucy was her best friend at camp. Lois had other friends in winter, when there was school and itchy woolen clothing and darkness in the afternoons, but Lucy was her summer friend.

She turned up the second year, when Lois was ten, and a Bluejay. (Chickadees, Bluejays, Ravens, and Kingfishers—these were the names Camp Manitou assigned to the different age groups, a sort of totemic clan system. In those days, thinks Lois, it was birds for girls, animals for boys: wolves, and so forth. Though some animals and birds were suitable and some were not. Never vultures, for instance; never skunks, or rats.)

Lois helped Lucy to unpack her tin trunk and place the folded clothes on the wooden shelves, and to make up her bed. She put her in the top bunk right above her, where she could keep an eye on her. Already she knew that Lucy was an exception, to a good many rules; already she felt proprietorial.

Lucy was from the United States, where the comic books came from, and the movies. She wasn't from New York or Hollywood or Buffalo, the only American cities Lois knew the names of, but from Chicago. Her house was on the lake shore and had gates to it, and grounds. They had a maid, all of the time. Lois's family only had a cleaning lady twice a week.

The only reason Lucy was being sent to *this* camp (she cast a look of minor scorn around the cabin, diminishing it and also offending Lois, while at the same time daunting her) was that her mother had been a camper here. Her mother had been a Canadian once, but had married her father, who had a patch over one eye, like a pirate. She showed Lois the picture of him in her wallet. He got the patch in the war. "Shrapnel," said Lucy. Lois, who was unsure about shrapnel, was so impressed she could only grunt. Her own two-eyed, unwounded father was tame by comparison.

"My father plays golf," she ventured at last.

"*Everyone* plays golf," said Lucy. "My *mother* plays golf."

Lois's mother did not. Lois took Lucy to see the outhouses and the swimming dock and the dining hall with Monty Manitou's baleful head, knowing in advance they would not measure up.

This was a bad beginning; but Lucy was good-natured, and accepted Camp Manitou with the same casual shrug with which she seemed to accept everything. She would make the best of it, without letting Lois forget that this was what she was doing.

However, there were things Lois knew that Lucy did not. Lucy scratched the tops off all her mosquito bites and had to be taken to the infirmary to be daubed with Ozonol. She took her T-shirt off while sailing, and although the counselor spotted her after a while and made her put it back on, she burnt spectacularly, bright red, with the X of her bathing-suit straps standing out in alarming white; she let Lois peel the sheets of whispery-thin burned skin off her shoulders. When they sang "Alouette" around the campfire, she did not know any of the French words. The difference was that Lucy did not care about the things she didn't know, whereas Lois did.

During the next winter, and subsequent winters, Lucy and Lois wrote to each other. They were both only children, at a time when this was thought to be a disadvantage, so in their letters they pretended to be sisters, or even twins. Lois had to strain a little over this, because Lucy was so blond, with translucent skin and large blue eyes like a doll's, and Lois was nothing out of the ordinary—just a tallish, thinnish, brownish person with freckles. They signed their letters LL, with the L's entwined together like the monograms on a towel. (Lois and Lucy, thinks Lois. How our names date us. Lois Lane, Superman's girlfriend, enterprising female reporter; "I Love Lucy." Now we are obsolete, and it's little Jennifers, little Emilys, little Alexandras and Carolines and Tiffanys.)

They were more effusive in their letters than they ever were in person.

They bordered their pages with X's and O's, but when they met again in the summers it was always a shock. They had changed so much, or Lucy had. It was like watching someone grow up in jolts. At first it would be hard to think up things to say.

But Lucy always had a surprise or two, something to show, some marvel to reveal. The first year she had a picture of herself in a tutu, her hair in a ballerina's knot on the top of her head; she pirouetted around the swimming dock, to show Lois how it was done, and almost fell off. The next year she had given that up and was taking horseback riding. (Camp Manitou did not have horses.) The next year her mother and father had been divorced, and she had a new stepfather, one with both eyes, and a new house, although the maid was the same. The next year, when they had graduated from Bluejays and entered Ravens, she got her period, right in the first week of camp. The two of them snitched some matches from their counselor, who smoked illegally, and made a small fire out behind the farthest outhouse, at dusk, using their flashlights. They could set all kinds of fires by now; they had learned how in Campcraft. On this fire they burned one of Lucy's used sanitary napkins. Lois is not sure why they did this, or whose idea it was. But she can remember the feeling of deep satisfaction it gave her as the white fluff singed and the blood sizzled, as if some wordless ritual had been fulfilled.

They did not get caught, but then they rarely got caught at any of their camp transgressions. Lucy had such large eyes, and was such an accomplished liar.

This year Lucy is different again: slower, more languorous. She is no longer interested in sneaking around after dark, purloining cigarettes from the counselor, dealing in black-market candy bars. She is pensive, and hard to wake in the mornings. She doesn't like her stepfather, but she doesn't want to live with her real father either, who has a new wife. She thinks her mother may be having a love affair with a doctor; she doesn't know for sure, but she's seen them smooching in his car, out on the driveway, when her stepfather wasn't there. It serves him right. She hates her private school. She has a boyfriend, who is sixteen and works as a gardener's assistant. This is how she met him: in the garden. She describes to Lois what it is like when he kisses her—rubbery at first, but then your knees go limp. She has been forbidden to see him, and threatened with boarding school. She wants to run away from home.

Lois has little to offer in return. Her own life is placid and satisfactory, but there is nothing much that can be said about happiness. "You're so lucky," Lucy tells her, a little smugly. She might as well say *boring* because this is how it makes Lois feel.

* * *

Lucy is apathetic about the canoe trip, so Lois has to disguise her own excitement. The evening before they are to leave, she slouches into the campfire ring as if coerced, and sits down with a sigh of endurance, just as Lucy does.

Every canoe trip that went out of camp was given a special send-off by Cappie and the section leader and counselors, with the whole section in attendance. Cappie painted three streaks of red across each of her cheeks with a lipstick. They looked like three-fingered claw marks. She put a blue circle on her forehead with fountain-pen ink, and tied a twisted bandanna around her head and stuck a row of frazzle-ended feathers around it, and wrapped herself in a red-and-black Hudson's Bay blanket. The counselors, also in blankets but with only two streaks of red, beat on tom-toms made of round wooden cheese boxes with leather stretched over the top and nailed in place. Cappie was Chief Cappeosota. They all had to say "How!" when she walked into the circle and stood there with one hand raised.

Looking back on this, Lois finds it disquieting. She knows too much about Indians: this is why. She knows, for instance, that they should not even be called Indians, and that they have enough worries without other people taking their names and dressing up as them. It has all been a form of stealing.

But she remembers, too, that she was once ignorant of this. Once she loved the campfire, the flickering of light on the ring of faces, the sound of the fake tom-toms, heavy and fast like a scared heartbeat; she loved Cappie in a red blanket and feathers, solemn, as a chief should be, raising her hand and saying, "Greetings, my Ravens." It was not funny, it was not making fun. She wanted to be an Indian. She wanted to be adventurous and pure, and aboriginal.

"You go on big water," says Cappie. This is her idea—all their ideas—of how Indians talk. "You go where no man has ever trod. You go many moons." This is not true. They are only going for a week, not many moons. The canoe route is clearly marked, they have gone over it on a map, and there are prepared campsites with names which are used year after year. But when Cappie says this—and despite the way Lucy rolls up her eyes—Lois can feel the water stretching out, with the shores twisting away on either side, immense and a little frightening.

"You bring back much wampum," says Cappie. "Do good in war, my braves, and capture many scalps." This is another of her pretenses: that they are boys, and bloodthirsty. But such a game cannot be played by substituting the word "squaw." It would not work at all.

Each of them has to stand up and step forward and have a red line drawn across her cheeks by Cappie. She tells them they must follow in the paths of their ancestors (who most certainly, thinks Lois, looking out the window of her apartment and remembering the family stash of daguerreotypes and sepia-colored portraits on her mother's dressing table, the stiff-shirted, black-coated, grim-faced men and the beflounced women with their severe hair and their corseted respectability, would never have considered heading off onto an open lake, in a canoe, just for fun).

At the end of the ceremony they all stood and held hands around the circle, and sang taps. This did not sound very Indian, thinks Lois. It sounded like a bugle call at a military post, in a movie. But Cappie was never one to be much concerned with consistency, or with archeology.

After breakfast the next morning they set out from the main dock, in four canoes, three in each. The lipstick stripes have not come off completely, and still show faintly pink, like healing burns. They wear their white denim sailing hats, because of the sun, and thin-striped T-shirts, and pale baggy shorts with the cuffs rolled up. The middle one kneels, propping her rear end against the rolled sleeping bags. The counselors going with them are Pat and Kip. Kip is no-nonsense; Pat is easier to wheedle, or fool.

There are white puffy clouds and a small breeze. Glints come from the little waves. Lois is in the bow of Kip's canoe. She still can't do a J-stroke very well, and she will have to be in the bow or the middle for the whole trip. Lucy is behind her; her own J-stroke is even worse. She splashes Lois with her paddle, quite a big splash.

"I'll get you back," says Lois.

"There was a stable fly on your shoulder," Lucy says.

Lois turns to look at her, to see if she's grinning. They're in the habit of splashing each other. Back there, the camp has vanished behind the first long point of rock and rough trees. Lois feels as if an invisible rope has broken. They're floating free, on their own, cut loose. Beneath the canoe the lake goes down, deeper and colder than it was a minute before.

"No horsing around in the canoe," says Kip. She's rolled her T-shirt sleeves up to the shoulder; her arms are brown and sinewy, her jaw determined, her stroke perfect. She looks as if she knows exactly what she is doing.

The four canoes keep close together. They sing, raucously and with defiance; they sing "The Quartermaster's Store," and "Clementine," and "Alouette." It is more like bellowing than singing.

After that the wind grows stronger, blowing slantwise against the bows, and they have to put all their energy into shoving themselves through the water.

Was there anything important, anything that would provide some sort of reason or clue to what happened next? Lois can remember everything, every detail; but it does her no good.

They stopped at noon for a swim and lunch, and went on in the afternoon. At last they reached Little Birch, which was the first campsite for overnight. Lois and Lucy made the fire, while the others pitched the heavy canvas tents. The fireplace was already there, flat stones piled into a U. A burned tin can and a beer bottle had been left in it. Their fire went out, and they had to restart it. "Hustle your bustle," said Kip. "We're starving."

The sun went down, and in the pink sunset light they brushed their teeth and spat the toothpaste froth into the lake. Kip and Pat put all the food that wasn't in cans into a packsack and slung it into a tree, in case of bears.

Lois and Lucy weren't sleeping in a tent. They'd begged to be allowed to sleep out; that way they could talk without the others hearing. If it rained, they told Kip, they promised not to crawl dripping into the tent over everyone's legs: they would get under the canoes. So they were out on the point.

Lois tried to get comfortable inside her sleeping bag, which smelled of musty storage and of earlier campers, a stale salty sweetness. She curled herself up, with her sweater rolled up under her head for a pillow and her flashlight inside her sleeping bag so it wouldn't roll away. The muscles of her sore arms were making small pings, like rubber bands breaking.

Beside her Lucy was rustling around. Lois could see the glimmering oval of her white face.

"I've got a rock poking into my back," said Lucy.

"So do I," said Lois. "You want to go into the tent?" She herself didn't, but it was right to ask.

"No," said Lucy. She subsided into her sleeping bag. After a moment she said, "It would be nice not to go back."

"To camp?" said Lois.

"To Chicago," said Lucy. "I hate it there."

"What about your boyfriend?" said Lois. Lucy didn't answer. She was either asleep or pretending to be.

There was a moon, and a movement of the trees. In the sky there were stars, layers of stars that went down and down. Kip said that when the stars were bright like that instead of hazy it meant bad weather later on. Out on the lake there were two loons, calling to each other in their insane, mournful voices. At the time it did not sound like grief. It was just background.

The lake in the morning was flat calm. They skimmed along over the glassy surface, leaving V-shaped trails behind them; it felt like flying. As the sun rose higher it got hot, almost too hot. There were stable flies in the canoes, landing on a bare arm or leg for a quick sting. Lois hoped for wind.

They stopped for lunch at the next of the named campsites, Lookout Point. It was called this because, although the site itself was down near the water on a flat shelf of rock, there was a sheer cliff nearby and a trail that led up to the top. The top was the lookout, although what you were supposed to see from there was not clear. Kip said it was just a view.

Lois and Lucy decided to make the climb anyway. They didn't want to hang around waiting for lunch. It wasn't their turn to cook, though they hadn't avoided much by not doing it, because cooking lunch was no big deal, it was just unwrapping the cheese and getting out the bread and peanut butter, but Pat and Kip always had to do their woodsy act and boil up a billy tin for their own tea.

They told Kip where they were going. You had to tell Kip where you were going, even if it was only a little way into the woods to get dry twigs for kindling. You could never go anywhere without a buddy.

"Sure," said Kip, who was crouching over the fire, feeding driftwood into it. "Fifteen minutes to lunch."

"Where are they off to?" said Pat. She was bringing their billy tin of water from the lake.

"Lookout," said Kip.

"Be careful," said Pat. She said it as an afterthought, because it was what she always said.

"They're old hands," Kip said.

Lois looks at her watch: it's ten to twelve. She is the watch-minder; Lucy is careless of time. They walk up the path, which is dry earth and rocks, big rounded pinky-gray boulders or split-open ones with jagged edges. Spindly balsam and spruce trees grow to either side, the lake is blue fragments to the left. The sun is right overhead; there are no shadows anywhere. The heat comes up at them as well as down. The forest is dry and crackly.

It isn't far, but it's a steep climb and they're sweating when they reach the top. They wipe their faces with their bare arms, sit gingerly down on a scorching-hot rock, five feet from the edge but too close for Lois. It's a lookout all right, a sheer drop to the lake and a long view over the water, back the way they've come. It's amazing to Lois that they've traveled so far, over all that water, with nothing to propel them but their own arms. It makes her feel strong. There are all kinds of things she is capable of doing.

"It would be quite a dive off here," says Lucy.

"You'd have to be nuts," says Lois.

"Why?" says Lucy. "It's really deep. It goes straight down." She stands up and takes a step nearer the edge. Lois gets a stab in her midriff, the kind she gets when a car goes too fast over a bump. "Don't," she says.

"Don't what?" says Lucy, glancing around at her mischievously. She knows how Lois feels about heights. But she turns back. "I really have to pee," she says.

"You have toilet paper?" says Lois, who is never without it. She digs in her shorts pocket.

"Thanks," says Lucy.

They are both adept at peeing in the woods: doing it fast so the mosquitoes don't get you, the underwear pulled up between the knees, the squat with the feet apart so you don't wet your legs, facing downhill. The exposed feeling of your bum, as if someone is looking at you from behind. The etiquette when you're with someone else is not to look. Lois stands up and starts to walk back down the path, to be out of sight.

"Wait for me?" says Lucy.

Lois climbed down, over and around the boulders, until she could not see Lucy; she waited. She could hear the voices of the others, talking and laughing, down near the shore. One voice was yelling, "Ants! Ants!" Someone must have sat on an ant hill. Off to the side, in the woods, a raven was croaking, a hoarse single note.

She looked at her watch: it was noon. This is when she heard the shout.

She has gone over and over it in her mind since, so many times that the first, real shout has been obliterated, like a footprint trampled by other footprints. But she is sure (she is almost positive, she is nearly certain) that it was not a shout of fear. Not a scream. More like a cry of surprise, cut off too soon. Short, like a dog's bark.

"Lucy?" Lois said. Then she called "Lucy!" By now she was clambering back up, over the stones of the path. Lucy was not up there. Or she was not in sight.

"Stop fooling around," Lois said. "It's lunchtime." But Lucy did not rise from behind a rock or step out, smiling, from behind a tree. The sunlight was all around; the rocks looked white. "This isn't funny!" Lois said, and it wasn't, panic was rising in her, the panic of a small child who does not know where the bigger ones are hidden. She could hear her own heart. She looked quickly around; she lay down on the ground and looked over the edge of the cliff. It made her feel cold. There was nothing.

She went back down the path, stumbling; she was breathing too quickly; she was too frightened to cry. She felt terrible—guilty and dismayed, as if she had done something very bad, by mistake. Something that could never be repaired. "Lucy's gone," she told Kip.

Kip looked up from her fire, annoyed. The water in the billy can was boiling. "What do you mean, gone?" she said. "Where did she go?"

"I don't know," said Lois. "She's just gone."

No one had heard the shout, but then no one had heard Lois calling, either. They had been talking among themselves, by the water.

Kip and Pat went up to the lookout and searched and called, and blew their whistles. Nothing answered.

Then they came back down, and Lois had to tell exactly what had happened. The other girls all sat in a circle and listened to her. Nobody said anything. They all looked frightened, especially Pat and Kip. They were the leaders. You did not just lose a camper like this, for no reason at all.

"Why did you leave her alone?" said Kip.

"I was just down the path," said Lois. "I told you. She had to go to the bathroom." She did not say *pee* in front of people older than herself.

Kip looked disgusted.

"Maybe she just walked off into the woods and got turned around," said one of the girls.

"Maybe she's doing it on purpose," said another.

Nobody believed either of these theories.

They took the canoes and searched around the base of the cliff, and peered down into the water. But there had been no sound of falling rock; there had been no splash. There was no clue, nothing at all. Lucy had simply vanished.

That was the end of the canoe trip. It took them the same two days to go back that it had taken coming in, even though they were short a paddler. They did not sing.

After that, the police went in a motorboat, with dogs; they were the Mounties and the dogs were German shepherds, trained to follow trails in the woods. But it had rained since, and they could find nothing.

Lois is sitting in Cappie's office. Her face is bloated with crying, she's seen that in the mirror. By now she feels numbed; she feels as if she has drowned. She can't stay here. It has been too much of a shock. Tomorrow her parents are coming to take her away. Several of the other girls who were on the canoe trip are also being collected. The others will have to stay, because their parents are in Europe, or cannot be reached.

Cappie is grim. They've tried to hush it up, but of course everyone in camp knows. Soon the papers will know too. You can't keep it quiet, but what can be said? What can be said that makes any sense? "Girl vanishes in broad daylight, without a trace." It can't be believed. Other things, worse things, will be suspected. Negligence, at the very least. But they have always taken such care. Bad luck will gather around Camp Manitou like a fog; parents will avoid it, in favor of other, luckier places. Lois can see Cappie thinking all this, even through her numbness. It's what anyone would think.

Lois sits on the hard wooden chair in Cappie's office, beside the old wooden desk, over which hangs the thumbtacked bulletin board of normal camp routine, and gazes at Cappie through her puffy eyelids. Cappie is now smiling what is supposed to be a reassuring smile. Her manner is too casual: she's after something. Lois has seen this look on Cappie's face when she's been sniffing out contraband chocolate bars, hunting down those rumored to have snuck out of their cabins at night.

"Tell me again," says Cappie, "from the beginning."

Lois has told her story so many times by now, to Pat and Kip, to Cappie, to the police, that she knows it word for word. She knows it, but she no longer believes it. It has become a story. "I told you," she said. "She wanted to go to the bathroom. I gave her my toilet paper. I went down the path, I waited for her. I heard this kind of shout . . ."

"Yes," says Cappie, smiling confidingly, "but before that. What did you say to one another?"

Lois thinks. Nobody has asked her this before. "She said you could dive off there. She said it went straight down."

"And what did you say?"

"I said you'd have to be nuts."

"Were you mad at Lucy?" says Cappie, in an encouraging voice.

"No," says Lois. "Why would I be mad at Lucy? I wasn't ever mad at Lucy." She feels like crying again. The times when she has in fact been mad at Lucy have been erased already. Lucy was always perfect.

"Sometimes we're angry when we don't know we're angry," says Cappie, as if to herself. "Sometimes we get really mad and we don't even know it. Sometimes we might do a thing without meaning to, or without knowing what will happen. We lose our tempers."

Lois is only thirteen, but it doesn't take her long to figure out that Cappie is not including herself in any of this. By *we* she means Lois. She is accusing Lois of pushing Lucy off the cliff. The unfairness of this hits her like a slap. "I didn't!" she says.

"Didn't what?" says Cappie softly. "Didn't what, Lois?"

Lois does the worst thing, she begins to cry. Cappie gives her a look like a pounce. She's got what she wanted.

Later, when she was grown up, Lois was able to understand what this interview had been about. She could see Cappie's desperation, her need for a story, a real story with a reason in it; anything but the senseless vacancy Lucy had left for her to deal with. Cappie wanted Lois to supply the reason, to be the reason. It wasn't even for the newspapers or the parents, because she could never make such an accusation without proof. It was for herself: something to explain the loss of Camp Manitou and of all she had worked for, the years of entertaining spoiled children and buttering up parents and making a fool of herself with feathers stuck in her hair. Camp Manitou was in fact lost. It did not survive.

Lois worked all this out, twenty years later. But it was far too late. It was too late even ten minutes afterwards, when she'd left Cappie's office and was walking slowly back to her cabin to pack. Lucy's clothes were still there, folded on the shelves, as if waiting. She felt the other girls in the cabin watching her with speculation in their eyes. *Could she have done it? She must have done it.* For the rest of her life, she has caught people watching her in this way.

Maybe they weren't thinking this. Maybe they were merely sorry for her. But she felt she had been tried and sentenced, and this is what has stayed with her: the knowledge that she had been singled out, condemned for something that was not her fault.

Lois sits in the living room of her apartment, drinking a cup of tea. Through the knee-to-ceiling window she has a wide view of Lake Ontario, with its skin of wrinkled blue-gray light, and of the willows of Centre Island shaken by a wind, which is silent at this distance, and on this side of the glass. When there isn't too much pollution she can see the far shore, the foreign shore; though today it is obscured.

Possibly she could go out, go downstairs, do some shopping; there isn't much in the refrigerator. The boys say she doesn't get out enough. But she isn't hungry, and moving, stirring from this space, is increasingly an effort.

She can hardly remember, now, having her two boys in the hospital, nursing them as babies; she can hardly remember getting married, or what Rob looked like. Even at the time she never felt she was paying full attention. She was tired a lot, as if she was living not one life but two: her own, and another, shadowy life that hovered around her and would not let itself be realized—the life of what would have happened if Lucy had not stepped sideways, and disappeared from time.

She would never go up north, to Rob's family cottage or to any place with wild lakes and wild trees and the calls of loons. She would never go anywhere near. Still, it was as if she was always listening for another voice, the voice of a person who should have been there but was not. An echo.

While Rob was alive, while the boys were growing up, she could pretend she didn't hear it, this empty space in sound. But now there is nothing much left to distract her.

She turns away from the window and looks at her pictures. There is the pinkish island, in the lake, with the intertwisted trees. It's the same landscape they paddled through, that distant summer. She's seen travelogues of this country, aerial photographs; it looks different from above, bigger, more hopeless: lake after lake, random blue puddles in dark green bush, the trees like bristles.

How could you ever find anything there, once it was lost? Maybe if they cut it all down, drained it all away, they might find Lucy's bones, some time, wherever they are hidden. A few bones, some buttons, the buckle from her shorts.

But a dead person is a body; a body occupies space, it exists somewhere. You can see it; you put it in a box and bury it in the ground, and then it's in a box in the ground. But Lucy is not in a box, or in the ground. Because she is nowhere definite, she could be anywhere.

And these paintings are not landscape paintings. Because there aren't any landscapes up there, not in the old, tidy European sense, with a gentle hill, a curving river, a cottage, a mountain in the background, a golden evening sky. Instead there's a tangle, a receding maze, in which you can become lost almost as soon as you step off the path. There are no backgrounds in any of these paintings, no vistas; only a great deal of foreground that goes back and back, endlessly, involving you in its twists and turns of tree and branch and rock. No matter how far back in you go, there will be more. And the trees themselves are hardly trees; they are currents of energy, charged with violent color.

Who knows how many trees there were on the cliff just before Lucy disappeared? Who counted? Maybe there was one more, afterwards.

Lois sits in her chair and does not move. Her hand with the cup is raised halfway to her mouth. She hears something, almost hears it: a shout of recognition, or of joy.

She looks at the paintings, she looks into them. Every one of them is a picture of Lucy. You can't see her exactly, but she's there, in behind the pink stone island or the one behind that. In the picture of the cliff she is hidden by the clutch of fallen rocks towards the bottom, in the one of the river shore she is crouching beneath the overturned canoe. In the yellow autumn woods she's behind the tree that cannot be seen because of the other trees, over beside the blue sliver of pond; but if you walked into the picture and found the tree, it would be the wrong one, because the right one would be further on.

Everyone has to be somewhere, and this is where Lucy is. She is in Lois's apartment, in the holes that open inwards on the wall, not like windows but like doors. She is here. She is entirely alive.

TONI CADE BAMBARA

Raymond's Run

TONI CADE BAMBARA (1939–1995) was a professor at Rutgers University. She lectured extensively in the Northeast and on the West Coast and lived with her daughter, Karma, in Atlanta, Georgia. Bambara edited *The Black Woman* and *Tales and Short Stories for Black Folk* anthologies and was the author of *Gorilla, My Love, The Sea Birds Are Still Alive, If Blessing Comes, The Salt Eaters,* and *Deep Sightings and Rescue Missions: Fiction, Essays, and Conversations.* She died of cancer in 1995 at the age of fifty-six.

I don't have much work to do around the house like some girls. My mother does that. And I don't have to earn my pocket money by hustling; George runs errands for the big boys and sells Christmas cards. And anything else that's got to get done, my father does. All I have to do in life is mind my brother Raymond, which is enough.

Sometimes I slip and say my little brother Raymond. But as any fool can see he's much bigger and he's older too. But a lot of people call him my little brother cause he needs looking after cause he's not quite right. And a lot of smart mouths got lots to say about that too, especially when George was minding him. But now, if anybody has anything to say to Raymond, anything to say about his big head, they have to come by me. And I don't play the dozens or believe in standing around with somebody in my face doing a lot of talking. I much rather just knock you down and take my chances even if I am a little girl with skinny arms and a squeaky voice, which is how I got the name Squeaky. And if things get too rough, I run. And as anybody can tell you, I'm the fastest thing on two feet.

There is no track meet that I don't win the first place medal. I used to win the twenty-yard dash when I was a little kid in kindergarten. Nowadays, it's the fifty-yard dash. And tomorrow I'm subject to run the quarter-meter relay all by myself and come in first, second, and third. The big kids call me Mercury cause I'm the swiftest thing in the neighborhood. Everybody knows that—except two people who know better, my father and me. He can beat me to Amsterdam Avenue with me having a two fire-hydrant headstart and him running with his hands in his pockets and whistling. But that's private information. Cause can you imagine some thirty-five-year-old man stuffing himself into PAL shorts to race little kids? So as far as everyone's concerned, I'm the fastest and that goes for Gretchen, too, who has put out the tale that she is going to win the first-place medal this year. Ridiculous. In the second place, she's got short legs. In the third place, she's got freckles. In the first place, no one can beat me and that's all there is to it.

I'm standing on the corner admiring the weather and about to take a stroll down Broadway so I can practice my breathing exercises, and I've got Raymond walking on the inside close to the buildings, cause he's subject to fits of fantasy and starts thinking he's a circus performer and that the curb is a tightrope strung high in the air. And sometimes after a rain he likes to step down off his tightrope right into the gutter and slosh around getting his shoes and cuffs wet. Then I get hit when I get home. Or sometimes if you don't watch him he'll dash across traffic to the island in the middle of Broadway and give the pigeons a fit. Then I have to go behind him apologizing to all the old people sitting around trying to get some sun and getting all upset with the pigeons fluttering around them, scattering their newspapers and upsetting the waxpaper lunches in their laps. So I keep Raymond on the inside of me, and he plays like he's driving a stage coach which is O.K. by me so long as he doesn't run me over or interrupt my breathing exercises, which I have to do on account of I'm serious about my running, and I don't care who knows it.

Now some people like to act like things come easy to them, won't let on that they practice. Not me. I'll high-prance down 34th Street like a rodeo pony to keep my knees strong even if it does get my mother uptight so that she walks ahead like she's not with me, don't know me, is all by herself on a shopping trip, and I am somebody else's crazy child. Now you take Cynthia Procter for instance. She's just the opposite. If there's a test tomorrow, she'll say something like, "Oh, I guess I'll play handball this afternoon and watch television tonight," just to let you know she ain't thinking about the test. Or like last week when she won the spelling bee for the millionth time, "A good thing you got 'receive,' Squeaky, cause I would have got it wrong. I completely forgot about the spelling bee." And she'll clutch the lace on her blouse like it was a narrow escape. Oh, brother. But of course when I pass her house on my early morning trots around the block, she is practicing the scales on the piano over and over and over and over. Then in music class she always lets herself get bumped around so she falls accidently on purpose onto the piano stool and is so surprised to find herself sitting there that she decides just for fun to try out the ole keys. And what do you know—Chopin's waltzes just spring out of her fingertips and she's the most surprised thing in the world. A regular prodigy. I could kill people like that. I stay up all night studying the words for the spelling bee. And you can see me any time of day practicing running. I never walk if I can trot, and shame on Raymond if he can't keep up. But of course he does, cause if he hangs back someone's liable to walk up to him and get smart, or take his allowance from him, or ask him where he got that great big pumpkin head. People are so stupid sometimes.

So I'm strolling down Broadway breathing out and breathing in on counts of seven, which is my lucky number, and here comes Gretchen and her sidekicks: Mary Louise, who used to be a friend of mine when she first moved to Harlem from Baltimore and got beat up by everybody till I took up for her on account of her mother and my mother used to sing in the same choir when they were young girls, but people ain't grateful, so now she hangs out with the new girl Gretchen and talks about me like a dog; and Rosie, who is as fat as I am skinny and has a big mouth where Raymond is concerned and is too stupid to know that there is not a big deal of difference between herself and Raymond and that she can't afford to throw stones. So they are steady coming up Broadway and I see right away that it's going to be one of those Dodge City scenes cause the street ain't that big and they're close to the buildings just as we are. First I think I'll step into the candy store and look over the new comics and let them pass. But that's chicken and I've got a reputation to consider. So then I think I'll just walk straight on through them or even over them if necessary. But as they get to me, they slow down. I'm ready to fight, cause like I said I don't feature a whole lot of chit-chat, I much prefer to just knock you down right from the jump and save everybody a lotta precious time.

"You signing up for the May Day races?" smiles Mary Louise, only it's not a smile at all. A dumb question like that doesn't deserve an answer. Besides, there's just me and Gretchen standing there really, so no use wasting my breath talking to shadows.

"I don't think you're going to win this time," says Rosie, trying to signify with her hands on her hips all salty, completely forgetting that I have whupped her behind many times for less salt than that.

"I always win cause I'm the best," I say straight at Gretchen who is, as far as I'm concerned, the only one talking in this ventriloquist-dummy routine. Gretchen smiles, but it's not a smile, and I'm thinking that girls never really smile at each other because they don't know how and don't want to know how and there's probably no one to teach us how, cause grown-up girls don't know either. Then they all look at Raymond who has just brought his mule team to a standstill. And they're about to see what trouble they can get into through him.

"What grade you in now, Raymond?"

"You got anything to say to my brother, you say it to me, Mary Louise Williams of Raggedy Town, Baltimore."

"What are you, his mother?" sasses Rosie.

"That's right, Fatso. And the next word out of anybody and I'll be *their* mother too." So they just stand there and Gretchen shifts from one leg to the other and so do they. Then Gretchen puts her hands on her hips and is about to say something with her freckle-face self but doesn't. Then she walks around me looking me up and down but keeps walking up Broadway, and her sidekicks follow her. So me and Raymond smile at each other and he says, "Gidyap" to his team and I continue with my breathing exercises, strolling down Broadway toward the ice man on 145th with not a care in the world cause I am Miss Quicksilver herself.

I take my time getting to the park on May Day because the track meet is the last thing on the program. The biggest thing on the program is the May Pole dancing, which I can do without, thank you, even if my mother thinks it's a shame I don't take part and act like a girl for a change. You'd think my mother'd be grateful not to have to make me a white organdy dress with a big satin sash and buy me new white baby-doll shoes that can't be taken out of the box till the big day. You'd think she'd be glad her daughter ain't out there prancing around a May Pole getting the new clothes all dirty and sweaty and trying to act like a fairy or a flower or whatever you're supposed to be when you should be trying to be yourself, whatever that is, which is, as far as I am concerned, a poor Black girl who really can't afford to buy shoes and a new dress you only wear once a lifetime cause it won't fit next year.

I was once a strawberry in a Hansel and Gretel pageant when I was in nursery school and didn't have no better sense than to dance on tiptoe with my arms in a circle over my head doing umbrella steps and being a perfect fool just so my mother and father could come dressed up and clap. You'd think they'd know better than to encourage that kind of nonsense. I am not a strawberry. I do not dance on my toes. I run. That is what I am all about. So I always come late to the May Day program, just in time to get my number pinned on and lay in the grass till they announce the fifty-yard dash.

I put Raymond in the little swings, which is a tight squeeze this year and will be impossible next year. Then I look around for Mr. Pearson, who pins the numbers on. I'm really looking for Gretchen if you want to know the truth, but she's not around. The park is jam-packed. Parents in hats and corsages and breast-pocket handkerchiefs peeking up. Kids in white dresses and light-blue suits. The parkees unfolding chairs and chasing the rowdy kids from Lenox as if they had no right to be there. The big guys with their caps on backwards, leaning against the fence swirling the basketballs on the tips of their fingers, waiting for all these crazy people to clear out the park so they can play. Most of the kids in my class are carrying bass drums and glockenspiels and flutes. You'd think they'd put in a few bongos or something for real like that.

Then here comes Mr. Pearson with his clipboard and his cards and pencils and whistles and safety pins and fifty million other things he's always dropping all over the place with his clumsy self. He sticks out in a crowd because he's on stilts. We used to call him Jack and the Beanstalk to get him mad. But I'm the only one that can outrun him and get away, and I'm too grown for that silliness now.

"Well, Squeaky," he says, checking my name off the list and handing me number seven and two pins. And I'm thinking he's got no right to call me Squeaky, if I can't call him Beanstalk.

"Hazel Elizabeth Deborah Parker," I correct him and tell him to write it down on his board.

"Well, Hazel Elizabeth Deborah Parker, going to give someone else a break this year?" I squint at him real hard to see if he is seriously thinking I should lose the race on purpose just to give someone else a break. "Only six girls running this time," he continues, shaking his head sadly like it's my fault all of New York didn't turn out in sneakers. "That new girl should give you a run for your money." He looks around the park for Gretchen like a periscope in a submarine movie. "Wouldn't it be a nice gesture if you were . . . to ahhh . . ."

I give him such a look he couldn't finish putting that idea into words. Grownups got a lot of nerve sometimes. I pin number seven to myself and stomp away, I'm so burnt. And I go straight for the track and stretch out on the grass while the band winds up with "Oh, the Monkey Wrapped His Tail Around the Flag Pole," which my teacher calls by some other name. The man on the loudspeaker is calling everyone over to the track and I'm on my back looking at the sky, trying to pretend I'm in the country, but I can't, because even grass in the city feels hard as sidewalk, and there's just no pretending you are anywhere but in a "concrete jungle" as my grandfather says.

The twenty-yard dash takes all of two minutes cause most of the little kids don't know no better than to run off the track or run the wrong way or run smack into the fence and fall down and cry. One little kid, though, has got the good sense to run straight for the white ribbon up ahead so he wins. Then the second-graders line up for the thirty-yard dash and I don't even bother to turn my head to watch cause Raphael Perez always wins. He wins before he even begins by psyching the runners, telling them they're going to trip on their shoelaces and fall on their faces or lose their shorts or something, which he doesn't really have to do since he is very fast, almost as fast as I am. After that is the forty-yard dash which I use to run when I was in first grade. Raymond is hollering from the swings cause he knows I'm about to do my thing cause the man on the loudspeaker has just announced the fifty-yard dash, although he might just as well be giving a recipe for angel food cake cause you can hardly make out what he's sayin for the static. I get up and slip off my sweat pants and then I see Gretchen standing at the starting line, kicking her legs out like a pro. Then as I get into place I see that ole Raymond is on line on the other side of the fence, bending down with his fingers on the ground just like he knew what he was doing. I was going to yell at him but then I didn't. It burns up your energy to holler.

Every time, just before I take off in a race, I always feel like I'm in a dream, the kind of dream you have when you're sick with fever and feel all hot and weightless. I dream I'm flying over a sandy beach in the early morning sun, kissing the leaves of the trees as I fly by. And there's always the smell of apples, just like in the country when I was little and used to think I was a choo-choo train, running through the fields of corn and chugging up the hill to the orchard. And all the time I'm dreaming this, I get lighter and lighter until I'm flying over the beach again, getting blown through the sky like a feather that weighs nothing at all. But once I spread my fingers in the dirt and crouch over the Get on Your Mark, the dream goes and I am solid again and am telling myself, Squeaky you must win, you must win, you are the fastest thing in the world, you can even beat your father up Amsterdam if you really try. And then I feel my weight coming back just behind my knees then down to my feet then into the earth and the pistol shot explodes in my blood and I am off and weightless again, flying past the other runners, my arms pumping up and down and the whole world is quiet except for the crunch as I zoom over the gravel in the track. I glance to my left and there is no one. To the right, a blurred Gretchen, who's got her chin jutting out as if it would win the race all by itself. And on the other side of the fence is Raymond with his arms down to his side and the palms tucked up behind him, running in his very own style, and it's the first time I ever saw that and I almost stop to watch my brother Raymond on his first run. But the white ribbon is bouncing toward me and I tear past it, racing into the distance till my feet with a mind of their own start digging up footfuls of dirt and brake me short. Then all the kids standing on the side pile on me, banging me on the back and slapping my head with their May Day programs, for I have won again and everybody on 151st Street can walk tall for another year.

"In first place . . ." the man on the loudspeaker is clear as a bell now. But then he pauses and the loudspeaker starts to whine. Then static. And I lean down to catch my breath and here comes Gretchen walking back, for she's overshot the finish line too, huffing and puffing with her hands on her hips taking it slow, breathing in steady time like a real pro and I sort of like her a little for the first time. "In first place . . ." and then three or four voices get all mixed up on the loudspeaker and I dig my sneaker into the grass and stare at Gretchen who's staring back, we both wondering just who did win. I can hear old Beanstalk arguing with the man on the loudspeaker and then a few others running their mouths about what the stopwatches say. Then I hear Raymond yanking at the fence to call me and I wave to shush him, but he keeps rattling the fence like a gorilla in a cage like in them gorilla movies, but then like a dancer or something he starts climbing up nice and easy but very fast. And it occurs to me, watching how smoothly he climbs hand over hand and remembering how he looked running with his arms down to his side and with the wind pulling his mouth back and his teeth showing and all, it occurred to me that Raymond would make a very fine runner. Doesn't he always keep up with me on my trots? And he surely knows how to breathe in counts of seven cause he's always doing it at the dinner table, which drives my brother George up the wall. And I'm smiling to beat the band cause if I've lost this race, or if me and Gretchen tied, or even if I've won, I can always retire as a runner and begin a whole new career as a coach with Raymond as my champion. After all, with a little more study I can beat Cynthia and her phony self at the spelling bee. And if I bugged my mother, I could get piano lessons and become a star. And I have a big rep as the baddest thing around. And I've got a roomful of ribbons and medals and awards. But what has Raymond got to call his own?

So I stand there with my new plans, laughing out loud by this time as Raymond jumps down from the fence and runs over with his teeth showing and his arms down to the side, which no one before him has quite mastered as a running style. And by the time he comes over I'm jumping up and down so glad to see him—my brother Raymond, a great runner in the family tradition. But of course everyone thinks I'm jumping up and down because the men on the loudspeaker have finally gotten themselves together and compared notes and are announcing "In first place—Miss Hazel Elizabeth Deborah Parker." (Dig that.) "In second place—Miss Gretchen P. Lewis." And I look over at Gretchen wondering what the "P" stands for. And I smile. Cause she's good, no doubt about it. Maybe she'd like to help me coach Raymond; she obviously is serious about running, as any fool can see. And she nods to congratulate me and then she smiles. And I smile. We stand there with this big smile of respect between us. It's about as real a smile as girls can do for each other, considering we don't practice real smiling every day, you know, cause maybe we too busy being flowers or fairies or strawberries instead of something honest and worthy of respect . . . you know . . . like being people.

RUSSELL BANKS

Sarah Cole: A Type of Love Story

RUSSELL BANKS (1940–), author of four collections of short stories and at work on his tenth novel, has taught at various colleges and universities, including Columbia University and Princeton. His most recent work, *Cloudsplitter,* a historical novel about abolitionist John Brown, is set near Banks's home in the Adirondacks, where Brown lived and was buried. Several of the author's novels have been translated into film. In 1997 *The Sweet Hereafter,* directed by Atom Egoyan, received critical acclaim and two Oscar nominations. Most recently, *Affliction,* directed by Paul Schrader, was released, for which James Coburn won an Oscar as Best Supporting Actor. Banks is the father of four daughters and the husband of poet Chase Twitchell.

To begin, then, here is a scene in which I am the man and my friend Sarah Cole is the woman. I don't mind describing it now, because I'm a decade older and don't look the same now as I did then, and Sarah is dead. That is to say, on hearing this story you might think me vain if I looked the same now as I did then, because I must tell you that I was extremely handsome then. And if Sarah were not dead, you'd think I was cruel, for I must tell you that Sarah was very homely. In fact, she was the homeliest woman I have ever known. Personally, I mean. I've *seen* a few women who were more unattractive than Sarah, but they were clearly freaks of nature or had been badly injured or had been victimized by some grotesque, disfiguring disease. Sarah, however, was quite normal, and I knew her well, because for three and a half months we were lovers.

Here is the scene. You can put it in the present, even though it took place ten years ago, because nothing that matters to the story depends on when it took place, and you can put it in Concord, New Hampshire, even though that is indeed where it took place, because it doesn't matter where it took place, so it might as well be Concord, New Hampshire, a place I happen to know well and can therefore describe with sufficient detail to make the story believable. Around six o'clock on a Wednesday evening in late May a man enters a bar. The place, a cocktail lounge at street level with a restaurant upstairs, is decorated with hanging plants and unfinished wood paneling, butcher-block tables and captain's chairs, with a half dozen darkened, thickly upholstered booths along one wall. Three or four men between the ages of twenty-five and thirty-five are drinking at the bar, and they, like the man who has just entered, wear three-piece suits and loosened neckties. They are probably lawyers, young, unmarried lawyers gossiping with their brethren over martinis so as to postpone arriving home alone at their whitewashed town-house apartments, where they will fix their evening meals in Radaranges and, afterwards, while their TVs chuckle quietly in front of them, sit on their couches and do a little extra work for tomorrow. They are, for the most part, honorable, educated, hard-working, shallow, and moderately unhappy young men. Our man, call him Ronald, Ron, in most ways is like these men, except that he is unusually good-looking, and that makes him a little less unhappy than they. Ron is effortlessly attractive, a genetic wonder, tall, slender, symmetrical, and clean. His flaws, a small mole on the left corner of his square but not-too-prominent chin, a slight excess of blond hair on the tops of his tanned hands, and somewhat underdeveloped buttocks, insofar as they keep him from resembling too closely a men's store mannequin, only contribute to his beauty, for he is beautiful, the way we usually think of a woman as being beautiful. And he is nice, too, the consequence, perhaps, of his seeming not to know how beautiful he is, to men as well as women, to young people, even children, as well as old, to attractive people, who realize immediately that he is so much more attractive than they as not to be competitive with them, as well as unattractive people, who see him and gain thereby a comforting perspective on those they have heretofore envied for their good looks.

Ron takes a seat at the bar, unfolds the evening paper in front of him, and before he can start reading, the bartender asks to help him, calling him "Sir," even though Ron has come into this bar numerous times at this time of day, especially since his divorce last fall. Ron got divorced because, after three years of marriage, his wife had chosen to pursue the career that his had interrupted, that of a fashion designer, which meant that she had to live in New York City while he had to continue to live in New Hampshire, where his career had got its start. They agreed to live apart until he could continue his career near New York City, but after a few months, between conjugal visits, he started sleeping with other women, and she started sleeping with other men, and that was that. "No big deal," he explained to friends, who liked both Ron and his wife, even though he was slightly more beautiful than she. "We really were too young when we got married, college sweethearts. But we're still best friends," he assured them. They understood. Most of Ron's friends were divorced by then too.

Ron orders a scotch and soda, with a twist, and goes back to reading his paper. When his drink comes, before he takes a sip of it, he first carefully finishes reading an article about the recent re-appearance of coyotes in northern New Hampshire and Vermont. He lights a cigarette. He goes on reading. He takes a second sip of his drink. Everyone in the room, the three or four men scattered along the bar, the tall, thin bartender, and several people in the booths at the back, watches him do these ordinary things.

He has got to the classified section, is perhaps searching for someone willing to come in once a week and clean his apartment, when the woman who will turn out to be Sarah Cole leaves a booth in the back and approaches him. She comes up from the side and sits next to him. She's wearing heavy, tan cowboy boots and a dark brown, suede cowboy hat, lumpy jeans and a yellow tee shirt that clings to her arms, breasts, and round belly like the skin of a sausage. Though he will later learn that she is thirty-eight years old, she looks older by about ten years, which makes her look about twenty years older than he actually is. (It's difficult to guess accurately how old Ron is; he looks anywhere from a mature twenty-five to a youthful forty, so his actual age doesn't seem to matter.)

"It's not bad here at the bar," she says looking around. "More light, anyhow. Whatcha readin'?" she asks brightly, planting both elbows on the bar.

Ron looks up from his paper with a slight smile on his lips, sees the face of a woman homelier than any he has ever seen or imagined before, and goes on smiling lightly. He feels himself falling into her tiny, slightly crossed, dark brown eyes, pulls himself back, and studies for a few seconds her mottled, pocked complexion, bulbous nose, loose mouth, twisted and gapped teeth, and heavy but receding chin. He casts a glance over her thatch of dun-colored hair and along her neck and throat, where acne burns against gray skin, and returns to her eyes, and again feels himself falling into her.

"What did you say?" he asks.

She knocks a mentholated cigarette from her pack, and Ron swiftly lights it. Blowing smoke from her large, wing-shaped nostrils, she speaks again. Her voice is thick and nasal, a chocolate-colored voice. "I asked you whatcha readin', but I can see now." She belts out a single, loud laugh. "The paper!"

Ron laughs, too. "The paper! *The Concord Monitor!*" He is not hallucinating, he clearly sees what is before him and admits—no, he asserts—to himself that he is speaking to the most unattractive woman he has ever seen, a fact which fascinates him, as if instead he were speaking to the most beautiful woman he has ever seen or perhaps ever will see, so he treasures the moment, attempts to hold it as if it were a golden ball, a disproportionately heavy object which—if he doesn't hold it lightly yet with precision and firmness—will slip from his hand and roll across the lawn to the lip of the well and down, down to the bottom of the well, lost to him forever. It will be merely a memory, something to speak of wistfully and with wonder as over the years the image fades and comes in the end to exist only in the telling. His mind and body waken from their sleepy self-absorption, and all his attention focuses on the woman, Sarah Cole, her ugly face, like a warthog's, her thick, rapid voice, her dumpy, off-center wreck of a body, and to keep this moment here before him, he begins to ask questions of her, he buys her a drink, he smiles, until soon it seems, even to him, that he is taking her and her life, its vicissitudes and woe, quite seriously.

He learns her name, of course, and she volunteers the information that she spoke to him on a dare from one of the two women still sitting in the booth behind her. She turns on her stool and smiles brazenly, triumphantly, at her friends, two women, also homely (though nowhere as homely as she) and dressed, like her, in cowboy boots, hats and jeans. One of the women, a blonde with an underslung jaw and wearing heavy eye makeup, flips a little wave at her, and as if embarrassed, she and the other woman at the booth turn back to their drinks and sip fiercely at straws.

Sarah returns to Ron and goes on telling him what he wants to know, about her job at the Rumford Press, about her divorced husband who was a bastard and stupid and "sick," she says, as if filling suddenly with sympathy for the man. She tells Ron about her three children, the youngest, a girl, in junior high school and boy-crazy, the other two, boys, in high school and almost never at home anymore. She speaks of her children with genuine tenderness and concern, and Ron is touched. He can see with what pleasure and pain she speaks of her children; he watches her tiny eyes light up and water over when he asks their names.

"You're a nice woman," he informs her.

She smiles, looks at her empty glass. "No. No, I'm not. But you're a nice man, to tell me that."

Ron, with a gesture, asks the bartender to refill Sarah's glass. She is drinking white Russians. Perhaps she has been drinking them for an hour or two, for she seems very relaxed, more relaxed than women usually do when they come up and without introduction or invitation speak to him.

She asks him about himself, his job, his divorce, how long he has lived in Concord, but he finds that he is not at all interested in telling her about himself. He wants to know about her, even though what she has to tell him about herself is predictable and ordinary and the way she tells it unadorned and clichéd. He wonders about her husband. What kind of man would fall in love with Sarah Cole?

II

That scene, at Osgood's Lounge in Concord, ended with Ron's departure, alone, after having bought Sarah's second drink, and Sarah's return to her friends in the booth. I don't know what she told them, but it's not hard to imagine. The three women were not close friends, merely fellow workers at Rumford Press, where they stood at the end of a long conveyor belt day after day packing *TV Guide*s into cartons. They all hated their jobs, and frequently after work, when they worked the day shift, they would put on their cowboy hats and boots, which they kept all day in their lockers, and stop for a drink or two on their way home. This had been their first visit to Osgood's, a place that, prior to this, they had avoided out of a sneering belief that no one went there but lawyers and insurance men. It had been Sarah who had asked the others why that should keep them away, and when they had no answer for her, the three had decided to stop at Osgood's. Ron was right, they had been there over an hour when he came in, and Sarah was a little drunk. "We'll hafta come in here again," she said to her friends, her voice rising slightly.

Which they did, that Friday, and once again Ron appeared with his evening newspaper. He put his briefcase down next to his stool and ordered a drink and proceeded to read the front page, slowly, deliberately, clearly a weary, unhurried, solitary man. He did not notice the three women in cowboy hats and boots in the booth in back, but they saw him, and after a few minutes Sarah was once again at his side.

"Hi."

He turned, saw her, and instantly regained the moment he had lost when, the previous night, once outside the bar, he had forgotten about the ugliest woman he had ever seen. She seemed even more grotesque to him now than before, which made the moment all the more precious to him, and so once again he held the moment as if in his hands and began to speak with her, to ask questions, to offer his opinions and solicit hers.

I said earlier that I am the man in this story and my friend Sarah Cole, now dead, is the woman. I think back to that night, the second time I had seen Sarah, and I tremble, not with fear but in shame. My concern then, when I was first becoming involved with Sarah, was merely with the moment, holding on to it, grasping it wholly as if its beginning did not grow out of some other prior moment in her life and my life separately and at the same time did not lead into future moments in our separate lives. She talked more easily than she had the night before, and I listened as eagerly and carefully as I had before, again, with the same motives, to keep her in front of me, to draw her forward from the context of her life and place her, as if she were an object, into the context of mine. I did not know how cruel this was. When you have never done a thing before and that thing is not simply and clearly right or wrong, you frequently do not know if it is a cruel thing, you just go ahead and do it, and maybe later you'll be able to determine whether you acted cruelly. That way you'll know if it was right or wrong of you to have done it in the first place.

While we drank, Sarah told me that she hated her ex-husband because of the way he treated the children. "It's not so much the money," she said, nervously wagging her booted feet from her perch on the high barstool. "I mean, I get by, barely, but I get them fed and clothed on my own okay. It's because he won't even write them a letter or anything. He won't call them on the phone, all he calls for is to bitch at me because I'm trying to get the state to take him to court so I can get some of the money he's s'posed to be paying for child support. And he won't even think to talk to the kids when he calls. Won't even ask about them."

"He sounds like a bastard," I said.

"He is, he is," she said. "I don't know why I married him. Or stayed married. Fourteen years, for Christ's sake. He put a spell over me or something, I don't know," she said with a note of wistfulness in her voice. "He wasn't what you'd call good-looking."

After her second drink, she decided she had to leave. Her children were at home, it was Friday night and she liked to make sure she ate supper with them and knew where they were going and who they were with when they went out on their dates. "No dates on schoolnights," she said to me. "I mean, you gotta have rules, you know."

I agreed, and we left together, everyone in the place following us with his or her gaze. I was aware of that, I knew what they were thinking, and I didn't care, because I was simply walking her to her car.

It was a cool evening, dusk settling onto the lot like a gray blanket. Her car, a huge, dark green Buick sedan at least ten years old, was battered, scratched, and almost beyond use. She reached for the door handle on the driver's side and yanked. Nothing. The door wouldn't open. She tried again. Then I tried. Still nothing.

Then I saw it, a V-shaped dent in the left front fender creasing the fender where the door joined it, binding the metal of the door against the metal of the fender in a large crimp that held the door fast. "Someone must've backed into you while you were inside," I said to her.

She came forward and studied the crimp for a few seconds, and when she looked back at me, she was weeping. "Jesus, Jesus, Jesus!" she wailed, her large, frog-like mouth wide open and wet with spit, her red tongue flopping loosely over gapped teeth. "I can't pay for this! I *can't!*" Her face was red, and even in the dusky light I could see it puff out with weeping, her tiny eyes seeming almost to disappear behind wet cheeks. Her shoulders slumped, and her hands fell limply to her sides.

Placing my briefcase on the ground, I reached out to her and put my arms around her body and held her close to me, while she cried wetly into my shoulder. After a few seconds, she started pulling herself back together and her weeping got reduced to sniffling. Her cowboy hat had been pushed back and now clung to her head at a precarious, absurdly jaunty angle. She took a step away from me and said, "I'll get in the other side."

"Okay," I said almost in a whisper. "That's fine."

Slowly, she walked around the front of the huge, ugly vehicle and opened the door on the passenger's side and slid awkwardly across the seat until she had positioned herself behind the steering wheel. Then she started the motor, which came to life with a roar. The muffler was shot. Without saying another word to me, or even waving, she dropped the car into reverse gear and backed it loudly out of the parking space and headed out the lot to the street.

I turned and started for my car, when I happened to glance toward the door of the bar, and there, staring after me, were the bartender, the two women who had come in with Sarah, and two of the men who had been sitting at the bar. They were lawyers, and I knew them slightly. They were grinning at me. I grinned back and got into my car, and then, without looking at them again, I left the place and drove straight to my apartment.

III

One night several weeks later, Ron meets Sarah at Osgood's, and after buying her three white Russians and drinking three scotches himself, he takes her back to his apartment in his car —a Datsun fastback coupe that she says she admires—for the sole purpose of making love to her.

I'm still the man in this story, and Sarah is still the woman, but I'm telling it this way because what I have to tell you now confuses me, embarrasses me, and makes me sad, and consequently, I'm likely to tell it falsely. I'm likely to cover the truth by making Sarah a better woman than she actually was, while making myself appear worse than I actually was or am; or else I'll do the opposite, make Sarah worse than she was and me better. The truth is, I was pretty, extremely so, and she was not, extremely so, and I knew it and she knew it. She walked out the door of Osgood's determined to make love to a man much prettier than any she had seen up close before, and I walked out determined to make love to a woman much homelier than any I had made love to before. We were, in a sense, equals.

No, that's not exactly true. (You see? This is why I have to tell the story the way I'm telling it.) I'm not at all sure she feels as Ron does. That is to say, perhaps she genuinely likes the man, in spite of his being the most physically attractive man she has ever known. Perhaps she is more aware of her homeliness than of his beauty, just as he is more aware of her homeliness than of his beauty, for Ron, despite what I may have implied, does not think of himself as especially beautiful. He merely knows that other people think of him that way. As I said before, he is a nice man.

Ron unlocks the door to his apartment, walks in ahead of her, and flicks on the lamp beside the couch. It's a small, single bedroom, modern apartment, one of thirty identical apartments in a large brick building on the heights just east of downtown Concord. Sarah stands nervously at the door, peering in.

"Come in, come in," he says.

She steps timidly in and closes the door behind her. She removes her cowboy hat, then quickly puts it back on, crosses the livingroom, and plops down in a blond easy chair, seeming to shrink in its hug out of sight to safety. Ron, behind her, at the entry to the kitchen, places one hand on her shoulder, and she stiffens. He removes his hand.

"Would you like a drink?"

"No . . . I guess not," she says, staring straight ahead at the wall opposite where a large framed photograph of a bicyclist advertises in French the Tour de France. Around a corner, in an alcove off the living room, a silver-gray ten-speed bicycle leans casually against the wall, glistening and poised, slender as a thoroughbred racehorse.

"I don't know," she says. Ron is in the kitchen now, making himself a drink. "I don't know . . . I don't know."

"What? Change your mind? I can make a white Russian for you. Vodka, cream, Kahlúa, and ice, right?"

Sarah tries to cross her legs, but she is sitting too low in the chair and her legs are too thick at the thigh, so she ends, after a struggle, with one leg in the air and the other twisted on its side. She looks as if she has fallen from a great height.

Ron steps out from the kitchen, peers over the back of the chair, and watches her untangle herself, then ducks back into the kitchen. After a few seconds, he returns. "Seriously. Want me to fix you a white Russian?"

"No."

Ron, again from behind, places one hand on Sarah's shoulder, and this time she does not stiffen, though she does not exactly relax, either. She sits there, a block of wood, staring straight ahead.

"Are you scared?" he asks gently. Then he adds, "*I* am."

"Well, no, I'm not scared." She remains silent for a moment. "You're scared? Of what?" She turns to face him but avoids his eyes.

"Well . . . I don't do this all the time, you know. Bring home a woman I . . . ," he trails off.

"Picked up in a bar."

"No. I mean, I like you, Sarah, I really do. And I didn't just pick you up in a bar, you know that. We've gotten to be friends, you and me."

"You want to sleep with me?" she asks, still not meeting his steady gaze.

"Yes." He seems to mean it. He does not take a gulp or even a sip from his drink. He just says, "Yes," straight out, and cleanly, not too quickly, either, and not after a hesitant delay. A simple statement of a simple fact. The man wants to make love to the woman. She asked him, and he told her. What could be simpler?

"Do you want to sleep with *me?*" he asks.

She turns around in the chair, faces the wall again, and says in a low voice, "Sure I do, but . . . it's hard to explain."

"What? But what?" Placing his glass down on the table between the chair and the sofa, he puts both hands on her shoulders and lightly kneads them. He knows he can be discouraged from pursuing this, but he is not sure how easily. Having got this far without bumping against obstacles (except the ones he has placed in his way himself), he is not sure what it will take to turn him back. He does not know, therefore, how assertive or how seductive he should be with her. He suspects that he can be stopped very easily, so he is reluctant to give her a chance to try. He goes on kneading her doughy shoulders.

"You and me . . . we're real different." She glances at the bicycle in the corner.

"A man . . . and a woman," he says.

"No, not that. I mean, different. That's all. Real different. More than you . . . you're nice, but you don't know what I mean, and that's one of the things that makes you so nice. But we're different. Listen," she says, "I gotta go. I gotta leave now."

The man removes his hands and retrieves his glass, takes a sip, and watches her over the rim of the glass, as, not without difficulty, she rises from the chair and moves swiftly toward the door. She stops at the door, squares her hat on her head, and glances back at him.

"We can be friends. Okay?"

"Okay. Friends."

"I'll see you again down at Osgood's, right?"

"Oh, yeah, sure."

"Good. See you," she says, opening the door.

The door closes. The man walks around the sofa, snaps on the television set, and sits down in front of it. He picks up a *TV Guide* from the coffee table and flips through it, stops, runs a finger down the listings, stops, puts down the magazine and changes the channel. He does not once connect the magazine in his hand to the woman who has just left his apartment, even though he knows she spends her days packing *TV Guide*s into cartons that get shipped to warehouses in distant parts of New England. He'll think of the connection some other night; but by then the connection will be merely sentimental. It'll be too late for him to understand what she meant by "different."

IV

But that's not the point of my story. Certainly it's an aspect of the story, the political aspect, if you want, but it's not the reason I'm trying to tell the story in the first place. I'm trying to tell the story so that I can understand what happened between me and Sarah Cole that summer and early autumn ten years ago. To say we were lovers says very little about what happened; to say we were friends says even less. No, if I'm to understand the whole thing, I have to say the whole thing, for, in the end, what I need to know is whether what happened between me and Sarah Cole was right or wrong. Character is fate, which suggests that if a man can know and then to some degree control his character, he can know and to that same degree control his fate.

But let me go on with my story. The next time Sarah and I were together we were at her apartment in the south end of Concord, a second-floor flat in a tenement building on Perley Street. I had stayed away from Osgood's for several weeks, deliberately trying to avoid running into Sarah there, though I never quite put it that way to myself. I found excuses and generated interests in and reasons for going elsewhere after work. Yet I was obsessed with Sarah by then, obsessed with the idea of making love to her, which, because it was not an actual *desire* to make love to her, was an unusually complex obsession. Passion without desire, if it gets expressed, may in fact be a kind of rape, and perhaps I sensed the danger that lay behind my obsession and for that reason went out of my way to avoid meeting Sarah again.

Yet I did meet her, inadvertently, of course. After picking up shirts at the cleaner's on South Main and Perley streets, I'd gone down Perley on my way to South State and the post office. It was a Saturday morning, and this trip on my bicycle was part of my regular Saturday routine. I did not remember that Sarah lived on Perley Street, although she had told me several times in a complaining way—it's a rough neighborhood, packed dirt yards, shabby apartment buildings, the carcasses of old, half-stripped cars on cinderblocks in the driveways, broken red and yellow plastic tricycles on the cracked sidewalks—but as soon as I saw her, I remembered. It was too late to avoid meeting her, I was riding my bike, wearing shorts and tee shirt, the package containing my folded and starched shirts hooked to the carrier behind me, and she was walking toward me along the sidewalk, lugging two large bags of groceries. She saw me, and I stopped. We talked, and I offered to carry her groceries for her. I took the bags while she led the bike, handling it carefully as if she were afraid she might break it.

At the stoop we came to a halt. The wooden steps were cluttered with half-opened garbage bags spilling eggshells, coffee grounds, and old food wrappers to the walkway. "I can't get the people downstairs to take care of their garbage," she explained. She leaned the bike against the banister and reached for her groceries.

"I'll carry them up for you," I said. I directed her to loop the chain lock from the bike to the banister rail and snap it shut and told her to bring my shirts up with her.

"Maybe you'd like a beer?" she said as she opened the door to the darkened hallway. Narrow stairs disappeared in front of me into heavy, damp darkness, and the air smelled like old newspapers.

"Sure," I said and followed her up.

"Sorry there's no light. I can't get them to fix it."

"No matter, I can see you and follow along," I said, and even in the dim light of the hall I could see the large, dark blue veins that cascaded thickly down the backs of her legs. She wore tight, white-duck bermuda shorts, rubber shower sandals, and a pink sleeveless sweater. I pictured her in the cashier's line at the supermarket. I would have been behind her, a stranger, and on seeing her, I would have turned away and studied the covers of the magazines, *TV Guide, People, The National Enquirer,* for there was nothing of interest in her appearance that in the hard light of day would not have slightly embarrassed me. Yet here I was inviting myself into her home, eagerly staring at the backs of her ravaged legs, her sad, tasteless clothing, her poverty. I was not detached, however, was not staring at her with scientific curiosity, and because of my passion, did not feel or believe that what I was doing was perverse. I felt warmed by her presence and was flirtatious and bold, a little pushy, even.

Picture this. The man, tanned, limber, wearing red jogging shorts, Italian leather sandals, a clinging net tee shirt of Scandinavian design and manufacture, enters the apartment behind the woman, whose dough-colored skin, thick, short body, and homely, uncomfortable face all try, but fail, to hide themselves. She waves him toward the table in the kitchen, where he sets down the bags and looks good-naturedly around the room. "What about the beer you bribed me with?" he asks. The apartment is dark and cluttered with old, oversized furniture, yard sale and second-hand stuff bought originally for a large house in the country or a spacious apartment on a boulevard forty or fifty years ago, passed down from antique dealer to used furniture store to yard sale to thrift shop, where it finally gets purchased by Sarah Cole and gets lugged over to Perley Street and shoved up the narrow stairs, she and her children grunting and sweating in the darkness of the hallway—overstuffed armchairs and couch, huge, ungainly dressers, upholstered rocking chairs, and in the kitchen, an old maple desk for a table, a half dozen heavy oak diningroom chairs, a high, glass-fronted cabinet, all peeling, stained, chipped and squatting heavily on a dark green linoleum floor.

The place is neat and arranged in a more or less orderly way, however, and the man seems comfortable there. He strolls from the kitchen to the livingroom and peeks into the three small bedrooms that branch off a hallway behind the livingroom. "Nice place!" he calls to the woman. He is studying the framed pictures of her three children arranged like an altar atop the buffet. "Nice-looking kids!" he calls out. They are. Blond, round-faced, clean, and utterly ordinary-looking, their pleasant faces glance, as instructed, slightly off camera and down to the right, as if they are trying to remember the name of the capital of Montana.

When he returns to the kitchen, the woman is putting away her groceries, her back to him. "Where's that beer you bribed me with?" he asks again. He takes a position against the doorframe, his weight on one hip, like a dancer resting. "You sure are quiet today, Sarah," he says in a low voice. "Everything okay?"

Silently, she turns away from the grocery bags, crosses the room to the man, reaches up to him, and holding him by the head, kisses his mouth, rolls her torso against his, drops her hands to his hips and yanks him tightly to her, and goes on kissing him, eyes closed, working her face furiously against his. The man places his hands on her shoulders and pulls away, and they face each other, wide-eyed, as if amazed and frightened. The man drops his hands, and the woman lets go of his hips. Then, after a few seconds, the man silently turns, goes to the door, and leaves. The last thing he sees as he closes the door behind him is the woman standing in the kitchen doorframe, her face looking down and slightly to one side, wearing the same pleasant expression on her face as her children in their photographs, trying to remember the capital of Montana.

V

Sarah appeared at my apartment door the following morning, a Sunday, cool and rainy. She had brought me the package of freshly laundered shirts I'd left in her kitchen, and when I opened the door to her, she simply held the package out to me as if it were a penitent's gift. She wore a yellow rain slicker and cap and looked more like a disconsolate schoolgirl facing an angry teacher than a grown woman dropping a package off at a friend's apartment. After all, she had nothing to be ashamed of.

I invited her inside, and she accepted my invitation. I had been reading the Sunday *New York Times* on the couch and drinking coffee, lounging through the gray morning in bathrobe and pajamas. I told her to take off her wet raincoat and hat and hang them in the closet by the door and started for the kitchen to get her a cup of coffee, when I stopped, turned, and looked at her. She closed the closet door on her yellow raincoat and hat, turned around, and faced me.

What else can I do? I must describe it. I remember that moment of ten years ago as if it occurred ten minutes ago, the package of shirts on the table behind her, the newspapers scattered over the couch and floor, the sound of windblown rain washing the sides of the building outside, and the silence of the room, as we stood across from one another and watched, while we each simultaneously removed our own clothing, my robe, her blouse and skirt, my pajama top, her slip and bra, my pajama bottom, her underpants, until we were both standing naked in the harsh, gray light, two naked members of the same species, a male and a female, the male somewhat younger and less scarred than the female, the female somewhat less delicately constructed than the male, both individuals pale-skinned with dark thatches of hair in the area of their genitals, both individuals standing slackly, as if a great, protracted tension between them had at last been released.

VI

We made love that morning in my bed for long hours that drifted easily into afternoon. And we talked, as people usually do when they spend half a day or half a night in bed together. I told her of my past, named and described the people I had loved and had loved me, my ex-wife in New York, my brother in the Air Force, my father and mother in their condominium in Florida, and I told her of my ambitions and dreams and even confessed some of my fears. She listened patiently and intelligently throughout and talked much less than I. She had already told me many of these things about herself, and perhaps whatever she had to say to me now lay on the next inner circle of intimacy or else could not be spoken of at all.

During the next few weeks we met and made love often and always at my apartment. On arriving home from work, I would phone her, or if not, she would phone me, and after a few feints and dodges, one would suggest to the other that we get together tonight, and a half hour later she'd be at my door. Our lovemaking was passionate, skillful, kindly, and deeply satisfying. We didn't often speak of it to one another or brag about it, the way some couples do when they are surprised by the ease with which they have become contented lovers. We did occasionally joke and tease each other, however, playfully acknowledging that the only thing we did together was make love but that we did it so frequently there was no time for anything else.

Then one hot night, a Saturday in August, we were lying in bed atop the tangled sheets, smoking cigarettes and chatting idly, and Sarah suggested that we go out for a drink.

"Now?"

"Sure. It's early. What time is it?"

I scanned the digital clock next to the bed. "Nine forty-nine."

"There. See?"

"That's not so early. You usually go home by eleven, you know. It's almost ten."

"No, it's only a little after nine. Depends on how you look at things. Besides, Ron, it's Saturday night. Don't you want to go out and dance or something? Or is this the only thing you know how to do?" she teased and poked me in the ribs. "You know how to dance? You like to dance?"

"Yeah, sure . . . sure, but not tonight. It's too hot. And I'm tired."

But she persisted, happily pointing out that an air-conditioned bar would be cooler than my apartment, and we didn't have to go to a dance bar, we could go to Osgood's. "As a compromise," she said.

I suggested a place called the El Rancho, a restaurant with a large, dark cocktail lounge and dance bar located several miles from town on the old Portsmouth highway. Around nine the restaurant closed and the bar became something of a roadhouse, with a small country-western houseband and a clientele drawn from the four or five villages that adjoined Concord on the north and east. I had eaten at the restaurant once but had never gone to the bar, and I didn't know anyone who had.

Sarah was silent for a moment. Then she lit a cigarette and drew the sheet over her naked body. "You don't want anybody to know about us, do you? Do you?"

"That's not it . . . I just don't like gossip, and I work with a lot of people who show up sometimes at Osgood's. On a Saturday night especially."

"No," she said firmly. "You're ashamed of being seen with me. You'll sleep with me, but you won't go out in public with me."

"That's not true, Sarah."

She was silent again. Relieved, I reached across her to the bedtable and got my cigarettes and lighter.

"You owe me, Ron," she said suddenly, as I passed over her. "You owe me."

"What?" I lay back, lit a cigarette, and covered my body with the sheet.

"I said, 'You owe me.' "

"I don't know what you're talking about, Sarah. I just don't like a lot of gossip going around, that's all. I like keeping my private life private, that's all. I don't *owe* you anything."

"Friendship you owe me. And respect. Friendship and respect. A person can't do what you've done with me without owing them friendship and respect."

"Sarah, I really don't know what you're talking about," I said. "I am your friend, you know that. And I respect you. I really do."

"You really think so, don't you?"

"Yes."

She said nothing for several long moments. Then she sighed and in a low, almost inaudible voice said, "Then you'll have to go out in public with me. I don't care about Osgood's or the people you work with, we don't have to go there or see any of them," she said. "But you're gonna have to go to places like the El Rancho with me, and a few other places I know, too, where there's people *I* work with, people *I* know, and maybe we'll even go to a couple of parties, because *I* get invited to parties sometimes, you know. I have friends, and I have some family, too, and you're gonna have to meet my family. My kids think I'm just going around bar-hopping when I'm over here with you, and I don't like that, so you're gonna have to meet them so I can tell them where I am when I'm not at home nights. And sometimes you're gonna come over and spend the evening at my place!" Her voice had risen as she heard her demands and felt their rightness, until now she was almost shouting at me. "You *owe* that to me. Or else you're a bad man. It's that simple."

It was.

VII

The handsome man is over-dressed. He is wearing a navy blue blazer, taupe shirt open at the throat, white slacks, white loafers. Everyone else, including the homely woman with the handsome man, is dressed appropriately, dressed, that is, like everyone else—jeans and cowboy boots, blouses or cowboy shirts or tee shirts with catchy sayings printed across the front, and many of the women are wearing cowboy hats pushed back and tied under their chins. The man doesn't know anyone at the bar or, if they're at a party, in the room, but the woman knows most of the people there, and she gladly introduces him. The men grin and shake his hand, slap him on his jacketed shoulder, ask him where he works, what's his line, after which they lapse into silence. The women flirt briefly with their faces, but they lapse into silence even before the men do. The woman with the man in the blazer does most of the talking for everyone. She talks for the man in the blazer, for the men standing around the refrigerator, or if they're at a bar, for the other men at the table, and for the other women, too. She chats and rambles aimlessly through loud monologues, laughs uproariously at trivial jokes, and drinks too much, until soon she is drunk, thick-tongued, clumsy, and the man has to say her goodbyes and ease her out the door to his car and drive her home to her apartment on Perley Street.

This happens twice in one week, and then three times the next—at the El Rancho, at the Ox Bow in Northwood, at Rita's and Jimmy's apartment on Thorndike Street, out in Warner at Betsy Beeler's new house, and, the last time, at a cottage on Lake Sunapee rented by some kids in shipping at Rumford Press. Ron no longer calls Sarah when he gets home from work; he waits for her call, and sometimes, when he knows it's she, he doesn't answer the phone. Usually, he lets it ring five or six times, and then he reaches down and picks up the receiver. He has taken his jacket and vest off and loosened his tie and is about to put supper, frozen manicotti, into the Radarange.

"Hello?"

"*Hi.*"

"How're you doing?"

"*Okay, I guess. A little tired.*"

"Still hung over?"

"*No. Not really. Just tired. I hate Mondays.*"

"You have fun last night?"

"*Well, yeah, sorta. It's nice out there, at the lake. Listen,*" she says, brightening. "*Whyn't you come over here tonight? The kids're all going out later, but if you come over before eight, you can meet them. They really want to meet you.*"

"You told them about me?"

"*Sure. Long time ago. I'm not supposed to tell my own kids?*"

Ron is silent.

"*You don't want to come over here tonight. You don't want to meet my kids. No, you don't want my kids to meet you, that's it.*"

"No, no, it's just . . . I've got a lot of work to do . . ."

"*We should talk,*" she announces in a flat voice.

"Yes," he says, "we should talk."

They agree that she will meet him at his apartment, and they'll talk, and they say goodbye and hang up.

While Ron is heating his supper and then eating alone at his kitchen table and Sarah is feeding her children, perhaps I should admit, since we are nearing the end of my story, that I don't actually know that Sarah Cole is dead. A few years ago I happened to run into one of her friends from the press, a blond woman with an underslung jaw. Her name, she reminded me, was Glenda; she had seen me at Osgood's a couple of times, and we had met at the El Rancho once when I had gone there with Sarah. I was amazed that she could remember me and a little embarrassed that I did not recognize her at all, and she laughed at that and said, "You haven't changed much, mister!" I pretended to recognize her, but I think she knew she was a stranger to me. We were standing outside the Sears store on South Main Street, where I had gone to buy paint. I had recently remarried, and my wife and I were redecorating my apartment.

"Whatever happened to Sarah?" I asked Glenda. "Is she still down at the press?"

"Jeez, no! She left a long time ago. Way back. I heard she went back with her ex-husband. I can't remember his name. Something Cole."

I asked her if she was sure of that, and she said no, she had only heard it around the bars and down at the press, but she had assumed it was true. People said Sarah had moved back with her ex-husband and was living in a trailer in a park near Hooksett, and the whole family had moved down to Florida that winter because he was out of work. He was a carpenter, she said.

"I thought he was mean to her. I thought he beat her up and everything. I thought she hated him," I said.

"Oh, well, yeah, he was a bastard, all right. I met him a couple of times, and I didn't like him. Short, ugly, and mean when he got drunk. But you know what they say."

"What do they say?"

"Oh, you know, about water seeking its own level."

"Sarah wasn't mean when she was drunk."

The woman laughed. "Naw, but she sure was short and ugly!"

I said nothing.

"Hey, don't get me wrong, I liked Sarah. But you and her . . . well, you sure made a funny-looking couple. She probably didn't feel so self-conscious and all with her husband," the woman said seriously. "I mean, with you . . . all tall and blond, and poor old Sarah . . . I mean, the way them kids in the press room used to kid her about her looks, it was embarrassing just to hear it."

"Well . . . I loved her," I said.

The woman raised her plucked eyebrows in disbelief. She smiled. "Sure, you did, honey," she said, and she patted me on the arm. "Sure, you did." Then she let the smile drift off her face, turned and walked away.

When someone you have loved dies, you accept the fact of his or her death, but then the person goes on living in your memory, dreams, and reveries. You have imaginary conversations with him or her, you see something striking and remind yourself to tell your loved one about it and then get brought up short by the knowledge of the fact of his or her death, and at night, in your sleep, the dead person visits you. With Sarah, none of that happened. When she was gone from my life, she was gone absolutely, as if she had never existed in the first place. It was only later, when I could think of her as dead and could come out and say it, my friend Sarah Cole is dead, that I was able to tell this story, for that is when she began to enter my memories, my dreams, and my reveries. In that way I learned that I truly did love her, and now I have begun to grieve over her death, to wish her alive again, so that I can say to her the things I could not know or say when she was alive, when I did not know that I loved her.

VIII

The woman arrives at Ron's apartment around eight. He hears her car, because of the broken muffler, blat and rumble into the parking lot below, and he crosses quickly from the kitchen and peers out the livingroom window and, as if through a telescope, watches her shove herself across the seat to the passenger's side to get out of the car, then walk slowly in the dusky light toward the apartment building. It's a warm evening, and she's wearing her white bermuda shorts, pink sleeveless sweater, and shower sandals. Ron hates those clothes. He hates the way the shorts cut into her flesh at the crotch and thigh, hates the large, dark caves below her arms that get exposed by the sweater, hates the flapping noise made by the sandals.

Shortly, there is a soft knock at his door. He opens it, turns away and crosses to the kitchen, where he turns back, lights a cigarette, and watches her. She closes the door. He offers her a drink, which she declines, and somewhat formally, he invites her to sit down. She sits carefully on the sofa, in the middle, with her feet close together on the floor, as if she were being interviewed for a job. Then he comes around and sits in the easy chair, relaxed, one leg slung over the other at the knee, as if he were interviewing her for the job.

"Well," he says, "you wanted to talk."

"Yes. But now you're mad at me. I can see that. I didn't do anything, Ron."

"I'm not mad at you."

They are silent for a moment. Ron goes on smoking his cigarette.

Finally, she sighs and says, "You don't want to see me anymore, do you?"

He waits a few seconds and answers, "Yes. That's right." Getting up from the chair, he walks to the silver-gray bicycle and stands before it, running a fingertip along the slender cross-bar from the saddle to the chrome-plated handlebars.

"You're a son of a bitch," she says in a low voice. "You're worse than my ex-husband." Then she smiles meanly, almost sneers, and soon he realizes that she is telling him that she won't leave. He's stuck with her, she informs him with cold precision. "You think I'm just so much meat, and all you got to do is call up the butcher shop and cancel your order. Well, now you're going to find out different. You *can't* cancel your order. I'm not meat, I'm not one of your pretty little girlfriends who come running when you want them and go away when you get tired of them. I'm *different.* I got nothing to lose, Ron. Nothing. You're stuck with me, Ron."

He continues stroking his bicycle. "No, I'm not."

She sits back in the couch and crosses her legs at the ankles. "I think I *will* have that drink you offered."

"Look, Sarah, it would be better if you go now."

"No," she says flatly. "You offered me a drink when I came in. Nothing's changed since I've been here. Not for me, and not for you. I'd like that drink you offered," she says haughtily.

Ron turns away from the bicycle and takes a step toward her. His face has stiffened into a mask. "Enough is enough," he says through clenched teeth. "I've given you enough."

"Fix me a drink, will you, honey?" she says with a phony smile.

Ron orders her to leave.

She refuses.

He grabs her by the arm and yanks her to her feet.

She starts crying lightly. She stands there and looks up into his face and weeps, but she does not move toward the door, so he pushes her. She regains her balance and goes on weeping.

He stands back and places his fists on his hips and looks at her. "Go on and leave, you ugly bitch," he says to her, and as he says the words, as one by one they leave his mouth, she's transformed into the most beautiful woman he has ever seen. He says the words again, almost tenderly. "Leave, you ugly bitch." Her hair is golden, her brown eyes deep and sad, her mouth full and affectionate, her tears the tears of love and loss, and her pleading, outstretched arms, her entire body, the arms and body of a devoted woman's cruelly rejected love. A third time he says the words. "Leave me, you disgusting, ugly bitch." She is wrapped in an envelope of golden light, a warm, dense haze that she seems to have stepped into, as into a carriage. And then she is gone, and he is alone again.

He looks around the room, as if searching for her. Sitting down in the easy chair, he places his face in his hands. It's not as if she has died; it's as if he has killed her.

JOHN BARTH

Click

JOHN BARTH (1930–) is the author of nine novels as well as a series of short fictions, a volume of novellas, and two collections of nonfiction. His works *The Floating Opera* and *Lost in the Funhouse* were finalists for the National Book Award in fiction; his *Chimera* won that award in 1973. Most recently his fiction has won the F. Scott Fitzgerald Award, the Lannan Foundation Lifetime Achievement Award, and the PEN/Malamud Award for Excellence in the Short Story. He is Professor Emeritus in the Writing Seminars at Johns Hopkins University.

"Click?"

So (sans question mark) reads the computer monitor when, in time, "Fred" and "Irma" haul themselves out of bed, wash up a bit, slip back into their undies, and—still nuzzling, patting, chuckling, sighing—go to check their E-mail on Fred's already booted up machine. Just that single uppercase imperative verb or sound-noun floating midscreen, where normally the desktop would appear, with its icons of their several files: HERS, HIS, SYSTEM, APPLICATIONS, FINANCES, HOUSE STUFF, INTERNET, and ETC (their catchall file). Surprised Irma, having pressed a key to disperse the screen-saver program and repeated aloud the word that oddly then appeared, calls Fred over to check it out, but the house cybercoach is as puzzled thereby as she. Since the thing's onscreen, however, and framed in a bordered box, they take it to be a command or an invitation—anyhow an option button, like SAVE or CANCEL, not merely the name of the sound that their computer mouse makes when . . . well, when clicked.

So they click (Irm does) on <u>Click</u>, and up comes a familiar title, or in this case maybe subtitle—<u>The</u> <u>Hypertextuality</u> <u>of</u> <u>Everyday</u> <u>Life</u>—followed this time by a parenthesized instruction: (*Click on any word of the above*).

"Your turn," declares our Irma. That's not the woman's real name, any more than the man's is Fred; those are their "online" names, in a manner of speaking, for reasons presently to be made clear. Never mind, just now, their "real" names: they would involve us in too much background, personal history, all the things that real names import; we would never get on with the story. Sufficient to say that although these two are unmarried, they're coupled housemates of some years' standing, a pair of Baby Boomer TINKs ("two incomes, no kids") of some ethnicity or other, not necessarily the same, and profession ditto—but never mind those either. Sufficient to say that what they've just rolled out of the sack from (one of them perhaps more reluctantly than the other) is an extended session of makeup sex after an extended lovers' quarrel, the most serious of their coupleship—a quarrel currently truced but by no means yet resolved and maybe inherently unresolvable, although they're really working on it, fingers crossed.

A bit of background here, perhaps? That's Fred's uncharacteristic suggestion, to which Irma, uncharacteristically, forces herself to reply, "Nope: Your turn is your turn. On with the story."

And so her friend—partner, mate, whatever—reaches from behind her to the mouse and, kissing her (glossy walnut) hair, clicks on <u>Hypertextuality</u>. (This parenthesized matter, they agree, is stuff that might be left out of or cut from The Fred and Irma Story—see below—but that they've agreed to leave in, at least for the present.) (In the opinion of one of them, there could be much more of it.) (In the opinion of the other, much less—but never mind.)

No surprise, Fred's selection: <u>Hypertextuality</u> is that (sub)title's obvious topic word, modified by the innocuous-seeming article before it and the homely prepositional phrase after (containing its own unexotic substantive [<u>Life</u>] with adjectival modifier [<u>Everyday</u>]). This man, one infers correctly, is the sort who gets right down to business, to the meat of the matter. Everybody knows, after all (or believes that he or she knows), what "everyday life" is, different as may be the everyday lives of, say, Kuwaiti oil sheikhs and American felons serving life sentences in maximum-security prisons without possibility of parole (different, for that matter, as may be the everyday lives of FWFs ["friends who fornicate"] when they're at their separate businesses between F'ly Fs). The term "hypertextuality" itself may or may not interest our Fred; he's computer-knowledgeable but not computer-addicted. The phrase "everyday life," however, most certainly doesn't in itself interest him. The fellow's too busy *leading* (perhaps being led by?) his everyday life to be attracted to it as a subject. With the woman it's another story (possibly to come). But precisely because he hasn't associated something as fancy-sounding as "hypertextuality" with something as ordinary as "everyday life," the juxtaposition of the two piques Fred's curiosity. Not impossibly, for the man's no ignoramus (nor is his companion), he hears in it an echo of Sigmund Freud's provocatively titled

1904 essay "The Psychopathology of Everyday Life." Everyday life psychopathological? (Try asking Irma, Fred.) (He will—another time.) Everyday life hypertextual? How so? In what sense? To find out, Fred has clicked on the implied proposition's most prominent but least certain term.

Some (the computer script now declares in effect, along with much of the paragraph above) out of mere orneriness will select one of the phrase's apparently insignificant elements—the The, for example, or the of—as if to say "Gotcha! You said 'Click on any word' . . ." The joke, however, if any, is on them: A good desk dictionary will list at least eight several senses of the homely word "the" in its adjectival function, plus a ninth in its adverbial ("the sooner the better," etc.)—twenty lines of fine-print definition in all, whereas the comparatively technical term just after it, "theanthropic," is nailed down in a mere three and a half. As for "of": no fewer than nineteen several definitions, in twenty-five lines of text, whereas the fancy word "oeuvre," just before it, is dispatched in a line and a half. Try "as," Fred, as in "As for 'of' "; try "for," Irm, or "or": the "simple" words you'll find hardest to define, whereas such technoglossy ones as "hypertextuality" . . .

Well, F and friend have just been shown an example of it, no? The further texts that lie behind any presenting text. Look up (that is, click on) the innocent word "of," and you get a couple hundred words of explanation. Click on any one of those or any one of their several phrases and clauses, such as "phrases and clauses," and get hundreds more. Click on any of *those,* etc. etc.—until, given time and clicks enough, you will have "accessed" virtually the sum of language, the entire expressible world. That's "hypertext," guys, in the sense meant here (there are other senses: see Hypertext): not the literal menus-of-menus and texts-behind-texts that one finds on CD-ROMs and other computer applications but rather the all-but-infinite array of potential explanations, illustrations, associations, glosses and exempla, even stories, that may be said to lie not only behind any verbal formulation but also behind any real-world image, scene, action, interaction. Enough said?

(If so, click on EXIT; *otherwise select any one of the four foregoing—image, scene, etc.—for further amplification.)*

Restless Fred moves to click on action but defers to Irma (their joint mood is, as mentioned, still tentative just now: he's being more deferential than is his wont), who clicks on scene and sees what the Author/Narrator sees as he pens this: a (white adult male right) hand moving a (black MontBlanc Meisterstück 146 fountain) pen (left to right) across the (blue) lines of (three-ring loose-leaf) paper in a (battered old) binder on a (large wooden former grade-school) worktable all but covered with implements and detritus of the writer's trade. (Parenthesized elements in this case = amplifications that might indeed be cut but might instead well be "hypertexted" behind the bare-bones description, to be accessed on demand, just as yet further amplifications [not given, but perhaps hypertexted] might lie behind "white," "adult male," "MontBlanc," "Meisterstück," etc.) For example, to mention only some of the more conspicuous items: miscellaneous printed and manuscript pages, (thermal) coffee mug (of a certain design) on (cork) coaster, (annotated) desk calendar (displaying MAY), notebooks and notepads, the aforeconsulted (*American Heritage*) desk dictionary open to the "the" page (1,333) on its (intricately hand-carved Indian) table stand, (Panasonic autostop electric) pencil sharpener (in need of emptying), (Sunbeam digital) clock (reading 9:47 A.M.), (AT&T 5500 cordless) telephone (in place on base unit), Kleenex box (ScotTissue, actually) half full (half empty?) . . . etc. Beyond the table is the workroom's farther wall: two (curtained and venetian-blinded double-hung) windows, between them a (three-shelf) bookcase (not quite filled with books, framed photos, and knickknacks and) topped by a wall mirror. The mirror (left of center) gives back a view not of the viewer—fortunately, or we'd never get out of the loop and on with the story—but of the workroom door (now closed against interruption) in the wall behind. (The two windows are closed, their figured curtains tied back, their blinds raised. Through them one sees first the green tops of foundation shrubbery [from which Irm infers, correctly, that the room is on the ground floor], and then assorted trees [L] and a sward of lawn [R] in the middle distance, beyond which lies a substantial body of [currently gray] water. Two [wooded] points of land can be seen extending into this waterway from the right-hand window's right-hand side, the first perhaps half a mile distant, an [uncamouflaged] goose blind at its outer end, the second perhaps a mile distant and all but obscured now by a light drizzle that also blurs the yet-more-distant horizontal where [gray] water meets [gray] sky.)

(Click on any of these items, including those in brackets.)

But "Enough already," says nudgy Fred, and he commandeers the mouse to click on <u>action</u>, whereupon some of the leaves on some of those trees move slightly in some breeze from some direction, the water surface ripples, and across it a large waterfowl flaps languidly left to right, just clearing some sort of orange marker-float out there on his or her way . . . upstream, one reasonably supposes, given that the stretch beyond that bird and those two points seems to be open water.

"That's action?" Fred scoffs, and moves to click again, but determined Irma stays his mouse-hand with her free right (Irm's a southpaw) while she registers yet a few further details. Atop that bookcase, for example (and therefore doubled in the mirror), are (L to R:) a (ceramic-based) lamp, the carapace of a (medium-size horseshoe) crab, and a (Lucite-box-framed) photograph of three (well-dressed) people (L to R: an elderly man, a middle-aged man, and a younger woman) in (animated) conversation (at some sort of social function).

(*Click on any detail, parenthesized or non-, in this scene.*)

Irma springs for well-dressed—not nearly specific enough, by her lights, as a description of three people "at some sort of social function" (!) in the photograph on the bookcase in the not yet fully identified scene on their computer's video-display terminal. With a really quite commendable effort of will, Fred restrains his impulse to utter some exasperated imprecation and snatch the freaking mouse from his freaking partner to freaking click on Fast Freaking Forward, On With the Story, EXIT, QUIT, Whatever. Instead he busses again his lover's (glossy) (walnut) hair, bids her "Have fun; I'll be futzing around outside, okay?" and (having slipped into jeans and T-shirt) clicks with his feet, so to speak, on the scene beyond his own workroom window.

Which twilit scene happens to be a small suburban back yard near the edge of the nation's troubled capital city, where this occasionally dysfunctional pair pursue their separate occupations: Mark the Expediter, as he has lately come to call himself; Valerie the Enhancer, ditto. Those are their "real" given names, if not really the real names of their jobs, and with the reader's permission (because all these digressions, suspensions, parentheses, and brackets are setting this Narrator's teeth on edge as well as Mark's) we'll just follow him out there for a bit while Val explores to her still-bruised heart's content the hypertextuality of everyday life.

Okay. How they got into that "Fred and Irma" business (Mark and I can reconstruct less distractedly now, as he waves to a neighbor lady and idly deadheads a few finished rhododendron blooms along their open side porch) was as follows: They having pretty well burned out, through this late-May Sunday, their scorching quarrel of the day before (enough, anyhow, to make and eat together a weary but entirely civil dinner), after cleanup Mark volunteered to show Valerie, as he had several times previously promised, some things he'd lately learned about accessing the Internet for purposes other than E-mail: more specifically, about navigating the World Wide Web (WWW), and in particular (Valerie being Valerie, Mark Mark) about the deployment of "bookmarks" as shortcuts through that electronic labyrinth, the black hole of leisure and very antidote to spare time. Mark is, as aforenoted, no computer freak; the PC in his Expediter's office, their Macintosh at home, are tools, not toys, more versatile than fax machine and phone but more time-expensive, too, and—like dictionaries, encyclopedias, and hardware stores (this last in Mark's case; substitute department stores and supermarkets in Val's)—easier to get into than out of. Tactfully, tactfully (by his lights, anyhow) (the only lights he can finally steer by)—for they really were and still are burned, and their armistice is as fragile as it is heartfelt—he led her through the flashy home page of their Web-server program, actually encouraging her to sidetrack here and there in the What's New? and What's Cool? departments (she trying just as determinedly to blind her peripheral vision, as it were, and walk straight down the aisles, as it were, of those enticing menus) and then sampling a curious Web site that he had "bookmarked" two days earlier, before their disastrous Saturday excursion to the National Aquarium, in Baltimore.

http://www.epiphs.art, it was addressed: the home page of an anonymous oddball (Net-named "CNG") who offered a shifting menu of what he or she called "electronic epiphanies," or "E-piphs." On the Friday, that menu had comprised three entrées: 1) Infinite Regression v. All but Interminable Digression, 2) "Flower in the Crannied Wall," and 3) The Hypertextuality of Everyday Life. Mark had clicked on the curious-sounding second option and downloaded a spiel that at first interested but soon bored him, having to do with the relation between a short poem by Tennyson—

Flower in the crannied wall,
I pluck you out of the crannies.
I hold you here, root and all, in my hand.
Little flower—but *if* I could understand
What you are, root and all, and all in all,
I should know what God and man is.

—and the virtually endless reticulations of the World Wide Web. This time (that is, on this postmeridianal, postprandial, post-quarrel but ante-makeup-sexual Sunday) the menu read 1) The Coastline Measurement Problem and the Web, 2) "The Marquise went out at five" (CNG seemed to favor quotations as second entries; this one was familiar to neither of our characters), and 3) The Hypertextuality of Everyday Life. That third item being the only carry-over, M suggested they see what it was. V clicked on it—the entire title, as no option was then offered to select from among its component terms—and they found themselves involved in a bit of interactive "E-fiction" called "Fred and Irma Go Shopping," of which I'll make the same short work that they did.

Onscreen the underlined items were "hot"—that is, highlighted as hypertext links to be clicked on as the interacting reader chose. Methodical Mark would have started with Fred and worked his way L to R, but Valerie, left-handing the mouse, went straight for Irma:

> Irma V., 43, art-school graduate, divorced, no children, currently employed as enhancer by small but thriving graphics firm in Annapolis MD while preparing show of her own computer-inspired fractal art for small but well-regarded gallery in Baltimore. Commutes to work from modest but comfortable and

well-appointed rowhouse in latter city's Bolton Hill neighborhood, 2 doors up from her latest lover, Fred M.

(more on Irma) (on with story)

"My turn?" Mark had asked at this point, and clicked on Fred M. before Valerie could choose from among divorced, no children, enhancer, well-appointed rowhouse, latest, and more.

Fred M., software expediter and current lover of Irma V.

(more on Fred) (on with story)

"That's the ticket," in Mark's opinion: "Who cares how old the stud is or where he majored in what? On with their story already."

"My friend the Expediter," Val had murmured warningly, having raised her free hand at his "Who cares?" Whereat her friend the Expediter (it was from here that they borrowed those job titles for themselves; Valerie in fact does interior design and decoration for a suburban D.C. housing developer; Mark, a not yet-successful novelist, writes capsule texts on everything under the sun for a CD-ROM operation in College Park, distilling masses of info into style-free paragraphs of a couple hundred words), duly warned, had replied, "Sorry there: Enhance, enhance."

But she had humored him by clicking on on, whereupon the title reappeared with only its last term now highlighted: "Fred and Irma Go Shopping."

"Off we go," had invited M. But when the clicked link called up a three-option menu—Department Store, Supermarket, Other—V had said "Uh-oh," and even Mark had recognized the too-perilous analogy to their debacle of the day before. Expediter and Enhancer in Supermarket, he with grocery list in one hand, pencil in other, and eye on watch, she already examining the (unlisted) radicchio and improvising new menu plans down the line . . .

"Unh-unh," he had agreed, and kissed her mouse-hand, then her mouth, then her throat. By unspoken agreement, bedward they'd headed, leaving the Mac to its screen-saver program (tropical fish, with bubbly sound effects). Somewhile later Valerie/Irma, re-undied, had returned to check for E-mail; the marine fauna dispersed into cyberspace; there floated Click in place of CNG's unpursued interactive E-tale—and here we all are.

Rather, here's Valerie at Mark's workstation in their (detached suburban) house (V's studio is across the hall; unlike those FWFs Irma and Fred, our couple are committed [though unsanctified and unlegalized] life partners, each with half equity in their jointly owned [commodious, well-appointed, 1960s-vintage] split-level in Silver Spring [MD]), and here are Mark and I, out on the dusky porch, deadheading the rhodos while thinking hard and more or less in sync about certain similarities among 1) the sore subject of their Saturday set-to, 2) a certain aspect of their recent makeup sex, 3) the so-called Coastline Measurement Problem aforeoptioned by CNG, 4) an analogous problem or aspect of storytelling, and 5) how it is, after all, to be a self, not on the World Wide Web but in the wide web of the world. Can M think hard about five things at once? He can, more or less expeditiously, when his attention's engaged, plus 6) Zeno's famous paradox of Achilles and the Tortoise, plus 7) the difference between Socrates' trances and the Buddha's. Our chap is nothing if not efficient—a phrase worth pondering—and I'm enhancing his efficiency as worst I can, by impeding it. Valerie, meanwhile (at my offscreen prodding), has reluctantly torn her attention away from that photograph on that bookshelf in that creekside scriptorium in that onscreen scene hypertexted behind the word "scene" in the definition hypertexted behind Hypertextuality in CNG's menu option 3) The Hypertextuality of Everyday Life, itself hypertexted the second time up behind the word Click. The twenty-year-old wedding-reception photo, she has learned it is, of (present) Narrator with (present) wife and (late) father at (post-)wedding do for (now divorced) daughter and (then) new son-in-law—and nothing accessible beyond. Interactivity is one thing, restless reader; prying's another. Having lingered briefly on the shrub outside the RH window (*Viburnum burkwoodii:* grows to 6 ft [but here cropped to 4 for the sake of view and ventilation], clusters 3 in. wide, blooms in spring, zone 4, and it's a lucky wonder her professional eye didn't fix on those figured curtains, or we'd never have gotten her outside) and then on that waterfowl (Great Blue Heron [*Ardea herodias,* not *Coerulea*]) flapping languidly up-creek (west fork of Langford, off the Chester River, off Chesapeake Bay, on Maryland's Eastern Shore, where Narrator pens these words as he has penned many others), she's "progressing" unhurriedly toward those two intriguing points of land in the farther distance but can't resist clicking en route on that orange marker-float out yonder near the creek channel.

> Marks an eel pot, 1 of 50 deployed in this particular tidal creek at this particular season by waterman Travis Pritchett of nearby Rock Hall MD in pursuit, so to speak, of "elvers": young eels born thousands of miles hence in the Sargasso Sea and now thronging instinctively back to the very same freshwater tributaries of the Chesapeake from which their parents migrated several years earlier to spawn them in midocean: one of nature's most mysterious and powerful reproductive phenomena. The eels among Pritchett's catch will be processed locally for marketing either as seafood in Europe and Japan or as crab bait for Chesapeake watermen later in the season.

Travel-loving Val goes for Sargasso Sea, and there we'll leave her to circulate indefinitely with the spawning eels and other denizens of the Sargassum while we click on item 1) some distance above: the sore subject of their Saturday set-to.

They love and cherish each other, this pair. Although neither is a physical knockout, each regards the other and her- or him-self as satisfactorily attractive in face and form. Although neither can be called outstanding in his or her profession, both are entirely competent, and neither is particularly career-ambitious in her or his salaried job. Both enjoy their work and take an interest in their partner's. Most important, perhaps, although neither has a history of successful long-term relations with significant others, both have enough experience, insight, and humility to have smoothed their rougher edges, tempered their temperaments, developed their reciprocal forbearance, and in general recognized that at their ages and stages neither is likely to do better than he or she has currently done in the mate-finding way; indeed, that despite their sundry differences (at least some of which they've learned to regard as compensations for each other's shortcomings: see below), they are fortunately well matched in disposition, taste, and values. Neither drinks more than an occasional glass of wine at dinner, or smokes tobacco, or sleeps around, or fancies house pets; both are borderline vegetarian, environmentally concerned, morally serious but unsanctimonious secular unenthusiastic Democrats. Mark has perhaps the quicker intelligence, the duller sensibility, the more various knowledge; Valerie perhaps the deeper understanding, the readier human insight, the sounder education. They've never quarreled over sex or money. Both wish they had children, but neither finally wants them. (etc.—although that's really enough background for their Saturday set-to, no?)

They do have differences, of course: M enjoys socializing with others more than V does; she enjoys traveling more than he. He's more liberal (or less frugal) with money; she's more generous in the good-works way. He's less ready to take offense, but also slower to put their occasional tiffs behind him. She leaves closet and cabinet doors ajar and will not learn how to load their dishwasher properly (by *his* standards) (and the user's manual's); he wears his socks and underwear for two days before changing (turning his briefs inside out the second day) and often makes no effort to stifle his burps and farts when it's just the two of them. (etc., although [etc.]) These lapses or anyhow disharmonies they've learned to live with, by and large. The difference that really drives each up her or his wall is the one herein amply hinted at already, if scarcely yet demonstrated: at its mildest, a tease- or sigh-provoker, a prompter of rolled eyes and of fingertips drummed on dashboard, chair arm, desk- or thigh-top; at its sorest . . .

Saturday. Their week's official work done and essential house chores attended to, they had planned a drive up to nearby Baltimore to tour that city's Inner Harbor development, which they hadn't done in a while, and in particular the National Aquarium, which they'd never. After a not unreasonable detour to an upscale dry-goods emporium in the vast shopping complex at Four Corners, a quick shot from their house, where Val really did need to check patterns and prices of a certain sort of figured drapery material for a job in the works (and, having done so, pointed out to Mark that there across the mall was a Radio Shack outlet where he could conveniently pick up the whatchamacallit-adapter that he, not she, insisted they needed for their sound system's FM antenna [while she popped into the next-door Hallmark place for just a sec to replenish their supply of oddball greeting cards, which was running low]), they zipped from the D.C. Beltway up I-95 to Baltimore and reached Harbor Place in time for a pickup lunch about an hour past noon (no matter, as they'd had a latish breakfast)—an hour and a half past noon, more like, since the main parking lots were full by that time, as Mark had fretfully predicted, and so they had to park (quite) a few blocks away, and it wouldn't've made sense not to take a quick look-see at the new Oriole Park at Camden Yards stadium that was such a hit with baseball fans and civic-architecture buffs alike, inasmuch as there it stood between their parking garage and the harbor, and since their objective, after all (she reminded him when he put on his Fidget Face), wasn't to grab a sandwich, see a fish, and bolt for home but to *tour* Harbor Place, right? Which really meant the city's harbor area, which surely included the erstwhile haunts of Babe Ruth and Edgar Allan Poe. They weren't on a timetable, for pity's sake!

Agreed, agreed—but he *was* a touch hungry, was Mr. Mark, and therefore maybe a touch off his feed, as it were, especially after that unscheduled and extended stop at Four Corners; and it was to be expected that the ticket line at the Aquarium might well be considerable, the day being both so fine and so advanced . . .

"So we'll catch the flight flick at the IMAX theater in the Science Center instead," Val verbally shrugged, "or I'll stand in the Aquarium line while you fetch us something from the food pavilion, and then you stand while I do The Nature Company. What's the problem?"

The problem, in Mark's ever-warmer opinion, was—rather, the problems were—that *a)* this constant sidetracking, this what's-the-rush digression, can take the edge off the main event by the time one gets to it, the way some restaurants lay on so many introductory courses and side dishes that one has no appetite for the entrée, or the way foreplay can sometimes be so protracted that (etc.). Having no timetable or deadlines doesn't mean having no agenda or priorities, wouldn't she agree? And *b)* it wasn't as if this were just something that happened to happen today, or he'd have no grounds to grouse; it was the way certain people went at *everything,* from leaving for work in the morning to telling an anecdote. How often had he waited in their Volvo wagon to get going in time to drop her off at her Metro stop on the way to his office and finally come back into the house and found her with one earring and one shoe on, making an impulsive last-minute phone call while simultaneously revising her DO list with one hand and rummaging in her purse with the other? (Valerie is a whiz at cradling the phone between ear and shoulder, a trick Mark can't manage even with one of those gizmos designed for the purpose.) How often had he been obliged to remind her, or to fight the urge to remind her, in mid-narrative in mid–dinner party, that the point of her story-in-regress was her little niece's *response* to what Val's sister's husband's mother had said when the tot had walked in on her in the guest-bath shower stall, not what that widow lady's new Cuban-American boyfriend (whom she hadn't even met yet at the time of the incident) apparently does for a living? And c) . . .

But he never reached c) (*click on it if you're curious*), because by this time V was giving as good as she got, right there on the promenade under the old *USS Constellation*'s bowsprit, where their progress toward the distant tail of the National Aquarium ticket queue caesura'd for this exchange. As for *a),* damn it to hell, if in his (wrongheaded) opinion she was a Gemini who preferred hors d'oeuvres to entrées both at table and (as he had more than once intimated) in bed, then *he* was a bullheaded whambamthankyouma'amer of a Taurus whose idea of foreplay was three minutes of heavyweight humping to ejaculation instead of two; and *b)* because he himself had his hands full thinking and breathing simultaneously, he couldn't imagine anyone's doing five things at once better than he could manage one; for the reason that *c)* . . .

But she never reached *c),* for the reason that *b)* (now *b1)*) reminded her that *b2)* his idea of a joke was the punch line, his idea of a whodunit the last page, revealing who done it (no wonder he couldn't place his Middle-less novels even with an agent, much less with a publisher); and *a2)* if she might presume to back up a bit, now that it occurred to her, his idea of a full agenda was a single item, his top priority always and only the bottom line, his eternal (and infernal) *Let's get on with the story* in fact a *Let's get* done *with the story,* for the reason that—*b3),* she guessed, or maybe *a3),* who gave a damn?—his idea of living life was the same, *Let's get done with it,* and every time she saw him ready and fidgeting in the car a full ten minutes earlier than he knew as well as she they needed to leave for work, she was tempted to suggest that they drive straight to the funeral parlor instead and *get done with it* (etc., okay? On to the freaking fish already!).

But they never reached the FF ticket line, far less the marine exhibits themselves, and that's a pity, inasmuch as in the two-million-plus recirculating gallons of scrupulously monitored exhibit water in the National Aquarium's numerous tanks and pools are to be found some 10,000 aquatic animals (eels included), concerning every one of which much of natural-historical interest might be said. Under the volatile circumstances, however, it is no doubt as well they didn't, for how could they imaginably have moved and paused harmoniously through the exhibits (Valerie tranced at the very first of them, Mark glancing already to see what's next, and next after that) without reopening their quarrel? Which quarrel, mind, was still in noisy progress, if that's the right word, there under the *Constellation*'s mighty bowsprit—which bowsprit, at the time I tell of, extended halfway across the promenade from the vessel's prow toward the second-floor Indian restaurant above the first-floor Greek one in Harbor Place's Pratt Street pavilion, but which at the time of this telling is alas no longer there, nor are those restaurants, nor is the formidable old warship whose bow that bowsprit sprits, or spritted, said vessel having been removed indefinitely for a much-needed, long-overdue, and staggeringly expensive major overhaul—to the tsking amusement of passersby (the lovers' spectacular, hang-it-all-out quarrel, I mean, of course, not the *Constellation*'s shifting to some marine-repair limbo) including Yours Truly, who happened just then to be passing by and sympathetically so saw and heard them, or a couple not unlike them, toe-to-toeing it, and who then or subsequently was inspired to imagine (etc.).

Embarrassed, wasted, desperate, and sore, tear-faced Valerie anon turned her back on the dear, congenitally blinkered bastard whom she so loves and just then despised and stomped off back toward the Light Street food pavilion and their parking garage, no objective in mind except breathing space and weeping room. Mark was damned if he'd go chasing after the beloved, indispensable, impossible, darling bitch, but he did so after all, sort of; anyhow he trudged off in the same general direction, but made himself pause—Valerie-like, though in part to spite her—to half attend a juggling act in progress at the promenade's central plaza, where street musicians and performers entertain. Although he was as aware as was V (and no less alarmed) that the heavy artillery just fired could never be unfired, and that it had perilously, perhaps mortally, wounded their connection, he nonetheless registered with glum admiration the jugglers' so-skillful routine: their incremental accumulation of difficulties and complications at a pace adroitly timed to maximize dramatic effect without straining audience attention past the point of diminishing returns, a business as tricky in its way as the juggling itself—and now he couldn't refind Valerie among the promenaders. Well, there was The Nature Company yonder; she had mentioned that. And beyond it were the food concessions; she must have been as hungry by then as he, but probably as appetiteless, too, from their wring-out. And somewhere beyond or among those concessions were the public restrooms, whereto she might have retreated to collect herself (V is better than M at self-collection), and beyond them the parking ramp. Did she have her car keys? Probably, in her purse; anyhow there were spares in a magnetic holder under the rear bumper brace. Would she drive off without him, for spite? He doubted it, although she seemed more hurt and angry than he'd ever known her to be; anyhow, the lot ticket was in his wallet—not that she mightn't pay the hefty lost-ticket fee just to strand him, or, more likely, just to get out of there, with no thought of him either way. Most probably, however, she would collapse in furious tears in the Volvo's passenger seat, poor sweetheart, and then lay into him with more of her inexcusable even if not wholly off-the-mark insults when he tried to make peace with her, the bitch.

Well, she wasn't in The Nature Company, where among the coruscating geodes and "Save the Rain Forest" stuff his attention was caught by one of those illuminated flat-projection Earth-map clocks that show which parts of the planet are currently daylit and which in darkness (the East Coast of North America was just then correctly mid-afternoonish; dusk was racing across Asia Minor, dawn approaching Kamchatka and Polynesia). What (momentarily) arrested him in this instance was not that vertiginous reminder of onstreaming time and the world's all-at-onceness but rather the profusion of continental coastlines, necessarily much stylized in so small-scale a rendering but considerably articulated all the same. Chesapeake Bay, for example (180-some miles in straight-line length, but with upwards of 9,600 miles of tidal shoreline in its forty major rivers and their all but innumerable creeks and coves), was a simple small nick up there between Washington and Philadelphia, yet quite distinguishable in shape and position from Delaware Bay, just above it; even the Delmarva Peninsula, between them, no bigger here than a grain of rice, had overall its characteristic sand-flea shape. Framed nearby, as if to invite speculation on the contrast, was a large-scale, fine-grained aerial photo map of Baltimore's Inner Harbor, every pier and building sharply resolved, including the no-longer-present-as-I-write-this *Constellation.* One could distinguish not only individual small watercraft paddling about or moored at the harbor bulkheads but their occupants as well, and strollers like varicolored sand grains on the promenade.

One could not, however (Mark duly reflected, looking now for the exit to the food court and/or for a glimpse of Valerie's . . . yellow blouse, was it? Yes, he was almost certain: her yellow whatchamacallit blouse with those thingamajigs on it and either a white skirt or white culottes, he couldn't recall which and saw no sign of either), even with so fine a resolution, distinguish male from female, for example, or black from white from Asian, much less identify himself and Valerie having it out under the warship's bowsprit if they'd happened to be there doing that at that moment, much less yet see the thingamabobs on her whatchamacallits and much less yet the individual whatsits on each thingamabob (etc.)—any more than the most finely drawn map of the Chesapeake could show every barnacle on every pile of every pier on every creeklet (etc.): the famous Coastline Measurement Problem aforereferred to, in terms whereof the estuary's shore length could as well be put at 96 million miles as 9,600 (etc.). Which all led him to, but not yet across, the verge of recognizing . . .

Yellow blouse? Yes, out there by the Polish-sausage stand, but minus thingamajiggies and blousing a red-faced matron whose steatopygous buttocks were hugely sheathed in pink cotton warm-up pants (though there might, to be sure, he reminded himself, be a truly saintly spirit under all that [maybe helplessly genetic] grossness). *No Middles to his novels,* V had told him! His eye ever on the destination, not the getting there! Already figuring the server's tip while she lingered over the appetizer! No greater evidence of the degree of Pal Val's present pissed-offness than that she had been sidetracked neither in The Nature Company, as even he had briefly been, nor in the food court (where she would normally have been provisioning the pair of them, bless her, with goodies both for present consumption and for future enjoyment at home), nor on the pedestrian overpass to the parking lot, where in other circumstances she was entirely capable of dawdling to contemplate at length the vehicular traffic below, the cumulus formations overhead, the observation elevators up-and-downing the Hyatt Regency façade nearby. Unless she had indeed withdrawn into a women's room (he had forgotten to locate the WCs; couldn't've done anything in that precinct anyhow except dumbly stand by), she must have beelined for the car, as did he now finally.

No Valerie. Well, she was more liable than he to forget the level and pillar numbers of their parking slot. Not impossibly, in her present troubled state, she was wandering the ramps in a weepy rage. Plenty troubled himself, he walked up one level and down one, gave up the search as counterproductive, leaned against the Volvo's tailgate for some minutes, arms crossed, and then trudged back, *faute de mieux,* toward the walkway/footbridge/overpass/whatever. Halfway across it he stopped, disconsolate, and simply stood—facing uptown, as it happened, but really seeing nothing beyond his distress.

Which let's consider himwith for just a paragraph. A physically healthy, mentally sound, well-educated, (usually) well-fed, comfortably housed and clothed, gainfully employed, not unattractive early-fortyish middle-class male WASP American is at least temporarily on the outs with his housemate/girlfriend, a comparably advantaged and not unattractive professional who has declared her opinion that he hasn't the talent to achieve his heart-of-hearts career aim and that this deficit is of a piece with a certain general characteristic of his that she finds objectionable. So Mr. Mark's pride is bruised, his self-respect ruffled, the future of his closest and most valued personal relationship uncertain indeed. *So what?* he has asked himself before any of us can ask him. The world comprises approximately 4.7 zillion more mattersome matters, from saving the tropical rain forests to finding money enough in the chaotic post-Soviet Russian economy to bring that country's fiscally stranded cosmonauts back to Earth. Not that love and loss, or commitment and (potential) estrangement, aren't serious even among Volvo-driving yuppies, but really . . . What of real consequence is at stake here? If this were fiction (the wannabe writer asked himself), a made-up story, why should anyone give a damn?

Well, it *wasn't* fiction from Mark's perspective, although out of aspirant-professional habit he couldn't help considering (as he resumed his troubled path-retracement back to and through the Light Street pavilion in search of his dear damned Valerie) how, if it were, it ought properly to end. Reconciliation? On what terms? Uneasy armistice? Virtual divorce? In each case signifying what of interest to a reader who presumes the characters and situation to be imaginary?

From *our* point of view, of course, they *are* imaginary, and so these questions immediately apply (in a proper story they would never have come up; bear in mind that it was heart-hurt Mark who raised them) and shall be duly though not immediately addressed. Even their allegedly Middle-challenged poser, however, understood—as he rescanned in vain the food concessions and monitored for a fruitless while the traffic to and from the women's room after availing himself of the men's—that more's at stake here than the ups and downs of early-middle-aged Baby Boomer love. Not until "tomorrow" (the Sun following this sore Sat) will CNG's interactive E-fiction serendipitously supply the terms "Expediter" and "Enhancer" to shorthand the characterological differences that erupted under the *Constellation*'s awesome bowsprit; but already back there on the footbridge Mark sensed that the conflict here is larger than any temperamental incompatibility between Fred and Irma, or himself and Val: it's between fundamentally opposite views of and modes of dealing with the infinitely complex nature of reality.

Valerie sensed that too; she was, indeed, already deep into the pondering thereof when, almost simultaneously, she espied him approaching from the second-level fooderies, and he her at a railingside table on the open deck out there overlooking the promenade. Far from roaming the ramps in a weepy blind rage, or storming off alone in the Volvo (Val's better than Mark, we remember, at shrugging off their infrequent blowups; he tends to forget that and to project from his own distress), our yellow-bloused Enhancer, her chair tipped back and feet propped on the balcony rail, was finishing off a chocolate-chocolate-chip frozen-yogurt waffle cone while simultaneously *a)* teaching her sumbitch lover a lesson by neither fleeing nor chasing after him, *b)* facilitating their reunion by staying put, as her mother had taught her to do in little-girlhood if "lost" in, say, a department store or supermarket, and *c)* calming her still-roused adrenaline with a spot of yogurt while keeping an eye out for friend M and at the same time considering, in a preliminary way, his criticisms of her and the differences, as she saw them, between Socrates' famous occasional "trances," the Buddha's, and her own. They had in common, those trances, a self-forgetfulness, a putting of circumambient busyness on hold in favor of extraordinary concentration. But the Buddha under the bo tree was transcendentally *meditating,* thinking *about* nothing in particular while subsuming his ego-self into the cosmic "Buddha self"; Socrates, tranced in the agora or come upon by his protégés stock-still in some Athenian side street, was strenuously *contemplating,* presumably in finely honed logical terms, such uppercase concepts as Knowledge, Reality, Justice, and Virtue. She, however, beguiled indefinitely by . . . by the hypertextuality of everyday life, we might as well say, as encountered in the very first fish tank in the National Aquarium, or in the book beside the book upshelf from the book that she had gone to fetch from the library stacks, or on the counter across from the counter in the department en route to the department that she had been vectored toward in the department store downplaza from the supermarket that she was finally aiming for, was not so much meditating or contemplating as *fascinating:* being bemused and fascinated by the contiguities, complexities, interscalar resonances, and virtually endless multifariousness of the world, while at the same time often doing pretty damned efficiently several things at once.

"*Damn,*" said Mark, hands on hips on deck beside her. "Damn and damn."

"The same," came back his unfazed friend. "That said, is it on with our day or on with our spat?"

"Spat!" had all but spat more-than-ever-now-pissed-off M.

"Pity." Val gave her (glossy walnut) hair a toss and licked a drip from her (waffle) cone. "I thought *you* were the big mover-onner and I was the over-dweller-on-things. Lick?"

"No, thank you. There's a difference between moving on and hit-and-run driving, Val."

"Shall we discuss that difference?" More a challenge than a cordial invitation.

"No, thank you. Because what happened back there was no accident."

"So let's discuss *that:* its non-accidentality."

"No, thank you very much," the fire gone out of him. "Because there'd be no bloody end to it. Let's go the hell home."

But "Not so fast, Buster," had countered Ms. Valerie, and although they did in fact then go the hell home after all, they ventilated reciprocally all the way, each charging the other now with spoiling the day in addition to his or her more basic grievances. Through that evening, too, they had kept scarifyingly at it, heartsick Mark from time to time declaring "What it all comes down to . . ." and tearful Valerie being damned if she'd let him shortcut to that bottom line before he'd had his nose thoroughly rubbed en route in this, that, and the other. Exhausted half-sleep, as far apart as manageable in their king-size bed. Then a grumpy, burned-out Sunday, both parties by that time more saddened and alarmed than angry, each therapeutically pursuing her or his separate business till Happy Hour—which wasn't, but which at least brought them civilly together as was their custom for their (single) glass of wine with a bit of an hors d'oeuvre, over which they exchanged tentative, strained apologies, and then apologies less strained and tentative. Through dinner prep each guardedly conceded a measure of truth in the other's bill of complaints; through dinner itself (with, uncharacteristically, a second glass of wine, much diluted with club soda) a measure less guarded and more generous. Thereafter, by way of goodwill respite from the subject, M had offered to show V that business he'd mentioned sometime earlier about navigating the World Wide Web. She had welcomed the diversion; they had booted up Mark's Macintosh, had shortcut to CNG's E-piphanies home page with its E-tale of Expediter Fred and Enhancer Irma, had aborted it early in favor of makeup sex (etc.)—and here they are.

Mm-hm. And where is that, exactly?

That exactly is in separate rooms of their (jointly owned, jointly tenanted) Silver Spring house and likewise in their extraordinarily strained but by no means severed connection. More exactly yet, it is *a)* in Mark's case, on their pleasant, now dark side porch, where—having thought hard and efficiently about those five or seven interrelated matters aforelisted (Saturday set to, makeup sex, Coastline Measurement Problem, analogous aspect of storytelling, selfhood in the world's wide web, etc.)—in a sudden access of loving appreciation of his companion and their indispensable differences he turns from his idle rhododendron-tending to hurry herward with the aim of embracing her and ardently reaffirming that she is not only to him indispensable but by him treasured, and that he is determined to temper his maddening get-on-with-itness with as much of her wait-let's-explore-the-associationsness as his nature permits. And *b)* in Valerie's case, in Mark's workroom, where—having floated a fascinated while in the Sargasso Sea of everyday life's virtual hypertextuality (but at no time so bemused thereby as to lose sight of the subject of their Saturday set-to)—in a sudden access of loving etc. she bolts up from Mark's Mac to hurry himward with corresponding intent. The physical halfway point thembetween happens to be the fourth-from-bottom step of the staircase connecting their house's ground floor (living room, dining room, kitchen/breakfast room, lavatory, front and rear entry halls, side porch, attached garage) and its second (main bedroom and bath, V's and M's separate workrooms with hallway and No. 2 bath between, library-loft [accessible from main BR] over garage) (additionally, in basement and thus irrelevant to their projectible rendezvous: TV/guest room, workshop, utility room). Where they'll actually meet is another matter, perhaps suspendable while Narrator tidies a few loose ends. To wit:

• Any reasonable reader's suspicions to the contrary notwithstanding, "CNG" stands in this context not for Compressed Natural Gas but rather for Center of Narrative Gravity: in a made-up story, the author's narrative viewpoint; in real life-in-the-world, however, the self itself, of which more presently unless it's clicked on now . . .

• Presently, then. Meanwhile, as to the aforedemonstrated essential difference between Ms. Valerie's sensibility and Mr. Mark's, it is nowhere more manifest than in the way each, in the other's opinion, tells a story. "Anna train squish," is how Val claims Mark would render Leo Tolstoy's *Anna Karenina;* indeed, given the man's Middle-challengedness, she suspects he might skip the train. She, on the other hand (claims he, whether teasingly or in their Saturday set-to mode), would never get beyond Count Tolstoy's famous opening sentence, "Happy families are all alike;" etc.—indeed, would never get through, much less past, it, inasmuch as she would need to pause to explore such counterevidence as that her family and Mark's, for example, while both prevailingly quite "happy," are as different in nearly every other respect as aardvarks and zebras; and once having clicked on Mark's family, or equally on hers (or, for that matter, on aardvarks or zebras), she would most likely never get *back* to Tolstoy's proposition, not to mention on to its second half and the eight-part novel therebeyond.

• Myself, I'm on both their sides in this matter, not only because M and V seem equally reasonable, decent, harmless souls, but also because their tendencies represent contrary narrative impulses of equal validity and importance. A satisfyingly told story requires enough "Valerie"—that is, enough detail, amplification, and analysis—to give it clarity, texture, solidity, verisimilitude, and empathetic effect. It requires equally enough "Mark"—that is, efficiently directed forward motion, "profluence," on-with-the-storyness—for coherence, anti-tedium, and dramatic effect. In successful instances a right balance is found for the purpose (and adjusted for alternative purposes). In unsuccessful instances . . .

Friend of Valerie and Mark's: So, how'd your vacation go, guys?

M: Cool—Spain in ten days.

V: Really terrific, what little we got to see. The very first morning, for example, in Avila—Do you know Avila? Saint Teresa and all that?—we were in the Parador Nacional, just outside the old city wall. You've stayed in the Spanish paradors, right? So, anyhow, the one in Avila's this fifteenth-century palace called Piedras Albas ('cause that's what it's made of, white stones from [etc., *never getting past the breakfast* churros, *inasmuch as hypertexted behind them, for Valerie, lie all of Spanish history, culture, geography, and the rest, inseparable from the rest of Europe's and the world's. Mark had had practically to drag the rapt, protesting woman out of that stern and splendid place, to get on with their itinerary*]) . . .

• So what? you ask, unless one happens to take some professional interest in storytelling, which you for one do not? Thanks for clicking on that Frequently Asked Question, reply CNG and I: The "so what" is that that same right-balance-for-the-purpose finding applies to the measurement of coastlines, the appropriate scaling of maps, and—Hold that clicker—not only interpersonal relations, Q.E.D., but *intra*personal ones as well.

Intrapersonal relations?

Thanks again, and yes indeed. For what is Valerie, finally, what is Mark, what are you, and what am I—in short, what is the self itself—if not what has been aptly called a "posited center of narrative gravity" that, in order to function in and not be overwhelmed by the chaotically instreaming flood of sense data, continuously notices, ignores, associates, distinguishes, categorizes, prioritizes, hypothesizes, and selectively remembers and forgets; that continuously spins trial scenarios, telling itself stories about who it is and what it's up to, who others are and what they're up to; that finally *is,* if it is anything, those continuously revised, continuously edited stories? In sum, what we're dealing with here is no trifling or merely academic matter, friends: finding, maintaining, and forever adjusting from occasion to occasion an appropriate balance between the "Mark" in each of us and the "Valerie" ditto is of the very essence of our selfhood, our being in the world. We warmly therefore hope, do CNG & I (click on that & and see it turn into an =, + much more on intrapersonal relations), that that couple works things out, whenever and wherever they recouple.

When. One short paragraph from now, it will turn out, although given the infinite subdivisibility of time, space, and narrative (not to mention The Hypertextuality of Everyday Life), it could as readily be ten novels hence or never. See Zeno's paradoxes of time and motion; see swift Achilles close forever upon the tortoise; see Spot run . . .

Where. Not on that fourth-step-from-the-bottom *Mittelpunkt,* it turns out, but back where this story of them started. Mark (inescapably himself even when determined to be more Valish) is off the porch and through the dining room and up the staircase and into the upstairs hallway by the time Valerie (who, decidedly herself even after deciding to be more Marklike, has stepped from M's workroom first into the No. 2 bathroom to do a thing to her hair or face before hurrying porchward, then into their bedroom to slip a thigh-length T-shirt over her undies in case the neighbor lady's out there gardening by streetlight, then back into M's workroom to exit the Internet so that their access meter won't run on while they finish making up, which could take a happy while), hearing him hurrying herward, re-rises from Mark's Macintosh to meet its open-armed owner with open arms.

To her (glossy) (walnut) hair he groans, "I love you so damned much!"

To his (right) collarbone she murmurs, "I love you more."

They then vow (etc.), and one thing sweetly segues to another right there on the workroom's (Berber) wall-to-wall, while the screen saver's tropical fish and seahorses burble soothingly per program themabove.

• *The Marquise Went Out at Five (La Marquise sortit à cinq heures)* is the title of a 1961 novel by the French writer Claude Mauriac and a refrain in the Chilean novelist José Donoso's 1984 opus *Casa de Campo (A House in the Country).* The line comes from the French poet and critic Paul Valéry, who remarked in effect that he could never write a novel because of the *arbitrariness,* the vertiginous *contingency,* of such a "prosaic" but inescapable opening line as, say, "The Marquise went out at five"—for the rigorous M. Valéry, a paralyzing toe-dip into what might be called the hypertextuality of everyday life.

Not too fast there, Mark. Not too slow there, Val. That's got it, guys; that's got it . . . (so "CNG" [= I/you/eachandallofus] encourages them from the hyperspatial wings, until agile Valerie lifts one [long] [lithe] [cinnamon-tan] leg up and with her [left] [great] toe gives the Mac's master switch a

DONALD BARTHELME

The School

DONALD BARTHELME (1931–1989) published twelve books, including two novels and a prizewinning children's book. He was a regular contributor to *The New Yorker* and divided his time between New York and Houston, where he taught creative writing at the University of Houston. In his career, he won a Guggenheim Fellowship, a National Book Award, and a National Institute of Arts and Letters Award, among other honors. Mr. Barthelme died in July 1989.

Well, we had all these children out planting trees, see, because we figured that . . . that was part of their education, to see how, you know, the root systems . . . and also the sense of responsibility, taking care of things, being individually responsible. You know what I mean. And the trees all died. They were orange trees. I don't know why they died, they just died. Something wrong with the soil possibly or maybe the stuff we got from the nursery wasn't the best. We complained about it. So we've got thirty kids there, each kid had his or her own little tree to plant, and we've got these thirty dead trees. All these kids looking at these little brown sticks, it was depressing.

It wouldn't have been so bad except that just a couple of weeks before the thing with the trees, the snakes all died. But I think that the snakes—well, the reason that the snakes kicked off was that . . . you remember, the boiler was shut off for four days because of the strike, and that was explicable. It was something you could explain to the kids because of the strike. I mean, none of their parents would let them cross the picket line and they knew there was a strike going on and what it meant. So when things got started up again and we found the snakes they weren't too disturbed.

With the herb gardens it was probably a case of overwatering, and at least now they know not to overwater. The children were very conscientious with the herb gardens and some of them probably . . . you know, slipped them a little extra water when we weren't looking. Or maybe . . . well, I don't like to think about sabotage, although it did occur to us. I mean, it was something that crossed our minds. We were thinking that way probably because before that the gerbils had died, and the white mice had died, and the salamander . . . well, now they know not to carry them around in plastic bags.

Of course we *expected* the tropical fish to die, that was no surprise. Those numbers, you look at them crooked and they're belly-up on the surface. But the lesson plan called for a tropical-fish input at that point, there was nothing we could do, it happens every year, you just have to hurry past it.

We weren't even supposed to have a puppy.

We weren't even supposed to have one, it was just a puppy the Murdoch girl found under a Gristede's truck one day and she was afraid the truck would run over it when the driver had finished making his delivery, so she stuck it in her knapsack and brought it to school with her. So we had this puppy. As soon as I saw the puppy I thought, Oh Christ, I bet it will live for about two weeks and then . . . And that's what it did. It wasn't supposed to be in the classroom at all, there's some kind of regulation about it, but you can't tell them they can't have a puppy when the puppy is already there, right in front of them, running around on the floor and yap yap yapping. They named it Edgar—that is, they named it after me. They had a lot of fun running after it and yelling, "Here, Edgar! Nice Edgar!" Then they'd laugh like hell. They enjoyed the ambiguity. I enjoyed it myself. I don't mind being kidded. They made a little house for it in the supply closet and all that. I don't know what it died of. Distemper, I guess. It probably hadn't had any shots. I got it out of there before the kids got to school. I checked the supply closet each morning, routinely, because I knew what was going to happen. I gave it to the custodian.

And then there was this Korean orphan that the class adopted through the Help the Children program, all the kids brought in a quarter a month, that was the idea. It was an unfortunate thing, the kid's name was Kim and maybe we adopted him too late or something. The cause of death was not stated in the letter we got, they suggested we adopt another child instead and sent us some interesting case histories, but we didn't have the heart. The class took it pretty hard, they began (I think; nobody ever said anything to me directly) to feel that maybe there was something wrong with the school. But I don't think there's anything wrong with the school, particularly, I've seen better and I've seen worse. It was just a run of bad luck. We had an extraordinary number of parents passing away, for instance. There were I think two heart attacks and two suicides, one drowning, and four killed together in a car accident. One stroke. And we had the usual heavy mortality rate among the grandparents, or maybe it was heavier this year, it seemed so. And finally the tragedy.

The tragedy occurred when Matthew Wein and Tony Mavrogordo were playing over where they're excavating for the new federal office building. There were all these big wooden beams stacked, you know, at the edge of the excavation. There's a court case coming out of that, the parents are claiming that the beams were poorly stacked. I don't know what's true and what's not. It's been a strange year.

I forgot to mention Billy Brandt's father, who was knifed fatally when he grappled with a masked intruder in his home.

One day, we had a discussion in class. They asked me, where did they go? The trees, the salamander, the tropical fish, Edgar, the poppas and mommas, Matthew and Tony, where did they go? And I said, I don't know, I don't know. And they said, who knows? and I said, nobody knows. And they said, is death that which gives meaning to life? and I said, no, life is that which gives meaning to life. Then they said, but isn't death, considered as a fundamental datum, the means by which the taken-for-granted mundanity of the everyday may be transcended in the direction of—

I said, yes, maybe.

They said, we don't like it.

I said, that's sound.

They said, it's a bloody shame!

I said, it is.

They said, will you make love now with Helen (our teaching assistant) so that we can see how it is done? We know you like Helen.

I do like Helen but I said that I would not.

We've heard so much about it, they said, but we've never seen it.

I said I would be fired and that it was never, or almost never, done as a demonstration. Helen looked out of the window.

They said, please, please make love with Helen, we require an assertion of value, we are frightened.

I said that they shouldn't be frightened (although I am often frightened) and that there was value everywhere. Helen came and embraced me. I kissed her a few times on the brow. We held each other. The children were excited. Then there was a knock on the door, I opened the door, and the new gerbil walked in. The children cheered wildly.

RICK BASS

Wild Horses

RICK BASS (1958–) is the author of fifteen works of fiction and nonfiction, including the novel *Where the Sea Used to Be.*

Karen was twenty-six. She had been engaged twice, married once. Her husband had run away with another woman after only six months. It still made her angry when she thought about it, which was not often.

The second man she had loved more, the most. He was the one she had been engaged to, but had not married. His name was Henry. He had drowned in the Mississippi the day before they were to be married. They never even found the body. He had a marker in the cemetery, but it was a sham. All her life, Karen had heard those stories about fiancés dying the day before the wedding; and then it had happened to her.

Henry and some of his friends, including his best friend, Sydney Bean, had been sitting up on the old railroad trestle, the old highway that ran so far and across that river, above the wide muddiness. Louisiana and trees on one side; Mississippi and trees, and some farms, on the other side—the place from which they had come. There had been a full moon and no wind, and they had been sitting above the water, maybe a hundred feet above it, laughing, and drinking Psychos from the Daiquiri World over in Delta, Louisiana. The Psychos contained rum and Coca-Cola and various fruit juices and blue food coloring. They came in styrofoam cups the size of small trash cans, so large they had to be held with both hands. They had had too many of them: two, maybe three apiece.

Henry had stood up, beaten his chest like Tarzan, shouted, and then dived in. It had taken him forever, just to hit the water; the light from the moon was good, and they had been able to watch him, all the way down.

Sometimes Sydney Bean still came by to visit Karen. Sydney was gentle and sad, her own age, and he worked somewhere on a farm, out past Utica, back to the east, where he broke and sometimes trained horses.

Once a month—at the end of each month—Sydney would stay over on Karen's farm, and they would go into her big empty closet, and he would let her hit him: striking him with her fists, kicking him, kneeing him, slapping his face until his ears rang and his nose bled; slapping and swinging at him until she was crying and her hair was wild and in her eyes, and the palms of her hands hurt too much to hit him any more.

It built up, the ache and the anger in Karen; and then, hitting Sydney, it went away for a while. He was a good friend. But the trouble was that it always came back.

Sometimes Sydney would try to help her in other ways. He would tell her that someday she was going to have to realize that Henry would not be coming back. Not ever—not in any form—but to remember what she had had, to keep *that* from going away.

Sydney would stand there, in the closet, and let her strike him. But the rules were strict: she had to keep her mouth closed. He would not let her call him names while she was hitting him.

Though she wanted to.

After it was over, and she was crying, more drained than she had felt since the last time, sobbing, her feelings laid bare, Sydney would help her up. He would take her into the bedroom and towel her forehead with a cool washcloth. Karen would be crying in a child's gulping sobs, and he would brush her hair, hold her hand, even hold her against him, and pat her back while she moaned.

Farm sounds would come from the field, and when she looked out the window, she might see her neighbor, old Dr. Lynly, the vet, driving along in his ancient blue truck, moving along the bayou, down along the trees, with his dog, Buster, running alongside, barking, herding the cows together for vaccinations.

"I can still feel the hurt," Karen would tell Sydney sometimes, when Sydney came over, not to be beaten up, but to cook supper for her, or to just sit on the back porch with her, and to watch the fields.

Sydney would nod whenever Karen said that she still hurt, and he would study his hands.

"I could have grabbed him," he'd say, and then look up and out at the field some more. "I keep thinking that one of these years, I'm going to get a second chance." Sydney would shake his head again. "I think I could have grabbed him," he'd say.

"Or you could have dived in after him," Karen would say, hopefully, wistfully. "Maybe you could have dived in after him."

Her voice would trail off, and her face would be flat and weary.

On these occasions, Sydney Bean wanted the beatings to come once a week, or even daily. But they hurt, too, almost as much as the loss of his friend, and he said nothing. He still felt as if he owed Henry something. He didn't know what.

Sometimes, when he was down on his knees, and Karen was kicking him or elbowing him, he felt close to it—and he almost felt angry at Karen—but he could never catch the shape of it, only the feeling.

He wanted to know what was owed, so he could go on.

On his own farm, there were cattle down in the fields, and they would get lost, separated from one another, and would low all through the night. It was a sound like soft thunder in the night, before the rain comes, and he liked it.

He raised the cattle, and trained horses too: he saddle-broke the young ones that had never been ridden before, the one- and two-year-olds, the stallions, the wild mares. That pounding, and the evil, four-footed stamp-and-spin they went into when they could not shake him; when they began to do that, he knew he had them beaten. He charged $250 a horse, and sometimes it took him a month.

Old Dr. Lynly needed a helper, but couldn't pay much, and Sydney, who had done some business with the vet, helped Karen get the job. She needed something to do besides sitting around on her back porch, waiting for the end of each month.

Dr. Lynly was older than Karen had thought he would be, when she met him up close. He had that look to him that told her it might be the last year of his life. It wasn't so much any illness or feebleness or disability. It was just a finished look.

He and Buster—an Airedale, six years old—lived within the city limits of Vicksburg, down below the battlefield, hidden in one of the ravines—his house was up on blocks, the yard flooded with almost every rain—and in his yard, in various corrals and pens, were chickens, ducks, goats, sheep, ponies, horses, cows, and an ostrich. It was illegal to keep them as pets, and the city newspaper editor was after him to get rid of them, but Dr. Lynly claimed they were all being treated by his tiny clinic.

"You're keeping these animals too long, Doc," the editor told him. Dr. Lynly would pretend to be senile, and would pretend to think the editor was asking for a prescription, and would begin quoting various and random chemical names.

The Airedale minded Dr. Lynly exquisitely. He brought the paper, the slippers, he left the room on command, and he brought the chickens' eggs, daily, into the kitchen, making several trips for his and Dr. Lynly's breakfast. Dr. Lynly would have six eggs, fried for himself, and Buster would get a dozen or so, broken into his bowl raw. Any extras went into the refrigerator for Dr. Lynly to take on his rounds, though he no longer had many; only the very oldest people, who remembered him, and the very poorest, who knew he worked for free. They knew he would charge them only for the medicine.

Buster's coat was glossy from the eggs, and burnished, black and tan. His eyes, deep in the curls, were bright, sometimes like the brightest things in the world. He watched Dr. Lynly all the time.

Sometimes Karen watched Dr. Lynly play with Buster, bending down and swatting him in the chest, slapping his shoulders. She had thought it would be mostly kittens and lambs. Mostly, though, he told her, it would be the horses.

The strongest creatures were the ones that got the sickest, and their pain was unspeakable when they finally did yield to it. On the rounds with Dr. Lynly, Karen forgot to think about Henry at all. Though she was horrified by the pain, and almost wished it were hers, bearing it rather than watching it, when the horses suffered.

Once, when Sydney was with her, he had reached out and taken her hand in his. When she looked down and saw it, she had at first been puzzled, not recognizing what it was, and then repulsed, as if it were a giant slug: and she threw Sydney's hand off hers quickly, and ran into her room.

Sydney stayed out on the porch. It was heavy blue twilight and all the cattle down in the fields were feeding.

"I'm sorry," he called out. "But I can't bring him back!" He waited for her to answer, but could only hear her sobs. It had been three years, he thought.

He knew he was wrong to have caught her off-balance like that: but he was tired of her unhappiness, and frustrated that he could do nothing to end it. The sounds of her crying carried, and the cows down in the fields began to move closer, with interest. The light had dimmed, there were only dark shadows and pale lights, and a low gold thumbnail of a moon—a wet moon—came up over the ragged tear of trees by the bayou.

The beauty of the evening, being on Karen's back porch and in her life, when it should have been Henry, flooded Sydney with a sudden guilt. He had been fighting it, and holding it back, constantly: and then, suddenly, the quietness of the evening, and the stillness, released it.

He heard himself saying a crazy thing.

"I pushed him off, you know," he said, loudly enough so she could hear. "I finished my drink, and put both hands on his skinny-ass little shoulders, and said, 'Take a deep breath, Henry.' I just pushed him off," said Sydney.

It felt good, making up the lie. He was surprised at the relief he felt: it was as if he had control of the situation. It was like when he was on the horses, breaking them, trying to stay on.

Presently, Karen came back out with a small blue pistol, a .38, and she went down the steps and out to where he was standing, and she put it next to his head.

"Let's get in the truck," she said.

He knew where they were going.

The river was about ten miles away, and they drove slowly. There was fog flowing across the low parts of the road and through the fields and meadows like smoke, coming from the woods, and he was thinking about how cold and hard the water would be when he finally hit.

He felt as if he were already falling towards it, the way it had taken Henry forever to fall. But he didn't say anything, and though it didn't feel right, he wondered if perhaps it was this simple, as if this was what was owed after all.

They drove on, past the blue fields and the great spills of fog. The roofs of the hay barns were bright silver polished tin, under the little moon and stars. There were small lakes, cattle stock tanks, and steam rose from them.

They drove with the windows down; it was a hot night, full of flying bugs, and about two miles from the river, Karen told him to stop.

He pulled off to the side of the road, and wondered what she was going to do with his body. A cattle egret flew by, ghostly white and large, flying slowly, and Sydney was amazed that he had never recognized their beauty before, though he had seen millions. It flew right across their windshield, from across the road, and it startled both of them.

The radiator ticked.

"You didn't really push him off, did you?" Karen asked. She still had the pistol against his head, and had switched hands.

Like frost burning off the grass in a bright morning sun, there was in his mind a sudden, sugary, watery feeling—like something dissolving. She was not going to kill him after all.

"No," he said.

"But you could have saved him," she said, for the thousandth time.

"I could have reached out and grabbed him," Sydney agreed. He was going to live. He was going to get to keep feeling things, was going to get to keep seeing things.

He kept his hands in his lap, not wanting to alarm Karen, but his eyes moved all around as he looked for more egrets. He was eager to see another one.

Karen watched him for a while, still holding the pistol against him, and then turned it around and looked at the open barrel of it, cross-eyed, and held it there, right in her face, for several seconds. Then she reached out and put it in the glove box.

Sydney Bean was shuddering.

"Thank you," he said. "Thank you for not shooting yourself."

He put his head down on the steering wheel, in the moonlight, and shuddered again. There were crickets calling all around them. They sat like that for a long time, Sydney leaning against the wheel, and Karen sitting up straight, just looking out at the fields.

Then the cattle began to move up the hill towards them, thinking that Karen's old truck was the one that had come to feed them, and slowly, drifting up the hill from all over the fields, coming from out of the woods, and from their nearby resting spots on the sandbars along the little dry creek that ran down into the bayou—eventually, they all assembled around the truck, like schoolchildren.

They stood there in the moonlight, some with white faces like skulls, all about the same size, and chewed grass and watched the truck. One, bolder than the rest—a yearling black Angus—moved in close, bumped the grille of the truck with his nose, playing, and then leapt back again, scattering some of the others.

"How much would you say that one weighs?" Karen asked. "How much, Sydney?"

They drove the last two miles to the river slowly. It was about four A.M. The yearling cow was bleating and trying to break free; Sydney had tied him up with his belt, and with jumper cables and shoelaces, and an old shirt. His lip was bloody from where the calf had butted him.

But he had wrestled larger steers than that before.

They parked at the old bridge, the one across which the trains still ran. Farther downriver, they could see an occasional car, two round spots of headlight moving slowly and steadily across the new bridge, so far above the river, going very slowly. Sydney put his shoulders under the calf's belly and lifted it with his back and legs, and like a prisoner in the stock, he carried it out to the center of the bridge. Karen followed. It took about fifteen minutes to get there, and Sydney was trembling, dripping with sweat, when finally they gauged they had reached the middle. The deepest part.

They sat there, soothing the frightened calf, stroking its ears, patting its flanks, and waited for the sun to come up. When it did, pale orange behind the great steaminess of the trees and river below—the fog from the river and trees a gunmetal gray, the whole world washed in gray flatness, except for the fruit of the sun—they untied the calf, and pushed him over.

They watched him forever and forever, a black object and then a black spot against the great background of no-colored river, and then there was a tiny white splash, lost almost immediately in the river's current. Logs, which looked like twigs from up on the bridge, swept across the spot. Everything headed south, moving south, and there were no eddies, no pauses.

"I am halfway over him," Karen said.

And then, walking back, she said: "So that was really what it was like?"

She had a good appetite, and they stopped at the Waffle House and ate eggs and pancakes, and had sausage and biscuits and bacon and orange juice. She excused herself to go to the restroom, and when she came back out, her face was washed, her hair brushed and clean-looking. Sydney paid for the meal, and when they stepped outside, the morning was growing hot.

"I have to work today," Karen said, when they got back to her house. "We have to go see about a mule."

"Me, too," said Sydney. "I've got a stallion who thinks he's a bad-ass."

She studied him for a second, and felt like telling him to be careful, but didn't. Something was in her, a thing like hope stirring, and she felt guilty for it.

Sydney whistled, driving home, and tapped his hands on the steering wheel, though the radio did not work.

Dr. Lynly and Karen drove until the truck wouldn't go any farther, bogged down in the clay, and then they got out and walked. It was cool beneath all the big trees, and the forest seemed to be trying to press in on them. Dr. Lynly carried his heavy bag, stopping and switching arms frequently. Buster trotted slightly ahead, between the two of them, looking left and right, and up the road, and even up into the tops of the trees.

There was a sawmill, deep in the woods, where the delta's farmland in the northern part of the county settled at the river and then went into dark mystery; hardwoods, and muddy roads, then no roads. The men at the sawmill used mules to drag their trees to the cutting. There had never been money for bulldozers, or even tractors. The woods were quiet, and foreboding; it seemed to be a place without sound or light.

When they got near the sawmill, they could hear the sound of axes. Four men, shirtless, in muddy boots with the laces undone, were working on the biggest tree Karen had ever seen. It was a tree too big for chain saws. Had any of the men owned one, the tree would have ruined the saw.

One of the men kept swinging at the tree: putting his back into it, with rhythmic, stroking cuts. The other three stepped back, hitched their pants, and wiped their faces with their forearms.

The fourth man stopped cutting finally. There was no fat on him and he was pale, even standing in the beam of sunlight that was coming down through an opening in the trees—and he looked old; fifty, maybe, or sixty. Some of his fingers were missing.

"The mule'll be back in a minute," he said. He wasn't even breathing hard. "He's gone to bring a load up out of the bottom." He pointed with his ax, down into the swamp.

"We'll just wait," said Dr. Lynly. He bent back and tried to look up at the top of the trees. "Y'all just go right ahead with your cutting."

But the pale muscled man was already swinging again, and the other three, with another tug at their beltless pants, joined in: an odd, pausing drumbeat, as four successive whacks hit the tree; then four more again; and then, almost immediately, the cadence stretching out, growing irregular, as the older man chopped faster.

All around them were the soft pittings, like hail, of tree chips, raining into the bushes. One of the chips hit Buster in the nose, and he rubbed it with his paw, and turned and looked up at Dr. Lynly.

They heard the mule before they saw him: he was groaning, like a person. He was coming up the hill that led out of the swamp; he was coming towards them.

They could see the tops of small trees and saplings shaking as he dragged his load through them. Then they could see the tops of his ears; then his huge head, and after that they saw his chest. Veins raced against the chestnut thickness of it.

Then the tops of his legs.

Then his knee. Karen stared at it and then she started to tremble. She sat down in the mud, and hugged herself—the men stopped swinging, for just a moment—and Dr. Lynly had to help her up.

It was the mule's right knee that was injured, and it had swollen to the size of a basketball. It buckled, with every step he took, pulling the sled up the slick and muddy hill, but he kept his footing and he did not stop. Flies buzzed around the knee, around the infections, where the loggers had pierced the skin with nails and the ends of their knives, trying to drain the pus. Dried blood ran down in streaks to the mule's hoof, to the mud.

The sawlogs on the back of the sled smelled good, fresh. They smelled like they were still alive.

Dr. Lynly walked over to the mule and touched the knee. The mule closed his eyes and trembled slightly, as Karen had done, or even as if in ecstasy, at the chance to rest. The three younger men, plus the sledder, gathered around.

"We can't stop workin' him," the sledder said. "We can't shoot him, either. We've got to keep him alive. He's all we've got. If he dies, it's us that'll have to pull them logs up here."

A cedar moth, from the woods, passed over the mule's ears, fluttering blindly. It rested on the mule's forehead briefly, and then flew off. The mule did not open his eyes. Dr. Lynly frowned and rubbed his chin. Karen felt faint again, and leaned against the mule's sweaty back to keep from falling.

"You sure you've got to keep working him?" Dr. Lynly asked.

"Yes, sir."

The pale logger was still swinging: tiny chips flying in batches.

Dr. Lynly opened his bag. He took out a needle and rag, and a bottle of alcohol. He cleaned the mule's infections. The mule drooled a little when the needle went in, but did not open his eyes. The needle was slender, and it bent and flexed, and slowly Dr. Lynly drained the fluid.

Karen held onto the mule's wet back and vomited into the mud: both her hands on the mule as if she were being arrested against the hood of a car, and her feet spread out wide. The men gripped their axes awkwardly.

Dr. Lynly gave one of them a large plastic jug of pills.

"These will kill his pain," he said. "The knee will get big again, though. I'll be back out, to drain it again." He handed Karen a clean rag from his satchel, and led her away from the mule, away from the mess.

One of the ax men carried their satchel all the way back to the truck. Dr. Lynly let Karen get up into the truck first, and then Buster; then the ax man rocked and shoved, pushing on the hood of the truck as the tires spun, and helped them back it out of the mud: their payment for healing the mule. A smell of burning rubber and smoke hung in the trees after they left.

They didn't talk much. Dr. Lynly was thinking about the painkillers: how for a moment, he had almost given the death pills instead.

Karen was thinking how she would not let him pay her for that day's work. Also she was thinking about Sydney Bean: she would sit on the porch with him again, and maybe drink a beer and watch the fields.

He was sitting on the back porch, when she got in; he was on the wooden bench next to the hammock, and he had a tray set up for her with a pitcher of cold orange juice. There was froth in the pitcher, a light creamy foaminess from where he had been stirring it, and the ice cubes were circling around. Beads of condensation slid down the pitcher, rolling slowly, then quickly, like tears. She could feel her heart giving. The field was rich summer green, and then, past the field, the dark line of trees. A long string of cattle egrets flew past, headed down to their rookery in the swamp.

Sydney poured her a small glass of orange juice. He had a metal pail of cold water and a clean washcloth. It was hot on the back porch, even for evening. He helped her get into the hammock; then he wrung the washcloth out and put it across her forehead, her eyes. Sydney smelled as if he had just gotten out of the shower, and he was wearing clean white duckcloth pants and a bright blue shirt.

She felt dizzy, and leaned back in the hammock. The washcloth over her eyes felt so good. She sipped the orange juice, not looking at it, and licked the light foam of it from her lips. Owls were beginning to call, down in the swamp.

She felt as if she were younger, going back to a place, some place she had not been in a long time but could remember fondly. It felt like she was in love. She knew that she could not be, but that was what it felt like.

Sydney sat behind her and rubbed her temples.

It grew dark, and the moon came up.

"It was a rough day," she said, around ten o'clock.

But he just kept rubbing.

Around eleven o'clock, she dozed off, and he woke her, helped her from the hammock, and led her inside, not turning on any lights, and helped her get in bed.

Then he went back outside, locking the door behind him. He sat on the porch a little longer, watching the moon, so high above him, and then he drove home, slowly, cautiously, as ever. Accidents were everywhere; they could happen at any time, from any direction.

Sydney moved carefully, and tried to look ahead and be ready for the next one.

He really wanted her. He wanted her in his life. Sydney didn't know if the guilt was there for that—the wanting—or because he was alive, still seeing things, still feeling. He wanted someone in his life, and it didn't seem right to feel guilty about it. But he did.

Sometimes, at night, he would hear the horses running, thundering across the hard summer-baked flatness of his pasture, running wild—and he would imagine they were laughing at him for wasting his time feeling guilty, but it was a feeling he could not shake, could not ride down, and his sleep was often poor and restless.

Sydney often wondered if horses were even meant to be ridden at all.

It was always such a struggle.

The thing about the broncs, he realized—and he never realized it until they were rolling on top of him in the dust, or rubbing him off against a tree, or against the side of a barn, trying to break his leg—was that if the horses didn't get broken, tamed, they'd get wilder. There was nothing as wild as a horse that had never been broken. It just got meaner, each day.

So he held on. He bucked and spun and arched and twisted, shooting up and down with the mad horses' leaps; and when the horse tried to hurt itself, by running straight into something—a fence, a barn, the lake—he stayed on.

If there was, once in a blue moon, a horse not only stronger, but more stubborn than he, then he would have to destroy it.

The cattle were easy to work with, they would do anything for food, and once one did it, they would all follow; but working with the horses made him think ahead, and sometimes he wondered, in streaks and bits of paranoia, if perhaps all the horses in the world did not have some battle against him, and were destined, all of them, to pass through his corrals, each one testing him before he was allowed to stop.

Because like all bronc-busters, that was what Sydney someday allowed himself to consider and savor, in moments of rest: the day when he could stop. A run of successes. A string of wins so satisfying and continuous that it would seem—even though he would be sore, and tired—that a horse would never beat him again, and he would be convinced of it, and then he could quit.

Mornings in summers past, Henry used to come over, and sit on the railing and watch. He had been an elementary school teacher, and frail, almost anemic: but he had loved to watch Sydney Bean ride the horses. He taught only a few classes in the summers, and he would sip coffee and grade a few papers while Sydney and the horse fought out in the center.

Sometimes Henry had set a broken bone for Sydney—Sydney had shown him how—and other times Sydney, if he was alone, would set his own bones, if he even bothered with them. Then he would wrap them up and keep riding. Dr. Lynly had set some of his bones, on the bad breaks.

Sydney was feeling old, since Henry had drowned. Not so much in the mornings, when everything was new and cool, and had promise; but in the evenings, he could feel the crooked shapes of his bones, within him. He would drink beers, and watch his horses, and other people's horses in his pasture, as they ran. The horses never seemed to feel old, not even in the evenings, and he was jealous of them, of their strength.

He called Karen one weekend. "Come out and watch me break horses," he said.

He was feeling particularly sore and tired. For some reason he wanted her to see that he could always do it; that the horses were always broken. He wanted her to see what it looked like, and how it always turned out.

"Oh, I don't know," she said, after she had considered it. "I'm just so *tired.*" It was a bad and crooked road, bumpy, from her house to his, and it took nearly an hour to drive it.

"I'll come get you . . . ?" he said. He wanted to shake her. But he said nothing; he nodded, and then remembered he was on the phone and said, "I understand."

She did let him sit on the porch with her, whenever he drove over to her farm. She had to have someone.

"Do you want to hit me?" he asked one evening, almost hopefully.

But she just shook her head sadly.

He saw that she was getting comfortable with her sorrow, was settling down into it, like an old way of life, and he wanted to shock her out of it, but felt paralyzed and mute, like the dumbest of animals.

Sydney stared at his crooked hands, with the scars from the cuts, made over the years by the fencing tools. Silently, he cursed all the many things he did not know. He could lift bales of hay. He could string barbed-wire fences. He could lift things. That was all he knew. He wished he were a chemist, an electrician, a poet, or a preacher. The things he had—what little of them there were—wouldn't help her.

She had never thought to ask how drunk Henry had been. Sydney thought that made a difference: whether you jumped off the bridge with one beer in you, or two, or a six-pack; or with a sea of purple Psychos rolling around in your stomach—but she never asked.

He admired her confidence, and doubted his ability to be as strong, as stubborn. She never considered that it might have been her fault, or Henry's; that some little spat might have prompted it, or general disillusionment.

It was his fault, Sydney's, square and simple, and she seemed comfortable, if not happy, with the fact.

Dr. Lynly treated horses, but he did not seem to love them, thought Karen.

"Stupid creatures," he would grumble, when they would not do as he wanted, when he was trying to doctor them. "Utter idiots." He and Buster and Karen would try to herd the horse into the trailer, or the corral, pulling on the reins and swatting the horse with green branches.

"Brickheads," Dr. Lynly would growl, pulling the reins and then walking around and slapping, feebly, the horse's flank. "Brickheads and fatheads." He had been loading horses for fifty years, and Karen would giggle, because the horses' stupidity always seemed to surprise, and then anger Dr. Lynly, and she thought it was sweet.

It was as if he had not yet really learned that that was how they always were.

But Karen had seen that right away. She knew that a lot of girls, and women, were infatuated with horses, in love with them even, for their great size and strength, and for their wildness—but Karen, as she saw more and more of the sick horses, the ailing ones, the ones most people did not see regularly, knew that all horses were dumb, simple and trusting, and that even the smartest ones could be made to do as they were told.

And they could be so dumb, so loyal, and so oblivious to pain. It was as if—even if they could feel it—they could never, ever acknowledge it.

It was sweet, she thought, and dumb.

Karen let Sydney rub her temples and brush her hair. She would go into the bathroom, and wash it while he sat on the porch. He had taken up whittling; one of the stallions had broken Sydney's leg by throwing him into a fence and then trampling him, and the leg was in a heavy cast. So Sydney had decided to take a break for a few days.

He had bought a whittling kit at the hardware store, and was going to try hard to learn how to do it. There were instructions. The kit had a square, light piece of balsa wood, almost the weight of nothing, and a plain curved whittling knife. There was a dotted outline in the shape of a duck's head on the balsa wood that showed what the shape of his finished work would be.

After he learned to whittle, Sydney wanted to learn to play the harmonica. That was next, after whittling.

He would hear the water running, and hear Karen splashing, as she put her head under the faucet and rinsed.

She would come out in her robe, drying her hair, and then would let him sit in the hammock with her and brush her hair. It was September, and the cottonwoods were tinging, were making the skies hazy, soft and frozen. Nothing seemed to move.

Her hair came down to the middle of her back. She had stopped cutting it. The robe was old and worn, the color of an old blue dish. Something about the shampoo she used reminded him of apples. She wore moccasins that had a shearling lining in them, and Sydney and Karen would rock in the hammock, slightly. Sometimes Karen would get up and bring out two Cokes from the refrigerator, and they would drink those.

"Be sure to clean up those shavings when you go," she told him. There were little balsa wood curls all over the porch. Her hair, almost dry, would be light and soft. "Be sure not to leave a mess when you go," she would say.

It would be dark then, Venus out beyond them.

"Yes," he said.

Before he left, she reached out from the hammock, and caught his hand. She squeezed it, and then let go.

He drove home slowly, thinking of Henry, and of how he had once taken Henry fishing for the first time. They had caught a catfish so large that it had scared Henry. They drank beers, and sat in the boat, and talked.

One of Sydney Bean's headlights faltered, on the drive home, then went out, and it took him an hour and a half to get home.

The days got cold and brittle. It was hard, working with the horses: Sydney's leg hurt all the time. Sometimes the horse would leap, and come down with all four hooves bunched in close together, and the pain and shock of it would travel all the way up Sydney's leg and into his shoulder, and down into his wrists: the break was in his ankle.

He was sleeping past sun-up, some days, and was being thrown, now, nearly every day; sometimes several times in the same day.

There was always a strong wind. Rains began to blow in. It was cool, getting cold, crisp as apples, and it was the weather that in the summer everyone said they would be looking forward to. One night there was a frost, and a full moon.

On her back porch, sitting in the hammock by herself with a heavy blanket around her, Karen saw a stray balsa shaving caught between the cracks of her porch floor. It was white, in the moonlight—the whole porch was—and the field was blue—the cattle stood out in the moonlight like blue statues—and she almost called Sydney.

She even went as far as to get up and call information, to find out his number; it was that close.

But then the silence and absence of a thing—she presumed it was Henry, but did not know for sure what it was—closed in around her, and the field beyond her porch, like the inside of her heart, seemed to be deathly still—and she did not call.

She thought angrily, I can love who I want to love. But she was angry at Sydney Bean, for having tried to pull her so far out, into a place where she did not want to go.

She fell asleep in the hammock, and dreamed that Dr. Lynly was trying to wake her up, and was taking her blood pressure, feeling her forehead, and, craziest of all, swatting at her with green branches.

She awoke from the dream, and decided to call him after all. Sydney answered the phone as if he, too, had been awake.

"Hello?" he said. She could tell by the true questioning in his voice that he did not get many phone calls.

"Hello," said Karen. "I just—wanted to call, and tell you hello." She paused; almost a falter. "And that I feel better. That I feel good, I mean. That's all."

"Well," said Sydney Bean, "Well, good. I mean, great."

"That's all," said Karen. "Bye," she said.

"Good-bye," said Sydney.

On Thanksgiving Day, Karen and Dr. Lynly headed back out to the swamp, to check up on the loggers' mule. It was the hardest cold of the year, and there was bright ice on the bridges, and it was not thawing, even in the sun. The inside of Dr. Lynly's old truck was no warmer than the air outside. Buster, in his wooliness, lay across Karen to keep her warm.

They turned onto a gravel road, and started down into the swamp. Smoke, low and spreading, was all in the woods, like a fog. The men had little fires going all throughout the woods; they were each working on a different tree, and had small warming fires where they stood and shivered when resting.

Karen found herself looking for the pale ugly logger.

He was swinging the ax, but he only had one arm, he was swinging at the tree with one arm. The left arm was gone, and there was a sort of a sleeve over it, like a sock. The man was sweating, and a small boy stepped up and quickly toweled him dry each time the pale man stepped back to take a rest.

They stopped the truck and got out and walked up to him, and he stepped back—wet, already, again; the boy toweled him off, standing on a low stool and starting with the man's neck and shoulders, and then going down the great back—and the man told them that the mule was better but that if they wanted to see him, he was lower in the swamp.

They followed the little path towards the river. All around them were downed trees, and stumps, and stacks of logs, but the woods looked no different. The haze from the fires made it seem colder. Acorns popped under their feet.

About halfway down the road, they met the mule. He was coming back up towards them, and he was pulling a good load. A small boy was in front of him, holding out a carrot, only partially eaten. The mule's knee looked much better, though it was still a little swollen, and probably always would be.

The boy stopped, and let the mule take another bite of carrot, making him lean far forward in the trace. His great rubbery lips stretched and quavered, and then flapped, as he tried to get it, and then there was the crunch when he did.

They could smell the carrot as the mule ground it with his old teeth. It was a wild carrot, dug from the woods, and not very big: but it smelled good.

Karen had brought an apple and some sugar cubes, and she started forward to give them to the mule, but instead, handed them to the little boy, who ate the sugar cubes himself, and put the apple in his pocket.

The mule was wearing an old straw hat, and looked casual, out-of-place. The boy switched him, and he shut his eyes and started up: his chest swelled, tight and sweaty, to fit the dark soft stained leather harness, and the big load behind him started in motion, too.

Buster whined, as the mule went by.

It was spring again then, the month in which Henry had left them, and they were on the back porch. Karen had purchased a Clydesdale yearling, a great and huge animal, whose mane and fur she had shaved to keep it cool in the warming weather, and she had asked a little boy from a nearby farm with time on his hands to train it, in the afternoons. The horse was already gentled, but needed to be stronger. She was having the boy walk him around in the fields, pulling a makeshift sled of stones and tree stumps and old rotten bales of hay.

In the fall, when the Clydesdale was strong enough, she and Dr. Lynly were going to trailer it out to the swamp, and trade it for the mule.

Sydney Bean's leg had healed, been broken again, and was now healing once more. The stallion he was trying to break was showing signs of weakening. There was something in the whites of his eyes, Sydney thought, when he reared up, and he was not slamming himself into the barn—so it seemed to Sydney, anyway—with quite as much anger. Sydney thought that perhaps this coming summer would be the one in which he broke all of his horses, day after day, week after week.

They sat in the hammock and drank Cokes and nibbled radishes, celery, which Karen had washed and put on a little tray. They watched the boy, or one of his friends, his blue shirt a tiny spot against the treeline, as he followed the big dark form of the Clydesdale. The sky was a wide spread of crimson, all along the western trees, towards the river. They couldn't tell which of the local children it was, behind the big horse; it could have been any of them.

"I really miss him," said Sydney Bean. "I really hurt."

"I know," Karen said. She put her hand on Sydney's, and rested it there. "I will help you," she said.

Out in the field, a few cattle egrets fluttered and hopped behind the horse and boy. The great young draft horse lifted his thick legs high and free of the mud with each step, free from the mud made soft by the rains of spring, and slowly—they could tell—he was skidding the sled forward.

The egrets hopped and danced, following at a slight distance, but neither the boy nor the horse seemed to notice. They kept their heads down, and moved forward.

RICHARD BAUSCH

The Man Who Knew Belle Starr

RICHARD BAUSCH (1945–) is the author of twelve volumes of fiction, including the novels *Rebel Powers, Violence, Good Evening Mr. & Mrs. America and All the Ships at Sea,* and *In the Night Season;* and the story collections *Spirits, The Fireman's Wife, Rare & Endangered Species,* and *Selected Stories.* He was recently elected to membership in the Fellowship of Southern Writers. He is Heritage Professor of Writing at George Mason University and lives in rural Virginia with his wife, Karen, and their five children.

On his way west McRae picked up a hitcher, a young woman carrying a paper bag and a leather purse, wearing jeans and a shawl—which she didn't take off, though it was more than ninety degrees out and McRae had no air-conditioning. He was driving an old Dodge Charger with a bad exhaust system and one long crack in the wraparound windshield. He pulled over for her, and she got right in, put the leather purse on the seat between them, and settled herself with the paper bag on her lap between her hands. He had just crossed into Texas from Oklahoma. This was the third day of the trip.

"Where you headed?" he asked.

She said, "What about you?"

"Nevada, maybe."

"Why maybe?"

And that fast he was answering *her* questions. "I just got out of the Air Force," he told her, though this wasn't exactly true. The Air Force had given him a dishonorable discharge, after four years at Leavenworth for assaulting a staff sergeant. He was a bad character. He had a bad temper that had got him into a load of trouble already, and he just wanted to get out west, out to the wide open spaces. Just to see it, really. He had the feeling that people didn't require as much from a person way out where there was that kind of room.

He didn't have any family now. He had five thousand dollars from his father's insurance policy, and he was going to make the money last a while. He said, "I'm sort of undecided about a lot of things."

"Not me," she said.

"You figured out where you're going?"

"You could say that."

"So where might that be?"

She made a fist and then extended her thumb, and turned it over. "Under," she said. "Down."

"Excuse me?"

"Does the radio work?" she asked, reaching for it.

"It's on the blink," he said.

She turned the knob anyway. Then she sat back and folded her arms over the paper bag.

He took a glance at her. She was skinny and long-necked, and her hair was the color of water in a metal pail. She looked just old enough for high school.

"What's in the bag?" he said.

She sat up a little. "Nothing. Another blouse."

"Well, so what did you mean back there?"

"Back where?"

"Look," he said, "we don't have to do any talking if you don't want to."

"Then what will we do?"

"Anything you want," he said.

"What if I just want to sit here and let you drive me all the way to Nevada?"

"That's fine," he said. "That's just fine."

"Well, I won't do that. We can talk."

"Are you going to Nevada?" he asked.

She gave a little shrug of her shoulders. "Why not?"

"All right," he said, and for some reason he offered her his hand. She looked at it and then smiled at him, and he put his hand back on the wheel.

It got a little awkward almost right away. The heat was awful, and she sat there sweating, not saying much. He never thought he was very smooth or anything, and he had been in prison; it had been a long time since he had found himself in the company of a woman. Finally she fell asleep, and for a few miles he could look at her without worrying about anything but staying on the road. He decided that she was kind of good-looking around the eyes and mouth. If she ever filled out, she might be something. He caught himself wondering what might happen, thinking of sex. A girl who traveled alone like this was probably pretty loose. Without quite realizing it, he began to daydream about her, and when he got aroused by the daydream he tried to concentrate on figuring his chances, playing his cards right, not messing up any opportunities—but being gentlemanly, too. He was not the sort of man who forced himself on young women. She slept very quietly, not breathing loudly or sighing or moving much; and then she simply sat up and folded her arms over the bag again and stared out at the road.

"God," she said. "I went out."

"You hungry?" he asked.

"No."

"What's your name? I never got your name."

"Belle Starr," she said, and, winking at him, she made a clicking sound out of the side of her mouth.

"Belle Starr," he said.

"Don't you know who Belle Starr was?"

All he knew was that it was a familiar-sounding name. "Belle Starr."

She put her index finger to the side of his head and said, "Bang."

"Belle Starr," he said.

"Come on," she said. "Annie Oakley. Wild Bill Hickok."

"Oh," McRae said. "Okay."

"That's me," she said, sliding down in the seat. "Belle Starr."

"That's not your real name."

"It's the only one I go by these days."

They rode on in silence for a time.

"What's *your* name?" she asked.

He told her.

"Irish?"

"I never thought about it."

"Where you from, McRae?"

"Washington, D.C."

"Long way from home."

"I haven't been there in years."

"Where *have* you been?"

"Prison," he said. He hadn't known he would say it, and now that he had, he kept his eyes on the road. He might as well have been posing for her; he had an image of himself as he must look from the side, and he shifted his weight a little, sucked in his belly. When he stole a glance at her, he saw that she was simply gazing out at the Panhandle, one hand up like a visor to shade her eyes.

"What about you?" he asked, and felt like somebody in a movie—two people with a past come together on the open road. He wondered how he could get the talk around to the subject of love.

"What *about* me?"

"Where you from?"

"I don't want to bore you with all the facts," she said.

"I don't mind," McRae said. "I got nothing else to do."

"I'm from way up north."

"Okay," he said, "you want me to guess?"

"Maine," she said. "Land of moose and lobster."

He said, "Maine. Well, now."

"See?" she said. "The facts are just a lot of things that don't change."

"Unless you change them," McRae said.

She reached down and, with elaborate care, as if it were fragile, put the paper bag on the floor. Then she leaned back and put her feet up on the dash. She was wearing low-cut tennis shoes.

"You going to sleep?" he asked.

"Just relaxing," she said. But a moment later, when he asked if she wanted to stop and eat, she didn't answer. He looked over and saw that she was sound asleep.

His father had died while he was at Leavenworth. The last time McRae saw him, he was lying on a gurney in one of the bays of D.C. General's emergency ward, a plastic tube in his mouth, an IV set into an ugly yellow-blue bruise on his wrist. McRae had come home on leave from the Air Force—which he had joined on the suggestion of a juvenile judge—to find his father on the floor in the living room, in a pile of old newspapers and bottles, wearing his good suit, with no socks or shoes and no shirt. He looked like he was dead. But the ambulance drivers found a pulse and rushed him off to the hospital. McRae cleaned the house up a little and then followed in the Charger. The old man had been going steadily downhill from the time McRae was a boy, so this latest trouble wasn't new. In the hospital they got the tube in his mouth and hooked him to the IV, and then left him there on the gurney. McRae stood at his side, still in uniform, and when the old man opened his eyes and looked at him, it was clear that he didn't know who it was. The old man blinked, stared, and then sat up, took the tube out of his mouth, and spit something terrible-looking into a small metal dish that was suspended from the complicated apparatus of the room, which made a continual water-dropping sound, like a leaking sink. He looked at McRae again, and then he looked at the tube. "Jesus Christ," he said.

"Hey," McRae said.

"What."

"It's me."

The old man put the tube back in his mouth and looked away.

"Pops," McRae said. He didn't feel anything.

The tube came out. "Don't look at me, boy. You got yourself into it. Getting into trouble, stealing and running around. You got yourself into it."

"I don't mind it, Pops. It's three meals a day and a place to sleep."

"Yeah," the old man said, and then seemed to gargle something. He spit into the little metal dish again.

"I got thirty days of leave, Pops."

"Eh?"

"I don't have to go back for a month."

"Where you going?"

"Around," McRae said.

The truth was that he hated the Air Force, and he was thinking of taking the Charger and driving to Canada or someplace like that, and hiding out for the rest of his life. The Air Force felt like punishment—it *was* punishment—and he had already been in trouble for his quick temper and his attitude. That afternoon he left his father to whatever would happen, got in the Charger, and started north. But he didn't make it. He lost heart a few miles south of New York City, and he turned around and came back. The old man had been moved to a room in the alcoholic ward, but McRae didn't go to see him. He stayed in the house, watching television and drinking beer, and when old high school buddies came by he went around with them a little. Mostly he stayed home, though, and at the end of his leave he locked the place and drove back to Chanute, in Illinois, where he was stationed. He hadn't been there two months before he got into the scrape that landed him in prison. A staff sergeant caught him drinking beer in the dayroom of one of the training barracks and asked for his name. McRae walked over to him, said, "My name is trouble," and, at the word *trouble,* struck the other man in the face. He'd had a lot of beer, and he had been sitting there in the dark, going over everything in his mind, and the staff sergeant, a baby-faced man with a spare tire of flesh around his waist and an attitude about the stripes on his sleeves, had just walked into it. McRae didn't even know him. Yet he stood over the sergeant where he had fallen and started kicking him. The poor man wound up in the hospital with a broken jaw (the first punch had done it), a few cracked ribs, and multiple lacerations and bruises. The court-martial was swift. The sentence was four years at hard labor, along with a dishonorable discharge. He'd had less than a month on the sentence when he got the news about his father. He felt no surprise, nor, really, any grief, yet there was a little thrill of something like fear; he was in his cell, and for an instant some part of him actually wanted to remain there, inside walls, where things were certain and no decisions had to be made. A week later he learned of the money from the insurance, which would have been more than the five thousand except that his father had been a few months behind on the rent and on other payments. McRae settled what he had to of those things, and kept the rest. He had started to feel like a happy man, out of Leavenworth and the Air Force. And now he was on his way to Nevada, or someplace like that—and he had picked up a girl.

He drove on until dusk, stopping only for gas, and the girl slept right through. Just past the line into New Mexico he pulled off the interstate and went north for a mile or so, looking for some place other than a chain restaurant to eat. She sat up straight and pushed the hair back from her face. "Where are we?"

"New Mexico," he said. "I'm looking for a place to eat."

"I'm not hungry."

"Well," he said, "you might be able to go all day without eating, but I got a three-meal-a-day habit to support."

She brought the paper bag up from the floor and held it in her lap.

"You got food in there?"

"No."

"You're very pretty—childlike, sort of, when you sleep."

"I didn't snore?"

"You were quiet as a mouse."

"And you think I'm pretty."

"I guess you know a thing like that. I hope I didn't offend you."

"I don't like dirty remarks," she said. "But I guess you don't mean to be dirty."

"Dirty."

"Sometimes people can say a thing like that and mean it very dirty, but I could tell you didn't."

He pulled in at a roadside diner and turned the ignition off. "Well?" he said.

She sat there with the bag on her lap. "I don't think I'll go in with you."

"You can have a cold drink or something," he said.

"You go in. I'll wait out here."

"Come on in there with me and have a cold drink," McRae said. "I'll buy it for you. I'll buy you dinner, if you want."

"I don't want to," she said.

He got out and started for the entrance, and before he reached it, he heard her door open and close, and turned to watch her come toward him, thin and waiflike in the shawl, which hid her arms and hands.

The diner was empty. A long, low counter ran along one side, with soda fountains and glass cases in which pies and cakes were set. There were booths along one wall. Everything seemed in order, except that no one was around.

McRae and the girl stood in the doorway for a moment and waited, and finally she stepped in and took a seat in the first booth. "I guess we're supposed to seat ourselves," she said.

"This is weird," McRae said.

"Hey," she said, rising. "A jukebox." She strode over to it and leaned on it, crossing one leg behind the other at the ankle, her hair falling down to hide her face.

"Hello?" McRae said. "Anybody here?"

"Got any change?" the girl asked.

He gave her a quarter and then sat at the counter. A door at the far end of the diner swung in and a big, red-faced man entered, wearing a white cook's apron over a sweat-stained baby-blue shirt, the sleeves of which he had rolled up past the meaty curve of his elbows. "Yeah?" he said.

"You open?" McRae asked.

"That jukebox don't work, honey," the man said.

"You open?" McRae said, as the girl came and sat down beside him.

"I guess maybe I am."

"Place is kind of empty."

"What do you want to eat?"

"You got a menu?"

"You want a menu?"

"Sure," McRae said. "Why not."

"Truth is," the big man said, "I'm selling this place. I don't have menus anymore. I make hamburgers and breakfast stuff. Some french fries and cold drinks. A hot dog, maybe. I'm not keeping track."

"Let's go somewhere else," the girl said.

"Yeah," the big man said, "why don't you do that."

"Look," McRae said, "what's the story here?"

The other man shrugged. "You came in at the end of the run, you know what I mean? I'm going out of business. Sit down and I'll make you a hamburger, on the house."

McRae looked at the girl.

"Okay," she said, in a tone that made it clear that she would've been happier to leave.

The big man put his hands on the bar and leaned toward her. "Miss, if I were you, I wouldn't look a gift horse in the mouth."

"I don't like hamburger," she said.

"You want a hot dog?" the man said. "I got a hot dog for you. Guaranteed to please."

"I'll have some french fries," she said.

The big man turned to the grill and opened the metal drawer under it. He was very wide at the hips, and his legs were like tree trunks. "I get out of the Army after twenty years," he said, "and I got a little money put aside. The wife and I decide we want to get into the restaurant business. The government's going to be paying me a nice pension, and we got the savings, so we sink it all in this Goddamn diner. Six and a half miles from the interstate. You get the picture? The guy's selling us this diner at a great price, you know? A terrific price. For a song, I'm in the restaurant business. The wife will cook the food and I'll wait tables, you know, until we start to make a little extra, and then we'll hire somebody—a high school kid, or somebody like that. We might even open another restaurant, if the going gets good enough. But, of course, this is New Mexico. This is six and a half miles from the interstate. You know what's up the road? Nothing." He had put the hamburger on, and a basket of frozen french fries. "Now the wife decides she's had enough of life on the border, and off she goes to Seattle to sit in the rain with her mother, and here I am trying to sell a place nobody else is dumb enough to buy. You know what I mean?"

"That's rough," McRae said.

"You're the second customer I've had all *week,* bub."

The girl said, "I guess that cash register's empty, then, huh."

"It ain't full, honey."

She got up and wandered across the room. For a while she stood gazing out the windows over the booths, her hands invisible under the woolen shawl. When she came back to sit next to McRae again, the hamburger and french fries were ready.

"On the house," the big man said.

And the girl brought a gun out from under the shawl—a pistol that looked like a toy. "Suppose you open up that register, Mr. Poor Mouth," she said.

The big man looked at her, then at McRae, who had taken a large bite of his hamburger and had it bulging in his cheeks.

"This thing is loaded, and I'll use it."

"Well, for Christ's sake," the big man said.

McRae started to get off the stool. "Hold on a minute," he said to them both, his words garbled by the mouthful of food, and then everything started happening at once. The girl aimed the pistol. There was a popping sound—a single small pop, not much louder than the sound of a cap gun—and the big man took a step back, into the dishes and pans. He stared at the girl, wide-eyed, for what seemed like a long time, and then went down, pulling dishes with him in a tremendous shattering.

"Jesus Christ," McRae said, swallowing, standing back far from her, raising his hands.

She put the pistol back in her jeans, under the shawl, and then went around the counter and opened the cash register. "Damn," she said.

McRae said, low, "Jesus Christ."

And now she looked at him; it was as if she had forgotten he was there. "What're you standing there with your hands up like that?"

"God," he said, "oh, God."

"Stop it," she said. "Put your hands down."

He did so.

"Cash register's empty." She sat down on one of the stools and gazed over at the body of the man where it had fallen. "Damn."

"Look," McRae said, "take my car. You can have my car."

She seemed puzzled. "I don't want your car. What do I want your car for?"

"You—" he said. He couldn't talk, couldn't focus clearly, or think. He looked at the man, who lay very still, and then he began to cry.

"Will you stop it?" she said, coming off the stool, reaching under the shawl and bringing out the pistol again.

"Jesus," he said. "Good Jesus."

She pointed the pistol at his forehead. "Bang," she said. "What's my name?"

"Your—name?"

"My name."

"Belle—" he managed.

"Come on," she said. "The whole thing. You remember."

"Belle—Belle Starr."

"Right." She let the gun hand drop to her side, into one of the folds of the shawl. "I like that so much better than Annie Oakley."

"Please," McRae said.

She took a few steps away from him and then whirled and aimed the gun. "I think we better get out of here. What do you think?"

"Take the car," he said, almost with exasperation; he was frightened to hear it in his voice.

"I can't drive," she said simply. "Never learned."

"Jesus," he said. It went out of him like a sigh.

"Lordy," she said, gesturing with the pistol for him to move to the door, "it's hard to believe you were ever in *prison.*"

The interstate went on into the dark, beyond the glow of the headlights. He lost track of miles, road signs, other traffic, time; trucks came by and surprised him, and other cars seemed to materialize as they started the lane change that would bring them over in front of him. He saw their taillights grow small in the distance, and all the while the girl sat watching him, her hands somewhere under the shawl. For a long time he heard only the sound of the rushing night air at the windows, and then she moved a little, shifted her weight, bringing one leg up on the seat.

"What were you in prison for, anyway?"

Her voice startled him, and for a moment he couldn't think of an answer.

"Come on," she said. "I'm getting bored with all this quiet. What were you in prison for?"

"I—beat up a guy."

"That's all?"

"Yes, that's all." He couldn't keep the irritation out of his voice.

"Tell me about it."

"It was just—I just beat up a guy. It wasn't anything."

"I didn't shoot that man for money, you know."

McRae said nothing.

"I shot him because he made a nasty remark to me about the hot dog."

"I didn't hear any nasty remark."

"If he hadn't said it, he'd still be alive."

McRae held tight to the wheel.

"Don't you wish it was the Wild West?" she said.

"Wild West," he said. "Yeah." He could barely speak for the dryness in his mouth and the deep ache of his own breathing.

"You know," she said, "I'm not really from Maine."

He nodded

"I'm from Florida."

"Florida," he managed.

"Yes, only I don't have a southern accent, so people think I'm not from there. Do you hear any trace of a southern accent at all when I talk?"

"No," he said.

"Now you—you've got an accent. A definite southern accent."

He was silent.

"Talk to me," she said.

"What do you want me to say?" he said. "Jesus."

"You could ask me things."

"Ask you things—"

"Ask me what my name is."

Without hesitating, McRae said, "What's your name?"

"You know."

"No, really," he said, trying to play along.

"It's Belle Starr."

"Belle Starr," he said.

"Nobody *but,*" she said.

"Good," he said.

"And I don't care about money, either," she said. "That's not what I'm after."

"No," McRae said.

"What I'm after is adventure."

"Right," McRae said.

"Fast living."

"Fast living, right."

"A good time."

"Good," he said.

"I'm going to live a ton before I die."

"A ton, yes."

"What about you?"

"Yes," he said. "Me too."

"Want to join up with me?"

"Join up," he said. "Right." He was watching the road.

She leaned toward him a little. "Do you think I'm lying about my name?"

"No."

"Good," she said.

He had begun to feel as though he might start throwing up what he'd had of the hamburger. His stomach was cramping on him, and he was dizzy. He might even be having a heart attack.

"Your eyes are as big as saucers," she said.

He tried to narrow them a little. His whole body was shaking now.

"You know how old I am, McRae? I'm nineteen."

He nodded, glanced at her and then at the road again.

"How old are you?"

"Twenty-three."

"Do you believe people go to heaven when they die?"

"Oh, God," he said.

"Look, I'm not going to shoot you while you're driving the car. We'd crash if I did that."

"Oh," he said. "Oh, Jesus, please—look, I never saw anybody shot before—"

"Will you *stop it?*"

He put one hand to his mouth. He was soaked: he felt the sweat on his upper lip, and then he felt the dampness all through his clothes.

She said, "I don't kill everybody I meet, you know."

"No," he said. "Of course not." The absurdity of this exchange almost brought a laugh up out of him. How astonishing, that a laugh could be anywhere in him at such a time, but here it was, rising up in his throat like some loosened part of his anatomy. He held on with his whole mind, and a moment passed before he realized that *she* was laughing.

"Actually," she said, "I haven't killed all that many people."

"How—" he began. Then he had to stop to breathe. "How many?"

"Take a guess."

"I don't have any idea," he said.

"Well," she said, "you'll just have to guess. And you'll notice that I haven't spent any time in prison."

He was quiet.

"*Guess,*" she said.

McRae said, "Ten?"

"No."

He waited.

"Come on, keep guessing."

"More than ten?"

"Maybe."

"More than ten," he said.

"Well, all right. Less than ten."

"Less than ten," he said.

"Guess," she said.

"Nine."

"No."

"Eight."

"No, not eight."

"Six?"

"Not six."

"Five?"

"Five and a half people," she said. "You almost hit it right on the button."

"Five and a half people," McRae said.

"Right. A kid who was hitchhiking, like me; a guy at a gas station; a dog that must've got lost—I count him as the half; another guy at a gas station; a guy that took me to a motel and made an obscene gesture to me; and the guy at the diner. That makes five and a half."

"Five and a half," McRae said.

"You keep repeating everything I say. I wish you'd quit that."

He wiped his hand across his mouth and then feigned a cough to keep from having to speak.

"Five and a half people," she said, turning a little in the seat, putting her knees up on the dash. "Have you ever met anybody like me? Tell the truth."

"No," McRae said, "nobody."

"Just think about it, McRae. You can say you rode with Belle Starr. You can tell your grandchildren."

He was afraid to say anything to this, for fear of changing the delicate balance of the thought. Yet he knew the worst mistake would be to say nothing at all. He was beginning to sense something of the cunning that he would need to survive, even as he knew that the slightest miscalculation might mean the end of him. He said, with fake wonder, "I knew Belle Starr."

She said, "Think of it."

"Something," he said.

And she sat farther down in the seat. "Amazing."

He kept to fifty-five miles an hour, and everyone else was speeding. The girl sat straight up now, nearly facing him on the seat. For long periods she had been quiet, simply watching him drive. Soon they were going to need gas; they had less than half a tank.

"Look at those people speeding," she said. "We're the only ones obeying the speed limit. Look at them."

"Do you want me to speed up?"

"I think they ought to get tickets for speeding, that's what I think. Sometimes I wish I were a policeman."

"Look," McRae said, "we're going to need gas pretty soon."

"No, let's just run it until it quits. We can always hitch a ride with somebody."

"This car's got a great engine," McRae said. "We might have to outrun the police, and I wouldn't want to do that in any other car."

"This old thing? It's got a crack in the windshield. The radio doesn't work."

"Right. But it's a fast car. It'll outrun a police car."

She put one arm over the seat back and looked out the rear window. "You really think the police are chasing us?"

"They might be," he said.

She stared at him a moment. "No. There's no reason. Nobody saw us."

"But if somebody did—this car, I mean, it'll go like crazy."

"I'm afraid of speeding, though," she said. "Besides, you know what I found out? If you run slow enough, the cops go right past you. Right on past you, looking for somebody who's in a hurry. No, I think it's best if we just let it run until it quits and then get out and hitch."

McRae thought he knew what might happen when the gas ran out: she would make him push the car to the side of the road, and then she would walk him back into the cactus and brush there, and when they were far enough from the road, she would shoot him. He knew this as if she had spelled it all out, and he began again to try for the cunning he would need. "Belle," he said. "Why don't we lay low for a few days in Albuquerque?"

"Is that an obscene gesture?" she asked.

"No!" he said, almost shouted. "No! That's—it's outlaw talk. You know. Hide out from the cops—lay low. It's—it's prison talk."

"Well, I've never been in prison."

"That's all I meant."

"You want to hide out."

"Right," he said.

"You and me?"

"You—you asked if I wanted to join up with you."

"Did I?" She seemed puzzled by this.

"Yes," he said, feeling himself press it a little. "Don't you remember?"

"I guess I do."

"You did," he said.

"I don't know."

"Belle Starr had a gang," he said.

"She did?"

"I could be the first member of your gang."

She sat there thinking this over. McRae's blood moved at the thought that she was deciding whether or not he would live. "Well," she said, "maybe."

"You've got to have a gang, Belle."

"We'll see," she said.

A moment later she said, "How much money do you have?"

"I have enough to start a gang."

"It takes money to start a gang?"

"Well—" He was at a loss.

"How much do you have?"

He said, "A few hundred."

"Really?" she said. "That much?"

"Just enough to—just enough to get to Nevada."

"Can I have it?"

He said, "Sure." He was holding the wheel and looking out into the night.

"And we'll be a gang?"

"Right," he said.

"I like the idea. Belle Starr and her gang."

McRae started talking about what the gang could do, making it up as he went along, trying to sound like all the gangster movies he'd seen. He heard himself talking about things like robbery and getaway cars and not getting nabbed and staying out of prison, and then, as she sat there staring at him, he started talking about being at Leavenworth, what it was like. He went on about it, the hours of forced work and the time alone, the harsh day-to-day routines, the bad food. Before he was through, feeling the necessity of deepening her sense of him as her new accomplice—and feeling strangely as though in some way he had indeed become exactly that—he was telling her everything, all the bad times he'd had: his father's alcoholism, and growing up wanting to hit something for the anger that was in him; the years of getting into trouble; the fighting and the kicking and what it had got him. He embellished it all, made it sound worse than it really was, because she seemed to be going for it and because, telling it to her, he felt oddly sorry for himself; a version of this story of pain and neglect and lonely rage was true. He had been through a lot. And as he finished describing for her the scene at the hospital the last time he saw his father, he was almost certain he had struck a chord in her. He thought he saw it in the rapt expression on her face.

"Anyway," he said, and smiled at her.

"McRae?" she said.

"Yeah?"

"Can you pull over?"

"Well," he said, his voice shaking, "why don't we wait until it runs out of gas?"

She was silent.

"We'll be that much farther down the road," he said.

"I don't really want a gang," she said. "I don't like dealing with other people that much. I mean, I don't think I'm a leader."

"Oh, yes," McRae said. "No—you're a leader. You're definitely a leader. I was in the Air Force and I know leaders, and you are definitely what I'd call a leader."

"Really?"

"Absolutely. You are leadership material all the way."

"I wouldn't have thought so."

"Definitely," he said. "Definitely a leader."

"But I don't really like people around, you know."

"That's a leadership quality. Not wanting people around. It is definitely a leadership quality."

"Boy," she said, "the things you learn."

He waited. If he could only think himself through to the way out. If he could get her to trust him, get the car stopped—be there when she turned her back.

"You want to be in my gang, huh?"

"I sure do," he said.

"Well, I guess I'll have to think about it."

"I'm surprised nobody's mentioned it to you before."

"You're just saying that."

"No, really."

"Were you ever married?" she asked.

"Married?" he said, and then stammered over the answer. "Ah—uh, no."

"You ever been in a gang before?"

"A couple times, but—they never had good leadership."

"You're giving me a line, huh."

"No," he said, "it's true. No good leadership. It was always a problem."

"I'm tired," she said, shifting toward him a little. "I'm tired of talking."

The steering wheel was hurting the insides of his hands. He held tight, looking at the coming-on of the white stripes in the road. There were no other cars now, and not a glimmer of light anywhere beyond the headlights.

"Don't you ever get tired of talking?"

"I never was much of a talker," he said.

"I guess I don't mind talking as much as I mind listening," she said.

He made a sound in his throat which he hoped she took for agreement.

"That's just when I'm tired, though."

"Why don't you take a nap?" he said.

She leaned back against the door and regarded him. "There's plenty of time for that later."

"So," he wanted to say, "you're not going to kill me—we're a gang?"

They had gone for a long time without speaking, an excruciating hour of minutes, during which the gas gauge had sunk to just above empty, and finally she had begun talking about herself, mostly in the third person. It was hard to make sense of most of it, yet he listened as if to instructions concerning how to extricate himself. She talked about growing up in Florida, in the country, and owning a horse; she remembered when she was taught to swim by somebody she called Bill, as if McRae would know who that was; and then she told him how when her father ran away with her mother's sister, her mother started having men friends over all the time. "There was a lot of obscene things going on," she said, and her voice tightened a little.

"Some people don't care what happens to their kids," McRae said.

"Isn't it the truth?" she said. Then she took the pistol out of the shawl. "Take this exit."

He pulled onto the ramp and up an incline to a two-lane road that went off through the desert, toward a glow that burned on the horizon. For perhaps five miles the road was straight as a plumb line, and then it curved into long, low undulations of sand and mesquite and cactus.

"My mother's men friends used to do whatever they wanted to me," she said. "It went on all the time. All sorts of obscene goings-on."

McRae said, "I'm sorry that happened to you, Belle." And for an instant he was surprised by the sincerity of his feeling: it was as if he couldn't feel sorry enough. Yet it was genuine: it had to do with his own unhappy story. The whole world seemed very, very sad to him. "I'm really very sorry," he said.

She was quiet a moment, as if thinking about this. Then she said, "Let's pull over now. I'm tired of riding."

"It's almost out of gas," he said.

"I know, but pull it over anyway."

"You sure you want to do that?"

"See?" she said. "That's what I mean—I wouldn't like being told what I should do all the time, or asked if I was sure of what I wanted or not."

He pulled the car over and slowed to a stop. "You're right," he said. "See? Leadership. I'm just not used to somebody with leadership qualities."

She held the gun a little toward him. He was looking at the small, dark, perfect circle at the end of the barrel. "I guess we should get out," she said.

"I guess so," he said.

"Do you have any relatives left anywhere?"

"No."

"Your folks are both dead?"

"Right, yes."

"Which one died first?"

"I told you," he said. "Didn't I? My mother, my mother died first."

"Do you feel like an orphan?"

He sighed. "Sometimes." The whole thing was slipping away from him.

"I guess I do too." She reached back and opened her door. "Let's get out now."

And when he reached for the door handle, she aimed the gun at his head. "Get out slow."

"Aw, Jesus," he said. "Look, you're not going to do this, are you? I mean, I thought we were friends and all."

"Just get out real slow, like I said to."

"Okay," he said. "I'm getting out." He opened his door, and the ceiling light surprised and frightened him. Some wordless part of him understood that this was it, and all his talk had come to nothing: all the questions she had asked him, and everything he had told her—it was all completely useless. This was going to happen to him, and it wouldn't mean anything; it would just be what happened.

"Real slow," she said. "Come on."

"Why are you doing this?" he asked. "You've got to tell me that before you do it."

"Will you please get out of the car now?"

He just stared at her.

"All right, I'll shoot you where you sit."

"Okay," he said. "Don't shoot."

She said in an irritable voice, as though she were talking to a recalcitrant child, "You're just putting it off."

He was backing himself out, keeping his eyes on the little barrel of the gun, and he could hear something coming, seemed to notice it in the same instant that she said, "Wait." He stood half in and half out of the car, doing as she said, and a truck came over the hill ahead of them, a tractor trailer, all white light and roaring.

"Stay still," she said, crouching, aiming the gun at him.

The truck came fast, was only fifty yards away, and without having to decide about it, without even knowing that he would do it, McRae bolted into the road. He was running; he heard the exhausted sound of his own breath, the truck horn blaring, coming on, louder, the thing bearing down on him, something buzzing past his head. Time slowed. His legs faltered under him, were heavy, all the nerves gone out of them. In the light of the oncoming truck he saw his own white hands outstretched as if to grasp something in the air before him, and then the truck was past him, the blast of air from it propelling him over the side of the road and down an embankment, in high, dry grass, which pricked his skin and crackled like hay.

He was alive. He lay very still. Above him was the long shape of the road, curving off in the distance, the light of the truck going on. The noise faded and was nothing. A little wind stirred. He heard the car door close. Carefully he got to all fours and crawled a few yards away from where he had fallen. He couldn't be sure of which direction—he only knew he couldn't stay where he was. Then he heard what he thought were her footsteps in the road, and he froze. He lay on his side, facing the embankment. When she appeared there he almost cried out.

"McRae?" she said. "Did I get you?" She was looking right at where he was in the dark, and he stopped breathing. "McRae?"

He watched her move along the edge of the embankment.

"McRae?" She put one hand over her eyes and stared at a place a few feet over from him, and then she turned and went back out of sight. He heard the car door again, and again he began to crawl farther away. The ground was cold and rough, sandy.

He heard her put the key in the trunk. He stood up, tried to run, but something went wrong in his leg, something sent him sprawling, and a sound came out of him that seemed to echo, to stay on the air, as if to call her to him. He tried to be perfectly still, tried not to breathe, hearing now the small pop of the gun. He counted the reports: one, two, three. She was standing there at the edge of the road, firing into the dark, toward where she must have thought she heard the sound. Then she was rattling the paper bag. She was reloading—he could hear the click of the gun. He tried to get up and couldn't. He had sprained his ankle, had done something very bad to it. Now he was crawling wildly, blindly, through the tall grass, hearing again the small report of the pistol. At last he rolled into a shallow gully. He lay there with his face down, breathing the dust, his own voice leaving him in a whimpering, animal-like sound that he couldn't stop, even as he held both shaking hands over his mouth.

"McRae?" She sounded so close. "Hey," she said. "McRae?"

He didn't move. He lay there perfectly still, trying to stop himself from crying. He was sorry for everything he had ever done. He didn't care about the money, or the car, or going out west, or anything. When he lifted his head to peer over the lip of the gully and saw that she had started down the embankment with his flashlight, moving like someone with time and the patience to use it, he lost his sense of himself as McRae; he was just something crippled and breathing in the dark, lying flat in a little winding gully of weeds and sand. McRae was gone, was someone far, far away, from ages ago—a man fresh out of prison, with the whole country to wander in and insurance money in his pocket, who had headed west with the idea that maybe his luck, at long last, had changed.

CHARLES BAXTER

Gryphon

CHARLES BAXTER (1947–) is the author of two novels and four books of short stories of which his most recent work is *Believers,* published by Pantheon. Baxter is also the author of a book of essays, *Burning Down the House,* published by Graywolf. He lives in Ann Arbor and teaches at the University of Michigan.

On Wednesday afternoon, between the geography lesson on ancient Egypt's hand-operated irrigation system and an art project that involved drawing a model city next to a mountain, our fourth-grade teacher, Mr. Hibler, developed a cough. This cough began with a series of muffled throat-clearings and progressed to propulsive noises contained within Mr. Hibler's closed mouth. "Listen to him," Carol Peterson whispered to me. "He's gonna blow up." Mr. Hibler's laughter—dazed and infrequent—sounded a bit like his cough, but as we worked on our model cities we would look up, thinking he was enjoying a joke, and see Mr. Hibler's face turning red, his cheeks puffed out. This was not laughter. Twice he bent over, and his loose tie, like a plumb line, hung down straight from his neck as he exploded himself into a Kleenex. He would excuse himself, then go on coughing. "I'll bet you a dime," Carol Peterson whispered, "we get a substitute tomorrow."

Carol sat at the desk in front of mine and was a bad person—when she thought no one was looking she would blow her nose on notebook paper, then crumple it up and throw it into the wastebasket—but at times of crisis she spoke the truth. I knew I'd lose the dime.

"No deal," I said.

When Mr. Hibler stood us in formation at the door just prior to the final bell, he was almost incapable of speech. "I'm sorry, boys and girls," he said. "I seem to be coming down with something."

"I hope you feel better tomorrow, Mr. Hibler," Bobby Kryzanowicz, the faultless brown-noser, said, and I heard Carol Peterson's evil giggle. Then Mr. Hibler opened the door and we walked out to the buses, a clique of us starting noisily to hawk and raugh as soon as we thought we were a few feet beyond Mr. Hibler's earshot.

Since Five Oaks was a rural community, and in Michigan, the supply of substitute teachers was limited to the town's unemployed community college graduates, a pool of about four mothers. These ladies fluttered, provided easeful class days, and nervously covered material we had mastered weeks earlier. Therefore it was a surprise when a woman we had never seen came into the class the next day, carrying a purple purse, a checkerboard lunchbox, and a few books. She put the books on one side of Mr. Hibler's desk and the lunchbox on the other, next to the Voice of Music phonograph. Three of us in the back of the room were playing with Heever, the chameleon that lived in a terrarium and on one of the plastic drapes, when she walked in.

She clapped her hands at us. "Little boys," she said, "why are you bent over together like that?" She didn't wait for us to answer. "Are you tormenting an animal? Put it back. Please sit down at your desks. I want no cabals this time of the day." We just stared at her. "Boys," she repeated, "I asked you to sit down."

I put the chameleon in his terrarium and felt my way to my desk, never taking my eyes off the woman. With white and green chalk, she had started to draw a tree on the left side of the blackboard. She didn't look usual. Furthermore, her tree was outsized, disproportionate, for some reason.

"This room needs a tree," she said, with one line drawing the suggestion of a leaf. "A large, leafy, shady, deciduous . . . oak."

Her fine, light hair had been done up in what I would learn years later was called a chignon, and she wore gold-rimmed glasses whose lenses seemed to have the faintest blue tint. Harold Knardahl, who sat across from me, whispered, "Mars," and I nodded slowly, savoring the imminent weirdness of the day. The substitute drew another branch with an extravagant arm gesture, then turned around and said, "Good morning. I don't believe I said good morning to all of you yet."

Facing us, she was no special age—an adult is an adult—but her face had two prominent lines, descending vertically from the sides of her mouth to her chin. I knew where I had seen those lines before: *Pinocchio.* They were marionette lines. "You may stare at me," she said to us, as a few more kids from the last bus came into the room, their eyes fixed on her, "for a few more seconds, until the bell rings. Then I will permit no more staring. Looking I will permit. Staring, no. It is impolite to stare, and a sign of bad breeding. You cannot make a social effort while staring."

Harold Knardahl did not glance at me, or nudge, but I heard him whisper

"Mars" again, trying to get more mileage out of his single joke with the kids who had just come in.

When everyone was seated, the substitute teacher finished her tree, put down her chalk fastidiously on the phonograph, brushed her hands, and faced us. "Good morning," she said. "I am Miss Ferenczi, your teacher for the day. I am fairly new to your community, and I don't believe any of you know me. I will therefore start by telling you a story about myself."

While we settled back, she launched into her tale. She said her grandfather had been a Hungarian prince; her mother had been born in some place called Flanders, had been a pianist, and had played concerts for people Miss Ferenczi referred to as "crowned heads." She gave us a knowing look. "Grieg," she said, "the Norwegian master, wrote a concerto for piano that was . . ."—she paused—"my mother's triumph at her debut concert in London." Her eyes searched the ceiling. Our eyes followed. Nothing up there but ceiling tile. "For reasons that I shall not go into, my family's fortunes took us to Detroit, then north to dreadful Saginaw, and now here I am in Five Oaks, as your substitute teacher, for today, Thursday, October the eleventh. I believe it will be a good day: all the forecasts coincide. We shall start with your reading lesson. Take out your reading book. I believe it is called *Broad Horizons*, or something along those lines."

Jeannie Vermeesch raised her hand. Miss Ferenczi nodded at her. "Mr. Hibler always starts the day with the Pledge of Allegiance," Jeannie whined.

"Oh, does he? In that case," Miss Ferenczi said, "you must know it *very* well by now, and we certainly need not spend our time on it. No, no allegiance pledging on the premises today, by my reckoning. Not with so much sunlight coming into the room. A pledge does not suit my mood." She glanced at her watch. "Time *is* flying. Take out *Broad Horizons*."

She disappointed us by giving us an ordinary lesson, complete with vocabulary and drills, comprehension questions, and recitation. She didn't seem to care for the material, however. She sighed every few minutes and rubbed her glasses with a frilly handkerchief that she withdrew, magician-style, from her left sleeve.

After reading we moved on to arithmetic. It was my favorite time of the morning, when the lazy autumn sunlight dazzled its way through ribbons of clouds past the windows on the east side of the classroom and crept across the linoleum floor. On the playground the first group of children, the kindergartners, were running on the quack grass just beyond the monkey bars. We were doing multiplication tables. Miss Ferenczi had made John Wazny stand up at his desk in the front row. He was supposed to go through the tables of six. From where I was sitting, I could smell the Vitalis soaked into John's plastered hair. He was doing fine until he came to six times eleven and six times twelve. "Six times eleven," he said, "is sixty-eight. Six times twelve is . . ." He put his fingers to his head, quickly and secretly sniffed his fingertips, and said, ". . . seventy-two." Then he sat down.

"Fine," Miss Ferenczi said. "Well now. That was very good."

"Miss Ferenczi!" One of the Eddy twins was waving her hand desperately in the air. "Miss Ferenczi! Miss Ferenczi!"

"Yes?"

"John said that six times eleven is sixty-eight and you said he was right!"

"*Did* I?" She gazed at the class with a jolly look breaking across her marionette's face. "Did I say that? Well, what *is* six times eleven?"

"It's sixty-six!"

She nodded. "Yes. So it is. But, and I know some people will not entirely agree with me, at some times it is sixty-eight."

"When? When is it sixty-eight?"

We were all waiting.

"In higher mathematics, which you children do not yet understand, six times eleven can be considered to be sixty-eight." She laughed through her nose. "In higher mathematics numbers are . . . more fluid. The only thing a number does is contain a certain amount of something. Think of water. A cup is not the only way to measure a certain amount of water, is it?" We were staring, shaking our heads. "You could use saucepans or thimbles. In either case, the water *would be the same.* Perhaps," she started again, "it would be better for you to think that six times eleven is sixty-eight only when I am in the room."

"Why is it sixty-eight," Mark Poole asked, "when you're in the room?"

"Because it's more interesting that way," she said, smiling very rapidly behind her blue-tinted glasses. "Besides, I'm your substitute teacher, am I not?" We all nodded. "Well, then, think of six times eleven equals sixty-eight as a substitute fact."

"A substitute fact?"

"Yes." Then she looked at us carefully. "Do you think," she asked, "that anyone is going to be hurt by a substitute fact?"

We looked back at her.

"Will the plants on the windowsill be hurt?" We glanced at them. There were sensitive plants thriving in a green plastic tray, and several wilted ferns in small clay pots. "Your dogs and cats, or your moms and dads?" She waited. "So," she concluded, "what's the problem?"

"But it's wrong," Janice Weber said, "isn't it?"

"What's your name, young lady?"

"Janice Weber."

"And you think it's wrong, Janice?"

"I was just asking."

"Well, all right. You were just asking. I think we've spent enough time on this matter by now, don't you, class? You are free to think what you like. When your teacher, Mr. Hibler, returns, six times eleven will be sixty-six again, you can rest assured. And it will be that for the rest of your lives in Five Oaks. Too bad, eh?" She raised her eyebrows and glinted herself at us. "But for now, it wasn't. So much for that. Let us go on to your assigned problems for today, as painstakingly outlined, I see, in Mr. Hibler's lesson plan. Take out a sheet of paper and write your names on the upper left-hand corner."

For the next half hour we did the rest of our arithmetic problems. We handed them in and then went on to spelling, my worst subject. Spelling always came before lunch. We were taking spelling dictation and looking at the clock. "Thorough," Miss Ferenczi said. "Boundary." She walked in the aisles between the desks, holding the spelling book open and looking down at our papers. "Balcony." I clutched my pencil. Somehow, the way she said those words, they seemed foreign, mis-voweled and mis-consonanted. I stared down at what I had spelled. *Balconie.* I turned the pencil upside down and erased my mistake. *Balconey.* That looked better, but still incorrect. I cursed the world of spelling and tried erasing it again and saw the paper beginning to wear away. *Balkony.* Suddenly I felt a hand on my shoulder.

"I don't like that word either," Miss Ferenczi whispered, bent over, her mouth near my ear. "It's ugly. My feeling is, if you don't like a word, you don't have to use it." She straightened up, leaving behind a slight odor of Clorets.

At lunchtime we went out to get our trays of sloppy joes, peaches in heavy syrup, coconut cookies, and milk, and brought them back to the classroom, where Miss Ferenczi was sitting at the desk, eating a brown sticky thing she had unwrapped from tightly rubber-banded waxed paper. "Miss Ferenczi," I said, raising my hand. "You don't have to eat with us. You can eat with the other teachers. There's a teacher's lounge," I ended up, "next to the principal's office."

"No, thank you," she said. "I prefer it here."

"We've got a room monitor," I said. "Mrs. Eddy." I pointed to where Mrs. Eddy, Joyce and Judy's mother, sat silently at the back of the room, doing her knitting.

"That's fine," Miss Ferenczi said. "But I shall continue to eat here, with you children. I prefer it," she repeated.

"How come?" Wayne Razmer asked without raising his hand.

"I talked to the other teachers before class this morning," Miss Ferenczi said, biting into her brown food. "There was a great rattling of the words for the fewness of the ideas. I didn't care for their brand of hilarity. I don't like ditto-machine jokes."

"Oh," Wayne said.

"What's that you're eating?" Maxine Sylvester asked, twitching her nose. "Is it food?"

"It most certainly *is* food. It's a stuffed fig. I had to drive almost down to Detroit to get it. I also brought some smoked sturgeon. And this," she said, lifting some green leaves out of her lunchbox, "is raw spinach, cleaned this morning."

"Why're you eating raw spinach?" Maxine asked.

"It's good for you," Miss Ferenczi said. "More stimulating than soda pop or smelling salts." I bit into my sloppy joe and stared blankly out the window. An almost invisible moon was faintly silvered in the daytime autumn sky. "As far as food is concerned," Miss Ferenczi was saying, "you have to shuffle the pack. Mix it up. Too many people eat . . . well, never mind."

"Miss Ferenczi," Carol Peterson said, "what are we going to do this afternoon?"

"Well," she said, looking down at Mr. Hibler's lesson plan, "I see that your teacher, Mr. Hibler, has you scheduled for a unit on the Egyptians." Carol groaned. "Yessss," Miss Ferenczi continued, "that is what we will do: the Egyptians. A remarkable people. Almost as remarkable as the Americans. But not quite." She lowered her head, did her quick smile, and went back to eating her spinach.

After noon recess we came back into the classroom and saw that Miss Ferenczi had drawn a pyramid on the blackboard close to her oak tree. Some of us who had been playing baseball were messing around in the back of the room, dropping the bats and gloves into the playground box, and Ray Schontzeler had just slugged me when I heard Miss Ferenczi's high-pitched voice, quavering with emotions. "Boys," she said, "come to order right this minute and take your seats. I do not wish to waste a minute of class time. Take out your geography books." We trudged to our desks and, still sweating, pulled out *Distant Lands and Their People.* "Turn to page forty-two." She waited for thirty seconds, then looked over at Kelly Munger. "Young man," she said, "why are you still fossicking in your desk?"

Kelly looked as if his foot had been stepped on. "Why am I what?"

"Why are you . . . burrowing in your desk like that?"

"I'm lookin' for the book, Miss Ferenczi."

Bobby Kryzanowicz, the faultless brown-noser who sat in the first row by choice, softly said, "His name is Kelly Munger. He can't ever find his stuff. He always does that."

"I don't care what his name is, especially after lunch," Miss Ferenczi said. "*Where is your book?*"

"I just found it." Kelly was peering into his desk and with both hands pulled at the book, shoveling along in front of it several pencils and crayons, which fell into his lap and then to the floor.

"I hate a mess," Miss Ferenczi said. "I hate a mess in a desk or a mind. It's . . . unsanitary. You wouldn't want your house at home to look like your desk at school, now, would you?" She didn't wait for an answer. "I should think not. A house at home should be as neat as human hands can make it. What were we talking about? Egypt. Page forty-two. I note from Mr. Hibler's lesson plan that you have been discussing the modes of Egyptian irrigation. Interesting, in my view, but not so interesting as what we are about to cover. The pyramids, and Egyptian slave labor. A plus on one side, a minus on the other." We had our books open to page forty-two, where there was a picture of a pyramid, but Miss Ferenczi wasn't looking at the book. Instead, she was staring at some object just outside the window.

"Pyramids," Miss Ferenczi said, still looking past the window. "I want you to think about pyramids. And what was inside. The bodies of the pharaohs, of course, and their attendant treasures. Scrolls. Perhaps," Miss Ferenczi said, her face gleeful but unsmiling, "these scrolls were novels for the pharaohs, helping them to pass the time in their long voyage through the centuries. But then, I am joking." I was looking at the lines on Miss Ferenczi's skin. "Pyramids," Miss Ferenczi went on, "were the repositories of special cosmic powers. The nature of a pyramid is to guide cosmic energy forces into a concentrated point. The Egyptians knew that; we have generally forgotten it. Did you know," she asked, walking to the side of the room so that she was standing by the coat closet, "that George Washington had Egyptian blood, from his grandmother? Certain features of the Constitution of the United States are notable for their Egyptian ideas."

Without glancing down at the book, she began to talk about the movement of souls in Egyptian religion. She said that when people die, their souls return to Earth in the form of carpenter ants or walnut trees, depending on how they behaved—"well or ill"—in life. She said that the Egyptians believed that people act the way they do because of magnetism produced by tidal forces in the solar system, forces produced by the sun and by its "planetary ally," Jupiter. Jupiter, she said, was a planet, as we had been told, but had "certain properties of stars." She was speaking very fast. She said that the Egyptians were great explorers and conquerors. She said that the greatest of all the conquerors, Genghis Khan, had had forty horses and forty young women killed on the site of his grave. We listened. No one tried to stop her. "I myself have been in Egypt," she said, "and have witnessed much dust and many brutalities." She said that an old man in Egypt who worked for a circus had personally shown her an animal in a cage, a monster, half bird and half lion. She said that this monster was called a gryphon and that she had heard about them but never seen them until she traveled to the outskirts of Cairo. She wrote the word out on the blackboard in large capital letters: GRYPHON. She said that Egyptian astronomers had discovered the planet Saturn but had not seen its rings. She said that the Egyptians were the first to discover that dogs, when they are ill, will not drink from rivers, but wait for rain, and hold their jaws open to catch it.

"She lies."

We were on the school bus home. I was sitting next to Carl Whiteside, who had bad breath and a huge collection of marbles. We were arguing. Carl thought she was lying. I said she wasn't, probably.

"I didn't believe that stuff about the bird," Carl said, "and what she told us about the pyramids? I didn't believe that, either. She didn't know what she was talking about."

"Oh yeah?" I had liked her. She was strange. I thought I could nail him. "If she was lying," I said, "what'd she say that was a lie?"

"Six times eleven isn't sixty-eight. It isn't ever. It's sixty-six, I know for a fact."

"She said so. She admitted it. What else did she lie about?"

"I don't know," he said. "Stuff."

"What stuff?"

"Well." He swung his legs back and forth. "You ever see an animal that was half lion and half bird?" He crossed his arms. "It sounded real fakey to me."

"It could happen," I said. I had to improvise, to outrage him. "I read in this newspaper my mom bought in the IGA about this scientist, this mad scientist in the Swiss Alps, and he's been putting genes and chromosomes and stuff together in test tubes, and he combined a human being and a hamster." I waited, for effect. "It's called a humster."

"You never." Carl was staring at me, his mouth open, his terrible bad breath making its way toward me. "What newspaper was it?"

"*The National Enquirer,*" I said, "that they sell next to the cash registers." When I saw his look of recognition, I knew I had him. "And this mad scientist," I said, "his name was, um, Dr. Frankenbush." I realized belatedly that this name was a mistake and waited for Carl to notice its resemblance to the name of the other famous mad master of permutations, but he only sat there.

"A man and a hamster?" He was staring at me, squinting, his mouth opening in distaste. "Jeez. What'd it look like?"

When the bus reached my stop, I took off down our dirt road and ran up through the backyard, kicking the tire swing for good luck. I dropped my books on the back steps so I could hug and kiss our dog, Mr. Selby. Then I hurried inside. I could smell brussels sprouts cooking, my unfavorite vegetable. My mother was washing other vegetables in the kitchen sink, and my baby brother was hollering in his yellow playpen on the kitchen floor.

"Hi, Mom," I said, hopping around the playpen to kiss her. "Guess what?"

"I have no idea."

"We had this substitute today, Miss Ferenczi, and I'd never seen her before, and she had all these stories and ideas and stuff."

"Well. That's good." My mother looked out the window in front of the sink, her eyes on the pine woods west of our house. That time of the afternoon her skin always looked so white to me. Strangers always said my mother looked like Betty Crocker, framed by the giant spoon on the side of the Bisquick box. "Listen, Tommy," she said. "Would you please go upstairs and pick your clothes off the floor in the bathroom, and then go outside to the shed and put the shovel and ax away that your father left outside this morning?"

"She said that six times eleven was sometimes sixty-eight!" I said. "And she said she once saw a monster that was half lion and half bird." I waited. "In Egypt."

"Did you hear me?" my mother asked, raising her arm to wipe her forehead with the back of her hand. "You have chores to do."

"I know," I said. "I was just telling you about the substitute."

"It's very interesting," my mother said, quickly glancing down at me, "and we can talk about it later when your father gets home. But right now you have some work to do."

"Okay, Mom." I took a cookie out of the jar on the counter and was about to go outside when I had a thought. I ran into the living room, pulled out a dictionary next to the TV stand, and opened it to the Gs. After five minutes I found it. *Gryphon:* variant of griffin. *Griffin:* "a fabulous beast with the head and wings of an eagle and the body of a lion." Fabulous was right. I shouted with triumph and ran outside to put my father's tools in their proper places.

Miss Ferenczi was back the next day, slightly altered. She had pulled her hair down and twisted it into pigtails, with red rubber bands holding them tight one inch from the ends. She was wearing a green blouse and pink scarf, making her difficult to look at for a full class day. This time there was no pretense of doing a reading lesson or moving on to arithmetic. As soon as the bell rang, she simply began to talk.

She talked for forty minutes straight. There seemed to be less connection between her ideas, but the ideas themselves were, as the dictionary would say, fabulous. She said she had heard of a huge jewel, in what she called the antipodes, that was so brilliant that when light shone into it at a certain angle it would blind whoever was looking at its center. She said the biggest diamond in the world was cursed and had killed everyone who owned it, and that by a trick of fate it was called the Hope Diamond. Diamonds are magic, she said, and this is why women wear them on their fingers, as a sign of the magic of womanhood. Men have strength, Miss Ferenczi said, but no true magic. That is why men fall in love with women but women do not fall in love with men: they just love being loved. George Washington had died because of a mistake he made about a diamond. Washington was not the first *true* President, but she didn't say who was. In some places in the world, she said, men and women still live in the trees and eat monkeys for breakfast. Their doctors are magicians. At the bottom of the sea are creatures thin as pancakes who have never been studied by scientists because when you take them up to air, the fish explode.

There was not a sound in the classroom, except for Miss Ferenczi's voice, and Donna DeShano's coughing. No one even went to the bathroom.

Beethoven, she said, had not been deaf; it was a trick to make himself famous, and it worked. As she talked, Miss Ferenczi's pigtails swung back and forth. There are trees in the world, she said, that eat meat: their leaves are sticky and close up on bugs like hands. She lifted her hands and brought them together, palm to palm. Venus, which most people think is the next closest planet to the sun, is not always closer, and, besides, it is the planet of greatest mystery because of its thick cloud cover. "I know what lies underneath those clouds," Miss Ferenczi said, and waited. After the silence, she said, "Angels. Angels live under those clouds." She said that angels were not invisible to everyone and were in fact smarter than most people. They did not dress in robes as was often claimed but instead wore formal evening clothes, as if they were about to attend a concert. Often angels *do* attend concerts and sit in the aisles, where, she said, most people pay no attention to them. She said the most terrible angel had the shape of the Sphinx. "There is no running away from that one," she said. She said that unquenchable fires burn just under the surface of the earth in Ohio, and that the baby Mozart fainted dead away in his cradle when he first heard the sound of a trumpet. She said that someone named Narzim al Harrardim was the greatest writer who ever lived. She said that planets control behavior, and anyone conceived during a solar eclipse would be born with webbed feet.

"I know you children like to hear these things," she said, "these secrets, and that is why I am telling you all this." We nodded. It was better than doing comprehension questions for the readings in *Broad Horizons.*

"I will tell you one more story," she said, "and then we will have to do arithmetic." She leaned over, and her voice grew soft. "There is no death," she said. "You must never be afraid. Never. That which is, cannot die. It will change into different earthly and unearthly elements, but I know this as sure as I stand here in front of you, and I swear it: you must not be afraid. I have seen this truth with these eyes. I know it because in a dream God kissed me. Here." And she pointed with her right index finger to the side of her head, below the mouth where the vertical lines were carved into her skin.

Absentmindedly we all did our arithmetic problems. At recess the class was out on the playground, but no one was playing. We were all standing in small groups, talking about Miss Ferenczi. We didn't know if she was crazy, or what. I looked out beyond the playground, at the rusted cars piled in a small heap behind a clump of sumac, and I wanted to see shapes there, approaching me.

On the way home, Carl sat next to me again. He didn't say much, and I didn't either. At last he turned to me. "You know what she said about the leaves that close up on bugs?"

"Huh?"

"The leaves," Carl insisted. "The meat-eating plants. I know it's true. I saw it on television. The leaves have this icky glue that the plants have got smeared all over them and the insects can't get off 'cause they're stuck. I saw it." He seemed demoralized. "She's tellin' the truth."

"Yeah."

"You think she's seen all those angels?"

I shrugged.

"I don't think she has," Carl informed me. "I think she made that part up."

"There's a tree," I suddenly said. I was looking out the window at the farms along County Road H. I knew every barn, every broken windmill, every fence, every anhydrous ammonia tank, by heart. "There's a tree that's . . . that I've seen . . ."

"Don't you try to do it," Carl said. "You'll just sound like a jerk."

I kissed my mother. She was standing in front of the stove. "How was your day?" she asked.

"Fine."

"Did you have Miss Ferenczi again?"

"Yeah."

"Well?"

"She was fine. Mom," I asked, "can I go to my room?"

"No," she said, "not until you've gone out to the vegetable garden and picked me a few tomatoes." She glanced at the sky. "I think it's going to rain. Skedaddle and do it now. Then you come back inside and watch your brother for a few minutes while I go upstairs. I need to clean up before dinner." She looked down at me. "You're looking a little pale, Tommy." She touched the back of her hand to my forehead and I felt her diamond ring against my skin. "Do you feel all right?"

"I'm fine," I said, and went out to pick the tomatoes.

Coughing mutedly, Mr. Hibler was back the next day, slipping lozenges into his mouth when his back was turned at forty-five-minute intervals and asking us how much of his prepared lesson plan Miss Ferenczi had followed. Edith Atwater took the responsibility for the class of explaining to Mr. Hibler that the substitute hadn't always done exactly what he, Mr. Hibler, would have done, but we had worked hard even though she talked a lot. About what? he asked. All kinds of things, Edith said. I sort of forgot. To our relief, Mr. Hibler seemed not at all interested in what Miss Ferenczi had said to fill the day. He probably thought it was woman's talk: unserious and not suited for school. It was enough that he had a pile of arithmetic problems from us to correct.

For the next month, the sumac turned a distracting red in the field, and the sun traveled toward the southern sky, so that its rays reached Mr. Hibler's Halloween display on the bulletin board in the back of the room, fading the pumpkin head scarecrow from orange to tan. Every three days I measured how much farther the sun had moved toward the southern horizon by making small marks with my black Crayola on the north wall, ant-sized marks only I knew were there.

And then in early December, four days after the first permanent snowfall, she appeared again in our classroom. The minute she came in the door, I felt my heart begin to pound. Once again, she was different: this time, her hair hung straight down and seemed hardly to have been combed. She hadn't brought her lunchbox with her, but she was carrying what seemed to be a small box. She greeted all of us and talked about the weather. Donna DeShano had to remind her to take her overcoat off.

When the bell to start the day finally rang, Miss Ferenczi looked out at all of us and said, "Children, I have enjoyed your company in the past, and today I am going to reward you." She held up the small box. "Do you know what this is?" She waited. "Of course you don't. It is a Tarot pack."

Edith Atwater raised her hand. "What's a Tarot pack, Miss Ferenczi?"

"It is used to tell fortunes," she said. "And that is what I shall do this morning. I shall tell your fortunes, as I have been taught to do."

"What's fortune?" Bobby Kryzanowicz asked.

"The future, young man. I shall tell you what your future will be. I can't do your whole future, of course. I shall have to limit myself to the five-card system, the wands, cups, swords, pentacles, and the higher arcanes. Now who wants to be first?"

There was a long silence. Then Carol Peterson raised her hand.

"All right," Miss Ferenczi said. She divided the pack into five smaller packs and walked back to Carol's desk, in front of mine. "Pick one card from each one of these packs," she said. I saw that Carol had a four of cups and a six of swords, but I couldn't see the other cards. Miss Ferenczi studied the cards on Carol's desk for a minute. "Not bad," she said. "I do not see much higher education. Probably an early marriage. Many children. There's something bleak and dreary here, but I can't tell what. Perhaps just the tasks of a housewife life. I think you'll do very well, for the most part." She smiled at Carol, a smile with a certain lack of interest. "Who wants to be next?"

Carl Whiteside raised his hand slowly.

"Yes," Miss Ferenczi said, "let's do a boy." She walked over to where Carl sat. After he picked his five cards, she gazed at them for a long time. "Travel," she said. "Much distant travel. You might go into the army. Not too much romantic interest here. A late marriage, if at all. But the Sun in your major arcana, that's a very good card." She giggled. "You'll have a happy life."

Next I raised my hand. She told me my future. She did the same with Bobby Kryzanowicz, Kelly Munger, Edith Atwater, and Kim Foor. Then she came to Wayne Razmer. He picked his five cards, and I could see that the Death card was one of them.

"What's your name?" Miss Ferenczi asked.

"Wayne."

"Well, Wayne," she said, "you will undergo a great metamorphosis, a change, before you become an adult. Your earthly element will no doubt leap higher, because you seem to be a sweet boy. This card, this nine of swords, tells me of suffering and desolation. And this ten of wands, well, that's a heavy load."

"What about this one?" Wayne pointed at the Death card.

"It means, my sweet, that you will die soon." She gathered up the cards. We were all looking at Wayne. "But do not fear," she said. "It is not really death. Just change. Out of your earthly shape." She put the cards on Mr. Hibler's desk. "And now, let's do some arithmetic."

At lunchtime Wayne went to Mr. Faegre, the principal, and informed him of what Miss Ferenczi had done. During the noon recess, we saw Miss Ferenczi drive out of the parking lot in her rusting green Rambler American. I stood under the slide, listening to the other kids coasting down and landing in the little depressive bowls at the bottom. I was kicking stones and tugging at my hair right up to the moment when I saw Wayne come out to the playground. He smiled, the dead fool, and with the fingers of his right hand he was showing everyone how he had told on Miss Ferenczi.

I made my way toward Wayne, pushing myself past two girls from another class. He was watching me with his little pinhead eyes.

"You told," I shouted at him. "She was just kidding."

"She shouldn't have," he shouted back. "We were supposed to be doing arithmetic."

"She just scared you," I said. "You're a chicken. You're a chicken, Wayne. You are. Scared of a little card," I singsonged.

Wayne fell at me, his two fists hammering down on my nose. I gave him a good one in the stomach and then I tried for his head. Aiming my fist, I saw that he was crying. I slugged him.

"She was right," I yelled. "She was always right! She told the truth!" Other kids were whooping. "You were just scared, that's all!"

And then large hands pulled at us, and it was my turn to speak to Mr. Faegre.

In the afternoon Miss Ferenczi was gone, and my nose was stuffed with cotton clotted with blood, and my lip had swelled, and our class had been combined with Mrs. Mantei's sixth-grade class for a crowded afternoon science unit on insect life in ditches and swamps. I knew where Mrs. Mantei lived: she had a new house trailer just down the road from us, at the Clearwater Park. She was no mystery. Somehow she and Mr. Bodine, the other fourth-grade teacher, had managed to fit forty-five desks into the room. Kelly Munger asked if Miss Ferenczi had been arrested, and Mrs. Mantei said no, of course not. All that afternoon, until the buses came to pick us up, we learned about field crickets and two-striped grasshoppers, water bugs, cicadas, mosquitoes, flies, and moths. We learned about insects' hard outer shell, the exoskeleton, and the usual parts of the mouth, including the labrum, mandible, maxilla, and glossa. We learned about compound eyes, and the four-stage metamorphosis from egg to larva to pupa to adult. We learned something, but not much, about mating. Mrs. Mantei drew, very skillfully, the internal anatomy of the grasshopper on the blackboard. We learned about the dance of the honeybee, directing other bees in the hive to pollen. We found out about which insects were pests to man, and which were not. On lined white pieces of paper we made lists of insects we might actually see, then a list of insects too small to be clearly visible, such as fleas; Mrs. Mantei said that our assignment would be to memorize these lists for the next day, when Mr. Hibler would certainly return and test us on our knowledge.

MADISON SMARTT BELL

Customs of the Country

MADISON SMARTT BELL (1957–) is the author of nine novels, including *The Washington Square Ensemble, Waiting for the End of the World, Straight Cut, The Year of Silence, Doctor Sleep, Save Me, Joe Louis,* and *Soldier's Joy,* which received the Lillian Smith Award in 1989. Bell has also published two collections of short stories: *Zero db* and *Barking Man.* His eighth novel, *All Souls' Rising,* was a finalist for the 1995 National Book Award and the 1996 PEN/Faulkner Award. His ninth novel, *Ten Indians,* was published by Pantheon in 1997. Born and raised in Tennessee, he now lives in Baltimore, Maryland. A graduate of Princeton and Hollins College, he has taught in various writing programs, including the Iowa Writers' Workshop and the Johns Hopkins University Writing Seminars. He is currently Writer in Residence at Goucher College, along with his wife, the poet Elizabeth Spires.

I don't know how much I remember about that place anymore. It was nothing but somewhere I came to put in some pretty bad time, though that was not what I had planned on when I went there. I had it in mind to improve things, but I don't think you could fairly claim that's what I did. So that's one reason I might just as soon forget about it. And I didn't stay there all that long, not more than nine months or so, about the same time, come to think, that the child I'd come to try and get back had lived inside my body.

It was a cluster-housing thing called Spring Valley, I wouldn't know why, just over the Botetourt County line on the highway going north out of Roanoke. I suppose it must have been there ten or fifteen years, long enough to lose that raw look they have when they're new built, but not too rundown yet, so long as you didn't look close. There were five or six long two-story buildings running in rows back up the hillside. You got to the upstairs apartments by an outside balcony, like you would in a motel. The one I rented was in the lowest building down the hill, upstairs on the northwest corner. There was a patch of grass out front beyond the gravel of the parking lot, but the manager didn't take much trouble over it. He kept it cut, but it was weedy, and a few yards past the buildings it began to go to brush. By my corner there was a young apple tree that never made anything but small sour green apples, knotted up like little fists. Apart from that there was nothing nearby that the eye would care to dwell on. But upstairs, out my front windows, I could look way out beyond the interstate to where the mountains were.

You got there driving about two miles up a bumpy two-lane from the state road. It was mostly wooded land along the way, with a couple of pastures spotted in, and one little store. About halfway you crossed the railroad cut, and from the apartment I could hear the trains pulling north out of town, though it wasn't near enough I could see them. I listened to them often enough, though, nights I couldn't sleep, and bad times I might pull a chair out on the concrete slab of balcony so I could hear them better.

The apartment was nothing more than the least I needed, some place that would look all right and yet cost little enough to leave me something to give the lawyer. Two rooms and a bath and a fair-sized kitchen. It would have been better if there'd been one more room for Davey but I couldn't stretch my money far enough to cover that. It did have fresh paint on the walls and the trim in the kitchen and bathroom was in good enough shape. And it was real quiet mostly, except that the man next door would beat up his wife about two or three times a week. The place was close enough to soundproof I couldn't usually hear talk but I could hear yelling plain as day, and when he got going good he would slam her bang into our common wall. If she hit in just the right spot it would send all my pots and pans flying off the pegboard where I'd hung them there above the stove.

Not that it mattered to me that the pots fell down, except for the noise and the time it took to pick them up again. Living alone like I was I didn't have heart to do much cooking, and if I did fix myself something I mostly used a plain old iron skillet that hung there on the same wall. The rest was a set of Revereware my family give me when Patrick and I got married. They had copper bottoms, and when I first moved in that apartment I polished them to where it practically hurt to look at them head on, but it was all for show.

The whole apartment was done about the same way, made into something I kept spotless and didn't much care to use. A piece of dirt never got a fair chance to settle there, that much was for sure. I wore down the kitchen counters scrubbing out the old stains, I went at the grout between the bathroom tiles with a toothbrush, I did all that kind of thing. Spring Valley was the kind of place where people would sometimes leave too fast to take their furniture along, so I was able to get most everything I needed from the manager, who saved it up to try selling it to whatever new people moved in. Then I bought fabric and sewed covers to where everything matched, and I sewed curtains and got posters to put up on the walls, but I can't say I ever felt at home there. It was an act, and I wasn't putting it on for me or Davey, but for those other people who would come to see it and judge it. And however good I could get it looking, it never felt quite right.

I'd step into the place with the same cross feeling I had when I got in my car, an old Malibu I'd bought a body and paint job for, instead of the new clutch and brakes it really needed. But one way or another I could run the thing, and six days a week I would climb in it and go back down to the state road, turn north and drive up to the interstate crossing. There was a Truckstops of America up there, and that was where my job was at. I worked the three snake bends of the counter and it was enough to keep me run off my feet most days. Or nights, since I was on a swing shift that rolled over every ten days. I wouldn't have ate the food myself but the place was usually busy and the tips were fair. I'd have made a lot more money working in a bar somewhere, being a cocktail waitress or what have you, but that would have been another case of it not looking the way it was supposed to.

The supervisor out there was a man named Tim that used to know Patrick a little, back from before we split. He was how I got the job, and he was good about letting me have time off when I needed it for the lawyer or something, and he let me take my calls there too. By and large he was an easy enough man to work for except that about once a week he would have a tantrum over something or other and try to scream the walls down for a while. Still, it never went anywhere beyond yelling, and he always acted sorry once he got through.

The other waitress on my shift was about old enough to be my mother, I would guess. Her name was Priscilla but she wanted you to call her Prissy, though it didn't suit her a bit. She was kind of dumpy and she had to wear support hose and she had the worst dye job on her hair I just about ever saw, some kind of home brew that turned her hair the color of French's mustard. But she was good-natured, really a kindly person, and we got along good and helped each other out whenever one of us looked like getting behind.

Well, I was tired all the time with the shifts changing the way they did. The six-to-two I hated the worst because it would have me getting back to my apartment building around three in the morning, which was not the time the place looked its best. It was a pretty sorry lot of people living there, I hadn't quite realized when I moved in, a lot of small-time criminals, dope dealers and thieves, and none of them too good at whatever crime they did. So when I came in off that graveyard shift there was a fair chance I'd find the sheriff's car out there looking for somebody. I suppose they felt like if they came at that time of night they would stand a better chance of catching whoever they were after asleep.

I didn't get to know the neighbors any too well, it didn't seem like a good idea. The man downstairs was a drunk and a check forger. Sometimes he would break into the other apartments looking for whiskey, but he never managed to get into mine. I didn't keep whiskey anyhow, maybe he had some sense for that. The manager liked to make passes at whatever women were home in the day. He even got around to trying me, though not but the one time.

The man next door, the one that beat up his wife, didn't do crimes or work either that I ever could tell. He just seemed to lay around the place, maybe drawing some kind of welfare. There wasn't a whole lot to him, he was just a stringy little fellow, hair and mustache a dishwater brown, cheap green tattoos running up his arms. Maybe he was stronger than he looked, but I did wonder how come his wife would take it from him, since she was about a head taller and must have outweighed him an easy ten pounds. I might have thought she was whipping on *him*—stranger things have been known to go on—but she was the one that seemed like she might break out crying if you looked at her crooked. She was a big fine-looking girl with a lovely shape, and long brown hair real smooth and straight and shiny. I guess she was too hammered down most of the time to pay much attention to the way she dressed, but she still had pretty brown eyes, big and long-lashed and soft, kind of like a cow's eyes are, except I never saw a cow that looked that miserable.

At first I thought maybe I might make a friend of her, she was about the only one around there I felt like I might want to. Our paths crossed pretty frequent, either around the apartment buildings or in the Quik-Sak back toward town, where I'd find her running the register some days. But she was shy of me—shy of anybody, I suppose. She would flinch if you did so much as say hello. So after a while, I quit trying. She'd get hers about twice a week, maybe other times I wasn't around to hear it happen. It's a wonder all the things you can learn to ignore, and after a month or so I was so accustomed I barely noticed when they would start in. I would just wait till I thought they were good and through, and then get up and hang those pans back on the wall where they were supposed to go.

What with the way the shifts kept rolling over out there at the TOA, I had a lot of trouble sleeping. I never did learn to sleep in the daytime worth a damn. I would just lie down when I got back till some of the ache drained out of me, and then get up and try to think of some way to pass the time. There wasn't a whole lot to do around that apartment. I didn't have any TV, only a radio, and that didn't work too well itself. After the first few weeks I sent off to one of those places that say they'll pay you to stuff envelopes at your own house. My thought was it would be some extra money, but it never amounted to anything much of that. It just killed me some time and gave me something to do with my hands, in between smoking cigarettes. Something to do with myself while I was worrying, and I used to worry a good deal in those days.

The place where Davey had been fostered out was not all that far away, just about ten or twelve miles on up the road, out there in the farm country. The people were named Baker, I never got to first names with them, just called them Mr. and Mrs. They were some older than me, just into their forties, and they didn't have children of their own. The place was just a small farm but Mr. Baker grew tobacco on the most of it and I'm told he made it a paying thing. Mrs. Baker kept a milk cow or two and she grew a garden and canned. Thrifty people, in the old-time way. They were real sweet to Davey and he seemed to like being with them pretty well. It was a place a little boy would expect to enjoy, except there weren't any neighbors too near. And he had been staying there almost the whole two years, which was lucky too, since most children usually got moved around a whole lot more than that.

But that was the trouble, like the lawyer explained to me, it was just too good. Davey was doing too well out there. He'd made out better in the first grade too than anybody would have thought. So nobody really felt like he needed to be moved. The worst of it was the Bakers had got to like him well enough they were saying they wanted to adopt him if they could, and that was what plagued my mind the most. If I thought about that while I was doing those envelopes, it would start me giving myself paper cuts.

Even though he was so close, I didn't go out to see Davey near as much as I would have liked to. The lawyer kept on telling me it wasn't a good idea to look like I was pressing too hard. Better take it easy till all the evaluations came in and we had our court date and all. Still, I would call and go on out there maybe a little more than once a month, most usually on the weekends since that seemed to suit the Bakers better. They never acted like it was any trouble, and they were always pleasant to me, or polite might be the better word. They wanted what I wanted, so I never expected us to turn out good friends. The way it sometimes seemed they didn't trust me, that bothered me a little more. I would have liked to take him out to the movies a time or two, but I could see plain enough the Bakers wouldn't have been easy about me having him off their place.

Still, I can't remember us having a bad time, not any of those times I went. He was always happy to see me, though he'd be quiet when we were in the house, with Mrs. Baker hovering. So I would get us outside quick as ever I could, and once we were out, we would just play like both of us were children. There was an open pasture, a creek with a patch of woods, and a hay barn where we would play hide-and-go-seek. I don't know what all else we did—silly things, mostly. That was how I could get near him the easiest, he didn't get a whole lot of playing in way out there. The Bakers weren't what you would call playful and there weren't any other children living near. So that was the thing I could give him that was all mine to give. When the weather was good we would stay outside together most all the day and he would just wear me out. After it turned cold we couldn't stay outside so long, though one of our best days of all was when I showed him how to make a snowman. But over the winter those visits seemed to get shorter and shorter, like the days.

Davey called me Momma still, but I suppose he had come to think your mother was something more like a big sister or just some kind of a friend. Mrs. Baker was the one doing for him all the time. I don't know just what he remembered from before, or if he remembered any of the bad part. He would always mind me but he never acted scared around me, and if anybody says he did, they lie. But I never really did get to know what he had going on in the back of his mind about the past. At first I worried the Bakers might have been talking against me, but after I had seen a little more of them I knew they wouldn't have done anything like that, wouldn't have thought it right. So I expect whatever Davey knew about that other time he remembered all on his own. He never mentioned Patrick hardly and I think he really had forgotten about him. Thinking back, I guess he never really saw that much of Patrick even where we all were living together. But Davey had Patrick's mark all over him, the same eyes and the same red hair.

Patrick had thick wavy hair the shade of an Irish setter's and a big rolling mustache the same color. Maybe that was his best feature, but he was a good-looking man altogether—still is, I suppose, though the prison haircut don't suit him. If he ever had much of a thought in his head, I suspect he had knocked it clean out with dope, yet he was always fun to be around. I wasn't but seventeen when I married him and I didn't have any better sense myself. Right through to the end I never thought anything much was the matter, his vices looked so small to me. He was good-tempered almost all the time, and good with Davey when he did notice him. Never one time did he raise his hand to either one of us. In little ways he was unreliable—late, not showing up at all, gone out of the house for days together sometimes. Hindsight shows me he ran with other women, but I managed not to know anything about that at the time. He had not quite finished high school and the best job he could hold was being an orderly down at the hospital, but he made a good deal of extra money stealing pills out of there and selling them on the street.

That was something else I didn't allow myself to think on much back then. Patrick never told me a lot about it anyhow, always acted real mysterious about whatever he was up to in that line. He would disappear on one of his trips and come back with a whole mess of money, and I would spend up my share and be glad I had it too. Never thought much about where it was coming from, the money or the pills, either one. He used to keep all manner of pills around the house, Valium and ludes and a lot of different kinds of speed, and we both took what we felt like whenever we felt in the mood. But what Patrick made the most on was Dilaudid. I used to take that without ever knowing what it really was, but once everything fell in on us I found out it was a bad thing, bad as heroin they said, and not much different, and that was what they gave Patrick most of his time for.

I truly was surprised to find out that was the strongest dope we had, because I never really felt like it made me all that high. It sure didn't have anything like the punch the speed did. Yet you could fall into the habit of taking a good bit of it, never noticing how much. You would just take one and kick back on a long slow stroke and whatever trouble you might have, it would not be able to find you. It came on like nothing but it was the hardest habit to lose, and I was a long time shaking it. I might be thinking about it yet if I would let myself, and there were times, all through the winter I spent in that apartment, I'd catch myself remembering the feeling.

I had come just before the leaves started turning, and then I believed it was all going to happen quick. I thought to have Davey back with me inside of a month or six weeks. But pretty soon the lawyer was singing me a different tune, delaying it all for this reason or that. He had a whole lot of different schemes in his mind, having to do with which judge, which social worker, which doctor might help us out the most. I got excited over everything he told me, in the beginning I did at least, but then nothing ever seemed to come of it at all. It turned off cold, the leaves came down, that poor little apple tree underneath my window was bare as a stick, and still nothing had happened.

You couldn't call it a real bad winter, there wasn't much snow or anything, but I was cold just about all the time, except when I was at work. The TOA was hot as a steam bath, especially back around the kitchen, and when I was there I'd sweat until I smelled. In the apartment, though, all I had was some electric baseboard heaters, and they cost too much for me to leave them running very long at a stretch. I'd keep it just warm enough I couldn't see my breath, and spend my time in a hot bathtub or under a big pile of blankets on the bed. Or else I would just be cold.

Outside wasn't all that much colder than in, and I spent a lot of time sitting there on that balcony, looking way out yonder toward the mountains. I got a pair of those gloves with the fingers out so I could keep on stuffing my envelopes while I was sitting out there. Day or night, it didn't matter, I was so familiar with it I could do it in the dark. I'd sit there sometimes for hours on end, counting the time by the trains that went by. Sound seemed to carry better in the cold, and I felt like I could hear every clack of the rails when a train was coming, and when they let the horn off it rang that whole valley like a bell.

But inside the apartment it was mostly dead quiet. I might hear the pipes moaning now and again and that was all. If the phone rang it would make me jump. Didn't seem like there was any TV or radio next door. The only sound coming out of there was Susan getting beat up once in a while. That was her name—a sweet name, I think. I found it out from hearing him say it, which he used to do almost every time before he started in on her. "Su*san,*" he'd call out, loud enough I could just hear him through the wall. He'd do it a time or two, he might have been calling her to him, I don't know. After that would come a bad silence that reminded you of a snake being somewhere around. Then a few minutes' worth of hitting sounds and then the big slam as she hit the wall and the clatter of my pots falling down on the floor. He'd throw her at the wall maybe once or twice, usually when he was about to get through. By the time the pots had quit spinning on the floor it would be real quiet over there again, and the next time I saw Susan she'd be walking in that ginger way people have when they're hiding a hurt, and if I said hello to her she'd give a little jump and look away.

After a while I quit paying it much mind, it didn't feel any different to me than hearing the news. All their carrying on was not any more than one wall of the rut I had worked myself into, going back and forth from the job, cleaning that apartment till it hurt, calling up the lawyer about once a week to find out about the next postponement. I made a lot of those calls from the TOA, and Tim and Prissy got pretty interested in the whole business. I would tell them all about it, too. Sometimes, when our shift was done, Prissy and I would pour coffee and sit in a booth for as much as a couple of hours, just chewing that subject over and over, with Tim passing by now and again to chip in his opinion of what was going to happen. But nothing much ever did happen, and after a while I got to where I didn't want to discuss it anymore. I kept ahead making those calls but every one of them just wore down my hope a little more, like a drip of water wearing down a stone. And little by little I got in the habit of thinking that nothing really was going to change.

It was spring already by the time things finally did begin to move. That sad little apple tree was beginning to try and put out some leaves, and the weather was getting warmer every day, and I was starting to feel it inside me too, the way you do. That was when the lawyer called *me,* for a change, and told me he had some people lined up to see me at last.

Well, I was all ready for them to come visit, come see how I'd fixed up my house and all the rest of my business to get set for having Davey back with me again. But as it turned out, nobody seemed to feel like they were called on to make that trip. "I don't think that will be necessary," was what one of them said, I don't recall which. They both talked about the same, in voices that sounded like filling out forms.

So all I had to do was drive downtown a couple of times and see them in their offices. The child psychologist was the first and I doubt he kept me more than half an hour. I couldn't even tell the point of most of the questions he asked. My second trip I saw the social worker, who turned out to be a black lady once I got down there, though I never could have told it over the phone. Her voice sounded like it was coming out of the TV. She looked me in the eye while she was asking her questions, but I couldn't make out a thing about what she thought. It wasn't till afterward, when I was back in the apartment, that I understood she must have already had her mind made up.

That came to me in a sort of flash, while I was standing in the kitchen washing out a cup. Soon as I walked back in the door I'd seen my coffee mug left over from breakfast, and kicked myself for letting it sit out. I was giving it a hard scrub with a scouring pad when I realized it didn't matter anymore. I might just as well have dropped it on the floor and got what kick I could out of watching it smash, because it wasn't going to make any difference to anybody now. But all the same I rinsed it and set it in the drainer, careful as if it might have been an eggshell. Then I stepped backward out of the kitchen and took a long look around that cold shabby place and thought it might be for the best that nobody was coming. How could I have expected it to fool anybody else when it wasn't even good enough to fool me? A lonesomeness came over me, I felt like I was floating all alone in the middle of the cold air, and then I began to remember some things I would just as soon have not.

No, I never did like to think about this part, but I have had to think about it time and again, with never a break for a long, long time, because I needed to get to understand it at least well enough to believe it never would ever happen anymore. And I had come to believe that, in the end. If I hadn't I never would have come back at all. I had found a way to trust myself again, though it took me a full two years to do it, and though of course it still didn't mean that anybody else would trust me.

What had happened was that Patrick went off on one of his mystery trips and stayed gone a deal longer than usual. Two nights away, I was used to that, but on the third I did start to wonder. He normally would have called, at least, if he meant to be gone that long of a stretch. But I didn't hear a peep until about halfway through the fourth day. And it wasn't Patrick himself that called, but one of those public assistance lawyers from downtown.

Seemed like the night before Patrick had got himself stopped on the interstate loop down there. The troopers said he was driving like a blind man, and he was so messed up on whiskey and ludes I suppose he must have been pretty near blind. Well, maybe he would have just lost his license or something like that, only that the back seat of the car was loaded up with all he had lately stole out of the hospital.

So it was bad. It was so bad my mind just could not contain it, and every hour it seemed to get worse. I spent the next couple of days running back and forth between the jail and that lawyer, and I had to haul Davey along with me wherever I went. He was too little for school and I couldn't find anybody to take him right then, though all that running around made him awful cranky. Patrick was just grim, he would barely speak. He already knew for pretty well sure he'd be going to prison. The lawyer had told him there wasn't no use in getting a bondsman, he might just as well sit in there and start pulling his time. I don't know how much he really saved himself that way, though, since what they ended up giving him was twenty-five years.

That was when all my troubles found me, quick. The second day after Patrick got arrested, I came down real sick with something. I thought at first it was a bad cold or the flu. My nose kept running and I felt so wore out I couldn't hardly get up off the bed and yet at the same time I felt real restless, like all my nerves had been scraped raw. Well, I didn't really connect it up to the fact that I'd popped the last pill in the house about two days before. What was really the matter was me coming off that Dilaudid, but I didn't have any notion of that at the time.

I was laying there in the bed not able to get up, and about ready to jump right out of my skin at the same time, when Davey got the drawer underneath the stove open. Of course he was getting restless himself with everything that had been going on, and me not able to pay him much attention. All our pots and pans were down in that drawer then, and he began to take them out one at a time and throw them on the floor. It made a hell of a racket, and the shape I was in I started feeling like he must be doing it on purpose, to devil me. I called out to him and asked him to quit. Nice at first: "You stop that now, Davey. Momma don't feel good." But he kept right ahead. All he wanted was a little noticing, I know, but my mind wasn't working like it should. I knew I should get up and just go lead him away from there, but I couldn't seem to get myself to move. I had a picture of myself doing what I ought to do, but I just wasn't doing it. I was still laying there calling for him to quit and he was still banging those pots around, and before long I was screaming at him outright, and starting to cry at the same time. But he never stopped a minute. I guess I had scared him some already and he was just locked into doing it, or maybe he wanted to drown me out. Every time he flung a pot it felt like I was getting shot at. And the next thing I knew, I had got myself in the kitchen somehow and was snatching him up off the floor.

To this day I don't remember doing it, though I have tried and tried. I thought if I could call it back, then maybe I could root it out of myself and be rid of it for good. But all I ever knew was, one minute I was grabbing hold of him and the next he was laying on the far side of the room with his right leg folded up funny where it was broke, not even crying, just looking surprised.

And I knew it had to be me that threw him over there because sure as hell is real, there was nobody else around that could have done it.

I drove him to the hospital myself. I laid him out straight on the front seat beside me and drove with one hand all the way so I could hold on to him with the other. He was real quiet and real brave the whole time, never cried the least bit, just kept a tight hold of my hand with his. I was crying a river myself, couldn't hardly see the road. It's a wonder we didn't crash, I suppose. Well, we got there and they ran him off somewhere to get his leg set and pretty soon this doctor came back out and asked me how it had happened.

It was the same hospital where Patrick had worked and I even knew that doctor a little bit. Not that being connected to Patrick would have done me a whole lot of good around there at that time. Still, I've often thought since that things might have come out better for me and Davey if I only could have lied to that man, but I was not up to telling a lie that anybody would be apt to believe. All I could do was start to scream and jabber like a crazy person, and it ended up I stayed in that hospital a good few days myself. They took me for a junkie and I guess I really was one too, though that was the first time I'd known it. And I never saw Davey again for a whole two years, not till the first time they let me go out to the Bakers'.

Sometimes you don't get but one mistake, if the one you pick is bad enough. Do as much as step in the road the wrong time without looking, and your life could be over with then and there. But during those two years I taught myself to believe that this mistake of mine could be wiped out, that if I struggled hard enough with myself and the world I could make it like it never had been.

Three weeks went by after I went to see that social worker, and I didn't have any idea what was happening, or if anything was. Didn't call anybody, I expect I was afraid to. Then one day the phone rang for me out there at the TOA. It was that lawyer and I could tell right off from the sound of his voice that I wasn't going to care for his news. Well, he told me all the evaluations had come in now, sure enough, and they weren't running in our favor. They weren't against *me*—he made sure to say that—it was more like they were *for* the Bakers. And his judgment was, it wouldn't pay me anything if we went on to court. It looked like the Bakers would get Davey for good, and they were likely to be easier about visitation if there wasn't any big tussle. But if I drug them into court, then we would have to start going back over that whole case history—

That was the word he used, *case history,* and it was around about there that I hung up. I went walking stiff-legged back across to the counter and just let myself sort of drop on a stool. Prissy had been covering the counter while I was on the phone and she came right over to me then.

"What is it?" she said. I guess she could tell it was something by the look on my face.

"I lost him," I said.

"Oh, hon, you know I'm so sorry," she said. She reached out for my hand but I snatched it back. I know she meant well but I was just not in the mood to be touched.

"There's no forgiveness," I said. I felt bitter about it. It had been a hard road for me to come as near forgiving myself as ever I could. And Davey forgave me, I really knew that, I could tell it in the way he behaved when we were together. And if us two could do it, I didn't feel like it ought to be anybody's business but ours. Tim walked up then and Prissy whispered something to him, and then he took a step nearer to me.

"I'm sorry," he told me.

"Not like I am," I said.

"Go ahead and take off the rest of your shift if you feel like it," he said. "I'll wait on these tables myself, need be."

"I don't know it would make any difference," I said.

"Better take it easy on yourself," he said. "No use in taking it so hard. You're just going to have to get used to it."

"Is that a fact," I said. And I lit myself a cigarette and turned my face away. We had been pretty busy, it was lunchtime, and the people were getting restless seeing us all bunched up there and not doing a whole lot about bringing them their food. Somebody called out something to Tim, I didn't hear too well what it was, but it set off one of his temper fits.

"Go on and get out of here if that's how you feel," he said. "You think you're the most important thing to us in here? Well, you're wrong." He was getting red in the face and waving his arms at the whole restaurant, including them all in what he was saying. "Go on and clear out of here, every last one of you, and we don't care if you never come back. We don't need your kind in here and never did. There's not a one of you couldn't stand to miss a meal anyhow. Take a look at yourselves, you're all fat as hogs . . ."

And he kept on, looked like he meant to go for the record. He had already said I could leave, so I hung up my apron and got my purse and I left. It was the first time he ever blew up at the customers that way, it had always been me or Prissy or one of the cooks. I never did find out what came of it all because I never went back to that place again.

I drove home in a poison mood. The brakes on the car were so bad by that time I had to pump like crazy to get the thing stopped, but I didn't really care all that much if I got killed or not. I kept thinking about what Tim had said about having to get used to it. It came to me that I was used to it already, I hadn't really been all that surprised. That's what I'd really been doing all those months, just gradually getting used to losing my child forever.

When I got back to the apartment I just fell in a chair and sat there staring across at the kitchen wall. It was in my mind to pack my traps and leave that place, but I hadn't yet figured out what place I would go to. I sat there a good while, I guess. The door was ajar from me not paying attention, it wasn't cold enough out to make any difference. If I turned my head that way I could see a slice of the parking lot. I saw Susan drive up and come limping toward the building with an armload of groceries. Because of the angle I couldn't see her go into their apartment but I heard the door open and shut, and after that it was quiet as the tomb. I kept on sitting there thinking about how used to everything I had got. There must have been God's plenty of other people too, I thought, who had got themselves accustomed to all kinds of things. Some were used to taking the pain and the rest were used to serving it up. About half the world was screaming in misery, and it wasn't anything but a habit.

When I started to hear the hitting sounds come through the wall, a smile came on my face like it was cut there with a knife. I'd been expecting it, you see, and the mood I was in I felt satisfied to see what I expected was going to happen. So I listened a little more carefully than I'd been inclined to do before. It was *hit hit hit* going along together with a groan and a hiss of the wind being knocked out of her. I had to strain pretty hard to hear that breathing part, and I could hear him grunt, too, when he got in a good one. There was about three minutes of that with some little breaks, and then a longer pause. When she hit that wall it was the hardest she had yet, I think. It brought all my pots down at one time, including that big iron skillet that was the only one I ever used.

It was the first time they'd ever managed to knock that skillet down, and I was so impressed I went over and stood looking down at it like I needed to make sure it was a real thing. I stared at that skillet so long it went out of focus and started looking more like a big black hole in the floor. That's when it dawned on me that this was one thing I didn't really have to keep on being used to.

It took three or four knocks before he came to the door, but that didn't worry me at all. I had faith, I knew he was going to come. I meant to stay right there until he did. When he came, he opened the door wide and stood there with his arms folded and his face all stiff with his secrets. It was fairly dark behind him, they had all the curtains drawn. I had that skillet held out in front of me in both my hands, like maybe I had come over to borrow a little hot grease or something. It was so heavy it kept wanting to dip down toward the floor like a water witch's rod. When I saw he wasn't expecting anything, I twisted the skillet back over my shoulder like baseball players do their bats, and I hit him bang across the face as hard as I knew how. He went down and out at the same time and fetched up on his back clear in the middle of the room.

Then I went in after him, with the skillet cocked and ready in case he made to get up. But he didn't look like there was a whole lot of fight left in him right then. He was awake, at least partly awake, but his nose was just spouting blood and it seemed like I'd knocked out a few of his teeth. I wish I could tell you I was sorry or glad, but I didn't feel much of anything, really, just that high lonesome whistle in the blood I used to get when I took that Dilaudid. Susan was sitting on the floor against the wall, leaning down on her knees and sniveling. Her eyes were red but she didn't have any bruises where they showed. He never did hit her on the face, that was the kind he was. There was a big crack coming down the wall behind her and I remember thinking it probably wouldn't be too much longer before it worked through to my side.

"I'm going to pack and drive over to Norfolk," I told her. I hadn't thought of it till I spoke but just then it came to me as the thing I would do. "You can ride along with me if you want to. With your looks you could make enough money serving drinks to the sailors to buy that Quik-Sak and blow it up."

She didn't say anything, just raised her head up and stared at me kind of bug-eyed. And after a minute I turned around and went out. It didn't take me any time at all to get ready. All I had was two boxes of kitchen stuff and a suitcase and another box of clothes. The sheets and blankets I just yanked off the bed and stuffed in the trunk in one big wad. I didn't care a damn about that furniture, I would have lit it on fire for a dare.

When I was done I stuck my head back into the other apartment. The door was still open like I had left it. What was she doing but kneeling down over that son of a bitch and trying to clean his face off with a washrag. I noticed he was making a funny sound when he breathed, and his nose was still bleeding pretty quick, so I thought maybe I had broke it. Well, I can't say that worried me much.

"Come on now if you're coming, girl," I said.

She looked up at me, not telling me one word, just giving me a stare out of those big cow eyes of hers like I was the one had been beating on her that whole winter through. And I saw then that they were both stuck in their groove and that she would not be the one to step out of it. So I pulled back out of the doorway and went on down the steps to my car.

I was speeding down the road to Norfolk, doing seventy, seventy-five. I'd have liked to go faster if the car had been up to it. It didn't matter to me that I didn't have any brakes. Anybody wanted to keep out of a wreck had better just keep the hell out of my way. I can't say I felt sorry for busting that guy, though I didn't enjoy the thought of it either. I just didn't know what difference it had made, and chances were it had made none at all. Kind of a funny thing, when you thought about it that way. It was the second time in my life I'd hurt somebody bad, and the other time I hadn't meant to do it at all. This time I'd known what I was doing for sure, but I still didn't know what I'd done.

AMY BLOOM

Silver Water

AMY BLOOM (1953–) is the author of the novel *Love Invents Us* and the collection of stories *Come to Me,* which was nominated for both the National Book Award and the *Los Angeles Times* First Fiction Award. Her stories and articles have appeared in *The New Yorker, Story, Zoetrope, Antaeus, River City, Room of One's Own,* and *Vogue* and have been included in *The Best American Short Stories 1991* and *1992* as well as *Prize Stories: The O. Henry Awards 1994.*

My sister's voice was like mountain water in a silver pitcher; the clear, blue beauty of it cools you and lifts you up beyond your heat, beyond your body. After we went to see *La Traviata,* when she was fourteen and I was twelve, she elbowed me in the parking lot and said, "Check this out." And she opened her mouth unnaturally wide and her voice came out, so crystalline and bright, that all the departing operagoers stood frozen by their cars, unable to take out their keys or open their doors until she had finished and then they cheered like hell.

That's what I like to remember and that's the story I told to all of her therapists. I wanted them to know her, to know that who they saw was not all there was to see. That before the constant tinkling of commercials and fast-food jingles, there had been Puccini and Mozart and hymns so sweet and mighty, you expected Jesus to come down off his cross and clap. That before there was a mountain of Thorazined fat, swaying down the halls in nylon maternity tops and sweatpants, there had been the prettiest girl in Arrandale Elementary School, the belle of Landmark Junior High. Maybe there were other pretty girls, but I didn't see them. To me, Rose, my beautiful blond defender, my guide to Tampax and my mother's moods, was perfect.

She had her first psychotic break when she was fifteen. She had been coming home moody and tearful, then quietly beaming, then she stopped coming home. She would go out into the woods behind our house and not come in until my mother would go out at dusk, and step gently into the briars and saplings and pull her out, blank-faced, her pale blue pullover covered with crumbled leaves, her white jeans smeared with dirt. After three weeks of this, my mother, who is a musician and widely regarded as eccentric, said to my father, who is a psychiatrist and a kind, sad man, "She's going off."

"What is that, your professional opinion?" He picked up the newspaper and put it down again, sighing. "I'm sorry, I didn't mean to snap at you. I know something's bothering her. Have you talked to her?"

"What's there to say? David, she's going crazy, she doesn't need a heart-to-heart talk with Mom, she needs a hospital."

They went back and forth and my father sat down with Rose for a few hours and she sat there, licking the hairs on her forearm, first one way, then the other. My mother stood in the hallway, dry-eyed and pale, watching the two of them. She had already packed Rose's bag and when three of my father's friends dropped by to offer free consultations and recommendations, my mother and Rose's suitcase were already in the car. My mother hugged me and told me that they would be back that night, but not with Rose. She also said, divining my worst fear, "It won't happen to you, honey. Some people go crazy and some people never do. You never will." She smiled and stroked my hair. "Not even when you want to."

Rose was in hospitals, great and small, for the next ten years. She had lots of terrible therapists and a few good ones. One place had no pictures on the walls, no windows, and the patients all wore slippers with the hospital crest on them. My mother didn't even bother to go to Admissions. She turned Rose around and the two of them marched out, my father, trailing behind them, apologizing to his colleagues. My mother ignored the psychiatrists, the social workers and the nurses and she played Handel and Bessie Smith for the patients on whatever piano was available. At some places, she had a Steinway donated by a grateful, or optimistic, family; at others, she banged out "Gimme a Pigfoot" on an old, scarred box that hadn't been tuned since there'd been English-speaking physicians on the grounds. My father talked in serious, appreciative voices to the administrators and unit chiefs and tried to be friendly with whoever was managing Rose's case. We all hated the family therapists.

The worst family therapist we ever had sat in a pale green room with us, visibly taking stock of my mother's ethereal beauty and her faded blue T-shirt and girl-sized jeans, my father's rumpled suit and stained tie and my own unreadable, sixteen-year-old fashion statement. Rose was beyond fashion that year, in one of her dancing-teddy-bear smocks and extra-extra-large Celtics sweatpants. Mr. Walker read Rose's file in front of us and then watched, in alarm, as Rose began crooning, beautifully, and slowly massaging her breasts.

My mother and I started to laugh and even my father started to smile. This was Rose's usual opening salvo for new therapists.

Mr. Walker said, "I wonder why it is that everyone is so entertained by Rose behaving inappropriately."

Rose burped and then we all laughed. This was the seventh family therapist we had seen and none of them had lasted very long. Mr. Walker, unfortunately, was determined to do right by us.

"What do you think of Rose's behavior, Violet?" They did this sometimes. In their manual, it must say, if you think the parents are too weird, try talking to the sister.

"I don't know. Maybe she's trying to get you to stop talking about her in the third person."

"Nicely put," my father said.

"Indeed," my mother said.

"Fuckin' A," Rose said.

"Well, this is something that the whole family agrees upon," Mr. Walker said, trying to act as if he understood, or even liked us.

"That was not a successful intervention, Ferret Face." Rose tended to function better when she was angry. He did look like a blond ferret and we all laughed again. Even my father, who tried to give these people a chance out of some sense of collegiality, had given it up.

Mr. Walker decided, after fourteen minutes, that our time was up and walked out, leaving us grinning at each other. Rose was still nuts, but at least we'd all had a little fun.

Our best family therapist started out almost as badly. We scared off a resident and then scared off her supervisor, who sent us Dr. Thorne. Three hundred pounds of Texas chili, cornbread and Lone Star beer, finished off with big black cowboy boots and a little string tie around the area of his neck.

"Oh, frabjous day, it's Big Nut." Rose was in heaven and stopped massaging her breasts immediately.

"Hey, Little Nut." You have to understand how big a man would have to be to call my sister "little." He christened us all, right away. "And it's the good Doctor Nut, and Madame Hickory Nut, 'cause they are the hardest damn nuts to crack, and over here in the overalls and not much else, is No One's Nut"—a name which summed up both my sanity and my loneliness. We all relaxed.

Dr. Thorne was good for us. Rose moved into a halfway house, whose director loved Big Nut so much she kept Rose even when Rose went through a period of having sex with everyone who passed her door. She was in a fever for a while, trying to still the voices by fucking her brains out.

Big Nut said, "Darlin', I can't. I cannot make love to every beautiful woman I meet and, furthermore, I can't do that and be your therapist, too. It's a great shame, but I think you might be able to find a really nice guy, someone who treats you just as sweet and kind as I would, if I were lucky enough to be your beau. I don't want you to settle for less." And she stopped propositioning the crack addicts and the alcoholics and the guys at the shelter. We loved Dr. Thorne.

My father cut back on seeing rich neurotics and helped out one day a week at Dr. Thorne's walk-in clinic. My mother finished a record of Mozart concerti and played at fund-raisers for Rose's halfway house. I went back to college and found a wonderful linebacker from Texas to sleep with. In the dark, I would make him call me "darlin'." Rose took her meds, lost about fifty pounds and began singing at the A.M.E. Zion Church, down the street from the halfway house.

At first, they didn't know what to do with this big, blond lady, dressed funny and hovering wistfully in the doorway during their rehearsals, but she gave them a few bars of "Precious Lord" and the choir director felt God's hand and saw that, with the help of His sweet child, Rose, the Prospect Street Choir was going all the way to the Gospel Olympics.

Amidst a sea of beige, umber, cinnamon and espresso faces, there was Rose, bigger, blonder and pinker than any two white women could be. And Rose and the choir's contralto, Addie Robicheaux, laid out their gold and silver voices and wove them together in strands as fine as silk, as strong as steel. And we wept as Rose and Addie, in their billowing garnet robes, swayed together, clasping hands until the last perfect note floated up to God and then they smiled down at us.

Rose would still go off from time to time and the voices would tell her to do bad things, but Dr. Thorne or Addie or my mother could usually bring her back. After five good years, Big Nut died. Stuffing his face with a chili dog, sitting in his un-air-conditioned office in the middle of July, he had one big, Texas-sized aneurism and died.

Rose held on tight for seven days; she took her meds, went to choir practice and rearranged her room about a hundred times. His funeral was a Lourdes for the mentally ill. If you were psychotic, borderline, bad-off neurotic, or just very hard to get along with, you were there. People shaking so bad from years of heavy meds that they fell out of the pews. People holding hands, crying, moaning, talking to themselves; the crazy and the not-so-crazy were all huddled together, like puppies at the pound.

Rose stopped taking her meds and the halfway house wouldn't keep her after she pitched another patient down the stairs. My father called the insurance company and found out that Rose's new, improved psychiatric coverage wouldn't begin for forty-five days. I put all of her stuff in a garbage bag and we walked out of the halfway house, Rose winking at the poor, drooling boy on the couch.

"This is going to be difficult—not all bad, but difficult—for the whole family and I thought we should discuss everybody's expectations. I know I have some concerns." My father had convened a family meeting as soon as Rose had finished putting each one of her thirty stuffed bears in its own special place.

"No meds," Rose said, her eyes lowered, her stubby fingers, those fingers that had braided my hair and painted tulips on my cheeks, pulling hard on the hem of her dirty smock.

My father looked in despair at my mother.

"Rosie, do you want to drive the new car?" my mother asked.

Rose's face lit up. "I'd love to drive that car. I'd drive to California, I'd go see the bears at the San Diego Zoo. I would take you, Violet, but you always hated the zoo. Remember how she cried at the Bronx Zoo when she found out that the animals didn't get to go home at closing?" Rose put her damp hand on mine and squeezed it, sympathetically. "Poor Vi."

"If you take your medication, after a while, you'll be able to drive the car. That's the deal. Meds, car." My mother sounded accommodating but unenthusiastic, careful not to heat up Rose's paranoia.

"You got yourself a deal, darlin'."

I was living about an hour away then, teaching English during the day, writing poetry at night. I went home every few days, for dinner. I called every night.

My father said, quietly, "It's very hard. We're doing all right, I think. Rose has been walking in the mornings with your mother and she watches a lot of TV. She won't go to the day hospital and she won't go back to the choir. Her friend, Mrs. Robicheaux, came by a couple of times. What a sweet woman. Rose wouldn't even talk to her; she just sat there, staring at the wall and humming. We're not doing all that well, actually, but I guess we're getting by. I'm sorry, sweetheart, I don't mean to depress you."

My mother said, emphatically, "We're doing fine. We've got our routine and we stick to it and we're fine. You don't need to come home so often, you know. Wait till Sunday, just come for the day. Lead your life, Vi. She's leading hers."

I stayed away until Sunday, afraid to pick up my phone, grateful to my mother for her harsh calm and her reticence, the qualities that had enraged me throughout my childhood.

I came on a Sunday, in the early afternoon, to help my father garden, something we had always enjoyed together. We weeded and staked tomatoes and killed aphids while my mother and Rose were down at the lake. I didn't even get into the house until four, when I needed a glass of water.

Someone had broken the piano bench into five neatly stacked pieces and placed them where the piano bench usually was.

"We were having such a nice time, I couldn't bear to bring it up," my father said, standing in the doorway, carefully keeping his gardening boots out of the kitchen.

"What did Mommy say?"

"She said, 'Better the bench than the piano.' And your sister lay down on the floor and just wept. Then, your mother took her down to the lake. This can't go on, Vi. We have twenty-seven days left, your mother gets no sleep because Rose doesn't sleep and if I could just pay twenty-seven thousand dollars to keep her in the hospital until the insurance takes over, I'd do it."

"All right. Do it. Pay the money and take her back to Hartley-Rees. It was the prettiest place and she liked the art therapy there."

"I would if I could. The policy states that she must be symptom-free for at least forty-five days before her coverage begins. Symptom-free means no hospitalization."

"Jesus, Daddy, how could you get that kind of policy? She hasn't been symptom-free for forty-five minutes."

"It's the only one I could get for long-term psychiatric." He put his hand over his mouth to block whatever he was about to say and went back out to the garden. I couldn't see if he was crying.

He stayed outside and I stayed inside, until Rose and my mother came home from the lake. Rose's soggy sweatpants were rolled up to her knees and she had a bucketful of shells and gray stones, which my mother persuaded her to leave on the back porch. My mother kissed me lightly and told Rose to go up to her room and change out of her wet pants.

Rose's eyes grew very wide. "Never. I will never . . ." she began banging her head with rhythmic intensity, against the kitchen floor, throwing all of her weight behind each attack. My mother put her arms around Rose's waist and tried to hold her back. Rose shook her off, not even looking around to see what was slowing her down. My mother crumpled next to the refrigerator.

"Violet, please . . ."

I threw myself onto the kitchen floor, becoming the spot that Rose was smacking her head against. She stopped a fraction of an inch short of my stomach.

"Oh, Vi, Mommy, I'm sorry. I'm sorry, don't hate me." She staggered to her feet and ran, wailing, to her room.

My mother got up and washed her face, brusquely, rubbing it dry with a dishcloth. My father heard the wailing and came running in, slipping his long bare feet out of his rubber boots.

"Galen, Galen, let me see." He held her head and looked closely for bruises on her pale, small face. "What happened?" My mother looked at me. "Violet, what happened? Where's Rose?"

"Rose got upset and when she went running upstairs, she pushed Mommy out of the way." I've only told three lies in my life and that was my second.

"She must feel terrible, pushing you, of all people. It would have to be you, but I know she didn't want it to be." He made my mother a cup of tea and all the love he had for her, despite her silent rages and her vague stares, came pouring through the teapot, warming her cup, filling her small, long-fingered hands. He stood by her and she rested her head against his hip. I looked away.

"Let's make dinner, then I'll call her. Or you call her, David, maybe she'd rather see your face first."

Dinner was filled with all of our starts and stops and Rose's desperate efforts to control herself. She could barely eat and hummed the McDonald's theme song over and over again, pausing only to spill her juice down the front of her smock and begin weeping. My father looked at my mother and handed Rose his napkin. She dabbed at herself, listlessly, but the tears stopped.

"I want to go to bed. I want to go to bed and be in my head. I want to go to bed and be in my bed and in my head and just wear red. For red is the color that my baby wore and once more, it's true, yes, it is, it's true. Please don't wear red tonight, ohh, ohh, please don't wear red tonight, for red is the color—"

"Okay, okay, Rose. It's okay. I'll go upstairs with you and you can get ready for bed. Then, Mommy will come up and say good night, too. It's okay, Rose." My father reached out his hand and Rose grasped it and they walked out of the dining room together, his long arm around her middle.

My mother sat at the table for a moment, her face in her hands, and then she began clearing the table. We cleared without talking, my mother humming Schubert's "Schlummerlied," a lullaby about the woods and the river calling to the child to go to sleep. She sang it to us every night, when we were small.

My father came back into the kitchen and signaled to my mother. She went upstairs and they came back down together, a few minutes later.

"She's asleep," they said and we went to sit on the porch and listen to the crickets. I don't remember the rest of the evening, but I remember it as quietly sad and I remember the rare sight of my parents holding hands, sitting on the picnic table, watching the sunset.

I woke up at three o'clock in the morning, feeling the cool night air through my sheet. I went down the hall for another blanket and looked into Rose's room, for no reason. She wasn't there. I put on my jeans and a sweater and went downstairs. I could feel her absence. I went outside and saw her wide, draggy footprints darkening the wet grass, into the woods.

"Rosie," I called, too softly, not wanting to wake my parents, not wanting to startle Rose. "Rosie, it's me. Are you here? Are you all right?"

I almost fell over her. Huge and white in the moonlight, her flowered smock bleached in the light and shadow, her sweatpants now completely wet. Her head was flung back, her white, white neck exposed like a lost Greek column.

"Rosie, Rosie—" Her breathing was very slow and her lips were not as pink as they usually were. Her eyelids fluttered.

"Closing time," she whispered. I believe that's what she said.

I sat with her, uncovering the bottle of white pills by her hand, and watched the stars fade.

When the stars were invisible and the sun was warming the air, I went back to the house. My mother was standing on the porch, wrapped in a blanket, watching me. Every step I took overwhelmed me; I could picture my mother slapping me, shooting me for letting her favorite die.

"Warrior queens," she said, wrapping her thin strong arms around me. "I raised warrior queens." She kissed me fiercely and went into the woods by herself.

A little later, she woke my father, who could not go into the woods, and still later she called the police and the funeral parlor. She hung up the phone, lay down, and didn't get back out of bed until the day of the funeral. My father fed us both and called the people who needed to be called and picked out Rose's coffin by himself.

My mother played the piano and Addie sang her pure gold notes and I closed my eyes and saw my sister, fourteen years old, lion's mane thrown back and her eyes tightly closed against the glare of the parking lot lights. That sweet sound held us tight, flowing around us, eddying through our hearts, rising, still rising.

KATE BRAVERMAN

Tall Tales from the Mekong Delta

KATE BRAVERMAN (1950–) was born in Los Angeles and educated at Berkeley during the sixties. She has published four poetry collections, and a trilogy of novels about Los Angeles—*Lithium for Medea, Palm Latitudes,* and *Wonders of the West.* Her books of short stories are *Squandering the Blue* and the recent *Small Craft Warnings* (University of Nevada Press, 1998). Braverman writes that she has "spent her career writing about women defying the travesty of their traditional 'roles.' Women on narcotics, women alone, abandoned with children, women who refuse to be defined by their relationships with men. Women who despise fashion, a new 20th century crime. The artist is an arsonist, juggling with fire. . . . [A]rt must be an act of insurrection. For her convictions, she has been psychologically brutalized and mutilated by the publishing/fashion industry." She now lives in semiseclusion with her husband, Alan, and daughter, Gabrielle, in the remote northwestern Allegheny Mountains.

It was in the fifth month of her sobriety. It was after the hospital. It was after her divorce. It was autumn. She had even stopped smoking. She was wearing pink aerobic pants, a pink T-shirt with KAUAI written in lilac across the chest, and tennis shoes. She had just come from the gym. She was walking across a parking lot bordering a city park in West Hollywood. She was carrying cookies for the AA meeting. She was in charge of bringing the food for the meeting. He fell into step with her. He was short, fat, pale. He had bad teeth. His hair was dirty. Later, she would freeze this frame in her mind and study it. She would say he seemed frightened and defeated and trapped, "cagey" was the word she used to describe his eyes, how he measured and evaluated something in the air between them. The way he squinted through hazel eyes, it had nothing to do with the sunlight.

"I'm Lenny," he said, extending his hand. "What's your name?"

She told him. She was holding a bag with packages of cookies in it. After the meeting, she had an appointment with her psychiatrist, then a manicure. She kept walking.

"You a teacher? You look like a teacher," he said.

"I'm a writer," she told him. "I teach creative writing."

"You look like a teacher," Lenny said.

"I'm not just a teacher," she told him. She was annoyed.

"Okay. You're a writer. And you're bad. You're one of those bad girls from Beverly Hills. I've had my eye on you," Lenny said.

She didn't say anything. He was wearing blue jeans, a black leather jacket zipped to his throat, a long red wool scarf around his neck, and a Dodgers baseball cap. It was too hot a day for the leather jacket and scarf. She didn't find that detail significant. It caught her attention, she touched it briefly and then let it go. She looked but did not see. They were standing on a curb. The meeting was in a community room across the boulevard. She wasn't afraid yet.

"You do drugs? What do you do? Drink too much?" he asked.

"I'm a cocaine addict," she told him.

"Me too. Let's see your tracks. Show me your tracks." Lenny reached out for her arm.

"I don't have any now." She glanced at her arm. She extended her arm into the yellow air between them. The air was already becoming charged and disturbed. "They're gone."

"I see them," Lenny told her, inspecting her arm, turning it over, holding it in the sunlight. He touched the part of her arm behind her elbow where the vein rose. "They're beautiful."

"But there's nothing there," she said.

"Yeah, there is. There always is if you know how to look," Lenny told her. "How many people by the door? How many steps?"

He was talking about the door across the boulevard. His back was turned. She didn't know.

"Four steps," Lenny said. "Nine people. Four women. One old man. I look. I see."

She was counting the people on the steps in front of the meeting. She didn't say anything.

"Let's get a coffee later. That's what you do, right? You can't get a drink? You go out for coffee?" Lenny was studying her face.

"I don't think so," she said.

"You don't think so? Come on. I'll buy you coffee. You can explain AA to me. You like that Italian shit? That French shit? The little cups?" Lenny was staring at her.

"No, thank you. I'm sorry," she said. He was short and fat and sweating. He looked like he was laughing at her with his eyes.

"You're sorry. I'll show you sorry. Listen. I know what you want. You're one of those smart-ass teachers from Beverly Hills," Lenny said.

"Right," she said. She didn't know why she bothered talking to him.

"You want to get in over your head. You want to see what's on the other side. I'll show you. I'll take you there. It'll be the ride of your life," Lenny said.

"Goodbye," she answered.

Lenny was at her noon meeting the next day. She saw him immediately as she walked through the door. She wondered how he knew that she would be there. As she approached her usual chair, she saw a bouquet of long-stemmed pink roses.

"You look beautiful," Lenny said. "You knew I'd be here. That's why you put that crap on your face. You didn't have that paint on yesterday. Don't do that. You don't need that. Those whores from Beverly Hills need it. Not you. You're a teacher. I like that. Sit down." He picked the roses up. "Sit next to me. You glad to see me?"

"I don't think so." She sat down. Lenny handed the roses to her. She put them on the floor.

"Yeah. You're glad to see me. You were hoping I'd be here. And here I am. You want me to chase you? I'll chase you. Then I'll catch you. Then I'll show you what being in over your head means." Lenny was smiling.

She turned away. When the meeting was over, she stood up quickly and began moving, even before the prayer was finished. "I have to go," she said, softly, over her shoulder. She felt she had to apologize. She felt she had to be careful.

"You don't have to go," Lenny said. He caught up with her on the steps. "Yeah. Don't look surprised. Lenny's fast, real fast. And you're lying. Don't ever lie to me. You think I'm stupid? Yeah, you think Lenny's stupid. You think you can get away from me? You can't get away. You got an hour. You don't pick that kid up for the dance school until four. Come on. I'll buy you coffee."

"What are you talking about?" She stopped. Her breath felt sharp and fierce. It was a warm November. The air felt like glass.

"I know all about you. I know your routine. I been watching you for two weeks. Ever since I got to town. I saw you my first day. You think I'd ask you out on a date and not know your routine?" Lenny stared at her.

She felt her eyes widen. She started to say something but she changed her mind.

"You live at the top of the hill, off of Doheny. You pick up that kid, what's her name, Annie something? You pick her up and take her to dance school.

You get coffee next door. Table by the window. You read the paper. Then you go home. Just the two of you. And that Mex cleaning lady. Maria. That her name? Maria? They're all called Maria. And the gardener Friday afternoons. That's it." Lenny lit a cigarette.

"You've been following me?" She was stunned. Her mouth opened.

"Recon," Lenny said.

"I beg your pardon?"

"In Nam. We called it recon. Fly over, get a lay of the land. Or stand behind some trees. Count the personnel. People look but they don't see. I'll tell you about it. Get coffee. You got an hour. Want to hear about Vietnam? I got stories. Choppers? I like choppers. You can take your time, aim. You can hit anything, even dogs. Some days we'd go out just aiming at dogs. Or the black market? Want to hear about that? Profiteering in smack? You're a writer, right? You like stories. I got some tall tales from the Mekong Delta for you, sweetheart. Knock your socks off. Come on." He reached out and touched her arm. "Later you can have your own war stories. I can be one of your tall tales. I can be the tallest."

The sun was strong. The world was washed with white. The day seemed somehow clarified. He was wearing a leather jacket and shaking. It occurred to her that he was sick.

"Excuse me. I must go," she said. "If you follow me, I shall have someone call the police."

"Okay. Okay. Calm down," Lenny was saying behind her. "I'll save you a seat tomorrow, okay?"

She didn't reply. She sat in her car. It was strange how blue the sky seemed, etched with the blue of radium or narcotics. Or China blue, perhaps. Was that a color? The blue of the China Sea? The blue of Vietnam. When he talked about Asia, she could imagine that blue, luminescent with ancient fever, with promises and bridges broken, with the harvest lost in blue flame. Always there were barbarians, shooting the children and dogs.

She locked her car and began driving. It occurred to her, suddenly, that the Chinese took poets as concubines. Their poets slept with warlords. They wrote with gold ink. They ate orchids and smoked opium. They were consecrated by nuance, by birds and silk and the ritual birthdays of gods, and nothing changed for a thousand years. And afternoon was absinthe yellow and almond, burnt orange and chrysanthemum. And in the abstract sky, a litany of kites.

She felt herself look for him as she walked into the meeting the next day at noon. The meeting was in the basement of a church. Lenny was standing near the coffeepot with his back to the wall. He was holding two cups of coffee as if he was expecting her. He handed one to her.

"I got seats," he said. He motioned for her to follow. She followed. He pointed to a chair. She sat in it. An older woman was standing at the podium, telling the story of her life. Lenny was wearing a white warm-up suit with a green neon stripe down the sides of the pants and the arms of the jacket. He was wearing a baseball cap. His face seemed younger and tanner than she had remembered.

"Like how I look? I look like a lawyer on his way to tennis, right? I even got a tan. Fit right in. Chameleon Lenny. The best, too." He lit a cigarette. He held the pack out to her.

She shook her head, no. She was staring at the cigarette in his mouth, in his fingers. She could lean her head closer, part her lips, take just one puff.

"I got something to show you," Lenny said.

The meeting was over. They were walking up the stairs from the basement of the church. The sun was strong. She blinked in the light. It was the yellow of a hot autumn, a yellow that seemed amplified and redeemed. She glanced at her watch.

"Don't do that," Lenny said. He was touching the small of her back with his hand. He was helping her walk.

"What?"

"Looking at that fucking watch all the time. Take it off," Lenny said.

"My watch?" She was looking at her wrist as if she had never seen it before.

"Give it here, come on." Lenny put his hand out. He motioned with his fingers. She placed her watch in the palm of his hand.

"That's a good girl," Lenny was saying. "You don't need it. You don't have to know what time it is. You're with me. Don't you get it? You're hungry, I feed you. You're tired, I find a hotel. You're in a structured environment now. You're protected. I protect you. It doesn't matter what time it is." He put her watch in his pocket. "Forget it. I'll buy you a new one. A better one. That was junk. I was embarrassed for you to wear junk like that. Want a Rolex?"

"You can't afford a Rolex," she said. She felt intelligent. She looked into his face.

"I got a drawerful," Lenny told her. "I got all the colors. Red. Black. Gold."

"Where?" She studied his face. They were walking on a side street in Hollywood. The air was a pale blue, bleeding into the horizon, taking the sky.

"In the bank," Lenny said. "In the safety deposit with everything else. All the cash that isn't buried." Lenny smiled.

"What else?" She put her hands on her hips.

"Let's go for a ride," Lenny said.

They were standing at the curb. They were two blocks from the church. A motorcycle was parked there. Lenny took out a key.

"Get on," he said.

"I don't want to get on a motorcycle." She was afraid.

"Yes, you do," Lenny told her. "Sit down on it. Wrap your arms around me. Just lean into me. Nothing else. You'll like it. You'll be surprised. It's a beautiful day. It looks like Hong Kong today. Want to go to the beach? Want lunch? I know a place in Malibu. You like seafood? Crab? Scampi? Watch the waves?" Lenny was doing something to the motorcycle. He looked at her face.

"No," she said.

"How about Italian? I got a place near the Marina. Owner owes for ten kilos. We'll get a good table. You like linguini?" Lenny sat down on the motorcycle.

She shook her head, no.

"Okay. You're not hungry. You're skinny. You should eat. Come on. We'll go around the block. Get on. Once around the block and I'll bring you back to the church." Lenny reached out his hand through the warm white air.

She looked at his hand and how the air seemed blue near his fingers. It's simply a blue glaze, she was thinking. In Malibu, in Hilo, in the China Sea, forms of blue, confusion and remorse, a dancing dress, a daughter with a mouth precisely your own and it's done, all of it. Somewhere it was carnival night in the blue wash of a village on the China Sea. On the river, boats passed with low-slung antique masts sliding silently to the blue of the ocean, to the inverted delta where the horizon concluded itself in a rapture of orchid and pewter. That's what she was thinking when she took his hand.

She did not see him for a week. She changed her meeting schedule. She went to women's meetings in the Pacific Palisades and the Valley. She went to meetings she had never been to before. She trembled when she thought about him.

She stopped her car at a red light. It occurred to her that it was an early afternoon in autumn in her thirty-eighth year. Then she found herself driving to the community center. The meeting was over. There was no one left on the street. Just one man, sitting alone on the front steps, smoking. Lenny looked up at her and smiled.

"I was expecting you," Lenny said. "I told you. You can't get away from me."

She could feel his eyes on her face, the way when she lived with a painter, she had learned to feel lamplight on her skin. When she had learned to perceive light as an entity. She began to cry.

"Don't cry," Lenny said, his voice soft. "I can't stand you crying. Let's make up. I'll buy you dinner."

"I can't." She didn't look at him.

"Yeah. You can. I'll take you someplace good. Spago? You like those little pizzas with the duck and shit? Lobster? You want the Palm? The Rangoon

Racket Club? Yeah. Don't look surprised. I know the places. I made deals in all those places. What did you think?" He was lighting a cigarette and she could feel his eyes on her skin.

She didn't say anything. They were walking across a parking lot. The autumn made everything ache. Later, it would be worse. At dusk, with the subtle irritation of lamps.

"Yeah. I know what you think. You think Lenny looks like he just crawled out from a rock. This is a disguise. Blue jeans, sneakers. I fit right in. I got a gang of angry Colombians on my ass. Forget it." Lenny stared at her. "You got a boyfriend?"

"What's it to you?"

"What's it to me? That's sharp. I want to date you. I probably want to marry you. You got a boyfriend, I got to hurt him." Lenny smiled.

"I can't believe you said that." She put her hands on her hips.

"You got a boyfriend? I'm going to cut off his arm and beat him with it. Here. Look at this." He was bending over and removing something from his sock. He held it in the palm of his hand.

"Know what this is?" Lenny asked.

She shook her head, no.

"It's a knife, sweetheart," Lenny said.

She could see that now, even before he opened it. A push-button knife. Lenny was reaching behind to his back. He was pulling out something from behind his belt, under his shirt. It was another knife.

"Want to see the guns?"

She felt dizzy. They were standing near her car. It was early in December. The Santa Anas had been blowing. She felt that it had been exceptionally warm for months.

"Don't get in the car," Lenny said. "I can't take it when you leave. Stay near me. Just let me breathe the same air as you. I love you."

"You don't even know me," she said.

"But you know me. You been dreaming me. I'm your ticket to the other side, remember?" Lenny had put his knives away. "Want to hear some more Nam stories? How we ran smack into Honolulu? You'll like this. You like the dope stories. You want to get loaded?"

She shook her head, no.

"You kidding me? You don't want to get high?" Lenny smiled.

"I like being sober," she said.

"Sure," Lenny said. "Let me know when that changes. One phone call. I got the best dope in the world."

They were standing in front of her car. The street beyond the parking lot seemed estranged, the air was tarnished. She hadn't thought about drugs in months. Lenny was handing her something, thin circles of metal. She looked down at her hand. Two dimes seemed to glare in her palm.

"For when you change your mind," Lenny said. He was still smiling.

They were sitting on the grass of a public park after a meeting. Lenny was wearing Bermuda shorts and a green T-shirt that said CANCUN. They were sitting in a corner of the park with a stucco wall behind them.

"It's our anniversary," Lenny told her. "We been in love four weeks."

"I've lost track of time," she said. She didn't have a watch anymore. The air felt humid, green, stalled. It was December in West Hollywood. She was thinking that the palms were livid with green death. They could be the palms of Vietnam.

"I want to fuck you," Lenny said. "Let's go to your house."

She shook her head, no. She turned away from him. She began to stand up.

"Okay. Okay. You got the kid. I understand that. Let's go to a hotel. You want the Beverly Wilshire? I can't go to the Beverly Hills Hotel. I got a problem there. What about the Four Seasons? You want to fuck in the Four Seasons?"

"You need to get an AIDS test," she said.

"Why?" Lenny looked amused.

"Because you're a heroin addict. Because you've been in jail," she began.

"Who told you that?" Lenny sat up.

"You told me," she said. "Terminal Island. Chino. Folsom? Is it true?"

"Uh-huh," Lenny said. He lit a cigarette. "Five years in Folsom. Consecutive. Sixty months. I topped out."

She stared at him. She thought how easy it would be, to reach and take a cigarette. Just one, once.

"Means I finished my whole sentence. No time off for good behavior. Lenny did the whole sixty." He smiled. "I don't need an AIDS test."

"You're a heroin addict. You shoot cocaine. You're crazy. Who knows what you do or who you do it with?" She was beginning to be afraid.

"You think I'd give you a disease?" Lenny looked hurt.

Silence. She was looking at Lenny's legs, how white the exposed skin was. She was thinking that he brought his sick body to her, that he was bloated enormous with pathology and bad history, with jails and demented resentments.

"Listen. You got nothing to worry about. I don't need a fucking AIDS test. Listen to me. Are you hearing me? You get that disease, I take care of you. I take you to Bangkok. I keep a place there, on the river. Best smack in the world. Fifty cents. I keep you loaded. You'll never suffer. You start hurting, I'll take you out. I'll kill you myself. With my own hands. I promise," Lenny said.

Silence. She was thinking that he must be drawn to her vast emptiness, could he sense that she was aching and hot and always listening? There is always a garish carnival across the boulevard. We are born, we eat and sleep, conspire and mourn, a birth, a betrayal, an excursion to the harbor, and it's done. All of it, done.

"Come here." Lenny extended his arm. "Come here. You're like a child. Don't be afraid. I want to give you something."

She moved her body closer to his. There are blue enormities, she was thinking, horizons and boulevards. Somewhere, there are blue rocks and they burn.

"Close your eyes," Lenny said. "Open your mouth."

She closed her eyes. She opened her mouth. There was something pressing against her lip. Perhaps it was a flower.

"Close your mouth and breathe," Lenny said.

It was a cigarette. She felt the smoke in her lungs. It had been six months since she smoked. Her hand began to tremble.

"There," Lenny was saying. "You need to smoke. I can tell. It's okay. You can't give up everything at once. Here. Share it. Give me a hit."

They smoked quietly. They passed the cigarette back and forth. She was thinking that she was like a sacked capital. Nothing worked in her plazas. The palm trees were on fire. The air was smoky and blue. No one seemed to notice.

"Sit on my lap. Come on. Sit down. Closer. On my lap," Lenny was saying. "Good. Yeah. Good. I'm not going to bite you. I love you. Want to get married? Want to have a baby? Closer. Let me kiss you. You don't do anything. Let me do it. Now your arms. Yeah. Around my neck. Tighter. Tighter. You worried? You got nothing to worry about. You get sick, I keep you whacked on smack. Then I kill you. So what are you worried? Closer. Yeah. Want to hear about R and R in Bangkok? Want to hear about what you get for a hundred bucks on the river? You'll like this. Lean right up against me. Yeah. Close your eyes."

"Look. It's hot. You want to swim. You like that? Swimming? You know how to swim?" Lenny looked at her. "Yeah? Let's go. I got a place in Bel Air."

"You have a place in Bel Air?" she asked. It was after the meeting. It was the week before Christmas. It was early afternoon.

"Guy I used to know. I did a little work for him. I introduced him to his wife. He owes me some money. He gave me the keys." Lenny reached in his pocket. He was wearing a white-and-yellow warm-up suit. He produced a key ring. It hung in the hot air between them. "It's got everything there. Food. Booze. Dope. Pool. Tennis court. Computer games. You like that? Pac-Man?"

She didn't say anything. She felt she couldn't move. She lit a cigarette. She was buying two packages at a time again. She would be buying cartons soon.

"Look. We'll go for a drive. I'll tell you some more war stories. Come on. I got a nice car today. I got a brand-new red Ferrari. Want to see it? Just take a look. One look. It's at the curb. Give me your hand." Lenny reached out for her hand.

She could remember being a child. It was a child's game in a child's afternoon, before time or distance were factors. When you were told you couldn't move or couldn't see. And for those moments you are paralyzed or blind. You freeze in place. You don't move. You feel that you have been there for years. It does not occur to you that you can move. It does not occur to you that you can break the rules. The world is a collection of absolutes and spells. You know words have a power. You are entranced. The world is a soft blue.

"There. See. I'm not crazy. A red Ferrari. A hundred forty grand. Get in. We'll go around the block. Sit down. Nice interior, huh? Nice stereo. But I got no fucking tapes. Go to the record store with me? You pick out the tapes, okay? Then we'll go to Bel Air. Swim a little. Watch the sunset. Listen to some music. Want to dance? I love to dance. You can't get a disease doing that, right?" Lenny was holding the car door open for her.

She sat down. The ground seemed enormous. It seemed to leap up at her face.

"Yeah. I'm a good driver. Lean back. Relax. I used to drive for a living," Lenny told her.

"What did you drive? A bus?" She smiled.

"A bus? That's sharp. You're sharp. You're one of those sharp little Jewish girls from Beverly Hills with a cocaine problem. Yeah. I know what you're about. All of you. I drove some cars on a few jobs. Couple of jewelry stores, a few banks. Now I fly," Lenny said.

Lenny turned the car onto Sunset Boulevard. In the gardens of the houses behind the gates, everything was in bloom. Patches of color slid past so fast she thought they might be hallucinations. Azaleas and camellias and hibiscus. The green seemed sullen and half asleep. Or perhaps it was opiated, dazed, exhausted from pleasure.

"You fly?" she repeated.

"Planes. You like planes? I'll take you up. I got a plane. Company plane," Lenny told her. "It's in Arizona."

"You're a pilot?" She put out her cigarette and immediately lit another.

"I fly planes for money. Want to fly? I'm going next week. Every second Tuesday. Want to come?" Lenny looked at her.

"Maybe," she said. They had turned on a street north of Sunset. They were winding up a hill. The street was narrow. The bougainvillea was a kind of net near her face. The air smelled of petals and heat.

"Yeah. You'll come with me. I'll show you what I do. I fly over a stretch of desert looks like the moon. There's a small manufacturing business down there. Camouflaged. You'd never see it. I drop some boxes off. I pick some boxes up. Three hours' work. Fifteen grand," Lenny said. "Know what I'm talking about?"

"No."

"Yeah. You don't want to know anything about this. Distribution," Lenny said. "That's federal."

"You do that twice a month?" she asked. They were above Sunset Boulevard. The bougainvillea was a magenta web. There were sounds of birds and insects. They were winding through pine trees. "That's thirty thousand dollars a month."

"That's nothing. The real money's the Bogota run," Lenny said. "Mountains leap up out of the ground, out of nowhere. The Bogota run drove me crazy. Took me a month to come down. Then the Colombians got mad. You know what I'm talking about?"

"No."

"That's good. You don't want to know anything about the Colombians," Lenny said again.

She was thinking about the Colombians and Bogota and the town where Lenny said he had a house, Medellin. She was thinking they would have called her *gitana,* with her long black hair and bare feet. She could have fanned herself with handfuls of hundred-dollar bills like a green river. She could have borne sons for men crossing borders, searching for the definitive run, the one you don't return from. She would dance in bars in the permanently hot nights. They would say she was intoxicated with grief and dead husbands. Sadness made her dance. When she thought about this, she laughed.

The driveway seemed sudden and steep. They were approaching a walled villa. Lenny pushed numbers on a console. The gate opened.

He parked the red Ferrari. He opened the car door for her. She followed him up a flight of stone steps. The house looked like a Spanish fortress.

A large Christmas wreath with pine cones and a red ribbon hung on the door. The door was unlocked. The floor was tile. They were walking on an Oriental silk carpet, past a piano, a fireplace, a bar. There were ceiling-high glass cabinets in which Chinese artifacts were displayed, vases and bowls and carvings. They were walking through a library, then a room with a huge television, stereo equipment, a billiard table. She followed him out a side door.

The pool was built on the edge of the hill. The city below seemed like a sketch for a village, something not quite formed beneath the greenery. Pink and yellow roses had been planted around two sides of the pool. There were beds of azaleas with ferns between them and red camellias, yellow lilies, white daisies, and birds-of-paradise.

"Time to swim," Lenny said.

She was standing near the pool, motionless. "We don't have suits," she said.

"Don't tell nobody, okay?" Lenny was pulling his shirt over his head. He stared at her, a cigarette in his mouth. "It's private. It's walled. Just a cliff out here. And Bernie and Phyllis aren't coming back. Come on. Take off your clothes. What are you? Scared? You're like a child. Come here. I'll help you. Daddy'll help you. Just stand near me. Here. See? Over your head. Over baby's head. Did that hurt? What's that? One of those goddamn French jobs with the hooks in front? You do it. What are you looking at? I put on a few pounds. Okay? I'm a little out of shape. I need some weights. I got to buy some weights. What are you? Skinny? You're so skinny. You one of those vomiters? I'm not going to bite. Come here. Reach down. Take off my necklace. Unlock the chain. Yeah. Good. Now we swim."

The water felt strange and icy. It was nothing like she expected. There were shadows on the far side of the pool. The shadows were hideous. There was nothing ambiguous about them. The water beneath the shadows looked remote and troubled and green. It looked contaminated. The more she swam, the more the infected blue particles clustered on her skin. There would be no way to remove them.

"I have to leave," she said.

The sun was going down. It was an unusual sunset for Los Angeles, red and protracted. Clouds formed islands in the red sky. The sprinklers came on. The air smelled damp and green like a forest. There were pine trees beyond the rose garden. She thought of the smell of camp at nightfall, when she was a child.

"What are you? Crazy? You kidding me? I want to take you out," Lenny said. He wrapped a towel around his waist. Then he wrapped a towel around her shoulders. "Don't just stand there. Dry off. Come on. You'll get sick. Dry yourself."

He lit a cigarette for her. "You want to get dressed up, right? I know you skinny broads from Beverly Hills. You want to get dressed up. Look. Let me show you something. You'll like it. I know. Come on." He put out his hand for her. She took it.

They were walking up a marble stairway to the bedroom. The bedroom windows opened onto a tile balcony. There were sunken tubs in the bathroom. Everything was black marble. The faucets were gold. There were gold chandeliers hanging above them. Every wall had mirrors bordered by bulbs and gold. Lenny was standing in front of a closet.

"Pick something out. Go on. Walk in. Pink. You like pink? No. You like it darker. Yeah. Keep walking. Closet big as a tennis court. They got no taste, right? Looks like Vegas, right? You like red? No. Black. That's you. Here.

Black silk." Lenny came out of the closet. He was holding an evening gown. "This your size? All you skinny broads wear the same size."

Lenny handed the dress to her. He stretched out on the bed. "Yeah. Let go of the towel. That's right. Only slower."

He was watching her. He lit a cigarette. His towel had come apart. He was holding something near his lap. It was a jewelry box.

"After you put that crap on your face, the paint, the lipstick, we'll pick out a little something nice for you. Phyllis won't need it. She's not coming back. Yeah." Lenny laughed. "Bernie and Phyllis are entertaining the Colombians by now. Give those boys from the jungle something to chew on. Don't look like that. You like diamonds? I know you like diamonds."

Lenny was stretched out on the bed. The bed belonged to Bernie and Phyllis but they weren't coming back. Lenny was holding a diamond necklace out to her. She wanted it more than she could remember wanting anything.

"I'll put it on you. Come here. Sit down. I won't touch you. Not unless you ask me. I can see you're all dressed up. Just sit near me. I'll do the clasp for you," Lenny offered.

She sat down. She could feel the stones around her throat, cool, individual, like the essence of something that lives in the night. Or something more ancient, part of the fabric of the night itself.

"Now you kiss me. Come on. You want to. I can tell. Kiss me. Know what this costs?" Lenny touched the necklace at her throat with his fingertips. He studied the stones. He left his fingers on her throat. "Sixty, seventy grand maybe. You can kiss me now."

She turned her face toward him. She opened her lips. Outside, the Santa Ana winds were startling, howling as if from a mouth. The air smelled of scorched lemons and oranges, of something delirious and intoxicated. When she closed her eyes, everything was blue.

She didn't see him at her noon meeting the next day or the day after. She thought, Well, that's it. She wasn't sorry. She got a manicure. She went to her psychiatrist. She began taking a steam bath after her aerobics class at the gym. She went Christmas shopping. She bought her daughter a white rabbit coat trimmed with blue fox. She was spending too much money. She didn't care. It was Christmas Eve when the doorbell rang. There were carols on the radio. She was wearing a silk robe and smoking. She told Maria that she would answer the door.

"You promised never to come here." She was angry. "You promised to respect my life. To recognize my discrete borders."

"Discrete borders?" Lenny repeated. "I'm in serious trouble. Look at me. Can't you see there's something wrong? You look but you don't see."

There was nothing unusual about him. He was wearing blue jeans and a black leather jacket. He was carrying an overnight bag. She could see the motorcycle near the curb. Maybe the Colombians had the red Ferrari. Maybe they were chewing on that now. She didn't ask him in.

"This is it," Lenny was saying. He brushed past her and walked into the living room. He was talking quickly. He was telling her what had happened in the desert, what the Colombians had done. She felt like she was being electrocuted, that her hair was standing on end. It occurred to her that it was a sensation so singular that she might come to enjoy it. There were small blue wounded sounds in the room now. She wondered if they were coming from her.

"I disappear in about five minutes." Lenny looked at her. "You coming?"

She thought about it. "I can't come, no," she said finally. "I have a child."

"We take her," Lenny offered.

She shook her head, no. The room was going dark at the edges, she noticed. Like a field of blue asters, perhaps. Or ice when the sun strikes it. And how curious the blue becomes when clouds cross the sun, when the blue becomes broken, tawdry.

"I had plans for you. I was going to introduce you to some people. I should have met you fifteen years ago. I could have retired. Get me some ice," Lenny said. "Let's have a drink."

"We're in AA. Are you crazy?" She was annoyed.

"I need a drink. I need a fix. I need an automatic weapon. I need a plane," he said. He looked past her to the den. Maria was watching television and wrapping Christmas presents.

"You need a drink, too," Lenny said. "Don't even think about it. The phone. You're an accessory after the fact. You can go to jail. What about your kid then?"

They were standing in her living room. There was a noble pine tree near the fireplace. There were wrapped boxes beneath the branches. Maria asked in Spanish if she needed anything. She said not at the moment. Two glasses with ice, that was all.

"Have a drink," Lenny said. "You can always go back to the meetings. They take you back. They don't mind. I do it all the time. All over the world. I been doing it for ten years."

"I didn't know that," she said. It was almost impossible to talk. It occurred to her that her sanity was becoming intermittent, like a sudden stretch of intact road in an abandoned region. Or radio music, blatant after months of static.

"Give me the bottle. I'll pour you one. Don't look like that. You look like you're going down for the count. Here." Lenny handed the glass to her. She could smell the vodka. "Open your mouth, goddamn it."

She opened her mouth. She took a sip. Then she lit a cigarette.

"Wash the glass when I leave," Lenny said. "They can't prove shit. You don't know me. You were never anywhere. Nothing happened. You listening? You don't look like you're listening. You look like you're on tilt. Come on, baby. Listen to Daddy. That's good. Take another sip."

She took another sip. Lenny was standing near the door. "You're getting off easy, you know that? I ran out of time. I had plans for you," he was saying.

He was opening the door. "Some ride, huh? Did Daddy do like he said? Get you to the other side? You catch a glimpse? See what's there? I think you're starting to see. Can't say Lenny lied to you, right?"

She took another sip. "Right," she agreed. When this glass was finished she would pour another. When the bottle was empty, she would buy another.

Lenny closed the door. The night stayed outside. She was surprised. She opened her mouth but no sound came out. Instead, blue things flew in, pieces of glass or tin, or necklaces of blue diamonds, perhaps. The air was the blue of a pool when there are shadows, when clouds cross the turquoise surface, when you suspect something contagious is leaking, something camouflaged and disrupted. There is only this infected blue enormity elongating defiantly. The blue that knows you and where you live and it's never going to forget.

ROBERT OLEN BUTLER

A Good Scent from a Strange Mountain

ROBERT OLEN BUTLER (1945–) has published ten books since 1981, eight novels—*The Alleys of Eden, Sun Dogs, Countrymen of Bones, On Distant Ground, Wabash, The Deuce, They Whisper,* and *The Deep Green Sea*—and two volumes of short fiction, *Tabloid Dreams* and *A Good Scent from a Strange Mountain,* which won the 1993 Pulitzer Prize in fiction. His stories have appeared widely in such publications as *The New Yorker, Esquire, The Paris Review, Harper's, GQ, The Hudson Review, The Virginia Quarterly Review,* and *The Sewanee Review* and have been chosen for inclusion in four annual editions of The Best American Short Stories and six annual editions of New Stories from the South. A recipient of both a Guggenheim Fellowship in fiction and a National Endowment for the Arts grant, he also won the Richard and Hilda Rosenthal Foundation Award from the American Academy and Institute of Arts and Letters and was a finalist for the PEN/Faulkner Award. He has recently written screenplays for Twentieth Century-Fox, Warner Brothers, Paramount, Disney, and Universal Pictures. He teaches creative writing at McNeese State University in Lake Charles, Louisiana, where he lives with his wife, the novelist and playwright Elizabeth Dewberry.

Ho Chi Minh came to me again last night, his hands covered with confectioners' sugar. This was something of a surprise to me, the first time I saw him beside my bed, in the dim light from the open shade. My oldest daughter leaves my shades open, I think so that I will not forget that the sun has risen again in the morning. I am a very old man. She seems to expect that one morning I will simply forget to keep living. This is very foolish. I will one night rise up from my bed and slip into her room and open the shade there.

Let *her* see the sun in the morning. She is sixty-four years old and she should worry for herself. I could never die from forgetting.

But the light from the street was enough to let me recognize Ho when I woke, and he said to me, "Dao, my old friend, I have heard it is time to visit you." Already on that first night there was a sweet smell about him, very strong in the dark, even before I could see his hands. I said nothing, but I stretched to the nightstand beside me and I turned on the light to see if he would go away. And he did not. He stood there beside the bed—I could even see him reflected in the window—and I knew it was real because he did not appear as he was when I'd known him but as he was when he'd died. This was Uncle Ho before me, the thin old man with the dewlap beard wearing the dark clothes of a peasant and the rubber sandals, just like in the news pictures I studied with such a strange feeling for all those years. Strange because when I knew him, he was not yet Ho Chi Minh. It was 1917 and he was Nguyen Ai Quoc and we were both young men with clean-shaven faces, the best of friends, and we worked at the Carlton Hotel in London, where I was a dishwasher and he was a pastry cook under the great Escoffier. We were the best of friends and we saw snow for the first time together. This was before we began to work at the hotel. We shoveled snow and Ho would stop for a moment and blow his breath out before him and it would make him smile, to see what was inside him, as if it was the casting of bones to tell the future.

On that first night when he came to me in my house in New Orleans, I finally saw what it was that smelled so sweet and I said to him, "Your hands are covered with sugar."

He looked at them with a kind of sadness.

I have received that look myself in the past week. It is time now for me to see my family, and the friends I have made who are still alive. This is our custom from Vietnam. When you are very old, you put aside a week or two to receive the people of your life so that you can tell one another your feelings, or try at last to understand one another, or simply say good-bye. It is a formal leave-taking, and with good luck you can do this before you have your final illness. I have lived almost a century and perhaps I should have called them all to me sooner, but at last I felt a deep weariness and I said to my oldest daughter that it was time.

They look at me with sadness, some of them. Usually the dull-witted ones, or the insincere ones. But Ho's look was, of course, not dull-witted or insincere. He considered his hands and said, "The glaze. Maestro's glaze."

There was the soft edge of yearning in his voice and I had the thought that perhaps he had come to me for some sort of help. I said to him, "I don't remember. I only washed dishes." As soon as the words were out of my mouth, I decided it was foolish for me to think he had come to ask me about the glaze.

But Ho did not treat me as foolish. He looked at me and shook his head. "It's all right," he said. "I remember the temperature now. Two hundred and thirty degrees, when the sugar is between the large thread stage and the small orb stage. The Maestro was very clear about that and I remember." I knew from his eyes, however, that there was much more that still eluded him. His eyes did not seem to move at all from my face, but there was some little shifting of them, a restlessness that perhaps only I could see, since I was his close friend from the days when the world did not know him.

I am nearly one hundred years old, but I can still read a man's face. Perhaps better than I ever have. I sit in the overstuffed chair in my living room and I receive my visitors and I want these people, even the dull-witted and insincere ones—please excuse an old man's ill temper for calling them that—I want them all to be good with one another. A Vietnamese family is extended as far as the bloodline strings us together, like so many paper lanterns around a village square. And we all give off light together. That's the way it has always been in our culture. But these people who come to visit me have been in America for a long time and there are very strange things going on that I can see in their faces.

None stranger than this morning. I was in my overstuffed chair and with me there were four of the many members of my family: my son-in-law Thang, a former colonel in the Army of the Republic of Vietnam and one of the insincere ones, sitting on my Castro convertible couch; his youngest son, Loi, who had come in late, just a few minutes earlier, and had thrown himself down on the couch as well, youngest but a man old enough to have served as a lieutenant under his father as our country fell to the communists more than a decade ago; my daughter Lam, who is Thang's wife, hovering behind the both of them and refusing all invitations to sit down; and my oldest daughter, leaning against the door frame, having no doubt just returned from my room, where she had opened the shade that I had closed when I awoke.

It was Thang who gave me the sad look I have grown accustomed to, and I perhaps seemed to him at that moment a little weak, a little distant. I had stopped listening to the small talk of these people and I had let my eyes half close, though I could still see them clearly and I was very alert. Thang has a steady face and the quick eyes of a man who is ready to come under fire, but I have always read much more there, in spite of his efforts to show nothing. So after he thought I'd faded from the room, it was with slow eyes, not quick, that he moved to his son and began to speak of the killing.

You should understand that Mr. Nguyen Bich Le had been shot dead in our community here in New Orleans just last week. There are many of us Vietnamese living in New Orleans and one man, Mr. Le, published a little newspaper for all of us. He had recently made the fatal error—though it should not be that in America—of writing that it was time to accept the reality of the communist government in Vietnam and begin to talk with them. We had to work now with those who controlled our country. He said that he remained a patriot to the Republic of Vietnam, and I believed him. If anyone had asked an old man's opinion on this whole matter, I would not have been afraid to say that Mr. Le was right.

But he was shot dead last week. He was forty-five years old and he had a wife and three children and he was shot as he sat behind the wheel of his Chevrolet pickup truck. I find a detail like that especially moving, that this man was killed in his Chevrolet, which I understand is a strongly American thing. We knew this in Saigon. In Saigon it was very American to own a Chevrolet, just as it was French to own a Citroën.

And Mr. Le had taken one more step in his trusting embrace of this new culture. He had bought not only a Chevrolet but a Chevrolet pickup truck, which made him not only American but also a man of Louisiana, where there are many pickup trucks. He did not, however, also purchase a gun rack for the back window, another sign of this place. Perhaps it would have been well if he had, for it was through the back window that the bullet was fired. Someone had hidden in the bed of his truck and had killed him from behind in his Chevrolet and the reason for this act was made very clear in a phone call to the newspaper office by a nameless representative of the Vietnamese Party for the Annihilation of Communism and for the National Restoration.

And Thang, my son-in-law, said to his youngest son, Loi, "There is no murder weapon." What I saw was a faint lift of his eyebrows as he said this, like he was inviting his son to listen beneath his words. Then he said it again, more slowly, like it was code. "There is *no weapon.*" My grandson nodded his head once, a crisp little snap. Then my daughter Lam said in a very loud voice, with her eyes on me, "That was a terrible thing, the death of Mr. Le." She nudged her husband and son, and both men turned their faces sharply to me and they looked at me squarely and said, also in very loud voices, "Yes, it was terrible."

I am not deaf, and I closed my eyes further, having seen enough and wanting them to think that their loud talk had not only failed to awake me but had put me more completely to sleep. I did not like to deceive them, however, even though I have already spoken critically of these members of my family. I am a Hoa Hao Buddhist and I believe in harmony among all living things, especially the members of a Vietnamese family.

After Ho had reassured me, on that first visit, about the temperature needed to heat Maestro Escoffier's glaze, he said, "Dao, my old friend, do you still follow the path you chose in Paris?"

He meant by this my religion. It was in Paris that I embraced the Buddha and disappointed Ho. We went to France in early 1918, with the war still on, and we lived in the poorest street of the poorest part of the Seventeenth Arrondissement. Number nine, Impasse Compoint, a blind alley with a few crumbling houses, all but ours rented out for storage. The cobblestones were littered with fallen roof tiles and Quoc and I each had a tiny single room with only an iron bedstead and a crate to sit on. I could see my friend Quoc in the light of the tallow candle and he was dressed in a dark suit and a bowler hat and he looked very foolish. I did not say so, but he knew it himself and he kept seating and reseating the hat and shaking his head very slowly, with a loudly silent anger. This was near the end of our time together, for I was visiting daily with a Buddhist monk and he was drawing me back to the religion of my father. I had run from my father, gone to sea, and that was where I had met Nguyen Ai Quoc and we had gone to London and to Paris and now my father was calling me back, through a Vietnamese monk I met in the Tuileries.

Quoc, on the other hand, was being called not from his past but from his future. He had rented the dark suit and bowler and he would spend the following weeks in Versailles, walking up and down the mirrored corridors of the Palace trying to gain an audience with Woodrow Wilson. Quoc had eight requests for the Western world concerning Indochina. Simple things. Equal rights, freedom of assembly, freedom of the press. The essential things that he knew Wilson would understand, based as they were on Wilson's own Fourteen Points. And Quoc did not even intend to ask for independence. He wanted Vietnamese representatives in the French Parliament. That was all he would ask. But his bowler made him angry. He wrenched out of the puddle of candlelight, both his hands clutching the bowler, and I heard him muttering in the darkness and I felt that this was a bad sign already, even before he had set foot in Versailles. And as it turned out, he never saw Wilson, or Lloyd George either, or even Clemenceau. But somehow his frustration with his hat was what made me sad, even now, and I reached out from my bedside and said, "Uncle Ho, it's all right."

He was still beside me. This was not an awakening, as you might expect, this was not a dream ending with the bowler in Paris and I awaking to find that Ho was never there. He was still beside my bed, though he was just beyond my outstretched hand and he did not move to me. He smiled on one side of his mouth, a smile full of irony, as if he, too, was thinking about the night he'd tried on his rented clothes. He said, "Do you remember how I worked in Paris?"

I thought about this and I did remember, with the words of his advertisement in the newspaper "La Vie Ouvrière": "If you would like a lifelong memento of your family, have your photos retouched at Nguyen Ai Quoc's." This was his work in Paris; he retouched photos with a very delicate hand, the same fine hand that Monsieur Escoffier had admired in London. I said, "Yes, I remember."

Ho nodded gravely. "I painted the blush into the cheeks of Frenchmen."

I said, "A lovely portrait in a lovely frame for forty francs," another phrase from his advertisement.

"Forty-five," Ho said.

I thought now of his question that I had not answered. I motioned to the far corner of the room where the prayer table stood. "I still follow the path."

He looked and said, "At least you became a Hoa Hao."

He could tell this from the simplicity of the table. There was only a red cloth upon it and four Chinese characters: Bao Son Ky Huong. This is the saying of the Hoa Haos. We follow the teachings of a monk who broke away from the fancy rituals of the other Buddhists. We do not need elaborate pagodas or rituals. The Hoa Hao believes that the maintenance of our spirits is very simple, and the mystery of joy is simple, too. The four characters mean "A good scent from a strange mountain."

I had always admired the sense of humor of my friend Quoc, so I said, "You never did stop painting the blush into the faces of Westerners."

Ho looked back to me but he did not smile. I was surprised at this but more surprised at my little joke seeming to remind him of his hands. He raised them and studied them and said, "After the heating, what was the surface for the glaze?"

"My old friend," I said, "you worry me now."

But Ho did not seem to hear. He turned away and crossed the room and I knew he was real because he did not vanish from my sight but opened the door and went out and closed the door behind him with a loud click.

I rang for my daughter. She had given me a porcelain bell, and after allowing Ho enough time to go down the stairs and out the front door, if that was where he was headed, I rang the bell, and my daughter, who is a very light sleeper, soon appeared.

"What is it, Father?" she asked with great patience in her voice. She is a good girl. She understands about Vietnamese families and she is a smart girl.

"Please feel the doorknob," I said.

She did so without the slightest hesitation and this was a lovely gesture on her part, a thing that made me wish to rise up and embrace her, though I was very tired and did not move.

"Yes?" she asked after touching the knob.

"Is it sticky?"

She touched it again. "Ever so slightly," she said. "Would you like me to clean it?"

"In the morning," I said.

She smiled and crossed the room and kissed me on the forehead. She smelled of lavender and fresh bedclothes and there are so many who have gone on before me into the world of spirits and I yearn for them all, yearn to find them all together in a village square, my wife there smelling of lavender and our own sweat, like on a night in Saigon soon after the terrible fighting in 1968 when we finally opened the windows onto the night and there were sounds of bombs falling on the horizon and there was no breeze at all, just the heavy stillness of the time between the dry season and the wet, and Saigon smelled of tar and motorcycle exhaust and cordite but when I opened the window and turned to my wife, the room was full of a wonderful scent, a sweet smell that made her sit up, for she sensed it, too. This was a smell that had nothing to do with flowers but instead reminded us that flowers were always ready to fall into dust, while this smell was as if a gemstone had begun to give off a scent, as if a mountain of emerald had found its own scent. I crossed the room to my wife and we were already old, we had already buried children and grandchildren that we prayed waited for us in that village square at the foot of the strange mountain, but when I came near the bed, she lifted her silk gown and threw it aside and I pressed close to her and our own sweat smelled sweet on that night. I want to be with her in that square and with the rest of those we'd buried, the tiny limbs and the sullen eyes and the gray faces of the puzzled children and the surprised adults and the weary old people who have gone before us, who know the secrets now. And the sweet smell of the glaze on Ho's hands reminds me of others that I would want in the square, the people from the ship, too, the Vietnamese boy from a village near my own who died of a fever in the Indian Ocean and the natives in Dakar who were forced by colonial officials to swim out to our ship in shark-infested waters to secure the moorings and two were killed before our eyes without a French regret. Ho was very moved by this, and I want those men in our square and I want the Frenchman, too, who called Ho "monsieur" for the first time. A man on the dock in Marseilles. Ho spoke of him twice more during our years together and I want that Frenchman there. And, of course, Ho. Was he in the village square even now, waiting? Heating his glaze fondant? My daughter was smoothing my covers around me and the smell of lavender on her was still strong.

"He was in this room," I said to her to explain the sticky doorknob.

"Who was?"

But I was very sleepy and I could say no more, though perhaps she would not have understood anyway, in spite of being the smart girl that she is.

The next night I left my light on to watch for Ho's arrival, but I dozed off and he had to wake me. He was sitting in a chair that he'd brought from across the room. He said to me, "Dao. Wake up, my old friend."

I must have awakened when he pulled the chair near to me, for I heard each of these words. "I am awake," I said. "I was thinking of the poor men who had to swim out to our ship."

"They are already among those I have served," Ho said. "Before I forgot." And he raised his hands and they were still covered with sugar.

I said, "Wasn't it a marble slab?" I had a memory, strangely clear after these many years, as strange as my memory of Ho's Paris business card.

"A marble slab," Ho repeated, puzzled.

"That you poured the heated sugar on."

"Yes." Ho's sweet-smelling hands came forward but they did not quite touch me. I thought to reach out from beneath the covers and take them in my own hands, but Ho leaped up and paced about the room. "The marble slab, moderately oiled. Of course. I am to let the sugar half cool and then use the spatula to move it about in all directions, every bit of it, so that it doesn't harden and form lumps."

I asked, "Have you seen my wife?"

Ho had wandered to the far side of the room, but he turned and crossed back to me at this. "I'm sorry, my friend. I never knew her."

I must have shown some disappointment in my face, for Ho sat down and brought his own face near mine. "I'm sorry," he said. "There are many other people that I must find here."

"Are you very disappointed in me?" I asked. "For not having traveled the road with you?"

"It's very complicated," Ho said softly. "You felt that you'd taken action. I am no longer in a position to question another soul's choice."

"Are you at peace, where you are?" I asked this knowing of his worry over the recipe for the glaze, but I hoped that this was only a minor difficulty in the afterlife, like the natural anticipation of the good cook expecting guests when everything always turns out fine in the end.

But Ho said, "I am not at peace."

"Is Monsieur Escoffier over there?"

"I have not seen him. This has nothing to do with him, directly."

"What is it about?"

"I don't know."

"You won the country. You know that, don't you?"

Ho shrugged. "There are no countries here."

I should have remembered Ho's shrug when I began to see things in the faces of my son-in-law and grandson this morning. But something quickened in me, a suspicion. I kept my eyes shut and laid my head to the side, as if I was fast asleep, encouraging them to talk more.

My daughter said, "This is not the place to speak."

But the men did not regard her. "How?" Loi asked his father, referring to the missing murder weapon.

"It's best not to know too much," Thang said.

Then there was a silence. For all the quickness I'd felt at the first suspicion, I was very slow now. In fact, I did think of Ho from that second night. Not his shrug. He had fallen silent for a long time and I had closed my eyes, for the light seemed very bright. I listened to his silence just as I listened to the silence of these two conspirators before me.

And then Ho said, "They were fools, but I can't bring myself to grow angry anymore."

I opened my eyes in the bedroom and the light was off. Ho had turned it off, knowing that it was bothering me. "Who were fools?" I asked.

"We had fought together to throw out the Japanese. I had very good friends among them. I smoked their lovely Salem cigarettes. They had been repressed by colonialists themselves. Did they not know their own history?"

"Do you mean the Americans?"

"There are a million souls here with me, the young men of our country, and they are all dressed in black suits and bowler hats. In the mirrors they are made ten million, a hundred million."

"I chose my path, my dear friend Quoc, so that there might be harmony."

And even with that yearning for harmony I could not overlook what my mind made of what my ears had heard this morning. Thang was telling Loi that the murder weapon had been disposed of. Thang and Loi both knew the killers, were in sympathy with them, perhaps were part of the killing. The father and son had been airborne rangers and I had several times heard them talk bitterly of the exile of our people. We were fools for trusting the Americans all along, they said. We should have taken matters forward and disposed of the infinitely corrupt Thieu and done what needed to be done. Whenever they spoke like this in front of me, there was soon a quick exchange of sideways glances at me and then a turn and an apology. "We're sorry, Grandfather. Old times often bring old anger. We are happy our family is living a new life."

I would wave my hand at this, glad to have the peace of the family restored. Glad to turn my face and smell the dogwood tree or even smell the coffee plant across the highway. These things had come to be the new smells of our family. But then a weakness often came upon me. The others would drift away, the men, and perhaps one of my daughters would come to me and stroke my head and not say a word and none of them ever would ask why I was weeping. I would smell the rich blood smells of the afterbirth and I would hold our first son, still slippery in my arms, and there was the smell of dust from the square and the smell of the South China Sea just over the rise of the hill and there was the smell of the blood and of the inner flesh from my wife as my son's own private sea flowed from this woman that I loved, flowed and carried him into the life that would disappear from him so soon. In the afterlife would he stand before me on unsteady child's legs? Would I have to bend low to greet him or would he be a man now?

My grandson said, after the silence had nearly carried me into real sleep, troubled sleep, my grandson Loi said to his father, "I would be a coward not to know."

Thang laughed and said, "You have proved yourself no coward."

And I wished then to sleep, I wished to fall asleep and let go of life somewhere in my dreams and seek my village square. I have lived too long, I thought. My daughter was saying, "Are you both mad?" And then she changed her voice, making the words very precise. "Let Grandfather sleep."

So when Ho came tonight for the third time, I wanted to ask his advice. His hands were still covered with sugar and his mind was, as it had been for the past two nights, very much distracted. "There's something still wrong with the glaze," he said to me in the dark, and I pulled back the covers and swung my legs around to get up. He did not try to stop me, but he did draw back quietly into the shadows.

"I want to pace the room with you," I said. "As we did in Paris, those tiny rooms of ours. We would talk about Marx and about Buddha and I must pace with you now."

"Very well," he said. "Perhaps it will help me remember."

I slipped on my sandals and I stood up and Ho's shadow moved past me, through the spill of streetlight and into the dark near the door. I followed him, smelling the sugar on his hands, first before me and then moving past me as I went on into the darkness he'd just left. I stopped as I turned and I could see Ho outlined before the window and I said, "I believe my son-in-law and grandson are involved in the killing of a man. A political killing."

Ho stayed where he was, a dark shape against the light, and he said nothing and I could not smell his hands from across the room and I smelled only the sourness of Loi as he laid his head on my shoulder. He was a baby and my daughter Lam retreated to our balcony window after handing him to me and the boy turned his head and I turned mine to him and I could smell his mother's milk, sour on his breath, he had a sour smell and there was incense burning in the room, jasmine, the smoke of souls, and the boy sighed on my shoulder, and I turned my face away from the smell of him. Thang was across the room and his eyes were quick to find his wife and he was waiting for her to take the child from me.

"You have never done the political thing," Ho said.

"Is this true?"

"Of course."

I asked, "Are there politics where you are now, my friend?"

I did not see him moving toward me, but the smell of the sugar on his hands grew stronger, very strong, and I felt Ho Chi Minh very close to me, though I could not see him. He was very close and the smell was strong and sweet and it was filling my lungs as if from the inside, as if Ho was passing through my very body, and I heard the door open behind me and then close softly shut.

I moved across the room to the bed. I turned to sit down but I was facing the window, the scattering of a streetlamp on the window like a nova in some far part of the universe. I stepped to the window and touched the reflected light there, wondering if there was a great smell when a star explodes, a great burning smell of gas and dust. Then I closed the shade and slipped into bed, quite gracefully, I felt, I was quite wonderfully graceful, and I lie here now waiting for sleep. Ho is right, of course. I will never say a word about my grandson. And perhaps I will be as restless as Ho when I join him. But that will be all right. He and I will be together again and perhaps we can help each other. I know now what it is that he has forgotten. He has used confectioners' sugar for his glaze fondant and he should be using granulated sugar. I was only a washer of dishes but I did listen carefully when Monsieur Escoffier spoke. I wanted to understand everything. His kitchen was full of such smells that you knew you had to understand everything or you would be incomplete forever.

ETHAN CANIN

The Year of Getting to Know Us

ETHAN CANIN (1961–) is the author of *Emperor of the Air, Blue River, The Palace Thief,* and *For Kings and Planets.* A physician, he is also on the faculty of the Iowa Writers' Workshop. He lives in California and Iowa.

I told my father not to worry, that love is what matters, and that in the end, when he is loosed from his body, he can look back and say without blinking that he did all right by me, his son, and that I loved him.

And he said, "Don't talk about things you know nothing about."

We were in San Francisco, in a hospital room. IV tubes were plugged into my father's arms; little round Band-Aids were on his chest. Next to his bed was a table with a vase of yellow roses and a card that my wife, Anne, had brought him. On the front of the card was a photograph of a golf green. On the wall above my father's head an electric monitor traced his heartbeat. He was watching the news on a TV that stood in the corner next to his girlfriend, Lorraine. Lorraine was reading a magazine.

I was watching his heartbeat. It seemed all right to me: the blips made steady peaks and drops, moved across the screen, went out at one end, and then came back at the other. It seemed that this was all a heart could do. I'm an English teacher, though, and I don't know much about it.

"It looks strong," I'd said to my mother that afternoon over the phone. She was in Pasadena. "It's going right across, pretty steady. Big bumps. Solid."

"Is he eating all right?"

"I think so."

"Is *she* there?"

"Is Lorraine here, you mean?"

She paused. "Yes, Lorraine."

"No," I said. "She's not."

"Your poor father," she whispered.

I'm an only child, and I grew up in a big wood-frame house on Huron Avenue in Pasadena, California. The house had three empty bedrooms and in the back yard a section of grass that had been stripped and leveled, then seeded and mowed like a putting green. Twice a week a Mexican gardener came to trim it, wearing special moccasins my father had bought him. They had soft hide soles that left no imprints.

My father was in love with golf. He played seven times every week and talked about the game as if it were a science that he was about to figure out. "Cut through the outer rim for a high iron," he used to say at dinner, looking out the window into the yard while my mother passed him the carved-wood salad bowl, or "In hot weather hit a high-compression ball." When conversations paused, he made little putting motions with his hands. He was a top amateur and in another situation might have been a pro. When I was sixteen, the year I was arrested, he let me caddie for the first time. Before that all I knew about golf was his clubs—the Spalding made-to-measure woods and irons, Dynamiter sand wedge, St. Andrews putter—which he kept in an Abercrombie & Fitch bag in the trunk of his Lincoln, and the white leather shoes with long tongues and screw-in spikes, which he stored upside down in the hall closet. When he wasn't playing, he covered the club heads with socks that had little yellow dingo balls on the ends.

He never taught me to play. I was a decent athlete—could run, catch, throw a perfect spiral—but he never took me to the golf course. In the summer he played every day. Sometimes my mother asked if he would take me along with him. "Why should I?" he answered. "Neither of us would like it."

Every afternoon after work he played nine holes; he played eighteen on Saturday, and nine again on Sunday morning. On Sunday afternoon, at four o'clock, he went for a drive by himself in his white Lincoln Continental. Nobody was allowed to come with him on the drives. He was usually gone for a couple of hours. "Today I drove in the country," he would say at dinner, as he put out his cigarette, or "This afternoon I looked at the ocean," and we were to take from this that he had driven north on the coastal highway. He almost never said more, and across our blue-and-white tablecloth, when I looked at him, my silent father, I imagined in his eyes a pure gaze with which he read the waves and currents of the sea. He had made a fortune in business and owed it to being able to see the truth in any situation. For this reason, he said, he liked to drive with all the windows down. When he returned from his trips his face was red from the wind and his thinning hair lay fitfully on his head. My mother baked on

Sunday afternoons while he was gone, walnut pies or macaroons that she prepared on the kitchen counter, which looked out over his putting green.

I teach English in a high school now, and my wife, Anne, is a journalist. I've played golf a half-dozen times in ten years and don't like it any more than most beginners, though the two or three times I've hit a drive that sails, that takes flight with its own power, I've felt something that I think must be unique to the game. These were the drives my father used to hit. Explosions off the tee, bird flights. But golf isn't my game, and it never has been, and I wouldn't think about it at all if not for my father.

Anne and I were visiting in California, first my mother, in Los Angeles, and then my father and Lorraine, north in Sausalito, and Anne suggested that I ask him to play nine holes one morning. She'd been wanting me to talk to him. It's part of the project we've started, part of her theory of what's wrong—although I don't think that much is. She had told me that twenty-five years changes things, and since we had the time, why not go out to California.

She said, "It's not too late to talk to him."

My best friend in high school was named Nickie Apple. Nickie had a thick chest and a voice that had been damaged somehow, made a little hoarse, and sometimes people thought he was twenty years old. He lived in a four-story house that had a separate floor for the kids. It was the top story, and his father, who was divorced and a lawyer, had agreed never to come up there. That was where we sat around after school. Because of the agreement, no parents were there, only kids. Nine or ten of us, usually. Some of them had slept the night on the big pillows that were scattered against the walls: friends of his older brothers', in Stetson hats and flannel shirts; girls I had never seen before.

Nickie and I went to Shrier Academy, where all the students carried around blue-and-gray notebooks embossed with the school's heraldic seal. SUMUS PRIMI the seal said. Our gray wool sweaters said it; our green exam books said it; the rear window decal my mother brought home said it. My father wouldn't put the sticker on the Lincoln, so she pressed it onto the window above her kitchen sink instead. ƧUMUƧ IMIЯꟼ I read whenever I washed my hands. At Shrier we learned Latin in the eighth grade and art history in the ninth, and in the tenth I started getting into some trouble. Little things: cigarettes, graffiti. Mr. Goldman, the student counselor, called my mother in for a premonition visit. "I have a premonition about Leonard," he told her in the counseling office one afternoon in the warm October when I was sixteen. The office was full of plants and had five floor-to-ceiling windows that let in sun like a greenhouse. They looked over grassy, bushless knolls. "I just have a feeling about him."

That October he started talking to me about it. He called me in and asked me why I was friends with Nickie Apple, a boy going nowhere. I was looking out the big windows, opening and closing my fists beneath the desk top. He said, "Lenny, you're a bright kid—what are you trying to tell us?" And I said, "Nothing. I'm not trying to tell you anything."

Then we started stealing, Nickie and I. He did it first, and took things I didn't expect: steaks, expensive cuts that we cooked on a grill by the window in the top story of his house; garden machinery; luggage. We didn't sell it and we didn't use it, but every afternoon we went someplace new. In November he distracted a store clerk and I took a necklace that we thought was diamonds. In December we went for a ride in someone else's car, and over Christmas vacation, when only gardeners were on the school grounds, we threw ten rocks, one by one, as if we'd paid for them at a carnival stand, through the five windows in Mr. Goldman's office.

"You look like a train station," I said to my father as he lay in the hospital bed. "All those lines coming and going everywhere."

He looked at me. I put some things down, tried to make a little bustle. I could see Anne standing in the hall just beyond the door.

"Are you comfortable, Dad?"

"What do you mean, 'comfortable'? My heart's full of holes, leaking all over the place. Am I comfortable? No, I'm dying."

"You're not dying," I said, and I sat down next to him. "You'll be swinging the five iron in two weeks."

I touched one of the tubes in his arm. Where it entered the vein, the needle disappeared under a piece of tape. I hated the sight of this. I moved the bedsheets a little bit, tucked them in. Anne had wanted me to be alone with him. She was in the hall, waiting to head off Lorraine.

"What's the matter with her?" he asked, pointing at Anne.

"She thought we might want to talk."

"What's so urgent?"

Anne and I had discussed it the night before. "Tell him what you feel," she said. "Tell him you love him." We were eating dinner in a fish restaurant. "Or if you don't love him, tell him you don't."

"Look, Pop," I said now.

"What?"

I was forty-two years old. We were in a hospital and he had tubes in his arms. All kinds of everything: needles, air, tape. I said it again.

"Look, Pop."

Anne and I have seen a counselor, who told me that I had to learn to accept kindness from people. He saw Anne and me together, then Anne alone, then me. Children's toys were scattered on the floor of his office. "You sound as if you don't want to let people near you," he said. "Right?"

"I'm a reasonably happy man," I answered.

I hadn't wanted to see the counselor. Anne and I have been married seven years, and sometimes I think the history of marriage can be written like this: People Want Too Much. Anne and I have suffered no plague; we sleep late two mornings a week; we laugh at most of the same things; we have a decent house in a suburb of Boston, where, after the commuter traffic has eased, a quiet descends and the world is at peace. She writes for a newspaper, and I teach the children of lawyers and insurance men. At times I'm alone, and need to be alone; at times she does too. But I can always count on a moment, sometimes once in a day, sometimes more, when I see her patting down the sheets on the bed, or watering the front window violets, and I am struck by the good fortune of my life.

Still, Anne says I don't feel things.

It comes up at dinner, outside in the yard, in airports as we wait for planes. You don't let yourself feel, she tells me; and I tell her that I think it's a crazy thing, all this talk about feeling. What do the African Bushmen say? They say, Will we eat tomorrow? Will there be rain?

When I was sixteen, sitting in the back seat of a squad car, the policeman stopped in front of our house on Huron Avenue, turned around against the headrest, and asked me if I was sure this was where I lived.

"Yes, sir," I said.

He spoke through a metal grate. "Your daddy owns this house?"

"Yes, sir."

"But for some reason you don't like windows."

He got out and opened my door, and we walked up the porch steps. The swirling lights on the squad car were making crazy patterns in the French panes of the living room bays. He knocked. "What's your daddy do?"

I heard lights snapping on, my mother moving through the house. "He's in business," I said. "But he won't be home now." The policeman wrote something on his notepad. I saw my mother's eye through the glass in the door, and then the locks were being unlatched, one by one, from the top.

When Anne and I came to California to visit, we stayed at my mother's for three days. On her refrigerator door was a calendar with men's names marked on it—dinner dates, theater—and I knew this was done for our benefit. My mother has been alone for fifteen years. She's still thin, and her eyes still water, and I noticed that books were lying open all through the house. Thick paperbacks—*Doctor Zhivago, The Thorn Birds*—in the bathroom and the studio and the bedroom. We never mentioned my father, but at the end of our stay, when we had packed the car for our drive north along the coast, after she'd hugged us both and we'd backed out of the driveway, she came down off the lawn into the street, her arms crossed over her chest, leaned into the window, and said, "You might say hello to your father for me."

We made the drive north on Highway 1. We passed mission towns, fields of butter lettuce, long stretches of pumpkin farms south of San Francisco. It was the first time we were going to see my father with Lorraine. She was a hairdresser. He'd met her a few years after coming north, and one of the first things they'd done together was take a trip around the world. We got postcards from the Nile delta and Bangkok. When I was young, my father had never taken us out of California.

His house in Sausalito was on a cliff above a finger of San Francisco Bay. A new Lincoln stood in the carport. In his bedroom was a teak-framed king-size waterbed, and on the walls were bits of African artwork—opium pipes, metal figurines. Lorraine looked the same age as Anne. One wall of the living room was glass, and after the first night's dinner, while we sat on the leather sofa watching tankers and yachts move under the Golden Gate Bridge, my father put down his Scotch and water, touched his jaw, and said, "Lenny, call Dr. Farmer."

It was his second one. The first had been two years earlier, on the golf course in Monterey, where he'd had to kneel, then sit, then lie down on the fairway.

At dinner the night after I was arrested, my mother introduced her idea. "We're going to try something," she said. She had brought out a chicken casserole, and it was steaming in front of her. "That's what we're going to do. Max, are you listening? This next year, starting tonight, is going to be the year of getting to know us better." She stopped speaking and dished my father some chicken.

"What do you mean?" I asked.

"I mean it will be to a small extent a theme year. Nothing that's going to change every day of our lives, but in this next year I thought we'd all make an attempt to get to know each other better. Especially you, Leonard. Dad and I are going to make a better effort to know you."

"I'm not sure what you mean," said my father.

"All kinds of things, Max. We'll go to movies together, and Lenny can throw a party here at the house. And I personally would like to take a trip, all of us together, to the American Southwest."

"Sounds all right to me," I said.

"And Max," she said, "you can take Lenny with you to play golf. For example." She looked at my father.

"Neither of us would like it," he said.

"Lenny never sees you."

I looked out the window. The trees were turning, dropping their leaves onto the putting green. I didn't care what he said, one way or the other. My mother spooned a chicken thigh onto my plate and covered it with sauce. "All right," my father said. "He can caddie."

"And as preparation for our trip," my mother said, "can you take him on your Sunday rides?"

My father took off his glasses. "The Southwest," he said, wiping the lenses with a napkin, "is exactly like any other part of the country."

Anne had an affair once with a man she met on an assignment. He was young, much younger than either of us—in his late twenties, I would say from the one time I saw him. I saw them because one day on the road home I passed Anne's car in the lot of a Denny's restaurant. I parked around the block and went in to surprise her. I took a table at the back, but from my seat in the corner I didn't realize for several minutes that the youngish-looking woman leaning forward and whispering to the man with a beard was my wife.

I didn't get up and pull the man out with me into the parking lot, or even join them at the table, as I have since thought might have been a good idea. Instead I sat and watched them. I could see that under the table they were holding hands. His back was to me, and I noticed that it was broad, as mine is not. I remember thinking that she probably liked this broadness. Other than that, though, I didn't feel very much. I ordered another cup of coffee just to hear myself talk, but my voice wasn't quavering or fearful. When the waitress left, I took out a napkin and wrote on it, "You are a forty-year-old man with no children and your wife is having an affair." Then I put some money on the table and left the restaurant.

"I think we should see somebody," Anne said to me a few weeks later. It was a Sunday morning, and we were eating breakfast on the porch.

"About what?" I asked.

On a Sunday afternoon when I was sixteen I went out to the garage with a plan my mother had given me. That morning my father had washed the Lincoln. He had detergent-scrubbed the finish and then sun-dried it on Huron Avenue, so that in the workshop light of the garage its highlights shone. The windshield molding, the grille, the chrome side markers, had been cloth-dried to erase water spots. The keys hung from their magnetic sling near the door to the kitchen. I took them out and opened the trunk. Then I hung them up again and sat on the rear quarter panel to consider what to do. It was almost four o'clock. The trunk of my father's car was large enough for a half-dozen suitcases and had been upholstered in a gray medium-pile carpet that was cut to hug the wheel wells and the spare-tire berth. In one corner, fastened down by straps, was his toolbox, and along the back lay the golf bag. In the shadows the yellow dingos of the club socks looked like baby chicks. He was going to come out in a few minutes. I reached in, took off four of the club socks, and made a pillow for my head. Then I stepped into the trunk. The shocks bounced once and stopped. I lay down with my head propped on the quarter panel and my feet resting in the taillight berth, and then I reached up, slammed down the trunk, and was in the dark.

This didn't frighten me. When I was very young, I liked to sleep with the shades drawn and the door closed so that no light entered my room. I used to hold my hand in front of my eyes and see if I could imagine its presence. It was too dark to see anything. I was blind then, lying in my bed, listening for every sound. I used to move my hand back and forth, close to my eyes, until I had the sensation that it was there but had in some way been amputated. I had heard of soldiers who had lost limbs but still felt them attached. Now I held my open hand before my eyes. It was dense black inside the trunk, colorless, without light.

When my father started the car, all the sounds were huge, magnified as if they were inside my own skull. The metal scratched, creaked, slammed when he got in; the bolt of the starter shook all the way through to the trunk; the idle rose and leveled; then the gears changed and the car lurched. I heard the garage door glide up. Then it curled into its housing, bumped once, began descending again. The seams of the trunk lid lightened in the sun. We were in the street now, heading downhill. I lay back and felt the road, listened to the gravel pocking in the wheel wells.

I followed our route in my mind. Left off Huron onto Telscher, where the car bottomed in the rain gulley as we turned, then up the hill to Santa Ana. As we waited for the light, the idle made its change, shifting down, so that below my head I heard the individual piston blasts in the exhaust pipe. Left on Santa Ana, counting the flat stretches where I felt my father tap the brakes, numbering the intersections as we headed west toward the ocean. I heard cars pull up next to us, accelerate, slow down, make turns. Bits of gravel echoed inside the quarter panels. I pulled off more club socks and enlarged my pillow. We slowed down, stopped, and then we accelerated, the soft piston explosions becoming a hiss as we turned onto the Pasadena freeway.

"Dad's rides," my mother had said to me the night before, as I lay in bed, "would be a good way for him to get to know you." It was the first week of the year of getting to know us better. She was sitting at my desk.

"But he won't let me go," I said.

"You're right." She moved some things around on a shelf. The room wasn't quite dark, and I could see the outline of her white blouse. "I talked to Mr. Goldman," she said.

"Mr. Goldman doesn't know me."

"He says you're angry." My mother stood up, and I watched her white blouse move to the window. She pulled back the shade until a triangle of light from the streetlamp fell on my sheets. "Are you angry?"

"I don't know," I said. "I don't think so."

"I don't think so either." She replaced the shade, came over and kissed me on the forehead, and then went out into the hall. In the dark I looked for my hand.

A few minutes later the door opened again. She put her head in. "If he won't let you come," she said, "sneak along."

On the freeway the thermal seams whizzed and popped in my ears. The ride had smoothed out now, as the shocks settled into the high speed, hardly dipping on curves, muffling everything as if we were under water. As far as I could tell, we were still driving west, toward the ocean. I sat halfway up and rested my back against the golf bag. I could see shapes now inside the trunk. When we slowed down and the blinker went on, I attempted bearings, but the sun was the same in all directions and the trunk lid was without shadow. We braked hard. I felt the car leave the freeway. We made turns. We went straight. Then more turns, and as we slowed down and I was stretching out, uncurling my body along the diagonal, we made a sharp right onto gravel and pulled over and stopped.

My father opened the door. The car dipped and rocked, shuddered. The engine clicked. Then the passenger door opened. I waited.

If I heard her voice today, twenty-six years later, I would recognize it.

"Angel," she said.

I heard the weight of their bodies sliding across the back seat, first hers, then his. They weren't three feet away. I curled up, crouched into the low space between the golf bag and the back of the passenger compartment. There were two firm points in the cushion where it was displaced. As I lay there, I went over the voice again in my head: it was nobody I knew. I heard a laugh from her, and then something low from him. I felt the shift of the trunk's false rear, and then, as I lay behind them, I heard the contact: the crinkle of clothing, arms wrapping, and the half-delicate, muscular sounds. It was like hearing a television in the next room. His voice once more, and then the rising of their breath, slow; a minute of this, maybe another; then shifting again, the friction of cloth on the leather seat and the car's soft rocking. "Dad," I whispered. Then rocking again; my father's sudden panting, harder and harder, his half-words. The car shook violently. "Dad," I whispered. I shouted, "Dad!"

The door opened.

His steps kicked up gravel. I heard jingling metal, the sound of the key in the trunk lock. He was standing over me in an explosion of light.

He said, "Put back the club socks."

I did and got out of the car to stand next to him. He rubbed his hands down the front of his shirt.

"What the hell," he said.

"I was in the trunk."

"I know," he said. "What the goddamn."

The year I graduated from college, I found a job teaching junior high school in Boston. The school was a cement building with small windows well up from the street, and dark classrooms in which I spent a lot of time maintaining discipline. In the middle of an afternoon that first winter a boy knocked on my door to tell me I had a phone call. I knew who it was going to be.

"Dad's gone," my mother said.

He'd taken his things in the Lincoln, she told me, and driven away that morning before dawn. On the kitchen table he'd left a note and some cash. "A lot of cash," my mother added, lowering her voice. "Twenty thousand dollars."

I imagined the sheaf of bills on our breakfast table, held down by the ceramic butter dish, the bank notes ruffling in the breeze from the louvered windows that opened onto his green. In the note he said he had gone north and would call her when he'd settled. It was December. I told my mother that I would visit in a week, when school was out for Christmas. I told her to go to her sister's and stay there, and then I said that I was working and had to get back to my class. She didn't say anything on the other end of the line, and in the silence I imagined my father crisscrossing the state of California, driving north, stopping in Palm Springs and Carmel, the Lincoln riding low with the weight.

"Leonard," my mother said, "did you know anything like this was happening?"

During the spring of the year of getting to know us better I caddied for him a few times. On Saturdays he played early in the morning, when the course was mostly empty and the grass was still wet from the night. I learned to fetch the higher irons as the sun rose over the back nine and the ball, on drying ground, rolled farther. He hit skybound approach shots with backspin, chips that bit into the green and stopped. He played in a foursome with three other men, and in the locker room, as they changed their shoes, they told jokes and poked one another in the belly. The lockers were shiny green metal, the floor clean white tiles that clicked under the shoe spikes. Beneath the mirrors were jars of combs in green disinfectant. When I combed my hair with them it stayed in place and smelled like limes.

We were on the course at dawn. At the first fairway the other men dug in their spikes, shifted their weight from leg to leg, dummy-swung at an empty tee while my father lit a cigarette and looked out over the hole. "The big gun," he said to me, or, if it was a par three, "The lady." He stepped on his cigarette. I wiped the head with the club sock before I handed it to him. When he took the club, he felt its balance point, rested it on one finger, and then, in slow motion, he gripped the shaft. Left hand first, then right, the fingers wrapping pinkie to index. Then he leaned down over the ball. On a perfect drive the tee flew straight up in the air and landed in front of his feet.

Over the weekend his heart lost its rhythm for a few seconds. It happened Saturday night, when Anne and I were at the house in Sausalito, and we didn't hear about it until Sunday. "Ventricular fibrillation," the intern said. "Circus movements." The condition was always a danger after a heart attack. He had been given a shock and his heartbeat had returned to normal.

"But I'll be honest with you," the intern said. We were in the hall. He looked down, touched his stethoscope. "It isn't a good sign."

The heart gets bigger as it dies, he told me. Soon it spreads across the x-ray. He brought me with him to a room and showed me strips of paper with the electric tracings: certain formations. The muscle was dying in patches, he said. He said things might get better, they might not.

My mother called that afternoon. "Should I come up?"

"He was a bastard to you," I said.

When Lorraine and Anne were eating dinner, I found the intern again. "I want to know," I said. "Tell me the truth." The intern was tall and thin, sick-looking himself. So were the other doctors I had seen around the place. Everything in that hospital was pale—the walls, the coats, the skin.

He said, "What truth?"

I told him that I'd been reading about heart disease. I'd read about EKGs, knew about the medicines—lidocaine, propranolol. I knew that the lungs filled up with water, that heart failure was death by drowning. I said, "The truth about my father."

The afternoon I had hidden in the trunk, we came home while my mother was cooking dinner. I walked up the path from the garage behind my father, watching the pearls of sweat on his neck. He was whistling a tune. At the door he kissed my mother's cheek. He touched the small of her back. She was cooking vegetables, and the steam had fogged up the kitchen windows and dampened her hair. My father sat down in the chair by the window and opened the newspaper. I thought of the way the trunk rear had shifted when he and the woman had moved into the back of the Lincoln. My mother was smiling.

"Well?" she said.

"What's for dinner?" I asked.

"Well?" she said again.

"It's chicken," I said. "Isn't it?"

"Max, aren't you going to tell me if anything unusual happened today?"

My father didn't look up from the newspaper. "Did anything unusual happen today?" he said. He turned the page, folded it back smartly. "Why don't you ask Lenny?"

She smiled at me.

"I surprised him," I said. Then I turned and looked out the window.

"I have something to tell you," Anne said to me one Sunday morning in the fifth year of our marriage. We were lying in bed. I knew what was coming.

"I already know," I said.

"What do you already know?"

"I know about your lover."

She didn't say anything.

"It's all right," I said.

It was winter. The sky was gray, and although the sun had risen only a few hours earlier, it seemed like late afternoon. I waited for Anne to say something more. We were silent for several minutes. Then she said, "I wanted to hurt you." She got out of bed and began straightening out the bureau. She pulled my sweaters from the drawer and refolded them. She returned all our shoes to the closet. Then she came back to the bed, sat down, and began to cry. Her back was toward me. It shook with her gasps, and I put my hand out and touched her. "It's all right," I said.

"We only saw each other a few times," she answered. "I'd take it back if I could. I'd make it never happen."

"I know you would."

"For some reason I thought I couldn't really hurt you."

She had stopped crying. I looked out the window at the tree branches hung low with snow. It didn't seem I had to say anything.

"I don't know why I thought I couldn't hurt you," she said. "Of course I can hurt you."

"I forgive you."

Her back was still toward me. Outside, a few snowflakes drifted up in the air.

"*Did* I hurt you?"

"Yes, you did. I saw you two in a restaurant."

"Where?"

"At Denny's."

"No," she said. "I mean, where did I hurt you?"

* * *

The night he died, Anne stayed awake with me in bed. "Tell me about him," she said.

"What about?"

"Stories. Tell me what it was like growing up, things you did together."

"We didn't do that much," I said. "I caddied for him. He taught me things about golf."

That night I never went to sleep. Lorraine was at a friend's apartment and we were alone in my father's empty house, but we pulled out the sheets anyway, and the two wool blankets, and we lay on the fold-out sofa in the den. I told stories about my father until I couldn't think of any more, and then I talked about my mother until Anne fell asleep.

In the middle of the night I got up and went into the living room. Through the glass I could see lights across the water, the bridges, Belvedere and San Francisco, ships. It was clear outside, and when I walked out to the cement carport the sky was lit with stars. The breeze moved inside my nightclothes. Next to the garage the Lincoln stood half-lit in the porch floodlight. I opened the door and got in. The seats were red leather and smelled of limes and cigarettes. I rolled down the window and took the key from the glove compartment. I thought of writing a note for Anne, but didn't. Instead I coasted down the driveway in neutral and didn't close the door or turn on the lights until the bottom of the hill, or start the engine until I had swung around the corner, so that the house was out of sight and the brine smell of the marina was coming through the open windows of the car. The pistons were almost silent.

I felt urgent, though I had no route in mind. I ran one stop sign, then one red light, and when I reached the ramp onto Highway 101, I squeezed the accelerator and felt the surge of the fuel-injected, computer-sparked V-8. The dash lights glowed. I drove south and crossed over the Golden Gate Bridge at seventy miles an hour, its suspension cables swaying in the wind and the span rocking slowly, ocean to bay. The lanes were narrow. Reflectors zinged when the wheels strayed. If Anne woke, she might come out to the living room and then check for me outside. A light rain began to fall. Drops wet my knees, splattered my cheek. I kept the window open and turned on the radio; the car filled up with wind and music. Brass sounds. Trumpets. Sounds that filled my heart.

The Lincoln drove like a dream. South of San Francisco the road opened up, and in the gulley of a shallow hill I took it up over a hundred. The arrow nosed rightward in the dash. Shapes flattened out. "Dad," I said. The wind sounds changed pitch. I said, "The year of getting to know us." Signposts and power poles were flying by. Only a few cars were on the road, and most moved over before I arrived. In the mirror I could see the faces as I passed. I went through San Mateo, Pacifica, Redwood City, until, underneath a concrete overpass, the radio began pulling in static and I realized that I might die at this speed. I slowed down. At seventy drizzle wandered in the windows again. At fifty-five the scenery stopped moving. In Menlo Park I got off the freeway.

It was dark still, and off the interstate I found myself on a road without streetlights. It entered the center of town and then left again, curving up into shallow hills. The houses were large on either side. They were spaced far apart, three and four stories tall, with white shutters or ornament work that shone in the perimeter of the Lincoln's headlamps. The yards were large, dotted with eucalyptus and laurel. Here and there a light was on. Sometimes I saw faces: someone on an upstairs balcony; a man inside the breakfast room, awake at this hour, peering through the glass to see what car could be passing. I drove slowly, and when I came to a high school with its low buildings and long athletic field I pulled over and stopped.

The drizzle had become mist. I left the headlights on and got out and stood on the grass. I thought, This is the night your father has passed. I looked up at the lightening sky. I said it, "This is the night your father has passed," but I didn't feel what I thought I would. Just the wind on my throat, the chill of the morning. A pickup drove by and flashed its lights at me on the lawn. Then I went to the trunk of the Lincoln, because this was what my father would have done, and I got out the golf bag. It was heavier than I remembered, and the leather was stiff in the cool air. On the damp sod I set up: dimpled white ball, yellow tee. My father would have swung, would have hit drives the length of the football field, high irons that disappeared into the gray sky, but as I stood there I didn't even take the clubs out of the bag. Instead I imagined his stance. I pictured the even weight, the deliberate grip, and after I had stood there for a few moments, I picked up the ball and tee, replaced them in the bag, and drove home to my wife.

The year I was sixteen we never made it to the American Southwest. My mother bought maps anyway, and planned our trip, talking to me about it at night in the dark, taking us in her mind across the Colorado River at the California border, where the water was opal green, into Arizona and along the stretch of desert highway to New Mexico. There, she said, the canyons were a mile deep. The road was lined with sagebrush and a type of cactus, jumping cholla, that launched its spines. Above the desert, where a man could die of dehydration in an afternoon and a morning, the peaks of the Rocky Mountains turned blue with sun and ice.

We didn't ever go. Every weekend my father played golf, and at last, in August, my parents agreed to a compromise. One Sunday morning, before I started the eleventh grade, we drove north in the Lincoln to a state park along the ocean. Above the shore the cliffs were planted with ice plant to resist erosion. Pelicans soared in the thermal currents. My mother had made chicken sandwiches, which we ate on the beach, and after lunch, while I looked at the crabs and swaying fronds in the tide pools, my parents walked to the base of the cliffs. I watched their progress on the shallow dunes. Once when I looked, my father was holding her in his arms and they were kissing.

She bent backward in his hands. I looked into the tide pool where, on the surface, the blue sky, the clouds, the reddish cliffs, were shining. Below them rock crabs scurried between submerged stones. The afternoon my father found me in the trunk, he introduced me to the woman in the back seat. Her name was Christine. She smelled of perfume. The gravel drive where we had parked was behind a warehouse, and after we shook hands through the open window of the car, she got out and went inside. It was low and long, and the metal door slammed behind her. On the drive home, wind blowing all around us in the car, my father and I didn't say much. I watched his hands on the steering wheel. They were big and red-knuckled, the hands of a butcher or a carpenter, and I tried to imagine them on the bend of Christine's back.

Later that afternoon on the beach, while my mother walked along the shore, my father and I climbed a steep trail up the cliffs. From above, where we stood in the carpet of ice plant, we could see the hue of the Pacific change to a more translucent blue—the drop-off and the outline of the shoal where the breakers rose. I tried to see what my father was seeing as he gazed out over the water. He picked up a rock and tossed it over the cliff. "You know," he said without looking at me, "you could be all right on the course." We approached the edge of the palisade, where the ice plant thinned into eroded cuts of sand. "Listen," he said. "We're here on this trip so we can get to know each other a little bit." A hundred yards below us waves broke on the rocks. He lowered his voice. "But I'm not sure about that. Anyway, you don't *have* to get to know me. You know why?"

"Why?" I asked.

"You don't have to get to know me," he said, "because one day you're going to grow up and then you're going to *be* me." He looked at me and then out over the water. "So what I'm going to do is teach you how to hit." He picked up a long stick and put it in my hand. Then he showed me the backswing. "You've got to know one thing to drive a golf ball," he told me, "and that's that the club is part of you." He stood behind me and showed me how to keep the left arm still. "The club is your hand," he said. "It's your bone. It's your whole arm and your skeleton and your heart." Below us on the beach I could see my mother walking the waterline. We took cut after cut, and he taught me to visualize the impact, to sense it. He told me to whittle down the point of energy so that the ball would fly. When I swung he held my head in position. "Don't just watch," he said. "*See.*" I looked. The ice plant was watery-looking and fat, and at the edge of my vision I could see the tips of my father's shoes. I was sixteen years old and waiting for the next thing he would tell me.

RAYMOND CARVER

Errand

RAYMOND CARVER (1938–1988) was born in Clatskanie, Oregon, and died, at fifty, from lung cancer shortly after he married writer Tess Gallagher. He is the author of five books of stories: *Will You Please Be Quiet, Please?,* nominated for the National Book Award; *Furious Seasons and Other Stories; What We Talk About When We Talk About Love; Cathedral,* nominated for the National Book Critics Circle Award and runner-up for the Pulitzer Prize; and *Where I'm Calling From.* Carver also wrote six books of poems, including *All of Us, A New Path to the Waterfall, Ultramarine,* and *Where Water Comes Together with Other Water.* One of the first Mildred and Harold Strauss Living Award recipients (he received the award in 1983), Carver was also inducted into the American Academy and Institute of Arts and Letters in 1988. Other awards included two NEA grants, a Guggenheim Fellowship, and an honorary Doctor of Letters degree from the University of Hartford.

Chekhov. On the evening of March 22, 1897, he went to dinner in Moscow with his friend and confidant Alexei Suvorin. This Suvorin was a very rich newspaper and book publisher, a reactionary, a self-made man whose father was a private at the battle of Borodino. Like Chekhov, he was the grandson of a serf. They had that in common: each had peasant's blood in his veins. Otherwise, politically and temperamentally, they were miles apart. Nevertheless, Suvorin was one of Chekhov's few intimates, and Chekhov enjoyed his company.

Naturally, they went to the best restaurant in the city, a former town house called the Hermitage—a place where it could take hours, half the night even, to get through a ten-course meal that would, of course, include several wines, liqueurs, and coffee. Chekhov was impeccably dressed, as always—a dark suit and waistcoat, his usual pince-nez. He looked that night very much as he looks in the photographs taken of him during this period. He was relaxed, jovial. He shook hands with the maître d', and with a glance took in the large dining room. It was brilliantly illuminated by ornate chandeliers, the tables occupied by elegantly dressed men and women. Waiters came and went ceaselessly. He had just been seated across the table from Suvorin when suddenly, without warning, blood began gushing from his mouth. Suvorin and two waiters helped him to the gentlemen's room and tried to stanch the flow of blood with ice packs. Suvorin saw him back to his own hotel and had a bed prepared for Chekhov in one of the rooms of the suite. Later, after another hemorrhage, Chekhov allowed himself to be moved to a clinic that specialized in the treatment of tuberculosis and related respiratory infections. When Suvorin visited him there, Chekhov apologized for the "scandal" at the restaurant three nights earlier but continued to insist there was nothing seriously wrong. "He laughed and jested as usual," Suvorin noted in his diary, "while spitting blood into a large vessel."

Maria Chekhov, his younger sister, visited Chekhov in the clinic during the last days of March. The weather was miserable; a sleet storm was in progress, and frozen heaps of snow lay everywhere. It was hard for her to wave down a carriage to take her to the hospital. By the time she arrived she was filled with dread and anxiety.

"Anton Pavlovich lay on his back," Maria wrote in her *Memoirs.* "He was not allowed to speak. After greeting him, I went over to the table to hide my emotions." There, among bottles of champagne, jars of caviar, bouquets of flowers from well-wishers, she saw something that terrified her: a freehand drawing, obviously done by a specialist in these matters, of Chekhov's lungs. It was the kind of sketch a doctor often makes in order to show his patient what he thinks is taking place. The lungs were outlined in blue, but the upper parts were filled in with red. "I realized they were diseased," Maria wrote.

Leo Tolstoy was another visitor. The hospital staff were awed to find themselves in the presence of the country's greatest writer. The most famous man in Russia? Of course they had to let him in to see Chekhov, even though "nonessential" visitors were forbidden. With much obsequiousness on the part of the nurses and resident doctors, the bearded, fierce-looking old man was shown into Chekhov's room. Despite his low opinion of Chekhov's abilities as a playwright (Tolstoy felt the plays were static and lacking in any moral vision. "Where do your characters take you?" he once demanded of Chekhov. "From the sofa to the junk room and back"), Tolstoy liked Chekhov's short stories. Furthermore, and quite simply, he loved the man. He told Gorky, "What a beautiful, magnificent man: modest and quiet, like a girl. He even walks like a girl. He's simply wonderful." And Tolstoy wrote in his journal (everyone kept a journal or a diary in those days), "I am glad I love . . . Chekhov."

Tolstoy removed his woollen scarf and bearskin coat, then lowered himself into a chair next to Chekhov's bed. Never mind that Chekhov was taking medication and not permitted to talk, much less carry on a conversation. He had to listen, amazedly, as the Count began to discourse on his theories of the immortality of the soul. Concerning that visit, Chekhov later wrote, "Tolstoy assumes that all of us (humans and animals alike) will live on in a principle (such as reason or love) the essence and goals of which are a mystery to us. . . . I have no use for that kind of immortality. I don't understand it, and Lev Nikolayevich was astonished I didn't."

Nevertheless, Chekhov was impressed with the solicitude shown by Tolstoy's visit. But, unlike Tolstoy, Chekhov didn't believe in an afterlife and never had. He didn't believe in anything that couldn't be apprehended by one or more of his five senses. And as far as his outlook on life and writing went, he once told someone that he lacked "a political, religious, and philosophical world view. I change it every month, so I'll have to limit myself to the description of how my heroes love, marry, give birth, die, and how they speak."

Earlier, before his t.b. was diagnosed, Chekhov had remarked, "When a peasant has consumption, he says, 'There's nothing I can do. I'll go off in the spring with the melting of the snows.' " (Chekhov himself died in the summer, during a heat wave.) But once Chekhov's own tuberculosis was discovered he continually tried to minimize the seriousness of his condition. To all appearances, it was as if he felt, right up to the end, that he might be able to throw off the disease as he would a lingering catarrh. Well into his final days, he spoke with seeming conviction of the possibility of an improvement. In fact, in a letter written shortly before his end, he went so far as to tell his sister that he was "getting fat" and felt much better now that he was in Badenweiler.

Badenweiler is a spa and resort city in the western area of the Black Forest, not far from Basel. The Vosges are visible from nearly anywhere in the city, and in those days the air was pure and invigorating. Russians had been going there for years to soak in the hot mineral baths and promenade on the boulevards. In June, 1904, Chekhov went there to die.

Earlier that month, he'd made a difficult journey by train from Moscow to Berlin. He traveled with his wife, the actress Olga Knipper, a woman he'd met in 1898 during rehearsals for "The Seagull." Her contemporaries describe her as an excellent actress. She was talented, pretty, and almost ten years younger than the playwright. Chekhov had been immediately attracted to her, but was slow to act on his feelings. As always, he preferred a flirtation to marriage. Finally, after a three-year courtship involving many separations, letters, and the inevitable misunderstandings, they were at last married, in a private ceremony in Moscow, on May 25, 1901. Chekhov was enormously happy. He called Olga his "pony," and sometimes "dog" or "puppy." He was also fond of addressing her as "little turkey" or simply as "my joy."

In Berlin, Chekhov consulted with a renowned specialist in pulmonary disorders, a Dr. Karl Ewald. But, according to an eyewitness, after the doctor examined Chekhov he threw up his hands and left the room without a word. Chekhov was too far gone for help: this Dr. Ewald was furious with himself for not being able to work miracles, and with Chekhov for being so ill.

A Russian journalist happened to visit the Chekhovs at their hotel and sent back this dispatch to his editor: "Chekhov's days are numbered. He seems mortally ill, is terribly thin, coughs all the time, gasps for breath at the slightest movement, and is running a high temperature." This same journalist saw the Chekhovs off at Potsdam Station when they boarded their train for Badenweiler. According to his account, "Chekhov had trouble making his way up the small staircase at the station. He had to sit down for several minutes to catch his breath." In fact, it was painful for Chekhov to move: his legs ached continually and his insides hurt. The disease had attacked his intestines and spinal cord. At this point he had less than a month to live. When Chekhov spoke of his condition now, it was, according to Olga, "with an almost reckless indifference."

Dr. Schwöhrer was one of the many Badenweiler physicians who earned a good living by treating the well-to-do who came to the spa seeking relief from various maladies. Some of his patients were ill and infirm, others simply old and hypochondriacal. But Chekhov's was a special case: he was clearly beyond help and in his last days. He was also very famous. Even Dr. Schwöhrer knew his name: he'd read some of Chekhov's stories in a German magazine. When he examined the writer early in June, he voiced his appreciation of Chekhov's art but kept his medical opinions to himself. Instead, he prescribed a diet of cocoa, oatmeal drenched in butter, and strawberry tea. This last was supposed to help Chekhov sleep at night.

On June 13, less than three weeks before he died, Chekhov wrote a letter to his mother in which he told her his health was on the mend. In it he said, "It's likely that I'll be completely cured in a week." Who knows why he said this? What could he have been thinking? He was a doctor himself, and he knew better. He was dying, it was as simple and as unavoidable as that. Nevertheless, he sat out on the balcony of his hotel room and read railway timetables. He asked for information on sailings of boats bound for Odessa from Marseilles. But he *knew.* At this stage he had to have known. Yet in one of the last letters he ever wrote he told his sister he was growing stronger by the day.

He no longer had any appetite for literary work, and hadn't for a long time. In fact, he had very nearly failed to complete *The Cherry Orchard* the year before. Writing that play was the hardest thing he'd ever done in his life.

Toward the end, he was able to manage only six or seven lines a day. "I've started losing heart," he wrote Olga. "I feel I'm finished as a writer, and every sentence strikes me as worthless and of no use whatever." But he didn't stop. He finished his play in October, 1903. It was the last thing he ever wrote, except for letters and a few entries in his notebook.

A little after midnight on July 2, 1904, Olga sent someone to fetch Dr. Schwöhrer. It was an emergency: Chekhov was delirious. Two young Russians on holiday happened to have the adjacent room, and Olga hurried next door to explain what was happening. One of the youths was in his bed asleep, but the other was still awake, smoking and reading. He left the hotel at a run to find Dr. Schwöhrer. "I can still hear the sound of the gravel under his shoes in the silence of that stifling July night," Olga wrote later on in her memoirs. Chekhov was hallucinating, talking about sailors, and there were snatches of something about the Japanese. "You don't put ice on an empty stomach," he said when she tried to place an ice pack on his chest.

Dr. Schwöhrer arrived and unpacked his bag, all the while keeping his gaze fastened on Chekhov, who lay gasping in the bed. The sick man's pupils were dilated and his temples glistened with sweat. Dr. Schwöhrer's face didn't register anything. He was not an emotional man, but he knew Chekhov's end was near. Still, he was a doctor, sworn to do his utmost, and Chekhov held on to life, however tenuously. Dr. Schwöhrer prepared a hypodermic and administered an injection of camphor, something that was supposed to speed up the heart. But the injection didn't help—nothing, of course, could have helped. Nevertheless, the doctor made known to Olga his intention of sending for oxygen. Suddenly, Chekhov roused himself, became lucid, and said quietly, "What's the use? Before it arrives I'll be a corpse."

Dr. Schwöhrer pulled on his big moustache and stared at Chekhov. The writer's cheeks were sunken and gray, his complexion waxen; his breath was raspy. Dr. Schwöhrer knew the time could be reckoned in minutes. Without a word, without conferring with Olga, he went over to an alcove where there was a telephone on the wall. He read the instructions for using the device. If he activated it by holding his finger on a button and turning a handle on the side of the phone, he could reach the lower regions of the hotel—the kitchen. He picked up the receiver, held it to his ear, and did as the instructions told him. When someone finally answered, Dr. Schwöhrer ordered a bottle of the hotel's best champagne. "How many glasses?" he was asked. "Three glasses!" the doctor shouted into the mouthpiece. "And hurry, do you hear?" It was one of those rare moments of inspiration that can easily enough be overlooked later on, because the action is so entirely appropriate it seems inevitable.

The champagne was brought to the door by a tired-looking young man whose blond hair was standing up. The trousers of his uniform were wrinkled, the creases gone, and in his haste he'd missed a loop while buttoning his jacket. His appearance was that of someone who'd been resting (slumped in a chair, say, dozing a little), when off in the distance the phone had clamored in the early-morning hours—great God in Heaven!—and the next thing he knew he was being shaken awake by a superior and told to deliver a bottle of Moët to Room 211. "And hurry, do you hear?"

The young man entered the room carrying a silver ice bucket with the champagne in it and a silver tray with three cut-crystal glasses. He found a place on the table for the bucket and glasses, all the while craning his neck, trying to see into the other room, where someone panted ferociously for breath. It was a dreadful, harrowing sound, and the young man lowered his chin into his collar and turned away as the ratchety breathing worsened. Forgetting himself, he stared out the open window toward the darkened city. Then this big imposing man with a thick moustache pressed some coins into his hand—a large tip, by the feel of it—and suddenly the young man saw the door open. He took some steps and found himself on the landing, where he opened his hand and looked at the coins in amazement.

Methodically, the way he did everything, the doctor went about the business of working the cork out of the bottle. He did it in such a way as to minimize, as much as possible, the festive explosion. He poured three glasses and, out of habit, pushed the cork back into the neck of the bottle. He then took the glasses of champagne over to the bed. Olga momentarily released her grip on Chekhov's hand—a hand, she said later, that burned her fingers. She arranged another pillow behind his head. Then she put the cool glass of champagne against Chekov's palm and made sure his fingers closed around the stem. They exchanged looks—Chekhov, Olga, Dr. Schwöhrer. They didn't touch glasses. There was no toast. What on earth was there to drink to? To death? Chekhov summoned his remaining strength and said, "It's been so long since I've had champagne." He brought the glass to his lips and drank. In a minute or two Olga took the empty glass from his hand and set it on the nightstand. Then Chekhov turned onto his side. He closed his eyes and sighed. A minute later, his breathing stopped.

Dr. Schwöhrer picked up Chekhov's hand from the bedsheet. He held his fingers to Chekhov's wrist and drew a gold watch from his vest pocket, opening the lid of the watch as he did so. The second hand on the watch moved slowly, very slowly. He let it move around the face of the watch three times while he waited for signs of a pulse. It was three o'clock in the morning and still sultry in the room. Badenweiler was in the grip of its worst heat wave in years. All the windows in both rooms stood open, but there was no sign of a breeze. A large, black-winged moth flew through a window and banged wildly against the electric lamp. Dr. Schwöhrer let go of Chekhov's wrist. "It's over," he said. He closed the lid of his watch and returned it to his vest pocket.

At once Olga dried her eyes and set about composing herself. She thanked the doctor for coming. He asked if she wanted some medication—laudanum, perhaps, or a few drops of valerian. She shook her head. She did have one request, though: before the authorities were notified and the newspapers found out, before the time came when Chekhov was no longer in her keeping, she wanted to be alone with him for a while. Could the doctor help with this? Could he withhold, for a while anyway, news of what had just occurred?

Dr. Schwöhrer stroked his moustache with the back of a finger. Why not? After all, what difference would it make to anyone whether this matter became known now or a few hours from now? The only detail that remained was to fill out a death certificate, and this could be done at his office later on in the morning, after he'd slept a few hours. Dr. Schwöhrer nodded his agreement and prepared to leave. He murmured a few words of condolence. Olga inclined her head. "An honor," Dr. Schwöhrer said. He picked up his bag and left the room and, for that matter, history.

It was at this moment that the cork popped out of the champagne bottle; foam spilled down onto the table. Olga went back to Chekhov's bedside. She sat on a footstool, holding his hand, from time to time stroking his face. "There were no human voices, no everyday sounds," she wrote. "There was only beauty, peace, and the grandeur of death."

She stayed with Chekhov until daybreak, when thrushes began to call from the garden below. Then came the sound of tables and chairs being moved about down there. Before long, voices carried up to her. It was then a knock sounded at the door. Of course she thought it must be an official of some sort—the medical examiner, say, or someone from the police who had questions to ask and forms for her to fill out, or maybe, just maybe, it could be Dr. Schwöhrer returning with a mortician to render assistance in embalming and transporting Chekhov's remains back to Russia.

But, instead, it was the same blond young man who'd brought the champagne a few hours earlier. This time, however, his uniform trousers were neatly pressed, with stiff creases in front, and every button on his snug green jacket was fastened. He seemed quite another person. Not only was he wide awake but his plump cheeks were smooth-shaven, his hair was in place, and he appeared anxious to please. He was holding a porcelain vase with three long-stemmed yellow roses. He presented these to Olga with a smart click of his heels. She stepped back and let him into the room. He was there, he said, to collect the glasses, ice bucket, and tray, yes. But he also wanted to say that, because of the extreme heat, breakfast would be served in the garden this morning. He hoped this weather wasn't too bothersome; he apologized for it.

The woman seemed distracted. While he talked, she turned her eyes away and looked down at something in the carpet. She crossed her arms and held her elbows. Meanwhile, still holding his vase, waiting for a sign, the young man took in the details of the room. Bright sunlight flooded through the open windows. The room was tidy and seemed undisturbed, almost untouched. No garments were flung over chairs, no shoes, stockings, braces, or stays were in evidence, no open suitcases. In short, there was no clutter, nothing but the usual heavy pieces of hotel-room furniture. Then, because the woman was still looking down, he looked down, too, and at once spied a cork near the toe of his shoe. The woman did not see it—she was looking somewhere else. The young man wanted to bend over and pick up the cork, but he was still holding the roses and was afraid of seeming to intrude even more by drawing any further attention to himself. Reluctantly, he left the cork where it was and raised his eyes. Everything was in order except for the uncorked, half-empty bottle of champagne that stood alongside two crystal glasses over on the little table. He cast his gaze about once more. Through an open door he saw that the third glass was in the bedroom, on the nightstand. But someone still occupied the bed! He couldn't see a face, but the figure under the covers lay perfectly motionless and quiet. He noted the figure and looked elsewhere. Then, for a reason he couldn't understand, a feeling of uneasiness took hold of him. He cleared his throat and moved his weight to the other leg. The woman still didn't look up or break her silence. The young man felt his cheeks grow warm. It occurred to him, quite without his having thought it through, that he should perhaps suggest an alternative to breakfast in the garden. He coughed, hoping to focus the woman's attention, but she didn't look at him. The distinguished foreign guests could, he said, take breakfast in their rooms this morning if they wished. The young man (his name hasn't survived, and it's likely he perished in the Great War) said he would be happy to bring up a tray. Two trays, he added, glancing uncertainly once again in the direction of the bedroom.

He fell silent and ran a finger around the inside of his collar. He didn't understand. He wasn't even sure the woman had been listening. He didn't know what else to do now; he was still holding the vase. The sweet odor of the roses filled his nostrils and inexplicably caused a pang of regret. The entire time he'd been waiting, the woman had apparently been lost in thought. It was as if all the while he'd been standing there, talking, shifting his weight, holding his flowers, she had been someplace else, somewhere far from Badenweiler. But now she came back to herself, and her face assumed another expression. She raised her eyes, looked at him, and then shook her head. She seemed to be struggling to understand what on earth this young man could be doing there in the room holding a vase with three yellow roses. Flowers? She hadn't ordered flowers.

The moment passed. She went over to her handbag and scooped up some coins. She drew out a number of banknotes as well. The young man touched his lips with his tongue; another large tip was forthcoming, but for what? What did she want him to do? He'd never before waited on such guests. He cleared his throat once more.

No breakfast, the woman said. Not yet, at any rate. Breakfast wasn't the important thing this morning. She required something else. She needed him to go out and bring back a mortician. Did he understand her? Herr Chekhov was dead, you see. *Comprenez-vous?* Young man? Anton Chekhov was dead. Now listen carefully to me, she said. She wanted him to go downstairs and ask someone at the front desk where he could go to find the most respected mortician in the city. Someone reliable, who took great pains in his work and whose manner was appropriately reserved. A mortician, in short, worthy of a great artist. Here, she said, and pressed the money on him. Tell them downstairs that I have specifically requested you to perform this duty for me. Are you listening? Do you understand what I'm saying to you?

The young man grappled to take in what she was saying. He chose not to look again in the direction of the other room. He had sensed that something was not right. He became aware of his heart beating rapidly under his jacket, and he felt perspiration break out on his forehead. He didn't know where he should turn his eyes. He wanted to put the vase down.

Please do this for me, the woman said. I'll remember you with gratitude. Tell them downstairs that I insist. Say that. But don't call any unnecessary attention to yourself or to the situation. Just say that this is necessary, that I request it—and that's all. Do you hear me? Nod if you understand. Above all, don't raise an alarm. Everything else, all the rest, the commotion—that'll come soon enough. The worst is over. Do we understand each other?

The young man's face had grown pale. He stood rigid, clasping the vase. He managed to nod his head.

After securing permission to leave the hotel he was to proceed quietly and resolutely, though without any unbecoming haste, to the mortician's. He was to behave exactly as if he were engaged on a very important errand, nothing more. He *was* engaged on an important errand, she said. And if it would help keep his movements purposeful he should imagine himself as someone moving down the busy sidewalk carrying in his arms a porcelain vase of roses that he had to deliver to an important man. (She spoke quietly, almost confidentially, as if to a relative or a friend.) He could even tell himself that the man he was going to see was expecting him, was perhaps impatient for him to arrive with his flowers. Nevertheless, the young man was not to become excited and run, or otherwise break his stride. Remember the vase he was carrying! He was to walk briskly, comporting himself at all times in as dignified a manner as possible. He should keep walking until he came to the mortician's house and stood before the door. He would then raise the brass knocker and let it fall, once, twice, three times. In a minute the mortician himself would answer.

This mortician would be in his forties, no doubt, or maybe early fifties—bald, solidly built, wearing steel-frame spectacles set very low on his nose. He would be modest, unassuming, a man who would ask only the most direct and necessary questions. An apron. Probably he would be wearing an apron. He might even be wiping his hands on a dark towel while he listened to what was being said. There'd be a faint whiff of formaldehyde on his clothes. But it was all right, and the young man shouldn't worry. He was nearly a grown-up now and shouldn't be frightened or repelled by any of this. The mortician would hear him out. He was a man of restraint and bearing, this mortician, someone who could help allay people's fears in this situation, not increase them. Long ago he'd acquainted himself with death in all its various guises and forms; death held no surprises for him any longer, no hidden secrets. It was this man whose services were required this morning.

The mortician takes the vase of roses. Only once while the young man is speaking does the mortician betray the least flicker of interest, or indicate that he's heard anything out of the ordinary. But the one time the young man mentions the name of the deceased, the mortician's eyebrows rise just a little. Chekhov, you say? Just a minute, and I'll be with you.

Do you understand what I'm saying, Olga said to the young man. Leave the glasses. Don't worry about them. Forget about crystal wineglasses and such. Leave the room as it is. Everything is ready now. We're ready. Will you go?

But at that moment the young man was thinking of the cork still resting near the toe of his shoe. To retrieve it he would have to bend over, still gripping the vase. He would do this. He leaned over. Without looking down, he reached out and closed it into his hand.

SANDRA CISNEROS

Woman Hollering Creek

SANDRA CISNEROS (1954–) is a novelist, poet, short-story writer, and essayist. Her novel, *The House on Mango Street,* won the Before Columbus Foundation's American Book Award in 1985. *Woman Hollering Creek and Other Stories* won the PEN Center USA West Award for Best Fiction of 1991, the Quality Paperback Book Club New Voices Award, the Anisfield-Wolf Book Award, the Lannan Foundation Literary Award, and was selected as a noteworthy book of the year by *The New York Times* and the *American Library Journal.* It was also nominated for Best Book of Fiction for 1991 by the *Los Angeles Times.* Cisneros has written three volumes of poetry—*Bad Boys*; *My Wicked, Wicked Ways*; and *Loose Woman*—and she was awarded the MacArthur Foundation Fellowship and other literary honors, including two fellowships, for fiction and poetry, respectively, from the NEA. Her work has appeared in *The New York Times, Los Angeles Times, The New Yorker, Glamour, Elle, Ms., Story, Grand Street,* and *The Village Voice.* Cisneros received her B.A. from Loyola University and her M.F.A. from the University of Iowa. She shares a home in San Antonio, Texas, with several cats, dogs, parrots, and guest writers.

The day Don Serafín gave Juan Pedro Martínez Sánchez permission to take Cleófilas Enriqueta DeLeón Hernández as his bride, across her father's threshold, over several miles of dirt road and several miles of paved, over one border and beyond to a town *en el otro lado*—on the other side—already did he divine the morning his daughter would raise her hand over her eyes, look south, and dream of returning to the chores that never ended, six good-for-nothing brothers, and one old man's complaints.

He had said, after all, in the hubbub of parting: I am your father, I will never abandon you. He *had* said that, hadn't he, when he hugged and then let her go. But at the moment Cleófilas was busy looking for Chela, her maid of honor, to fulfill their bouquet conspiracy. She would not remember her father's parting words until later. *I am your father, I will never abandon you.*

Only now as a mother did she remember. Now, when she and Juan Pedrito sat by the creek's edge. How when a man and a woman love each other, sometimes that love sours. But a parent's love for a child, a child's for its parents, is another thing entirely.

This is what Cleófilas thought evenings when Juan Pedro did not come home, and she lay on her side of the bed listening to the hollow roar of the interstate, a distant dog barking, the pecan trees rustling like ladies in stiff petticoats—*shh-shh-shh, shh-shh-shh*—soothing her to sleep.

In the town where she grew up, there isn't very much to do except accompany the aunts and godmothers to the house of one or the other to play cards. Or walk to the cinema to see this week's film again, speckled and with one hair quivering annoyingly on the screen. Or to the center of town to order a milk shake that will appear in a day and a half as a pimple on her backside. Or to the girlfriend's house to watch the latest *telenovela* episode and try to copy the way the women comb their hair, wear their makeup.

But what Cleófilas has been waiting for, has been whispering and sighing and giggling for, has been anticipating since she was old enough to lean against the window displays of gauze and butterflies and lace, is passion. Not the kind on the cover of the *¡Alarma!* magazines, mind you, where the lover is photographed with the bloody fork she used to salvage her good name. But passion in its purest crystalline essence. The kind the books and songs and *telenovelas* describe when one finds, finally, the great love of one's life, and does whatever one can, must do, at whatever the cost.

Tú o Nadie. "You or No One." The title of the current favorite *telenovela.* The beautiful Lucía Méndez having to put up with all kinds of hardships of the heart, separation and betrayal, and loving, always loving no matter what, because *that* is the most important thing, and did you see Lucía Méndez on the Bayer aspirin commercials—wasn't she lovely? Does she dye her hair do you think? Cleófilas is going to go to the *farmacía* and buy a hair rinse; her girlfriend Chela will apply it—it's not that difficult at all.

Because you didn't watch last night's episode when Lucía confessed she loved him more than anyone in her life. In her life! And she sings the song "You or No One" in the beginning and end of the show. *Tú o Nadie.* Somehow one ought to live one's life like that, don't you think? You or no one. Because to suffer for love is good. The pain all sweet somehow. In the end.

Seguín. She had liked the sound of it. Far away and lovely. Not like *Monclova. Coahuia.* Ugly.

Seguín, Tejas. A nice sterling ring to it. The tinkle of money. She would get to wear outfits like the women on the *tele,* like Lucía Méndez. And have a lovely house, and wouldn't Chela be jealous.

And yes, they will drive all the way to Laredo to get her wedding dress. That's what they say. Because Juan Pedro wants to get married right away, without a long engagement since he can't take off too much time from work. He has a very important position in Seguin with, with . . . a beer company, I think. Or was it tires? Yes, he has to be back. So they will get married in the spring when he can take off work, and then they will drive off in his new pickup—did you see it?—to their new home in Seguin. Well, not exactly new, but they're going to repaint the house. You know newlyweds. New paint and new furniture. Why not? He can afford it. And later on add maybe a room or two for the children. May they be blessed with many.

Well, you'll see. Cleófilas has always been so good with her sewing machine. A little *rrrr, rrrr, rrrr* of the machine and *¡zas!* Miracles. She's always been so clever, that girl. Poor thing. And without even a mama to advise her on things like her wedding night. Well, may God help her. What with a father with a head like a burro, and those six clumsy brothers. Well, what do you think! Yes, I'm going to the wedding. Of course! The dress I want to wear just needs to be altered a teensy bit to bring it up to date. See, I saw a new style last night that I thought would suit me. Did you watch last night's episode of *The Rich Also Cry*? Well, did you notice the dress the mother was wearing?

La Gritona. Such a funny name for such a lovely *arroyo.* But that's what they called the creek that ran behind the house. Though no one could say whether the woman had hollered from anger or pain. The natives only knew the *arroyo* one crossed on the way to San Antonio, and then once again on the way back, was called Woman Hollering, a name no one from these parts questioned, little less understood. *Pues, allá de los indios, quién sabe*—who knows, the townspeople shrugged, because it was of no concern to their lives how this trickle of water received its curious name.

"What do you want to know for?" Trini the laundromat attendant asked in the same gruff Spanish she always used whenever she gave Cleófilas change or yelled at her for something. First for putting too much soap in the machines. Later, for sitting on a washer. And still later, after Juan Pedrito was born, for not understanding that in this country you cannot let your baby walk around with no diaper and his pee-pee hanging out, it wasn't nice, *¿entiendes? Pues.*

How could Cleófilas explain to a woman like this why the name Woman Hollering fascinated her. Well, there was no sense talking to Trini.

On the other hand there were the neighbor ladies, one on either side of the house they rented near the *arroyo.* The woman Soledad on the left, the woman Dolores on the right.

The neighbor lady Soledad liked to call herself a widow, though how she came to be one was a mystery. Her husband had either died, or run away with an ice-house floozie, or simply gone out for cigarettes one afternoon and never came back. It was hard to say which since Soledad, as a rule, didn't mention him.

In the other house lived *la señora* Dolores, kind and very sweet, but her house smelled too much of incense and candles from the altars that burned continuously in memory of two sons who had died in the last war and one husband who had died shortly after from grief. The neighbor lady Dolores divided her time between the memory of these men and her garden, famous for its sunflowers—so tall they had to be supported with broom handles and old boards; red red cockscombs, fringed and bleeding a thick menstrual color; and, especially, roses whose sad scent reminded Cleófilas of the dead. Each Sunday *la señora* Dolores clipped the most beautiful of these flowers and arranged them on three modest headstones at the Seguin cemetery.

The neighbor ladies, Soledad, Dolores, they might've known once the name of the *arroyo* before it turned English but they did not know now. They were too busy remembering the men who had left through either choice or circumstance and would never come back.

Pain or rage, Cleófilas wondered when she drove over the bridge the first time as a newlywed and Juan Pedro had pointed it out. *La Gritona,* he had said, and she had laughed. Such a funny name for a creek so pretty and full of happily ever after.

The first time she had been so surprised she didn't cry out or try to defend herself. She had always said she would strike back if a man, any man, were to strike her.

But when the moment came, and he slapped her once, and then again, and again, until the lip split and bled an orchid of blood, she didn't fight back, she didn't break into tears, she didn't run away as she imagined she might when she saw such things in the *telenovelas.*

In her own home her parents had never raised a hand to each other or to their children. Although she admitted she may have been brought up a little leniently as an only daughter—*la consentida,* the princess—there were some things she would never tolerate. Ever.

Instead, when it happened the first time, when they were barely man and wife, she had been so stunned, it left her speechless, motionless, numb. She had done nothing but reach up to the heat on her mouth and stare at the blood on her hand as if even then she didn't understand.

She could think of nothing to say, said nothing. Just stroked the dark curls of the man who wept and would weep like a child, his tears of repentance and shame, this time and each.

The men at the ice house. From what she can tell, from the times during her first year when still a newlywed she is invited and accompanies her husband, sits mute beside their conversation, waits and sips a beer until it grows warm, twists a paper napkin into a knot, then another into a fan, one into a rose, nods her head, smiles, yawns, politely grins, laughs at the appropriate moments, leans against her husband's sleeve, tugs at his elbow, and finally becomes good at predicting where the talk will lead, from this Cleófilas concludes each is nightly trying to find the truth lying at the bottom of the bottle like a gold doubloon on the sea floor.

They want to tell each other what they want to tell themselves. But what is bumping like a helium balloon at the ceiling of the brain never finds its way out. It bubbles and rises, it gurgles in the throat, it rolls across the surface of the tongue, and erupts from the lips—a belch.

If they are lucky, there are tears at the end of the long night. At any given moment, the fists try to speak. They are dogs chasing their own tails before lying down to sleep, trying to find a way, a route, an out, and—finally—get some peace.

In the morning sometimes before he opens his eyes. Or after they have finished loving. Or at times when he is simply across from her at the table putting pieces of food into his mouth and chewing. Cleófilas thinks, This is the man I have waited my whole life for.

Not that he isn't a good man. She has to remind herself why she loves him when she changes the baby's Pampers, or when she mops the bathroom floor, or tries to make the curtains for the doorways without doors, or whiten the linen. Or wonder a little when he kicks the refrigerator and says he hates this shitty house and is going out where he won't be bothered with the baby's howling and her suspicious questions, and her requests to fix this and this and this because if she had any brains in her head she'd realize he's been up before the rooster earning his living to pay for the food in her belly and the roof over her head and would have to wake up again early the next day so why can't you just leave me in peace, woman.

He is not very tall, no, and he doesn't look like the men on the *telenovelas.* His face still scarred from acne. And he has a bit of a belly from all the beer he drinks. Well, he's always been husky.

This man who farts and belches and snores as well as laughs and kisses and holds her. Somehow this husband whose whiskers she finds each morning in the sink, whose shoes she must air each evening on the porch, this husband who cuts his fingernails in public, laughs loudly, curses like a man, and demands each course of dinner be served on a separate plate like at his mother's, as soon as he gets home, on time or late, and who doesn't care at all for music or *telenovelas* or romance or roses or the moon floating pearly over the *arroyo,* or through the bedroom window for that matter, shut the blinds and go back to sleep, this man, this father, this rival, this keeper, this lord, this master, this husband till kingdom come.

A doubt. Slender as a hair. A washed cup set back on the shelf wrong-side-up. Her lipstick, and body talc, and hairbrush all arranged in the bathroom a different way.

No. Her imagination. The house the same as always. Nothing.

Coming home from the hospital with her new son, her husband. Something comforting in discovering her house slippers beneath the bed, the faded housecoat where she left it on the bathroom hook. Her pillow. Their bed.

Sweet sweet homecoming. Sweet as the scent of face powder in the air, jasmine, sticky liquor.

Smudged fingerprint on the door. Crushed cigarette in a glass. Wrinkle in the brain crumpling to a crease.

Sometimes she thinks of her father's house. But how could she go back there? What a disgrace. What would the neighbors say? Coming home like that with one baby on her hip and one in the oven. Where's your husband?

The town of gossips. The town of dust and despair. Which she has traded for this town of gossips. This town of dust, despair. Houses farther apart perhaps, though no more privacy because of it. No leafy *zócalo* in the center of the town, though the murmur of talk is clear enough all the same. No huddled whispering on the church steps each Sunday. Because here the whispering begins at sunset at the ice house instead.

This town with its silly pride for a bronze pecan the size of a baby carriage in front of the city hall. TV repair shop, drugstore, hardware, dry cleaner's, chiropractor's, liquor store, bail bonds, empty storefront, and nothing, nothing, nothing of interest. Nothing one could walk to, at any rate. Because the towns here are built so that you have to depend on husbands. Or you stay home. Or you drive. If you're rich enough to own, allowed to drive, your own car.

There is no place to go. Unless one counts the neighbor ladies. Soledad on one side, Dolores on the other. Or the creek.

Don't go out there after dark, *mi'jita.* Stay near the house. *No es bueno para la salud. Mala suerte.* Bad luck. *Mal aire.* You'll get sick and the baby too.

You'll catch a fright wandering about in the dark, and then you'll see how right we were.

The stream sometimes only a muddy puddle in the summer, though now in the springtime, because of the rains, a good-size alive thing, a thing with a voice all its own, all day and all night calling in its high, silver voice. Is it La Llorona, the weeping woman? La Llorona, who drowned her own children. Perhaps La Llorona is the one they named the creek after, she thinks, remembering all the stories she learned as a child.

La Llorona calling to her. She is sure of it. Cleófilas sets the baby's Donald Duck blanket on the grass. Listens. The day sky turning to night. The baby pulling up fistfuls of grass and laughing. La Llorona. Wonders if something as quiet as this drives a woman to the darkness under the trees.

What she needs is . . . and made a gesture as if to yank a woman's buttocks to his groin. Maximiliano, the foul-smelling fool from across the road, said this and set the men laughing, but Cleófilas just muttered, *Grosera,* and went on washing dishes.

She knew he said it not because it was true, but more because it was he who needed to sleep with a woman, instead of drinking each night at the ice house and stumbling home alone.

Maximiliano who was said to have killed his wife in an ice-house brawl when she came at him with a mop. I had to shoot, he had said—she was armed.

Their laughter outside the kitchen window. Her husband's, his friends'. Manolo, Beto, Efraín, el Perico. Maximiliano.

Was Cleófilas just exaggerating as her husband always said? It seemed the newspapers were full of such stories. This woman found on the side of the interstate. This one pushed from a moving car. This one's cadaver, this one unconscious, this one beaten blue. Her ex-husband, her husband, her lover, her father, her brother, her uncle, her friend, her co-worker. Always. The same grisly news in the pages of the dailies. She dunked a glass under the soapy water for a moment—shivered.

He had thrown a book. Hers. From across the room. A hot welt across the cheek. She could forgive that. But what stung more was the fact it was *her* book, a love story by Corín Tellado, what she loved most now that she lived in the U.S., without a television set, without the *telenovelas.*

Except now and again when her husband was away and she could manage it, the few episodes glimpsed at the neighbor lady Soledad's house because Dolores didn't care for that sort of thing, though Soledad was often kind enough to retell what had happened on what episode of *María de Nadie,* the poor Argentine country girl who had the ill fortune of falling in love with the beautiful son of the Arrocha family, the very family she worked for, whose roof she slept under and whose floors she vacuumed, while in that same house, with the dust brooms and floor cleaners as witnesses, the square-jawed Juan Carlos Arrocha had uttered words of love, I love you, María, listen to me, *mi querida,* but it was she who had to say No, no, we are not of the same class, and remind him it was not his place nor hers to fall in love, while all the while her heart was breaking, can you imagine.

Cleófilas thought her life would have to be like that, like a *telenovela,* only now the episodes got sadder and sadder. And there were no commercials in between for comic relief. And no happy ending in sight. She thought this when she sat with the baby out by the creek behind the house. Cleófilas de . . . ? But somehow she would have to change her name to Topazio, or Yesenia, Cristal, Adriana, Stefania, Andrea, something more poetic than Cleófilas. Everything happened to women with names like jewels. But what happened to a Cleófilas? Nothing. But a crack in the face.

Because the doctor has said so. She has to go. To make sure the new baby is all right, so there won't be any problems when he's born, and the appointment card says next Tuesday. Could he please take her. And that's all.

No, she won't mention it. She promises. If the doctor asks she can say she fell down the front steps or slipped when she was out in the backyard, slipped out back, she could tell him that. She has to go back next Tuesday, Juan Pedro, please, for the new baby. For their child.

She could write to her father and ask maybe for money, just a loan, for the new baby's medical expenses. Well then if he'd rather she didn't. All right, she won't. Please don't anymore. Please don't. She knows it's difficult saving money with all the bills they have, but how else are they going to get out of debt with the truck payments? And after the rent and the food and the electricity and the gas and the water and the who-knows-what, well, there's hardly anything left. But please, at least for the doctor visit. She won't ask for anything else. She has to. Why is she so anxious? Because.

Because she is going to make sure the baby is not turned around backward this time to split her down the center. Yes. Next Tuesday at five-thirty. I'll have Juan Pedrito dressed and ready. But those are the only shoes he has. I'll polish them, and we'll be ready. As soon as you come from work. We won't make you ashamed.

Felice? It's me, Graciela.

No, I can't talk louder. I'm at work.

Look, I need kind of a favor. There's a patient, a lady here who's got a problem.

Well, wait a minute. Are you listening to me or what?

I can't talk real loud 'cause her husband's in the next room.

Well, would you just listen?

I was going to do this sonogram on her—she's pregnant, right?—and she just starts crying on me. *Híjole,* Felice! This poor lady's got black-and-blue marks all over. I'm not kidding.

From her husband. Who else? Another one of those brides from across the border. And her family's all in Mexico.

Shit. You think they're going to help her? Give me a break. This lady doesn't even speak English. She hasn't been allowed to call home or write or nothing. That's why I'm calling you.

She needs a ride.

Not to Mexico, you goof. Just to the Greyhound. In San Anto.

No, just a ride. She's got her own money. All you'd have to do is drop her off in San Antonio on your way home. Come on, Felice. Please? If we don't help her, who will? I'd drive her myself, but she needs to be on that bus before her husband gets home from work. What do you say?

I don't know. Wait.

Right away, tomorrow even.

Well, if tomorrow's no good for you . . .

It's a date, Felice. Thursday. At the Cash N Carry off I-10. Noon. She'll be ready.

Oh, and her name's Cleófilas.

I don't know. One of those Mexican saints, I guess. A martyr or something.

Cleófilas. C-L-E-O-F-I-L-A-S. Cle. O. Fi. Las. Write it down.

Thanks, Felice. When her kid's born she'll have to name her after us, right?

Yeah, you got it. A regular soap opera sometimes. *Qué vida, comadre. Bueno* bye.

All morning that flutter of half-fear, half-doubt. At any moment Juan Pedro might appear in the doorway. On the street. At the Cash N Carry. Like in the dreams she dreamed.

There was that to think about, yes, until the woman in the pickup drove up. Then there wasn't time to think about anything but the pickup pointed toward San Antonio. Put your bags in the back and get in.

But when they drove across the *arroyo,* the driver opened her mouth and let out a yell as loud as any mariachi. Which startled not only Cleófilas, but Juan Pedrito as well.

Pues, look how cute. I scared you two, right? Sorry. Should've warned you. Every time I cross that bridge I do that. Because of the name, you know. Woman Hollering. *Pues,* I holler. She said this in a Spanish pocked with

English and laughed. Did you ever notice, Felice continued, how nothing around here is named after a woman? Really. Unless she's the Virgin. I guess you're only famous if you're a virgin. She was laughing again.

That's why I like the name of that *arroyo.* Makes you want to holler like Tarzan, right?

Everything about this woman, this Felice, amazed Cleófilas. The fact that she drove a pickup. A pickup, mind you, but when Cleófilas asked if it was her husband's, she said she didn't have a husband. The pickup was hers. She herself had chosen it. She herself was paying for it.

I used to have a Pontiac Sunbird. But those cars are for *viejas.* Pussy cars. Now this here is a *real* car.

What kind of talk was that coming from a woman? Cleófilas thought. But then again, Felice was like no woman she'd ever met. Can you imagine, when we crossed the *arroyo* she just started yelling like a crazy, she would say later to her father and brothers. Just like that. Who would've thought?

Who would've? Pain or rage, perhaps, but not a hoot like the one Felice had just let go. Makes you want to holler like Tarzan, Felice had said.

Then Felice began laughing again, but it wasn't Felice laughing. It was gurgling out of her own throat, a long ribbon of laughter, like water.

MICHAEL CUNNINGHAM

White Angel

MICHAEL CUNNINGHAM (1952–) was born in Cincinnati, Ohio, and grew up in Pasadena, California. He received his B.A. in English literature from Stanford University and his M.F.A. from the University of Iowa. His novels are *A Home at the End of the World* and *Flesh and Blood.* His work has appeared in *The Atlantic Monthly, Redbook, Esquire, The Paris Review, The New Yorker, Vogue,* and *Metropolitan Home.* His story "White Angel" was chosen for *The Best American Short Stories 1989.* He received a Guggenheim Fellowship in 1993, a National Endowment for the Arts Fellowship in 1988, and a Michener Fellowship from the University of Iowa in 1982. He currently lives in New York City.

We lived then in Cleveland, in the middle of everything. It was the sixties—our radios sang out love all day long. This of course is history. It happened before the city of Cleveland went broke, before its river caught fire. We were four. My mother and father, Carlton, and me. Carlton turned sixteen the year I turned nine. Between us were several brothers and sisters, weak flames quenched in our mother's womb. We are not a fruitful or many-branched line. Our family name is Morrow.

Our father was a high school music teacher. Our mother taught children called "exceptional," which meant that some could name the day Christmas would fall in the year 2000 but couldn't remember to drop their pants when they peed. We lived in a tract called Woodlawn—neat one- and two-story houses painted optimistic colors. Our tract bordered a cemetery. Behind our back yard was a gully choked with brush, and beyond that, the field of smooth, polished stones. I grew up with the cemetery, and didn't mind it. It could be beautiful. A single stone angel, small-breasted and determined, rose amid the more conservative markers close to our house. Farther away, in a richer section, miniature mosques and Parthenons spoke silently to Cleveland of man's enduring accomplishments. Carlton and I played in the cemetery as children and, with a little more age, smoked joints and drank Southern Comfort there. I was, thanks to Carlton, the most criminally advanced nine-year-old in my fourth-grade class. I was going places. I made no move without his counsel.

Here is Carlton several months before his death, in an hour so alive with snow that earth and sky are identically white. He labors among the markers and I run after, stung by snow, following the light of his red knitted cap. Carlton's hair is pulled back into a ponytail, neat and economical, a perfect pinecone of hair. He is thrifty, in his way.

We have taken hits of acid with our breakfast juice. Or rather, Carlton has taken a hit and I, considering my youth, have been allowed half. This acid is called windowpane. It is for clarity of vision, as Vicks is for decongestion of the nose. Our parents are at work, earning the daily bread. We have come out into the cold so that the house, when we reenter it, will shock us with its warmth and righteousness. Carlton believes in shocks.

"I think I'm coming on to it," I call out. Carlton has on his buckskin jacket, which is worn down to the shine. On the back, across his shoulder blades, his girlfriend has stitched an electric-blue eye. As we walk I speak into the eye. "I think I feel something," I say.

"Too soon," Carlton calls back. "Stay loose, Frisco. You'll know when the time comes."

I am excited and terrified. We are into serious stuff. Carlton has done acid half a dozen times before, but I am new at it. We slipped the tabs into our mouths at breakfast, while our mother paused over the bacon. Carlton likes taking risks.

Snow collects in the engraved letters on the headstones. I lean into the wind, trying to decide whether everything around me seems strange because of the drug, or just because everything truly is strange. Three weeks earlier, a family across town had been sitting at home, watching television, when a single-engine plane fell on them. Snow swirls around us, seeming to fall up as well as down.

Carlton leads the way to our spot, the pillared entrance to a society tomb. This tomb is a palace. Stone cupids cluster on the peaked roof, with stunted, frozen wings and matrons' faces. Under the roof is a veranda, backed by cast-iron doors that lead to the house of the dead proper. In summer this veranda is cool. In winter it blocks the wind. We keep a bottle of Southern Comfort there.

Carlton finds the bottle, unscrews the cap, and takes a good, long draw. He is studded with snowflakes. He hands me the bottle and I take a more conservative drink. Even in winter, the tomb smells mossy as a well. Dead leaves and a yellow M & M's wrapper, worried by the wind, scrape on the marble floor.

"Are you scared?" Carlton asks me.

I nod. I never think of lying to him.

"Don't be, man," he says. "Fear will screw you right up. Drugs can't hurt you if you feel no fear."

I nod. We stand sheltered, passing the bottle. I lean into Carlton's certainty as if it gave off heat.

"We can do acid all the time at Woodstock," I say.

"Right on. Woodstock Nation. Yow."

"Do people really *live* there?" I ask.

"Man, you've got to stop asking that. The concert's over, but people are still there. It's the new nation. Have faith."

I nod again, satisfied. There is a different country for us to live in. I am already a new person, renamed Frisco. My old name was Robert.

"We'll do acid all the time," I say.

"You better believe we will." Carlton's face, surrounded by snow and marble, is lit. His eyes are bright as neon. Something in them tells me he can see the future, a ghost that hovers over everybody's head. In Carlton's future we all get released from our jobs and schooling. Awaiting us all, and soon, is a bright, perfect simplicity. A life among the trees by the river.

"How are you feeling, man?" he asks me.

"Great," I tell him, and it is purely the truth. Doves clatter up out of a bare tree and turn at the same instant, transforming themselves from steel to silver in the snow-blown light. I know at that moment that the drug is working. Everything before me has become suddenly, radiantly itself. How could Carlton have known this was about to happen? "Oh," I whisper. His hand settles on my shoulder.

"Stay loose, Frisco," he says. "There's not a thing in this pretty world to be afraid of. I'm here."

I am not afraid. I am astonished. I had not realized until this moment how real everything is. A twig lies on the marble at my feet, bearing a cluster of hard brown berries. The broken-off end is raw, white, fleshly. Trees are alive.

"I'm here," Carlton says again, and he is.

Hours later, we are sprawled on the sofa in front of the television, ordinary as Wally and the Beav. Our mother makes dinner in the kitchen. A pot lid clangs. We are undercover agents. I am trying to conceal my amazement.

Our father is building a grandfather clock from a kit. He wants to have something to leave us, something for us to pass along. We can hear him in the basement, sawing and pounding. I know what is laid out on his sawhorses—a long raw wooden box, onto which he glues fancy moldings. A single pearl of sweat meanders down his forehead as he works. Tonight I have discovered my ability to see every room of the house at once, to know every single thing that goes on. A mouse nibbles inside the wall. Electrical wires curl behind the plaster, hidden and patient as snakes.

"Shhh," I say to Carlton, who has not said anything. He is watching television through his splayed fingers. Gunshots ping. Bullets raise chalk dust on a concrete wall. I have no idea what we are watching.

"Boys?" our mother calls from the kitchen. I can, with my new ears, hear her slap hamburger into patties. "Set the table like good citizens," she calls.

"Okay, Ma," Carlton replies, in a gorgeous imitation of normality. Our father hammers in the basement. I can feel Carlton's heart ticking. He pats my hand, to assure me that everything's perfect.

We set the table, spoon fork knife, paper napkins triangled to one side. We know the moves cold. After we are done I pause to notice the dining-room wallpaper: a golden farm, backed by mountains. Cows graze, autumn trees cast golden shade. This scene repeats itself three times, on three walls.

"Zap," Carlton whispers. "Zzzzzoom."

"Did we do it right?" I ask him.

"We did everything perfect, little son. How are you doing in there, anyway?" He raps lightly on my head.

"Perfect, I guess." I am staring at the wallpaper as if I were thinking of stepping into it.

"You guess. You guess? You and I are going to other planets, man. Come over here."

"Where?"

"Here. Come here." He leads me to the window. Outside the snow skitters, nervous and silver, under streetlamps. Ranch-style houses hoard their warmth, bleed light into the gathering snow. It is a street in Cleveland. It is our street.

"You and I are going to fly, man," Carlton whispers, close to my ear. He opens the window. Snow blows in, sparking on the carpet. "Fly," he says, and we do. For a moment we strain up and out, the black night wind blowing in our faces—we raise ourselves up off the cocoa-colored deep-pile wool-and-polyester carpet by a sliver of an inch. Sweet glory. The secret of flight is this—you have to do it immediately, before your body realizes it is defying the laws. I swear it to this day.

We both know we have taken momentary leave of the earth. It does not strike either of us as remarkable, any more than does the fact that airplanes sometimes fall from the sky, or that we have always lived in these rooms and will soon leave them. We settle back down. Carlton touches my shoulder.

"You wait, Frisco," he says. "Miracles are happening. Fucking miracles."

I nod. He pulls down the window, which reseals itself with a sucking sound. Our own faces look back at us from the cold, dark glass. Behind us, our mother drops the hamburgers sizzling into the skillet. Our father bends to his work under a hooded lightbulb, preparing the long box into which he will lay clockworks, pendulum, a face. A plane drones by overhead, invisible in the clouds. I glance nervously at Carlton. He smiles his assurance and squeezes the back of my neck.

March. After the thaw. I am walking through the cemetery, thinking about my endless life. One of the beauties of living in Cleveland is that any direction feels like progress. I've memorized the map. We are by my calculations three hundred and fifty miles shy of Woodstock, New York. On this raw new day I am walking east, to the place where Carlton and I keep our bottle. I am going to have an early nip, to celebrate my bright future.

When I get to our spot I hear low moans coming from behind the tomb. I freeze, considering my choices. The sound is a long-drawn-out agony with a whip at the end, a final high C, something like "ooooooOw." A wolf's cry run backward. What decides me on investigation rather than flight is the need to make a story. In the stories my brother likes best, people always do the foolish, risky thing. I find I can reach decisions this way, by thinking of myself as a character in a story told by Carlton.

I creep around the side of the monument, cautious as a badger, pressed up close to the marble. I peer over a cherub's girlish shoulder. What I find is Carlton on the ground with his girlfriend, in an uncertain jumble of clothes and bare flesh. Carlton's jacket, the one with the embroidered eye, is draped over the stone, keeping watch.

I hunch behind the statue. I can see the girl's naked arms, and the familiar bones of Carlton's spine. The two of them moan together in the dry winter grass. Though I can't make out the girl's expression, Carlton's face is twisted and grimacing, the cords of his neck pulled tight. I had never thought the experience might be painful. I watch, trying to learn. I hold on to the cherub's cold wings.

It isn't long before Carlton catches sight of me. His eyes rove briefly, ecstatically skyward, and what do they light on but his brother's small head, sticking up next to a cherub's. We lock eyes and spend a moment in mutual decision. The girl keeps on clutching at Carlton's skinny back. He decides to smile at me. He decides to wink.

I am out of there so fast I tear up divots. I dodge among the stones, jump the gully, clear the fence into the swing-set-and-picnic-table sanctity of the back yard. Something about that wink. My heart beats fast as a sparrow's.

I go into the kitchen and find our mother washing fruit. She asks what's going on. I tell her nothing is. Nothing at all.

She sighs over an apple's imperfection. The curtains sport blue teapots. Our mother works the apple with a scrub brush. She believes they come coated with poison.

"Where's Carlton?" she asks.

"Don't know," I tell her.

"Bobby?"

"Huh?"

"What exactly is going on?"

"Nothing," I say. My heart works itself up to a humingbird's rate, more buzz than beat.

"I think something is. Will you answer a question?"

"Okay."

"Is your brother taking drugs?"

I relax a bit. It is only drugs. I know why she's asking. Lately police cars have been browsing our house like sharks. They pause, take note, glide on. Some neighborhood crackdown. Carlton is famous in these parts.

"No," I tell her.

She faces me with the brush in one hand, an apple in the other. "You wouldn't lie to me, would you?" She knows something is up. Her nerves run through this house. She can feel dust settling on the tabletops, milk starting to turn in the refrigerator.

"No," I say.

"Something's going on," she sighs. She is a small, efficient woman who looks at things as if they give off a painful light. She grew up on a farm in Wisconsin and spent her girlhood tying up bean rows, worrying over the sun and rain. She is still trying to overcome her habit of modest expectations.

I leave the kitchen, pretending sudden interest in the cat. Our mother follows, holding her brush. She means to scrub the truth out of me. I follow the cat, his erect black tail and pink anus.

"Don't walk away when I'm talking to you," our mother says.

I keep walking, to see how far I'll get, calling, "Kittykittykitty." In the front hall, our father's homemade clock chimes the half hour. I make for the clock. I get as far as the rubber plant before she collars me.

"I told you not to walk away," she says, and cuffs me a good one with the brush. She catches me on the ear and sets it ringing. The cat is out of there quick as a quarter note.

I stand for a minute, to let her know I've received the message. Then I resume walking. She hits me again, this time on the back of the head, hard enough to make me see colors. "Will you *stop?*" she screams. Still, I keep walking. Our house runs west to east. With every step I get closer to Yasgur's farm.

* * *

Carlton comes home whistling. Our mother treats him like a guest who's overstayed. He doesn't care. He is lost in optimism. He pats her cheek and calls her "Professor." He treats her as if she were harmless, and so she is.

She never hits Carlton. She suffers him the way farm girls suffer a thieving crow, with a grudge so old and endless it borders on reverence. She gives him a scrubbed apple, and tells him what she'll do if he tracks mud on the carpet.

I am waiting in our room. He brings the smell of the cemetery with him, its old snow and wet pine needles. He rolls his eyes at me, takes a crunch of his apple. "What's happening, Frisco?" he says.

I have arranged myself loosely on my bed, trying to pull a Dylan riff out of my harmonica. I have always figured I can bluff my way into wisdom. I offer Carlton a dignified nod.

He drops onto his own bed. I can see a crushed crocus, the first of the year, stuck to the black rubber sole of his boot.

"Well, Frisco," he says. "Today you are a man."

I nod again. Is that all there is to it?

"*You,*" Carlton says. He laughs, pleased with himself and the world. "That was so perfect."

I pick out what I can of "Blowin' in the Wind."

Carlton says, "Man, when I saw you out there spying on us I thought to myself, *yes.* Now *I'm* really here. You know what I'm saying?" He waves his apple core.

"Uh-huh," I say.

"Frisco, that was the first time her and I ever did it. I mean, we'd talked. But when we finally got down to it, there you were. My brother. Like you *knew.*"

I nod, and this time for real. What happened was an adventure we had together. All right. The story is beginning to make sense.

"Aw, Frisco," Carlton says. "I'm gonna find you a girl, too. You're nine. You been a virgin too long."

"Really?" I say.

"*Man.* We'll find you a woman from the sixth grade, somebody with a little experience. We'll get stoned and all make out under the trees in the boneyard. I want to be present at your deflowering, man. You're gonna need a brother there."

I am about to ask, as casually as I can manage, about the relationship between love and bodily pain, when our mother's voice cuts into the room. "You did it," she screams. "You tracked mud all over the rug."

A family entanglement follows. Our mother brings our father, who comes and stands in the doorway with her, taking in evidence. He is a formerly handsome man. His face has been worn down by too much patience. He has lately taken up some sporty touches—a goatee, a pair of calfskin boots.

Our mother points out the trail of muddy half-moons that lead from the door to Carlton's bed. Dangling over the foot of the bed are the culprits themselves, voluptuously muddy, with Carlton's criminal feet still in them.

"You see?" she says. "You see what he thinks of me?"

Our father, a reasonable man, suggests that Carlton clean it up. Our mother finds that too small a gesture. She wants Carlton not to have done it in the first place. "I don't ask for much," she says. "I don't ask where he goes. I don't ask why the police are suddenly so interested in our house. I ask that he not track mud all over the floor. That's all." She squints in the glare of her own outrage.

"Better clean it right up," our father says to Carlton.

"And that's it?" our mother says. "He cleans up the mess, and all's forgiven?"

"Well, what do you want him to do? Lick it up?"

"I want some consideration," she says, turning helplessly to me. "That's what I want."

I shrug, at a loss. I sympathize with our mother, but am not on her team.

"All right," she says. "I just won't bother cleaning the house anymore. I'll let you men handle it. I'll sit and watch television and throw my candy wrappers on the floor."

She starts out, cutting the air like a blade. On her way she picks up a jar of pencils, looks at it and tosses the pencils on the floor. They fall like fortune-telling sticks, in pairs and crisscrosses.

Our father goes after her, calling her name. Her name is Isabel. We can hear them making their way across the house, our father calling, "Isabel, Isabel, Isabel," while our mother, pleased with the way the pencils had looked, dumps more things onto the floor.

"I hope she doesn't break the TV," I say.

"She'll do what she needs to do," Carlton tells me.

"I hate her," I say. I am not certain about that. I want to test the sound of it, to see if it's true.

"She's got more balls than any of us, Frisco," he says. "Better watch what you say about her."

I keep quiet. Soon I get up and start gathering pencils, because I prefer that to lying around trying to follow the shifting lines of allegiance. Carlton goes for a sponge and starts in on the mud.

"You get shit on the carpet, you clean it up," he says. "Simple."

The time for all my questions about love has passed, and I am not so unhip as to force a subject. I know it will come up again. I make a neat bouquet of pencils. Our mother rages through the house.

Later, after she has thrown enough and we three have picked it all up, I lie on my bed thinking things over. Carlton is on the phone to his girlfriend, talking low. Our mother, becalmed but still dangerous, cooks dinner. She sings as she cooks, some slow forties number that must have been all over the jukes when her first husband's plane went down in the Pacific. Our father plays his clarinet in the basement. That is where he goes to practice, down among his woodworking tools, the neatly hung hammers and awls that throw oversized shadows in the light of the single bulb. If I put my ear to the floor I can hear him, pulling a long low tomcat moan out of that horn. There is some strange comfort in pressing my ear to the carpet and hearing our father's music leaking up through the floorboards. Lying down, with my ear to the floor, I join in on my harmonica.

That spring our parents have a party to celebrate the sun's return. It has been a long, bitter winter and now the first wild daisies are poking up on the lawns and among the graves.

Our parents' parties are mannerly affairs. Their friends, schoolteachers all, bring wine jugs and guitars. They are Ohio hip. Though they hold jobs and meet mortgages, they think of themselves as independent spirits on a spying mission. They have agreed to impersonate teachers until they write their novels, finish their dissertations, or just save up enough money to set themselves free.

Carlton and I are the lackeys. We take coats, fetch drinks. We have done this at every party since we were small, trading on our precocity, doing a brother act. We know the moves. A big, lipsticked woman who has devoted her maidenhood to ninth-grade math calls me Mr. Right. An assistant vice principal in a Russian fur hat asks us both whether we expect to vote Democratic or Socialist. By sneaking sips I manage to get myself semi-crocked.

The reliability of the evening is derailed halfway through, however, by a half dozen of Carlton's friends. They rap on the door and I go for it, anxious as a carnival sharp to see who will step up next and swallow the illusion that I'm a kindly, sober nine-year-old child. I'm expecting callow adults and who do I find but a pack of young outlaws, big-booted and wild-haired. Carlton's girlfriend stands in front, in an outfit made up almost entirely of fringe.

"Hi, Bobby," she says confidently. She comes from New York, and is more than just locally smart.

"Hi," I say. I let them all in despite a retrograde urge to lock the door and phone the police. Three are girls, four boys. They pass me in a cloud of dope smoke and sly-eyed greeting.

What they do is invade the party. Carlton is standing on the far side of the rumpus room, picking the next album, and his girl cuts straight through the crowd to his side. She has the bones and the loose, liquid moves some people consider beautiful. She walks through that room as if she'd been sent to teach the whole party a lesson.

Carlton's face tips me off that this was planned. Our mother demands to know what's going on here. She is wearing a long dark-red dress that doesn't interfere with her shoulders. When she dresses up you can see what it is about her, or what it was. She is responsible for Carlton's beauty. I have our father's face.

Carlton does some quick talking. Though it's against our mother's better judgment, the invaders are suffered to stay. One of them, an Eddie Haskell for all his leather and hair, tells her she is looking good. She is willing to hear it.

So the outlaws, house-sanctioned, start to mingle. I work my way over to Carlton's side, the side unoccupied by his girlfriend. I would like to say something ironic and wised-up, something that will band Carlton and me against every other person in the room. I can feel the shape of the comment I have in mind but, being a tipsy nine-year-old, can't get my mouth around it. What I say is, "Shit, man."

Carlton's girl laughs at me. She considers it amusing that a little boy says "shit." I would like to tell her what I have figured out about her, but I am nine, and three-quarters gone on Tom Collinses. Even sober, I can only imagine a sharp-tongued wit.

"Hang on, Frisco," Carlton tells me. "This could turn into a real party."

I can see by the light in his eyes what is going down. He has arranged a blind date between our parents' friends and his own. It's a Woodstock move—he is plotting a future in which young and old have business together. I agree to hang on, and go to the kitchen, hoping to sneak a few knocks of gin.

There I find our father leaning up against the refrigerator. A line of butterfly-shaped magnets hovers around his head. "Are you enjoying this party?" he asks, touching his goatee. He is still getting used to being a man with a beard.

"Uh-huh."

"I am, too," he says sadly. He never meant to be a high school music teacher. The money question caught up with him.

"What do you think of this music?" he asks. Carlton has put the Stones on the turntable. Mick Jagger sings "19th Nervous Breakdown." Our father gestures in an openhanded way that takes in the room, the party, the whole house—everything the music touches.

"I like it," I say.

"So do I." He stirs his drink with his finger, and sucks on the finger.

"I *love* it," I say, too loud. Something about our father leads me to raise my voice. I want to grab handfuls of music out of the air and stuff them into my mouth.

"I'm not sure I could say I love it," he says. "I'm not sure if I could say that, no. I would say I'm friendly to its intentions. I would say that if this is the direction music is going in, I won't stand in its way."

"Uh-huh," I say. I am already anxious to get back to the party, but don't want to hurt his feelings. If he senses he's being avoided he can fall into fits of apology more terrifying than our mother's rages.

"I think I may have been too rigid with my students," our father says. "Maybe over the summer you boys could teach me a few things about the music people are listening to these days."

"Sure," I say, loudly. We spend a minute waiting for the next thing to say.

"You boys are happy, aren't you?" he asks. "Are you enjoying this party?"

"We're having a great time," I say.

"I thought you were. I am, too."

I have by this time gotten myself to within jumping distance of the door. I call out, "Well, goodbye," and dive back into the party.

Something has happened in my small absence. The party has started to roll. Call it an accident of history and the weather. Carlton's friends are on decent behavior, and our parents' friends have decided to give up some of their wine-and-folk-song propriety to see what they can learn. Carlton is dancing with a vice principal's wife. Carlton's friend Frank, with his ancient-child face and IQ in the low sixties, dances with our mother. I see that our father has followed me out of the kitchen. He positions himself at the party's edge; I jump into its center. I invite the fuchsia-lipped math teacher to dance. She is only too happy. She is big and graceful as a parade float, and I steer her effortlessly out into the middle of everything. My mother, who is known around school for Sicilian discipline, dances freely, which is news to everybody. There is no getting around her beauty.

The night rises higher and higher. A wildness sets in. Carlton throws new music on the turntable—Janis Joplin, the Doors, the Dead. The future shines for everyone, rich with the possibility of more nights exactly like this. Even our father is pressed into dancing, which he does like a flightless bird, all flapping arms and potbelly. Still, he dances. Our mother has a kiss for him.

Finally I nod out on the sofa, blissful under the drinks. I am dreaming of flight when our mother comes and touches my shoulder. I smile up into her flushed, smiling face.

"It's hours past your bedtime," she says, all velvet motherliness. I nod. I can't dispute the fact.

She keeps on nudging my shoulder. I am a moment or two apprehending the fact that she actually wants me to leave the party and go to bed. "No," I tell her.

"Yes," she smiles.

"No," I say cordially, experimentally. This new mother can dance, and flirt. Who knows what else she might allow?

"Yes." The velvet motherliness leaves her voice. She means business, business of the usual kind. I get myself out of there and no excuses this time. I am exactly nine and running from my bedtime as I'd run from death.

I run to Carlton for protection. He is laughing with his girl, a sweaty question mark of hair plastered to his forehead. I plow into him so hard he nearly goes over.

"Whoa, Frisco," he says. He takes me up under the arms and swings me a half-turn. Our mother plucks me out of his hands and sets me down, with a good farm-style hold on the back of my neck.

"Say good night, Bobby," she says. She adds, for the benefit of Carlton's girl, "He should have been in bed before this party started."

"*No,*" I holler. I try to twist loose, but our mother has a grip that could crack walnuts.

Carlton's girl tosses her hair and says, "Good night, baby." She smiles a victor's smile. She smooths the stray hair off Carlton's forehead.

"*No,*" I scream again. Something about the way she touches his hair. Our mother calls our father, who comes and scoops me up and starts out of the room with me, holding me like the live bomb I am. Before I go I lock eyes with Carlton. He shrugs and says, "Night, man." Our father hustles me out. I do not take it bravely. I leave flailing, too furious to cry, dribbling a slimy thread of horrible-child's spittle.

Later I lie alone on my narrow bed, feeling the music hum in the coiled springs. Life is cracking open right there in our house. People are changing. By tomorrow, no one will be quite the same. How can they let me miss it? I dream up revenge against our parents, and worse for Carlton. He is the one who could have saved me. He could have banded with me against them. What I can't forgive is his shrug, his mild-eyed "Night, man." He has joined the adults. He has made himself bigger, and taken size from me. As the Doors thump "Strange Days," I hope something awful happens to him. I say so to myself.

Around midnight, dim-witted Frank announces he has seen a flying saucer hovering over the back yard. I can hear his deep, excited voice all the way in my room. He says it's like a blinking, luminous cloud. I hear half the party struggling out through the sliding glass door in a disorganized, whooping knot. By that time everyone is so delirious a flying saucer would be just what was expected. That much celebration would logically attract an answering happiness from across the stars.

I get out of bed and sneak down the hall. I will not miss alien visitors for anyone, not even at the cost of our mother's wrath or our father's disappointment. I stop at the end of the hallway, though, embarrassed to be in pajamas.

If there really are aliens, they will think I'm the lowest member of the house. While I hesitate over whether to go back to my room to change, people start coming back inside, talking about a trick of the mist and an airplane. People resume their dancing.

Carlton must have jumped the back fence. He must have wanted to be there alone, singular, in case they decided to take somebody with them. A few nights later I will go out and stand where he would have been standing. On the far side of the gully, now a river swollen with melted snow, the cemetery will gleam like a lost city. The moon will be full. I will hang around just as Carlton must have, hypnotized by the silver light on the stones, the white angel raising her arms up across the river.

According to our parents the mystery is why he ran back to the house full tilt. Something in the graveyard may have scared him, he may have needed to break its spell, but I think it's more likely that when he came back to himself he just couldn't wait to get back to the music and the people, the noisy disorder of continuing life.

Somebody has shut the sliding glass door. Carlton's girlfriend looks lazily out, touching base with her own reflection. I look, too. Carlton is running toward the house. I hesitate. Then I figure he can bump his nose. It will be a good joke on him. I let him keep coming. His girlfriend sees him through her own reflection, starts to scream a warning just as Carlton hits the glass.

It is an explosion. Triangles of glass fly brightly through the room. I think for him it must be more surprising than painful, like hitting water from a great height. He stands blinking for a moment. The whole party stops, stares, getting its bearings. Bob Dylan sings "Just Like a Woman." Carlton reaches up curiously to take out the shard of glass that is stuck in his neck, and that is when the blood starts. It shoots out of him. Our mother screams. Carlton steps forward into his girlfriend's arms and the two of them fall together. Our mother throws herself down on top of him and the girl. People shout their accident wisdom. Don't lift him. Call an ambulance. I watch from the hallway. Carlton's blood spurts, soaking into the carpet, spattering people's clothes. Our mother and father both try to plug the wound with their hands, but the blood just shoots between their fingers. Carlton looks more puzzled than anything, as if he can't quite follow this turn of events. "It's all right," our father tells him, trying to stop the blood. "It's all right, just don't move, it's all right." Carlton nods, and holds our father's hand. His eyes take on an astonished light. Our mother screams, "Is anybody *doing* anything?" What comes out of Carlton grows darker, almost black. I watch. Our father tries to get a hold on Carlton's neck while Carlton keeps trying to take his hand. Our mother's hair is matted with blood. It runs down her face. Carlton's girl holds him to her breasts, touches his hair, whispers in his ear.

He is gone by the time the ambulance gets there. You can see the life drain out of him. When his face goes slack our mother wails. A part of her flies wailing through the house, where it will wail and rage forever. I feel our mother pass through me on her way out. She covers Carlton's body with her own.

He is buried in the cemetery out back. Years have passed—we are living in the future, and it's turned out differently from what we'd planned. Our mother has established her life of separateness behind the guest-room door. Our father mutters his greetings to the door as he passes.

One April night, almost a year to the day after Carlton's accident, I hear cautious footsteps shuffling across the living-room floor after midnight. I run out eagerly, thinking of ghosts, but find only our father in moth-colored pajamas. He looks unsteadily at the dark air in front of him.

"Hi, Dad," I say from the doorway.

He looks in my direction. "Yes?"

"It's me. Bobby."

"Oh, Bobby," he says. "What are you doing up, young man?"

"Nothing," I tell him. "Dad?"

"Yes, son."

"Maybe you better come back to bed. Okay?"

"Maybe I had," he says. "I just came out here for a drink of water, but I seem to have gotten turned around in the darkness. Yes, maybe I better had."

I take his hand and lead him down the hall to his room. The grandfather clock chimes the quarter hour.

"Sorry," our father says.

I get him into bed. "There," I say. "Okay?"

"Perfect. Could not be better."

"Okay. Good night."

"Good night. Bobby?"

"Uh-huh?"

"Why don't you stay a minute?" he says. "We could have ourselves a talk, you and me. How would that be?"

"Okay," I say. I sit on the edge of his mattress. His bedside clock ticks off the minutes.

I can hear the low rasp of his breathing. Around our house, the Ohio night chirps and buzzes. The small gray finger of Carlton's stone pokes up among the others, within sight of the angel's blank white eyes. Above us, airplanes and satellites sparkle. People are flying even now toward New York or California, to take up lives of risk and invention.

I stay until our father has worked his way into a muttering sleep.

Carlton's girlfriend moved to Denver with her family a month before. I never learned what it was she'd whispered to him. Though she'd kept her head admirably during the accident, she lost her head afterward. She cried so hard at the funeral that she had to be taken away by her mother—an older, redder-haired version of her. She started seeing a psychiatrist three times a week. Everyone, including my parents, talked about how hard it was for her, to have held a dying boy in her arms at that age. I'm grateful to her for holding my brother while he died, but I never once heard her mention the fact that though she had been through something terrible, at least she was still alive and going places. At least she had protected herself by trying to warn him. I can appreciate the intricacies of her pain. But as long as she was in Cleveland, I could never look her straight in the face. I couldn't talk about the wounds she suffered. I can't even write her name.

JUNOT DIAZ

Fiesta 1980

JUNOT DIAZ (1968–) is the author of the 1996 short-story collection *Drown* . He lives in New York City, teaches creative writing at Syracuse University, and is at work on his first novel. He is the recipient of the 1998 Eugene McDermott Award and his stories have appeared in *The New Yorker, Story, The Paris Review, Glimmer Train,* and *African Voices.*

Mami's youngest sister—my tía Yrma—finally made it to the United States that year. She and tío Miguel got themselves an apartment in the Bronx, off the Grand Concourse and everybody decided that we should have a party. Actually, my pops decided, but everybody—meaning Mami, tía Yrma, tío Miguel and their neighbors—thought it a dope idea. On the afternoon of the party Papi came back from work around six. Right on time. We were all dressed by then, which was a smart move on our part. If Papi had walked in and caught us lounging around in our underwear, he would have kicked our asses something serious.

He didn't say nothing to nobody, not even my moms. He just pushed past her, held up his hand when she tried to talk to him and headed right into the shower. Rafa gave me the look and I gave it back to him; we both knew Papi had been with that Puerto Rican woman he was seeing and wanted to wash off the evidence quick.

Mami looked really nice that day. The United States had finally put some meat on her; she was no longer the same flaca who had arrived here three years before. She had cut her hair short and was wearing tons of cheap-ass jewelry which on her didn't look too lousy. She smelled like herself, like the wind through a tree. She always waited until the last possible minute to put on her perfume because she said it was a waste to spray it on early and then have to spray it on again once you got to the party.

We—meaning me, my brother, my little sister and Mami—waited for

Papi to finish his shower. Mami seemed anxious, in her usual dispassionate way. Her hands adjusted the buckle of her belt over and over again. That morning, when she had gotten us up for school, Mami told us that she wanted to have a good time at the party. I want to dance, she said, but now, with the sun sliding out of the sky like spit off a wall, she seemed ready just to get this over with.

Rafa didn't much want to go to no party either, and me, I never wanted to go anywhere with my family. There was a baseball game in the parking lot outside and we could hear our friends, yelling, Hey, and, Cabrón, to one another. We heard the pop of a ball as it sailed over the cars, the clatter of an aluminum bat dropping to the concrete. Not that me or Rafa loved baseball; we just liked playing with the local kids, thrashing them at anything they were doing. By the sounds of the shouting, we both knew the game was close, either of us could have made a difference. Rafa frowned and when I frowned back, he put up his fist. Don't you mirror me, he said.

Don't you mirror me, I said.

He punched me—I would have hit him back but Papi marched into the living room with his towel around his waist, looking a lot smaller than he did when he was dressed. He had a few strands of hair around his nipples and a surly closed-mouth expression, like maybe he'd scalded his tongue or something.

Have they eaten? he asked Mami.

She nodded. I made you something.

You didn't let him eat, did you?

Ay, Dios mío, she said, letting her arms fall to her side.

Ay, Dios mío is right, Papi said.

I was never supposed to eat before our car trips, but earlier, when she had put out our dinner of rice, beans and sweet platanos, guess who had been the first one to clean his plate? You couldn't blame Mami really, she had been busy—cooking, getting ready, dressing my sister Madai. I should have reminded her not to feed me but I wasn't that sort of son.

Papi turned to me. Coño, muchacho, why did you eat?

Rafa had already started inching away from me. I'd once told him I considered him a low-down chickenshit for moving out of the way every time Papi was going to smack me.

Collateral damage, Rafa had said. Ever heard of it?

No.

Look it up.

Chickenshit or not, I didn't dare glance at him. Papi was old-fashioned; he expected your undivided attention when you were getting your ass whupped. You couldn't look him in the eye either—that wasn't allowed. Better to stare at his belly button, which was perfectly round and immaculate. Papi pulled me to my feet by my ear.

If you throw up—

I won't, I cried, tears in my eyes, more out of reflex than pain.

Ya, Ramón, ya. It's not his fault, Mami said.

They've known about this party forever. How did they think we were going to get there? Fly?

He finally let go of my ear and I sat back down. Madai was too scared to open her eyes. Being around Papi all her life had turned her into a major-league wuss. Anytime Papi raised his voice her lip would start trembling, like some specialized tuning fork. Rafa pretended that he had knuckles to crack and when I shoved him, he gave me a *Don't start* look. But even that little bit of recognition made me feel better.

I was the one who was always in trouble with my dad. It was like my God-given duty to piss him off, to do everything the way he hated. Our fights didn't bother me too much. I still wanted him to love me, something that never seemed strange or contradictory until years later, when he was out of our lives.

By the time my ear stopped stinging Papi was dressed and Mami was crossing each one of us, solemnly, like we were heading off to war. We said, in turn, Bendición, Mami, and she poked us in our five cardinal spots while saying, Que Dios te bendiga.

This was how all our trips began, the words that followed me every time I left the house.

None of us spoke until we were inside Papi's Volkswagen van. Brand-new, lime-green and bought to impress. Oh, we were impressed, but me, every time I was in that VW and Papi went above twenty miles an hour, I vomited. I'd never had trouble with cars before—that van was like my curse. Mami suspected it was the upholstery. In her mind, American things—appliances, mouthwash, funny-looking upholstery—all seemed to have an intrinsic badness about them. Papi was careful about taking me anywhere in the VW, but when he had to, I rode up front in Mami's usual seat so I could throw up out a window.

¿Cómo te sientas? Mami asked over my shoulder when Papi pulled onto the turnpike. She had her hand on the base of my neck. One thing about Mami, her palms never sweated.

I'm OK, I said, keeping my eyes straight ahead. I definitely didn't want to trade glances with Papi. He had this one look, furious and sharp, that always left me feeling bruised.

Toma. Mami handed me four mentas. She had thrown three out her window at the beginning of our trip, an offering to Eshú; the rest were for me.

I took one and sucked it slowly, my tongue knocking it up against my teeth. We passed Newark Airport without any incident. If Madai had been awake she would have cried because the planes flew so close to the cars.

How's he feeling? Papi asked.

Fine, I said. I glanced back at Rafa and he pretended like he didn't see me. That was the way he was, at school and at home. When I was in trouble, he didn't know me. Madai was solidly asleep, but even with her face all wrinkled up and drooling she looked cute, her hair all separated into twists.

I turned around and concentrated on the candy. Papi even started to joke that we might not have to scrub the van out tonight. He was beginning to loosen up, not checking his watch too much. Maybe he was thinking about that Puerto Rican woman or maybe he was just happy that we were all together. I could never tell. At the toll, he was feeling positive enough to actually get out of the van and search around under the basket for dropped coins. It was something he had once done to amuse Madai, but now it was habit. Cars behind us honked their horns and I slid down in my seat. Rafa didn't care; he grinned back at the other cars and waved. His actual job was to make sure no cops were coming. Mami shook Madai awake and as soon as she saw Papi stooping for a couple of quarters she let out this screech of delight that almost took off the top of my head.

That was the end of the good times. Just outside the Washington Bridge, I started feeling woozy. The smell of the upholstery got all up inside my head and I found myself with a mouthful of saliva. Mami's hand tensed on my shoulder and when I caught Papi's eye, he was like, No way. Don't do it.

The first time I got sick in the van Papi was taking me to the library. Rafa was with us and he couldn't believe I threw up. I was famous for my steel-lined stomach. A third-world childhood could give you that. Papi was worried enough that just as quick as Rafa could drop off the books we were on our way home. Mami fixed me one of her honey-and-onion concoctions and that made my stomach feel better. A week later we tried the library again and on this go-around I couldn't get the window open in time. When Papi got me home, he went and cleaned out the van himself, an expression of askho on his face. This was a big deal, since Papi almost never cleaned anything himself. He came back inside and found me sitting on the couch feeling like hell.

It's the car, he said to Mami. It's making him sick.

This time the damage was pretty minimal, nothing Papi couldn't wash off the door with a blast of the hose. He was pissed, though; he jammed his finger into my cheek, a nice solid thrust. That was the way he was with his punishments: imaginative. Earlier that year I'd written an essay in school called "My Father the Torturer," but the teacher made me write a new one. She thought I was kidding.

We drove the rest of the way to the Bronx in silence. We only stopped once, so I could brush my teeth. Mami had brought along my toothbrush and a tube of toothpaste and while every car known to man sped by us she stood outside with me so I wouldn't feel alone.

Tío Miguel was about seven feet tall and had his hair combed up and out, into a demi-fro. He gave me and Rafa big spleen-crushing hugs and then kissed Mami and finally ended up with Madai on his shoulder. The last time I'd seen Tío was at the airport, his first day in the United States. I remembered how he hadn't seemed all that troubled to be in another country.

He looked down at me. Carajo, Yunior, you look horrible!

He threw up, my brother explained.

I pushed Rafa. Thanks a lot, ass-face.

Hey, he said. Tío asked.

Tío clapped a bricklayer's hand on my shoulder. Everybody gets sick sometimes, he said. You should have seen me on the plane over here. Dios mio! He rolled his Asian-looking eyes for emphasis. I thought we were all going to die.

Everybody could tell he was lying. I smiled like he was making me feel better.

Do you want me to get you a drink? Tío asked. We got beer and rum.

Miguel, Mami said. He's young.

Young? Back in Santo Domingo, he'd be getting laid by now.

Mami thinned her lips, which took some doing.

Well, it's true, Tío said.

So, Mami, I said. When do I get to go visit the D.R.?

That's enough, Yunior.

It's the only pussy you'll ever get, Rafa said to me in English.

Not counting your girlfriend, of course.

Rafa smiled. He had to give me that one.

Papi came in from parking the van. He and Miguel gave each other the sort of handshakes that would have turned my fingers into Wonder bread.

Coño, compa'i, ¿cómo va todo? they said to each other.

Tía came out then, with an apron on and maybe the longest Lee Press-On Nails I've ever seen in my life. There was this one guru motherfucker in the *Guinness Book of World Records* who had longer nails, but I tell you, it was close. She gave everybody kisses, told me and Rafa how guapo we were—Rafa, of course, believed her—told Madai how bella she was, but when she got to Papi, she froze a little, like maybe she'd seen a wasp on the tip of his nose, but then kissed him all the same.

Mami told us to join the other kids in the living room. Tío said, Wait a minute, I want to show you the apartment. I was glad Tía said, Hold on, because from what I'd seen so far, the place had been furnished in Contemporary Dominican Tacky. The less I saw, the better. I mean, I liked plastic sofa covers but damn, Tío and Tía had taken it to another level. They had a disco ball hanging in the living room and the type of stucco ceilings that looked like stalactite heaven. The sofas all had golden tassels dangling from their edges. Tía came out of the kitchen with some people I didn't know and by the time she got done introducing everybody, only Papi and Mami were given the guided tour of the four-room third-floor apartment. Me and Rafa joined the kids in the living room. They'd already started eating. We were hungry, one of the girls explained, a pastelito in hand. The boy was about three years younger than me but the girl who'd spoken, Leti, was my age. She and another girl were on the sofa together and they were cute as hell.

Leti introduced them: the boy was her brother Wilquins and the other girl was her neighbor Mari. Leti had some serious tetas and I could tell that my brother was going to gun for her. His taste in girls was predictable. He sat down right between Leti and Mari and by the way they were smiling at him I knew he'd do fine. Neither of the girls gave me more than a cursory one-two, which didn't bother me. Sure, I liked girls but I was always too terrified to speak to them unless we were arguing or I was calling them stupidos, which was one of my favorite words that year. I turned to Wilquins and asked him what there was to do around here. Mari, who had the lowest voice I'd ever heard, said, He can't speak.

What does that mean?

He's mute.

I looked at Wilquins incredulously. He smiled and nodded, as if he'd won a prize or something.

Does he understand? I asked.

Of course he understands, Rafa said. He's not dumb.

I could tell Rafa had said that just to score points with the girls. Both of them nodded. Low-voice Mari said, He's the best student in his grade.

I thought, Not bad for a mute. I sat next to Wilquins. After about two seconds of TV Wilquins whipped out a bag of dominos and motioned to me. Did I want to play? Sure. Me and him played Rafa and Leti and we whupped their collective asses twice, which put Rafa in a real bad mood. He looked at me like maybe he wanted to take a swing, just one to make him feel better. Leti kept whispering into Rafa's ear, telling him it was OK.

In the kitchen I could hear my parents slipping into their usual modes. Papi's voice was loud and argumentative; you didn't have to be anywhere near him to catch his drift. And Mami, you had to put cups to your ears to hear hers. I went into the kitchen a few times—once so the tíos could show off how much bullshit I'd been able to cram in my head the last few years; another time for a bucket-sized cup of soda. Mami and Tía were frying tostones and the last of the pastelitos. She appeared happier now and the way her hands worked on our dinner you would think she had a life somewhere else making rare and precious things. She nudged Tía every now and then, shit they must have been doing all their lives. As soon as Mami saw me though, she gave me the eye. Don't stay long, that eye said. Don't piss your old man off.

Papi was too busy arguing about Elvis to notice me. Then somebody mentioned María Montez and Papi barked, María Montez? Let me tell *you* about María Montez, compa'i.

Maybe I was used to him. His voice—louder than most adults'—didn't bother me none, though the other kids shifted uneasily in their seats. Wilquins was about to raise the volume on the TV, but Rafa said, I wouldn't do that. Muteboy had balls, though. He did it anyway and then sat down. Wilquins's pop came into the living room a second later, a bottle of Presidente in hand. That dude must have had Spider-senses or something. Did you raise that? he asked Wilquins and Wilquins nodded.

Is this your house? his pops asked. He looked ready to beat Wilquins silly but he lowered the volume instead.

See, Rafa said. You nearly got your ass *kicked.*

I met the Puerto Rican woman right after Papi had gotten the van. He was taking me on short trips, trying to cure me of my vomiting. It wasn't really working but I looked forward to our trips, even though at the end of each one I'd be sick. These were the only times me and Papi did anything together. When we were alone he treated me much better, like maybe I was his son or something.

Before each drive Mami would cross me.

Bendición, Mami, I'd say.

She'd kiss my forehead. Que Dios te bendiga. And then she would give me a handful of mentas because she wanted me to be OK. Mami didn't think these excursions would cure anything, but the one time she had brought it up to Papi he had told her to shut up, what did she know about anything anyway?

Me and Papi didn't talk much. We just drove around our neighborhood. Occasionally he'd ask, How is it?

And I'd nod, no matter how I felt.

One day I was sick outside of Perth Amboy. Instead of taking me home he went the other way on Industrial Avenue, stopping a few minutes later in front of a light blue house I didn't recognize. It reminded me of the Easter eggs we colored at school, the ones we threw out the bus windows at other cars.

The Puerto Rican woman was there and she helped me clean up. She had dry papery hands and when she rubbed the towel on my chest, she did it hard, like I was a bumper she was waxing. She was very thin and had a cloud of brown hair rising above her narrow face and the sharpest blackest eyes you've ever seen.

He's cute, she said to Papi.

Not when he's throwing up, Papi said.

What's your name? she asked me. Are you Rafa?

I shook my head.

Then it's Yunior, right?

I nodded.

You're the smart one, she said, suddenly happy with herself. Maybe you want to see my books?

They weren't hers. I recognized them as ones my father must have left in her house. Papi was a voracious reader, couldn't even go cheating without a paperback in his pocket.

Why don't you go watch TV? Papi suggested. He was looking at her like she was the last piece of chicken on earth.

We got plenty of channels, she said. Use the remote if you want.

The two of them went upstairs and I was too scared of what was happening to poke around. I just sat there, ashamed, expecting something big and fiery to crash down on our heads. I watched a whole hour of the news before Papi came downstairs and said, Let's go.

About two hours later the women laid out the food and like always nobody but the kids thanked them. It must be some Dominican tradition or something. There was everything I liked—chicharrones, fried chicken, tostones, sancocho, rice, fried cheese, yuca, avocado, potato salad, a meteor-sized hunk of pernil, even a tossed salad which I could do without—but when I joined the other kids around the serving table, Papi said, Oh no you don't, and took the paper plate out of my hand. His fingers weren't gentle.

What's wrong now? Tía asked, handing me another plate.

He ain't eating, Papi said. Mami pretended to help Rafa with the pernil.

Why can't he eat?

Because I said so.

The adults who didn't know us made like they hadn't heard a thing and Tío just smiled sheepishly and told everybody to go ahead and eat. All the kids—about ten of them now—trooped back into the living room with their plates a-heaping and all the adults ducked into the kitchen and the dining room, where the radio was playing loud-ass bachatas. I was the only one without a plate. Papi stopped me before I could get away from him. He kept his voice nice and low so nobody else could hear him.

If you eat anything, I'm going to beat you. ¿Entiendes?

I nodded.

And if your brother gives you any food, I'll beat him too. Right here in front of everybody. ¿Entiendes?

I nodded again. I wanted to kill him and he must have sensed it because he gave my head a little shove.

All the kids watched me come in and sit down in front of the TV.

What's wrong with your dad? Leti asked.

He's a dick, I said.

Rafa shook his head. Don't say that shit in front of people.

Easy for you to be nice when you're eating, I said.

Hey, if I was a pukey little baby, I wouldn't get no food either.

I almost said something back but I concentrated on the TV. I wasn't going to start it. No fucking way. So I watched Bruce Lee beat Chuck Norris into the floor of the Colosseum and tried to pretend that there was no food anywhere in the house. It was Tía who finally saved me. She came into the living room and said, Since you ain't eating, Yunior, you can at least help me get some ice.

I didn't want to, but she mistook my reluctance for something else.

I already asked your father.

She held my hand while we walked; Tía didn't have any kids but I could tell she wanted them. She was the sort of relative who always remembered your birthday but who you only went to visit because you had to. We didn't get past the first-floor landing before she opened her pocketbook and handed me the first of three pastelitos she had smuggled out of the apartment.

Go ahead, she said. And as soon as you get inside make sure you brush your teeth.

Thanks a lot, Tía, I said.

Those pastelitos didn't stand a chance.

She sat next to me on the stairs and smoked her cigarette. All the way down on the first floor and we could still hear the music and the adults and the television. Tía looked a ton like Mami; the two of them were both short and light-skinned. Tía smiled a lot and that was what set them apart the most.

How is it at home, Yunior?

What do you mean?

How's it going in the apartment? Are you kids OK?

I knew an interrogation when I heard one, no matter how sugar-coated it was. I didn't say anything. Don't get me wrong, I loved my tía, but something told me to keep my mouth shut. Maybe it was family loyalty, maybe I just wanted to protect Mami or I was afraid that Papi would find out—it could have been anything really.

Is your mom all right?

I shrugged.

Have there been lots of fights?

None, I said. Too many shrugs would have been just as bad as an answer. Papi's at work too much.

Work, Tía said, like it was somebody's name she didn't like.

Me and Rafa, we didn't talk much about the Puerto Rican woman. When we ate dinner at her house, the few times Papi had taken us over there, we still acted like nothing was out of the ordinary. Pass the ketchup, man. No sweat, bro. The affair was like a hole in our living room floor, one we'd gotten so used to circumnavigating that we sometimes forgot it was there.

By midnight all the adults were crazy dancing. I was sitting outside Tía's bedroom—where Madai was sleeping—trying not to attract attention. Rafa had me guarding the door; he and Leti were in there too, with some of the other kids, getting busy no doubt. Wilquins had gone across the hall to bed so I had me and the roaches to mess around with.

Whenever I peered into the main room I saw about twenty moms and dads dancing and drinking beers. Every now and then somebody yelled, Quisqueya! And then everybody else would yell and stomp their feet. From what I could see my parents seemed to be enjoying themselves.

Mami and Tía spent a lot of time side by side, whispering, and I kept expecting something to come of this, a brawl maybe. I'd never once been out with my family when it hadn't turned to shit. We weren't even theatrical or straight crazy like other families. We fought like sixth-graders, without any real dignity. I guess the whole night I'd been waiting for a blowup, something between Papi and Mami. This was how I always figured Papi would be exposed, out in public, where everybody would know.

You're a cheater!

But everything was calmer than usual. And Mami didn't look like she was about to say anything to Papi. The two of them danced every now and then but they never lasted more than a song before Mami joined Tía again in whatever conversation they were having.

I tried to imagine Mami before Papi. Maybe I was tired, or just sad, thinking about the way my family was. Maybe I already knew how it would all end up in a few years, Mami without Papi, and that was why I did it. Picturing her alone wasn't easy. It seemed like Papi had always been with her, even when we were waiting in Santo Domingo for him to send for us.

The only photograph our family had of Mami as a young woman, before she married Papi, was the one that somebody took of her at an election party that I found one day while rummaging for money to go to the arcade. Mami had it tucked into her immigration papers. In the photo, she's surrounded by laughing cousins I will never meet, who are all shiny from dancing, whose clothes are rumpled and loose. You can tell it's night and hot and that the mosquitos have been biting. She sits straight and even in a crowd she stands out, smiling quietly like maybe she's the one everybody's celebrating. You can't see her hands but I imagined they're knotting a straw or a bit of thread. This was the woman my father met a year later on the Malecón, the woman Mami thought she'd always be.

Mami must have caught me studying her because she stopped what she was doing and gave me a smile, maybe her first one of the night. Suddenly I wanted to go over and hug her, for no other reason than I loved her, but there were about eleven fat jiggling bodies between us. So I sat down on the tiled floor and waited.

I must have fallen asleep because the next thing I knew Rafa was kicking me and saying, Let's go. He looked like he'd been hitting those girls off; he was all smiles. I got to my feet in time to kiss Tía and Tío good-bye. Mami was holding the serving dish she had brought with her.

Where's Papi? I asked.

He's downstairs, bringing the van around. Mami leaned down to kiss me.

You were good today, she said.

And then Papi burst in and told us to get the hell downstairs before some pendejo cop gave him a ticket. More kisses, more handshakes and then we were gone.

I don't remember being out of sorts after I met the Puerto Rican woman, but I must have been because Mami only asked me questions when she thought something was wrong in my life. It took her about ten passes but finally she cornered me one afternoon when we were alone in the apartment. Our upstairs neighbors were beating the crap out of their kids, and me and her had been listening to it all afternoon. She put her hand on mine and said, Is everything OK, Yunior? Have you been fighting with your brother?

Me and Rafa had already talked. We'd been in the basement, where our parents couldn't hear us. He told me that yeah, he knew about her.

Papi's taken me there twice now, he said.

Why didn't you tell me? I asked.

What the hell was I going to say? *Hey, Yunior, guess what happened yesterday? I met Papi's sucia!*

I didn't say anything to Mami either. She watched me, very very closely. Later I would think, maybe if I had told her, she would have confronted him, would have done something, but who can know these things? I said I'd been having trouble in school and like that everything was back to normal between us. She put her hand on my shoulder and squeezed and that was that.

* * *

We were on the turnpike, just past Exit 11, when I started feeling it again. I sat up from leaning against Rafa. His fingers smelled and he'd gone to sleep almost as soon as he got into the van. Madai was out too but at least she wasn't snoring.

In the darkness, I saw that Papi had a hand on Mami's knee and that the two of them were quiet and still. They weren't slumped back or anything; they were both wide awake, bolted into their seats. I couldn't see either of their faces and no matter how hard I tried I could not imagine their expressions. Neither of them moved. Every now and then the van was filled with the bright rush of somebody else's headlights. Finally I said, Mami, and they both looked back, already knowing what was happening.

STUART DYBEK

Pet Milk

STUART DYBEK (1942–) is the author of three books: *Brass Knuckles, Childhood and Other Neighborhoods,* and *The Coast of Chicago.* His work has received numerous awards, including the PEN/Malamud Prize for "lifetime achievement in the short story form," an Academy-Institute Award from the Academy and Institute of Arts and Letters, a Whiting Writers' Award, four O. Henry Prizes, including an O. Henry First Prize, and fellowships from the NEA and the Guggenheim Foundation. He teaches writing at Western Michigan University.

Today I've been drinking instant coffee and Pet milk, and watching it snow. It's not that I enjoy the taste especially, but I like the way Pet milk swirls in the coffee. Actually, my favorite thing about Pet milk is what the can opener does to the top of the can. The can is unmistakable—compact, seamless looking, its very shape suggesting that it could condense milk without any trouble. The can opener bites in neatly, and the thick liquid spills from the triangular gouge with a different look and viscosity than milk. Pet milk isn't *real* milk. The color's off, to start with. There's almost something of the past about it, like old ivory. My grandmother always drank it in her coffee. When friends dropped over and sat around the kitchen table, my grandma would ask, "Do you take cream and sugar?" Pet milk was the cream.

There was a yellow plastic radio on her kitchen table, usually tuned to the polka station, though sometimes she'd miss it by half a notch and get the Greek station instead, or the Spanish, or the Ukrainian. In Chicago, where we lived, all the incompatible states of Europe were pressed together down at the staticky right end of the dial. She didn't seem to notice, as long as she wasn't hearing English. The radio, turned low, played constantly. Its top was warped and turning amber on the side where the tubes were. I remember the sound of it on winter afternoons after school, as I sat by her table watching the Pet milk swirl and cloud in the steaming coffee, and noticing, outside her window, the sky doing the same thing above the railroad yard across the street.

And I remember, much later, seeing the same swirling sky in tiny liqueur glasses containing a drink called a King Alphonse: the crème de cacao rising like smoke in repeated explosions, blooming in kaleidoscopic clouds through the layer of heavy cream. This was in the Pilsen, a little Czech restaurant where my girlfriend, Kate, and I would go sometimes in the evening. It was the first year out of college for both of us, and we had astonished ourselves by finding real jobs—no more waitressing or pumping gas, the way we'd done in school. I was investigating credit references at a bank, and she was doing something slightly above the rank of typist for Hornblower & Weeks, the investment firm. My bank showed training films that emphasized the importance of suitable dress, good grooming, and personal neatness, even for employees like me, who worked at the switchboard in the basement. Her firm issued directives on appropriate attire—skirts, for instance, should cover the knees. She had lovely knees.

Kate and I would sometimes meet after work at the Pilsen, dressed in our proper business clothes and still feeling both a little self-conscious and glamorous, as if we were impostors wearing disguises. The place had small, round oak tables, and we'd sit in a corner under a painting called "The Street Musicians of Prague" and trade future plans as if they were escape routes. She talked of going to grad school in Europe; I wanted to apply to the Peace Corps. Our plans for the future made us laugh and feel close, but those same plans somehow made anything more than temporary between us seem impossible. It was the first time I'd ever had the feeling of missing someone I was still with.

The waiters in the Pilsen wore short black jackets over long white aprons. They were old men from the old country. We went there often enough to have our own special waiter, Rudi, a name he pronounced with a rolled *R.* Rudi boned our trout and seasoned our salads, and at the end of the meal he'd bring the bottle of crème de cacao from the bar, along with two little glasses and a small pitcher of heavy cream, and make us each a King Alphonse right at our table. We'd watch as he'd fill the glasses halfway up with the syrupy brown liqueur, then carefully attempt to float a layer of cream on top. If he failed to float the cream, we'd get that one free.

"Who was King Alphonse anyway, Rudi?" I sometimes asked, trying to break his concentration, and if that didn't work I nudged the table with my foot so the glass would jiggle imperceptibly just as he was floating the cream. We'd usually get one on the house. Rudi knew what I was doing. In fact, serving the King Alphonses had been his idea, and he had also suggested the trick of jarring the table. I think it pleased him, though he seemed concerned about the way I'd stare into the liqueur glass, watching the patterns.

"It's not a microscope," he'd say. "Drink."

He liked us, and we tipped extra. It felt good to be there and to be able to pay for a meal.

Kate and I met at the Pilsen for supper on my twenty-second birthday. It was May, and unseasonably hot. I'd opened my tie. Even before looking at the dinner menu, we ordered a bottle of Mumm's and a dozen oysters apiece. Rudi made a sly remark when he brought the oysters on platters of ice. They were freshly opened and smelled of the sea. I'd heard people joke about oysters being aphrodisiac but never considered it anything but a myth—the kind of idea they still had in the old country.

We squeezed on lemon, added dabs of horseradish, slid the oysters into our mouths, and then rinsed the shells with champagne and drank the salty, cold juice. There was a beefy-looking couple eating schnitzel at the next table, and they stared at us with the repugnance that public oyster-eaters in the Midwest often encounter. We laughed and grandly sipped it all down. I was already half tipsy from drinking too fast, and starting to feel filled with a euphoric, aching energy. Kate raised a brimming oyster shell to me in a toast: "To the Peace Corps!"

"To Europe!" I replied, and we clunked shells.

She touched her wineglass to mine and whispered, "Happy birthday," and then suddenly leaned across the table and kissed me.

When she sat down again, she was flushed. I caught the reflection of her face in the glass-covered "The Street Musicians of Prague" above our table. I always loved seeing her in mirrors and windows. The reflections of her beauty startled me. I had told her that once, and she seemed to fend off the compliment, saying, "That's because you've learned what to look for," as if it were a secret I'd stumbled upon. But, this time, seeing her reflection hovering ghostlike upon an imaginary Prague was like seeing a future from which she had vanished. I knew I'd never meet anyone more beautiful to me.

We killed the champagne and sat twining fingers across the table. I was sweating. I could feel the warmth of her through her skirt under the table and I touched her leg. We still hadn't ordered dinner. I left money on the table and we steered each other out a little unsteadily.

"Rudi will understand," I said.

The street was blindingly bright. A reddish sun angled just above the rims of the tallest buildings. I took my suit coat off and flipped it over my shoulder. We stopped in the doorway of a shoe store to kiss.

"Let's go somewhere," she said.

My roommate would already be home at my place, which was closer. Kate lived up north, in Evanston. It seemed a long way away.

We cut down a side street, past a fire station, to a small park, but its gate was locked. I pressed close to her against the tall iron fence. We could smell the lilacs from a bush just inside the fence, and when I jumped for an overhanging branch my shirt sleeve hooked on a fence spike and tore, and petals rained down on us as the spring sprang from my hand.

We walked to the subway. The evening rush was winding down; we must have caught the last express heading toward Evanston. Once the train climbed from the tunnel to the elevated tracks, it wouldn't stop until the end of the line, on Howard. There weren't any seats together, so we stood swaying at the front of the car, beside the empty conductor's compartment. We wedged inside, and I clicked the door shut.

The train rocked and jounced, clattering north. We were kissing, trying to catch the rhythm of the ride with our bodies. The sun bronzed the windows on our side of the train. I lifted her skirt over her knees, hiked it higher so the sun shone off her thighs, and bunched it around her waist. She wouldn't stop kissing. She was moving her hips to pin us to each jolt of the train.

We were speeding past scorched brick walls, gray windows, back porches outlined in sun, roofs, and treetops—the landscape of the El I'd memorized from subway windows over a lifetime of rides: the podiatrist's foot sign past Fullerton; the bright pennants of Wrigley Field, at Addison; ancient hotels with TRANSIENTS WELCOME signs on their flaking back walls; peeling and graffiti-smudged billboards; the old cemetery just before Wilson Avenue. Even without looking, I knew almost exactly where we were. Within the compartment, the sound of our quick breathing was louder than the clatter of tracks. I was trying to slow down, to make it all last, and when she covered my mouth with her hand I turned my face to the window and looked out.

The train was braking a little from express speed, as it did each time it passed a local station. I could see blurred faces on the long wooden platform watching us pass—businessmen glancing up from folded newspapers, women clutching purses and shopping bags. I could see the expression on each face, momentarily arrested, as we flashed by. A high school kid in shirt sleeves, maybe sixteen, with books tucked under one arm and a cigarette in his mouth, caught sight of us, and in the instant before he disappeared he grinned and started to wave. Then he was gone, and I turned from the window, back to Kate, forgetting everything—the passing stations, the glowing late sky, even the sense of missing her—but that arrested wave stayed with me. It was as if I were standing on that platform, with my schoolbooks and a smoke, on one of those endlessly accumulated afternoons after school when I stood almost outside of time simply waiting for a train, and I thought how much I'd have loved seeing someone like us streaming by.

TONY EARLEY

The Prophet from Jupiter

TONY EARLEY is a native of North Carolina as well as a graduate of Warren Wilson College and the University of Alabama, where he received an M.F.A. in creative writing. A professor of English at Vanderbilt University, he has had fiction and nonfiction published in *The New Yorker, Harper's, Esquire, Story,* and *The Oxford American,* for which he is a contributing writer. He is the author of *Here We Are in Paradise,* a collection of short stories, and a forthcoming novel entitled *Jim the Boy.*

My house, the damkeeper's house, sits above the lake on Pierce-Arrow Point. The dam juts out of the end of the point and curves away across the cove into the ridge on the other side of the channel. On this side is the water, 115 feet deep at the base of the dam, and on the other side is air: the gorge, the river starting up again, rocks far down below, a vista. Seen from my windows, the dam looks like a bridge. There are houses on hundred-foot lots all the way around the lake, and too many real estate brokers. They all have jangling pockets full of keys, and four-wheel-drive station wagons with coffee cups sitting on the dashboards. The coffee cups are bigger at the bottom than they are at the top. Sometimes, at night, the real estate brokers pull up each other's signs and sling them into the lake.

A family on Tryon Bay has a Labrador retriever that swims in circles for hours, chasing ducks. Tourists stop on the bridge that crosses the bay and take the dog's picture. You can buy postcards in town with the dog on the front, swimming, swimming, the ducks always just out of reach. There is a red and white sign on the Tryon Bay Bridge that says NO JUMPING OR DIVING FROM BRIDGE, but teenage boys taunting each other and drunk on beer climb onto the rail and fling themselves off. I could drop the water level down a foot and a half any summer Saturday and paralyze all I wanted. Sometimes rednecks whoop and yell *Nigger!* and throw beer bottles at Junie Wilson, who walks up and down Highway 20 with a coat hanger around his neck. Junie drops a dollar bill into the water every time he crosses the bridge.

The Prophet from Jupiter brings his five young sons to the bridge to watch the Lab swim. The six of them stand in a line at the guardrail and clap and wave their arms and shout encouragement to the dog. The Prophet drives an ancient blue Lincoln that is big as a yacht. He says he drove it in another life, meaning Florida. Down in the water, the ducks let the dog get almost to them before they fly away. They fly maybe thirty, forty yards, that's all, and splash back down. The townies call the dog Shithead. You may not believe me, but I swear I have heard ducks laugh. Shithead, as he paddles around the bay, puffs like he is dying. This is where I live and this is what I think: a dam is an unnatural thing, like a diaphragm.

The most important part of my job is to maintain a constant pond level. But the lake rises all night, every night; the river never stops. This will worry you after a while. When I drive below town, coming back toward home, I'm afraid I'll meet the lake coming down through the gorge. When Lake Glen was built, it covered the old town of Uree with eighty-five feet of water. As the dam was raised higher and higher across the river, workmen cut the steeple off the Uree Baptist Church so it would not stick up through the water, but they did not tear down the houses. Fish swim in and out of the doors. Old Man Bill Burdette, who lived beside the church, left his 1916 chain-drive Reo truck parked beside his house when he moved away.

The diver who inspected the dam in 1961 told the Mayor that he saw a catfish as big as a man swimming by the floodgates. It is a local legend, the size of the catfish the diver saw. At night I fish for it, from the catwalk connecting the floodgates, using deep-sea tackle and cow guts for bait. It hangs in the water facing the dam, just above the lake's muddy bottom. Its tail moves slowly, and it listens to the faint sound of the river glittering on the other side of the concrete. The Prophet from Jupiter says, *When you pull your giant fish out of the water, it will speak true words.* When they tell history, people will remember me because of the fish, even if I don't catch it.

The Prophet from Jupiter's real name is Archie Simpson. He sold real estate, and made a fortune, in Jupiter, Florida, until nine years ago, when God told him—just as he closed a $4 million condominium deal in Port St. Lucie—that he was the one true prophet who would lead the Christians in the last days before the Rapture. The Prophet says his first words after God finished talking were, *Jesus Christ, you gotta be kidding.* He is not shy about telling the story, and does not seem crazy. He has a young wife who wears beaded Indian headbands and does not shave under her arms.

Old Man Bill Burdette's four sons hired divers and dragged their father's Reo truck out of the lake fifty years to the day after the water rose. It was almost buried in mud, and hadn't rusted at all. The Burdette boys spent six thousand dollars restoring the old Reo and then said to anyone who would listen, *I don't know why Daddy left it. It was just like new.* Bill Junior, the eldest son, drives it in the town parade every Fourth of July, the back loaded with waving grandchildren. The oldest ones look embarrassed.

Before I start fishing, I pour ripe blood from the bottom of my bait bucket into the water. I use treble hooks sharp as razors. A reel like a winch. Randy, the assistant damkeeper, is an orderly at the hospital in Hendersonville, and fishes with me after he gets off work. He does not believe the story about the fish as big as a man. I fish all night. Sometimes small catfish, ripping intestines from the treble hooks (they shake their heads like dogs, pulling), impale themselves and make a small noise like crying when I pull them out of the water. I hold them by the tail and hit their heads against the rail of the catwalk and toss them backward over the edge of the dam.

At dawn I open the small gate that lets water into the turbine house, throw the generator switches—there are four—and go to bed. The Town of Lake Glen makes a million dollars a year selling electricity. Everybody who works for the Town of Lake Glen has a town truck to drive. The trucks are traded for new ones every two years, and Lake Glen town employees use them like whores, driving at high speed through all the potholes they possibly can, because the trucks do not have to last. The Prophet from Jupiter makes miniature ladder-backed chairs that he sells wholesale to the gift shops on the highway. His young wife braids long bands of cowhide into bullwhips and attaches them to clean pine handles. With a hot tool she burns a small cross and the words LAKE GLEN, NORTH CAROLINA on the sides of the handles. She once said to me, *I know that what my husband says about God is true because every time we make love he fills me with the most incredible light.* The bullwhips she makes hang, moving in the draft from the cars on the highway, in front of the gift shops, and tourists stop and buy them by the dozen. It is inexplicable. In town, in front of the Rogue Mountain Restaurant, there is a plywood cutout of a cross-eyed bear wearing patched overalls. The bear holds up a red and white sign that says EAT. Once, during lunch in the Rogue Mountain Restaurant, the Prophet from Jupiter looked down into his bowl of vegetable soup and said, *You know, in the last days Christians won't be able to get corn.* LAKE GLEN, NORTH CAROLINA. The high-voltage wires leading away from the turbine house, you can actually hear them hum.

Sometime during the afternoon—cartoons are on television, the turbines have spun all day, in the Town Hall they are counting money, the skiers are sunburned in their shining boats, and the fishermen are drunk—the water level drops back down to full pond and the alarm goes off. I get out of bed and go down the narrow stairs to the turbine house and close the gate. The lake leans out over me. I feel better when I get back to the top of the stairs. All around Lake Glen it is brilliant summer: the town policemen park beside the beach and look out from under the brims of their Smokey the Bear hats at the college girls glistening in the sun. The night of the Fourth of July, the main channel of the lake fills up with boats, and seen from the dam, the running lights on the dark water glitter like stars. The fireworks draw lines on the sky like the ghosts of the veins in your eyes after you have stared into the sun.

People who should know better play jokes on Junie Wilson. If they tell him that hair spray will scare away ghosts, he carries a can with him everywhere he goes, like Mace, until the joke gets around and somebody tells him differently. If they tell him that ghosts live in ski-boat gas tanks, he will not walk by the marina for days or get within two hundred yards of a fast boat. The Prophet from Jupiter says that Junie has the gift of true sight. The Mayor gives Junie rides to keep him out of trouble.

This is what it's like to live on Lake Glen: in the spring, before the water is warm enough for the skiers to get on the lake, the sun shines all the way through you and you twist down inside yourself, like a seed, and think about growing. There are red and white signs on the water side of the dam that say DANGER MAINTAIN A DISTANCE OF 200 YARDS, but you can't read them from that far away. In April, the wind blows down out of the mountains and across the cove toward my house, and the sun and the water smell like my wife's hair. I don't know any other way to tell you about it. Along the western shore, in the campgrounds beside the highway, gas lanterns glow like ghosts against the mountain. Boys and girls who will never see one another again, and somehow know it, make desperate promises and rub against each other in the laurel; they wade in their underwear in the cold river. In the summer night bullwhips pop like rifles.

Lake Glen was built between the mountains—Rogue Mountain and Rumbling Caesar—in 1927 by the Lake Glen Development Company. They built the dam, the municipal building, and a hotel with two hundred rooms before the stock market crashed. My wife's name is Elisabeth. She lives, until I leave Lake Glen, with her mother in Monte Sano, Alabama, and has nothing to say to me. Twice a day the town gives guided pontoon-boat tours of the lake. The boat stops two hundred yards from the dam, and I can hear the guide over the tinny loudspeaker explain how it would be dangerous to get any closer. Two summers ago the town made a deal with the family on Tryon Bay to keep Shithead penned until the tour boat came to the bay at ten and two. The ducks, however, proved to be undependable. Shithead in his pen became despondent. Tourists pay two dollars a pop to take the tour. The problem was that the ducks swim on Tryon Bay every day, you just never know when. Elisabeth says that for years I had nothing to say to her, and that I shouldn't expect her to have much to say to me. I am ashamed to admit that this is true. There are hurricane-fence gates at each end of the dam, and only Randy and the Mayor and I have keys. When fishermen approach it in boats, I stand in the kitchen and ring the alarm bell until they leave. They shout at me perched on top of a cliff of water. This is something they do not consider.

The old people say that when Aunt Plutina Williams left her house for the last time before the lake was flooded, she closed her windows and shut and locked the doors. The Lake Glen Development Company planned, before Black Friday, to build four more two-hundred-room hotels and five eighteen-hole golf courses. Some of the streets in the town of Lake Glen still have the old development company names: Air Strip Road, Yacht Club Drive, H. L. Mencken Circle.

Elisabeth, before she left, taught the church preschool class every other Sunday, and when she got home from church repeated for me, word for word, everything the kids said. One Easter she brought her class here for an Easter-egg hunt, and when she unlatched the gate on the front porch, they tumbled in their new clothes down the grassy slope toward the lake. Elisabeth followed me down to the turbine house once, and over the roar of the generators screamed into my ear, *Why won't you talk to me? What are you holding back?* The new police chief asked for a key to the hurricane-fence gates, but the Mayor refused to give him one.

The Lake Glen Hotel is sold and renovated about every five years, and banners are hung across the front of it on the days it reopens. A crowd gathers and drinks free Cokes. Old men sit and watch from the shade under the arches of the municipal building. A Florida Yankee makes a speech about the coming renaissance in Lake Glen. The Mayor cuts the ribbon and everybody claps. Most of the old streets are dead ends. The town of Lake Glen doesn't have an air strip or a yacht club: the hotel never stays open longer than a season. Most of the time, the signs of every real estate broker in town are lined up in front of it like stiff flags.

Elisabeth stood in the lake that Easter in a new yellow dress; the water was up over her calves. With one hand, she pulled her skirt up slightly from the waist. She held a glass jar in the other hand and looked into the water. The children squealed on the bank. Maybe then, watching Elisabeth, I believed for a minute in the risen Christ. This is what has happened: my wife, Elisabeth, is pregnant with the new police chief's child. Randy never mentions my misfortune, unless I mention it first. I am grooming him to be the new damkeeper. From the catwalk at night we see in the distance across the channel the lights of the town. There is no reason to come here and stay in a hotel with two hundred rooms. There is no reason to stay here at all.

Randy fishes for crappie with an ultralight rod that is limber as a switch, and will some nights pull seventy-five, a hundred, out of the dark water, glittering, like nickels. He comes to the dam straight from work and fishes in his white orderly clothes. He smells disinfected and doesn't stay all night. This is what I have done: I took the passenger-side shoulder harness out of my Town of Lake Glen truck and bolted it with long screw anchors to the side of the dam, behind the catwalk. I buckle up when I fish. I don't want to be pulled into the water.

Randy is twenty years old and already has two children. He is not married. His girlfriend is tall and skinny and mean-looking. Randy says she fucks like a cat. The old people say that the morning of the day the water came up, they loaded Aunt Plutina Williams into the bed of Old Man Bill Burdette's new truck. Somebody asked Aunt Plutina why she closed her windows and locked her doors, and she said, *Why you never know, sometime I just might want to come back.* Junie Wilson has seen her. I am afraid that someday I will see her, too. Maintain a constant pond level. The last time I slept with Elisabeth, two hearts beat inside her.

Randy will go far in this town. He knows how to live here without making anyone mad, which is a considerable gift. Sometimes I can see Elisabeth bending her back into the new police chief. Randy says don't think about it. He is an ex-redneck who learned the value of cutting his hair and being nice to Floridians. He someday might be mayor. He brought his girlfriend to the town employee barbecue and swim party at the Mayor's glass house, and her nipples were stiff, like buttons. My shoulder harness is a good thing: sometimes late at night I doze, leaning forward against it, and dream of something huge, suspended in the water beneath me, its eyes yellow and open. At the party I saw Randy whisper something into his girlfriend's ear. She looked down at the front of her shirt and said out loud, *Well Jesus Christ, Randy. What Do You Want Me To Do About It?*

During the summers in the thirties the Lake Glen Hotel was a refuge for people who could not afford to summer in the Berkshires or the Catskills anymore. Down the road from the hotel, where the Community Center is now, there was a dance pavilion built on wooden pilings out over the bay. Elisabeth stood in the lake in a new yellow dress, holding a jar. The kids from the Sunday school squatted at the edge of the water and helped her look for tadpoles. The Mayor was diagnosed with testicular cancer in the spring, and waits to see if he had his operation in time. He owns a mile and a half of undeveloped shoreline. Real estate brokers lick their lips.

From my dam I have caught catfish that weighed eighteen, twenty-four, and thirty-one pounds: just babies. Randy said the thirty-one-pounder was big enough. He thinks I should stop. I think I scare him. I got my picture in the paper in Hendersonville, holding up the fish. My beard is long and significant; the catfish looks wise. I mailed a copy to Elisabeth in Monte Sano. The new police chief drives up to the hurricane-fence gate after Randy goes home and shines his spotlight on me. I don't even unbuckle my harness anymore. The Mayor is not running for reelection. I will stay until inauguration day. I learned this from the old men in the hardware store: the new police chief will live with Elisabeth and their child in the damkeeper's house; Randy's girlfriend is pregnant again, and the house isn't big enough for three kids. The Town of Lake Glen police cars are four-wheel-drive station wagons with blue lights on the dashboards. It is hard to tell the cops here from the real estate brokers.

The dance-pavilion orchestra was made up of college boys from Chapel Hill, and black musicians who had lost their summer hotel jobs up north. The college boys and the black men played nightly for tips, in their shirt-sleeves on the covered bandstand, tunes that had been popular during the twenties, and on the open wooden floor out over the water the refugees danced under paper lanterns and blazing mosquito torches. Bootleggers dressed in overalls and wide-brimmed hats drove their Model T's down out of the laurel and sold moonshine in the parking lot.

The new police chief came here from New York State and is greatly admired by the Florida Yankees for his courtesy and creased trousers. I try to hate him, but it is too much like hating myself for what I have done, for what I have left undone. I am the man who didn't miss his water. Florida Yankees have too much money and nothing to do. They bitch about the municipal government and run against each other for city council. They drive to Hendersonville wearing sweat suits and walk around and around the mall. Randy will not express a preference for city council candidates, not even to me. He will go far. His girlfriend will be the first lady of the town of Lake Glen.

The Mayor came here on summer break from Chapel Hill in 1931 and never went back. He played second trumpet in the Lake Glen orchestra. He took his trust fund and bought land all the way around the lake for eighteen cents on the dollar. He is the only rich man I can stand to be around. At the end of the night, the Mayor says—three, four o'clock in the morning—after the band had packed up their instruments and walked back to the hotel, the last of the dancers stood at the pavilion rail and looked out at the lake. Fog grew up out of the water. Frogs screeched in the cattails near the river channel, and there were cold places in the air. I can hear the new police chief's radio as he sits in his Jeep, outside the gates of the dam. The Mayor says that the last dancers would peel off their clothes and dive white and naked into the foggy lake. He says that when they laughed, he could hear it from the road as he walked away, or from his boat as it drifted between the mountains on the black lake, just before first light.

I hear laughter sometimes, when I am on the catwalk at night, or faint music, coming over the water, and it makes me think about ghosts, about those ruined dancers, looking out across the lake. Some nights I think that if I drove over to the Community Center and turned off my lights, I could see them dancing on the fog. Junie Wilson has taught me to believe in ghosts. The music I hear comes from a distance: I can never make out the tune. I remember that Elisabeth used to put her heels against the bed and raise herself up—she used to push her breasts together with her hands. *Ghosts is with us everywhere,* Junie Wilson says. Whenever I drop the lake down at the end of the season, the old, sawed-off pilings from the dance pavilion stick up out of the mud like the ribs of a sunken boat.

The old people say that the town of Uree held a square dance on the bank of the river the night before the water came up. They say that Jim Skipper, drunk on moonshine, shit in the middle of his kitchen floor and set his house on fire. The week before, the Lake Glen Development Company dug up the dead in the Uree Baptist Church graveyard and reburied them beside the new brick church on the ridge overlooking Buffalo Shoals. They even provided new coffins for the two Confederate soldiers who had been buried wrapped in canvas. The work crews stole their brass buttons. This is something that happened: Elisabeth and I tried to have a baby for seven years before we went to see a fertility specialist in Asheville.

The old people say that the whole town whooped and danced in circles in front of Jim Skipper's burning house, and that boys and girls desperate for each other sneaked off and humped urgently in the deserted buildings, that last night before the town began to sink. All the trees around the town of Uree had been cut. They lay tangled where they fell. The dead twisted and turned in their new holes, away from the sound of the river.

During the Second World War the government ran the Lake Glen Hotel as a retreat for Army Air Corps officers on leave from Europe. The Mayor says that the pilots—the ones who were not joined at the hotel by their wives—lay in still rows on the beach all day, sweating moonshine, and at night went either to the dance pavilion—where they tried to screw summer girls, and girls who walked in homemade dresses down out of the laurel—or to the whorehouse on the second floor of the Glen Haven Restaurant, a mile outside the city limits, where the whores were from Charleston, some of them exotic and Gullah, and the jukebox thumped with swing. The Mayor says that the Glen Haven during the war was like Havana before the revolution. The house specialty was fried catfish, and hush puppies made with beer. The Prophet from Jupiter and his young wife live with their five sons in the Glen Haven building because the rent is so cheap. There are ten rooms upstairs, five on each side of a narrow hall. One room, the Prophet says, always smells like catfish, even though they have scrubbed it. One Sunday morning in the early spring, the Prophet's son Zeke told Elisabeth that he dreamed Jesus came to his house and pulled a big bucket of water out of a well and everybody drank from it.

The fertility specialist, Dr. Suzanne Childress, said that I had lethargic sperm. *I knew it wasn't me,* Elisabeth said. *I knew it wasn't me.*

Dr. Suzanne Childress said, *Your sperm count is normal. They just do not swim well enough to reach and fertilize Elisabeth's ova.*

They say that Jim Skipper camped out under his wagon for three weeks beside the rising lake. He borrowed a boat from the Lake Glen Development Company and paddled around the sinking houses. He looked in the windows until they disappeared, and he banged on the tin roofs with his paddle. He collected all the trash that floated to the surface—bottles and porch planks and blue mason jars—and put it in his wagon and studied it at night by a fire. He said he did not know how to live anywhere else. They say that before Jim Skipper shot himself, he stood in his borrowed boat and pissed down Old Man Bill Burdette's chimney.

Elisabeth said, *You always thought it was me, didn't you?*

Dr. Suzanne Childress said, *I think that perhaps we can correct your problem with dietary supplements. Vitamins. Do you exercise?*

Elisabeth said, *I'm ovulating right now. I can tell.*

Dr. Suzanne Childress said, *I know.*

They closed the dance pavilion for good in 1944 when a moonshiner named Rudy Thomas, in a fight over a Glen Haven whore, stabbed a B-27 pilot from New York eleven times and pushed him into the lake. Rudy Thomas died of tuberculosis in Central Prison in Raleigh in 1951. They say that Jim Skipper was a good man but one crazy son of a bitch.

Several nights a week during his second summer in town, the Mayor leaned a chambermaid named Lavonia over the windscreen of his 1928 Chris-Craft and screwed her until his legs got so weak that he almost fell out of the boat. Junie Wilson says that the boxes on the sides of telephone poles—if the ghosts have turned them on—make him so drunk that he is afraid he is going to fall into the lake. The coat hanger around Junie's neck protects him from evil spirits.

Sweet Lavonia, the Mayor says, *had the kind of body that a young man would paint on the side of his airplane before he flew off to fight in a war.*

The young Mayor took his clothes off as he drove his boat fast across the dark lake. Lavonia waited between two boulders on the shore near Uree Shoals. The Mayor cut the engine and drifted into the cove. Lavonia stepped out from between the rocks, pulled her skirt up around her waist, and waded out to the boat. The white Mayor glowed in the darkness and played gospel songs on his trumpet while she walked through the water. There wasn't a house or a light in sight. Lavonia told him every night while he squeezed her breasts, *You're putting the devil inside of me.* The boat turned in the water, and the Mayor owned everything he could see.

Randy in his orderly clothes, jigging for crappie, tells me there is nothing wrong with me, that to make a woman pregnant you have to fuck her in a certain way, that's all. You have to put your seed where it will take.

Junie Wilson woke me up one morning yelling, *Open the gate, open the gate.* One of the town cops had told him that ghosts wouldn't walk across a dam, that walking across a dam while it made electricity was the way for a man to get rid of his ghosts once and for all. Junie sees three ghosts in his dreams: he sees a man standing in a boat, he sees a woman looking out the window of a house underwater, and he sees his mama wading out into the lake. This dream torments Junie most, because he doesn't know how to swim. He stands on the bank and yells for her to come back. We walked across the dam, the water up close beside Junie, the air falling away beside me. Junie said, *She better get out of that water if she knows what's good for her.* What my wife said is true: I never thought it was me. Elisabeth after we made love kept her legs squeezed tight together, even after she went to sleep. *Ghosts is keeping me awake,* Junie said. *I got to get rid of these ghosts so I can get me some sleep. Ghosts is crucifying me.* Out in the bay the new police chief watched from his boat. The siren whooped once.

Something's wrong with me, Elisabeth whispered. *I can't have a baby.*

I said, *I still love you. Shhh.*

Before we went to see Dr. Suzanne Childress, I liked to sit astride Elisabeth, hard and slick between her breasts. Lavonia tried to kill the baby inside her by drinking two quarts of moonshine that she bought in the pavilion parking lot from a bootlegger named Big Julie Cooper. Junie didn't speak until he was four. Ghosts began to chase him when he was twelve. The first time Lavonia saw Junie touching himself, she whipped him with a belt and told him that if he ever did that again, a white man would come with a big knife and cut it off. Elisabeth, when I was finished, wiped her chest and neck off with a towel.

Bugs fly like angels into the white light of the gas lantern and then spin and fall into the water. Randy jabs the air with his index finger: *It's special pussy, man, way back in the back. It burns like fire.* The Mayor gave Lavonia a little money every month until she died, three years ago. He does not give money to Junie because Junie drops dollar bills off the Tryon Bay Bridge. He does it so that the ghosts won't turn on their machines when he walks by telephone poles. The Mayor says, *Jesus Christ, if I gave that boy a million dollars, he'd throw every bit of it off that damn bridge.*

Randy says, *Man, women go crazy when you start hitting that baby spot. They'll scratch the hell out of you. You gotta time it right, that's all. You gotta let it go when you hit it.* He slaps the back of one hand into the other. *Bang. You gotta get the pussy they don't want you to have.*

Junie Wilson and I walked back and forth across the dam until the alarm went off and I had to close the gate and shut down the generators. I didn't tell Junie about the machines in the turbine house. The new police chief still watched from the bay. Elisabeth said over the phone from Monte Sano, *I know you won't believe it now, but all I ever wanted was for you to pay attention to me.* In a sterile men's room in the doctor's office, I put my hands against the wall and Elisabeth jerked me off into a glass bottle. The Mayor eats bananas to keep his weight up. Junie Wilson said that he did not feel any better, and I said that walking across the dam does not always work.

In August the air over the lake is so thick you can see it, and distances through the haze look impossible to cross. The mountains disappear before lunch, and even the skiers in their fast boats get discouraged. The water is smooth and gray, and the town of Lake Glen shimmers across the channel like the place it tried to be. At the beach, policemen sit in their station wagons with the air conditioners running. The college girls are tanned the color of good baseball gloves. Randy's girlfriend is starting to gain weight, and Randy fishes less; the crappie have all but stopped biting. When it is this hot, I have trouble sleeping, even during the day, and eat white ice cream straight out of the box with a fat spoon. The Prophet from Jupiter winks and says that in hot weather his wife smells like good earth, and that God has blessed him in more ways than one. The Prophet and his wife have made love in every room at the Glen Haven. In the hot summer, the ghosts keep their machines turned on all the time, and Junie Wilson staggers through town like a drunk. If there is one true thing I know to tell you, it is this: in North Carolina, even in the mountains, it takes more than a month of your life to live through August.

September is no cooler, but the sky begins to brighten, like a promise. Gradually it changes from white back to blue, and the town begins to pack itself up for leaving. The college girls go first, their tans already fading, and motor homes with bicycles strapped to their backs groan up out of the campgrounds to the shimmering highway. Boys and girls damp with sweat sneak away to say good-bye in the laurel and make promises one last time. Around the lake, family by family, summer people close up their houses and go back to where they came from in June. The Florida Yankees have mercifully decided among themselves who the new mayor will be—he is from Fort Lauderdale and is running unopposed—but the council candidates drive around town at night and tear down each other's campaign posters. My beard is down to the middle of my chest. Junie Wilson walks through town with his hands held up beside his face like blinders, to keep from seeing the bright faces stapled to the telephone poles. At night, the frogs hum one long, deep note, and one afternoon I slept in front of a fan and dreamed it was spring: Elisabeth waded in the lake and I sat on the porch and held a baby whose hair smelled like the sun. When I wake up now, my bathroom makes me sad because the mirror is so big. I dialed a 1-900 number for a date and charged it to the Town of Lake Glen. A woman named Betty said she wanted me to come in her mouth. In the closed-up summer houses, burglar alarms squeal in frequencies that only bats can hear, and the lights burn all night, turned on and off by automatic timers, but the rooms are empty and still.

In the fall, the wild ducks fly away after the summer people in great, glittering vees. Maples catch fire on the sides of the mountains around the lake, and weekend tourists drive up from Charlotte and Greenville to point at the leaves and buy pumpkins. The ducks skim low over the channel in front of my house, their wings whistling like blood, and then cross the dam, suddenly very high in the air. The Floridians burn leaves in their yards and inhale the smoke like Mentholatum. Randy said, *Man, I hope there ain't going to be any hard feelings,* and stopped coming to fish. Early one morning my line stiffened and moved through the water for twenty yards. When I set the hook, the stiff rod bent double against a great weight. And then it was gone. And that was it. The next night the new police chief sat outside the gate in his Jeep and played an easy-listening radio station over his loudspeaker. In the town of Uree, Aunt Plutina Williams sits and looks out the window of her house. The sun is never brighter than a distant lantern. Jim Skipper wanders in and out of the houses. A giant fish moves through the air like a zeppelin. The new police chief said over the loudspeaker, *Look, chief, I just want,* and then stopped talking and backed up and drove away.

In November 1928 the Lake Glen dam almost washed away. A flash flood, shot brown with mud, boiled down out of the mountains after a week of rain, and the damkeeper, new at the job, did not open the floodgates in time. The water rose and filled the lake bed like a bowl before it spilled over the top of the dam. Old Man Bill Burdette, who lived five miles away, drove down the mountain in his new truck to warn people downstream: the lake had turned itself back into a river and was cutting a channel through the earth around the side of the dam.

They say that the men of the Lake Glen Development Company construction crews hauled six heavy freight wagons of red roofing slate from the hotel site and threw it over the side of the gorge. Local men, when they heard, came down out of the laurel and worked in the rain filling sandbags and tossing them into the hole. But still the water ran muddy around the side of the dam and over the tops of the sandbags and the roofing. The workers, without waiting for orders, rolled the six empty wagons in on top of the pile. They say that they carried all of the furniture and both stoves out of the damkeeper's house and threw them in. They pushed three Model T Fords belonging to the company, as well as the superintendent's personal Pierce-Arrow, into the channel the river had cut around the side of the dam. But the water still snaked its way through the wreckage, downhill toward the riverbed.

This October, Town of Lake Glen workmen hung huge red and yellow banners shaped like leaves from wires stretched between the telephone poles. They built cider stands and arts and crafts booths and a small plywood stage in the parking lot in front of the Lake Glen Hotel. The Chamber of Commerce hired a small carnival for the third Saturday in the month, called the whole thing ColorFest!, and promoted it on the Asheville TV station. Hundreds of tourists showed up, wearing bright sweaters even though it was warm. I saw townies look at me when they thought I wasn't looking, and their eyes said I wonder what he's going to do. My beard is a torrent of hair. A high school clogging team from Hendersonville stomped on the wooden stage. Old men sat and watched from underneath the arches of the municipal building. Little boys stood at the edge of the stage and looked up through the swirling white petticoats of the girl dancers. Shithead's owners walked him through the crowd on a leash. The Prophet from Jupiter and his wife sold miniature ladder-backed chairs and bullwhips from a booth, and gave away spiritual tracts about the coming Rapture. An old Cherokee, wearing a Sioux war bonnet, for two dollars a pop posed for pictures with tourist kids. Junie Wilson, crying for somebody to help him before the white man came to get him, showed his erection to three of Old Man Bill Burdette's great-granddaughters, who were sitting in the back of the 1916 Reo truck.

In 1928 the workers at the collapsing dam looked at each other in the rain. Everything seemed lost. The superintendent of the Lake Glen Development Company produced a Colt revolver and a box of cartridges. Big Julie Cooper took the superintendent's gun when nobody else would and one at a time shot twenty-four development company mules right between the eyes. The workers threw the dead and dying mules in on top of the cars and the wagons and the red roofing slate and the furniture and the stoves, before the rain slacked and the water retreated back to the lake side of the dam. Then the superintendent threw his hat into the gorge and danced a jig and said, *Boys, you don't miss your water until your dam starts to go.* When the roads dried out, the development company brought in a steam shovel to cover the debris and the mules with dirt and rock blasted from the sides of the mountains, but not before the weather cleared and warmed and the mules swelled and rotted in the late-autumn sun. They say that you could smell the mules for miles—

some of them even exploded—and that workmen putting the roof on the hotel, at the other end of the channel, wore kerchiefs dipped in camphor tied around their faces. They say that a black funnel cloud of buzzards and crows spun in the air over the gorge, and that you could see it from a long way away. At night bears came down off of Rumbling Caesar and ate the rotting mules. It is all covered by a thick growth of kudzu now, and every winter, after the vines die, I think of digging into the still-visible spine in the gorge beside the dam to see what I can find. Big Julie Cooper says, *By God, now let me tell you something, that son of a bitch liked to of went.*

When Old Man Bill Burdette's three great-granddaughters screamed, the new police chief twisted Junie Wilson's arm behind his back. Junie screamed, *Jesus, Jesus, Oh God, Please Don't Cut Me,* and tried to get away. The whole ColorFest! crowd, including the Indian chief, ran up close and silently watched while Junie and the new police chief spun around and around. *I'm not going to hurt you, Junie,* the new police chief said. Two other town cops showed up and held Junie down while the new police chief very efficiently handcuffed him and tied his legs together with three bullwhips that the Mayor brought from the Prophet from Jupiter's booth. The new police chief covered Junie's erection with a red ColorFest! banner shaped like a leaf. Junie's coat hanger was bent and twisted around his face. The new police chief pulled it off and handed it to the Mayor. Junie screamed for his mother over and over until his eyes rolled back in his head and his body began to jerk. Shithead howled. The high school clogging team from Hendersonville the whole time stomped and spun, wild-eyed, on the flimsy plywood stage.

The first Monday after Thanksgiving, I raised one of the floodgates halfway and lowered the lake eight feet. Randy will fill the lake back up the first Monday in February. It will be his job to maintain a constant pond level, to hold the water in the air, to try to imagine what the weather will be four days or two weeks from now. Every day I try to piss off the river side of the dam in a stream that will reach from me to the bottom of the gorge, but it is impossible to do. The water comes apart in the air. When the lake level is down, the exposed pilings of the boathouses are spindly like the legs of old men. Randy's girlfriend has started to show, and her breasts are heavy. The new police chief spends three days in Monte Sano with my wife every other week. The hotel is dark and for sale and locked up tight.

When the water is down and the mud between the shore and the water dries out, the people who live here year-round rake the leaves and trash from the lake bottom in front of their houses, and replace the rotten boards on their docks and the rotten rungs on their uncovered ladders. All around the lake, circular saws squeal. The water over the town of Uree seems darker somehow than the rest of the lake, and I've always wanted to drop the lake down far enough to see what is down there. At the end of that last night, when Jim Skipper's house had burned down to a glowing pile of ashes, the people of the town of Uree sang, "Shall We Gather at the River Where Bright Angel Feet Have Trod," and then stood around, just looking at their houses and barns and sheds, wishing they had done more, until the sun came over the dam at the head of the gorge.

The Mayor stays mostly in his house now. His successor has been elected. Randy wore a tie and met with the mayor-elect to discuss ways to generate electricity more efficiently. The Mayor keeps his thermostat set at eighty-five and still cannot get warm. The word from the state hospital in Morganton is that Junie Wilson has no idea where he is or what has happened and screams every time he sees a white doctor.

The lake began to freeze during a cold snap the week before Christmas. There were circles of whiter ice over the deeper water where part of the lake thawed in the sun and then refroze again at night. The temperature dropped fast all day Christmas Eve, and the ice closed in and trapped a tame duck on Tryon Bay. Shithead, going out after the duck, broke through a soft spot in the ice and could not get back out.

Within fifteen minutes, most of the people who live in the town of Lake Glen were on the Tryon Bay Bridge, screaming, *Come On, Shithead, Come On, Boy, You Can Do It.* Nobody could remember who had a canoe, or think of how to rescue the dog. The Prophet from Jupiter, before anyone could stop him, ran across the frozen mud and slid headfirst like a baseball player out onto the ice. The duck frozen to the lake in the middle of the bay flailed its wings. I stood beside the new police chief on the bank and screamed to the Prophet, *Lie Still, Lie Still,* that we would find a way to save him.

The Prophet from Jupiter moved his lips and began to inch his way forward across the ice. It groaned under his weight. Cracks in the ice shot away from his body like frozen lightning. The Prophet kept going, an inch at a time, none of us breathing until he reached forward into the hole and grabbed Shithead by the collar and pulled him up onto the ice. It held. The dog quivered for a second and then skittered back toward shore, his belly low to the frozen lake.

We opened our mouths to cheer, but there was a crack like a gunshot, and the Prophet from Jupiter disappeared. He came up, once—he looked surprised more than anything else, his face deathly white, his mouth a black O—and then disappeared again and did not come back up. On the bridge the Prophet's five sons ran in place and screamed and held their arms toward the water. Randy's girlfriend kept her arms wrapped tight around the Prophet's wife, who shouted, *Oh Jesus, Oh Jesus,* and tried to jump off of the bridge. By the time we got boats onto the lake, and broke the ice with sledgehammers, and pulled grappling hooks on the ends of ropes through the dark water and hooked the Prophet and dragged him up, there was nothing even God could do. The duck frozen to the lake had beaten itself to death against the ice. The new police chief sat down on the bank and cried like a baby.

Elisabeth's water broke that night. The new police chief called the Mayor and left for Monte Sano, and the Mayor called me. I walked back and forth and back and forth across the dam until all the ghosts of Lake Glen buzzed in my ears like electricity: I saw the Prophet from Jupiter riding with Old Man Bill Burdette, down the streets of Uree in a 1916 Reo truck, toward the light in Aunt Plutina Williams's window; I saw catfish as big as men, with whiskers like bull-whips, lie down at the feet of the Prophet and speak in a thousand strange tongues; I saw dancers moving against each other in the air to music I had never heard; I saw Lavonia, naked and beautiful, bathing and healing Junie in a moonlit cove; I saw Elisabeth standing in the edge of the lake in the spring, nursing a child who smelled like the sun; I saw the new police chief in a boat watching over his family; I saw the Mayor on his knees praying in Gullah with Charleston whores; I saw Jim Skipper and Rudy Thomas and Big Julie Cooper driving a bleeding pilot beside the river in a wagon pulled by twenty-four mules; I saw the Prophet from Jupiter and his five young sons shoot out of the lake like Fourth of July rockets and shout with incredible light and tongues of fire, *Rise, Children of the Water, Rise, and Be Whole in the Kingdom of God.*

LOUISE ERDRICH

Saint Marie

LOUISE ERDRICH's (1954–) latest novels are *The Antelope Wife* and the forthcoming *The Last Report on the Miracles at Little No Horse.* She lives in Minnesota with her children.

So when I went there, I knew the dark fish must rise. Plumes of radiance had soldered on me. No reservation girl had ever prayed so hard. There was no use in trying to ignore me any longer. I was going up there on the hill with the black robe women. They were not any lighter than me. I was going up there to pray as good as they could. Because I don't have that much Indian blood. And they never thought they'd have a girl from this reservation as a saint they'd have to kneel to. But they'd have me. And I'd be carved in pure gold. With ruby lips. And my toenails would be little pink ocean shells, which they would have to stoop down off their high horse to kiss.

I was ignorant. I was near age fourteen. The length of sky is just about the size of my ignorance. Pure and wide. And it was just that—the pure and wideness of my ignorance—that got me up the hill to Sacred Heart Convent and brought me back down alive. For maybe Jesus did not take my bait, but them Sisters tried to cram me right down whole.

You ever see a walleye strike so bad the lure is practically out its back end before you reel it in? That is what they done with me. I don't like to make that low comparison, but I have seen a walleye do that once. And it's the same attempt as Sister Leopolda made to get me in her clutch.

I had the mail-order Catholic soul you get in a girl raised out in the bush, whose only thought is getting into town. For Sunday Mass is the only time my father brought his children in except for school, when we were harnessed. Our soul went cheap. We were so anxious to get there we would have walked in on our hands and knees. We just craved going to the store, slinging bottle caps in the dust, making fool eyes at each other. And of course we went to church.

Where they have the convent is on top of the highest hill, so that from its windows the Sisters can be looking into the marrow of the town. Recently a windbreak was planted before the bar "for the purposes of tornado insurance." Don't tell me that. That poplar stand was put up to hide the drinkers as they get the transformation. As they are served into the beast of their burden. While they're drinking, that body comes upon them, and then they stagger or crawl out the bar door, pulling a weight they can't move past the poplars. They don't want no holy witness to their fall.

Anyway, I climbed. That was a long-ago day. There was a road then for wagons that wound in ruts to the top of the hill where they had their buildings of painted brick. Gleaming white. So white the sun glanced off in dazzling display to set forms whirling behind your eyelids. The face of God you could hardly look at. But that day it drizzled, so I could look all I wanted. I saw the homelier side. The cracked whitewash and swallows nesting in the busted ends of eaves. I saw the boards sawed the size of broken windowpanes and the fruit trees, stripped. Only the tough wild rhubarb flourished. Goldenrod rubbed up their walls. It was a poor convent. I didn't see that then but I know that now. Compared to others it was humble, ragtag, out in the middle of no place. It was the end of the world to some. Where the maps stopped. Where God had only half a hand in the creation. Where the Dark One had put in thick bush, liquor, wild dogs, and Indians.

I heard later that the Sacred Heart Convent was a catchall place for nuns that don't get along elsewhere. Nuns that complain too much or lose their mind. I'll always wonder now, after hearing that, where they picked up Sister Leopolda. Perhaps she had scarred someone else, the way she left a mark on me. Perhaps she was just sent around to test her Sisters' faith, here and there, like the spot-checker in a factory. For she was the definite most-hard trial to anyone's endurance, even when they started out with veils of wretched love upon their eyes.

I was that girl who thought the black hem of her garment would help me rise. Veils of love which was only hate petrified by longing—that was me. I was like those bush Indians who stole the holy black hat of a Jesuit and swallowed little scraps of it to cure their fevers. But the hat itself carried smallpox and was killing them with belief. Veils of faith! I had this confidence in Leopolda. She was different. The other Sisters had long ago gone blank and given up on Satan. He slept for them. They never noticed his comings and goings. But Leopolda kept track of him and knew his habits, minds he burrowed in, deep spaces where he hid. She knew as much about him as my grandma, who called him by other names and was not afraid.

In her class, Sister Leopolda carried a long oak pole for opening high windows. It had a hook made of iron on one end that could jerk a patch of your hair out or throttle you by the collar—all from a distance. She used this deadly hook-pole for catching Satan by surprise. He could have entered without your knowing it—through your lips or your nose or any one of your seven openings—and gained your mind. But she would see him. That pole would brain you from behind. And he would gasp, dazzled, and take the first thing she offered, which was pain.

She had a stringer of children who could only breathe if she said the word. I was the worst of them. She always said the Dark One wanted me most of all, and I believed this. I stood out. Evil was a common thing I trusted. Before sleep sometimes he came and whispered conversation in the old language of the bush. I listened. He told me things he never told anyone but Indians. I was privy to both worlds of his knowledge. I listened to him, but I had confidence in Leopolda. She was the only one of the bunch he even noticed.

There came a day, though, when Leopolda turned the tide with her hook-pole.

It was a quiet day with everyone working at their desks, when I heard him. He had sneaked into the closets in the back of the room. He was scratching around, tasting crumbs in our pockets, stealing buttons, squirting his dark juice in the linings and the boots. I was the only one who heard him, and I got bold. I smiled. I glanced back and smiled and looked up at her sly to see if she had noticed. My heart jumped. For she was looking straight at me. And she sniffed. She had a big stark bony nose stuck to the front of her face for smelling out brimstone and evil thoughts. She had smelled him on me. She stood up. Tall, pale, a blackness leading into the deeper blackness of the slate wall behind her. Her oak pole had flown into her grip. She had seen me glance at the closet. Oh, she knew. She knew just where he was. I watched her watch him in her mind's eye. The whole class was watching now. She was staring, sizing, following his scuffle. And all of a sudden she tensed down, posed on her bent kneesprings, cocked her arm back. She threw the oak pole singing over my head, through my braincloud. It cracked through the thin wood door of the back closet, and the heavy pointed hook drove through his heart. I turned. She'd speared her own black rubber overboot where he'd taken refuge in the tip of her darkest toe.

Something howled in my mind. Loss and darkness. I understood. I was to suffer for my smile.

He rose up hard in my heart. I didn't blink when the pole cracked. My skull was tough. I didn't flinch when she shrieked in my ear. I only shrugged at the flowers of hell. He wanted me. More than anything he craved me. But then she did the worst. She did what broke my mind to her. She grabbed me by the collar and dragged me, feet flying, through the room and threw me in the closet with her dead black overboot. And I was there. The only light was a crack beneath the door. I asked the Dark One to enter into me and boost my mind. I asked him to restrain my tears, for they was pushing behind my eyes. But he was afraid to come back there. He was afraid of her sharp pole. And I was afraid of Leopolda's pole for the first time, too. I felt the cold hook in my heart. How it could crack through the door at any minute and drag me out, like a dead fish on a gaff, drop me on the floor like a gutshot squirrel.

I was nothing. I edged back to the wall as far as I could. I breathed the chalk dust. The hem of her full black cloak cut against my cheek. He had left me. Her spear could find me any time. Her keen ears would aim the hook into the beat of my heart.

What was that sound?

It filled the closet, filled it up until it spilled over, but I did not recognize the crying wailing voice as mine until the door cracked open, brightness, and she hoisted me to her camphor-smelling lips.

"He *wants* you," she said. "That's the difference. I give you love."

Love. The black hook. The spear singing through the mind. I saw that she had tracked the Dark One to my heart and flushed him out into the open. So now my heart was an empty nest where she could lurk.

Well, I was weak. I was weak when I let her in, but she got a foothold there. Hard to dislodge as the year passed. Sometimes I felt him—the brush of dim wings—but only rarely did his voice compel. It was between Marie and Leopolda now, and the struggle changed. I began to realize I had been on the wrong track with the fruits of hell. The real way to overcome Leopolda was this: I'd get to heaven first. And then, when I saw her coming, I'd shut the gate. She'd be out! That is why, besides the bowing and the scraping I'd be dealt, I wanted to sit on the altar as a saint.

To this end, I went up on the hill. Sister Leopolda was the consecrated nun who had sponsored me to come there.

"You're not vain," she said. "You're too honest, looking into the mirror, for that. You're not smart. You don't have the ambition to get clear. You have two choices. One, you can marry a no-good Indian, bear his brats, die like a dog. Or two, you can give yourself to God."

"I'll come up there," I said, "but not because of what you think."

I could have had any damn man on the reservation at the time. And I could have made him treat me like his own life. I looked good. And I looked white. But I wanted Sister Leopolda's heart. And here was the thing: sometimes I wanted her heart in love and admiration. Sometimes. And sometimes I wanted her heart to roast on a black stick.

She answered the back door where they had instructed me to call. I stood there with my bundle. She looked me up and down.

"All right," she said finally. "Come in."

She took my hand. Her fingers were like a bundle of broom straws, so thin and dry, but the strength of them was unnatural. I couldn't have tugged loose if she was leading me into rooms of white-hot coal. Her strength was a kind of perverse miracle, for she got it from fasting herself thin. Because of this hunger practice her lips were a wounded brown and her skin deadly pale. Her eye sockets were two deep lashless hollows in a taut skull. I told you about the nose already. It stuck out far and made the place her eyes moved even deeper, as if she stared out the wrong end of a gun barrel. She took the bundle from my hands and threw it in the corner.

"You'll be sleeping behind the stove, child."

It was immense, like a great furnace. There was a small cot close behind it.

"Looks like it could get warm there," I said.

"Hot. It does."

"Do I get a habit?"

I wanted something like the thing she wore. Flowing black cotton. Her face was strapped in white bandages, and a sharp crest of starched white cardboard hung over her forehead like a glaring beak. If possible, I wanted a bigger, longer, whiter beak than hers.

"No," she said, grinning her great skull grin. "You don't get one yet. Who knows, you might not like us. Or we might not like you."

But she had loved me, or offered me love. And she had tried to hunt the Dark One down. So I had this confidence.

"I'll inherit your keys from you," I said.

She looked at me sharply, and her grin turned strange. She hissed, taking in her breath. Then she turned to the door and took a key from her belt. It was a giant key, and it unlocked the larder where the food was stored.

Inside there was all kinds of good stuff. Things I'd tasted only once or twice in my life. I saw sticks of dried fruit, jars of orange peel, spice like cinnamon. I saw tins of crackers with ships painted on the side. I saw pickles. Jars of herring and the rind of pigs. There was cheese, a big brown block of it from the thick milk of goats. And besides that there was the everyday stuff, in great quantities, the flour and the coffee.

It was the cheese that got to me. When I saw it my stomach hollowed. My tongue dripped. I loved that goat-milk cheese better than anything I'd ever ate. I stared at it. The rich curve in the buttery cloth.

"When you inherit my keys," she said sourly, slamming the door in my face, "you can eat all you want of the priest's cheese."

Then she seemed to consider what she'd done. She looked at me. She took the key from her belt and went back, sliced a hunk off, and put it in my hand.

"If you're good you'll taste this cheese again. When I'm dead and gone," she said.

Then she dragged out the big sack of flour. When I finished that heaven stuff she told me to roll my sleeves up and begin doing God's labor. For a while we worked in silence, mixing up the dough and pounding it out on stone slabs.

"God's work," I said after a while. "If this is God's work, I've done it all my life."

"Well, you've done it with the Devil in your heart then," she said. "Not God."

"How do you know?" I asked. But I knew she did. And wished I had not brought up the subject.

"I see right into you like a clear glass," she said. "I always did."

"You don't know it," she continued after a while, "but he's come around here sulking. He's come around here brooding. You brought him in. He knows the smell of me, and he's going to make a last ditch try to get you back. Don't let him." She glared over at me. Her eyes were cold and lighted. "Don't let him touch you. We'll be a long time getting rid of him."

So I was careful. I was careful not to give him an inch. I said a rosary, two rosaries, three, underneath my breath. I said the Creed. I said every scrap of Latin I knew while we punched the dough with our fists. And still, I dropped the cup. It rolled under that monstrous iron stove, which was getting fired up for baking.

And she was on me. She saw he'd entered my distraction.

"Our good cup," she said. "Get it out of there, Marie."

I reached for the poker to snag it out from beneath the stove. But I had a sinking feel in my stomach as I did this. Sure enough, her long arm darted past me like a whip. The poker lighted in her hand.

"Reach," she said. "Reach with your arm for that cup. And when your flesh is hot, remember that the flames you feel are only one fraction of the heat you will feel in his hellish embrace."

She always did things this way, to teach you lessons. So I wasn't surprised. It was playacting, anyway, because a stove isn't very hot underneath right along the floor. They aren't made that way. Otherwise a wood floor would burn. So I said yes and got down on my stomach and reached under. I meant to grab it quick and jump up again, before she could think up another lesson, but here it happened. Although I groped for the cup, my hand closed on nothing. That cup was nowhere to be found. I heard her step toward me, a slow step. I heard the creak of thick shoe leather, the little *plat* as the folds of her heavy skirts met, a trickle of fine sand sifting, somewhere, perhaps in the bowels of her, and I was afraid. I tried to scramble up, but her foot came down lightly behind my ear, and I was lowered. The foot came down more firmly at the base of my neck, and I was held.

"You're like I was," she said. "He wants you very much."

"He doesn't want me no more," I said. "He had his fill. I got the cup!"

I heard the valve opening, the hissed intake of breath, and knew that I should not have spoke.

"You lie," she said. "You're cold. There is a wicked ice forming in your blood. You don't have a shred of devotion for God. Only wild cold dark lust. I know it. I know how you feel. I see the beast . . . the beast watches me out of your eyes sometimes. Cold."

The urgent scrape of metal. It took a moment to know from where. Top of the stove. Kettle. Lessons. She was steadying herself with the iron poker. I could feel it like pure certainty, driving into the wood floor. I would not remind her of pokers. I heard the water as it came, tipped from the spout, cooling as it fell but still scalding as it struck. I must have twitched beneath her foot, because she steadied me, and then the poker nudged up beside my arm as if to guide. "To warm your cold ash heart," she said. I felt how patient she would be. The water came. My mind went dead blank. Again. I could only think the kettle would be cooling slowly in her hand. I could not stand it. I bit my lip so as not to satisfy her with a sound. She gave me more reason to keep still.

"I will boil him from your mind if you make a peep," she said, "by filling up your ear."

Any sensible fool would have run back down the hill the minute Leopolda let them up from under her heel. But I was snared in her black intelligence by then. I could not think straight. I had prayed so hard I think I broke a cog in my mind. I prayed while her foot squeezed my throat. While my skin burst. I prayed even when I heard the wind come through, shrieking in the busted bird nests. I didn't stop when pure light fell, turning slowly behind my eyelids. God's face. Even that did not disrupt my continued praise. Words came. Words came from nowhere and flooded my mind.

Now I could pray much better than any one of them. Than all of them full force. This was proved. I turned to her in a daze when she let me up. My thoughts were gone, and yet I remember how surprised I was. Tears glittered in her eyes, deep down, like the sinking reflection in a well.

"It was so hard, Marie," she gasped. Her hands were shaking. The kettle clattered against the stove. "But I have used all the water up now. I think he is gone."

"I prayed," I said foolishly. "I prayed very hard."

"Yes," she said. "My dear one, I know."

We sat together quietly because we had no more words. We let the dough rise and punched it down once. She gave me a bowl of mush, unlocked the sausage from a special cupboard, and took that in to the Sisters. They sat down the hall, chewing their sausage, and I could hear them. I could hear their teeth bite through their bread and meat. I couldn't move. My shirt was dry but the cloth stuck to my back, and I couldn't think straight. I was losing the sense to understand how her mind worked. She'd gotten past me with her poker and I would never be a saint. I despaired. I felt I had no inside voice, nothing to direct me, no darkness, no Marie. I was about to throw that cornmeal mush out to the birds and make a run for it, when the vision rose up blazing in my mind.

I was rippling gold. My breasts were bare and my nipples flashed and winked. Diamonds tipped them. I could walk through panes of glass. I could walk through windows. She was at my feet, swallowing the glass after each step I took. I broke through another and another. The glass she swallowed ground and cut until her starved insides were only a subtle dust. She coughed. She coughed a cloud of dust. And then she was only a black rag that flapped off, snagged in bob wire, hung there for an age, and finally rotted into the breeze.

I saw this, mouth hanging open, gazing off into the flagged boughs of trees.

"Get up!" she cried. "Stop dreaming. It is time to bake."

Two other Sisters had come in with her, wide women with hands like paddles. They were evening and smoothing out the firebox beneath the great jaws of the oven.

"Who is this one?" they asked Leopolda. "Is she yours?"

"She is mine," said Leopolda. "A very good girl."

"What is your name?" one asked me.

"Marie."

"Marie. Star of the Sea."

"She will shine," said Leopolda, "when we have burned off the dark corrosion."

The others laughed, but uncertainly. They were mild and sturdy French, who did not understand Leopolda's twisted jokes, although they muttered respectfully at things she said. I knew they wouldn't believe what she had done with the kettle. There was no question. So I kept quiet.

"*Elle est docile,*" they said approvingly as they left to starch the linens.

"Does it pain?" Leopolda asked me as soon as they were out the door.

I did not answer. I felt sick with the hurt.

"Come along," she said.

The building was wholly quiet now. I followed her up the narrow staircase into a hall of little rooms, many doors. Her cell was the quietest, at the very end. Inside, the air smelled stale, as if the door had not been opened for years. There was a crude straw mattress, a tiny bookcase with a picture of Saint Francis hanging over it, a ragged palm, a stool for sitting on, a crucifix. She told me to remove my blouse and sit on the stool. I did so. She took a pot of salve from the bookcase and began to smooth it upon my burns. Her hands made slow, wide circles, stopping the pain. I closed my eyes. I expected to see blackness. Peace. But instead the vision reared up again. My chest was still tipped with diamonds. I was walking through windows. She was chewing up the broken litter I left behind.

"I am going," I said. "Let me go."

But she held me down.

"Don't go," she said quickly. "Don't. We have just begun."

I was weakening. My thoughts were whirling pitifully. The pain had kept me strong, and as it left me I began to forget it; I couldn't hold on. I began to wonder if she'd really scalded me with the kettle. I could not remember. To remember this seemed the most important thing in the world. But I was losing the memory. The scalding. The pouring. It began to vanish. I felt like my mind was coming off its hinge, flapping in the breeze, hanging by the hair of my own pain. I wrenched out of her grip.

"He was always in you," I said. "Even more than in me. He wanted you even more. And now he's got you. Get thee behind me!"

I shouted that, grabbed my shirt, and ran through the door throwing it on my body. I got down the stairs and into the kitchen, even, but no matter what I told myself, I couldn't get out the door. It wasn't finished. And she knew I would not leave. Her quiet step was immediately behind me.

"We must take the bread from the oven now," she said.

She was pretending nothing happened. But for the first time I had gotten through some chink she'd left in her darkness. Touched some doubt. Her voice was so low and brittle it cracked off at the end of her sentence.

"Help me, Marie," she said slowly.

But I was not going to help her, even though she had calmly buttoned the back of my shirt up and put the big cloth mittens in my hands for taking out the loaves. I could have bolted for it then. But I didn't. I knew that something was nearing completion. Something was about to happen. My back was a wall of singing flame. I was turning. I watched her take the long fork in one hand, to tap the loaves. In the other hand she gripped the black poker to hook the pans.

"Help me," she said again, and I thought, Yes, this is part of it. I put the mittens on my hands and swung the door open on its hinges. The oven gaped. She stood back a moment, letting the first blast of heat rush by. I moved behind her. I could feel the heat at my front and at my back. Before, behind. My skin was turning to beaten gold. It was coming quicker than I thought. The oven was like the gate of a personal hell. Just big enough and hot enough for one person, and that was her. One kick and Leopolda would fly in headfirst. And that would be one-millionth of the heat she would feel when she finally collapsed in his hellish embrace.

Saints know these numbers.

She bent forward with her fork held out. I kicked her with all my might. She flew in. But the outstretched poker hit the back wall first, so she rebounded. The oven was not so deep as I had thought.

There was a moment when I felt a sort of thin, hot disappointment, as when a fish slips off the line. Only I was the one going to be lost. She was fearfully silent. She whirled. Her veil had cutting edges. She had the poker in one hand. In the other she held that long sharp fork she used to tap the delicate crusts of loaves. Her face turned upside down on her shoulders. Her face turned blue. But saints are used to miracles. I felt no trace of fear.

If I was going to be lost, let the diamonds cut! Let her eat ground glass!

"Bitch of Jesus Christ!" I shouted. "Kneel and beg! Lick the floor!"

That was when she stabbed me through the hand with the fork, then took the poker up alongside my head, and knocked me out.

It must have been a half an hour later when I came around. Things were so strange. So strange I can hardly tell it for delight at the remembrance. For when I came around this was actually taking place. I was being worshiped. I had somehow gained the altar of a saint.

I was laying back on the stiff couch in the Mother Superior's office. I looked around me. It was as though my deepest dream had come to life. The Sisters of the convent were kneeling to me. Sister Bonaventure. Sister Dympna. Sister Cecilia Saint-Claire. The two French with hands like paddles. They were down on their knees. Black capes were slung over some of their heads. My name was buzzing up and down the room, like a fat autumn fly lighting on the tips of their tongues between Latin, humming up the heavy blood-dark curtains, circling their little cosseted heads. Marie! Marie! A girl thrown in a closet. Who was afraid of a rubber overboot. Who was half overcome. A girl who came in the back door where they threw their garbage. Marie! Who never found the cup. Who had to eat their cold mush. Marie! Leopolda had her face buried in her knuckles. Saint Marie of the Holy Slops! Saint Marie of the Bread Fork! Saint Marie of the Burnt Back and Scalded Butt!

I broke out and laughed.

They looked up. All holy hell burst loose when they saw I'd woke. I still did not understand what was happening. They were watching, talking, but not to me.

"The marks . . ."

"She has her hand closed."

"*Je ne peux pas voir.*"

I was not stupid enough to ask what they were talking about. I couldn't tell why I was laying in white sheets. I couldn't tell why they were praying to me. But I'll tell you this: it seemed entirely natural. It was me. I lifted up my hand as in my dream. It was completely limp with sacredness.

"Peace be with you."

My arm was dried blood from the wrist down to the elbow. And it hurt. Their faces turned like flat flowers of adoration to follow that hand's movements. I let it swing through the air, imparting a saint's blessing. I had practiced. I knew exactly how to act.

They murmured. I heaved a sigh, and a golden beam of light suddenly broke through the clouded window and flooded down directly on my face. A stroke of perfect luck! They had to be convinced.

Leopolda still knelt in the back of the room. Her knuckles were crammed halfway down her throat. Let me tell you, a saint has senses honed keen as a wolf. I knew that she was over my barrel now. How it happened did not matter. The last thing I remembered was how she flew from the oven and stabbed me. That one thing was most certainly true.

"Come forward, Sister Leopolda." I gestured with my heavenly wound. Oh, it hurt. It bled when I reopened the slight heal. "Kneel beside me," I said.

She kneeled, but her voice box evidently did not work, for her mouth opened, shut, opened, but no sound came out. My throat clenched in noble delight I had read of as befitting a saint. She could not speak. But she was beaten. It was in her eyes. She stared at me now with all the deep hate of the wheel of devilish dust that rolled wild within her emptiness.

"What is it you want to tell me?" I asked. And at last she spoke.

"I have told my Sisters of your passion," she managed to choke out. "How the stigmata . . . the marks of the nails . . . appeared in your palm and you swooned at the holy vision. . . ."

"Yes," I said curiously.

And then, after a moment, I understood.

Leopolda had saved herself with her quick brain. She had witnessed a miracle. She had hid the fork and told this to the others. And of course they believed her, because they never knew how Satan came and went or where he took refuge.

"I saw it from the first," said the large one who put the bread in the oven. "Humility of the spirit. So rare in these girls."

"I saw it too," said the other one with great satisfaction. She sighed quietly. "If only it was me."

Leopolda was kneeling bolt upright, face blazing and twitching, a barely held fountain of blasting poison.

"Christ has marked me," I agreed.

I smiled the saint's smirk into her face. And then I looked at her. That was my mistake.

For I saw her kneeling there. Leopolda with her soul like a rubber overboot. With her face of a starved rat. With the desperate eyes drowning in the deep wells of her wrongness. There would be no one else after me. And I would leave. I saw Leopolda kneeling within the shambles of her love.

My heart had been about to surge from my chest with the blackness of my joyous heat. Now it dropped. I pitied her. I pitied her. Pity twisted in my stomach like that hook-pole was driven through me. I was caught. It was a feeling more terrible than any amount of boiling water and worse than being forked. Still, still, I could not help what I did. I had already smiled in a saint's mealy forgiveness. I heard myself speaking gently.

"Receive the dispensation of my sacred blood," I whispered.

But there was no heart in it. No joy when she bent to touch the floor. No dark leaping. I fell back into the white pillows. Blank dust was whirling through the light shafts. My skin was dust. Dust my lips. Dust the dirty spoons on the ends of my feet.

Rise up! I thought. Rise up and walk! There is no limit to this dust!

RICHARD FORD

Rock Springs

RICHARD FORD (1944–) was born in Jackson, Mississippi, the only child of a traveling salesman for a starch company, and was raised in Mississippi and in Arkansas. He went to college at Michigan State University, where he met Kristina Hensley, to whom he has been married since 1968. Ford attended law school briefly before entering the University of California at Irvine, where he received his M.F.A. in fiction writing in 1970. His novels are *A Piece of My Heart, The Ultimate Good Luck, The Sportswriter, Wildlife,* and, most recently, *Women with Men* and *Independence Day,* the only novel to win both the Pulitzer Prize and the PEN/Faulkner Award for fiction. Ford has taught writing and literature at the University of Michigan at Ann Arbor, at Princeton University, and at Williams College. He lives in New Orleans, where Kristina, is the head of the city-planning commission. He travels frequently and also spends time on a plantation in the Mississippi Delta and at his cabin in Chinook, Montana.

Edna and I had started down from Kalispell, heading for Tampa-St. Pete where I still had some friends from the old glory days who wouldn't turn me in to the police. I had managed to scrape with the law in Kalispell over several bad checks—which is a prison crime in Montana. And I knew Edna was already looking at her cards and thinking about a move, since it wasn't the first time I'd been in law scrapes in my life. She herself had already had her own troubles, losing her kids and keeping her ex-husband, Danny, from breaking in her house and stealing her things while she was at work, which was really why I had moved in in the first place, that and needing to give my little daughter, Cheryl, a better shake in things.

I don't know what was between Edna and me, just beached by the same tides when you got down to it. Though love has been built on frailer ground than that, as I well know. And when I came in the house that afternoon, I just asked her if she wanted to go to Florida with me, leave things where they sat, and she said, "Why not? My datebook's not that full."

Edna and I had been a pair eight months, more or less man and wife, some of which time I had been out of work, and some when I'd worked at the dog track as a lead-out and could help with the rent and talk sense to Danny when he came around. Danny was afraid of me because Edna had told him I'd been in prison in Florida for killing a man, though that wasn't true. I had once been in jail in Tallahassee for stealing tires and had gotten into a fight on the county farm where a man had lost his eye. But I hadn't done the hurting, and Edna just wanted the story worse than it was so Danny wouldn't act crazy and make her have to take her kids back, since she had made a good adjustment to not having them, and I already had Cheryl with me. I'm not a violent person and would never put a man's eye out, much less kill someone. My former wife, Helen, would come all the way from Waikiki Beach to testify to that. We never had violence, and I believe in crossing the street to stay out of trouble's way. Though Danny didn't know that.

But we were half down through Wyoming, going toward I-80 and feeling good about things, when the oil light flashed on in the car I'd stolen, a sign I knew to be a bad one.

I'd gotten us a good car, a cranberry Mercedes I'd stolen out of an ophthalmologist's lot in Whitefish, Montana. I stole it because I thought it would be comfortable over a long haul, because I thought it got good mileage, which it didn't, and because I'd never had a good car in my life, just old Chevy junkers and used trucks back from when I was a kid swamping citrus with Cubans.

The car made us all high that day. I ran the windows up and down, and Edna told us some jokes and made faces. She could be lively. Her features would light up like a beacon and you could see her beauty, which wasn't ordinary. It all made me giddy, and I drove clear down to Bozeman, then straight on through the park to Jackson Hole. I rented us the bridal suite in the Quality Court in Jackson and left Cheryl and her little dog, Duke, sleeping while Edna and I drove to a rib barn and drank beer and laughed till after midnight.

It felt like a whole new beginning for us, bad memories left behind and a new horizon to build on. I got so worked up, I had a tattoo done on my arm that said FAMOUS TIMES, and Edna bought a Bailey hat with an Indian feather band and a little turquoise-and-silver bracelet for Cheryl, and we made love on the seat of the car in the Quality Court parking lot just as the sun was burning up on the Snake River, and everything seemed then like the end of the rainbow.

It was that very enthusiasm, in fact, that made me keep the car one day longer instead of driving it into the river and stealing another one, like I should've done and *had* done before.

Where the car went bad there wasn't a town in sight or even a house, just some low mountains maybe fifty miles away or maybe a hundred, a barbed-wire fence in both directions, hardpan prairie, and some hawks riding the evening air seizing insects.

I got out to look at the motor, and Edna got out with Cheryl and the dog to let them have a pee by the car. I checked the water and checked the oil stick, and both of them said perfect.

"What's that light mean, Earl?" Edna said. She had come and stood by the car with her hat on. She was just sizing things up for herself.

"We shouldn't run it," I said. "Something's not right in the oil."

She looked around at Cheryl and Little Duke, who were peeing on the hardtop side-by-side like two little dolls, then out at the mountains, which were becoming black and lost in the distance. "What're we doing?" she said. She wasn't worried yet, but she wanted to know what I was thinking about.

"Let me try it again."

"That's a good idea," she said, and we all got back in the car.

When I turned the motor over, it started right away and the red light stayed off and there weren't any noises to make you think something was wrong. I let it idle a minute, then pushed the accelerator down and watched the red bulb. But there wasn't any light on, and I started wondering if maybe I hadn't dreamed I saw it, or that it had been the sun catching an angle off the window chrome, or maybe I was scared of something and didn't know it.

"What's the matter with it, Daddy?" Cheryl said from the backseat. I looked back at her, and she had on her turquoise bracelet and Edna's hat set back on the back of her head and that little black-and-white Heinz dog on her lap. She looked like a little cowgirl in the movies.

"Nothing, honey, everything's fine now," I said.

"Little Duke tinkled where I tinkled," Cheryl said, and laughed.

"You're two of a kind," Edna said, not looking back. Edna was usually good with Cheryl, but I knew she was tired now. We hadn't had much sleep, and she had a tendency to get cranky when she didn't sleep. "We oughta ditch this damn car first chance we get," she said.

"What's the first chance we got?" I asked, because I knew she'd been at the map.

"Rock Springs, Wyoming," Edna said with conviction. "Thirty miles down this road." She pointed out ahead.

I had wanted all along to drive the car into Florida like a big success story. But I knew Edna was right about it, that we shouldn't take crazy chances. I had kept thinking of it as my car and not the ophthalmologist's, and that was how you got caught in these things.

"Then my belief is we ought to go to Rock Springs and negotiate ourselves a new car," I said. I wanted to stay upbeat, like everything was panning out right.

"That's a great idea," Edna said, and she leaned over and kissed me hard on the mouth.

"That's a great idea," Cheryl said. "Let's pull on out of here right now."

The sunset that day I remember as being the prettiest I'd ever seen. Just as it touched the rim of the horizon, it all at once fired the air into jewels and red sequins the precise likes of which I had never seen before and haven't seen since. The West has it all over everywhere for sunsets, even Florida, where it's supposedly flat but where half the time trees block your view.

"It's cocktail hour," Edna said after we'd driven awhile. "We ought to have a drink and celebrate something." She felt better thinking we were going to get rid of the car. It certainly had dark troubles and was something you'd want to put behind you.

Edna had out a whiskey bottle and some plastic cups and was measuring levels on the glove-box lid. She liked drinking, and she liked drinking in the car, which was something you got used to in Montana, where it wasn't against the law, but where, strangely enough, a bad check would land you in Deer Lodge Prison for a year.

"Did I ever tell you I once had a monkey?" Edna said, setting my drink on the dashboard where I could reach it when I was ready. Her spirits were already picked up. She was like that, up one minute and down the next.

"I don't think you ever did tell me that," I said. "Where were you then?"

"Missoula," she said. She put her bare feet on the dash and rested the cup on her breasts. "I was waitressing at the AmVets. This was before I met you. Some guy came in one day with a monkey. A spider monkey. And I said, just to be joking, 'I'll roll you for that monkey.' And the guy said, 'Just one roll?' And I said, 'Sure.' He put the monkey down on the bar, picked up the cup, and rolled out boxcars. I picked it up and rolled out three fives. And I just stood there looking at the guy. He was just some guy passing through, I guess a vet. He got a strange look on his face—I'm sure not as strange as the one I had—but he looked kind of sad and surprised and satisfied all at once. I said, 'We can roll again.' But he said, 'No, I never roll twice for anything.' And he sat and drank a beer and talked about one thing and another for a while, about nuclear war and building a stronghold somewhere up in the Bitterroot, whatever it was, while I just watched the monkey, wondering what I was going to do with it when the guy left. And pretty soon he got up and said, 'Well, good-bye, Chipper'—that was this monkey's name, of course. And then he left before I could say anything. And the monkey just sat on the bar all that night. I don't know what made me think of that, Earl. Just something weird. I'm letting my mind wander."

"That's perfectly fine," I said. I took a drink of my drink. "I'd never own a monkey," I said after a minute. "They're too nasty. I'm sure Cheryl would like a monkey, though, wouldn't you, honey?" Cheryl was down on the seat playing with Little Duke. She used to talk about monkeys all the time then. "What'd you ever do with that monkey?" I said, watching the speedometer. We were having to go slower now because the red light kept fluttering on. And all I could do to keep it off was go slower. We were going maybe thirty-five and it was an hour before dark, and I was hoping Rock Springs wasn't far away.

"You really want to know?" Edna said. She gave me a quick glance, then looked back at the empty desert as if she was brooding over it.

"Sure," I said. I was still upbeat. I figured I could worry about breaking down and let other people be happy for a change.

"I kept it a week." And she seemed gloomy all of a sudden, as if she saw some aspect of the story she had never seen before. "I took it home and back and forth to the AmVets on my shifts. And it didn't cause any trouble. I fixed a chair up for it to sit on, back of the bar, and people liked it. It made a nice little clicking noise. We changed its name to Mary because the bartender figured out it was a girl. Though I was never really comfortable with it at home. I felt like it watched me too much. Then one day a guy came in, some guy who'd been in Vietnam, still wore a fatigue coat. And he said to me, 'Don't you know that a monkey'll kill you? It's got more strength in its fingers than you got in your whole body.' He said people had been killed in Vietnam by monkeys, bunches of them marauding while you were asleep, killing you and covering you with leaves. I didn't believe a word of it, except that when I got home and got undressed I started looking over across the room at Mary on her chair in the dark watching me. And I got the creeps. And after a while I got up and went out to the car, got a length of clothesline wire, and came back in and wired her to the doorknob through her little silver collar, then went back and tried to sleep. And I guess I must've slept the sleep of the dead—though I don't remember it—because when I got up I found Mary had tipped off her chair-back and hanged herself on the wire line. I'd made it too short."

Edna seemed badly affected by that story and slid low in the seat so she couldn't see out over the dash. "Isn't that a shameful story, Earl, what happened to that poor little monkey?"

"I see a town! I see a town!" Cheryl started yelling from the backseat, and right up Little Duke started yapping and the whole car fell into a racket. And sure enough she had seen something I hadn't, which was Rock Springs, Wyoming, at the bottom of a long hill, a little glowing jewel in the desert with I-80 running on the north side and the black desert spread out behind.

"That's it, honey," I said. "That's where we're going. You saw it first."

"We're hungry," Cheryl said. "Little Duke wants some fish, and I want spaghetti." She put her arms around my neck and hugged me.

"Then you'll just get it," I said. "You can have anything you want. And so can Edna and so can Little Duke." I looked over at Edna, smiling, but she was staring at me with eyes that were fierce with anger. "What's wrong?" I said.

"Don't you care anything about that awful thing that happened to me?" Her mouth was drawn tight, and her eyes kept cutting back at Cheryl and Little Duke, as if they had been tormenting her.

"Of course I do," I said. "I thought that was an awful thing." I didn't want her to be unhappy. We were almost there, and pretty soon we could sit down and have a real meal without thinking somebody might be hurting us.

"You want to know what I did with that monkey?" Edna said.

"Sure I do," I said.

"I put her in a green garbage bag, put it in the trunk of my car, drove to the dump, and threw her in the trash." She was staring at me darkly, as if the story meant something to her that was real important but that only she could see and that the rest of the world was a fool for.

"Well, that's horrible," I said. "But I don't see what else you could do. You didn't mean to kill it. You'd have done it differently if you had. And then you had to get rid of it, and I don't know what else you could have done. Throwing it away might seem unsympathetic to somebody, probably, but not to me. Sometimes that's all you can do, and you can't worry about what somebody else thinks." I tried to smile at her, but the red light was staying on if I pushed the accelerator at all, and I was trying to gauge if we could coast to Rock Springs before the car gave out completely. I looked at Edna again. "What else can I say?" I said.

"Nothing," she said, and stared back at the dark highway. "I should've known that's what you'd think. You've got a character that leaves something out, Earl. I've known that a long time."

"And yet here you are," I said. "And you're not doing so bad. Things could be a lot worse. At least we're all together here."

"Things could always be worse," Edna said. "You could go to the electric chair tomorrow."

"That's right," I said. "And somewhere somebody probably will. Only it won't be you."

"I'm hungry," said Cheryl. "When're we gonna eat? Let's find a motel. I'm tired of this. Little Duke's tired of it too."

Where the car stopped rolling was some distance from the town, though you could see the clear outline of the interstate in the dark with Rock Springs lighting up the sky behind. You could hear the big tractors hitting the spacers in the overpass, revving up for the climb to the mountains.

I shut off the lights.

"What're we going to do now?" Edna said irritably, giving me a bitter look.

"I'm figuring it," I said. "It won't be hard, whatever it is. You won't have to do anything."

"I'd hope not," she said and looked the other way.

Across the road and across a dry wash a hundred yards was what looked like a huge mobile-home town, with a factory or a refinery of some kind lit up behind it and in full swing. There were lights on in a lot of the mobile homes, and there were cars moving along an access road that ended near the freeway overpass a mile the other way. The lights in the mobile homes seemed friendly to me, and I knew right then what I should do.

"Get out," I said, opening my door.

"Are we walking?" Edna said.

"We're pushing."

"I'm not pushing." Edna reached up and locked her door.

"All right," I said. "Then you just steer."

"You're pushing us to Rock Springs, are you, Earl? It doesn't look like it's more than about three miles."

"I'll push," Cheryl said from the back.

"No, hon. Daddy'll push. You just get out with Little Duke and move out of the way."

Edna gave me a threatening look, just as if I'd tried to hit her. But when I got out she slid into my seat and took the wheel, staring angrily ahead straight into the cottonwood scrub.

"Edna can't drive that car," Cheryl said from out in the dark. "She'll run it in the ditch."

"Yes, she can, hon. Edna can drive it as good as I can. Probably better."

"No she can't," Cheryl said. "No she can't either." And I thought she was about to cry, but she didn't.

I told Edna to keep the ignition on so it wouldn't lock up and to steer into the cottonwoods with the parking lights on so she could see. And when I started, she steered it straight off into the trees, and I kept pushing until we were twenty yards into the cover and the tires sank in the soft sand and nothing at all could be seen from the road.

"Now where are we?" she said, sitting at the wheel. Her voice was tired and hard, and I knew she could have put a good meal to use. She had a sweet nature, and I recognized that this wasn't her fault but mine. Only I wished she could be more hopeful.

"You stay right here, and I'll go over to that trailer park and call us a cab," I said.

"What cab?" Edna said, her mouth wrinkled as if she'd never heard anything like that in her life.

"There'll be cabs," I said, and tried to smile at her. "There's cabs everywhere."

"What're you going to tell him when he gets here? Our stolen car broke down and we need a ride to where we can steal another one? That'll be a big hit, Earl."

"I'll talk," I said. "You just listen to the radio for ten minutes and then walk on out to the shoulder like nothing was suspicious. And you and Cheryl act nice. She doesn't need to know about this car."

"Like we're not suspicious enough already, right?" Edna looked up at me out of the lighted car. "You don't think right, did you know that, Earl? You think the world's stupid and you're smart. But that's not how it is. I feel sorry for you. You might've *been* something, but things just went crazy someplace."

I had a thought about poor Danny. He was a vet and crazy as a shit-house mouse, and I was glad he wasn't in for all this. "Just get the baby in the car," I said, trying to be patient. "I'm hungry like you are."

"I'm tired of this," Edna said. "I wish I'd stayed in Montana."

"Then you can go back in the morning," I said. "I'll buy the ticket and put you on the bus. But not till then."

"Just get on with it, Earl." She slumped down in the seat, turning off the parking lights with one foot and the radio on with the other.

The mobile-home community was as big as any I'd ever seen. It was attached in some way to the plant that was lighted up behind it, because I could see a car once in a while leave one of the trailer streets, turn in the direction of the plant, then go slowly into it. Everything in the plant was white, and you could see that all the trailers were painted white and looked exactly alike. A deep hum came out of the plant, and I thought as I got closer that it wouldn't be a location I'd ever want to work in.

I went right to the first trailer where there was a light, and knocked on the metal door. Kids' toys were lying in the gravel around the little wood steps, and I could hear talking on TV that suddenly went off. I heard a woman's voice talking, and then the door opened wide.

A large Negro woman with a wide, friendly face stood in the doorway. She smiled at me and moved forward as if she was going to come out, but she stopped at the top step. There was a little Negro boy behind her peeping out from behind her legs, watching me with his eyes half closed. The trailer had that feeling that no one else was inside, which was a feeling I knew something about.

"I'm sorry to intrude," I said. "But I've run up on a little bad luck tonight. My name's Earl Middleton."

The woman looked at me, then out into the night toward the freeway as if what I had said was something she was going to be able to see. "What kind of bad luck?" she said, looking down at me again.

"My car broke down out on the highway," I said. "I can't fix it myself, and I wondered if I could use your phone to call for help."

The woman smiled down at me knowingly. "We can't live without cars, can we?"

"That's the honest truth," I said.

"They're like our hearts," she said, her face shining in the little bulb light that burned beside the door. "Where's your car situated?"

I turned and looked over into the dark, but I couldn't see anything because of where we'd put it. "It's over there," I said. "You can't see it in the dark."

"Who all's with you now?" the woman said. "Have you got your wife with you?"

"She's with my little girl and our dog in the car," I said. "My daughter's asleep or I would have brought them."

"They shouldn't be left in the dark by themselves," the woman said and frowned. "There's too much unsavoriness out there."

"The best I can do is hurry back." I tried to look sincere, since everything except Cheryl being asleep and Edna being my wife was the truth. The truth is meant to serve you if you'll let it, and I wanted it to serve me. "I'll pay for the phone call," I said. "If you'll bring the phone to the door I'll call from right here."

The woman looked at me again as if she was searching for a truth of her own, then back out into the night. She was maybe in her sixties, but I couldn't say for sure. "You're not going to rob me, are you, Mr. Middleton?" She smiled like it was a joke between us.

"Not tonight," I said, and smiled a genuine smile. "I'm not up to it tonight. Maybe another time."

"Then I guess Terrel and I can let you use our phone with Daddy not here, can't we, Terrel? This is my grandson, Terrel Junior, Mr. Middleton." She put her hand on the boy's head and looked down at him. "Terrel won't talk. Though if he did he'd tell you to use our phone. He's a sweet boy." She opened the screen for me to come in.

The trailer was a big one with a new rug and a new couch and a living room that expanded to give the space of a real house. Something good and sweet was cooking in the kitchen, and the trailer felt like it was somebody's comfortable new home instead of just temporary. I've lived in trailers, but they were just snailbacks with one room and no toilet, and they always felt cramped and unhappy—though I've thought maybe it might've been me that was unhappy in them.

There was a big Sony TV and a lot of kids' toys scattered on the floor. I recognized a Greyhound bus I'd gotten for Cheryl. The phone was beside a new leather recliner, and the Negro woman pointed for me to sit down and call and gave me the phone book. Terrel began fingering his toys and the woman sat on the couch while I called, watching me and smiling.

There were three listings for cab companies, all with one number different. I called the numbers in order and didn't get an answer until the last one, which answered with the name of the second company. I said I was on the highway beyond the interstate and that my wife and family needed to be taken to town and I would arrange for a tow later. While I was giving the location, I looked up the name of a tow service to tell the driver in case he asked.

When I hung up, the Negro woman was sitting looking at me with the same look she had been staring with into the dark, a look that seemed to want truth. She was smiling, though. Something pleased her and I reminded her of it.

"This is a very nice home," I said, resting in the recliner, which felt like the driver's seat of the Mercedes, and where I'd have been happy to stay.

"This isn't *our* house, Mr. Middleton," the Negro woman said. "The company owns these. They give them to us for nothing. We have our own home in Rockford, Illinois."

"That's wonderful," I said.

"It's never wonderful when you have to be away from home, Mr. Middleton, though we're only here three months, and it'll be easier when Terrel Junior begins his special school. You see, our son was killed in the war, and his wife ran off without Terrel Junior. Though you shouldn't worry. He can't understand us. His little feelings can't be hurt." The woman folded her hands in her lap and smiled in a satisfied way. She was an attractive woman, and had on a blue-and-pink floral dress that made her seem bigger than she could've been, just the right woman to sit on the couch she was sitting on. She was good nature's picture, and I was glad she could be, with her little brain-damaged boy, living in a place where no one in his right mind would want to live a minute. "Where do *you* live, Mr. Middleton?" she said politely, smiling in the same sympathetic way.

"My family and I are in transit," I said. "I'm an ophthalmologist, and we're moving back to Florida, where I'm from. I'm setting up practice in some little town where it's warm year-round. I haven't decided where."

"Florida's a wonderful place," the woman said. "I think Terrel would like it there."

"Could I ask you something?" I said.

"You certainly may," the woman said. Terrel had begun pushing his Greyhound across the front of the TV screen, making a scratch that no one watching the set could miss. "Stop that, Terrel Junior," the woman said quietly. But Terrel kept pushing his bus on the glass, and she smiled at me again as if we both understood something sad. Except I knew Cheryl would never damage a television set. She had respect for nice things, and I was sorry for the lady that Terrel didn't. "What did you want to ask?" the woman said.

"What goes on in that plant or whatever it is back there beyond these trailers, where all the lights are on?"

"Gold," the woman said and smiled.

"It's what?" I said.

"Gold," the Negro woman said, smiling as she had for almost all the time I'd been there. "It's a gold mine."

"They're mining gold back there?" I said, pointing.

"Every night and every day." She smiled in a pleased way.

"Does your husband work there?" I said.

"He's the assayer," she said. "He controls the quality. He works three months a year, and we live the rest of the time at home in Rockford. We've waited a long time for this. We've been happy to have our grandson, but I won't say I'll be sorry to have him go. We're ready to start our lives over." She smiled broadly at me and then at Terrel, who was giving her a spiteful look from the floor. "You said you had a daughter," the Negro woman said. "And what's her name?"

"Irma Cheryl," I said. "She's named for my mother."

"That's nice. And she's healthy, too. I can see it in your face." She looked at Terrel Junior with pity.

"I guess I'm lucky," I said.

"So far you are. But children bring you grief, the same way they bring you joy. We were unhappy for a long time before my husband got his job in the gold mine. Now, when Terrel starts to school, we'll be kids again." She stood up. "You might miss your cab, Mr. Middleton," she said, walking toward the door, though not to be forcing me out. She was too polite. "If *we* can't see your car, the cab surely won't be able to."

"That's true." I got up off the recliner, where I'd been so comfortable. "None of us have eaten yet, and your food makes me know how hungry we probably all are."

"There are fine restaurants in town, and you'll find them," the Negro woman said. "I'm sorry you didn't meet my husband. He's a wonderful man. He's everything to me."

"Tell him I appreciate the phone," I said. "You saved me."

"You weren't hard to save," the woman said. "Saving people is what we were all put on earth to do. I just passed you on to whatever's coming to you."

"Let's hope it's good," I said, stepping back into the dark.

"I'll be hoping, Mr. Middleton. Terrel and I will both be hoping."

I waved to her as I walked out into the darkness toward the car where it was hidden in the night.

The cab had already arrived when I got there. I could see its little red-and-green roof lights all the way across the dry wash, and it made me worry that Edna was already saying something to get us in trouble, something about the car or where we'd come from, something that would cast suspicion on us. I thought, then, how I never planned things well enough. There was always a gap between my plan and what happened, and I only responded to things as they came along and hoped I wouldn't get in trouble. I was an offender in the law's eyes. But I always *thought* differently, as if I weren't an offender and had no intention of being one, which was the truth. But as I read on a napkin once, between the idea and the act a whole kingdom lies. And I had a hard time with my acts, which were oftentimes offender's acts, and my ideas, which were as good as the gold they mined there where the bright lights were blazing.

"We're waiting for you, Daddy," Cheryl said when I crossed the road. "The taxicab's already here."

"I see, hon," I said, and gave Cheryl a big hug. The cabdriver was sitting in the driver's seat having a smoke with the lights on inside. Edna was leaning against the back of the cab between the taillights, wearing her Bailey hat. "What'd you tell him?" I said when I got close.

"Nothing," she said. "What's there to tell?"

"Did he see the car?"

She glanced over in the direction of the trees where we had hid the Mercedes. Nothing was visible in the darkness, though I could hear Little Duke combing around in the underbrush tracking something, his little collar tinkling. "Where're we going?" she said. "I'm so hungry I could pass out."

"Edna's in a terrible mood," Cheryl said. "She already snapped at me."

"We're tired, honey," I said. "So try to be nicer."

"She's never nice," Cheryl said.

"Run go get Little Duke," I said. "And hurry back."

"I guess *my* questions come last here, right?" Edna said.

I put my arm around her. "That's not true."

"Did you find somebody over there in the trailers you'd rather stay with? You were gone long enough."

"That's not a thing to say," I said. "I was just trying to make things look right, so we don't get put in jail."

"So *you* don't, you mean." Edna laughed a little laugh I didn't like hearing.

"That's right. So I don't," I said. "I'd be the one in Dutch." I stared out at the big, lighted assemblage of white buildings and white lights beyond the trailer community, plumes of white smoke escaping up into the heartless Wyoming sky, the whole company of buildings looking like some unbelievable castle, humming away in a distorted dream. "You know what all those buildings are there?" I said to Edna, who hadn't moved and who didn't really seem to care if she ever moved anymore ever.

"No. But I can't say it matters, because it isn't a motel and it isn't a restaurant."

"It's a gold mine," I said, staring at the gold mine, which, I knew now, was a greater distance from us than it seemed, though it seemed huge and near, up against the cold sky. I thought there should've been a wall around it with guards instead of just the lights and no fence. It seemed as if anyone could go in and take what they wanted, just the way I had gone up to that woman's trailer and used the telephone, though that obviously wasn't true.

Edna began to laugh then. Not the mean laugh I didn't like, but a laugh that had something caring behind it, a full laugh that enjoyed a joke, a laugh she was laughing the first time I laid eyes on her, in Missoula in the East Gate Bar in 1979, a laugh we used to laugh together when Cheryl was still with her mother and I was working steady at the track and not stealing cars or passing bogus checks to merchants. A better time all around. And for some reason it made me laugh just hearing her, and we both stood there behind the cab in the dark, laughing at the gold mine in the desert, me with my arm around her and Cheryl out rustling up Little Duke and the cabdriver smoking in the cab and our stolen Mercedes-Benz, which I'd had such hopes for in Florida, stuck up to its axle in sand, where I'd never get to see it again.

"I always wondered what a gold mine would look like when I saw it," Edna said, still laughing, wiping a tear from her eye.

"Me too," I said. "I was always curious about it."

"We're a couple of fools, aren't we, Earl?" she said, unable to quit laughing completely. "We're two of a kind."

"It might be a good sign, though," I said.

"How could it be? It's not our gold mine. There aren't any drive-up windows." She was still laughing.

"We've seen it," I said, pointing. "That's it right there. It may mean we're getting closer. Some people never see it at all."

"In a pig's eye, Earl," she said. "You and me see it in a pig's eye."

And she turned and got in the cab to go.

The cabdriver didn't ask anything about our car or where it was, to mean he'd noticed something queer. All of which made me feel like we had made a clean break from the car and couldn't be connected with it until it was too late, if ever. The driver told us a lot about Rock Springs while he drove, that because of the gold mine a lot of people had moved there in just six months, people from all over, including New York, and that most of them lived out in the trailers. Prostitutes from New York City, who he called "B-girls," had come into town, he said, on the prosperity tide, and Cadillacs with New York plates cruised the little streets every night, full of Negroes with big hats who ran the women. He told us that everybody who got in his cab now wanted to know where the women were, and when he got our call he almost didn't come because some of the trailers were brothels operated by the mine for engineers and computer people away from home. He said he got tired of running back and forth out there just for vile business. He said that *60 Minutes* had even done a program about Rock Springs and that a blow-up had resulted in Cheyenne, though nothing could be done unless the boom left town. "It's prosperity's fruit," the driver said. "I'd rather be poor, which is lucky for me."

He said all the motels were sky-high, but since we were a family he could show us a nice one that was affordable. But I told him we wanted a first-rate place where they took animals, and the money didn't matter because we had had a hard day and wanted to finish on a high note. I also knew that it was in the little nowhere places that the police look for you and find you. People I'd known were always being arrested in cheap hotels and tourist courts with names you'd never heard of before. Never in Holiday Inns or TraveLodges.

I asked him to drive us to the middle of town and back out again so Cheryl could see the train station, and while we were there I saw a pink Cadillac with New York plates and a TV aerial being driven slowly by a Negro in a big hat down a narrow street where there were just bars and a Chinese restaurant. It was an odd sight, nothing you could ever expect.

"There's your pure criminal element," the cabdriver said and seemed sad. "I'm sorry for people like you to see a thing like that. We've got a nice town here, but there're some that want to ruin it for everybody. There used to be a way to deal with trash and criminals, but those days are gone forever."

"You said it," Edna said.

"You shouldn't let it get *you* down," I said to him. "There's more of you than them. And there always will be. You're the best advertisement this town has. I know Cheryl will remember you and not *that* man, won't you, honey?" But Cheryl was asleep by then, holding Little Duke in her arms on the taxi seat.

The driver took us to the Ramada Inn on the interstate, not far from where we'd broken down. I had a small pain of regret as we drove under the Ramada awning that we hadn't driven up in a cranberry-colored Mercedes but instead in a beat-up old Chrysler taxi driven by an old man full of complaints.

Though I knew it was for the best. We were better off without that car; better, really, in any other car but that one, where the signs had turned bad.

I registered under another name and paid for the room in cash so there wouldn't be any questions. On the line where it said "Representing" I wrote "Ophthalmologist" and put "M.D." after the name. It had a nice look to it, even though it wasn't my name.

When we got to the room, which was in the back where I'd asked for it, I put Cheryl on one of the beds and Little Duke beside her so they'd sleep. She'd missed dinner, but it only meant she'd be hungry in the morning, when she could have anything she wanted. A few missed meals don't make a kid bad. I'd missed a lot of them myself and haven't turned out completely bad.

"Let's have some fried chicken," I said to Edna when she came out of the bathroom. "They have good fried chicken at Ramadas, and I noticed the buffet was still up. Cheryl can stay right here, where it's safe, till we're back."

"I guess I'm not hungry anymore," Edna said. She stood at the window staring out into the dark. I could see out the window past her some yellowish foggy glow in the sky. For a moment I thought it was the gold mine out in the distance lighting the night, though it was only the interstate.

"We could order up," I said. "Whatever you want. There's a menu on the phone book. You could just have a salad."

"You go ahead," she said. "I've lost my hungry spirit." She sat on the bed beside Cheryl and Little Duke and looked at them in a sweet way and put her hand on Cheryl's cheek just as if she'd had a fever. "Sweet little girl," she said. "Everybody loves you."

"What do you want to do?" I said. "I'd like to eat. Maybe *I'll* order up some chicken."

"Why don't you do that?" she said. "It's your favorite." And she smiled at me from the bed.

I sat on the other bed and dialed room service. I asked for chicken, garden salad, potato and a roll, plus a piece of hot apple pie and iced tea. I realized I hadn't eaten all day. When I put down the phone I saw that Edna was watching me, not in a hateful way or a loving way, just in a way that seemed to say she didn't understand something and was going to ask me about it.

"When did watching me get so entertaining?" I said and smiled at her. I was trying to be friendly. I knew how tired she must be. It was after nine o'clock.

"I was just thinking how much I hated being in a motel without a car that was mine to drive. Isn't that funny? I started feeling like that last night when that purple car wasn't mine. That purple car just gave me the willies, I guess, Earl."

"One of those cars *outside* is yours," I said. "Just stand right there and pick it out."

"I know," she said. "But that's different, isn't it?" She reached and got her blue Bailey hat, put it on her head, and set it way back like Dale Evans. She looked sweet. "I used to like to go to motels, you know," she said. "There's something secret about them and free—I was never paying, of course. But you felt safe from everything and free to do what you wanted because you'd made the decision to be there and paid that price, and all the rest was the good part. Fucking and everything, you know." She smiled at me in a good-natured way.

"Isn't that the way this is?" I was sitting on the bed, watching her, not knowing what to expect her to say next.

"I don't guess it is, Earl," she said and stared out the window. "I'm thirty-two and I'm going to have to give up on motels. I can't keep that fantasy going anymore."

"Don't you like this place?" I said and looked around at the room. I appreciated the modern paintings and the lowboy bureau and the big TV. It seemed like a plenty nice enough place to me, considering where we'd been.

"No, I don't," Edna said with real conviction. "There's no use in my getting mad at you about it. It isn't your fault. You do the best you can for everybody. But every trip teaches you something. And I've learned I need to give up on motels before some bad thing happens to me. I'm sorry."

"What does that mean?" I said, because I really didn't know what she had in mind to do, though I should've guessed.

"I guess I'll take that ticket you mentioned," she said, and got up and faced the window. "Tomorrow's soon enough. We haven't got a car to take me anyhow."

"Well, that's a fine thing," I said, sitting on the bed, feeling like I was in shock. I wanted to say something to her, to argue with her, but I couldn't think what to say that seemed right. I didn't want to be mad at her, but it made me mad.

"You've got a right to be mad at me, Earl," she said, "but I don't think you can really blame me." She turned around and faced me and sat on the windowsill, her hands on her knees. Someone knocked on the door, and I just yelled for them to set the tray down and put it on the bill.

"I guess I *do* blame you," I said, and I was angry. I thought about how I could've disappeared into that trailer community and hadn't, had come back to keep things going, had tried to take control of things for everybody when they looked bad.

"Don't. I wish you wouldn't," Edna said and smiled at me like she wanted me to hug her. "Anybody ought to have their choice in things if they can. Don't you believe that, Earl? Here I am out here in the desert where I don't know anything, in a stolen car, in a motel room under an assumed name, with no money of my own, a kid that's not mine, and the law after me. And I have a choice to get out of all of it by getting on a bus. What would you do? I know exactly what you'd do."

"You think you do," I said. But I didn't want to get into an argument about it and tell her all I could've done and didn't do. Because it wouldn't have done any good. When you get to the point of arguing, you're past the point of changing anybody's mind, even though it's supposed to be the other way, and maybe for some classes of people it is, just never mine.

Edna smiled at me and came across the room and put her arms around me where I was sitting on the bed. Cheryl rolled over and looked at us and smiled, then closed her eyes, and the room was quiet. I was beginning to think of Rock Springs in a way I knew I would always think of it, a lowdown city full of crimes and whores and disappointments, a place where a woman left me, instead of a place where I got things on the straight track once and for all, a place I saw a gold mine.

"Eat your chicken, Earl," Edna said. "Then we can go to bed. I'm tired, but I'd like to make love to you anyway. None of this is a matter of not loving you, you know that."

Sometime late in the night, after Edna was asleep, I got up and walked outside into the parking lot. It could've been anytime because there was still the light from the interstate frosting the low sky and the big red Ramada sign humming motionlessly in the night and no light at all in the east to indicate it might be morning. The lot was full of cars all nosed in, a couple of them with suitcases strapped to their roofs and their trunks weighed down with belongings the people were taking someplace, to a new home or a vacation resort in the mountains. I had laid in bed a long time after Edna was asleep, watching the Atlanta Braves on television, trying to get my mind off how I'd feel when I saw that bus pull away the next day, and how I'd feel when I turned around and there stood Cheryl and Little Duke and no one to see about them but me alone, and that the first thing I had to do was get hold of some automobile and get the plates switched, then get them some breakfast and get us all on the road to Florida, all in the space of probably two hours, since that Mercedes would certainly look less hid in the daytime than the night, and word travels fast. I've always taken care of Cheryl myself as long as I've had her with me. None of the women ever did. Most of them didn't even seem to like her, though they took care of me in a way so that I could take care of her. And I knew that once Edna left, all that was going to get harder. Though what I wanted most to do was not think about it just for a little while, try to let my mind go limp so it could be strong for the rest of what there was. I thought that the difference between a successful life and an unsuccessful one, between me at that moment and all the people who owned the cars that were nosed into their proper places in the lot, maybe between me and that woman out in the trailers by the gold mine, was how well you were able to put things like this out of your mind and not be bothered by them, and maybe, too, by how many troubles like this one you had to face in a lifetime. Through luck or design they had all faced fewer troubles, and by their own characters, they forgot them faster. And that's what I wanted for me. Fewer troubles, fewer memories of trouble.

I walked over to a car, a Pontiac with Ohio tags, one of the ones with bundles and suitcases strapped to the top and a lot more in the trunk, by the way it was riding. I looked inside the driver's window. There were maps and paperback books and sunglasses and the little plastic holders for cans that hang on the window wells. And in the back there were kids' toys and some pillows and a cat box with a cat sitting in it staring up at me like I was the face of the moon. It all looked familiar to me, the very same things I would have in my car if I had a car. Nothing seemed surprising, nothing different. Though I had a funny sensation at that moment and turned and looked up at the windows along the back of the motel. All were dark except two. Mine and another one. And I wondered, because it seemed funny, what would you think a man was doing if you saw him in the middle of the night looking in the windows of cars in the parking lot of the Ramada Inn? Would you think he was trying to get his head cleared? Would you think he was trying to get ready for a day when trouble would come down on him? Would you think his girlfriend was leaving him? Would you think he had a daughter? Would you think he was anybody like you?

DAVID GATES

The Mail Lady

DAVID GATES (1947–) is the author of a recent collection of stories, *The Wonders of the Invisible World,* and two novels, *Jernigan,* nominated for the Pulitzer Prize, and *Preston Falls,* named one of the *New York Times Book Review*'s Top Ten Books of 1998. His stories have appeared in *Esquire, GQ, Grand Street, TriQuarterly,* and *Ploughshares,* and have been anthologized in *The Best American Short Stories 1994* and *Prize Stories: The O. Henry Awards 1995.* His byline appears frequently in *Newsweek,* for which he is a staff writer on books and music.

I wake again in our bedroom, vouchsafed another day. May I use it to Thy greater glory. In the dimness, a throbbing line of sunlight along the bottom of the window shade stabs the eye. So the rain has stopped at last. (Memory spared. Reason spared, too, seemingly.) When I turn away, my sight is momentarily burned black, and I can't be certain whether I'm truly *seeing* Wylie's features in the photograph on the nightstand or simply remembering them. I close my eyes again, and in afterimage the fierce light reappears.

The radio's on downstairs and I hear that sweet song, now what on earth is that called? Sweet sweet song. Our station comes all the way from Boston, and seems to be the one certain refuge anywhere on the dial. We still try the classical station from time to time—back in Woburn, we never deviated from WCRB—but now find it awfully heavy going. (I have it: "Edelweiss.") Now I hear a rustle of sheets. Alice is in here, making her bed. And checking on me. I don't open my eyes. A pat to her pillow and she's gone.

In the first weeks after my shock, I slept fourteen, sixteen hours a day, they tell me. The brain, as they explain it, shutting down in order to repair itself. It's the queerest idea: one's body simply shoving one aside. Lately I'm down to eight or nine hours (plus my nap in the afternoon), so I assume that much of what could be done has now been done. The thing is to be thankful for what's come back. But try as I will, it frets me: I had been, for my age, an active man. Taking care that each season's duties be done. Trees and shrubs pruned in the spring, leaves raked and burned in the fall. I would sleep six hours a night, seldom more, and wake up—if not refreshed, at least ready for what might be required. Now, in effect, I'm a child again, put to bed early and hearing the grown-ups through a closed door. Like a child, too, with these sudden storms of weeping. I'm told they could still come under control.

Stroke: a stroke of the lash, for chastisement and correction. Yet something gentle in the word as well.

The next thing I hear is Alice down in the kitchen, so I must have dozed off again. Or, God help me, had a vastation. I can hear the stove making that snapping sound, like a dangerous thing. Then it goes silent again, or nearly so, when it lights. I say nearly so because I seem to hear the ceaseless exhale of gas and the rumble of blue flame burning. Just after my shock my hearing became strangely acute (unless I was imagining it), as if in compensation for what I can only describe as the cubist way I was seeing things. Yet although my eyesight has returned to normal (thank you, Lord), that acute sense of hearing seems not to have been repossessed. So perhaps something else is being compensated for. I pray it's not some cognitive function that I'm too damaged to understand has been damaged.

Still, sharp as my hearing may be, it's impossible, isn't it, that I could hear a gas stove burning all the way down in the kitchen? Or—terrible thought—is what I'm hearing (or think I'm hearing) the hiss of unignited gas racing out the ports, spreading, expanding, filling the house? Well, and what then? Would I shout for Alice—who, being downstairs, may have been overcome already? Would I struggle up out of bed and make my way down the stairs after my new fashion, bad foot scraping along after good foot and cane? Or would I simply lie here and breathe?

Well, hardly a cheerful reflection to begin the day.

And good cheer—not mere resignation—is required of us. *To be unhappy is to be in sin*—I'm certain I've read that somewhere or other, though perhaps it was the other way around. Certainly easier to swallow it the other way around—to be in sin is to be unhappy—but that makes it so trite I don't see why it would have made an impression. Now what was my point? Good cheer. I had wanted to say, it is available to us. Freely offered. We need to know where to look, is all. And where not to. Back when Wylie was a little girl and Alice and I would have our troubles (I would like to believe we never allowed them to darken her childhood), I used to say to myself, *But on the other hand, you have Wylie.* Though there were times when even that didn't mean what it ought to have meant, and at such times I would have to be stern with myself and say, *You must think of Wylie.* This was before the Lord came into my life.

It's been many years, of course, since Wylie has lived at home. And many years, too, since Alice and I have had words. So things happen as they were meant to, and in the Lord's good time. Though I dread sometimes that I will pass on before I know, with my whole heart, that this is true. When in a more hopeful frame of mind, I think the Lord would never allow it, and that His plan for me includes revelations yet in store.

Certainly Alice hasn't presumed to question (in my hearing) the dispensation that now binds her to a piece of statuary in the likeness of her husband. (Now that, I'm sorry to say, smacks of self-pity.) *In sickness and in health,* she must tell herself daily. She has never complained about being unable to leave me alone. Or about the friends who have stopped visiting. (We have seen the Petersons *once!*) Her strength shames me, much as I like to think that these past months have made shame a luxury. (I have even been, God help me, incontinent.) And from little things I overhear, I gather she's quietly making her plans for afterwards. I'm afraid to ask about the details, and ashamed that I'm afraid. Isn't this something she's owed: a chance to talk with her husband about what must be on her mind constantly? What may in fact have been on her mind for years, since even before my illness (as she calls it) the actuarial tables were on her side. Although we've always taken pride (I know it's blamable) in not being like the generality of people.

It was my conversion, of course, that made me odd man out for many of my working years. Research chemists tend to be a skeptical lot anyway, and our company was particularly forward-thinking. (We were one of the first, you know, to have moved out to Route 128.) Eventually I decided it was best to steer clear of certain discussions; *As much as lieth in you,* Paul tells us, *live peaceably with all men.* Poor Alice, meanwhile, has had to go from being the wife of a hot-tempered drinker to being the wife of a religious nut, so-called. I remember one day, shortly after my life had been transformed, I walked in on her ironing one of Wylie's school skirts with the telephone wedged between ear and shoulder. "I'll tell you, June," she was saying, "I don't get it quite, but I don't look a gift horse in the mouth." Then she noticed me in the doorway and drew a hissing in-breath as her arms shrank into her ribs and the receiver clunked to the floor.

Up here we've found our neighbors more congenial politically than the old crowd from work, if not so well informed. The mail lady has told Alice that no one in town gets so many magazines. The people we know here, other retirees mostly, take *Modern Maturity* and *Reader's Digest.* The younger people, I imagine, scarcely read a newspaper; Alice was dismayed to learn that only two families in town get *Time.* But of course she can make conversation with anybody, right down to the neighbor woman, that Mrs. Paquette, whose talk even in the summertime is mostly about how she can no longer stand New Hampshire winters. She was over again the other morning—or was it earlier this morning?—for coffee and chitchat. Which is what her life amounts to, as far as I can see, though what can my life seem in her eyes? I could hear them all the way downstairs.

"Well, if anything should happen to Lew," Alice was saying, "Florida's the *last* place I'd go. And I would certainly not go out and inflict myself on Wylie and Jeff."

I thought about the word *anything*.

I thought about the word *if*.

"I think I'd try and get myself one of those new little apartments over in Concord," she said. "Have you been by there?"

I knew the place she meant. Brown brick and brown window glass. I had had no idea it loomed so large for her.

I wake again when Alice comes in and sets my tray on the dresser. How long have I been asleep this time? I struggle up to a sitting position—now that's something I couldn't have done a while ago!—she wedges the triangular pillow behind me and I collapse back on it. She's taken to saying that I live the life of Riley, getting my breakfast in bed. Can she think I don't understand (and don't understand that *she* understands) the truth of what has happened to me? To which cheer is still the only adequate response—but true cheer, not this life-of-Riley business. She hands me my eyeglasses, then walks over and tugs down on the string with the lace-covered ring at the end. Up goes the shade, and there I sit blinking like a nasty old owl (I can picture myself), the white hairs of my knobby chest curling out between the lapels of my pajamas. How can she stand this, unless she looks with the eyes of love? Or unless she no longer truly looks. She places the tray across my thighs, the living and the dead. Orange juice, Postum, All-Bran, and half a pink grapefruit, its sections sliced away from the sides, ready for the spoon. And this morning, a gaudy blossom—from one of her gloxinias?—floating in a juice glass.

"Austerity breakfast," I say. Yesterday was a bacon-and-eggs day; I am not allowed two in a row.

"Posterity?" she says.

"Aus-ter-i-ty," I say, furious. I point to the food. "Austere," I say.

"Ah," she says, giving me a too energetic nod. Can't tell if she's understood or not.

"On in the world," I say, a question.

"The world?" she says. "The news? Oh, they had the most awful thing this morning."

"Hear TV going," I say, meaning *I didn't*.

"The TV?" she says. "Yes, they were talking more about that airplane."

"Jet with a bomb," I say. We'd seen the report last night.

"Well now they're saying that those people who were sucked out of that hole?" She makes parentheses in air to suggest a hole three feet across. "They're saying that they apparently were *not* killed when it went off. They found out they were alive all the way down."

"Out you're alive," I say. Meaning *Well that's one way to find out you're alive.* I was making a joke out of her *theys*. Which I suppose was heartless. Though whom, really, could it hurt? Who, for that matter, could understand it? Alice cocks her head and squints, then just barges on. "And that poor woman was pregnant," she says.

Enough and more than enough of the world news roundup. I want her out of here now. Smear my food all over my face in peace.

"I'm going to let you eat your breakfast before it gets cold," she says, though there's nothing to get cold but the Postum. "Do you need anything else, dear?"

I don't bother answering. But when I see her going through the door, going away from me, I find that I'm weeping. It's one of the peculiarities of this thing: my body's heaving with sobs, the tears are rolling down my cheeks and off my jaw, yet really I feel nothing. Or so it seems to me. I command the crying to stop: no use. Something undamaged inside me is observing all this, but can't get out of its own silent space to intervene. Quite a study in something, if I could get it across to anyone.

After the fit passes, I take my time eating. Obviously. (Now there's a joke at *my* expense!) What I mean is, I'm dawdling to put off the process of dressing myself and getting myself downstairs. Dr. Ngo (you pronounce it like the fellow in James Bond) had suggested to Alice that she convert the dining room into a bedroom, but I wouldn't hear of it. And Mrs. Midgely backed me right up. (These therapists call you by your first name, but as soon as I was able to make myself understood I let it be known that it was to be *Mr. Coley* and *Mrs. Midgely.*) "If he can do it once," Mrs. Midgely said, "he can do it every day." Going up and down stairs and dressing yourself are what they're keenest on your learning.

Most days, though, it hardly seems worth the struggle—a way I must fight against thinking. I'll sit in the living room and look at the television, or read a magazine, or work a crossword puzzle. A great mercy that my vision has straightened out again: at first I saw only parts of things, and letters and words refused to stay in their proper order. A mercy, too, that I was muddled enough in my thinking at the time so this didn't alarm me. Nowadays I'm able to read everything from the *National Review* to our local newspaper. I even read the Neighbors page, about people we don't know being visited by their grown children from out of state, and the notices of church suppers and bingo games we can no longer attend. Not that we ever attended them. To have ended up in a town where our next-door neighbors live in a trailer (it *is* kept up nicely) with a Virgin Mary sheltering in a half-buried bathtub—it's not what we had expected of life.

Now stop right there and listen to yourself: will you ever awaken to your abundant blessings? Which *continue* to be abundant. That, I have come to believe, is part of what the Lord means to tell me. My stroke is part of our long conversation.

I'm sitting on the bed trying to pull on my socks one-handed when I hear a car slow up. I grip the four-footed aluminum cane with my good hand, rock a little to get me going, shudder up to a standing position, and go thump-scrape, thump-scrape over to the window. When I finally get over there, I see the mail lady pulling away from our mailbox in her tall, big-tired pickup truck. Toolbox on it the size of a child's coffin. Sometime during the winter, I'm not clear just when, it was while I was still in the hospital, I remember Alice telling me about the mail lady towing that roughneck Bobby Paquette's car out of the snow on Lily Pond Road. (This is the neighbor woman's nephew.) Alice says her truck's equipped with a winch and I don't know what all. A male lady indeed. Mrs. Laffond looks like a movie cowboy, sun-scorched and slitty-eyed. And that short hair doesn't help matters. Now Wylie when she was growing up was something of a tomboy too, but always looked feminine. An outdoor girl, perhaps it's better to say. Always enjoyed bicycling, played softball on the girls' team. If back then there'd been the agitation you see today over the Little League (and now even on into the high schools in some places), Wylie would've been first in line, I'm sure. But for the sake of being modern, not mannish. This Mrs. Laffond, though. It's nothing to see her in garageman's getup: green gabardine shirt and the trousers to match. There was a Mr. Laffond, but he left for parts unknown. Supposedly he drank. (Small wonder, wouldn't you say?) It would be their own business, of course, if there weren't children involved. Two little girls and a boy, Alice says. The one thing these people seem able to do is breed, if that's not an un-Christian observation.

"The mail's here," Alice calls from down in the kitchen, over the top of the music. "Are you done your tray?"

She'll find out whether or not I'm *done my tray,* as she puts it, when she comes back upstairs, not sooner. I won't have all this hollering in the house.

2

When I finally do get myself down to the living room, I find Alice working away with her plant mister.

"Don't *you* look spruce this morning," she says. I have on a pink oxford shirt and my gray wool slacks, neither spruce nor otherwise. "You know," she says, "I was thinking. You've been cooped up in here for days with the rain and all. Why don't we bundle you up warm and walk down together and get the mail? I think the fresh air would do you good."

"Sea a mud," I say. Just look at that driveway. They ought to have brought a load of traprock last fall, but they didn't come and didn't come, which seems to be par for the course up here. And then the ground froze, and then I had my shock.

"Such a beautiful day," she says.

It's one of those early spring days when you begin to smell the earth again. Painfully bright blue sky and the sun giving a false warmth. The branches of the bare trees seem silvery. Once I get down the steps, I stop and work open the buttons of my overcoat to let the air at my body, though what's wrong has nothing to do with the body. Halfway down the driveway I stop to rest, take Alice's arm to steady me, and poke the muddy wheelrut with one of my cane's rubber-tipped spider legs.

"Get in out," I say, meaning *You'll never be able to.* "Moon vehicle need the moon vehicle."

"Moon vehicle?" says Alice. "Why are you saying a moon vehicle, dear?"

"Truck the truck," I say. What I'm trying to get across is the mail lady's pickup truck. I float my good hand up to show the tall tires. No use. Oh, I hate this business where Alice thinks I'm making no sense when I *am* making sense. But this is serious business, this situation here with the driveway. To keep out of the mud, Alice has been driving along the edge of the grass, which is tearing up the lawn, and now we're going to have *that* on our hands, getting someone in to reseed it and roll it. On *her* hands, I suppose I mean.

The mail lady has brought a telephone bill, a letter from Wylie, and the new *Smithsonian.* Good: there's this afternoon taken care of. Alice tucks the envelopes inside the *Smithsonian* and we start back. It's become our custom to save the opening of the mail for when we get back to the house.

"Why I think that's a robin," says Alice as we start for the house again. "See? In that maple tree? No, over there—that's an oak tree."

Something or other flies off in the direction of the Paquettes'.

"I'm certain that was a robin," she says.

"So be it," I say. The way my mouth works now, I seem to be saying *Soviet.* This walk will have been enough and more than enough. I make her stop to rest three times on the way back.

When we've finally gotten my things off—I manage the coat all right, but the overshoes prove too much—we go into the living room so we can sit comfortably over the mail. I open the telephone bill, and she opens Wylie's letter.

Our old division of responsibilities: the human side for her. Though my side is now only ceremonial.

The telephone bill is sixty-eight dollars!

I study it and study it. Most of the calls are to Wylie. One to Phoenix, which must be Alice's sister Sylvia. Framingham (her friend June Latham), Taunton (her brother Herb), Taunton again. Oh I suppose it's correct. I've long given up trying to make sense of all those pages in the phone bill. I lay the thing down and look out the window.

"Wylie say?" I ask Alice. It looks like such a long way down there to the mailbox. How had I managed it? The trees are dead motionless, even in their smallest branches, but beyond them, in the pure blue, a small cloud riddled with blue gaps is traveling steadily from left to right. Its shape slowly changes as it moves. On a high branch of our apple tree is perched a bird—a robin, if it pleases Alice to think so—lifting its throat and opening its beak. Singing, apparently. A tiny speck drops straight, swift, and silent from below its tail. This simple process is not an occasion for shame. At least among those of His creatures who are not accountable.

Alice has not answered me. I turn away from the window and she's holding the letter out to me with an expression I don't know what to make of. Glad, but something else, too. It's the expression she had when she first watched me, cheered on by Mrs. Midgely, lurch up a flight of steps. I take the letter with my good hand. Like all Wylie's letters, it is written in blue felt-tip on lined notebook paper. Since they never taught penmanship at that school of hers—I came near to pulling her out of there because of it—her handwriting, part script, part print, still looks like that of a child. Nearly as bad as mine now looks. As for her style, so-called, we also have progressive education to thank.

> Dear Mom & Dad,
>
> I thought I would tell you this in a letter instead of on the phone because I thought you might like having this letter to keep. Not to keep you in suspense anymore, you are going to be grandparents! I am having a baby sometime the beginning of December. We found out today and are so thrilled. I sort of wanted you to know right off by phone but thought this best. Please do phone though when you get this, but I decided you would like having this letter to keep. Jeffrey sends his love.
>
> Love you alot,
> Wylie

Well, my first reaction is, why all this folderol about sentimental keepsakes when the plain truth of it is, Wylie can no longer bear talking to me on the telephone. And of course such a piece of news might well have rendered me more than usually—what shall we say?—unpredictable.

I tried to feel something more appropriate. I mean, good heavens, a grandchild.

"Oh I'm so glad," says Alice. "I thought she didn't *want* children."

"Trend the trend now the trend," I say.

"The trend?" she says. "I don't like to think of Wylie as part of any trend," she says.

I wave my good hand and say, "Shining individual," meaning *Fine, have it your way.* Alice cocks her head: more gabble she won't bother trying to decode. She looks at her wristwatch.

"Almost noon," she says. "So it's about nine o'clock." She picks up the phone.

It's so quiet in our house that I can hear the purr of the telephone ringing on the other end. Save this letter! Save it for *when,* for pity's sake? Things like this make you realize that Wylie still thinks of us as we were when she was a child. Take the time, a couple of years ago, when she was still living in New York and we came down to visit and she walked Alice's legs off shopping. More to the point, look at her decision to move a continent away from us. The pace was slower out there, she said. The air was better. The air was better! I blame Jeffrey in part. Of course this was before my shock; would she make the same choice today? I don't know. I don't suppose I want to know.

As Alice listens to the phone ring and ring, her smile becomes less and less a smile. Finally it is not a smile at all. She lays the receiver back down. Here we are.

3

It's a thing I try not to dwell on, but at times—talk to myself as I will, pray as I will for understanding—I can see no spiritual significance whatever in my ruin. And let's for heaven's sake not be mealy-mouthed about it: I am ruined, in this life. No appeal, no going back. Dragging half a dead body from room to room, numb lips and steak-thick tongue refusing to move as I command. If I am of use at all anymore, it can only be as an example of patient endurance. Or, more likely, of the perils of cholesterol. Since I was neither a smoker nor (at least in recent years) a drinker, it keeps coming back to that, doesn't it? Apparently I have thrown away my birthright—the everyday miracle of a functioning human body—for the sake of two eggs, every morning for forty years, over easy. For the sake of two strips of bacon, wet with fat, laid parallel next to the eggs, and the whole thing set before me like the four-and-twenty blackbirds baked in a pie. Initially in love and ignorance, then later, as the magazine articles began to come out, in love alone.

"He's saying you can't teach an old dog new tricks," Alice said to Dr. Ngo, translating for me. "He hates the breakfasts."

"Ah," said Dr. Ngo, who plainly didn't know enough English to understand even our most common idioms. I sat there stony with shame.

"He's been so used to his bacon and eggs," she said.

"Ah," said Dr. Ngo. "Two time a week it not hurt him you understand?"

I understood. This meant: why not pop off a little sooner with a few familiar comforts, since pop off I must?

"I am of more value than my pleasures," I said, or tried to say. What drunken smear of vowels came out I'm unwilling to remember. What I meant was that I mattered and must persist.

"Say again, dear?" said Alice.

I shook my head no and swatted the air with my good hand, *Go away go away.* What I had tried to say bordered on blasphemy: it went without saying, did it not, that I was to have life everlasting?

4

But since my purchase on *this* life (though no one will say so) seems none too certain, it has been decided that we must waste no time in wishing Wylie joy in person. Decided, I need not add, by Alice and Wylie. These days I'm doing well to get a *What do you think, dear?* And since Wylie is not to travel—in fact, must spend much of her time lying down—we are to come to them. So it's heigh-ho for Seattle. What do you think, dear?

What I think is, I'll do as I'm bid. If I can be wheeled onto an airplane, I can certainly sit for six hours. What else do I do? These terrorists hold no terrors for me, not because I'm armed in faith particularly—I wish I could say I were—but because no place seems safer than any other anymore. When we left Woburn there was a bad element moving in. In Florida you have your drug lords, and people shooting at you from the overpasses on I–295. Our problem up here is the roughnecks who ride the back roads in loud cars. They listen to the metal music.

Alice keeps asking, aren't I looking forward to seeing Wylie. The aim is to keep me looking forward. Of course what can I say but yes. But much as I love her—and I *do* look forward—I must say that Wylie can be trying. She has become one of those people who put bumper stickers on their automobiles—at one point, I recall, she had replaced *Visualize Peace* with *Teach Peace,* which seemed to me at least a small step away from delusion—and who believe we can communicate with the plants and the dolphins. I blame Bard College. And I imagine Jeffrey encourages it. I used to tell her, *You'd best forget the dolphins and learn to talk to your Savior.* I've come to accept that these things sink in if and when He wills them to sink in, so I try to soft-pedal that. Now some Christians—our minister up here is one—will tell you that the whole what they call New Age is of the devil. We'll know someday: *Every man's work shall be made manifest.* But who can be sure today that it's a distraction and a time waster—spiritual danger enough right there, it seems to me. *The night cometh when no man can work.* Alice says that Wylie says she's already begun talking to the baby inside her. I hope it takes what it's hearing with a good-sized grain of salt! I think Wylie imagines that this visit will have given her child at least this much acquaintance with its grandfather. Covering herself, don't you see.

I'm ashamed to say I think about it too. As if I were clutching at a moving train, crying *At least remember me.* (Keep me mindful that another home is prepared for me and that I shall have a new body, incorruptible.) I remember my own grandfather. Or at least I remember remembering him. He used to tell about the Civil War; he was twelve, I believe, when it ended. Now *his* father had been an abolitionist—a Unitarian, he was—and when the news came that President Lincoln was dead he had all the children dressed up in mourning. And my grandfather had a fistfight with a neighbor boy whose family hated the colored. The Coleys lived in Westerly in those days. And still lived there, in the old house, until my father died in '41, and still went to the Unitarian church. You know the saying, how the Unitarians believe in one God at most. Supposed to be a joke. But it chills me now to remember that beautiful white church-house from which the Holy Spirit was so resoundingly absent. Back then, of course, I liked the hymn-singing and that was that.

I thought of my grandfather's story about President Lincoln the other night when we saw Aretha Franklin on the television, singing a song about the turnpike of love, I think it was, and lifting her fleshy arms above her head. A woman of her age and size ought not to be seen in a sleeveless dress. It seemed impossible that I could have lived so long as to have known someone who'd been alive when Abraham Lincoln freed the slaves. I don't recall how we came to be watching such a thing; Alice and I used to enjoy Mahalia Jackson, but this one is too screechy. Sometimes we'll be watching one program and then find ourselves watching the next program and the program after without meaning to. Up here we still get all three networks, of course. And PBS, if you can put up with their political slant. But those people on the local news programs! So young and so coarse-looking. And so poorly spoken, as if they had all just come out of two-year colleges. That's un-Christian of me, I suppose. My own ruined speech is appropriate chastisement.

Just as my having had no son—I've often thought this—may have been chastisement for my pride in family. (There is only one family: the family of His saints.) Though perhaps it's another, more malignant, form of pride to believe myself singled out for chastisement. But for whatever reason, I am the last of the Coleys. There are other people named Coley, of course, but of our Coleys I am the last. We have become a branch of the family tree of people named Gunderson. We're often asked—or *were* often asked, back when we socialized—if Wylie is a family name. I would always say *Why how'd you guess?* to make light of the unusualness. The Wylies are my mother's people. (Alice, of course, is a Stannard.) We knew the name might sound awkward with Coley, so we gave her the middle name Jane as a sort of buffer. When I was a boy I knew a Mary Carey who called herself Mary Jane—she hadn't been so christened—so we thought Wylie Jane Coley would sound all right. Naturally we couldn't have foreseen that the other children would call her Wylie Coyote and tease her by yelling "Beep-beep" and running away from her. (It had to do with some show on the television.) I'm afraid it didn't mollify her when I told her that one of her Wylie forebears had been at the first Constitutional Convention! From when she was eight or nine until she went away to college, she called herself Jane; by then, she must have decided that "Wylie" would put her one up on the Wendys and Jennifers.

Though she hardly needed such help: even as a little girl she was always the prettiest in a group. Or so her father always thought. She was almost plump in grade school. When I first went over to the Paquettes'—and if there's a silver lining to this whole business, it's that I'm no longer able to go over to the Paquettes'—I was reminded of her little belly by that wooden Buddha or whatever it is on top of their television set. (This is a supposedly Christian home! Naturally they're Roman Catholics.) When she was about twelve, though, she began to starve herself and hasn't stopped to this day. Now I don't mean that she was ever in danger of going the way of that other singer, Karen something. (Alice and I watched that poor soul on television along toward the last, and we could both see she wasn't well.) But even two summers ago, when Wylie came east, I noticed her ribs under her T-shirt when she bent to tie her running shoes. (Carpenter, of course. Now you wouldn't think a Christian would forget Carpenter!) Alice, in fact, is concerned about the baby on this account. Another reason for our trip, though naturally she's not saying so to Wylie.

The story I always tell about Wylie (or always told) is the time we went to Alice's brother's house down in Taunton for Christmas. Herb had married a Roman Catholic girl and nothing would do but we had to go to their Christmas Eve mass. Well when we got into the church they had the biggest darned crucifix you ever saw hanging over the altar. The Christ wasn't quite life-size, but it must have been a good three or four feet long, with skin the color of a Band-Aid and a white-painted loincloth. The eyes wide open on it. Believe you me, Wylie's eyes opened pretty wide too: we of course had just the plain gold cross in our church. "Mommy?" she said, loud enough for everybody in the place to hear. "How come he's got diapers on?" To this day, Wylie hates to have that one told on her, though it's a perfectly harmless story.

I now wear a diaper.

The story I never tell about Wylie is this. One afternoon I surprised her and a little girlfriend behind the garage, both of them with their pants down. (This was at our house in Woburn.) I can still remember that little girl's name, Myra Meyers. Speaking of names somebody ought to have thought twice about. I sent her about her business, and grabbed Wylie by the arm and marched her right inside and whaled the living daylights out of her. They say now, of course, that you're not accountable: that you are what you are and not what you make up your mind to be. That it's all genetic: drinkers, too, like the mail lady's husband. That you're helpless to change yourself and certainly can't do anything for anybody else and never mind what God tells us in His word. Well, I believe I changed Wylie that day. Or at least helped her on toward the life she has now, with a husband (though not someone we might have chosen) and about to begin a family (however late). And away from—the old-fashioned word is *abominations,* but I'll say *abnormalities.* (My own theory is, that's what's wrong with the mail lady, children or no children.) I don't imagine Wylie realizes to this day—if she ever thinks of it—that each stroke burned with my love for her. But the day is coming when all that is hidden shall be revealed.

5

When I think back about the first great intervention in my life (I count my shock as the second), I'm ashamed to remember how long I tried to hold out. I first sought the conventional remedy for a man of my background and education (Brown, '39). One takes one's child to see *Fantasia,* one dreams that night of the devil, one's terror does not abate the next morning, nor the next, nor the next. After two weeks of this, off one scurries to a psychiatrist. To whom one is induced to complain about one's own childhood. One is talked around into trying to believe one had such and such feelings about one's father and one's mother: the so-called family romance. (Oh yes, I know the jargon.) It is pointed out to one that the word *abate* is in itself a not insignificant choice. The terror still does not abate.

Then one has a quote unquote chance encounter with a friend who quote unquote just happens to be a Christian.

This was a fellow named John Milliken, whom I'd known when we were both graduate students at Stanford. He actually took his Ph.D.; I'd had to leave and go back to New England when my father died. The little money Alice made at the library was barely enough for the two of us, and now there was Mother to think of. Eventually I was lucky enough to catch on with what was then a scrappy new company (a shoestring operation really in those days, right after the war), willing to hire a young chemist without an advanced degree. Well, Milliken, to make a long story short, ended up working for an outfit we did some business with and living just over in Arlington. So he and I would get together two or three times in the course of a year. We might have seen more of each other, but I was a new father and he was a bachelor. And Alice never warmed up to him, before *or* after.

One Saturday night, probably a month into my troubles, Milliken and I sat late at the bar of the old Parker House and I opened up to him. Alice by this time had taken the baby and gone to stay with Herb and Evelyn in Taunton; we were not calling it a separation. Desperate as I was, I would hardly have told Milliken about it had I not been drinking. In fact, I was hoping he'd call it a night so I could slip over to Scollay Square, to a certain bar I had discovered and wanted to know more about. (The thought of which terrifies me to this day.) But Milliken kept sitting there, nursing his one Manhattan, nodding, putting in a word or two. More or less, I'm bound to say, in the manner of the doctor I'd been seeing. Except kindly.

"Well Lew," he said when I told him about my dream and the terror that wasn't going away, "has it occurred to you to take this thing seriously?"

"Christ sake, what do you *think* I'm doing?" I said.

He shook his head. "Why don't I swing by your house tomorrow morning," he said. "I've got the hangover cure to end all hangover cures. Are you all right to drive, by the way?"

I was not. The room, in fact, looked tilted and seemed to be going silent. I was not all right to live.

"I think you'd best let me drop you," he said. "We can always pick up your car tomorrow. Unless you're afraid to be by yourself tonight. In which case, I've a fold-out sofa you're welcome to."

Years later, when I came to read C. S. Lewis—so often a help to me, and I wish I had the strength of mind to read him now—I was struck by what he said about his conversion. I believe I still have it by heart. *When we set out*—he was riding to the zoo in London in the sidecar of somebody's motorcycle—*I did not believe that Jesus Christ was the Son of God, and when we reached the zoo I did.* That's what it was like, riding to John Milliken's house: it was like riding to John Milliken's house. True, he did begin to pray aloud as we were passing over the Longfellow Bridge, with its stone towers like a castle keep. But around me it was quiet, and the faraway tune his voice was making seemed to blend in with something else that was happening. Out Main Street we flew and onto Massachusetts Avenue, and the people on the sidewalks seemed to pass each other in comradely fashion, like the angels in Jacob's dream—a thing I hadn't thought about, I'm sure, since I was a boy in Sunday school—moving up and down the ladder which reached from earth to heaven. They began to be surrounded by a throbbing radiance, and I thought I saw some of them passing right through others. It didn't strike me as out of the ordinary. I looked over at John Milliken: his profile glowed along its edge from hairline to Adam's apple; light frosted his gnarly eyebrows. His lips were moving. I looked to his hands, gripping the wheel, his bulging knuckles imperfectly mirroring the wheel's knuckled underside, a patch of hair on the top of each finger. I closed my eyes, and sounds rushed back in: the rubbery rapid-fire whapping of tire treads on pavement, John Milliken's voice saying *And in Jesus Christ's name we* something something something, a sweet-toned car horn off somewhere. When I opened my eyes again, there we were: just a couple of fellows in a car heading out Massachusetts Avenue.

But the whole point of Jacob's dream, as I now understand it, is that it's a *dream.* The door between this world and the spiritual world has closed, I have come to believe, and will remain closed until the heaven and the earth shall be made new. This is where I part company, not just with the Wylies of the world, but with the John Millikens. I soon shied away from the so-called spirit-filled church he brought me to that morning, where grown men and women stood blinking and babbling in no language, and he and I lost touch. He must be an old man now. I ended up with the Baptists—imagine what Great-grandfather Coley would say to *that!*—and have mostly felt at home there. With the doctrine if not always with the people.

Of course there are Baptists and Baptists. The fellow up here, for instance, turned out to be—not a modernizer, exactly, but more missionary than pastor. Collecting cans of food is all well and good, but need we congratulate ourselves by stacking the cartons right there in the sanctuary? And where, meanwhile, was the spiritual food? Alice and I hardly need sermons against the metal music. I told him straight out, I said I'd sooner sit home and read God's word. His answer to that was that it was a changing world. Well there you go, I said. I said, Isn't that all the more reason? Talking to a wall. He's a young man, with the same haircut as the television people and a suit that's too tight on him. He shaves so close his jowls gleam. He was probably glad to see the back of me. I suppose he must have said to himself, *Talking to a wall.*

So that was more or less the end of our churchgoing, except for Easter Sunday, when you still stand a fighting chance of hearing a sermon instead of a public-service message. Easter falls early this year; we'll still be in Seattle. (God willing.) I wonder if Wylie couldn't be talked into going to services with us. How she used to plead, when she was a teenager, to be left at home: what if her friends saw her! I sometimes fought down a mean impulse to tell her it was like going to a bar where sailors met businessmen: anyone who saw you there had a guilty secret too.

But that secret was mine, to live with as best I could. They'll never persuade me I was wrong not to have burdened Alice with details of the danger I'd been in. *Bring it to the Lord in prayer,* the song says. It doesn't say, *Bring it to your wife in guilt.* Very much out of fashion, I know, the idea that certain things are between you and the Lord, period. And yes: that morning, in Everett, Massachusetts, in that shabby wainscoted church—the church smell comes back to me, the smell of varnish, the smell of musty hymnals—I made confession. But before a crowd of strangers, whose care was for a soul that could have been anybody's.

6

It's Wednesday morning, and we're about ready to be on our way. Alice has locked the cellar door and the toolshed, carried her gloxinias to the bathtub, plugged the reading lamp into the timer, and set the thermostats (except in the bathroom) down to forty. And I have spent the morning trying to compose a letter. It may be the last piece of business I'll do, formally handing down to my daughter what remains, and I chose to do this last thing without Alice's help. It may also be foolishness—our plane will probably not go down, I will probably live on until the cost of my care eats up all our money—but I felt the need.

Dearest Wylie,

Airplanes I think are not so dangers but I am put in this today what you need to know and send by itself. Our lawyer Mr. Plankey who can explain. He is our will and his card you put away when you need it.

A day goes by with you and my prayers. When you look after your own child you remember He died and still looks after.

Loving father,
Lewis Coley

Oh, this is all wrong, preaching away as I've sworn a hundred times not to do. But no time now: let it go as it is. I lick the envelope—even pulling an envelope across the tongue (and at the same time moving the head in the opposite direction) takes analytic thinking—and put it with the bills to be left in the mailbox.

In our forty years of marriage, Alice has always done our packing, but never before has she handled the bags. I sit at the kitchen table and watch her out the window, struggling, dragging her right leg along in unison with the avocado-green Samsonite suitcase braced against her calf, her head bowed to avoid the branches of the little cherry tree. I ought to have pruned it last year. I must have assumed there would be time.

And, again, I find that I am weeping. It's the sight of her walking away from me. I hear the car trunk slam: I must stop this before she comes back to get me, though I don't know the way to stop. Hardly a cheerful beginning to our trip.

She pulls the car up onto the grass by the back door, but lets me do the steps by myself. There are more steps here than at the front door, but these are easier: a couple of years ago, I had a fellow come around and put up a railing. Nothing fancy, just pressure-treated two-by-fours. Back when breaking a hip in icy weather was the worst I could imagine. Gripping the rail with my good hand and hanging the cane from the crook of my arm like some antique gentleman, I make it down the steps all right. But by the time I've gotten myself into the car and the door closed, I'm done in. Enough and more than enough. And now there's the ride all the way down to Logan yet to do, and after that whatever's involved in getting a crippled man through a modern terminal and after that the hours in the air and after that the journey's unimaginable other end.

We start down the driveway, Alice keeping one wheel up on the strip of grass between the muddy wheel ruts and the other wheel on the lawn.

"Forget the mailbox," I say, meaning *Don't.* I'm making a joke on myself, the joke being that I'm an old fussbudget.

Alice just fetches a sigh. So I sigh too, and look out the window, beating the fingers of my good hand on my good knee, for all the world like a stroke patient. Though deep down I can't believe it, I remind myself this may be the last time I'll see this lawn, such as it is, with its untrimmed shrubs and the rocks I used to hit with the lawn mower. I try to give it the looking-at it deserves. And fall short as always. This was what we had worked toward, and we came too late to love it.

"Why don't I pull over close to the mailbox," says Alice, "and you just put down your window and pop the things in."

"Get stuck," I say.

"Good heavens," she says, "Mrs. Laffond goes in and out of here every day."

She gets the car over so that my mirror almost scrapes the mailbox and I feel my whole side of the car go down. Oh brother. I roll down my window as if nothing were wrong—trying to work magic, in spite of all I know and believe!—pull open the mailbox, stick the envelopes in, push the thing shut, and flip up the flag. As I roll the window back up, I look over at Alice, who looks at her watch and then at the dashboard clock. Her mouth is twitching. She steps on the gas: the wheels just whine and spin. She cuts the steering hard to the left, guns it, and we sink deeper.

"No no no no," I say. Doesn't the woman know you want to keep your wheels straight?

She jams it into reverse, guns it again, and the back tires just spin deeper.

"Cut your wheels!" I cry, meaning *Don't.* So of course she does, except she can't because we're in so deep. "Rock have to rock." Damn it she has to rock the damn car if it'll even rock.

"I don't know what you're saying," she says.

"You car rocking!" I holler. She slams it back into drive, the wheels spin, and she glares over at me.

I say, "Damn fuck."

"Well why don't *you* try it then," she says. Then she says, "I'm sorry, Lew, I didn't mean that." Well the harm is done: the next thing you know I'm sitting here bawling like a big angry baby.

"Lew," she says. "I'm so sorry. It's truly my fault." I entertain the thought that I'm weeping to punish her. Which may be so, but I try and can't stop it now.

"Lew," she says. "Now listen to me a minute. Try and listen. Will you be all right to sit here while I go back up to the house?"

"Do what?" I say.

"I can't understand you, dear."

I try harder. "You what to you do?" I say.

"I guess I'm going to try to raise somebody on the phone," she says. "Maybe one of the boys from the Shell station would come up."

I've got the blubbering stopped now. "Plane make the plane," I say, meaning *We'll never.*

"Well, Lew, *I* don't know what else to do," she says. "I'll leave the motor running so you can have the heater."

I don't turn to watch her walking up the driveway for fear it'll set me off again. I put the radio on, just in time to catch the end of some bouncy tune from way way back. Can it have been "The Dipsy Doodle"? But then the announcer comes on to say it's 10:08 and I snap the thing off again: the last thing I need is to be hearing what time it is every two minutes. The dashboard clock says 10:07. What to believe. I take a glove out of my pocket, fold it over, and put it on the dashboard to block my view of the clock. I stare out the windshield at the road we should be on and listen to the motor humming away. We've been very happy with the Lumina.

An idling engine consumes a gallon of gasoline an hour: Or used to years ago. (It said so in the owner's manual of some car we had and it stuck in my mind for some reason.) An hour. Be a good hour before anybody got here if they ran true to form. Oh brother. Well, there's not a thing you can do about it. I go back to the hum of the motor.

But wait now. Sunk in mud, motor running: couldn't this clog the tailpipe, make carbon monoxide seep in? Isn't this what they do, trapped and Godless men going out to the garage with the hose from the vacuum? In fact it's beginning to seem to me that I'm starting to feel sleepy, that something's woozy with my thoughts. You better reach over, cut that switch.

I let it run.

Before shutting my eyes I decide I'll take a last look around at things. And when I turn my head I see somebody pulling up in front of the Paquettes'. I see them sit there a second, then pull out again, coming right at me. If it's a car full of roughnecks I'm helpless out here. I spot Alice, but she's far away, she's on the doorstep, she's opening the door. They're still coming. I stretch over with my good hand and blow the horn. But she's in the house. They're halfway here, coming fast now. And now I see this thing is too high up off the ground to be a car. Oh, I'd rather the roughnecks than what's going to happen now. It's the mail lady in her moon vehicle. And we are saved.

TIM GAUTREAUX

Same Place, Same Things

TIM GAUTREAUX (1947–) was born and raised in south Louisiana. His stories have appeared in *The Atlantic Monthly, Harper's, GQ, Story,* The Best American Short Stories, and New Stories from the South. He has won a National Magazine Award for fiction and a NEA Creative Fellowship. In 1996 he was appointed the John and Renee Grisham Visiting Southern Writer in Residence at Ole Miss. He is the author of the collection of short stories *Same Place, Same Things* and the novel *The Next Step in the Dance,* set in south Louisiana during the oil bust. Gautreaux will have another collection of stories out in 1999, and he is presently working on a movie script and another novel. He holds a doctorate in English from the University of South Carolina, and he is Writer in Residence at Southeastern Louisiana University in Hammond, where he lives with his wife and children.

The pump repairman was cautious. He saw the dry rut in the lane and geared the truck down so he could take it through slow. The thin wheels of his ancient Ford bounced heavily, the road ridge scraping the axles. A few blackbirds charged out of the dead brush along the road and wheeled through the sky like a thrown handful of gravel. He wondered how far down the farm lane the woman lived. When she had called him at the tourist court, she had not been confident about giving directions, seeming unsure where her own house was. On both sides of the road, fields of strawberries baked in the sun. It had not rained, the locals told him, for seven weeks.

Leafless branches reached out to snatch away his headlights. Billows of dust flew up behind the truck like a woman's face powder, settling on roadside dewberry bushes that resembled thickened fountains of lava. It was an awful drought.

After a while he arrived at a weatherboard farmhouse set behind a leaning barbed-wire fence. He pulled up and got out. No one came from the house, so he slammed the door of the truck and coughed loudly. He had been in this part of the country long enough to know that the farm people did not want you on their porches unless you were a relative or a neighbor. Now, in the Depression, life was so hard for them they trusted almost nobody. Finally he blew the truck's horn and was rewarded with a movement at one of the windows. In half a minute a woman in a thin cotton housedress came out.

"You the pump man?" she asked.

"Yes, ma'am. Name's Harry Lintel."

She looked him over as though he were a goat she might or might not buy. Walking to the edge of her porch, she looked back toward the field behind the house. "If you walk this trail here for a while, you'll find my husband trying to fix the pump." He did not like the way she made a face when she said "husband." He was uneasy around women who did not like their men. She walked off the porch and through the fifteen feet of thistle and clover that served as a front lawn, moving carefully toward the pump repairman, who regarded her warily. Poor people made him nervous. He was poor himself, at least as far as money goes, but he was not hangdog and spiritless like many of the people he'd met in this part of the state, beaten down and ruined inside by hard times. She looked at his eyes. "How old you think I am?"

She seemed about forty, four years younger than he was, but with farm women you could never tell. He looked at her sandy hair and gray eyes. She was thin, but something about the way she looked at him suggested toughness. "Lady, I've come to fix a pump. What kind do you have and what's wrong with it?"

"My husband, he'll be back in a minute. He'll know what all you need to find out. What I want to know is where you're from. I ain't heard nobody around here talk like you in a while." She had her hair tied back in a loose knot and reached up to touch it delicately. This motion caught his eye. He guessed she might be closer to thirty-five.

Harry Lintel put a hand in his right front pocket and leaned back against the door of his truck. Taking off his straw hat, he threw it over his shoulder into the front seat. "I'm from Missouri," he said, running a hand through a clump of short, brassy hair.

Her expression was still one of intense evaluation. "Ain't there no pump work in Missouri?" she asked. "Or did your woman run you off?"

"My wife died," he said. "As for pump work, when it's dry and the local pump repairmen can't keep up with their work, or there ain't any pump repairmen, I come around and take up the slack." He looked around her at the peeling house and its broken panes patched with cardboard.

"So why ain't you where you belong, taking up slack?"

He looked at her hard. That last remark showed some wit, something he had not seen in a woman for a while. "Where's your husband, lady? I've got cash jobs waiting for me up Highway Fifty-one."

"Keep your pants on. He'll be here, I said." She folded her arms and came a step closer. "I'm just curious why anyone would come to this part of Louisiana from somewheres else."

"I follow the droughts," he said, straightening up and walking along the fence to where it opened into a rutted drive. The woman followed him, sliding her hands down her hips to smooth her dress. "Last week I was in Texas. Was doing a good trade until an all-night rain came in from Mexico and put me out of business. Wasn't much of a pumping situation after that, and the local repairmen could keep things going." He looked down the path as far as he could see along the field of limp plants. "Month before that I was in north Georgia. Before that I fixed pumps over in Alabama. Those people had a time with their green peppers. Where the devil's your old man?"

"I never see anyone but my husband and two or three buyers that come back in here to deal with him." She began to look at his clothes, and this made him uneasy, because he knew she saw that they were clean and not patched. He wore a khaki shirt and trousers. Perhaps no one she knew wore unpatched clothes. Her housedress looked like it had been made from a faded window curtain. "Texas," she said. "I saw your ad in the paper and I figured you were a traveling man."

"No, ma'am," he said. "I'm a man who travels." He saw she did not understand that there was a difference. She seemed desperate and bored, but many people he met were that way. Very few were curious about where he came from, however. They cared only that he was Harry Lintel, who could fix any irrigation pump or engine ever made.

He walked into the field toward the tree line a quarter mile off, and the woman went quickly to the house. He saw a wire strung from the house into a chinaberry tree, and then through a long file of willows edging a ditch, and figured this led to an electric pump. He was almost disappointed that the woman wasn't following him.

As he walked, he looked around at the farm. It was typical of the worst. He came up on a Titan tractor stilted on wood blocks in the weeds, its head cracked. Behind it was a corroded disk harrow, which could still have been useful had it been taken care of. In the empty field to his right stood two cows suffering from the bloat.

He was sweating through his shirt by the time he reached a thin stand of bramble-infested loblolly edging the field. Two hundred feet down the row of trees, a man hunched over an electric motor, his back to the repairman. Calling out to him, Lintel walked in that direction, but the other man did not respond—he was absorbed in close inspection of a belt drive, the pump repairman guessed. The farmer was sprawled on a steel grid that hung over an open well. Harry walked up and said hello, but the farmer said nothing. He seemed to be asleep, even though he was out in the sun and his undershirt was wet as a dishcloth. Harry stooped down and looked over the pump and the way it was installed. He saw that it was bolted to the grid without insulation. Two stray wires dangled into the well. He watched for the rise and fall of the man's body, but the man was not breathing. Kneeling down, Harry touched the back of his knuckles to the steel grid. There was no shock, so he grabbed the man by his arms and pulled him off the motor, turning him over. He was dead, without a doubt: electrocuted. His fingers were burned, and a dark stain ran down his pants leg. He felt the man's neck for a pulse and, finding none, sat there for a long time, studying the man's broad, slick face, a face angry and stupid even in death. He looked around at the sorry farm as though it were responsible, then got up and walked back to the farmhouse.

The woman was sitting in a rocker on the porch, staring off into a parched, fallow field. She looked at the repairman and smiled, just barely.

Harry Lintel rubbed his chin. "You got a phone?"

"Nope," she said, smoothing her hair down with her right hand. "There's one at the store out on Fifty-one."

He did not want to tell her, feeling that it would be better for someone else to break the news. "You've got a lady friend lives around here?"

She looked at him sharply, her gray eyes round. "What you want to know that for?"

"I've got my reasons," he said. He began to get into his big dusty truck, trying to act as though nothing had happened. He wanted to put some distance between himself and her coming sorrow.

"The first house where you turned in, there's Mary. But she don't have no phone."

"See you in a few minutes," he said, cranking up the truck.

At the highway he found Mary and told her to go back and tell the woman that her husband was dead out by the pump. The old woman simply nodded, went back into her house, and got her son to go with her. Her lack of concern bothered him. Didn't she care about the death of her neighbor?

At the store he called the sheriff and waited. He rode with the deputies back to the farmhouse and told them what he knew. The lawmen stood over the body, looked up at the dry sky, and told the pump repairman to go back to his business, that they would take care of everything.

He and one of the deputies walked out of the field past the farmhouse, and he tried not to look at the porch as he passed, but he could not keep himself from listening. He heard nothing—no crying, no voices heavy with muted passion. The two women were on the porch step, talking calmly, as though they were discussing the price of berries. The widow watched him carefully as he got into the police car. He thought he detected a trace of perfume in the air and looked around inside the gritty sedan for its source.

That day he repaired six engines, saving little farms from turning back to sand. The repairs were hard ones that no one else could manage: broken timing gears, worn-out governors, cracked water jackets. At least one person on each farm asked him if he was the one who had found the dead man, and when he admitted that he was, each sullen farmer backed off and let him work alone. Late in the afternoon he was heating an engine head in his portable forge, watching the hue of the metal so that he could judge whether the temperature was right for brazing. He waited for the right color to rise like the blush on a woman's cheek, and when it did, he sealed a complex crack with a clean streak of molten brass. A wizened Italian farmer watched him like a chicken hawk, his arms folded across a washed-out denim shirt. "It's no gonna work," he said.

But when, near dusk, Harry pulled the flywheel and the engine sprang to life with a heavy, thudding exhaust, turning up a rill of sunset-tinged water into the field, the farmer cracked a faint smile. "If you couldna fixed it, we'da run you out the parish."

Harry began to clean his hands with care. "Why?"

"Stranger find a dead man, that's bad luck."

"It's better I found him than his wife, isn't it?"

The farmer poked a few bills at Harry, turned, and began walking toward his packing shed. "Nothin' surprise that woman," he said.

It was eight-thirty when he got back to the Bell Pepper Tourist Court, a collection of six pink stucco cabins with a large oval window embedded in each. The office, which also contained a small café, was open, but he was too tired to eat. He sat on his jittery bed, staring across the highway to the railroad, where a local passenger train trundled by, its whistle singing for a crossing. Beyond this was yet another truck farm, maybe twelve acres punctuated by a tin-roof shack. He wondered how many other women were stuck back in the woods living without husbands. The widow of the electrocuted man didn't even have children to take her mind off her loneliness. He had that. He had gotten married when he was seventeen and had raised two daughters and a son. He was now forty-four and on his own, his wife having died five years before. The small Missouri town he was raised in couldn't keep him provided with work, so he had struck out, roaming the South and the Southwest, looking for machines that nobody else could repair.

He stared through an oval window at his truck. At least he could move around and meet different people, being either sorry to leave them or glad to get away, depending. He gazed fondly at the Ford, its stake body loaded with blacksmith's tongs, welding tools, a portable forge, and boxes of parts, wrenches, sockets, coal, hardies, gasket material, all covered with a green tarp slung over the wooden sides. It could take him anywhere, and with his tools he could fix anything but the weather.

The next morning at dawn he headed out for the first job of the day, noticing that the early sky was like a piece of sheet metal heated to a blue-gray color. He pulled up to a farmhouse and a small man wearing a ponderous mustache came out from around back, cursing. Harry Lintel threw his hat into the truck and ran his hands through his hair. He had never seen people who disliked strangers so much. The little farmer spat on the Ford's tire and told him to drive into the field behind the farmhouse. "My McCormick won't throw no spark," he said.

Harry turned to get under way, but over the Ford's hood he saw, two hundred yards off, the back of a woman's head moving above the weeds in an idle field. "Who's that?" he asked, pointing two fields over.

The farmer craned his neck but could not recognize the figure, who disappeared behind a brier patch between two farms. "I don't know," the farmer said, scratching his three-day beard, "but a woman what walk around like that with nothing better to do is thinking up trouble." He pointed to Harry. "When a woman thinks too long, look out! Now, get to work, you."

The day turned hot as a furnace and his skin flamed with sweat. By noon he had worked on three machines within a half mile of one another. From little farms up and down Highway 51 he could hear the thud and pop of pump engines. He was in a field of berries finishing up with a balky International, when he saw a woman walking along the railroad embankment with a basket in the crook of her right arm. It was the wife of the dead farmer. He waited until she was several rows away and then looked up at her. She met his gaze head-on, her eyes the color of dull nickel. He admitted to himself then and there that it scared him, the way she looked at him. Harry Lintel could figure out any machine on earth, but with women, he wished for an instruction manual.

She walked up to him and set the basket on top of his wrenches. "You ready to eat?"

He wiped his hands on a kerosene-soaked rag. "Where'd you come from?"

"It's not far from my place," she said. He noticed that she was wearing a new cotton dress, which seemed to have been snagged in a few places by briers. She knelt down and opened the basket, pulling out a baby quilt and sandwiches. He sat on the parched grass next to her in a spot of shade thrown by a willow.

"I'm sorry about your man," he said. "I should have told you myself."

Her hands moved busily in the basket. "That woman and I get along all right. You did as good as you could." They ate in silence for a while. From the distance came the deep music of a big Illinois Central freight engine, its whistle filling the afternoon, swaying up and down a scale of frantic notes. The Crimson Flyer thundered north, trailing a hundred refrigerated cars of berries, the work of an entire year for many local farmers. "That train's off its time," she said. "Seems like everything's off schedule lately." She took a bite of ham sandwich and chewed absently.

"I asked the boys that own this engine about your man. They didn't want to talk about him." He took a bite of sandwich and tried not to make a face. It was dry, and the ham tasted like it had been in the icebox too long. He wondered if she had fed her husband any better.

"He was from New Orleans, not from around here. Nobody liked him much, because of his berries. He tried to ship bad Klondykes once, and the men at the loading dock broke his leg."

The pump man shook his head. "Breaking a farmer's leg's kind of rough treatment."

"He deserved it," she said matter-of-factly. "Shipping bad berries gives the local farmers a bad name." She looked at her sandwich as though she had seen it for the first time, and threw it into the basket. "He was too damned lazy to pick early enough to ship on time."

He was afraid she was going to cry, but her face remained as dry as the gravel road that ran along the track. He began to wonder what she had done about her husband. "What about the services for your old man?"

"Mary's pickers helped me put him in this morning after the coroner came out and give us the okay."

So that's it, he thought. Half your life working in the sun and then your woman plants you in back of the toolshed like a dog. He was tempted to toss his sandwich, but he was hungrier than he had been in weeks, so he bit at it again. The woman put her eyes all over him, and he knew what she was doing. He began to compare himself to her husband. He was bigger. People told him frequently that he had a pleasant face, which he figured was their way of telling him he wasn't outright ugly.

When she stared away at a noisy crow, he stole a long look at her. The dress fit her pretty well, and if she were another woman, one that hadn't just put her husband in the ground, he might have asked her for a date. A row of pale freckles fell across her nose, and today her hair was untied, hanging down over her shoulders. Something in the back of his mind bothered him.

"What's your name?" he asked.

"Ada," she said quickly, as though she had expected the question.

"I thank you for the sandwich, but I've got to get going up the road."

She looked along the railway. "Must be nice to take off whenever you've a mind to. I bet you travel all over."

"A lot travel more'n I do." He bent down and began to pick up box-end wrenches.

"What you in such a hurry for?" she asked, stretching out her long legs into the dead grass. Harry studied them a moment.

"Lady, people around here wonder what the trees are up to when they lean with the breeze. What you think someone that sees us is going to think?"

He walked over to his truck, placed his tools in the proper boxes, row-hopped over to the engine, slung the flywheel with a cast-iron crank, and backed off to hear the exhausts talk to him. The woman watched his moves, all of them. As he was driving out of the field, he felt her eyes on the back of his neck.

That evening after supper in the Bell Pepper Tourist Court Café Harry looked up from his coffee and saw Ada walk in through the screen door. She moved across the hard-scrubbed pine floor as if she came into the place all the time, then sat across from him in a booth and put on the table a bottle of bright red strawberry wine. She had washed her hair and put on a jasmine perfume.

Harry was embarrassed. A couple of farmers watched them and Marie, the owner, lifted her chin when she saw the wine. He was at first grouchy about the visit, not liking to be surprised, but as she asked him questions about his travels, he studied her skin, which was not as rough as he'd first thought, her sandy hair, and those eyes that seemed to drink him in. He wondered how she had passed her life so far, stuck on a mud lane in the most spiritless backwater he'd ever seen. He was as curious about her static world as she was about his wandering one.

Conversation was not his long suit, but the woman had an hour's worth of questions about Arkansas and Georgia, listening to his tales of mountains as though he were telling her of China or the moon. What he wanted to talk about was Missouri and his children, but her questions wouldn't let him. At one point in the conversation she looked over at Marie and said, "There's them around here that say if you hang around me, there's no telling what trouble you'll get into." She put her hands together and placed them in the middle of the green oilcloth.

He looked at them, realizing that she had told him almost nothing about herself. "You said your husband was from New Orleans, but you didn't say where you were from."

She took a swallow of wine from a water glass. "Let's just say I showed up here a few years ago. Nobody knows nothing much about me except I was kept back in that patch and never came in to drink or dance or nothing. Where I'm from's not so important, is it?" She took a sip and smiled at him over the rim of her glass. "You like to dance?" she asked quickly.

"I can glide around some," he said. "But about this afternoon—why'd you follow me with them sandwiches out in the field?"

Ada bit her lower lip and thought a moment. "Maybe I want to move on," she said flatly. Harry looked out the window and whistled.

They took their time finishing off the bottle. She went to the ladies' room and he walked outside, into the dark parking lot. He stood there, stretching the kinks out of his muscles. Ada came out with him, looked up and down 51 for cars, and threw her arms around his waist, giving him a hard kiss. Then she backed off, smiling, and began walking up the dark highway toward her place.

Oh my, he thought. Her mouth had tasted of strawberry wine, hot and sweet. Oh my.

Later that night he lay in his bed with the window open, listening to the pump engines running out in the fields, which stretched away on all sides of the tourist court for miles. They throbbed, as delicate as distant heartbeats. He could tell which type each was by the sound it made. He heard an International hit-and-miss engine fire once and then coast slower and slower through several cycles before firing again. Woven into that sound was a distant Fairbanks Morse with a bad magneto throbbing steadily, then cutting off, slowing, slowing almost to stillness before the spark built up again and the engine boomed back alive. Across the road, a little McCormick muttered in a ditch. In the quiet night the engines fought the drought, popping like the musketry of a losing army. Through the screen of his window drifted the scent of kerosene exhaust.

He thought of the farmer's widow and finally admitted to himself, there in the dark, that she was good-looking. What was she doing right now? he wondered. Reading? For some reason he doubted this. Sewing? What—traveling clothes? Was she planning how to sell the patch and move back, as many women had done, to wherever she had come from? If she had any sense, he thought, she'd be asleep, and he turned over and faced the wall, listening to the springs ring under him. He tried to remember what he had done at night when he was at home, when he was twenty-four and had three children and a wife, but nothing at all came to him. Then, slowly, thoughts of rocking sick babies and helping his wife can sweet corn came to him, and before two minutes had passed, he was asleep.

The next morning the sky was as hard and expressionless as a pawnbroker's face. At eight o'clock the temperature was ninety-one, and the repairman had already welded a piston rod in Amite and was headed south. When he passed the woman's lane, he forced himself not to look down its rutted surface. He had dreamed of her last night, and that was enough, he thought. Times were so hard he could afford only his dreams. A half mile down the road he began working at pouring new babbitt bearings for an old Dan Patch engine. The owners of the farm left him alone so they could oversee a group of inexperienced pickers, and at nine-thirty, while he was turning the blower for the forge, she came out of the brush to the north, carrying a clear glass jug of lemonade.

"I'll bet you're dry," she said, giving him the jug and a tin cup.

"You're an awful friendly lady," he said, pouring himself a drink and looking at her slim waist, her long hair.

"I can be friendly when I want to be." She rested her hand on his damp shoulder a moment and let it slide off slowly.

They talked while he worked the forge. He tried to tell her about his children, but she seemed not to be interested. She wanted to know where he had been and where he was going. She wanted to know how it was to live on the road, what people were like in different places. "Do you stay in tourist courts every night?" she asked, wide-eyed.

By the time he had finished his repair, she had told him that she had just buried her third husband, that she had never been a hundred miles from the spot they were standing in, and that she didn't care if she never saw another strawberry for the rest of her days. "Sometimes I think it's staying in the same place, doing the same things, day in, day out, that gets me down. Get up in the morning and look out the window and see that same rusty fence. Look out another window and see that same willow tree. Out another and see that field. Same place, same things, all my life." She heard a distant train whistle and looked off toward it, caught up in the haunting sound.

Harry Lintel was at a loss in dealing with unhappy people. He remembered that putting his big arms around his young wife years ago would stop her from crying, but he had no notion why this worked. Looking at the delicate hollow of Ada's cheek, he felt sorry he didn't know what to do for her. He wondered if she would take up with him in his truck if he asked her, would just go off with him up the highway to Tennessee or Georgia, wherever the next drought was needing him to fix engines or windmills. Would this heal what was wrong?

After a local freight train racketed by, three men in overalls drove across the track, got out of their pickup, and began telling him about a big engine in a dry field six miles west, and how nobody could get it to run all week. The men ignored the woman, and as the repairman packed his tools and dumped the forge, he watched her walk off. She went south, away from her place, along the dirt lane that sidled up to the railroad, keeping her thin brown shoes out of the heaped-up dust ridge. After he loaded the truck, he cranked it and headed not west, along the route given him by the three men, but north. Turning into her lane, he bumped down along the ruts to her farmhouse. He walked to the back of the property and noticed her berries blanched by the sun as if they'd had kettles of boiling water poured over them. Returning to the house, he opened the fuse box nailed to the rear outside wall and discovered that one fuse was blown, even though it was a special heavy-duty type. He used his pocketknife to pry off the faceplate and saw where a switch wire cut into the circuit and ran from the bottom of the box through a hole into the house.

He found the front door unlocked. Walking through the house, he noticed there was little furniture: only a set of dark varnished chairs, two small, rough tables, and a rickety, curled-up sofa. The windows were dirty. In the kitchen he found the wall switch that activated the pump, and, peering close, he saw that it had been turned on. He was sure that many farms with electric pumps also had inside switches. But surely the man would have killed the circuit before he went out to work on the thing. And then he remembered that he hadn't seen any switch out in the field.

He sat down at the oilcloth-covered kitchen table and squinted out the front window. He saw a rusty fence. Looking out a side window, he saw a willow tree. My God, he thought. He turned to look through the rear window, into a field. Near the broken tractor was a freshly dug mound of dirt. He put his face down into his hands and shook like a man who had just missed being in a terrible accident.

During the next ten days he worked the whole parish. Wild animals came out of the woods looking for water. Bottoms of drainage ditches cracked open and buckled. He saw pickers brought out of the field with heatstroke. The woman found him only twice, and he was polite, listening to her tell him about her nights and what she saw through her windows. She wore the same dress but kept it clean and ironed. Once, she asked him to come over for supper, but he said he had work to do past dark.

At the tourist court he avoided the café and went to bed early, putting himself to sleep by thinking of his wife, painfully, deliberately. He remembered the kindness of her meals in their kitchen and the fondness of her touch, which was on him still, teaching him.

On a Thursday morning, before dawn, he was awakened by a drumming sound to the northwest. At first he thought it was someone at the door, but when the sound rolled down on the parish again, he knew it was thunder. By first light the rain had started in earnest, and at eight o'clock he was still in his room, staring out at sheets of wind-tortured spray welling up in puddles along the highway—three inches at least, and more to come, by the looks of the sky. It was time to move on.

In the café, for the first time Marie had no repair calls for him. He paid up, gave her a hug, and headed out north in his groaning truck, rainwater spilling off the taut new tarp covering the back.

The highway followed the railroad up through a series of small towns, and he made good time despite a traffic of small truckloads of produce and an occasional horse-drawn farm wagon. He felt lighthearted for the first time in days, and whistled as he steered around slower vehicles navigating the rainy road. There was something good about getting out of this section of the country, he felt, something good about pointing his headlights toward Jackson or Memphis, where he would hole up in a boardinghouse and read a big-city paper until the weather reports would tell him where he'd find lots of dust, heat, worn-out pumps, and busted windmills.

About noon he pulled over at a café south of McComb. Walking to the back of the truck, he saw that one of the tarp ropes had come undone. When he raised the cloth to check inside, he saw the woman lift her face toward him, her eyes rusty and dark. "When I heard the rain start on my roof, I knew you'd be pulling out," she said. "You can go somewheres. I can't."

He stared at her for a long time, trying to figure what to say. He looked up and down the red-dirt highway lined with spindly telephone poles and then at the café, which was closed, he realized, the front door padlocked. Finally, he climbed in and sat on a toolbox lid next to her in the oily dark. "You can't come along with me."

"Don't say that," she said, putting her arms loosely around his neck. "You're the only person I ever met can go where he wants to go." She said this not in a pleading voice but as a statement of fact. "I can go with you. I'll be good to you, Mr. Lintel."

He looked at her eyes and guessed that she was desperate for his freedom of movement but not for him. The eyes seemed already to be looking ahead, looking at a whole world passing by a truck window. "Where you want to go," he said at last, "I can't take you."

She pulled her arms away quickly. "What you mean by that? You just going to toss me off on the side of the road like a wore-out machine? There's something in me what needs to get away with you."

Harry Lintel leaned toward her and took her hands, trying to remember the ways he had once brought solace to his wife. "If I could help you, I'd bring you along for the ride," he said. "But I can't do a thing for you." He half-expected her to cry when he said that, but she only shook her head.

"You've got a heart like a rock," she told him.

"No, ma'am," he said. "I loved a good woman once, and I could love another. You can't come with me because you killed your old man."

Her eyes seemed to pulse, and what softness lingered around the corners of her mouth disappeared into a flinty expression of fear and desperation.

He reached for his wallet. "I'm going to buy a ticket and put you on the southbound. You can walk home from the station."

She grabbed a bill from him before he offered it, then straightened up, throwing an arm in back of her as if she was searching for the handle of her cardboard suitcase. Harry stared at his empty hand for a moment and turned to climb out into the drizzle. He heard the music of a tempered wrench being picked up, and then a bomb went off in his head, and he was down on the floorboards, rolling in cinders and wire, his arms and legs uncontrolled, his eyes letting in a broken vision of the woman standing over him, looking down the way someone might examine a stunned fish. "I've never met a man I could put up with for long," she told him. "I'm glad I got shut of all of mine."

His head roared like a forge, and he tried to rise, his eyes flickering, his arms pushing him toward the woman's upraised fist, where his biggest box-end wrench glimmered like a thunderbolt. The blow was a star-giving ball of pain, and he felt the tailgate in the small of his back, the world going over like a flywheel, his face in collision with gravel and clay, a coppery rill coursing through his nose and mouth. The only thing in his head was the silver ring of a tool, and then the exhaust of a four-cylinder engine pulling away, fading into a clash of gears at the top of a hill, and then, for the longest time, nothing. Somewhere a cow bellowed, or a car passed without stopping, or wind blew through the grass around him like knowledge through an ear.

Near dusk he woke to a dove singing on the phone wires. He wondered where she would sell the truck, to what town she would ride on the train. It didn't matter. She was a woman who would never get where she wanted to go. He was always where he was going.

One eye began to work, and he watched clouds, the broken pieces of the world hanging above like tomorrow's big repair job, waiting.

RON HANSEN

Nebraska

RON HANSEN (1947–) is the author of the novels *Mariette in Ecstasy, The Assassination of Jesse James by the Coward Robert Ford, Desperadoes,* and *Atticus,* for which he was a finalist for the 1996 National Book Award. His short-story collection, *Nebraska,* earned him an award from the American Academy and Institute of Arts and Letters. His new novel, *Hitler's Niece,* was published in September 1999 (HarperCollins). He lives in northern California.

The town is Americus, Covenant, Denmark, Grange, Hooray, Jerusalem, Sweetwater—one of the lesser-known moons of the Platte, conceived in sickness and misery by European pioneers who took the path of least resistance and put down roots in an emptiness like the one they kept secret in their youth. In Swedish and Danish and German and Polish, in anxiety and fury and God's providence, they chopped at the Great Plains with spades, creating green sod houses that crumbled and collapsed in the rain and disappeared in the first persuasive snow and were so low the grown-ups stooped to go inside; and yet were places of ownership and a hard kind of happiness, the places their occupants gravely stood before on those plenary occasions when photographs were taken.

And then the Union Pacific stopped by, just a camp of white campaign tents and a boy playing his Harpoon at night, and then a supply store, a depot, a pine water tank, stockyards, and the mean prosperity of the twentieth century. The trains strolling into town to shed a boxcar in the depot sideyard, or crying past at sixty miles per hour, possibly interrupting a girl in her high-wire act, her arms looping up when she tips to one side, the railtop as slippery as a silver spoon. And then the yellow and red locomotive rises up from the heat shimmer over a mile away, the August noonday warping the sight of it, but cinders tapping away from the spikes and the iron rails already vibrating up inside the girl's shoes. She steps down to the roadbed and then into high weeds as the Union Pacific pulls Wyoming coal and Georgia-Pacific lumber and snowplow blades and aslant Japanese pickup trucks through the open countryside and on to Omaha. And when it passes by, a worker she knows is opposite her, like a pedestrian at a stoplight, the sun not letting up, the plainsong of grasshoppers going on and on between them until the worker says, "Hot."

Twice the Union Pacific tracks cross over the sidewinding Democrat, the water slow as an oxcart, green as silage, croplands to the east, yards and houses to the west, a green ceiling of leaves in some places, whirlpools showing up in it like spinning plates that lose speed and disappear. In winter and a week or more of just above zero, high-school couples walk the gray ice, kicking up snow as quiet words are passed between them, opinions are mildly compromised, sorrows are apportioned. And Emil Jedlicka unslings his blue-stocked .22 and slogs through high brown weeds and snow, hunting ring-necked pheasant, sidelong rabbits, and—always suddenly—quail, as his little brother Orin sprints across the Democrat in order to slide like an otter.

July in town is a gray highway and a Ford hay truck spraying by, the hay sailing like a yellow ribbon caught in the mouth of a prancing dog, and Billy Awalt up there on the camel's hump, eighteen years old and sweaty and dirty, peppered and dappled with hay dust, a lump of chew like an extra thumb under his lower lip, his blue eyes happening on a Dairy Queen and a pretty girl licking a pale trickle of ice cream from the cone. And Billy slaps his heart and cries, "Oh! I am pierced!"

And late October is orange on the ground and blue overhead and grain silos stacked up like white poker chips, and a high silver water tower belittled one night by the sloppy tattoo of one year's class at George W. Norris High. And below the silos and water tower are stripped treetops, their gray limbs still lifted up in alleluia, their yellow leaves crowding along yard fences and sheeping along the sidewalks and alleys under the shepherding wind.

Or January and a heavy snow partitioning the landscape, whiting out the highways and woods and cattle lots until there are only open spaces and steamed-up windowpanes, and a Nordstrom boy limping pitifully in the hard plaster of his clothes, the snow as deep as his hips when the boy tips over and cannot get up until a little Schumacher girl sitting by the stoop window, a spoon in her mouth, a bowl of Cheerios in her lap, says in plain voice, "There's a boy," and her mother looks out to the sidewalk.

Houses are big and white and two stories high, each a cousin to the next, with pigeon roosts in the attic gables, green storm windows on the upper floor, and a green screened porch, some as pillowed and couched as parlors or made into sleeping rooms for the boy whose next step will be the Navy and days spent on a ship with his hometown's own population, on gray water that rises up and is allayed like a geography of cornfields, sugar beets, soybeans, wheat, that stays there and says, in its own way, "Stay." Houses are turned away from the land and toward whatever is not always, sitting across from each other like dressed-up children at a party in daylight, their parents looking on with hopes and fond expectations. Overgrown elm and sycamore trees poach the sunlight from the lawns and keep petticoats of snow around them into April. In the deep lots out back are wire clotheslines with flapping white sheets pinned to them, property lines are hedged with sour green and purple grapes, or with rabbit wire and gardens of peonies, roses, gladiola, irises, marigolds, pansies. Fruit trees are so closely planted that they cannot sway without knitting. The apples and cherries drop and sweetly decompose until they're only slight brown bumps in the yards, but the pears stay up in the wind, drooping under the pecks of birds, withering down like peppers until their sorrow is justly noticed and they one day disappear.

Aligned against an alley of blue shale rock is a garage whose doors slash weeds and scrape up pebbles as an old man pokily swings them open, teetering with his last weak push. And then Victor Johnson rummages inside, being cautious about his gray sweater and high-topped shoes, looking over paint cans, junked electric motors, grass rakes and garden rakes and a pitchfork and sickles, gray doors and ladders piled overhead in the rafters, and an old windup Victrola and heavy platter records from the twenties, on one of them a soprano singing "I'm a Lonesome Melody." Under a green tarpaulin is a wooden movie projector he painted silver and big cans of tan celluloid, much of it orange and green with age, but one strip of it preserved: of an Army pilot in jodhpurs hopping from one biplane onto another's upper wing. Country people who'd paid to see the movie had been spellbound by the slight dip of the wings at the pilot's jump, the slap of his leather jacket, and how his hair strayed wild and was promptly sleeked back by the wind. But looking at the strip now, pulling a ribbon of it up to a windowpane and letting it unspool to the ground, Victor can make out only twenty frames of the leap, and then snapshot after snapshot of an Army pilot clinging to the biplane's wing. And yet Victor stays with it, as though that scene of one man staying alive were what he'd paid his nickel for.

Main Street is just a block away. Pickup trucks stop in it so their drivers can angle out over their brown left arms and speak about crops or praise the weather or make up sentences whose only real point is their lack of complication. And then a cattle truck comes up and they mosey along with a touch of their cap bills or a slap of the door metal. High-school girls in skintight jeans stay in one place on weekends, and jacked-up cars cruise past, rowdy farmboys overlapping inside, pulling over now and then in order to give the girls cigarettes and sips of pop and grief about their lipstick. And when the cars peel out, the girls say how a particular boy measured up or they swap gossip about Donna Moriarity and the scope she permitted Randy when he came back from boot camp.

Everyone is famous in this town. And everyone is necessary. Townspeople go to the Vaughn Grocery Store for the daily news, and to the Home Restaurant for history class, especially at evensong when the old people eat graveled pot roast and lemon meringue pie and calmly sip coffee from cups they tip to their mouths with both hands. The Kiwanis Club meets here on Tuesday nights, and hopes are made public, petty sins are tidily dispatched, the proceeds from the gumball machines are tallied up and poured into the upkeep of a playground. Yutesler's Hardware has picnic items and kitchen appliances in its one window, in the manner of those prosperous men who would prefer to be known for their hobbies. And there is one crisp, white, Protestant church with a steeple, of the sort pictured on calendars; and the Immaculate Conception Catholic Church, grayly holding the town at bay like a Gothic wolfhound. And there is an insurance agency, a county coroner and justice of the peace, a secondhand shop, a handsome chiropractor named Koch who coaches the Pony League baseball team, a post office approached on unpainted wood steps outside of a cheap mobile home, the Nighthawk tavern where there's Falstaff tap beer, a green pool table, a poster recording the Cornhuskers scores, a crazy man patiently tolerated, a gray-haired woman with an unmoored eye, a boy in spectacles thick as paperweights, a carpenter missing one index finger, a plump waitress whose day job is in a basement beauty shop, an old woman who creeps up to the side door at eight in order to purchase one shot glass of whiskey.

And yet passing by, and paying attention, an outsider is only aware of what isn't, that there's no bookshop, no picture show, no pharmacy or dry cleaners, no cocktail parties, extreme opinions, jewelry or piano stores, motels, hotels, hospital, political headquarters, philosophical theories about Being and the soul.

High importance is only attached to practicalities, and so there is the Batchelor Funeral Home, where a proud old gentleman is on display in a dark brown suit, his yellow fingernails finally clean, his smeared eyeglasses in his coat pocket, a grandchild on tiptoes by the casket, peering at the lips that will not move, the sparrow chest that will not rise. And there's Tommy Seymour's for Sinclair gasoline and mechanical repairs, a green balloon dinosaur bobbing from a string over the cash register, old tires piled beneath the cottonwood, For Sale in the sideyard a Case tractor, a John Deere reaper, a hay mower, a red manure spreader, and a rusty grain conveyor, green weeds overcoming them, standing up inside them, trying slyly and little by little to inherit machinery for the earth.

And beyond that are woods, a slope of pasture, six empty cattle pens, a driveway made of limestone pebbles, and the house where Alice Sorensen pages through a child's World Book Encyclopedia, stopping at the descriptions of California, Capetown, Ceylon, Colorado, Copenhagen, Corpus Christi, Costa Rica, Cyprus.

Widow Dworak has been watering the lawn in an open raincoat and apron, but at nine she walks the green hose around to the spigot and screws down the nozzle so that the spray is a misty crystal bowl softly baptizing the ivy. She says, "How about some camomile tea?" And she says, "Yum. Oh, boy. That hits the spot." And bends to shut the water off.

The Union Pacific night train rolls through town just after ten o'clock when a sixty-year-old man named Adolf Schooley is a boy again in bed, and when the huge weight of forty or fifty cars jostles his upstairs room like a motor he'd put a quarter in. And over the sighing industry of the train, he can hear the train saying *Nebraska, Nebraska, Nebraska, Nebraska.* And he cannot sleep.

Mrs. Antoinette Heft is at the Home Restaurant, placing frozen meat patties on waxed paper, pausing at times to clamp her fingers under her arms and press the sting from them. She stops when the Union Pacific passes, then picks a cigarette out of a pack of Kools and smokes it on the back porch, smelling air as crisp as Oxydol, looking up at stars the Pawnee Indians looked at, hearing the low harmonica of big rigs on the highway, in the town she knows like the palm of her hand, in the country she knows by heart.

AMY HEMPEL

In the Cemetery Where Al Jolson Is Buried

AMY HEMPEL (1951–) is the author of three collections of short stories: *Reasons to Live, At the Gates of the Animal Kingdom,* and *Tumble Home.* Her stories have been widely anthologized, appearing in such collections as The Best American Short Stories, The Pushcart Prize, and *The Norton Anthology of Short Fiction.* She teaches in the graduate writing program at Bennington College and the New School in New York City.

"Tell me things I won't mind forgetting," she said. "Make it useless stuff or skip it."

I began. I told her insects fly through rain, missing every drop, never getting wet. I told her no one in America owned a tape recorder before Bing Crosby did. I told her the shape of the moon is like a banana—you see it looking full, you're seeing it end-on.

The camera made me self-conscious and I stopped. It was trained on us from a ceiling mount—the kind of camera banks use to photograph robbers. It played us to the nurses down the hall in Intensive Care.

"Go on, girl," she said. "You get used to it."

I had my audience. I went on. Did she know that Tammy Wynette had changed her tune? Really. That now she sings "Stand by Your *Friends*"? That Paul Anka did it too, I said. Does "You're Having *Our* Baby." That he got sick of all that feminist bitching.

"What else?" she said. "Have you got something else?"

Oh, yes.

For her I would always have something else.

"Did you know that when they taught the first chimp to talk, it lied? That when they asked her who did it on the desk, she signed back the name of the janitor. And that when they pressed her, she said she was sorry, that it was really the project director. But she was a mother, so I guess she had her reasons."

"Oh, that's good," she said. "A parable."

"There's more about the chimp," I said. "But it will break your heart."

"No, thanks," she says, and scratches at her mask.

We look like good-guy outlaws. Good or bad, I am not used to the mask yet. I keep touching the warm spot where my breath, thank God, comes out. She is used to hers. She only ties the strings on top. The other ones—a pro by now—she lets hang loose.

We call this place the Marcus Welby Hospital. It's the white one with the palm trees under the opening credits of all those shows. A Hollywood hospital, though in fact it is several miles west. Off camera, there is a beach across the street.

She introduces me to a nurse as the Best Friend. The impersonal article is more intimate. It tells me that *they* are intimate, the nurse and my friend.

"I was telling her we used to drink Canada Dry ginger ale and pretend we were in Canada."

"That's how dumb we were," I say.

"You could be sisters," the nurse says.

So how come, I'll bet they are wondering, it took me so long to get to such a glamorous place? But do they ask?

They do not ask.

Two months, and how long is the drive?

The best I can explain it is this—I have a friend who worked one summer in a mortuary. He used to tell me stories. The one that really got to me was not the grisliest, but it's the one that did. A man wrecked his car on 101 going south. He did not lose consciousness. But his arm was taken down to the wet bone—and when he looked at it—it scared him to death.

I mean, he died.

So I hadn't dared to look any closer. But now I'm doing it—and hoping that I will live through it.

She shakes out a summer-weight blanket, showing a leg you did not want to see. Except for that, you look at her and understand the law that requires *two* people to be with the body at all times.

"I thought of something," she says. "I thought of it last night. I think there is a real and present need here. You know," she says, "like for someone to do it for you when you can't do it yourself. You call them up whenever you want—like when push comes to shove."

She grabs the bedside phone and loops the cord around her neck.

"Hey," she says, "the end o' the line."

She keeps on, giddy with something. But I don't know with what.

"I can't remember," she says. "What does Kübler-Ross say comes after Denial?"

It seems to me Anger must be next. Then Bargaining, Depression, and so on and so forth. But I keep my guesses to myself.

"The only thing is," she says, "is where's Resurrection? God knows, I want to do it by the book. But she left out Resurrection."

She laughs, and I cling to the sound the way someone dangling above a ravine holds fast to the thrown rope.

"Tell me," she says, "about that chimp with the talking hands. What do they do when the thing ends and the chimp says, 'I don't want to go back to the zoo'?"

When I don't say anything, she says, "Okay—then tell me another animal story. I like animal stories. But not a sick one—I don't want to know about all the seeing-eye dogs going blind."

No, I would not tell her a sick one.

"How about the hearing-ear dogs?" I say. "They're not going deaf, but they are getting very judgmental. For instance, there's this golden retriever in New Jersey, he wakes up the deaf mother and drags her into the daughter's room because the kid has got a flashlight and is reading under the covers."

"Oh, you're killing me," she says. "Yes, you're definitely killing me."

"They say the smart dog obeys, but the smarter dog knows when to disobey."

"Yes," she says, "the smarter anything knows when to disobey. Now, for example."

She is flirting with the Good Doctor, who has just appeared. Unlike the Bad Doctor, who checks the IV drip before saying good morning, the Good Doctor says things like "God didn't give epileptics a fair shake." The Good Doctor awards himself points for the cripples he could have hit in the parking lot. Because the Good Doctor is a little in love with her, he says maybe a year. He pulls a chair up to her bed and suggests I might like to spend an hour on the beach.

"Bring me something back," she says. "Anything from the beach. Or the gift shop. Taste is no object."

He draws the curtain around her bed.

"Wait!" she cries.

I look in at her.

"Anything," she says, "except a magazine subscription."

The doctor turns away.

I watch her mouth laugh.

What seems dangerous often is not—black snakes, for example, or clear-air turbulence. While things that just lie there, like this beach, are loaded with jeopardy. A yellow dust rising from the ground, the heat that ripens melons overnight—this is earthquake weather. You can sit here braiding the fringe on your towel and the sand will all of a sudden suck down like an hourglass. The air roars. In the cheap apartments on-shore, bathtubs fill themselves and gardens roll up and over like green waves. If nothing happens, the dust will drift and the heat deepen till fear turns to desire. Nerves like that are only bought off by catastrophe.

"It never happens when you're thinking about it," she once observed. "Earthquake, earthquake, earthquake," she said.

"Earthquake, earthquake, earthquake," I said.

Like the aviaphobe who keeps the plane aloft with prayer, we kept it up until an aftershock cracked the ceiling.

That was after the big one in seventy-two. We were in college; our dormitory was five miles from the epicenter. When the ride was over and my jabbering pulse began to slow, she served five parts champagne to one part orange juice, and joked about living in Ocean View, Kansas. I offered to drive her to Hawaii on the new world psychics predicted would surface the next time, or the next.

I could not say that now—next.

Whose next? she could ask.

Was I the only one who noticed that the experts had stopped saying *if* and now spoke of *when*? Of course not; the fearful ran to thousands. We watched the traffic of Japanese beetles for deviation. Deviation might mean more natural violence.

I wanted her to be afraid with me. But she said, "I don't know. I'm just not."

She was afraid of nothing, not even of flying.

I have this dream before a flight where we buckle in and the plane moves down the runway. It takes off at thirty-five miles an hour, and then we're airborne, skimming the tree tops. Still, we arrive in New York on time.

It is so pleasant.

One night I flew to Moscow this way.

* * *

She flew with me once. That time she flew with me she ate macadamia nuts while the wings bounced. She knows the wing tips can bend thirty feet up and thirty feet down without coming off. She believes it. She trusts the laws of aerodynamics. My mind stampedes. I can almost accept that a battleship floats when everybody knows steel sinks.

I see fear in her now, and am not going to try to talk her out of it. She is right to be afraid.

After a quake, the six o'clock news airs a film clip of first-graders yelling at the broken playground per their teacher's instructions.

"*Bad* earth!" they shout, because anger is stronger than fear.

But the beach is standing still today. Everyone on it is tranquilized, numb, or asleep. Teenaged girls rub coconut oil on each other's hard-to-reach places. They smell like macaroons. They pry open compacts like clamshells; mirrors catch the sun and throw a spray of white rays across glazed shoulders. The girls arrange their wet hair with silk flowers the way they learned in *Seventeen.* They pose.

A formation of low-riders pulls over to watch with a six-pack. They get vocal when the girls check their tan lines. When the beer is gone, so are they—flexing their cars on up the boulevard.

Above this aggressive health are the twin wrought-iron terraces, painted flamingo pink, of the Palm Royale. Someone dies there every time the sheets are changed. There's an ambulance in the driveway, so the remaining residents line the balconies, rocking and not talking, one-upped.

The ocean they stare at is dangerous, and not just the undertow. You can almost see the slapping tails of sand sharks keeping cruising bodies alive.

If she looked, she could see this, some of it, from her window. She would be the first to say how little it takes to make a thing all wrong.

There was a second bed in the room when I got back to it!

For two beats I didn't get it. Then it hit me like an open coffin.

She wants every minute, I thought. She wants my life.

"You missed Gussie," she said.

Gussie is her parents' three-hundred-pound narcoleptic maid. Her attacks often come at the ironing board. The pillowcases in that family are all bordered with scorch.

"It's a hard trip for her," I said. "How is she?"

"Well, she didn't fall asleep, if that's what you mean. Gussie's great—you know what she said? She said, 'Darlin', stop this worriation. Just keep prayin', down on your knees'—me, who can't even get out of bed."

She shrugged. "What am I missing?"

"It's earthquake weather," I told her.

"The best thing to do about earthquakes," she said, "is not to live in California."

"That's useful," I said. "You sound like Reverend Ike—'The best thing to do for the poor is not to be one of them.' "

We're crazy about Reverend Ike.

I noticed her face was bloated.

"You know," she said, "I feel like hell. I'm about to stop having fun."

"The ancients have a saying," I said. " 'There are times when the wolves are silent; there are times when the moon howls.' "

"What's that, Navaho?"

"Palm Royale lobby graffiti," I said. "I bought a paper there. I'll read you something."

"Even though I care about nothing?"

I turned to the page with the trivia column. I said, "Did you know the more shrimp flamingo birds eat, the pinker their feathers get?" I said, "Did you know that Eskimos need refrigerators? Do you know *why* Eskimos need refrigerators? Did you know that Eskimos need refrigerators because how else would they keep their food from freezing?"

I turned to page three, to a UPI filler datelined Mexico City. I read her MAN ROBS BANK WITH CHICKEN, about a man who bought a barbecued chicken at a stand down the block from a bank. Passing the bank, he got the idea. He walked in and approached a teller. He pointed the brown paper bag at her and she handed over the day's receipts. It was the smell of barbecue sauce that eventually led to his capture.

The story had made her hungry, she said—so I took the elevator down six floors to the cafeteria, and brought back all the ice cream she wanted. We lay side by side, adjustable beds cranked up for optimal TV-viewing, littering the sheets with Good Humor wrappers, picking toasted almonds out of the gauze. We were Lucy and Ethel, Mary and Rhoda in extremis. The blinds were closed to keep light off the screen.

We watched a movie starring men we used to think we wanted to sleep with. Hers was a tough cop out to stop mine, a vicious rapist who went after cocktail waitresses.

"This is a good movie," she said when snipers felled them both.

I missed her already.

A Filipino nurse tiptoed in and gave her an injection. The nurse removed the pile of popsicle sticks from the nightstand—enough to splint a small animal.

The injection made us both sleepy. We slept.

I dreamed she was a decorator, come to furnish my house. She worked in secret, singing to herself. When she finished, she guided me proudly to the door. "How do you like it?" she asked, easing me inside.

Every beam and sill and shelf and knob was draped in gay bunting, with streamers of pastel crepe looped around bright mirrors.

"I have to go home," I said when she woke up.

She thought I meant home to her house in the Canyon, and I had to say No, *home* home. I twisted my hands in the time-honored fashion of people in pain. I was supposed to offer something. The Best Friend. I could not even offer to come back.

I felt weak and small and failed.

Also exhilarated.

I had a convertible in the parking lot. Once out of that room, I would drive it too fast down the Coast highway through the crab-smelling air. A stop in Malibu for sangria. The music in the place would be sexy and loud. They'd serve papaya and shrimp and watermelon ice. After dinner I would shimmer with lust, buzz with heat, vibrate with life, and stay up all night.

Without a word, she yanked off her mask and threw it on the floor. She kicked at the blankets and moved to the door. She must have hated having to pause for breath and balance before slamming out of Isolation, and out of the second room, the one where you scrub and tie on the white masks.

A voice shouted her name in alarm, and people ran down the corridor. The Good Doctor was paged over the intercom. I opened the door and the nurses at the station stared hard, as if this flight had been my idea.

"Where is she?" I asked, and they nodded to the supply closet.

I looked in. Two nurses were kneeling beside her on the floor, talking to her in low voices. One held a mask over her nose and mouth, the other rubbed her back in slow circles. The nurses glanced up to see if I was the doctor—and when I wasn't, they went back to what they were doing.

"There, there, honey," they cooed.

On the morning she was moved to the cemetery, the one where Al Jolson is buried, I enrolled in a "Fear of Flying" class. "What is your worst fear?" the instructor asked, and I answered, "That I will finish this course and still be afraid."

I sleep with a glass of water on the nightstand so I can see by its level if the coastal earth is trembling or if the shaking is still me.

* * *

What do I remember?

I remember only the useless things I hear—that Bob Dylan's mother invented Wite-Out, that twenty-three people must be in a room before there is a fifty-fifty chance two will have the same birthday. Who cares whether or not it's true? In my head there are bath towels swaddling this stuff. Nothing else seeps through.

I review those things that will figure in the retelling: a kiss through surgical gauze, the pale hand correcting the position of the wig. I noted these gestures as they happened, not in any retrospect—though I don't know why looking back should show us more than looking *at.*

It is just possible I will say I stayed the night.

And who is there that can say that I did not?

I think of the chimp, the one with the talking hands.

In the course of the experiment, that chimp had a baby. Imagine how her trainers must have thrilled when the mother, without prompting, began to sign to her newborn.

Baby, drink milk.

Baby, play ball.

And when the baby died, the mother stood over the body, her wrinkled hands moving with animal grace, forming again and again the words: Baby, come hug, Baby, come hug, fluent now in the language of grief.

for Jessica Wolfson

DENIS JOHNSON

Emergency

DENIS JOHNSON (1949–) was born in Munich, West Germany. The son of a U.S. information agent, Johnson had lived in Tokyo, Washington, D.C., Manila, and Munich by the time he was eighteen. He received a B.A. from the University of Iowa and attended the Iowa Writers' Workshop. When he was nineteen, his first collection of poetry, *The Incognito Lounge,* was selected for the 1982 National Poetry Series. He is the author of the story collection *Jesus' Son* and the novels *Angels, Fiskadoro, The Stars at Noon,* and *Resuscitation of a Hanged Man.* He has received two National Endowment for the Arts Fellowships, a fellowship from the Fine Arts Work Center in Provincetown, Massachusetts, and a Whiting Writers' Award for excellence in fiction and poetry. Mr. Johnson has held a variety of jobs, including teaching at Lake Forest College outside Chicago, waiting tables in Seattle, and teaching creative writing at the state prison in Florence, Arizona. He currently lives in northern Idaho.

I'd been working in the emergency room for about three weeks, I guess. This was in 1973, before the summer ended. With nothing to do on the overnight shift but batch the insurance reports from the daytime shifts, I just started wandering around, over to the coronary-care unit, down to the cafeteria, et cetera, looking for Georgie, the orderly, a pretty good friend of mine. He often stole pills from the cabinets.

He was running over the tiled floor of the operating room with a mop. "Are you still doing that?" I said.

"Jesus, there's a lot of blood here," he complained.

"Where?" The floor looked clean enough to me.

"What the hell were they doing in here?" he asked me.

"They were performing surgery, Georgie," I told him.

"There's so much goop inside of us, man," he said, "and it all wants to get out." He leaned his mop against a cabinet.

"What are you crying for?" I didn't understand.

He stood still, raised both arms slowly behind his head, and tightened his ponytail. Then he grabbed the mop and started making broad random arcs with it, trembling and weeping and moving all around the place really fast. "What am I *crying* for?" he said. "Jesus. Wow, oh boy, perfect."

I was hanging out in the E.R. with fat, quivering Nurse. One of the Family Service doctors that nobody liked came in looking for Georgie to wipe up after him. "Where's Georgie?" this guy asked.

"Georgie's in O.R.," Nurse said.

"Again?"

"No," Nurse said. "Still."

"Still? Doing what?"

"Cleaning the floor."

"Again?"

"No," Nurse said again. "Still."

Back in O.R., Georgie dropped his mop and bent over in the posture of a child soiling its diapers. He stared down with his mouth open in terror.

He said, "What am I going to do about these fucking *shoes,* man?"

"Whatever you stole," I said, "I guess you already ate it all, right?"

"Listen to how they squish," he said, walking around carefully on his heels.

"Let me check your pockets, man."

He stood still a minute, and I found his stash. I left him two of each, whatever they were. "Shift is about half over," I told him.

"Good. Because I really, really, really need a drink," he said. "Will you please help me get this blood mopped up?"

Around 3:30 a.m. a guy with a knife in his eye came in, led by Georgie.

"I hope *you* didn't do that to him," Nurse said.

"Me?" Georgie said. "No. He was like this."

"My wife did it," the man said. The blade was buried to the hilt in the outside corner of his left eye. It was a hunting knife kind of thing.

"Who brought you in?" Nurse said.

"Nobody. I just walked down. It's only three blocks," the man said.

Nurse peered at him. "We'd better get you lying down."

"Okay, I'm certainly ready for something like that," the man said.

She peered a bit longer into his face.

"Is your other eye," she said, "a glass eye?"

"It's plastic, or something artificial like that," he said.

"And you can see out of *this* eye?" she asked, meaning the wounded one.

"I can see. But I can't make a fist out of my left hand because this knife is doing something to my brain."

"My God," Nurse said.

"I guess I'd better get the doctor," I said.

"There you go," Nurse agreed.

They got him lying down, and Georgie says to the patient, "Name?"

"Terrence Weber."

"Your face is dark. I can't see what you're saying."

"Georgie," I said.

"What are you saying, man? I can't see."

Nurse came over, and Georgie said to her, "His face is dark."

She leaned over the patient. "How long ago did this happen, Terry?" she shouted down into his face.

"Just a while ago. My wife did it. I was asleep," the patient said.

"Do you want the police?"

He thought about it and finally said, "Not unless I die."

Nurse went to the wall intercom and buzzed the doctor on duty, the Family Service person. "Got a surprise for you," she said over the intercom. He took his time getting down the hall to her, because he knew she hated Family Service and her happy tone of voice could only mean something beyond his competence and potentially humiliating.

He peeked into the trauma room and saw the situation: the clerk—that is, me—standing next to the orderly, Georgie, both of us on drugs, looking down at a patient with a knife sticking up out of his face.

"What seems to be the trouble?" he said.

The doctor gathered the three of us around him in the office and said, "Here's the situation. We've got to get a team here, an entire team. I want a good eye man. A great eye man. The best eye man. I want a brain surgeon. And I want a really good gas man, get me a genius. I'm not touching that head. I'm just going to watch this one. I know my limits. We'll just get him prepped and sit tight. Orderly!"

"Do you mean me?" Georgie said. "Should I get him prepped?"

"Is this a hospital?" the doctor asked. "Is this the emergency room? Is that a patient? Are you the orderly?"

I dialled the hospital operator and told her to get me the eye man and the brain man and the gas man.

Georgie could be heard across the hall, washing his hands and singing a Neil Young song that went "Hello, cowgirl in the sand. Is this place at your command?"

"That person is not right, not at all, not one bit," the doctor said.

"As long as my instructions are audible to him it doesn't concern me," Nurse insisted, spooning stuff up out of a little Dixie cup. "I've got my own life and the protection of my family to think of."

"Well, okay, okay. Don't chew my head off," the doctor said.

The eye man was on vacation or something. While the hospital's operator called around to find someone else just as good, the other specialists were hurrying through the night to join us. I stood around looking at charts and chewing up more of Georgie's pills. Some of them tasted the way urine smells, some of them burned, some of them tasted like chalk. Various nurses, and two physicians who'd been tending somebody in I.C.U., were hanging out down here with us now.

Everybody had a different idea about exactly how to approach the problem of removing the knife from Terrence Weber's brain. But when Georgie came in from prepping the patient—from shaving the patient's eyebrow and disinfecting the area around the wound, and so on—he seemed to be holding the hunting knife in his left hand.

The talk just dropped off a cliff.

"Where," the doctor asked finally, "did you get that?"

Nobody said one thing more, not for quite a long time.

After a while, one of the I.C.U. nurses said, "Your shoelace is untied." Georgie laid the knife on a chart and bent down to fix his shoe.

There were twenty more minutes left to get through.

"How's the guy doing?" I asked.

"Who?" Georgie said.

It turned out that Terrence Weber still had excellent vision in the one good eye, and acceptable motor and reflex, despite his earlier motor complaint. "His vitals are normal," Nurse said. "There's nothing wrong with the guy. It's one of those things."

After a while you forget it's summer. You don't remember what the morning is. I'd worked two doubles with eight hours off in between, which I'd spent sleeping on a gurney in the nurse's station. Georgie's pills were making me feel like a giant helium-filled balloon, but I was wide awake. Georgie and I went out to the lot, to his orange pickup.

We lay down on a stretch of dusty plywood in the back of the truck with the daylight knocking against our eyelids and the fragrance of alfalfa thickening on our tongues.

"I want to go to church," Georgie said.

"Let's go to the county fair."

"I'd like to worship. I would."

"They have these injured hawks and eagles there. From the Humane Society," I said.

"I need a quiet chapel about now."

Georgie and I had a terrific time driving around. For a while the day was clear and peaceful. It was one of the moments you stay in, to hell with all the troubles of before and after. The sky is blue and the dead are coming back. Later in the afternoon, with sad resignation, the county fair bares its breasts. A champion of the drug LSD, a very famous guru of the love generation, is being interviewed amid a TV crew off to the left of the poultry cages. His eyeballs look like he bought them in a joke shop. It doesn't occur to me, as I pity this extraterrestrial, that in my life I've taken as much as he has.

After that, we got lost. We drove for hours, literally hours, but we couldn't find the road back to town.

Georgie started to complain. "That was the worst fair I've been to. Where were the rides?"

"They had rides," I said.

"I didn't see one ride."

A jackrabbit scurried out in front of us, and we hit it.

"There was a merry-go-round, a Ferris wheel, and a thing called the Hammer that people were bent over vomiting from after they got off," I said. "Are you completely blind?"

"What was that?"

"A rabbit."

"Something thumped."

"You hit him. *He* thumped."

Georgie stood on the brake pedal. "Rabbit stew."

He threw the truck in reverse and zigzagged back toward the rabbit. "Where's my hunting knife?" He almost ran over the poor animal a second time.

"We'll camp in the wilderness," he said. "In the morning we'll breakfast on its haunches." He was waving Terrence Weber's hunting knife around in what I was sure was a dangerous way.

In a minute he was standing at the edge of the fields, cutting the scrawny little thing up, tossing away its organs. "I should have been a doctor," he cried.

A family in a big Dodge, the only car we'd seen for a long time, slowed down and gawked out the windows as they passed by. The father said, "What is it, a snake?"

"No, it's not a snake," Georgie said. "It's a rabbit with babies inside it."

"Babies!" the mother said, and the father sped the car forward, over the protests of several little kids in the back.

Georgie came back to my side of the truck with his shirtfront stretched out in front of him as if he were carrying apples in it, or some such, but they were, in fact, slimy miniature bunnies. "No way I'm eating those things," I told him.

"Take them, take them. I gotta drive, take them," he said, dumping them in my lap and getting in on his side of the truck. He started driving along faster and faster, with a look of glory on his face. "We killed the mother and saved the children," he said.

"It's getting late," I said. "Let's get back to town."

"You bet." Sixty, seventy, eighty-five, just topping ninety.

"These rabbits better be kept warm." One at a time I slid the little things in between my shirt buttons and nestled them against my belly. "They're hardly moving," I told Georgie.

"We'll get some milk and sugar and all that, and we'll raise them up ourselves. They'll get as big as gorillas."

The road we were lost on cut straight through the middle of the world. It was still daytime, but the sun had no more power than an ornament or a sponge. In this light the truck's hood, which had been bright orange, had turned a deep blue.

Georgie let us drift to the shoulder of the road, slowly, slowly, as if he'd fallen asleep or given up trying to find his way.

"What is it?"

"We can't go on. I don't have any headlights," Georgie said.

We parked under a strange sky with a faint image of a quarter-moon superimposed on it.

There was a little woods beside us. This day had been dry and hot, the buck pines and whatall simmering patiently, but as we sat there smoking cigarettes it started to get very cold.

"The summer's over," I said.

That was the year when arctic clouds moved down over the Midwest and we had two weeks of winter in September.

"Do you realize it's going to snow?" Georgie asked me.

He was right, a gun-blue storm was shaping up. We got out and walked around idiotically. The beautiful chill! That sudden crispness, and the tang of evergreen stabbing us!

The gusts of snow twisted themselves around our heads while the night fell. I couldn't find the truck. We just kept getting more and more lost. I kept calling, "Georgie, can you see?" and he kept saying, "See what? See what?"

The only light visible was a streak of sunset flickering below the hem of the clouds. We headed that way.

We bumped softly down a hill toward an open field that seemed to be a military graveyard, filled with rows and rows of austere, identical markers over soldiers' graves. I'd never before come across this cemetery. On the farther side of the field, just beyond the curtains of snow, the sky was torn away and the angels were descending out of a brilliant blue summer, their huge faces streaked with light and full of pity. The sight of them cut through my heart and down the knuckles of my spine, and if there'd been anything in my bowels I would have messed my pants from fear.

Georgie opened his arms and cried out, "It's the drive-in, man!"

"The drive-in . . ." I wasn't sure what these words meant.

"They're showing movies in a fucking blizzard!" Georgie screamed.

"I see. I thought it was something else," I said.

We walked carefully down there and climbed through the busted fence and stood in the very back. The speakers, which I'd mistaken for grave markers, muttered in unison. Then there was tinkly music, of which I could very nearly make out the tune. Famous movie stars rode bicycles beside a river, laughing out of their gigantic, lovely mouths. If anybody had come to see this show, they'd left when the weather started. Not one car remained, not even a broken-down one from last week, or one left here because it was out of gas. In a couple of minutes, in the middle of a whirling square dance, the screen turned black, the cinematic summer ended, the snow went dark, there was nothing but my breath.

"I'm starting to get my eyes back," Georgie said in another minute.

A general greyness was giving birth to various shapes, it was true. "But which ones are close and which ones are far off?" I begged him to tell me.

By trial and error, with a lot of walking back and forth in wet shoes, we found the truck and sat inside it shivering.

"Let's get out of here," I said.

"We can't go anywhere without headlights."

"We've gotta get back. We're a long way from home."

"No, we're not."

"We must have come three hundred miles."

"We're right outside town, Fuckhead. We've just been driving around and around."

"This is no place to camp. I hear the Interstate over there."

"We'll just stay here till it gets late. We can drive home late. We'll be invisible."

We listened to the big rigs going from San Francisco to Pennsylvania along the Interstate, like shudders down a long hacksaw blade, while the snow buried us.

Eventually Georgie said, "We better get some milk for those bunnies."

"We don't have *milk,*" I said.

"We'll mix sugar up with it."

"Will you forget about this milk all of a sudden?"

"They're mammals, man."

"Forget about those rabbits."

"Where are they, anyway?"

"You're not listening to me. I said, 'Forget the rabbits.' "

"Where are they?"

The truth was I'd forgotten all about them, and they were dead.

"They slid around behind me and got squashed," I said tearfully.

"They slid around *behind?*"

He watched while I pried them out from behind my back.

I picked them out one at a time and held them in my hands and we looked at them. There were eight. They weren't any bigger than my fingers, but everything was there.

Little feet! Eyelids! Even whiskers! "Deceased," I said.

Georgie asked, "Does everything you touch turn to shit? Does this happen to you every time?"

"No wonder they call me Fuckhead."

"It's a name that's going to stick."

"I realize that."

" 'Fuckhead' is gonna ride you to your grave."

"I just said so. I agreed with you in advance," I said.

Or maybe that wasn't the time it snowed. Maybe it was the time we slept in the truck and I rolled over on the bunnies and flattened them. It doesn't matter. What's important for me to remember now is that early the next morning the snow was melted off the windshield and the daylight woke me up. A mist covered everything and, with the sunshine, was beginning to grow sharp and strange. The bunnies weren't a problem yet, or they'd already been a problem and were already forgotten, and there was nothing on my mind. I felt the beauty of the morning. I could understand how a drowning man might suddenly feel a deep thirst being quenched. Or how the slave might become a friend to his master. Georgie slept with his face right on the steering wheel.

I saw bits of snow resembling an abundance of blossoms on the stems of the drive-in speakers—no, revealing the blossoms that were always there. A bull elk stood still in the pasture beyond the fence, giving off an air of authority and stupidity. And a coyote jogged across the pasture and faded away among the saplings.

That afternoon we got back to work in time to resume everything as if it had never stopped happening and we'd never been anywhere else.

"The Lord," the intercom said, "is my shepherd." It did that each evening because this was a Catholic hospital. "Our Father, who art in Heaven," and so on.

"Yeah, yeah," Nurse said.

The man with the knife in his head, Terrence Weber, was released around suppertime. They'd kept him overnight and given him an eyepatch—all for no reason, really.

He stopped off at E.R. to say goodbye. "Well, those pills they gave me make everything taste terrible," he said.

"It could have been worse," Nurse said.

"Even my tongue."

"It's just a miracle you didn't end up sightless or at least dead," she reminded him.

The patient recognized me. He acknowledged me with a smile. "I was peeping on the lady next door while she was out there sunbathing," he said. "My wife decided to blind me."

He shook Georgie's hand. Georgie didn't know him. "Who are you supposed to be?" he asked Terrence Weber.

Some hours before that, Georgie had said something that had suddenly and completely explained the difference between us. We'd been driving back toward town, along the Old Highway, through the flatness. We picked up a hitchhiker, a boy I knew. We stopped the truck and the boy climbed slowly up out of the fields as out of the mouth of a volcano. His name was Hardee. He looked even worse than we probably did.

"We got messed up and slept in the truck all night," I told Hardee.

"I had a feeling," Hardee said. "Either that or, you know, driving a thousand miles."

"That too," I said.

"Or you're sick or diseased or something."

"Who's this guy?" Georgie asked.

"This is Hardee. He lived with me last summer. I found him on the doorstep. What happened to your dog?" I asked Hardee.

"He's still down there."

"Yeah, I heard you went to Texas."

"I was working on a bee farm," Hardee said.

"Wow. Do those things sting you?"

"Not like you'd think," Hardee said. " You're part of their daily drill. It's all part of a harmony."

Outside, the same identical stretch of grass repeatedly rolled past our faces. The day was cloudless, blinding. But Georgie said, "Look at that," pointing straight ahead of us.

One star was so hot it showed, bright and blue in the empty sky.

"I recognized you right away," I told Hardee. "But what happened to your hair? Who chopped it off?"

"I hate to say."

"Don't tell me."

"They drafted me."

"Oh no."

"Oh yeah. I'm AWOL. I'm bad AWOL. I got to get to Canada."

"Oh, that's terrible," I said to Hardee.

"Don't worry," Georgie said. "We'll get you there."

"How?"

"Somehow. I think I know some people. Don't worry. You're on your way to Canada."

That world! These days it's all been erased and they've rolled it up like a scroll and put it away somewhere. Yes, I can touch it with my fingers. But where is it?

After a while Hardee asked Georgie, "What do you do for a job," and Georgie said, "I save lives."

EDWARD P. JONES

Marie

EDWARD P. JONES (1950–), the author of *Lost in the City,* has published stories in *The Paris Review, Ploughshares, Callaloo, Essence,* and elsewhere. A recipient of the M.F.A. of the University of Virginia, he has taught at Princeton University, George Mason University, Warren Wilson College, Hofstra University, American University, and the University of Virginia.

Every now and again, as if on a whim, the federal government people would write to Marie Delaveaux Wilson in one of those white, stampless envelopes and tell her to come in to their place so they could take another look at her. They, the Social Security people, wrote to her in a foreign language that she had learned to translate over the years, and for all the years she had been receiving the letters the same man had been signing them. Once, because she had something important to tell him, Marie called the number the man always put at the top of the letters, but a woman answered Mr. Smith's telephone and told Marie he was in an all-day meeting. Another time she called and a man said Mr. Smith was on vacation. And finally one day a woman answered and told Marie that Mr. Smith was deceased. The woman told her to wait and she would get someone new to talk to her about her case, but Marie thought it bad luck to have telephoned a dead man and she hung up.

Now, years after the woman had told her Mr. Smith was no more, the letters were still being signed by John Smith. Come into our office at 21st and M streets, Northwest, the letters said in that foreign language. Come in so we can see if you are still blind in one eye, come in so we can see if you are still old and getting older. Come in so we can see if you still deserve to get Supplemental Security Income payments.

She always obeyed the letters, even if the order now came from a dead man, for she knew people who had been temporarily cut off from SSI for not showing up or even for being late. And once cut off, you had to move heaven and earth to get back on.

So on a not unpleasant day in March, she rose in the dark in the morning, even before the day had any sort of character, to give herself plenty of time to bathe, eat, lay out money for the bus, dress, listen to the spirituals on the radio. She was eighty-six years old, and had learned that life was all chaos and painful uncertainty and that the only way to get through it was to expect chaos even in the most innocent of moments. Offer a crust of bread to a sick bird and you often drew back a bloody finger.

John Smith's letter had told her to come in at eleven o'clock, his favorite time, and by nine that morning she had had her bath and had eaten. Dressed by nine thirty. The walk from Claridge Towers at 12th and M down to the bus stop at 14th and K took her about ten minutes, more or less. There was a bus at about ten thirty, her schedule told her, but she preferred the one that came a half hour earlier, lest there be trouble with the ten thirty bus. After she dressed, she sat at her dining room table and went over still again what papers and all else she needed to take. Given the nature of life—particularly the questions asked by the Social Security people—she always took more than they might ask for—her birth certificate, her husband's death certificate, doctors' letters.

One of the last things she put in her pocketbook was a seven-inch or so knife that she had, with the use of a small saw borrowed from a neighbor, serrated on both edges. The knife, she was convinced now, had saved her life about two weeks before. Before then she had often been careless about when she took the knife out with her, and she had never taken it out in daylight, but now she never left her apartment without it, even when going down the hall to the trash drop.

She had gone out to buy a simple box of oatmeal, no more, no less. It was about seven in the evening, the streets with enough commuters driving up 13th Street to make her feel safe. Several yards before she reached the store, the young man came from behind her and tried to rip off her coat pocket where he thought she kept her money, for she carried no purse or pocketbook after five o'clock. The money was in the other pocket with the knife, and his hand caught in the empty pocket long enough for her to reach around with the knife and cut his hand as it came out of her pocket.

He screamed and called her an old bitch. He took a few steps up 13th Street and stood in front of Emerson's Market, examining the hand and shaking off blood. Except for the cars passing up and down 13th Street, they were alone, and she began to pray.

"You cut me," he said, as if he had only been minding his own business when she cut him. "Just look what you done to my hand," he said and looked around as if for some witness to her crime. There was not a great amount of blood, but there was enough for her to see it dripping to the pavement. He seemed to be about twenty, no more than twenty-five, dressed the way they were all dressed nowadays, as if a blind man had matched up all their colors. It occurred to her to say that she had seven grandchildren his age, that by telling him this he would leave her alone. But the more filth he spoke, the more she wanted him only to come toward her again.

"You done crippled me, you old bitch."

"I sure did," she said, without malice, without triumph, but simply the way she would have told him the time of day had he asked and had she known. She gripped the knife tighter, and as she did, she turned her body ever so slightly so that her good eye lined up with him. Her heart was making an awful racket, wanting to be away from him, wanting to be safe at home. I will not be moved, some organ in the neighborhood of the heart told the heart. "And I got plenty more where that come from."

The last words seemed to bring him down some and, still shaking the blood from his hand, he took a step or two back, which disappointed her. I will not be moved, that other organ kept telling the heart. "You just crazy, thas all," he said. "Just a crazy old hag." Then he turned and lumbered up toward Logan Circle, and several times he looked back over his shoulder as if afraid she might be following. A man came out of Emerson's, then a woman with two little boys. She wanted to grab each of them by the arm and tell them she had come close to losing her life. "I saved myself with this here thing," she would have said. She forgot about the oatmeal and took her raging heart back to the apartment. She told herself that she should, but she never washed the fellow's blood off the knife, and over the next few days it dried and then it began to flake off.

Toward ten o'clock that morning Wilamena Mason knocked and let herself in with a key Marie had given her.

"I see you all ready," Wilamena said.

"With the help of the Lord," Marie said. "Want a spot a coffee?"

"No thanks," Wilamena said, and dropped into a chair at the table. "Been drinkin so much coffee lately, I'm gonna turn into coffee. Was up all night with Calhoun."

"How he doin?"

Wilamena told her Calhoun was better that morning, his first good morning in over a week. Calhoun Lambeth was Wilamena's boyfriend, a seventy-five-year-old man she had taken up with six or so months before, not long after he moved in. He was the best-dressed old man Marie had ever known, but he had always appeared to be sickly, even while strutting about with his gold-tipped cane. And seeing that she could count his days on the fingers of her hands, Marie had avoided getting to know him. She could not understand why Wilamena, who could have had any man in Claridge Towers or any other senior citizen building for that matter, would take such a man into her bed. "True love," Wilamena had explained. "Avoid heartache," Marie had said, trying to be kind.

They left the apartment. Marie sought help from no one, lest she come to depend on a person too much. But since the encounter with the young man, Wilamena had insisted on escorting Marie. Marie, to avoid arguments, allowed Wilamena to walk with her from time to time to the bus stop, but no farther.

Nothing fit Marie's theory about life like the weather in Washington. Two days before the temperature had been in the forties, and yesterday it had dropped to the low twenties then warmed up a bit, with the afternoon bringing snow flurries. Today the weather people on the radio had said it would be warm enough to wear just a sweater, but Marie was wearing her coat. And tomorrow, the weather people said, it would be in the thirties, with maybe an inch or so of snow.

Appointments near twelve o'clock were always risky, because the Social Security people often took off for lunch long before noon and returned sometime after one. And except for a few employees who seemed to work through their lunch hours, the place shut down. Marie had never been interviewed by someone willing to work through the lunch hour. Today, though the appointment was for eleven, she waited until one thirty before the woman at the front of the waiting room told her she would have to come back another day, because the woman who handled her case was not in.

"You put my name down when I came in like everything was all right," Marie said after she had been called up to the woman's desk.

"I know," the woman said, "but I thought that Mrs. Brown was in. They told me she was in. I'm sorry." The woman began writing in a log book that rested between her telephone and a triptych of photographs. She handed Marie a slip and told her again she was sorry.

"Why you have me wait so long if she whatn't here?" She did not want to say too much, appear too upset, for the Social Security people could be unforgiving. And though she was used to waiting three and four hours, she found it especially unfair to wait when there was no one for her at all behind those panels the Social Security people used for offices. "I been here since before eleven."

"I know," the woman behind the desk said. "I know. I saw you there, ma'am, but I really didn't know Mrs. Brown wasn't here." There was a nameplate at the front of the woman's desk and it said Vernelle Wise. The name was surrounded by little hearts, the kind a child might have drawn.

Marie said nothing more and left.

The next appointment was two weeks later, eight thirty, a good hour, and the day before a letter signed by John Smith arrived to remind her. She expected to be out at least by twelve. Three times before eleven o'clock, Marie asked Vernelle Wise if the man, Mr. Green, who was handling her case, was in that day, and each time the woman assured her that he was. At twelve, Marie ate one of the two oranges and three of the five slices of cheese she had brought. At one, she asked again if Mr. Green was indeed in that day and politely reminded Vernelle Wise that she had been waiting since about eight that morning. Vernelle was just as polite and told her the wait would soon be over.

At one fifteen, Marie began to watch the clock hands creep around the dial. She had not paid much attention to the people about her, but more and more it seemed that others were being waited on who had arrived long after she had gotten there. After asking about Mr. Green at one, she had taken a seat near the front, and as more time went by, she found herself forced to listen to the conversation that Vernelle was having with the other receptionist next to her.

"I told him . . . I told him . . . I said just get your things and leave," said the other receptionist, who didn't have a nameplate.

"Did he leave?" Vernelle wanted to know.

"Oh, no," the other woman said. "Not at first. But I picked up some of his stuff, that Christian Dior jacket he worships. I picked up my cigarette lighter and that jacket, just like I was gonna do something bad to it, and he started movin then."

Vernelle began laughing. "I wish I was there to see that." She was filing her fingernails. Now and again she would look at her fingernails to inspect her work, and if it was satisfactory, she would blow on the nail and on the file. "He back?" Vernelle asked.

The other receptionist eyed her. "What you think?" and they both laughed.

Along about two o'clock Marie became hungry again, but she did not want to eat the rest of her food because she did not know how much longer she would be there. There was a soda machine in the corner, but all sodas gave her gas.

"You-know-who gonna call you again?" the other receptionist was asking Vernelle.

"I hope so," Vernelle said. "He pretty fly. Seemed decent too. It kinda put me off when he said he was a car mechanic. I kinda like kept tryin to take a peek at his fingernails and everything the whole evenin. See if they was dirty or what."

"Well, that mechanic stuff might be good when you get your car back. My cousin's boyfriend used to do that kinda work and he made good money, girl. I mean real good money."

"Hmmmm," Vernelle said. "Anyway, the kids like him, and you know how peculiar they can be."

"Tell me about it. They do the job your mother and father used to do, huh? Only on another level."

"You can say that again," Vernelle said.

Marie went to her and told her how long she had been waiting.

"Listen," Vernelle said, pointing her fingernail file at Marie. "I told you you'll be waited on as soon as possible. This is a busy day. So I think you should just go back to your seat until we call your name." The other receptionist began to giggle.

Marie reached across the desk and slapped Vernelle Wise with all her might. Vernelle dropped the file, which made a cheap tinny sound when it hit the plastic board her chair was on. But no one heard the file because she had begun to cry right away. She looked at Marie as if, in the moment of her greatest need, Marie had denied her. "Oh, oh," Vernelle Wise said through the tears. "Oh, my dear God . . ."

The other receptionist, in her chair on casters, rolled over to Vernelle and put her arm around her. "Security!" the other receptionist hollered. "We need security here!"

The guard at the front door came quickly around the corner, one hand on his holstered gun and the other pointing accusatorially at the people seated in the waiting area. Marie had sat down and was looking at the two women almost sympathetically, as if a stranger had come in, hit Vernelle Wise, and fled.

"She slapped Vernelle!" the other receptionist said.

"Who did it?" the guard said, reaching for the man sitting beside Marie. But when the other receptionist said it was the old lady in the blue coat, the guard held back for the longest time, as if to grab her would be like arresting his own grandmother. He stood blinking and he would have gone on blinking had Marie not stood up.

She was too flustered to wait for the bus and so took a cab home. With both chains, she locked herself in the apartment, refusing to answer the door or the telephone the rest of the day and most of the next. But she knew that if her family or friends received no answer at the door or on the telephone, they would think something had happened to her. So the next afternoon, she began answering the phone and spoke with the chains on, telling Wilamena and others that she had a toothache.

For days and days after the incident she ate very little, asked God to forgive her. She was haunted by the way Vernelle's cheek had felt, by what it was like to invade and actually touch the flesh of another person. And when she thought too hard, she imagined that she was slicing through the woman's cheek, the way she had sliced through the young man's hand. But as time went on she began to remember the man's curses and the purplish color of Vernelle's fingernails, and all remorse would momentarily take flight. Finally, one morning nearly two weeks after she slapped the woman, she woke with a phrase she had not used or heard since her children were small: You whatn't raised that way.

It was the next morning that the thin young man in the suit knocked and asked through the door chains if he could speak with her. She thought that he was a Social Security man come to tear up her card and papers and tell her that they would send her no more checks. Even when he pulled out an identification card showing that he was a Howard University student, she did not believe.

In the end, she told him she didn't want to buy anything, not magazines, not candy, not anything.

"No, no," he said. "I just want to talk to you for a bit. About your life and everything. It's for a project for my folklore course. I'm talking to everyone in the building who'll let me. Please . . . I won't be a bother. Just a little bit of your time."

"I don't have anything worth talkin about," she said. "And I don't keep well these days."

"Oh, ma'am, I'm sorry. But we all got something to say. I promise I won't be a bother."

After fifteen minutes of his pleas, she opened the door to him because of his suit and his tie clip with a bird in flight, and because his long dark-brown fingers reminded her of delicate twigs. But had he turned out to be death with a gun or a knife or fingers to crush her neck, she would not have been surprised. "My name's George. George Carter. Like the president." He had the kind of voice that old people in her young days would have called womanish. "But I was born right here in D.C. Born, bred, and buttered, my mother used to say."

He stayed the rest of the day and she fixed him dinner. It scared her to be able to talk so freely with him, and at first she thought that at long last, as she had always feared, senility had taken hold of her. A few hours after he left, she looked his name up in the telephone book, and when a man who sounded like him answered, she hung up immediately. And the next day she did the same thing. He came back at least twice a week for many weeks and would set his cassette recorder on her coffee table. "He's takin down my whole life," she told Wilamena, almost the way a woman might speak in awe of a new boyfriend.

One day he played back for the first time some of what she told the recorder:

> *. . . My father would be sittin there readin the paper. He'd say whenever they put in a new president, "Look like he got the chair for four years." And it got so that's what I saw—this poor man sittin in that chair for four long years while the rest of the world went on about its business. I don't know if I thought he ever did anything, the president. I just knew that he had to sit in that chair for four years. Maybe I thought that by his sittin in that chair and doin nothin else for four years he made the country what it was and that without him sittin there the country wouldn't be what it was. Maybe thas what I got from listenin to my father readin and to my mother askin him questions bout what he was readin. They was like that, you see. . . .*

George stopped the tape and was about to put the other side in when she touched his hand.

"No more, George," she said. "I can't listen to no more. Please . . . please, no more." She had never in her whole life heard her own voice. Nothing had been so stunning in a long, long while, and for a few moments before she found herself, her world turned upside down. There, rising from a machine no bigger than her Bible, was a voice frighteningly familiar and yet unfamiliar, talking about a man whom she knew as well as her husbands and her sons, a man dead and buried sixty years. She reached across to George and he handed her the tape. She turned it over and over, as if the mystery of everything could be discerned if she turned it enough times. She began to cry, and with her other hand she lightly touched the buttons of the machine.

Between the time Marie slapped the woman in the Social Security office and the day she heard her voice for the first time, Calhoun Lambeth, Wilamena's boyfriend, had been in and out of the hospital three times. Most evenings when Calhoun's son stayed the night with him, Wilamena would come up to Marie's and spend most of the evening, sitting on the couch that was catty-corner to the easy chair facing the big window. She said very little, which was unlike her, a woman with more friends than hairs on her head and who, at sixty-eight, loved a good party. The most attractive woman Marie knew would only curl her legs up under herself and sip whatever Marie put in her hand. She looked out at the city until she took herself to her apartment or went back down to Calhoun's place. In the beginning, after he returned from the hospital the first time, there was the desire in Marie to remind her friend that she wasn't married to Calhoun, that she should just get up and walk away, something Marie had seen her do with other men she had grown tired of.

Late one night, Wilamena called and asked her to come down to the man's apartment, for the man's son had had to work that night and she was there alone with him and she did not want to be alone with him. "Sit with me a spell," Wilamena said. Marie did not protest, even though she had not said more than ten words to the man in all the time she knew him. She threw on her bathrobe, picked up her keys and serrated knife, and went down to the second floor.

He was propped up on the bed, and he was surprisingly alert and spoke to Marie with an unforced friendliness. She had seen this in other dying people—a kindness and gentleness came over them that was often embarrassing for those around them. Wilamena sat on the side of the bed. Calhoun asked Marie to sit in a chair beside the bed and then he took her hand and held it for the rest of the night. He talked on throughout the night, not always understandable. Wilamena, exhausted, eventually lay across the foot of the bed. Almost everything the man had to say was about a time when he was young and was married for a year or so to a woman in Nicodemus, Kansas, a town where there were only black people. Whether the woman had died or whether he had left her, Marie could not make out. She only knew that the woman and Nicodemus seemed to have marked him for life.

"You should go to Nicodemus," he said at one point, as if the town was only around the corner. "I stumbled into the place by accident. But you should go on purpose. There ain't much to see, but you should go there and spend some time there."

Toward four o'clock that morning, he stopped talking and moments later he went home to his God. Marie continued holding the dead man's hand and she said the Lord's prayer over and over until it no longer made sense to her. She did not wake Wilamena. Eventually, the sun came through the man's venetian blinds and she heard the croaking of the pigeons congregating on the window ledge. When she finally placed his hand on his chest, the dead man expelled a burst of air that sounded to Marie like a sigh. It occurred to her that she, a complete stranger, was the last thing he had known in the world and that now that he was no longer in the world all she knew of him was that Nicodemus place and a lovesick woman asleep at the foot of his bed. She thought that she was hungry and thirsty, but the more she looked at the dead man and the sleeping woman, the more she realized that what she felt was a sense of loss.

Two days later, the Social Security people sent her a letter, again signed by John Smith, telling her to come to them one week hence. There was nothing in the letter about the slap, no threat to cut off her SSI payments because of what she had done. Indeed, it was the same sort of letter John Smith usually sent. She called the number at the top of the letter, and the woman who handled her case told her that Mrs. White would be expecting her on the day and time stated in the letter. Still, she suspected the Social Security people were planning something for her, something at the very least that would be humiliating. And, right up until the day before the appointment, she continued calling to confirm that it was okay to come in. Often, the person she spoke to after the switchboard woman and before the woman handling her case was Vernelle. "Social Security Administration. This is Vernelle Wise. May I help you?" And each time Marie heard the receptionist identify herself she wanted to apologize. "I whatn't raised that way," she wanted to tell the woman.

George Carter came the day she got the letter to present her with a cassette machine and copies of the tapes she had made about her life. It took quite some time for him to teach her how to use the machine, and after he was gone, she was certain it took so long because she really did not want to know how to use it. That evening, after her dinner, she steeled herself and put a tape marked "Parents; Early Childhood" in the machine.

> *. . . My mother had this idea that everything could be done in Washington, that a human bein could take all they troubles to Washington and things would be set right. I think that was all wrapped up with her notion of the govment, the Supreme Court and the president and the like. "Up there," she would say, "things can be made right." "Up there" was her only words for Washington. All them other cities had names, but Washington didn't need a name. It was just called "up there." I was real small and didn't know any better, so somehow I got to thinkin since things were on the perfect side in Washington, that maybe God lived there. God and his people. . . . When I went back home to visit that first time and told my mother all about my livin in Washington, she fell into such a cry, like maybe I had managed to make it to heaven without dyin. Thas how people was back in those days. . . .*

The next morning she looked for Vernelle Wise's name in the telephone book. And for several evenings she would call the number and hang up before the phone had rung three times. Finally, on a Sunday, two days before the appointment, she let it ring and what may have been a little boy answered. She could tell he was very young because he said "Hello" in a too-loud voice, as if he was not used to talking on the telephone.

"Hello," he said. "Hello, who this? Granddaddy, that you? Hello. Hello. I can see you."

Marie heard Vernelle tell him to put down the telephone, then another child, perhaps a girl somewhat older than the boy, came on the line. "Hello. Hello. Who is this?" she said with authority. The boy began to cry, apparently because he did not want the girl to talk if he couldn't. "Don't touch it," the girl said. "Leave it alone." The boy cried louder and only stopped when Vernelle came to the telephone.

"Yes?" Vernelle said. "Yes." Then she went off the line to calm the boy who had again begun to cry. "Loretta," she said, "go get his bottle. . . . Well, look for it. What you got eyes for?"

There seemed to be a second boy, because Vernelle told him to help Loretta look for the bottle. "He always losin things," Marie heard the second boy say. "You should tie everything to his arms." "Don't tell me what to do," Vernelle said. "Just look for that damn bottle."

"I don't lose nofin. I don't," the first boy said. "You got snot in your nose."

"Don't say that," Vernelle said before she came back on the line. "I'm sorry," she said to Marie. "Who is this? . . . Don't you dare touch it if you know what's good for you!" she said. "I wanna talk to Granddaddy," the first boy said. "Loretta, get me that bottle!"

Marie hung up. She washed her dinner dishes. She called Wilamena because she had not seen her all day, and Wilamena told her that she would be up later. The cassette tapes were on the coffee table beside the machine, and she began picking them up, one by one. She read the labels. "Husband No. 1." "Working." "Husband No. 2." "Children." "Race Relations." "Early D. C. Experiences." "Husband No. 3." She had not played another tape since the one about her mother's idea of what Washington was like, but she could still hear the voice, her voice. Without reading its label, she put a tape in the machine.

. . . I never planned to live in Washington, had no idea I would ever even step one foot in this city. This white family my mother worked for, they had a son married and gone to live in Baltimore. He wanted a maid, somebody to take care of his children. So he wrote to his mother and she asked my mother and my mother asked me about goin to live in Baltimore. Well, I was young. I guess I wanted to see the world, and Baltimore was as good a place to start as anywhere. This man sent me a train ticket and I went off to Baltimore. Hadn't ever been kissed, hadn't ever been anything, but here I was goin farther from home than my mother and father put together. . . . Well, sir, the train stopped in Washington, and I thought I heard the conductor say we would be stoppin a bit there, so I got off. I knew I probably wouldn't see no more than that Union Station, but I wanted to be able to say I'd done that, that I step foot in the capital of the United States. I walked down to the end of the platform and looked around, then I peeked into the station. Then I went in. And when I got back, the train and my suitcase was gone. Everything I had in the world on the way to Baltimore. . . .

. . . I couldn't calm myself anough to listen to when the redcap said another train would be leavin for Baltimore, I was just that upset. I had a buncha addresses

of people we knew all the way from home up to Boston, and I used one precious nickel to call a woman I hadn't seen in years, cause I didn't have the white people in Baltimore number. This woman come and got me, took me to her place. I member like it was yesterday, that we got on this streetcar marked 13th and D NE. The more I rode, the more brighter things got. You ain't lived till you been on a streetcar. The further we went on that streetcar—dead down in the middle of the street—the more I knowed I could never go live in Baltimore. I knowed I could never live in a place that didn't have that streetcar and them clackety-clack tracks. . . .

She wrapped the tapes in two plastic bags and put them in the dresser drawer that contained all that was valuable to her—birth and death certificates, silver dollars, life insurance policies, pictures of her husbands and the children they had given each other, and the grandchildren those children had given her and the great-grands whose names she had trouble remembering. She set the tapes in a back corner of the drawer, away from the things she needed to get her hands on regularly. She knew that however long she lived, she would not ever again listen to them, for in the end, despite all that was on the tapes, she could not stand the sound of her own voice.

THOM JONES

Cold Snap

THOM JONES (1945–) is the author of three short-story collections: *The Pugilist at Rest* (a National Book Award finalist), *Cold Snap,* and *Sonny Liston Was a Friend of Mine.* His stories have appeared in such magazines as *The New Yorker, Playboy, Esquire, GQ,* and *Harper's.* He lives in Olympia, Washington, with his wife and daughter.

Son of a bitch, there's a cold snap and I do this number where I leave all the faucets running because my house, and most houses out here on the West Coast, aren't "real"—they don't have windows that go up and down, or basements (which protect the pipes in a way that a crawl space can't), or sidewalks out in the front with a nice pair of towering oak trees or a couple of elms, which a real house will have, one of those good old Midwest houses. Out here the windows go side to side. You get no basement. No sidewalk and no real trees, just evergreens, and when it gets cold and snows nobody knows what to do. An inch of snow and they cancel school and the community is paralyzed. "Help me, I'm helpless!" Well, it's cold for a change and I guess that's not so bad, because all the fleas and mosquitoes will freeze, and also because any change is *something,* and maybe it will help snap me out of this bleak post-Africa depression—oh, baby, I'm so depressed—but I wake up at three in the morning and think, Oh, no, a pipe is gonna bust, so I run the water and let the faucets drip and I go outside and turn on the outdoor faucets, which are the most vulnerable. Sure enough, they were caking up, and I got to them just in the nick of time, which was good, since in my condition there was no way I could possibly cope with a broken water pipe. I just got back from Africa, where I was playing doctor to the natives, got hammered with a nasty case of malaria, and lost thirty pounds, but it was a manic episode I had that caused Global Aid to send me home. It was my worst attack to date, and on lithium I get such a bad case of psoriasis that I look like alligator man. You can take

Tegretol for mania but it once wiped out my white count and almost killed me, so what I like to do when I get all revved up is skin-pop some morphine, which I had with me by the gallon over there and which will keep you calm—and, unlike booze, it's something I can keep under control. Although I must confess I lost my medical license in the States for substance abuse and ended up with Global Aid when the dust settled over that one. God's will, really. Fate. Karma. Whatever. Anyhow, hypomania is a good thing in Africa, a real motivator, and you can do anything you want over there as long as you keep your feet on the ground and don't parade naked on the president's lawn in Nairobi and get expelled (which I did and which will get you expelled; O.K., I lied, you can't do *anything*—so sue me). On lithium, while you don't crash so bad, you never get high, either, and all you can do is sit around sucking on Primus beer bottles, bitching about how hot it is when there's so much work to do.

While I'm outside checking my faucets, I look my Oldsmobile over and wonder was it last year I changed the antifreeze? Back in bed, it strikes me that it's been three years, so I go out and run the engine and sit in the car with my teeth chattering—it's thirteen below, jeez! And pretty soon the warm air is defrosting the car and I drive over to the hardware section at Safeway and get one of those antifreeze testers with the little balls in it. At four in the morning I'm sitting in my kitchen trying to get it out of the plastic jacket, and it comes out in two parts, with the bulb upside down. No doubt some know-nothing Central American put it in upside down for twenty cents an hour in some slave factory. I know he's got problems—fact is, I've been there and could elucidate his problems—but how about me and my damn antifreeze? I mean, too bad about you, buddy, how about me? And I'm trying to jury-rig it when I realize there is a high potential for breaking the glass and cutting my thumb, and just as that voice that is me, that is always talking to me, my ego, I guess, tells me, "Be careful, Richard, so you don't cut your thumb"—at that instant, I slice my thumb down to the bone. So the next thing you know I'm driving to the hospital with a towel on my thumb thinking, A minute ago everything was just fine, and now I'm driving myself to the emergency room!

Some other guy comes in with this awful burn because a pressure cooker exploded in his face, and he's got this receding hairline, and you can see the way the skin is peeled back—poached-looking. The guy's going to need a hairpiece for sure. A doctor comes out eating a sandwich, and I hear him tell the nurse to set up an IV line and start running some Dilaudid for the guy, which he deserves, considering. I would like some for my thumb, but all I get is Novocain, and my doctor says, "You aren't going to get woozy on me, are you?" I tell him no, I'm not like that, but I have another problem, and he says, "What's that?" and I tell him I can't jack off left-handed. Everybody laughs, because it's the graveyard shift, when that kind of joke is appropriate—even in mixed company. Plus, it's true.

After he stitches me up, I'm in no pain, although I say, "I'll bet this is going to hurt tomorrow," and he says no, he'll give me some pain medication, and I'm thinking, What a great doctor. He's giving me *pain medication.* And while he's in a giving mood I hit him up for some prostate antibiotics because my left testicle feels very heavy.

"Your left testicle feels *heavy*?" he says skeptically.

Yeah, every guy gets it, shit; I tell him my left nut feels like an anvil. I mean, I want to cradle it in my hand when I'm out and about, or rest it on a little silk pillow when I'm stationary. It doesn't really hurt, but I'm very much conscious of having a left testicle, whereas I have teeth and a belly button and a right testicle and I don't even know. I tell him I don't want a finger wave, because I've been through this a thousand times. My prostate is backing up into the seminal vesicles, and if you don't jerk off it builds up and gets worse, and the doctor agrees—that does happen, and he doesn't really want to give me a finger wave, especially when I tell him that a urologist checked it out a couple of months back. He puts on a plastic glove and feels my testicle, pronounces it swollen, and writes a script for antibiotics, after which he tells me to quit drinking coffee. I was going to tell him that I don't jerk off because I'm a sex fiend; I have low sex drive, and it's actually not that much fun. I just do it to keep the prostate empty. Or should I tell him I'm a doctor myself, albeit defrocked, that I just got back from Africa and my nut could be infected with elephantiasis? Highly unlikely, but you never know. But he won't know diddle about tropical medicine—that's my department, and I decide I will just shut my mouth, which is a first for me.

The duty nurse is pretty good-looking, and she contradicts the doctor's orders—gives me a cup of coffee anyhow, plus a roll, and we're sitting there quietly, listening to the other doctor and a nurse fixing the guy with the burned forehead. A little human interaction is taking place and my depression is gone as I begin to feel sorry for the guy with the burn, who is explaining that he was up late with insomnia cooking sweet potatoes when the pressure cooker blew. He was going to candy them with brown sugar and eat them at six in the morning and he's laughing, too, because of the Dilaudid drip. After Linda Ronstadt sings "Just One Look" on the radio, the announcer comes on and says that we've set a record for cold—it's thirteen and a half below at the airport—and I notice that the announcer is happy, too; there's a kind of solidarity that occurs when suffering is inflicted on the community by nature.

My own thing is the Vincent van Gogh effect. I read where he "felt like a million" after he cut off his ear. It only lasted for a couple of days. They always show you the series of four cats that he painted at different times in his life as his mental condition went progressively downhill. Cat One is a realistic-looking cat, but as life goes on and his madness gets worse he paints Cat Four and it looks as though he's been doing some kind of bad LSD, which is how the world had been looking to me until I cut my thumb. It gave me a three-day respite from the blues, and clarity came into my life, and I have to remind myself by writing this down that all the bad stuff does pass if you can wait it out. You forget when you're in the middle of it, so during that three-day break, I slapped this note on the refrigerator door: "Richard, you are a good and loving person, and all the bad stuff does pass, so remember that the next time you get down and think that you've always been down and always will be down, since that's paranoia and it gets you nowhere. You're just in one of your Fyodor Dostoyevski moods—do yourself a favor and forget it!"

I felt so good I actually had the nerve to go out and buy a new set of clothes and see a movie, and then, on the last day before the depression came back, I drove out to Western State and checked my baby sister, Susan, out for a day trip. Susan was always a lot worse than me; she heard voices and pulled I don't know how many suicide attempts until she took my squirrel pistol and put a .22 long-rifle slug through the temple—not really the temple, because at the last minute you always flinch, but forward of the temple, and it was the most perfect lobotomy. I remember hearing the gun pop and how she came into my room (I was home from college for the summer) and said, "Richard, I just shot myself, how come I'm not dead?" Her voice was calm instead of the usual fingernails-on-the-chalkboard voice, the when-she-was-crazy (which was almost always) voice, and I realized later that she was instantly cured, the very moment the bullet zipped through her brain. Everyone said it was such a shame because she was so beautiful, but what good are looks if you are in hell? And she let her looks go at the hospital because she really didn't have a care in the world, but she was still probably the most beautiful patient at Western State. I had a fresh occasion to worry about her on this trip when I saw an attendant rough-handling an old man to stop him from whining, which it did. She'd go along with anything, and she had no advocate except me. And then I almost regretted going out there, in spite of my do-good mood, because Susan wanted to go to the Point Defiance Zoo to see Cindy, the elephant that was on the news after they transferred the attendant who took care of her, for defying orders and actually going into the elephant pen on the sly to be her friend.

There are three hundred elephants in North American zoos, and although Cindy is an Asian elephant and a female and small, she is still considered the most dangerous elephant in America. Last year alone, three people were killed by elephants in the United States, and this is what Susan had seen and heard on the color television in the ward dayroom, and she's like a child—she wants to go out and see an elephant when it's ten below zero. They originally had Cindy clamped up in a pen tighter than the one they've got John Gotti in down in Marion, Illinois, and I don't remember that the catalogue of Cindy's crimes included human murder. She was just a general troublemaker, and they were beating her with a two-by-four when some animal activist reported it and there was a big scandal that ended with Cindy getting shipped down to the San Diego Zoo, the best zoo in the world; I think there was some kind of escape (don't quote me on that) where Cindy was running around on a golf course in between moves, and then a capture involving tranquilizer darts, and when they couldn't control Cindy in San Diego they shipped her back up here to Tacoma and put her in maximum-security confinement. It was pretty awful. I told Susan that over in India Cindy would have a job hauling logs or something, and there would be an elephant boy to scrub her down at night with a big brush while she lay in the river, and the elephant boy would be with her at all times, her constant companion. Actually, the elephant would be more important than the boy, I told her, and that's how you should handle an elephant in America—import an experienced elephant boy for each one, give the kids a green card, pay them a lot of overtime, and have them stay with the elephants around the clock. You know, quality time. How could you blame Cindy for all the shit she pulled? And in the middle of this, Susan has a tear floating off her cheek and I don't know if it's a tear caused by the cold or if she was touched by Cindy's plight. The reason they sent my sister to the nuthouse was that you could light a fire on the floor in front of her and she would just sit there and watch it burn. When our parents died, I took her to my place in Washington state and hired helpers to look after her, but they would always quit—quit while I was over in the Third World, where it's impossible to do anything. It was like, *Meanwhile, back in the jungle / Meanwhile, back in the States* . . . Apart from her lack of affect, Susan was always logical and made perfect sense. She was kind of like a Mr. Spock who just didn't give a shit anymore except when it came to childish fun and games. All bundled up, with a scarf over her ears, in her innocence she looked like Eva Marie Saint in *On the Waterfront.*

We drove over to Nordstrom's in the University District and I bought Suz some new threads and then took her to a hair salon where she got this chic haircut, and she was looking so good that I almost regretted it, 'cause if those wacked-out freaks at the hospital weren't hitting on her before, they would be now. It was starting to get dark and time to head back when Susan spots the Space Needle from I-5—she's never been there, so I took her to the top and she wandered outside to the observation deck, where the wind was a walking razor blade at 518 feet, but Susan is grooving on the lights of Seattle and with her homemade lobotomy doesn't experience pain in quite the way a normal person does, and I want her to have a little fun, but I'm freezing out there, especially my thumb, which ached. I didn't want to pop back inside in the sheltered part and leave her out there, though, because she might want to pitch herself over the side. I mean, they've got safety nets, but what if she's still got some vestige of a death wish? We had dinner in the revolving dining room, and people were looking at us funny because of Susan's eating habits, which deteriorate when you live in a nuthouse, but we got through that and went back to my place to watch TV, and after that I was glad to go to sleep—but I couldn't sleep because of my thumb. I was thinking I still hadn't cashed in the script for the pain pills when Susan comes into my bedroom naked and sits down on the edge of the bed.

"Ever since I've been shot, I feel like those animals in the zoo. I want to set them free," she says, in a remarkable display of insight, since that scar in her frontal lobes has got more steel bars than all the prisons of the world, and, as a rule, folks with frontal-lobe damage don't have much insight. I get her to put on her pajamas, and I remember what it used to be like when she stayed at home—you always had to have someone watching her—and I wished I had gotten her back to the hospital that very night, because she was up prowling, and suddenly all my good feelings of the past few days were gone. I felt crappy, but I had to stay vigilant while my baby sister was tripping around the house with this bullet-induced, jocular euphoria.

At one point she went outside barefoot. Later I found her eating a cube of butter. Then she took out all the canned foods in my larder and stacked them up—Progresso black beans (*beaucoup*), beef-barley soup, and canned carrot juice—playing supermarket. I tell her, "Mrs. Ma'am, I'll take one of those, and one of those, and have you got any peachy pie?"

She says, "I'm sorry, Richard, we haven't got any peachy pie."

"But, baby, I would sure like a nice big piece of peachy pie, heated up, and some vanilla ice cream with some rum sauce and maybe something along the lines of a maraschino cherry to put on the top for a little garnish. Nutmeg would do. Or are you telling me this is just a soup, beans, and carrot-juice joint? Is that all you got here?"

"Yes, Richard. Just soup and beans. They're very filling, though."

"Ahhm gonna have to call Betty Crocker, 'cause I'm in the mood for some pie, darlin'."

Suzie looks at me sort of worried and says that she thinks Betty Crocker is dead. Fuck. I realized I just had to sit on the couch and watch her, and this goes on and on, and of course I think I hear someone crashing around in the yard, so I get my .357 out from under my pillow and walk around the perimeter of the house, my feet crunching on the frozen snow. There was nobody out there. Back inside I checked on Susan, who was asleep in my bed. When I finally saw the rising of the sun and heard birds chirping to greet the new day, I went to the refrigerator, where I saw my recent affirmation: "Richard, you are a good and loving person," etc. I ripped it off the refrigerator and tore it into a thousand tiny pieces. Only an idiot would write something like that. It was like, I can't hack it in Africa, can't hack it at home—all I can hack is dead. So I took all the bullets out of the .357 except one, spun the chamber, placed the barrel against my right temple, and squeezed the trigger. When I heard the click of the hammer—voilà! I instantly felt better. My thumb quit throbbing. My stomach did not burn. The dread of morning and of sunlight had vanished, and I saw the dawn as something good, the birdsong wonderful. Even the obscure, take-it-for-granted objects in my house—the little knickknacks covered in an inch of dust, a simple wooden chair, my morning coffee cup drying upside down on the drainboard—seemed so relevant, so alive and necessary. I was glad for life and glad to be alive, especially when I looked down at the gun and saw that my bullet had rotated to the firing chamber. The van Gogh effect again. I was back from Cat Four to Cat One.

They're calling from the hospital, because I kept Susan overnight: "Where is Susan?" "She's watching *Days of Our Lives,*" I say as I shove the .357 into a top drawer next to the phone book. "Is she taking her Stelazine?" "Yes," I say. "Absolutely. Thanks for your concern. Now, goodbye!"

Just then the doorbell rings, and what I've got is a pair of Jehovah's Witnesses. I've seen enough of them on the Dark Continent to overcome an instinctive dread, since they seem to be genuinely content, proportionately—like, if you measured a bunch of them against the general population they are very happy people, and so pretty soon we're drinking Sanka and Susan comes out and they are talking about Christ's Kingdom on Earth where the lion lies down with the lamb, and Susan buys every word of it, 'cause it's like that line "Unless they come to me as little children . . ." Susan is totally guileless and the two Witnesses are without much guile, and I, the king of agnostics, listen and think, How's a lion going to eat straw? It's got a GI system designed to consume flesh, bones, and viscera—it's got sharp teeth, claws, and predatory instincts, not twenty-seven stomachs, like some bovine Bossie the Cow or whatever. And while I'm paging through a copy of *Awake!,* I see a little article from the correspondent in Nigeria entitled "The Guinea Worm—Its Final Days." As a doctor of tropical medicine, I probably know more about *Dracunculus medinensis,* the "fiery serpent," or Guinea worm, than anyone in the country. Infection follows ingestion of water containing crustacea (*Cyclops*). The worms penetrate the gut wall and mature in the retroperitoneal space, where they can grow three feet in length, and then generally migrate to the lower legs, where they form a painful blister. What the Africans do is burst the ulcer and extract the adult worm by hooking a stick under it and ever so gently tugging it out, since if you break it off the dead body can become septic and the leg might have to be removed. The pain of the Guinea worm is on a par with the pain of gout, and it can take ten days to nudge one out. The bad part is they usually come not in singles but in multiples. I've seen seven come out of an old man's leg.

If and when Global Aid sends me back to Africa, I will help continue the worm-eradication program, and as the Witnesses delight Susan with tales of a Heaven on Earth I'm thinking of the heat and the bugs in the equatorial zone, and the muddy water that the villagers take from rivers—they pour it in jugs and let the sediment settle for an hour and then dip from the top, where it looks sort of clean; it's hard to get through to them that *Cyclops* crustacea may be floating about invisibly and one swallow could get you seven worms, a swallow you took three years ago. You can talk to the villagers until you're blue in the face and they'll drink it anyhow. So you have to poison the *Cyclops* without overpoisoning the water. I mean, it can be done, but, given the way things work over there, you have to do everything yourself if you want it done right, which is why I hate the idea of going back: you have to come on like a one-man band.

On the other hand, Brother Bogue and the other brothers in the home office of Global Aid don't trust me; they don't like it when I come into the office irrepressibly happy, like Maurice Chevalier in his tuxedo and straw hat—"*Jambo jambo, bwana, jambo bonjour!*"—and give everyone one of those African soft handshakes, and then maybe do a little turn at seventy-eight revolutions per minute: "Oh, *oui oui,* it's delightful for me, walking my baby back home!" or "Hey, ain't it great, after staying out late? Zangk heffen for leetle gorls." Etc. They hate it when I'm high and they hate it when I'm low, and they hate it most if I'm feeling crazy/paranoid and come in and say, "You won't believe what happened to me now!" To face those humorless brothers every day and stay forever in a job as a medical administrator, to wear a suit and tie and drive I-5 morning and night, to climb under the house and tape those pipes with insulation—you get in the crawl space and the dryer-hose vent is busted and there's lint up the ass, a time bomb for spontaneous combustion, funny the house hasn't blown already (and furthermore, no wonder the house is dusty), and, hey, what, carpenter ants, too? When I think of all that: Fair America, I bid you adieu!

But things are basically looking up when I get Suz back to the hospital. As luck has it, I meet an Indian psychiatrist who spent fifteen years in Kampala, Uganda—he was one of the three shrinks in the whole country—and I ask him how Big Daddy Idi Amin is doing. Apparently, he's doing fine, living in Saudi Arabia with paresis or something, and the next thing you know the doc is telling me he's going to review Susan's case file, which means he's going to put her in a better ward and look out for her, and that's a load off my mind. Before I go, Suz and I take a little stroll around the spacious hospital grounds—it's a tranquil place. I can't help thinking that if Brother Bogue fires me—though I'm determined to behave myself after my latest mishap—I could come here and take Haldol and lithium, watch color TV, and drool. Whatever happened to that deal where you just went off to the hospital for a "little rest," with no stigma attached? Maybe all I need is some rest.

Susan still has those Jehovah's Witnesses on her mind. As we sit on a bench, she pulls one of their booklets out of her coat and shows me scenes of cornucopias filled with fruit and bounty, rainbows, and vividly colored vistas of a heaven on earth. Vistas that I've seen in a way, however paradoxically, in these awful Third World places, and I'm thinking, Let them that have eyes see; and let them that have ears hear—that's how it is, and I start telling Suz about Africa, maybe someday I can take her there, and she gets excited and asks me what it's like. Can you see lions?

And I tell her, "Yeah, baby, you'll see lions, giraffes, zebras, monkeys, and parrots, and the Pygmies." And she really wants to see Pygmies. So I tell her about a Pygmy chief who likes to trade meat for tobacco, T-shirts, candy, and trinkets, and about how one time when I went manic and took to the bush I stayed with this tribe, and went on a hunt with them, and we found a honeycomb in the forest; one of the hunters climbed up the tree to knock it down, oblivious of all the bees that were biting him. There were about five of us in the party and maybe ten pounds of honey and we ate all of it on the spot, didn't save an ounce, because we had the munchies from smoking dope. I don't tell Suz how it feels to take an airplane to New York, wait four hours for a flight to London, spend six hours in a transient lounge, and then hop on a nine-hour flight to Nairobi, clear customs, and ride on the back of a feed truck driven by a kamikaze African over potholes, through thick red dust, mosquitoes, blackflies, tsetse flies, or about river blindness, bone-break fever, bilharziasis, dumdum fever, tropical ulcers, AIDS, leprosy, etc. To go through all that to save somebody's life and maybe have them spit in your eye for the favor—I don't tell her about it, the way you don't tell a little kid that Santa Claus is a fabrication. And anyhow if I had eyes and could see, and ears and could hear—it very well might *be* the Garden of Eden. I mean, I can fuck up a wet dream with my attitude. I don't tell her that lions don't eat straw, never have, and so she's happy. And it's a nice moment for me, too, in a funny-ass way. I'm beginning to feel that with her I might find another little island of stability.

Another hospital visit: winter has given way to spring and the cherry blossoms are out. In two weeks it's gone from ten below to sixty-five, my Elavil and lithium are kicking in, and I'm feeling fine, calm, feeling pretty good. (I'm ready to go back and rumble in the jungle, yeah! *Sha-lah la-la-la-lah.*) Susan tells me she had a prophetic dream. She's unusually focused and articulate. She tells me she dreamed the two of us were driving around Heaven in a blue '67 Dodge.

"A '67 Dodge. Baby, what were we, the losers of Heaven?"

"Maybe, but it didn't really matter because we were there and we were happy."

"What were the other people like? Who was there? Was Arthur Schopenhauer there?"

"You silly! We didn't see other people. Just the houses. We drove up this hill and everything was like in a Walt Disney cartoon and we looked at one another and smiled because we were in Heaven, because we made it, because there wasn't any more shit."

"Now, let me get this straight. We were driving around in a beat-up car—"

"Yes, Richard, but it didn't matter."

"Let me finish. You say people lived in houses. That means people have to build houses. Paint them, clean them, and maintain them. Are you telling me that people in Heaven have jobs?"

"Yes, but they like their jobs."

"Oh, God, does it never end? A *job!* What am I going to do? I'm a doctor. If people don't get sick there, they'll probably make me a coal miner or something."

"Yes, but you'll love it." She grabs my arm with both hands, pitches her forehead against my chest, and laughs. It's the first time I've heard Susan laugh, ever—since we were kids, I mean.

"Richard, it's just like Earth but with none of the bad stuff. You were happy, too. So please don't worry. Is Africa like the Garden of Eden, Richard?"

"It's lush all right, but there's lots and lots of dead time," I say. "It's a good place to read *Anna Karenina.* Do you get to read novels in Heaven, hon? Have they got a library? After I pull my shift in the coal mine, do I get to take a nice little shower, hop in the Dodge, and drive over to the library?"

Susan laughs for the second time. "We will travel from glory to glory, Richard, and you won't be asking existential questions all the time. You won't have to anymore. And Mom and Dad will be there. You and me, all of us in perfect health. No coal mining. No wars, no fighting, no discontent. Satan will be in the Big Pit. He's on the Earth now tormenting us, but these are his last days. Why do you think we are here?"

"I often ask myself that question."

"Just hold on for a little while longer, Richard. Can you do that? Will you do it for me, Richard? What good would Heaven be if you're not there? Please, Richard, tell me you'll come."

I said, "O.K., baby, anything for you. I repent."

"No more Fyodor Dostoyevski?"

"I'll be non-Dostoyevski. It's just that, in the meantime, we're just sitting around here—waiting for Godot?"

"No, Richard, don't be a smart-ass. In the meantime we eat lunch. What did you bring?"

I opened up a deli bag and laid out chicken-salad-sandwich halves on homemade bread wrapped in white butcher paper. The sandwiches were stuffed with alfalfa sprouts and grated cheese, impaled with toothpicks with red, blue, and green cellophane ribbons on them, and there were two large, perfect, crunchy garlic pickles on the side. And a couple of cartons of strawberry Yoplait, two tubs of fruit salad with fresh whipped cream and little wooden spoons, and two large cardboard cups of aromatic, steaming, fresh black coffee.

It begins to rain, and we have to haul ass into the front seat of my Olds, where Suz and I finish the best little lunch of a lifetime and suddenly the Shirelles are singing, "This is dedicated to the one I love," and I'm thinking that I'm gonna be all right, and in the meantime what can be better than a cool, breezy, fragrant day, rain-splatter diamonds on the wraparound windshield of a Ninety-eight Olds with a view of cherry trees blooming in the light spring rain?

DAVID MICHAEL KAPLAN

Doe Season

DAVID MICHAEL KAPLAN (1946–) is the author of a short-story collection, *Comfort,* a novel, *Skating in the Dark,* and *Revision: A Creative Approach to Writing and Rewriting Fiction.* His short stories have appeared in *The Atlantic Monthly, Playboy, Redbook, Mirabella, TriQuarterly, Doubletake,* and many other literary magazines, and have been anthologized in The Best American Short Stories, Prize Stories: The O. Henry Awards, and *Sudden Fiction International,* among other collections. He teaches fiction writing at Loyola University in Chicago.

They were always the same woods, she thought sleepily as they drove through the early morning darkness—deep and immense, covered with yesterday's snowfall which had frozen overnight. They were the same woods that lay behind her house, *and they stretch all the way to here,* she thought, *for miles and miles, longer than I could walk in a day, or a week even, but they are still the same woods.* The thought made her feel good: it was like thinking of God; it was like thinking of the space between here and the moon; it was like thinking of all the foreign countries from her geography book where even now, Andy knew, people were going to bed, while they—she and her father and Charlie Spoon and Mac, Charlie's eleven-year-old son—were driving deeper into the Pennsylvania countryside, to go hunting.

They had risen long before dawn. Her mother, yawning and not trying to hide her sleepiness, cooked them eggs and French toast. Her father smoked a cigarette and flicked ashes into his saucer while Andy listened, wondering *Why doesn't he come?* and *Won't he ever come?,* until at last a car pulled into the graveled drive and honked. "That will be Charlie Spoon," her father said; he always said "Charlie Spoon," even though his real name was Spreun, because Charlie was, in a sense, shaped like a spoon, with a large head and a narrow waist and chest.

Andy's mother kissed her and her father and said, "Well, have a good time" and "Be careful." Soon they were outside in the bitter dark, loading gear by the back-porch light, their breath steaming. The woods behind the house were then only a black streak against the wash of night.

Andy dozed in the car and woke to find that it was half-light. Mac—also sleeping—had slid against her. She pushed him away and looked out the window. Her breath clouded the glass, and she was cold; the car's heater didn't work right. They were riding over gentle hills, the woods on both sides now—the same woods, she knew, because she had been watching the whole way, even while she slept. They had been in her dreams, and she had never lost sight of them.

Charlie Spoon was driving. "I don't understand why she's coming," he said to her father. "How old is she anyway—eight?"

"Nine," her father replied. "She's small for her age."

"So—nine. What's the difference? She'll just add to the noise and get tired besides."

"No, she won't," her father said. "She can walk me to death. And she'll bring good luck, you'll see. Animals—I don't know how she does it, but they come right up to her. We go walking in the woods, and we'll spot more raccoons and possums and such than I ever see when I'm alone."

Charlie grunted.

"Besides, she's not a bad little shot, even if she doesn't hunt yet. She shoots the .22 real good."

"Popgun," Charlie snorted. "And target shooting ain't deer hunting."

"Well, she's not gonna be shooting anyway, Charlie," her father said. "Don't worry. She'll be no bother."

"I still don't know why she's coming," Charlie said.

"Because she wants to, and I want her to. Just like you and Mac. No difference."

Charlie turned onto a side road and after a mile or so slowed down. "That's it!" he cried. He stopped, backed up, and entered a narrow dirt road almost hidden by trees. Five hundred yards down, the road ran parallel to a fenced-in field. Charlie parked in a cleared area deeply rutted by frozen tractor tracks. The gate was locked. *In the spring,* Andy thought, *there will be cows here, and a dog that chases them,* but now the field was unmarked and bare.

"This is it," Charlie Spoon declared. "Me and Mac was up here just two weeks ago, scouting it out, and there's deer. Mac saw the tracks."

"That's right," Mac said.

"Well, we'll just see about that," her father said, putting on his gloves. He turned to Andy. "How you doing, honey-bun?"

"Just fine," she said.

Andy shivered and stamped as they unloaded: first the rifles, which they unsheathed and checked, sliding the bolts, sighting through scopes, adjusting the slings; then the gear, their food and tents and sleeping bags and stove stored in four backpacks—three big ones for Charlie Spoon and her father and Mac, and a day pack for her.

"That's about your size," Mac said, to tease her.

She reddened and said, "Mac, I can carry a pack big as yours any day." He laughed and pressed his knee against the back of hers, so that her leg buckled. "Cut it out," she said. She wanted to make an iceball and throw it at him, but she knew that her father and Charlie were anxious to get going, and she didn't want to displease them.

Mac slid under the gate, and they handed the packs over to him. Then they slid under and began walking across the field toward the same woods that ran all the way back to her home, where even now her mother was probably rising again to wash their breakfast dishes and make herself a fresh pot of coffee. *She is there, and we are here:* the thought satisfied Andy. There was no place else she would rather be.

Mac came up beside her. "Over there's Canada," he said, nodding toward the woods.

"Huh!" she said. "Not likely."

"I don't mean *right* over there. I mean further up north. You think I'm dumb?"

Dumb as your father, she thought.

"Look at that," Mac said, pointing to a piece of cow dung lying on a spot scraped bare of snow. "A frozen meadow muffin." He picked it up and sailed it at her. "Catch!"

"Mac!" she yelled. His laugh was as gawky as he was. She walked faster. He seemed different today somehow, bundled in his yellow-and-black-checkered coat, a rifle in hand, his silly floppy hat not quite covering his ears. They all seemed different as she watched them trudge through the snow—Mac and her father and Charlie Spoon—bigger, maybe, as if the cold landscape enlarged rather than diminished them, so that they, the only figures in that landscape, took on size and meaning just by being there. If they weren't there, everything would be quieter, and the woods would be the same as before. *But they are here,* Andy thought, looking behind her at the boot prints in the snow, *and I am too, and so it's all different.*

"We'll go down to the cut where we found those deer tracks," Charlie said as they entered the woods. "Maybe we'll get lucky and get a late one coming through."

The woods descended into a gully. The snow was softer and deeper here, so that often Andy sank to her knees. Charlie and Mac worked the top of the gully while she and her father walked along the base some thirty yards behind them. "If they miss the first shot, we'll get the second," her father said, and she nodded as if she had known this all the time. She listened to the crunch of their boots, their breathing, and the drumming of a distant woodpecker. And the crackling. In winter the woods crackled as if everything were straining, ready to snap like dried chicken bones.

We are hunting, Andy thought. The cold air burned her nostrils.

They stopped to make lunch by a rock outcropping that protected them from the wind. Her father heated the bean soup her mother had made for them, and they ate it with bread already stiff from the cold. He and Charlie took a few pulls from a flask of Jim Beam while she scoured the plates with snow and repacked them. Then they had coffee with sugar and powdered milk, and her father poured her a cup, too. "We won't tell your momma," he said, and Mac laughed. Andy held the cup the way her father did, not by the handle but around the rim. The coffee tasted smoky. She felt a little queasy, but she drank it all.

Charlie Spoon picked his teeth with a fingernail. "Now, you might've noticed one thing," he said.

"What's that?" her father asked.

"You might've noticed you don't hear no rifles. That's because there ain't no other hunters here. We've got the whole damn woods to ourselves. Now, I ask you—do I know how to find 'em?"

"We haven't seen deer yet, neither."

"Oh, we will," Charlie said, "but not for a while now." He leaned back against the rock. "Deer're sleeping, resting up for the evening feed."

"I seen a deer behind our house once, and it was afternoon," Andy said.

"Yeah, honey, but that was *before* deer season," Charlie said, grinning. "They know something now. They're smart that way."

"That's right," Mac said.

Andy looked at her father—had she said something stupid?

"Well, Charlie," he said, "if they know so much, how come so many get themselves shot?"

"Them's the ones that don't *believe* what they know," Charlie replied. The men laughed. Andy hesitated, and then laughed with them.

They moved on, as much to keep warm as to find a deer. The wind became even stronger. Blowing through the treetops, it sounded like the ocean, and once Andy thought she could smell salt air. But that was impossible; the ocean was *hundreds* of miles away, farther than Canada even. She and her parents had gone last summer to stay for a week at a motel on the New Jersey shore. That was the first time she'd seen the ocean, and it frightened her. It was huge and empty, yet always moving. Everything lay hidden. If you walked in it, you couldn't see how deep it was or what might be below; if you swam, something could pull you under and you'd never be seen again. Its musky, rank smell made her think of things dying. Her mother had floated beyond the breakers, calling to her to come in, but Andy wouldn't go farther than a few feet into the surf. Her mother swam and splashed with animal-like delight while her father, smiling shyly, held his white arms above the waist-deep water as if afraid to get them wet. Once a comber rolled over and sent them both tossing, and when her mother tried to stand up, the surf receding behind, Andy saw that her mother's swimsuit top had come off, so that her breasts swayed free, the nipples like two dark eyes. Embarrassed, Andy looked around: except for two women under a yellow umbrella farther up, the beach was empty. Her mother stood up unsteadily, regained her footing. Taking what seemed the longest time, she calmly refixed her top. Andy lay on the beach towel and closed her eyes. The sound of the surf made her head ache.

And now it was winter; the sky was already dimming, not just with the absence of light but with a mist that clung to the hunters' faces like cobwebs. They made camp early. Andy was chilled. When she stood still, she kept wiggling her toes to make sure they were there. Her father rubbed her arms and held her to him briefly, and that felt better. She unpacked the food while the others put up the tents.

"How about rounding us up some firewood, Mac?" Charlie asked.

"I'll do it," Andy said. Charlie looked at her thoughtfully and then handed her the canvas carrier.

There wasn't much wood on the ground, so it took her a while to get a good load. She was about a hundred yards from camp, near a cluster of high, lichen-covered boulders, when she saw through a crack in the rock a buck and two does walking gingerly, almost daintily, through the alder trees. She tried to hush her breathing as they passed not more than twenty yards away. There was nothing she could do. If she yelled, they'd be gone; by the time she got back to camp, they'd be gone. The buck stopped, nostrils quivering, tail up and alert. He looked directly at her. Still she didn't move, not one muscle. He was a beautiful buck, the color of late-turned maple leaves. Unafraid, he lowered his tail, and he and his does silently merged into the trees. Andy walked back to camp and dropped the firewood.

"I saw three deer," she said. "A buck and two does."

"Where?" Charlie Spoon cried, looking behind her as if they might have followed her into camp.

"In the woods yonder. They're gone now."

"Well, hell!" Charlie banged his coffee cup against his knee.

"Didn't I say she could find animals?" her father said, grinning.

"Too late to go after them," Charlie muttered. "It'll be dark in a quarter hour. Damn!"

"Damn," Mac echoed.

"They just walk right up to her," her father said.

"Well, leastwise this proves there's deer here." Charlie began snapping long branches into shorter ones. "You know, I think I'll stick with you," he told Andy, "since you're so good at finding deer and all. How'd that be?"

"Okay, I guess," Andy murmured. She hoped he was kidding: no way did she want to hunt with Charlie Spoon. Still, she was pleased he had said it.

Her father and Charlie took one tent, she and Mac the other. When they were in their sleeping bags, Mac said in the darkness, "I bet you really didn't see no deer, did you?"

She sighed. "I did, Mac. Why would I lie?"

"How big was the buck?"

"Four point. I counted."

Mac snorted.

"You just believe what you want, Mac," she said testily.

"Too bad it ain't buck season," he said. "Well, I got to go pee."

"So pee."

She heard him turn in his bag. "You ever see it?" he asked.

"It? What's 'it'?"

"It. A pecker."

"Sure," she lied.

"Whose? Your father's?"

She was uncomfortable. "No," she said.

"Well, whose, then?"

"Oh, I don't know! Leave me be, why don't you?"

"Didn't see a deer, didn't see a pecker," Mac said teasingly.

She didn't answer right away. Then she said, "My cousin Lewis. I saw his."

"Well, how old's he?"

"One and a half."

"Ha! A baby! A baby's is like a little worm. It ain't a real one at all."

If he says he'll show me his, she thought, *I'll kick him. I'll just get out of my bag and kick him.*

"I went hunting with my daddy and Versh and Danny Simmons last year in buck season," Mac said, "and we got ourselves one. And we hog-dressed the thing. You know what that is, don't you?"

"No," she said. She was confused. What was he talking about now?

"That's when you cut him open and take out all his guts, so the meat don't spoil. Makes him lighter to pack out, too."

She tried to imagine what the deer's guts might look like, pulled from the gaping hole. "What do you do with them?" she asked. "The guts?"

"Oh, just leave 'em for the bears."

She ran her finger like a knife blade along her belly.

"When we left them on the ground," Mac said, "they smoked. Like they were cooking."

"Huh," she said.

"They cut off the deer's pecker, too, you know."

Andy imagined Lewis's pecker and shuddered. "Mac, you're disgusting."

He laughed. "Well, I gotta go pee." She heard him rustle out of his bag. "Broo!" he cried, flapping his arms. "It's cold!"

He makes so much noise, she thought, *just noise and more noise.*

Her father woke them before first light. He warned them to talk softly and said that they were going to the place where Andy had seen the deer, to try to cut them off on their way back from their night feeding. Andy couldn't shake off her sleep. Stuffing her sleeping bag into its sack seemed to take an hour, and tying her boots was the strangest thing she'd ever done. Charlie Spoon made hot chocolate and oatmeal with raisins. Andy closed her eyes and, between beats of her heart, listened to the breathing of the forest. *When I open my eyes, it will be lighter,* she decided. But when she did, it was still just as dark, except for the swaths of their flashlights and the hissing blue flame of the stove. *There has to be just one moment when it all changes from dark to light,* Andy thought. She had missed it yesterday, in the car; today she would watch more closely.

But when she remembered again, it was already first light and they had moved to the rocks by the deer trail and had set up shooting positions—Mac and Charlie Spoon on the up-trail side, she and her father behind them, some six feet up on a ledge. The day became brighter, the sun piercing the tall pines, raking the hunters, yet providing little warmth. Andy now smelled alder and pine and the slightly rotten odor of rock lichen. She rubbed her hand over the stone and considered that it must be very old, had probably been here before the giant pines, *before anyone was in these woods at all.* A chipmunk sniffed on a nearby branch. She aimed an imaginary rifle and pressed the trigger. The chipmunk froze, then scurried away. Her legs were cramping on the narrow ledge. Her father seemed to doze, one hand in his parka, the other cupped lightly around the rifle. She could smell his scent of old wool and leather. His cheeks were speckled with gray-black whiskers, and he worked his jaws slightly, as if chewing a small piece of gum.

Please let us get a deer, she prayed.

A branch snapped on the other side of the rock face. Her father's hand stiffened on the rifle, startling her—*He hasn't been sleeping at all,* she marveled—

and then his jaw relaxed, as did the lines around his eyes, and she heard Charlie Spoon call, "Yo, don't shoot, it's us." He and Mac appeared from around the rock. They stopped beneath the ledge. Charlie solemnly crossed his arms.

"I don't believe we're gonna get any deer here," he said drily.

Andy's father lowered his rifle to Charlie and jumped down from the ledge. Then he reached up for Andy. She dropped into his arms and he set her gently on the ground.

Mac sidled up to her. "I knew you didn't see no deer," he said.

"Just because they don't come when you want 'em to don't mean she didn't see them," her father said.

Still, she felt bad. Her telling about the deer had caused them to spend the morning there, cold and expectant, with nothing to show for it.

They tramped through the woods for another two hours, not caring much about noise. Mac found some deer tracks, and they argued about how old they were. They split up for a while and then rejoined at an old logging road that deer might use, and followed it. The road crossed a stream, which had mostly frozen over but in a few spots still caught leaves and twigs in an icy swirl. They forded it by jumping from rock to rock. The road narrowed after that, and the woods thickened.

They stopped for lunch, heating up Charlie's wife's corn chowder. Andy's father cut squares of applesauce cake with his hunting knife and handed them to her and Mac, who ate his almost daintily. Andy could faintly taste knife oil on the cake. She was tired. She stretched her leg; the muscle that had cramped on the rock still ached.

"Might as well relax," her father said, as if reading her thoughts. "We won't find deer till suppertime."

Charlie Spoon leaned back against his pack and folded his hands across his stomach. "Well, even if we don't get a deer," he said expansively, "it's still great to be out here, breathe some fresh air, clomp around a bit. Get away from the house and the old lady." He winked at Mac, who looked away.

"That's what the woods are all about, anyway," Charlie said. "It's where the women don't want to go." He bowed his head toward Andy. "With your exception, of course, little lady." He helped himself to another piece of applesauce cake.

"She ain't a woman," Mac said.

"Well, she damn well's gonna be," Charlie said. He grinned at her. "Or will you? You're half a boy anyway. You go by a boy's name. What's your real name? Andrea, ain't it?"

"That's right," she said. She hoped that if she didn't look at him, Charlie would stop.

"Well, which do you like? Andy or Andrea?"

"Don't matter," she mumbled. "Either."

"She's always been Andy to me," her father said.

Charlie Spoon was still grinning. "So what are you gonna be, Andrea? A boy or a girl?"

"I'm a girl," she said.

"But you want to go hunting and fishing and everything, huh?"

"She can do whatever she likes," her father said.

"Hell, you might as well have just had a boy and be done with it!" Charlie exclaimed.

"That's funny," her father said, and chuckled. "That's just what her momma tells me."

They were looking at her, and she wanted to get away from them all, even from her father, who chose to joke with them.

"I'm going to walk a bit," she said.

She heard them laughing as she walked down the logging trail. She flapped her arms; she whistled. *I don't care how much noise I make,* she thought. Two grouse flew from the underbrush, startling her. A little farther down, the trail ended in a clearing that enlarged into a frozen meadow; beyond it the woods began again. A few moldering posts were all that was left of a fence that had once enclosed the field. The low afternoon sunlight reflected brightly off the snow, so that Andy's eyes hurt. She squinted hard. A gust of wind blew across the field, stinging her face. And then, as if it had been waiting for her, the doe emerged from the trees opposite and stepped cautiously into the field. Andy watched: it stopped and stood quietly for what seemed a long time and then ambled across. It stopped again about seventy yards away and began to browse in a patch of sugar grass uncovered by the wind. Carefully, slowly, never taking her eyes from the doe, Andy walked backward, trying to step into the boot prints she'd already made. When she was far enough back into the woods, she turned and walked faster, her heart racing. *Please let it stay,* she prayed.

"There's a doe in the field yonder," she told them.

They got their rifles and hurried down the trail.

"No use," her father said. "We're making too much noise any way you look at it."

"At least we got us the wind in our favor," Charlie Spoon said, breathing heavily.

But the doe was still there, grazing.

"Good Lord," Charlie whispered. He looked at her father. "Well, whose shot?"

"Andy spotted it," her father said in a low voice. "Let her shoot it."

"What!" Charlie's eyes widened.

Andy couldn't believe what her father had just said. She'd only shot tin cans and targets; she'd never even fired her father's .30–30, and she'd never killed anything.

"I can't," she whispered.

"That's right, she can't," Charlie Spoon insisted. "She's not old enough and she don't have a license even if she was!"

"Well, who's to tell?" her father said. "Nobody's going to know but us." He looked at her. "Do you want to shoot it, punkin?"

Why doesn't it hear us? she wondered. *Why doesn't it run away?* "I don't know," she said.

"Well, I'm sure as hell gonna shoot it," Charlie said. Her father grasped Charlie's rifle barrel and held it. His voice was steady.

"Andy's a good shot. It's her deer. She found it, not you. You'd still be sitting on your ass back in camp." He turned to her again. "Now—do you want to shoot it, Andy? Yes or no."

He was looking at her; they were all looking at her. Suddenly she was angry at the deer, who refused to hear them, who wouldn't run away even when it could. "I'll shoot it," she said. Charlie turned away in disgust.

She lay on the ground and pressed the rifle stock against her shoulder bone. The snow was cold through her parka; she smelled oil and wax and damp earth. She pulled off one glove with her teeth. "It sights just like the .22," her father said gently. "Cartridge's already chambered." As she had done so many times before, she sighted down the scope; now the doe was in the reticle. She moved the barrel until the cross hairs lined up. Her father was breathing beside her.

"Aim where the chest and legs meet, or a little above, punkin," he was saying calmly. "That's the killing shot."

But now, seeing it in the scope, Andy was hesitant. Her finger weakened on the trigger. Still, she nodded at what her father said and sighted again, the cross hairs lining up in exactly the same spot—the doe had hardly moved, its brownish gray body outlined starkly against the blue-backed snow. *It doesn't know,* Andy thought. *It just doesn't know.* And as she looked, deer and snow and faraway trees flattened within the circular frame to become like a picture on a calendar, not real, and she felt calm, as if she had been dreaming everything—the day, the deer, the hunt itself. And she, finger on trigger, was only a part of that dream.

"Shoot!" Charlie hissed.

Through the scope she saw the deer look up, ears high and straining.

Charlie groaned, and just as he did, and just at the moment when Andy knew—*knew*—the doe would bound away, as if she could feel its haunches tensing and gathering power, she pulled the trigger. Later she would think, *I felt the recoil, I smelled the smoke, but I don't remember pulling the trigger.* Through the scope the deer seemed to shrink into itself, and then slowly knelt, hind legs first, head raised as if to cry out. It trembled, still straining to keep its head high, as if that alone would save it; failing, it collapsed, shuddered, and lay still.

"Whoee!" Mac cried.

"One shot! One shot!" her father yelled, clapping her on the back. Charlie Spoon was shaking his head and smiling dumbly.

"I told you she was a great little shot!" her father said. "I told you!" Mac danced and clapped his hands. She was dazed, not quite understanding what had happened. And then they were crossing the field toward the fallen doe, she walking dreamlike, the men laughing and joking, released now from the tension of silence and anticipation. Suddenly Mac pointed and cried out, "Look at that!"

The doe was rising, legs unsteady. They stared at it, unable to comprehend, and in that moment the doe regained its feet and looked at them, as if it, too, were trying to understand. Her father whistled softly. Charlie Spoon unslung his rifle and raised it to his shoulder, but the doe was already bounding away. His hurried shot missed, and the deer disappeared into the woods.

"Damn, damn, damn," he moaned.

"I don't believe it," her father said. "That deer was dead."

"Dead, hell!" Charlie yelled. "It was gutshot, that's all. Stunned and gutshot. Clean shot, my ass!"

What have I done? Andy thought.

Her father slung his rifle over his shoulder. "Well, let's go. She can't get too far."

"Hell, I've seen deer run ten miles gutshot," Charlie said. He waved his arms. "We may never find her!"

As they crossed the field, Mac came up to her and said in a low voice, "Gutshoot a deer, you'll go to hell."

"Shut up, Mac," she said, her voice cracking. It was a terrible thing she had done, she knew. She couldn't bear to think of the doe in pain and frightened. *Please let it die,* she prayed.

But though they searched all the last hour of daylight, so that they had to recross the field and go up the logging trail in a twilight made even deeper by thick, smoky clouds, they didn't find the doe. They lost its trail almost immediately in the dense stands of alderberry and larch.

"I am cold, and I am tired," Charlie Spoon declared. "And if you ask me, that deer's in another county already."

"No one's asking you, Charlie," her father said.

They had a supper of hard salami and ham, bread, and the rest of the applesauce cake. It seemed a bother to heat the coffee, so they had cold chocolate instead. Everyone turned in early.

"We'll find it in the morning, honeybun," her father said, as she went to her tent.

"I don't like to think of it suffering." She was almost in tears.

"It's dead already, punkin. Don't even think about it." He kissed her, his breath sour and his beard rough against her cheek.

Andy was sure she wouldn't get to sleep; the image of the doe falling, falling, then rising again, repeated itself whenever she closed her eyes. Then she heard an owl hoot and realized that it had awakened her, so she must have been asleep after all. She hoped the owl would hush, but instead it hooted louder. She wished her father or Charlie Spoon would wake up and do something about it, but no one moved in the other tent, and suddenly she was afraid that they had all decamped, wanting nothing more to do with her. She whispered, "Mac, Mac," to the sleeping bag where he should be, but no one answered. She tried to find the flashlight she always kept by her side, but couldn't, and she cried in panic, "Mac, are you there?" He mumbled something, and immediately she felt foolish and hoped he wouldn't reply.

When she awoke again, everything had changed. The owl was gone, the woods were still, and she sensed light, blue and pale, light where before there had been none. *The moon must have come out,* she thought. And it was warm, too, warmer than it should have been. She got out of her sleeping bag and took off her parka—it was that warm. Mac was asleep, wheezing like an old man. She unzipped the tent and stepped outside.

The woods were more beautiful than she had ever seen them. The moon made everything ice-rimmed glimmer with a crystallized, immanent light, while underneath that ice the branches of trees were as stark as skeletons. She heard a crunching in the snow, the one sound in all that silence, and there, walking down the logging trail into their camp, was the doe. Its body, like everything around her, was silvered with frost and moonlight. It walked past the tent where her father and Charlie Spoon were sleeping and stopped no more than six feet from her. Andy saw that she had shot it, yes, had shot it cleanly, just where she thought she had, the wound a jagged, bloody hole in the doe's chest.

A heart shot, she thought.

The doe stepped closer, so that Andy, if she wished, could have reached out and touched it. It looked at her as if expecting her to do this, and so she did, running her hand, slowly at first, along the rough, matted fur, then down to the edge of the wound, where she stopped. The doe stood still. Hesitantly, Andy felt the edge of the wound. The torn flesh was sticky and warm. The wound parted under her touch. And then, almost without her knowing it, her fingers were within, probing, yet still the doe didn't move. Andy pressed deeper, through flesh and muscle and sinew, until her whole hand and more was inside the wound and she had found the doe's heart, warm and beating. She cupped it gently in her hand. *Alive,* she marveled. *Alive.*

The heart quickened under her touch, becoming warmer and warmer until it was hot enough to burn. In pain, Andy tried to remove her hand, but the wound closed about it and held her fast. Her hand was burning. She cried out in agony, sure they would all hear and come help, but they didn't. And then her hand pulled free, followed by a steaming rush of blood, more blood than she ever could have imagined—it covered her hand and arm, and she saw to her horror that her hand was steaming. She moaned and fell to her knees and plunged her hand into the snow. The doe looked at her gently and then turned and walked back up the trail.

In the morning, when she woke, Andy could still smell the blood, but she felt no pain. She looked at her hand. Even though it appeared unscathed, it felt weak and withered. She couldn't move it freely and was afraid the others would notice. *I will hide it in my jacket pocket,* she decided, *so nobody can see.* She ate the oatmeal that her father cooked and stayed apart from them all. No one spoke to her, and that suited her. A light snow began to fall. It was the last day of their hunting trip. She wanted to be home.

Her father dumped the dregs of his coffee. "Well, let's go look for her," he said.

Again they crossed the field. Andy lagged behind. She averted her eyes from the spot where the doe had fallen, already filling up with snow. Mac and Charlie entered the woods first, followed by her father. Andy remained in the field and considered the smear of gray sky, the nearby flock of crows pecking at unyielding stubble. *I will stay here,* she thought, *and not move for a long while.* But now someone—Mac—was yelling. Her father appeared at the woods' edge and waved for her to come. She ran and pushed through a brake of alderberry and larch. The thick underbrush scratched her face. For a moment she felt lost and looked wildly about. Then, where the brush thinned, she saw them standing quietly in the falling snow. They were staring down at the dead doe. A film covered its upturned eye, and its body was lightly dusted with snow.

"I told you she wouldn't get too far," Andy's father said triumphantly. "We must've just missed her yesterday. Too blind to see."

"We're just damn lucky no animal got to her last night," Charlie muttered.

Her father lifted the doe's foreleg. The wound was blood-clotted, brown, and caked like frozen mud. "Clean shot," he said to Charlie. He grinned. "My little girl."

Then he pulled out his knife, the blade gray as the morning. Mac whispered to Andy, "Now watch this," while Charlie Spoon lifted the doe from behind by its forelegs so that its head rested between his knees, its underside exposed. Her father's knife sliced thickly from chest to belly to crotch, and Andy was running from them, back to the field and across, scattering the crows who cawed and circled angrily. And now they were all calling to her—Charlie Spoon and Mac and her father—crying *Andy, Andy* (but that wasn't her name, she would no longer be called that); yet louder than any of them was the wind blowing through the treetops, like the ocean where her mother floated in green water, also calling *Come in, come in,* while all around her roared the mocking of the terrible, now inevitable, sea.

JANET KAUFFMAN

Patriotic

JANET KAUFFMAN (1945–) was born in Lancaster, Pennsylvania, and raised on a tobacco farm. She has published three books of short stories: *Characters on the Loose, Obscene Gestures for Women,* and *Places in the World a Woman Could Walk;* two novels, *Collaborators* and *The Body in Four Parts;* and three collections of poems, including *The Weather Book,* an AWP Award Series Selection. She teaches at Eastern Michigan University in Ypsilanti, Michigan, where her writing courses focus on visual/hybrid work and mixed-media pieces. Janet Kauffman has collaborated with artist Nancy Chalker-Tennant on two visual/hybrid books—*X Amount of Time/Lines* and *We Are Moving Words.* She lives in Hudson, Michigan, where she farmed hay for many years and is now working with the Federal Wetland Reserve Program on the farm to restore wetlands and wildlife habitat.

"Jesus, this is hard on me," says Floyd Dey.

He hooks a hay bale out of the chute and lifts it in front of him the way he would lift a girl cousin. He carries the hay, maybe sixty pounds, to the back of the wagon. There he starts a second tier, up and over, rolling the bale once—there it is.

After an hour's work on a hay wagon with a seventeen-year-old kid, who is shirtless and scratching his navel, I myself quit complaining. This isn't labor. If it's hot, I twist the sleeves of my T-shirt up on my shoulders in doughy rolls, and I say to myself, okay.

To be fair, Floyd doesn't take the work seriously. But he knows what looks good—and for his own sake, he fakes the complaint. And he leans his back, the long tan of it, against the hay to relax. His two dark tits, flat as stickers, face my way. Floyd is hairless. He seems to understand, his demeanor demonstrates that he understands—like the Oriental masterminds of pain who settle their bare skins down on steel spikes—how a grain of tolerance can look like bliss.

I take the next bale and hike it up against my hipbone. Floyd waits his turn, visibly at rest, involved in the dynamics of vertical pause. Once in a while, he closes his eyes. It has come and gone from Floyd's attention that under my V-neck shirt my breasts are smallish pegs, with nubbed blueberry nipples.

I don't wear a bra to bale—it would fill with leaves.

Maybe Floyd blinks at me. It is not discernible.

Floyd is a neighbor; he helps me out. Breezy, hay-drying days, my husband works, hammering at barn roofs and stapling together pre-fab constructions, across two counties. Sheds, garages go up overnight. It's seasonal work, which keeps him away from the sunny fields, and I find my own help.

Over the years, I've learned what to look for.

Floyd Dey is a high-school senior. I don't call him *boy* to his face; he never says *crone.* In other words, Floyd Dey and I get along. After three years, three cuttings of hay a year, we have fair-weather days down pat. I do this; he does that. Nobody shirks. Floyd Dey, by any measure, rates as goodhearted. When Floyd talks to me, he looks me straight in the eye.

He's the middle of three brothers, the only one blessed with the talent of health. Eugene, the older one, took a job this year with a mining company in Utah: a sour, sharp-witted boy who doesn't like sharing work and doesn't like rest. The youngest brother, Harry T., programmed a computer this year, Floyd says, with crop variables—soil types, seeds, moisture, fertility—and predicted the yields in several DeKalb test plots. Harry T. is thirteen. If he's strong enough to help next year, I'll probably find his facts useful.

"Floyd," I say, "I appreciate the fact that you look me in the eye."

"No foolin," he says, looking at me. "You're an appreciative person."

I am that. I am also thin, stripped with muscle, a Democrat.

For his birthday, Floyd bought a green-and-flesh '57 Ford, which he drives with care and which he always parks under the plum tree near the barn. Today, the second day of baling, he lifts himself out of the car, into the speckled shade, and right there pulls his T-shirt out from his jeans and peels it up like a skin over the top of his head. Then he slams the car door.

"Yo!" he calls on his way across the yard. He leaps, right foot up on the tongue of the hay wagon, left foot up on the flatbed. Here he kicks at the mounds of green and yellowing alfalfa dust from yesterday, and in that cloud he makes his way to the back latticework of two-by-fours that brace the bales.

It's the step of a man making himself at home.

He tosses his T-shirt up like a cap. The shirt snags where he wants it, on top of an upright, and a hot, cooperating wind lifts it dreamily.

Flag's up. The kid is ready to sail.

In the kitchen, I am on the phone with Mrs. Bagnoli, who in this lurch, in this perpetual lack of the able-bodied, I call on to help as tractor driver. I've heard about her; I've read her name in the papers.

"This is a Ford 4000," I say. "You know it?"

She plowed, she insists, in her springtimes in Oscoda, and last summer, when her nephew Rodney crushed himself under his Ford 4000 in mud, she was the one to bring some boards and the CPR people, and drive the sullied tractor home. Rodney's still saying thanks.

"I know the 4000," she swears. "I know it clean through."

Mrs. Bagnoli is also known to me as the woman whose husband survived eight hours in a moving cement mixer. I would never have thought it possible for a man to hang on, if what he did was hang on, or walk against the rotation, if he did walk against the rotation.

Although Mrs. Bagnoli lives on a farm three miles away, we have talked only a few times on the phone. She tells me her husband works at the Ford plant in Saline; *she* is the one who drives their wide-wheeled John Deere diesel.

"I'm on my way," she insists. "Glad to help. Happy to."

Through the screen door, I can see the hay wagon hitched in back of the red International 420 baler, and the blue Ford tractor in front. Seeing that display, seeing Floyd—like my own son on a flag-waving wagon, allowing the wind to mess his long hair—I decide that this is a day I could call myself—what is it?—patriotic? When the back of the neck is cool; the palms of the hands, tropical?

"Well, then," I say to Mrs. Bagnoli on the phone. "See you."

I fill a wide-mouthed jug with water and ice cubes, and cap it. From a shelf, I take the black hay hook, and halfway out the door, I reach back to the Kleenex box and stuff my pockets with yellow tissues.

Floyd is not one to carry Kleenex, even though his nostrils collect a leafy debris—even though he seems to enjoy making noises blowing his nose. I have told Floyd that Kleenex serves a working function, too. If the hay turns damp or wads up with weeds, we twist scraps of Kleenex as markers under the twine of wet bales.

In the barn, I set the wet bales aside. Floyd cooperates in these precautions, although he claims he has never seen steamy bales. "It happens," I say. "Spontaneous combustion."

Disaster has a cause, I try to tell him.

I cross the driveway, and I whistle the "Marseillaise" as far as I know it. When the tune gives out, I start again, mumbling the words that Floyd might or might not know in French. *Allons, enfants de la patrie*. . . .

Up on the wagon, Floyd, who is placid, always in the present moment, turns when he hears me. He stands, cross-armed, massaging both his shoulders. I greet him in sunlight that casts a bluish-gold sheen on every surface. It looks like the sun on the sea, like the sun in Hawaii on T.V.

"What luck," I say.

I swing a landowner's arm around, palm up.

From the wagon, Floyd surveys the landscape. What he sees are low, aquamarine hills of alfalfa, steep slopes, and gravelly glacial dumps with swamps in the sockets. Above it all, the sky is blue, top to bottom.

"You order this day?" he asks.

With the tips of his fingers, he rubs his belly lightly, using both hands, back and forth, along the line of his lower ribs.

A boy is not to be blamed for thoughtlessness.

I check twine; I push dust from the knotters; I count the shear pins glittering in the tool box.

Down the driveway, a black Chevy pickup rolls in and roars its engine. The driver downshifts twice and gravel smacks the siding of the house.

"Wild," says Floyd.

He jumps from the wagon to help me tighten the tension on the baler. We take the threaded handles either side of the chute, and we wind them down.

Mrs. Bagnoli drives the pickup, too fast, in the general direction of the barn. She runs off the driveway and cuts through the yard, aiming the grille right at us. I see her head, low in the cab, and her elbow out the driver's window. But I can't see where she's looking.

Floyd and I both take one step back.

At the last minute, the pickup veers, sharp to the left, toward the tractor, and Mrs. Bagnoli must pull the truck's emergency brake and smash the foot brake simultaneously, because the truck skids a couple of inches and stops, one tire kissing the tread of the tractor's rear tire. Mrs. Bagnoli pitches herself into the steering column. I see a twist of gray hair against the windshield.

"Jesus," says Floyd.

He takes in a breath and holds it. I don't notice what I do.

But Mrs. Bagnoli appears unharmed. With a motion that has to be called bobbing, she drops herself out of the truck, goes around the back end, and comes at us with a smile.

"It is *criminal,*" she says, in a festive voice, "farmers away from farms." She shakes my hand. "Criminal, husbands *working!* If *we* go"—she shakes my wrists—"*babies* will have to drive." She reaches a hand toward Floyd.

Floyd bends at the waist and brings his ankles together, politely. They shake hands.

I don't mind acknowledging Mrs. Bagnoli's energy. Her hair, which is thick and gray, a horsy sort of hair, is looped into a fountain effect on the top of her head. Small bobby pins catch the light and send out snappy flashes. She wears black tapered slacks and a black nylon blouse, over a body that is short-legged, thick-thighed, and enormously breasted. Now that she's out in the open, she looks reliable.

Floyd finishes inhaling the long breath he took in at her arrival, and lets out a low whistle. That easily, the day reassembles itself.

These are the United States, I chant in my heart. Floyd breathes with contentment, and I, for my part, am willing to take some risks. Maybe Mrs. Bagnoli was showing us she could drive.

We stand at the side of the wagon and sort out three pairs of brown cotton work gloves.

"Where's Floyd?" Mrs. Bagnoli asks me.

She means my husband, Lloyd.

"You mean *Lloyd,*" I say. "My husband is Lloyd. He's with the Marry brothers," I say. "Constructing. Pole barns. *This* is Floyd. Floyd Dey."

"Floyd! All right. Whatever. It's all the same. *You* won't farm either, will you?" She points at Floyd. She wears a large black-stoned ring on her index finger.

"Nah," he says. "This is it."

"There!" she says, and snaps the gloves in her hands and turns away.

"But I like it," Floyd explains.

Mrs. Bagnoli doesn't care whether he likes it or not. She goes to the tractor and she pats her gloved hand along the fender as she walks by.

"I like it," he says again.

"So," says Mrs. Bagnoli. "Let's go." With her hands on the steering wheel, she pulls herself up onto the tractor seat.

Without hesitation, without instruction, Mrs. Bagnoli starts up the engine. Floyd and I swing onto the wagon and dangle our legs off the side. Somehow, Mrs. Bagnoli knows the trick of the brake release, and Floyd nods at me, grinning.

It doesn't take long to see that Mrs. Bagnoli is a purposeful, serious-minded woman. It's clear she commands a world-view. Small things fall away. She sits up on the blue cushion seat, her back straight, her neck like a fine stalk, very slender and pearly above the black collar of the blouse. Her hair rises and rises, then falls in sprays. She doesn't look left or right, and—as soon as the clutch is released—we *glide,* around the barn, cutting right from the lane to make a path through the weed field. We hit high weeds—Queen Anne's lace, brittle and folded flat; flowering nettle. The stalks crumple under the tractor's tires, and bristled round seeds shoot up at the sides of the wagon. The roar of the tractor disappears in the smattering of weeds.

Tractor, baler, wagon, dry weeds—all of it stirs a considerable racket, a whirring that isn't mechanical.

"Lord!" Floyd says. He stretches out on his back and pretends he's floating.

Mrs. Bagnoli drives a path that hasn't a ripple. Our teeth don't rattle; our breath doesn't catch.

In the light wind, strands of Mrs. Bagnoli's hair whip out to the side and the tips point toward us. The ground unrolls like a carpet. We drive out of the weed field into the cleared hayfield, where the alfalfa lies in windrows, one beyond another in dark, continuous breakers. The air sweeps up from the hot field and the heat, an invisible wake, spreads out behind us.

At the first windrow, Mrs. Bagnoli pulls the silvery PTO knob and the baler flywheel spins, the pickup teeth swing around to feed in hay, and the plunger takes its first dive down, pushing leaf and stalk and flower together. It's the noise of a natural catastrophe. There's a sudden heat, as if the sun capped the field and folded everything in.

Floyd and I stand up to wait for the first bale.

"Smooth!" he shouts.

We have to shout.

"Look here!" I yell. I stand with my legs apart, on tiptoe.

Floyd cocks his head to watch. I touch my toes, right fingers to left foot, left fingers to right foot. The ride is so smooth I don't have to shift for balance. I don't topple. Floyd sees the proof.

"She's the best!" he shouts. "Hang on to her!"

"She's great!"

"We're sailin, ain't we? We get that woman to drive for the government, we'd be on our way, don't you think—sailin."

"You think she's driven these fields?" I ask.

"Nah, she's a *driver.* Make her Secretary of State!"

A good many things in this world are not possible. Floyd Dey, for instance, being goodhearted, will never deeply offend. It is possible he will know happiness.

"Will you be around next summer?" I shout.

In his loudest voice, his words come slowly through the heat. "Doubt it! I want to move myself out!"

"School?"

"Western, sure! It's a great place, Kalamazoo!"

Floyd takes the first bale, a lopsided one, very loose, which he has to hug to keep it from collapsing.

"It ain't all parties!" he says for my information. "I know a guy, Arnie. He says he'll get me work!"

"What'll you study?" It's my turn, and I hook a bale.

"Haven't the faintest!" he says.

"What about Debbie?" Debbie Ames is his girlfriend, an awestruck, intelligent girl.

Floyd doesn't hear.

"What about Debbie?"

"Debbie? Shit! I'll be on my own!"

Floyd snaps the twine on another bale; it's too loose. The bales are mushy.

"They got *fine* women in Kalamazoo, let me tell you!" he shouts. "I'll get me a fine woman! It's another place! You been there?"

Both of us jump down to tighten the handles. Mrs. Bagnoli, a driver with confidence in machinery, never looks back. Her hair sparkles, and she gazes ahead to the first steep slope, an arc of green in the blue sky ahead. Floyd and I know the requirements of the hill—we know the wagon is bolted and won't rear up—but we pull ourselves back in a hurry and stand at the front, counterbalancing. Standing sideways, a bend to the knee, we try to give ourselves weight, although my boots slip a little with the incline. Up the slope there's practically nothing but blue.

When the tractor goes over the top and everything evens out, I shout to Floyd, "I've never been to Kalamazoo!"

"Well, it ain't like this! There's ravines! Mists!" He waves his arms to create a murkiness. "They don't build in these ravines! So you get houses, jam-packed McDonald's, and then you step out the back door and it's the *wild!* I think it does something to the women!"

"You think?"

"They *look* wild! That suits *me!* When they get out of high school, they get apartments, buy their own furniture! Plants! Arnie's got a friend, nineteen, with her own place! Everything she wants!"

Floyd is as sweet as a foreigner. He travels along, never embarrassed, not oblivious, although women are as weird to him as hors d'oeuvres. Should he use a fork or his fingers? He checks out the world-at-large, and he doesn't take disappointment. He hardly blinks. Such is the mildness of sailors in Madagascar. What a place, they say.

Bales push up from the chute, heavy and solid, emerald-green. The smell of alfalfa bloom rushes in, and a thin puff of dust rises with each bale to shoulder height and then sinks as a film on the wagon. Loading the bales, lifting a measure of heat with each one, we breathe deep breaths, and of course the hairs in Floyd's nose pick up leaves, grit.

I give him a Kleenex.

Snorting a little, coughing, he rubs at the green dust and then sticks the Kleenex into the side of his shoe.

His back shows a pattern of dampness, beads of sweat organized either side of the backbone, and a fine moisture marks his face with dark streaks, just above and below his lips.

"It's hot!" I shout.

"So sweat!"

"I am!"

Floyd pushes my shoulder to turn me around. He is looking for sweat.

"Say, your shirt's soaked! Hang the thing up!"

I consider the idea. "I'd itch! It's sticky!"

"There's an air!" he says, flapping his arms.

I look at Floyd's face and I see a downright factual face.

"It's nothing to me!" he yells.

And it's true, I see that.

"Go on!" he says.

I pull the shirt out of my jeans and yank it off.

Floyd, my buddy, takes the shirt from me and aims for an upright. He pitches, and the thing catches.

Two flags flying. All-clear.

Great huffs, like breaths from enormous lungs, remote and chill, rush against my breasts and flow around my sides. I can feel my ribs, the bend of the bones, cooling.

There's not much to do. Floyd and I have the open air in common, nothing more. We ride along, arms out, ventilating.

"Cooler, ain't it?" is what Floyd says.

The day slips out of kilter. I don't tell Floyd. Crops, the flourishing hybrids, machinery, barns—all appear isolate, diminished, doll-pretty. I feel the shrinkage. Except for my arms, elbows to wrists, my skin is as white as a tusk. There are a few pale veins across my breasts, rivery; my navel is purple with some kind of leaf.

"Mrs. Bagnoli drives steady, don't she?" Floyd says. Then he looks at me. "You just let me know if you want that shirt."

"I will," I say.

Floyd Dey will be decent in death. I see that. He will use very predictable last words. His body in death will retain its beauty, a smoothness he's rubbed with his fingertips all his life.

On the tractor, Mrs. Bagnoli's magical accord with machinery signals the load is complete. She tosses her head the way people do to discard a knot of thoughts. She twists in her seat and looks back over her left shoulder. Her eyes are large and dark, the iris and pupil matching. She sees now, behind the baler, a full wagon, four tiers high, and two human bodies in jeans, bare-chested—one easygoing, one askew, armpits open to breezes. She takes note.

"Ahoy!" she yells.

She waves an arm and shows a set of wide teeth.

The next instant, she unbuttons her black nylon blouse and slips it off.

I hear the laughing. She looks ahead, but she waves to us once again, black blouse in hand. She wears a black bra, big as the top of a swimsuit. There's wide elastic right to the hooks. Across the round of her shoulders and the flat of her upper back, Mrs. Bagnoli's skin is phenomenally white.

All of the air in the field parts around her and flows away, drastically cooled.

"She's a go-getter!" Floyd shouts.

"A go-getter?"

Floyd pulls the last bale onto the wagon, throws the chute forward, and sits himself down.

"Just look at her," Floyd says. "She's going places."

With the wagon loaded, Mrs. Bagnoli punches the PTO knob and the baler winds down. The plunger drops heavily, lifts and drops, more slowly each time. Noises sink in the ground and go off with the heat.

The three of us ride in the quiet down a long slope toward the barn. Mrs. Bagnoli swings her blouse, an automatic motion, until it winds around her arm. She swings it the other way, unwinding it. After a time, she tosses the blouse, with an aim as sure as Floyd's, onto the muffler pipe that stands in the middle of the tractor's hood. The blouse catches the stack by a sleeve, and like the ill-assorted ship that we are, masted and rigged and fitted out, we drive on, signaling God knows what.

The black blouse clings to the muffler and twists around it. In another few seconds, the fabric smokes. A white steamy smoke. Another second, and Mrs. Bagnoli's blouse is a flame, tall and yellow and nearly invisible in the sun, obscured by the terrific glare off the field, out of the sky.

But the blouse is there, and the blouse burns.

We are slow to react. When we do, we are sensible. We stand up—Mrs. Bagnoli where she is, Floyd and I on the front two bales—and we call out, in chorus: *Get a stick—There ain't no stick—Get the blouse on the ground—Too dry, too dry—The gas tank!—No, don't move—Fumes—Watch out, it'll blow! Watch out!*

We sit down, abruptly, the three of us, to watch the flame and register the percussion that will blind us and deafen us and stop time just where it is. Mrs. Bagnoli drives straight ahead, as if she has blissfully ceased driving.

The flame rises and falls; a weak thread of gray smoke marks the wind's direction. Then the nylon cloth separates from itself and drips in small distinguishable fires down the muffler pipe. Flames pool and drop onto the hood of the tractor and drop again into the field.

Mrs. Bagnoli doesn't shift gears or brake.

I can see, without moving my eyes, too many things—the blouse burning, the black-and-white pattern of Mrs. Bagnoli's back; a flutter of remnant flames in the field.

It's a colorful afternoon, sweetly hushed, splashy. Disaster always feels brand-new.

But this, in the end, is the old story.

Nothing happens. The blouse burns itself out. I live to say so. We don't detonate.

When the last flames collapse, Mrs. Bagnoli stops the tractor. We're at the edge of the field and I can hear the rattle of grasshoppers and see flicks of them in the stubble. On my shoulder, I feel Floyd's breathing.

He climbs the bales and grabs our shirts. He understands civility very well—nobody runs bare-breasted to the aid of strangers.

While Floyd and I pull on our shirts and shake out our hair, Mrs. Bagnoli, up front, takes a screwdriver from the tool box and scrapes some ash off the muffler. She blows gray debris off the hood and picks up a black button or two.

"Good God! We should all be angels!" She swings herself down from the tractor.

"You okay?" Floyd calls.

"Sure," she says. "*You're* the pale one. *You* sit down."

But Floyd and I jump off the wagon and meet Mrs. Bagnoli by the side of the baler.

"Jesus," says Floyd, taking her hand. He keeps hold of Mrs. Bagnoli's hand, and he takes mine, too. The three of us do a little dance, in a circle. I catch Mrs. Bagnoli's eye.

"That was some driving!" Floyd says.

Mrs. Bagnoli frees her hands and claps a couple of times.

"I'd probably have stopped the tractor," Floyd says.

"Oh, a mistake!" Mrs. Bagnoli frowns.

Then she claps her hands again. "Let's get out of here!" In her black bra and slacks, she climbs on the tractor and starts it up. Floyd and I jump to our places on the front bales.

"No need to tell her a thing," Floyd says.

* * *

Mrs. Bagnoli drives to the barn, parks the tractor, and we walk, side by side, Mrs. Bagnoli in the middle, to the house. Inside, I hunt up one of my white blouses for her to wear, and we sit with gin-and-tonics at the white-painted kitchen table while Floyd calls up Debbie and sets a date for later. "I got news," he says into the phone.

Mrs. Bagnoli and I get acquainted. In answer to my questions, she tells me the story of her husband's ordeal in the cement mixer. Having been so close to death, she says, he eats only steaks now for supper. I learn how many of her kids live in California, and she gets the same sort of information from me.

I will wait until another time to ask her about her future, the plans she has.

"Bye-bye, Deb," Floyd says, and joins us. He sits down and crosses his legs at the ankles. He lifts his gin-and-tonic for a toast.

"To a hell of a driver!" he says.

"Hooray!" I say.

"Hear, hear!" says Mrs. Bagnoli.

Mrs. Bagnoli and I sip at our drinks. We watch Floyd drink down his glass and head outside to start up the motor on the hay elevator. On the back step, he peels off his shirt, rolls it in a ball, and as he goes by his car, he pitches it in through the open window.

"He's steady," I say to Mrs. Bagnoli. "Very helpful."

"And such a smooth back!" she remarks.

"Yes, indeed," I agree.

"Wouldn't you say," Mrs. Bagnoli says carefully, "that he is encouraged by what he has seen of womanhood?"

"I hope so," I say. "Time will tell."

We finish our drinks and step outside. When the wagon's unloaded, it will be nearly dusk and my husband, Lloyd, will be on his way home. By dark, Floyd Dey will be deep into kisses with Debbie, and Mrs. Bagnoli will have driven to and from Bob's Market for steaks.

Already, I'm looking forward to next summer's haying. With Floyd's brother Harry T. and Mrs. Bagnoli, everything should go like clockwork. But we won't forget Floyd. I'll tell her whatever I hear from Kalamazoo. After all, Floyd and I are good friends. He'll visit at Christmas and I'll write him sometimes to keep him informed of Mrs. Bagnoli's progress toward the office of Secretary of State. Floyd is not a boy to be mystified.

JAMAICA KINCAID

Girl

JAMAICA KINCAID (1946–) was born and educated in St. John's, Antigua, in the West Indies. Her first book, *At the Bottom of the River,* a collection of stories, received the Morton Dauwen Zabel Award of the American Academy and Institute of Arts and Letters and was nominated for the PEN/Faulkner Award. Ms. Kincaid's other books are *Annie John; A Small Place; Lucy; My Brother,* a finalist for the National Book Award; and *The Autobiography of My Mother,* a nominee for the National Book Critics Circle Award in fiction, a finalist for the PEN/Faulkner Award, and the winner of the Cleveland Foundation's Anisfield-Wolf Book Award as well as the *Boston Book Review*'s Fisk Fiction prize. Her stories have appeared in *The New Yorker, Rolling Stone,* and *The Paris Review.* She lives with her husband and two children in Bennington, Vermont.

Wash the white clothes on Monday and put them on the stone heap; wash the color clothes on Tuesday and put them on the clothesline to dry; don't walk barehead in the hot sun; cook pumpkin fritters in very hot sweet oil; soak your little cloths right after you take them off; when buying cotton to make yourself a nice blouse, be sure that it doesn't have gum on it, because that way it won't hold up well after a wash; soak salt fish overnight before you cook it; is it true that you sing benna in Sunday school?; always eat your food in such a way that it won't turn someone else's stomach; on Sundays try to walk like a lady and not like the slut you are so bent on becoming; don't sing benna in Sunday school; you mustn't speak to wharf-rat boys, not even to give directions; don't eat fruits on the street—flies will follow you; *but I don't sing benna on Sundays at all and never in Sunday school;* this is how to sew on a button; this is how to make a buttonhole for the button you have just sewed on; this is how to hem a dress when you see the hem coming down and so to prevent yourself from looking like the slut I know you are so bent on becoming; this is how you iron your father's khaki shirt so that it doesn't have a crease; this is how you iron your father's khaki pants so that they don't have a crease; this is how you grow okra—far from the house, because okra tree harbors red ants; when you are growing dasheen, make sure it gets plenty of water or else it makes your throat itch when you are eating it; this is how you sweep a corner; this is how you sweep a whole house; this is how you sweep a yard; this is how you smile to someone you don't like very much; this is how you smile to someone you don't like at all; this is how you smile to someone you like completely; this is how you set a table for tea; this is how you set a table for dinner; this is how you set a table for dinner with an important guest; this is how you set a table for lunch; this is how you set a table for breakfast; this is how to behave in the presence of men who don't know you very well, and this way they won't recognize immediately the slut I have warned you against becoming; be sure to wash every day, even if it is with your own spit; don't squat down to play marbles—you are not a boy, you know; don't pick people's flowers—you might catch something; don't throw stones at blackbirds, because it might not be a blackbird at all; this is how to make a bread pudding; this is how to make doukona; this is how to make pepper pot; this is how to make a good medicine for a cold; this is how to make a good medicine to throw away a child before it even becomes a child; this is how to catch a fish; this is how to throw back a fish you don't like, and that way something bad won't fall on you; this is how to bully a man; this is how a man bullies you; this is how to love a man, and if this doesn't work there are other ways, and if they don't work don't feel too bad about giving up; this is how to spit up in the air if you feel like it, and this is how to move quick so that it doesn't fall on you; this is how to make ends meet; always squeeze bread to make sure it's fresh; *but what if the baker won't let me feel the bread?;* you mean to say that after all you are really going to be the kind of woman who the baker won't let near the bread?

DAVID LEAVITT

Territory

DAVID LEAVITT (1961–) is the author of *Family Dancing,* a finalist for both the National Book Critics Circle Award and the PEN/Faulkner Prize; *The Lost Language of Cranes* (which became a BBC Film); *Equal Affections; A Place I've Never Been; While England Sleeps;* and *Arkansas.* With Mark Mitchell, he is coeditor of *The Penguin Book of Gay Short Stories* and *Pages Passed from Hand to Hand,* as well as coauthor of *Italian Pleasures.* He is a recipient of fellowships from both the Guggenheim Foundation and the National Endowment for the Arts. He lives in Italy.

Neil's mother, Mrs. Campbell, sits on her lawn chair behind a card table outside the food co-op. Every few minutes, as the sun shifts, she moves the chair and table several inches back so as to remain in the shade. It is a hundred degrees outside, and bright white. Each time someone goes in or out of the co-op a gust of air-conditioning flies out of the automatic doors, raising dust from the cement.

Neil stands just inside, poised over a water fountain, and watches her. She has on a sun hat, and a sweatshirt over her tennis dress; her legs are bare, and shiny with cocoa butter. In front of her, propped against the table, a sign proclaims: MOTHERS, FIGHT FOR YOUR CHILDREN'S RIGHTS—SUPPORT A NON-NUCLEAR FUTURE. Women dressed exactly like her pass by, notice the sign, listen to her brief spiel, finger pamphlets, sign petitions or don't sign petitions, never give money. Her weary eyes are masked by dark glasses. In the age of Reagan, she has declared, keeping up the causes of peace and justice is a futile, tiresome, and unrewarding effort; it is therefore an effort fit only for mothers to keep up. The sun bounces off the window glass through which Neil watches her. His own reflection lines up with her profile.

* * *

Later that afternoon, Neil spreads himself out alongside the pool and imagines he is being watched by the shirtless Chicano gardener. But the gardener, concentrating on his pruning, is neither seductive nor seducible. On the lawn, his mother's large Airedales—Abigail, Lucille, Fern—amble, sniff, urinate. Occasionally, they accost the gardener, who yells at them in Spanish.

After two years' absence, Neil reasons, he should feel nostalgia, regret, gladness upon returning home. He closes his eyes and tries to muster the proper background music for the cinematic scene of return. His rhapsody, however, is interrupted by the noises of his mother's trio—the scratchy cello, whining violin, stumbling piano—as she and Lillian Havalard and Charlotte Feder plunge through Mozart. The tune is cheery, in a Germanic sort of way, and utterly inappropriate to what Neil is trying to feel. Yet it *is* the music of his adolescence; they have played it for years, bent over the notes, their heads bobbing in silent time to the metronome.

It is getting darker. Every few minutes, he must move his towel so as to remain within the narrowing patch of sunlight. In four hours, Wayne, his lover of ten months and the only person he has ever imagined he could spend his life with, will be in this house, where no lover of his has ever set foot. The thought fills him with a sense of grand terror and curiosity. He stretches, tries to feel seductive, desirable. The gardener's shears whack at the ferns; the music above him rushes to a loud, premature conclusion. The women laugh and applaud themselves as they give up for the day. He hears Charlotte Feder's full nasal twang, the voice of a fat woman in a pink pants suit—odd, since she is a scrawny, arthritic old bird, rarely clad in anything other than tennis shorts and a blouse. Lillian is the fat woman in the pink pants suit; her voice is thin and warped by too much crying. Drink in hand, she calls out from the porch, "Hot enough!" and waves. He lifts himself up and nods to her.

The women sit on the porch and chatter; their voices blend with the clink of ice in glasses. They belong to a small circle of ladies all of whom, with the exception of Neil's mother, are widows and divorcées. Lillian's husband left her twenty-two years ago, and sends her a check every month to live on; Charlotte has been divorced twice as long as she was married, and has a daughter serving a long sentence for terrorist acts committed when she was nineteen. Only Neil's mother has a husband, a distant sort of husband, away often on business. He is away on business now. All of them feel betrayed—by husbands, by children, by history.

Neil closes his eyes, tries to hear the words only as sounds. Soon, a new noise accosts him: his mother arguing with the gardener in Spanish. He leans on his elbows and watches them; the syllables are loud, heated, and compressed, and seem on the verge of explosion. But the argument ends happily;

they shake hands. The gardener collects his check and walks out the gate without so much as looking at Neil.

He does not know the gardener's name; as his mother has reminded him, he does not know most of what has gone on since he moved away. Her life has gone on, unaffected by his absence. He flinches at his own egoism, the egoism of sons.

"Neil! Did you call the airport to make sure the plane's coming in on time?"

"Yes," he shouts to her. "It is."

"Good. Well, I'll have dinner ready when you get back."

"Mom—"

"What?" The word comes out in a weary wail that is more of an answer than a question.

"What's wrong?" he says, forgetting his original question.

"Nothing's wrong," she declares in a tone that indicates that everything is wrong. "The dogs have to be fed, dinner has to be made, and I've got people here. Nothing's wrong."

"I hope things will be as comfortable as possible when Wayne gets here."

"Is that a request or a threat?"

"Mom—"

Behind her sunglasses, her eyes are inscrutable. "I'm tired," she says. "It's been a long day. I . . . I'm anxious to meet Wayne. I'm sure he'll be wonderful, and we'll all have a wonderful, wonderful time. I'm sorry. I'm just tired."

She heads up the stairs. He suddenly feels an urge to cover himself; his body embarrasses him, as it has in her presence since the day she saw him shirtless and said with delight, "Neil! You're growing hair under your arms!"

Before he can get up, the dogs gather round him and begin to sniff and lick at him. He wriggles to get away from them, but Abigail, the largest and stupidest, straddles his stomach and nuzzles his mouth. He splutters and, laughing, throws her off. "Get away from me, you goddamn dogs," he shouts, and swats at them. They are new dogs, not the dog of his childhood, not dogs he trusts.

He stands, and the dogs circle him, looking up at his face expectantly. He feels renewed terror at the thought that Wayne will be here so soon: Will they sleep in the same room? Will they make love? He has never had sex in his parents' house. How can he be expected to be a lover here, in this place of his childhood, of his earliest shame, in this household of mothers and dogs?

"Dinnertime! Abbylucyferny, Abbylucyferny, dinnertime!" His mother's litany disperses the dogs, and they run for the door.

"Do you realize," he shouts to her, "that no matter how much those dogs love you they'd probably kill you for the leg of lamb in the freezer?"

* * *

Neil was twelve the first time he recognized in himself something like sexuality. He was lying outside, on the grass, when Rasputin—the dog, long dead, of his childhood—began licking his face. He felt a tingle he did not recognize, pulled off his shirt to give the dog access to more of him. Rasputin's tongue tickled coolly. A wet nose started to sniff down his body, toward his bathing suit. What he felt frightened him, but he couldn't bring himself to push the dog away. Then his mother called out, "Dinner," and Rasputin was gone, more interested in food than in him.

It was the day after Rasputin was put to sleep, years later, that Neil finally stood in the kitchen, his back turned to his parents, and said, with unexpected ease, "I'm a homosexual." The words seemed insufficient, reductive. For years, he had believed his sexuality to be detachable from the essential him, but now he realized that it was part of him. He had the sudden, despairing sensation that though the words had been easy to say, the fact of their having been aired was incurably damning. Only then, for the first time, did he admit that they were true, and he shook and wept in regret for what he would not be for his mother, for having failed her. His father hung back, silent; he was absent for that moment as he was mostly absent—a strong absence. Neil always thought of him sitting on the edge of the bed in his underwear, captivated by something on television. He said, "It's O.K., Neil." But his mother was resolute; her lower lip didn't quaver. She had enormous reserves of strength to which she only gained access at moments like this one. She hugged him from behind, wrapped him in the childhood smells of perfume and brownies, and whispered, "It's O.K., honey." For once, her words seemed as inadequate as his. Neil felt himself shrunk to an embarrassed adolescent, hating her sympathy, not wanting her to touch him. It was the way he would feel from then on whenever he was in her presence—even now, at twenty-three, bringing home his lover to meet her.

All through his childhood, she had packed only the most nutritious lunches, had served on the PTA, had volunteered at the children's library and at his school, had organized a successful campaign to ban a racist history textbook. The day after he told her, she located and got in touch with an organization called the Coalition of Parents of Lesbians and Gays. Within a year, she was president of it. On weekends, she and the other mothers drove their station wagons to San Francisco, set up their card tables in front of the Bulldog Baths, the Liberty Baths, passed out literature to men in leather and denim who were loath to admit they even had mothers. These men, who would habitually do violence to each other, were strangely cowed by the suburban ladies with their informational booklets, and bent their heads. Neil was a sophomore in college then, and lived in San Francisco. She brought him pamphlets detailing the dangers of bathhouses and back rooms, enemas and poppers, wordless sex in alleyways. His excursion into that world had been brief and lamentable, and was over. He winced at the thought that she knew all his sexual secrets, and vowed to move to the East Coast to escape her. It was not very different from the days when she had campaigned for a better playground, or tutored the Hispanic children in the audiovisual room. Those days, as well, he had run away from her concern. Even today, perched in front of the co-op, collecting signatures for nuclear disarmament, she was quintessentially a mother. And if the lot of mothers was to expect nothing in return, was the lot of sons to return nothing?

Driving across the Dumbarton Bridge on his way to the airport, Neil thinks, I have returned nothing; I have simply returned. He wonders if she would have given birth to him had she known what he would grow up to be.

Then he berates himself: Why should he assume himself to be the cause of her sorrow? She has told him that her life is full of secrets. She has changed since he left home—grown thinner, more rigid, harder to hug. She has given up baking, taken up tennis; her skin has browned and tightened. She is no longer the woman who hugged him and kissed him, who said, "As long as you're happy, that's all that's important to us."

The flats spread out around him; the bridge floats on purple and green silt, and spongy bay fill, not water at all. Only ten miles north, a whole city has been built on gunk dredged up from the bay.

He arrives at the airport ten minutes early, to discover that the plane has landed twenty minutes early. His first view of Wayne is from behind, by the baggage belt. Wayne looks as he always looks—slightly windblown—and is wearing the ratty leather jacket he was wearing the night they met. Neil sneaks up on him and puts his hands on his shoulders; when Wayne turns around, he looks relieved to see him.

They hug like brothers; only in the safety of Neil's mother's car do they dare to kiss. They recognize each other's smells, and grow comfortable again. "I never imagined I'd actually see you out here," Neil says, "but you're exactly the same here as there."

"It's only been a week."

They kiss again. Neil wants to go to a motel, but Wayne insists on being pragmatic. "We'll be there soon. Don't worry."

"We could go to one of the bathhouses in the city and take a room for a couple of aeons," Neil says. "Christ, I'm hard up. I don't even know if we're going to be in the same bedroom."

"Well, if we're not," Wayne says, "we'll sneak around. It'll be romantic."

They cling to each other for a few more minutes, until they realize that people are looking in the car window. Reluctantly, they pull apart. Neil reminds himself that he loves this man, that there is a reason for him to bring this man home.

He takes the scenic route on the way back. The car careers over foothills, through forests, along white four-lane highways high in the mountains. Wayne tells Neil that he sat next to a woman on the plane who was once Marilyn Monroe's psychiatrist's nurse. He slips his foot out of his shoe and nudges Neil's ankle, pulling Neil's sock down with his toe.

"I have to drive," Neil says. "I'm very glad you're here."

There is a comfort in the privacy of the car. They have a common fear of walking hand in hand, of publicly showing physical affection, even in the permissive West Seventies of New York—a fear that they have admitted only to one another. They slip through a pass between two hills, and are suddenly in residential Northern California, the land of expensive ranch-style houses.

As they pull into Neil's mother's driveway, the dogs run barking toward the car. When Wayne opens the door, they jump and lap at him, and he tries to close it again. "Don't worry. Abbylucyferny! Get in the house, damn it!"

His mother descends from the porch. She has changed into a blue flower-print dress, which Neil doesn't recognize. He gets out of the car and half-heartedly chastises the dogs. Crickets chirp in the trees. His mother looks radiant, even beautiful, illuminated by the headlights, surrounded by the now quiet dogs, like a Circe with her slaves. When she walks over to Wayne, offering her hand, and says, "Wayne, I'm Barbara," Neil forgets that she is his mother.

"Good to meet you, Barbara," Wayne says, and reaches out his hand. Craftier than she, he whirls her around to kiss her cheek.

Barbara! He is calling his mother Barbara! Then he remembers that Wayne is five years older than he is. They chat by the open car door, and Neil shrinks back—the embarrassed adolescent, uncomfortable, unwanted.

So the dreaded moment passes and he might as well not have been there. At dinner, Wayne keeps the conversation smooth, like a captivated courtier seeking Neil's mother's hand. A faggot son's sodomist—such words spit into Neil's head. She has prepared tiny meatballs with fresh coriander, fettucine with pesto. Wayne talks about the street people in New York; El Salvador is a tragedy; if only Sadat had lived; Phyllis Schlafly—what can you do?

"It's a losing battle," she tells him. "Every day I'm out there with my card table, me and the other mothers, but I tell you, Wayne, it's a losing battle. Sometimes I think us old ladies are the only ones with enough patience to fight."

Occasionally, Neil says something, but his comments seem stupid and clumsy. Wayne continues to call her Barbara. No one under forty has ever called her Barbara as long as Neil can remember. They drink wine; he does not.

Now is the time for drastic action. He contemplates taking Wayne's hand, then checks himself. He has never done anything in her presence to indicate that the sexuality he confessed to five years ago was a reality and not an invention. Even now, he and Wayne might as well be friends, college roommates. Then Wayne, his savior, with a single, sweeping gesture, reaches for his hand, and clasps it, in the midst of a joke he is telling about Saudi Arabians. By the time he is laughing, their hands are joined. Neil's throat contracts; his heart begins to beat violently. He notices his mother's eyes flicker, glance downward; she never breaks the stride of her sentence. The dinner goes on, and every taboo nurtured since childhood falls quietly away.

She removes the dishes. Their hands grow sticky; he cannot tell which fingers are his and which Wayne's. She clears the rest of the table and rounds up the dogs.

"Well, boys, I'm very tired, and I've got a long day ahead of me tomorrow, so I think I'll hit the sack. There are extra towels for you in Neil's bathroom, Wayne. Sleep well."

"Good night, Barbara," Wayne calls out. "It's been wonderful meeting you."

They are alone. Now they can disentangle their hands.

"No problem about where we sleep, is there?"

"No," Neil says. "I just can't imagine sleeping with someone in this house."

His leg shakes violently. Wayne takes Neil's hand in a firm grasp and hauls him up.

Later that night, they lie outside, under redwood trees, listening to the hysteria of the crickets, the hum of the pool cleaning itself. Redwood leaves prick their skin. They fell in love in bars and apartments, and this is the first time that they have made love outdoors. Neil is not sure he has enjoyed the experience. He kept sensing eyes, imagined that the neighborhood cats were staring at them from behind a fence of brambles. He remembers he once hid in this spot when he and some of the children from the neighborhood were playing sardines, remembers the intoxication of small bodies packed together, the warm breath of suppressed laughter on his neck. "The loser had to go through the spanking machine," he tells Wayne.

"Did you lose often?"

"Most of the time. The spanking machine never really hurt—just a whirl of hands. If you moved fast enough, no one could actually get you. Sometimes, though, late in the afternoon, we'd get naughty. We'd chase each other and pull each other's pants down. That was all. Boys and girls together!"

"Listen to the insects," Wayne says, and closes his eyes.

Neil turns to examine Wayne's face, notices a single, small pimple. Their lovemaking usually begins in a wrestle, a struggle for dominance, and ends with a somewhat confusing loss of identity—as now, when Neil sees a foot on the grass, resting against his leg, and tries to determine if it is his own or Wayne's.

From inside the house, the dogs begin to bark. Their yelps grow into alarmed falsettos. Neil lifts himself up. "I wonder if they smell something," he says.

"Probably just us," says Wayne.

"My mother will wake up. She hates getting waked up."

Lights go on in the house; the door to the porch opens.

"What's wrong, Abby? What's wrong?" his mother's voice calls softly.

Wayne clamps his hand over Neil's mouth. "Don't say anything," he whispers.

"I can't just—" Neil begins to say, but Wayne's hand closes over his mouth again. He bites it, and Wayne starts laughing.

"What was that?" Her voice projects into the garden. "Hello?" she says.

The dogs yelp louder. "Abbylucyferny, it's O.K., it's O.K." Her voice is soft and panicked. "Is anyone there?" she asks loudly.

The brambles shake. She takes a flashlight, shines it around the garden. Wayne and Neil duck down; the light lands on them and hovers for a few seconds. Then it clicks off and they are in the dark—a new dark, a darker dark, which their eyes must readjust to.

"Let's go to bed, Abbylucyferny," she says gently. Neil and Wayne hear her pad into the house. The dogs whimper as they follow her, and the lights go off.

Once before, Neil and his mother had stared at each other in the glare of bright lights. Four years ago, they stood in the arena created by the headlights of her car, waiting for the train. He was on his way back to San Francisco, where he was marching in a Gay Pride Parade the next day. The train station was next door to the food co-op and shared its parking lot. The co-op, familiar and boring by day, took on a certain mystery in the night. Neil recognized the spot where he had skidded on his bicycle and broken his leg. Through the glass doors, the brightly lit interior of the store glowed, its rows and rows of cans and boxes forming their own horizon, each can illuminated so that even from outside Neil could read the labels. All that was missing was the ladies in tennis dresses and sweatshirts, pushing their carts past bins of nuts and dried fruits.

"Your train is late," his mother said. Her hair fell loosely on her shoulders, and her legs were tanned. Neil looked at her and tried to imagine her in labor with him—bucking and struggling with his birth. He felt then the strange, sexless love for women which through his whole adolescence he had mistaken for heterosexual desire.

A single bright light approached them; it preceded the low, haunting sound of the whistle. Neil kissed his mother, and waved goodbye as he ran to meet the train. It was an old train, with windows tinted a sort of horrible lemon-lime. It stopped only long enough for him to hoist himself on board, and then it was moving again. He hurried to a window, hoping to see her drive off, but the tint of the window made it possible for him to make out only vague patches of light—street lamps, cars, the co-op.

He sank into the hard, green seat. The train was almost entirely empty; the only other passenger was a dark-skinned man wearing bluejeans and a leather jacket. He sat directly across the aisle from Neil, next to the window. He had rough skin and a thick mustache. Neil discovered that by pretending to look out the window he could study the man's reflection in the lemon-lime glass. It was only slightly hazy—the quality of a bad photograph. Neil felt his mouth open, felt sleep closing in on him. Hazy red and gold flashes through the glass pulsed in the face of the man in the window, giving the curious impression of muscle spasms. It took Neil a few minutes to realize that the man was staring at him, or, rather, staring at the back of his head—staring at his staring. The man smiled as though to say, I know exactly what you're staring at, and Neil felt the sickening sensation of desire rise in his throat.

Right before they reached the city, the man stood up and sat down in the seat next to Neil's. The man's thigh brushed deliberately against his own. Neil's eyes were watering; he felt sick to his stomach. Taking Neil's hand, the man said, "Why so nervous, honey? Relax."

Neil woke up the next morning with the taste of ashes in his mouth. He was lying on the floor, without blankets or sheets or pillows. Instinctively, he reached for his pants, and as he pulled them on came face to face with the man from the train. His name was Luis; he turned out to be a dog groomer. His apartment smelled of dog.

"Why such a hurry?" Luis said.

"The parade. The Gay Pride Parade. I'm meeting some friends to march."

"I'll come with you," Luis said. "I think I'm too old for these things, but why not?"

Neil did not want Luis to come with him, but he found it impossible to say so. Luis looked older by day, more likely to carry diseases. He dressed again in a torn T-shirt, leather jacket, bluejeans. "It's my everyday apparel," he said, and laughed. Neil buttoned his pants, aware that they had been washed by his mother the day before. Luis possessed the peculiar combination of hypermasculinity and effeminacy which exemplifies faggotry. Neil wanted to be rid of him, but Luis's mark was on him, he could see that much. They would become lovers whether Neil liked it or not.

They joined the parade midway. Neil hoped he wouldn't meet anyone he knew; he did not want to have to explain Luis, who clung to him. The parade was full of shirtless men with oiled, muscular shoulders. Neil's back ached. There were floats carrying garishly dressed prom queens and cheerleaders, some with beards, some actually looking like women. Luis said, "It makes me proud, makes me glad to be what I am." Neil supposed that by darting into the crowd ahead of him he might be able to lose Luis forever, but he found it difficult to let him go; the prospect of being alone seemed unbearable.

Neil was startled to see his mother watching the parade, holding up a sign. She was with the Coalition of Parents of Lesbians and Gays; they had posted a huge banner on the wall behind them proclaiming: OUR SONS AND DAUGHTERS, WE ARE PROUD OF YOU. She spotted him; she waved, and jumped up and down.

"Who's that woman?" Luis asked.

"My mother. I should go say hello to her."

"O.K.," Luis said. He followed Neil to the side of the parade. Neil kissed his mother. Luis took off his shirt, wiped his face with it, smiled.

"I'm glad you came," Neil said.

"I wouldn't have missed it, Neil. I wanted to show you I cared."

He smiled, and kissed her again. He showed no intention of introducing Luis, so Luis introduced himself.

"Hello, Luis," Mrs. Campbell said. Neil looked away. Luis shook her hand, and Neil wanted to warn his mother to wash it, warned himself to check with a V.D. clinic first thing Monday.

"Neil, this is Carmen Bologna, another one of the mothers," Mrs. Campbell said. She introduced him to a fat Italian woman with flushed cheeks, and hair arranged in the shape of a clamshell.

"Good to meet you, Neil, good to meet you," said Carmen Bologna. "You know my son, Michael? I'm so proud of Michael! He's doing so well now. I'm proud of him, proud to be his mother I am, and your mother's proud, too!"

The woman smiled at him, and Neil could think of nothing to say but "Thank you." He looked uncomfortably toward his mother, who stood listening to Luis. It occurred to him that the worst period of his life was probably about to begin and he had no way to stop it.

A group of drag queens ambled over to where the mothers were standing. "Michael! Michael!" shouted Carmen Bologna, and embraced a sticklike man wrapped in green satin. Michael's eyes were heavily dosed with green eyeshadow, and his lips were painted pink.

Neil turned and saw his mother staring, her mouth open. He marched over to where Luis was standing, and they moved back into the parade. He turned and waved to her. She waved back; he saw pain in her face, and then, briefly, regret. That day, he felt she would have traded him for any other son.

Later, she said to him, "Carmen Bologna really was proud, and, speaking as a mother, let me tell you, you have to be brave to feel such pride."

Neil was never proud. It took him a year to dump Luis, another year to leave California. The sick taste of ashes was still in his mouth. On the plane, he envisioned his mother sitting alone in the dark, smoking. She did not leave his mind until he was circling New York, staring down at the dawn rising over Queens. The song playing in his earphones would remain hovering on the edges of his memory, always associated with her absence. After collecting his baggage, he took a bus into the city. Boys were selling newspapers in the middle of highways, through the windows of stopped cars. It was seven in the morning when he reached Manhattan. He stood for ten minutes on East Thirty-fourth Street, breathed the cold air, and felt bubbles rising in his blood.

Neil got a job as a paralegal—a temporary job, he told himself. When he met Wayne a year later, the sensations of that first morning returned to him. They'd been up all night, and at six they walked across the park to Wayne's apartment with the nervous, deliberate gait of people aching to make love for the first time. Joggers ran by with their dogs. None of them knew what Wayne and he were about to do, and the secrecy excited him. His mother came to mind, and the song, and the whirling vision of Queens coming alive below him. His breath solidified into clouds, and he felt happier than he had ever felt before in his life.

The second day of Wayne's visit, he and Neil go with Mrs. Campbell to pick up the dogs at the dog parlor. The grooming establishment is decorated with pink ribbons and photographs of the owner's champion pit bulls. A fat, middle-aged woman appears from the back, leading the newly trimmed and fluffed Abigail, Lucille, and Fern by three leashes. The dogs struggle frantically when they see Neil's mother, tangling the woman up in their leashes. "Ladies, behave!" Mrs. Campbell commands, and collects the dogs. She gives Fern to Neil and Abigail to Wayne. In the car on the way back, Abigail begins pawing to get on Wayne's lap.

"Just push her off," Mrs. Campbell says. "She knows she's not supposed to do that."

"You never groomed Rasputin," Neil complains.

"Rasputin was a mutt."

"Rasputin was a beautiful dog, even if he did smell."

"Do you remember when you were a little kid, Neil, you used to make Rasputin dance with you? Once you tried to dress him up in one of my blouses."

"I don't remember that," Neil says.

"Yes. I remember," says Mrs. Campbell. "Then you tried to organize a dog beauty contest in the neighborhood. You wanted to have runners-up—everything."

"A dog beauty contest?" Wayne says.

"Mother, do we have to—"

"I think it's a mother's privilege to embarrass her son," Mrs. Campbell says, and smiles.

When they are about to pull into the driveway, Wayne starts screaming, and pushes Abigail off his lap. "Oh, my God!" he says. "The dog just pissed all over me."

Neil turns around and sees a puddle seeping into Wayne's slacks. He suppresses his laughter, and Mrs. Campbell hands him a rag.

"I'm sorry, Wayne," she says. "It goes with the territory."

"This is really disgusting," Wayne says, swatting at himself with the rag.

Neil keeps his eyes on his own reflection in the rearview mirror and smiles.

At home, while Wayne cleans himself in the bathroom, Neil watches his mother cook lunch—Japanese noodles in soup. "When you went off to college," she says, "I went to the grocery store. I was going to buy you ramen noodles, and I suddenly realized you weren't going to be around to eat them. I started crying right then, blubbering like an idiot."

Neil clenches his fists inside his pockets. She has a way of telling him little sad stories when he doesn't want to hear them—stories of dolls broken by her brothers, lunches stolen by neighborhood boys on the way to school. Now he has joined the ranks of male children who have made her cry.

"Mama, I'm sorry," he says.

She is bent over the noodles, which steam in her face. "I didn't want to say anything in front of Wayne, but I wish you had answered me last night. I was very frightened—and worried."

"I'm sorry," he says, but it's not convincing. His fingers prickle. He senses a great sorrow about to be born.

"I lead a quiet life," she says. "I don't want to be a disciplinarian. I just don't have the energy for these—shenanigans. Please don't frighten me that way again."

"If you were so upset, why didn't you say something?"

"I'd rather not discuss it. I lead a quiet life. I'm not used to getting woken up late at night. I'm not used—"

"To my having a lover?"

"No, I'm not used to having other people around, that's all. Wayne is charming. A wonderful young man."

"He likes you, too."

"I'm sure we'll get along fine."

She scoops the steaming noodles into ceramic bowls. Wayne returns, wearing shorts. His white, hairy legs are a shocking contrast to hers, which are brown and sleek.

"I'll wash those pants, Wayne," Mrs. Campbell says. "I have a special detergent that'll take out the stain."

She gives Neil a look to indicate that the subject should be dropped. He looks at Wayne, looks at his mother; his initial embarrassment gives way to a fierce pride—the arrogance of mastery. He is glad his mother knows that he is desired, glad it makes her flinch.

Later, he steps into the back yard; the gardener is back, whacking at the bushes with his shears. Neil walks by him in his bathing suit, imagining he is on parade.

That afternoon, he finds his mother's daily list on the kitchen table:

TUESDAY

7:00—breakfast
Take dogs to groomer
Groceries (?)

Campaign against Draft—4–7

Buy underwear
Trios—2:00
Spaghetti
Fruit
Asparagus if sale
Peanuts
Milk

Doctor's Appointment (make)
Write Cranston/Hayakawa
re disarmament

Handi-Wraps
Mozart
Abigail
Top Ramen
Pedro

Her desk and trash can are full of such lists; he remembers them from the earliest days of his childhood. He had learned to read from them. In his own life, too, there have been endless lists—covered with check marks and arrows, at least one item always spilling over onto the next day's agenda. From September to November, "Buy plane ticket for Christmas" floated from list to list to list.

The last item puzzles him: Pedro. Pedro must be the gardener. He observes the accretion of names, the arbitrary specifics that give a sense of his mother's life. He could make a list of his own selves: the child, the adolescent, the promiscuous faggot son, and finally the good son, settled, relatively successful. But the divisions wouldn't work; he is today and will always be the child being licked by the dog, the boy on the floor with Luis; he will still be everything he is ashamed of. The other lists—the lists of things done and undone—tell their own truth: that his life is measured more properly in objects than in stages. He knows himself as "jump rope," "book," "sunglasses," "underwear."

"Tell me about your family, Wayne," Mrs. Campbell says that night, as they drive toward town. They are going to see an Esther Williams movie at the local revival house: an underwater musical, populated by mermaids, underwater Rockettes.

"My father was a lawyer," Wayne says. "He had an office in Queens, with a neon sign. I think he's probably the only lawyer in the world who had a neon sign. Anyway, he died when I was ten. My mother never remarried. She lives in Queens. Her great claim to fame is that when she was twenty-two she went on 'The $64,000 Question.' Her category was mystery novels. She made it to sixteen thousand before she got tripped up."

"When I was about ten, I wanted you to go on 'Jeopardy,' " Neil says to his mother. "You really should have, you know. You would have won."

"You certainly loved 'Jeopardy,' " Mrs. Campbell says. "You used to watch it during dinner. Wayne, does your mother work?"

"No," he says. "She lives off investments."

"You're both only children," Mrs. Campbell says. Neil wonders if she is ruminating on the possible connection between that coincidence and their "alternative life style."

The movie theater is nearly empty. Neil sits between Wayne and his mother. There are pillows on the floor at the front of the theater, and a cat is prowling over them. It casts a monstrous shadow every now and then on the screen, disturbing the sedative effect of water ballet. Like a teenager, Neil cautiously reaches his arm around Wayne's shoulder. Wayne takes his hand immediately. Next to them, Neil's mother breathes in, out, in, out. Neil timorously moves his other arm and lifts it behind his mother's neck. He does not look at her, but he can tell from her breathing that she senses what he is doing. Slowly, carefully, he lets his hand drop on her shoulder; it twitches spasmodically, and he jumps, as if he had received an electric shock. His mother's quiet breathing is broken by a gasp; even Wayne notices. A sudden brightness on the screen illuminates the panic in her eyes, Neil's arm frozen above her, about to fall again.

Slowly, he lowers his arm until his fingertips touch her skin, the fabric of her dress. He has gone too far to go back now; they are all too far.

Wayne and Mrs. Campbell sink into their seats, but Neil remains stiff, holding up his arms, which rest on nothing. The movie ends, and they go on sitting just like that.

"I'm old," Mrs. Campbell says later, as they drive back home. "I remember when those films were new. Your father and I went to one on our first date. I loved them, because I could pretend that those women underwater were flying—they were so graceful. They really took advantage of Technicolor in those days. Color was something to appreciate. You can't know what it was like to see a color movie for the first time, after years of black-and-white. It's like trying to explain the surprise of snow to an East Coaster. Very little is new anymore, I fear."

Neil would like to tell her about his own nostalgia, but how can he explain that all of it revolves around her? The idea of her life before he was born pleases him. "Tell Wayne how you used to look like Esther Williams," he asks her.

She blushes. "I was told I looked like Esther Williams, but really more like Gene Tierney," she says. "Not beautiful, but interesting. I like to think I had a certain magnetism."

"You still do," Wayne says, and instantly recognizes the wrongness of his comment. Silence and a nervous laugh indicate that he has not yet mastered the family vocabulary.

When they get home, the night is once again full of the sound of crickets. Mrs. Campbell picks up a flashlight and calls the dogs. "Abbylucyferny, Abbylucyferny," she shouts, and the dogs amble from their various corners. She pushes them out the door to the back yard and follows them. Neil follows her. Wayne follows Neil, but hovers on the porch. Neil walks behind her as she tramps through the garden. She holds out her flashlight, and snails slide from behind bushes, from under rocks, to where she stands. When the snails become visible, she crushes them underfoot. They make a wet, cracking noise, like eggs being broken.

"Nights like this," she says, "I think of children without pants on, in hot South American countries. I have nightmares about tanks rolling down our street."

"The weather's never like this in New York," Neil says. "When it's hot, it's humid and sticky. You don't want to go outdoors."

"I could never live anywhere else but here. I think I'd die. I'm too used to the climate."

"Don't be silly."

"No, I mean it," she says. "I have adjusted too well to the weather."

The dogs bark and howl by the fence. "A cat, I suspect," she says. She aims her flashlight at a rock, and more snails emerge—uncountable numbers, too stupid to have learned not to trust light.

"I know what you were doing at the movie," she says.

"What?"

"I know what you were doing."

"What? I put my arm around you."

"I'm sorry, Neil," she says. "I can only take so much. Just so much."

"What do you mean?" he says. "I was only trying to show affection."

"Oh, affection—I know about affection."

He looks up at the porch, sees Wayne moving toward the door, trying not to listen.

"What do you mean?" Neil says to her.

She puts down the flashlight and wraps her arms around herself. "I remember when you were a little boy," she says. "I remember, and I have to stop remembering. I wanted you to grow up happy. And I'm very tolerant, very understanding. But I can only take so much."

His heart seems to have risen into his throat. "Mother," he says, "I think you know my life isn't your fault. But for God's sake, don't say that your life is my fault."

"It's not a question of fault," she says. She extracts a Kleenex from her pocket and blows her nose. "I'm sorry, Neil. I guess I'm just an old woman with too much on her mind and not enough to do." She laughs halfheartedly. "Don't worry. Don't say anything," she says. "Abbylucyferny, Abbylucyferny, time for bed!"

He watches her as she walks toward the porch, silent and regal. There is the pad of feet, the clinking of dog tags as the dogs run for the house.

He was twelve the first time she saw him march in a parade. He played the tuba, and as his elementary-school band lumbered down the streets of their then small town she stood on the sidelines and waved. Afterward, she had taken him out for ice cream. He spilled some on his red uniform, and she swiped at it with a napkin. She had been there for him that day, as well as years later, at that more memorable parade; she had been there for him every day.

Somewhere over Iowa, a week later, Neil remembers this scene, remembers other days, when he would find her sitting in the dark, crying. She had to take time out of her own private sorrow to appease his anxiety. "It was part of it," she told him later. "Part of being a mother."

"The scariest thing in the world is the thought that you could unknowingly ruin someone's life," Neil tells Wayne. "Or even change someone's life. I hate the thought of having such control. I'd make a rotten mother."

"You're crazy," Wayne says. "You have this great mother, and all you do is complain. I know people whose mothers have disowned them."

"Guilt goes with the territory," Neil says.

"Why?" Wayne asks, perfectly seriously.

Neil doesn't answer. He lies back in his seat, closes his eyes, imagines he grew up in a house in the mountains of Colorado, surrounded by snow—endless white snow on hills. No flat places, and no trees; just white hills. Every time he has flown away, she has come into his mind, usually sitting alone in the dark, smoking. Today she is outside at dusk, skimming leaves from the pool.

"I want to get a dog," Neil says.

Wayne laughs. "In the city? It'd suffocate."

The hum of the airplane is druglike, dazing. "I want to stay with you a long time," Neil says.

"I know." Imperceptibly, Wayne takes his hand.

"It's very hot there in the summer, too. You know, I'm not thinking about my mother now."

"It's O.K."

For a moment, Neil wonders what the stewardess or the old woman on the way to the bathroom will think, but then he laughs and relaxes.

Later, the plane makes a slow circle over New York City, and on it two men hold hands, eyes closed, and breathe in unison.

REGINALD McKNIGHT

The Kind of Light That Shines on Texas

REGINALD McKNIGHT (1956–) teaches at the University of Maryland, College Park. He has received an NEA Fellowship, an O. Henry Award, the PEN/Hemingway Special Citation, the Pushcart Prize, a Whiting Writers' Award, and the Drue Heinz Literature Prize. He is the author of *Moustapha's Eclipse, I Get on the Bus,* and *The Kind of Light That Shines on Texas.*

I never liked Marvin Pruitt. Never liked him, never knew him, even though there were only three of us in the class. Three black kids. In our school there were fourteen classrooms of thirty-odd white kids (in '66, they considered Chicanos provisionally white) and three or four black kids. Primary school in primary colors. Neat division. Alphabetized. They didn't stick us in the back, or arrange us by degrees of hue, apartheidlike. This was real integration, a ten-to-one ratio as tidy as upper-class landscaping. If it all worked, you could have ten white kids all to yourself. They could talk to you, get the feel of you, scrutinize you bone deep if they wanted to. They seldom wanted to, and that was fine with me for two reasons. The first was that their scrutiny was irritating. How do you comb your hair—why do you comb your hair—may I please touch your hair—were the kinds of questions they asked. This is no way to feel at home. The second reason was Marvin. He embarrassed me. He smelled bad, was at least two grades behind, was hostile, dark skinned, homely, close-mouthed. I feared him for his size, pitied him for his dress, watched him all the time. Marveled at him, mystified, astonished, uneasy.

He had the habit of spitting on his right arm, juicing it down till it would glisten. He would start in immediately after taking his seat when we'd finished with the Pledge of Allegiance, "The Yellow Rose of Texas," "The Eyes of

Texas Are upon You," and "Mistress Shady." Marvin would rub his spit-flecked arm with his left hand, rub and roll as if polishing an ebony pool cue. Then he would rest his head in the crook of his arm, sniffing, huffing deep like black-jacket boys huff bagsful of acrylics. After ten minutes or so, his eyes would close, heavy. He would sleep till recess. Mrs. Wickham would let him.

There was one other black kid in our class. A girl they called Ah-so. I never learned what she did to earn this name. There was nothing Asian about this big-shouldered girl. She was the tallest, heaviest kid in school. She was quiet, but I don't think any one of us was subtle or sophisticated enough to nickname our classmates according to any but physical attributes. Fat kids were called Porky or Butterball, skinny ones were called Stick or Ichabod. Ah-so was big, thick, and African. She would impassively sit, sullen, silent as Marvin. She wore the same dark blue pleated skirt every day, the same ruffled white blouse every day. Her skin always shone as if worked by Marvin's palms and fingers. I never spoke one word to her, nor she to me.

Of the three of us, Mrs. Wickham called only on Ah-so and me. Ah-so never answered one question, correctly or incorrectly, so far as I can recall. She wasn't stupid. When asked to read aloud she read well, seldom stumbling over long words, reading with humor and expression. But when Wickham asked her about Farmer Brown and how many cows, or the capital of Vermont, or the date of this war or that, Ah-so never spoke. Not one word. But you always felt she could have answered those questions if she'd wanted to. I sensed no tension, embarrassment, or anger in Ah-so's reticence. She simply refused to speak. There was something unshakable about her, some core so impenetrably solid, you got the feeling that if you stood too close to her she could eat your thoughts like a black star eats light. I didn't despise Ah-so as I despised Marvin. There was nothing malevolent about her. She sat like a great icon in the back of the classroom, tranquil, guarded, sealed up, watchful. She was close to sixteen, and it was my guess she'd given up on school. Perhaps she was just obliging the wishes of her family, sticking it out till the law could no longer reach her.

There were at least half a dozen older kids in our class. Besides Marvin and Ah-so there was Oakley, who sat behind me, whispering threats into my ear; Varna Willard with the large breasts; Eddie Limon, who played bass for a high school rock band; and Lawrence Ridderbeck, who everyone said had a kid and a wife. You couldn't expect me to know anything about Texan educational practices of the 1960s, so I never knew why there were so many older kids in my sixth-grade class. After all, I was just a boy and had transferred into the school around midyear. My father, an air force sergeant, had been sent to Viet Nam. The air force sent my mother, my sister, Claire, and me to Connolly Air Force Base, which during the war housed "unaccompanied wives." I'd been to so many different schools in my short life that I ceased wondering about their differences. All I knew about the Texas schools is that they weren't afraid to flunk you.

Yet though I was only twelve then, I had a good idea why Wickham never once called on Marvin, why she let him snooze in the crook of his polished arm. I knew why she would press her lips together, and narrow her eyes at me whenever I correctly answered a question, rare as that was. I know why she badgered Ah-so with questions everyone knew Ah-so would never even consider answering. Wickham didn't like us. She wasn't gross about it, but it was clear she didn't want us around. She would prove her dislike day after day with little stories and jokes. "I just want to share with you all," she would say, "a little riddle my daughter told me at the supper table th'other day. Now, where do you go when you injure your knee?" Then one, two, or all three of her pets would say for the rest of us, "We don't know, Miz Wickham," in that skin-chilling way suck-asses speak, "where?" "Why, to Africa," Wickham would say, "where the knee grows."

The thirty-odd white kids would laugh, and I would look across the room at Marvin. He'd be asleep. I would glance back at Ah-so. She'd be sitting still as a projected image, staring down at her desk. I, myself, would smile at Wickham's stupid jokes, sometimes fake a laugh. I tried to show her that at least one of us was alive and alert, even though her jokes hurt. I sucked ass, too, I suppose. But I wanted her to understand more than anything that I was not like her other nigra children, that I was worthy of more than the non-attention and the negative attention she paid Marvin and Ah-so. I hated her, but never showed it. No one could safely contradict that woman. She knew all kinds of tricks to demean, control, and punish you. And she could swing her two-foot paddle as fluidly as a big-league slugger swings a bat. You didn't speak in Wickham's class unless she spoke to you first. You didn't chew gum, or wear "hood" hair. You didn't drag your feet, curse, pass notes, hold hands with the opposite sex. Most especially, you didn't say anything bad about the Aggies, Governor Connolly, LBJ, Sam Houston, or Waco. You did the forbidden and she would get you. It was that simple.

She never got me, though. Never gave her reason to. But she could have invented reasons. She did a lot of that. I can't be sure, but I used to think she pitied me because my father was in Viet Nam and my uncle A.J. had recently died there. Whenever she would tell one of her racist jokes, she would always glance at me, preface the joke with, "Now don't you nigra children take offense. This is all in fun, you know. I just want to share with you all something Coach Gilchrest told me th'other day." She would tell her joke, and glance at me again. I'd giggle, feeling a little queasy. "I'm half Irish," she would chuckle, "and you should hear some of those Irish jokes." She never told any, and I never really expected her to. I just did my Tom-thing. I kept my shoes shined, my desk neat, answered her questions as best I could, never brought gum to school, never cursed, never slept in class. I wanted to show her we were not all the same.

I tried to show them all, all thirty-odd, that I was different. It worked to some degree, but not very well. When some article was stolen from someone's locker or desk, Marvin, not I, was the first accused. I'd be second. Neither Marvin, nor Ah-so nor I were ever chosen for certain classroom honors—"Pledge leader," "flag holder," "noise monitor," "paper passer outer," but Mrs. Wickham once let me be "eraser duster." I was proud. I didn't even care about the cracks my fellow students made about my finally having turned the right color. I had done something that Marvin, in the deeps of his never-ending sleep, couldn't even dream of doing. Jack Preston, a kid who sat in front of me, asked me one day at recess whether I was embarrassed about Marvin. "Can you believe that guy?" I said. "He's like a pig or something. Makes me sick."

"Does it make you ashamed to be colored?"

"No," I said, but I meant yes. Yes, if you insist on thinking us all the same. Yes, if his faults are mine, his weaknesses inherent in me.

"I'd be," said Jack.

I made no reply. I was ashamed. Ashamed for not defending Marvin and ashamed that Marvin even existed. But if it had occurred to me, I would have asked Jack whether he was ashamed of being white because of Oakley. Oakley, "Oak Tree," Kelvin "Oak Tree" Oakley. He was sixteen and proud of it. He made it clear to everyone, including Wickham, that his life's ambition was to stay in school one more year, till he'd be old enough to enlist in the army. "Them slopes got my brother," he would say. "I'mna sign up and git me a few slopes. Gonna kill them bastards deader'n shit." Oakley, so far as anyone knew, was and always had been the oldest kid in his family. But no one contradicted him. He would, as anyone would tell you, "snap yer neck jest as soon as look at you." Not a boy in class, excepting Marvin and myself, had been able to avoid Oakley's pink bellies, Texas titty twisters, moon pie punches, or worse. He didn't bother Marvin, I suppose, because Marvin was closer to his size and age, and because Marvin spent five sixths of the school day asleep. Marvin probably never crossed Oakley's mind. And to say that Oakley hadn't bothered me is not to say he had no intention of ever doing so. In fact, this haphazard sketch of hairy fingers, slash of eyebrow, explosion of acne, elbows, and crooked teeth, swore almost daily that he'd like to kill me.

Naturally, I feared him. Though we were about the same height, he outweighed me by no less than forty pounds. He talked, stood, smoked, and swore like a man. No one, except for Mrs. Wickham, the principal, and the coach, ever laid a finger on him. And even Wickham knew that the hot lines she laid on him merely amused him. He would smile out at the classroom, goofy and bashful, as she laid down the two, five, or maximum ten strokes on him. Often he would wink, or surreptitiously flash us the thumb as Wickham worked on him. When she was finished, Oakley would walk so cool back to his seat you'd think he was on wheels. He'd slide into his chair, sniff the air, and say, "Somethin's burnin. Do y'all smell smoke? I swanee, I smell smoke and fahr back here." If he had made these cracks and never threatened me, I might have grown to admire Oakley, even liked him a little. But he hated me, and took every opportunity during the six-hour school day to make me aware of this. "Some Sambo's gittin his ass broke open one of these days," he'd mumble. "I wanna fight somebody. Need to keep in shape till I git to Nam."

I never said anything to him for the longest time. I pretended not to hear him, pretended not to notice his sour breath on my neck and ear. "Yep," he'd whisper. "Coonies keep y' in good shape for slope killin." Day in, day out, that's the kind of thing I'd pretend not to hear. But one day when the rain dropped down like lead balls, and the cold air made your skin look plucked, Oakley whispered to me, "My brother tells me it rains like this in Nam. Maybe I oughta go out at recess and break your ass open today. Nice and cool so you don't sweat. Nice and wet to clean up the blood." I said nothing for at least half a minute, then I turned half right and said, "Thought you said your brother was dead." Oakley, silent himself, for a time, poked me in the back with his pencil and hissed, "*Yer* dead." Wickham cut her eyes our way, and it was over.

It was hardest avoiding him in gym class. Especially when we played murderball. Oakley always aimed his throws at me. He threw with unblinking intensity, his teeth gritting, his neck veining, his face flushing, his black hair sweeping over one eye. He could throw hard, but the balls were squishy and harmless. In fact, I found his misses more intimidating than his hits. The balls would whizz by, thunder against the folded bleachers. They rattled as though a locomotive were passing through them. I would duck, dodge, leap as if he were throwing grenades. But he always hit me, sooner or later. And after a while I noticed that the other boys would avoid throwing at me, as if I belonged to Oakley.

One day, however, I was surprised to see that Oakley was throwing at everyone else but me. He was uncommonly accurate, too; kids were falling like tin cans. Since no one was throwing at me, I spent most of the game watching Oakley cut this one and that one down. Finally, he and I were the only ones left on the court. Try as he would, he couldn't hit me, nor I him. Coach Gilchrest blew his whistle and told Oakley and me to bring the red rubber balls to the equipment locker. I was relieved I'd escaped Oakley's stinging throws for once. I was feeling triumphant, full of myself. As Oakley and I approached Gilchrest, I thought about saying something friendly to Oakley: Good game, Oak Tree, I would say. Before I could speak, though, Gilchrest said, "All right boys, there's five minutes left in the period. Y'all are so good, looks like, you're gonna have to play like men. No boundaries, no catch outs, and you gotta hit your opponent three times in order to win. Got me?"

We nodded.

"And you're gonna use these," said Gilchrest, pointing to three volleyballs at his feet. "And you better believe they're pumped full. Oates, you start at that end of the court. Oak Tree, you're at th'other end. Just like usual, I'll set the balls at mid-court, and when I blow my whistle I want y'all to haul your cheeks to the middle and th'ow for all you're worth. Got me?" Gilchrest nodded at our nods, then added, "Remember, no boundaries, right?"

I at my end, Oakley at his, Gilchrest blew his whistle. I was faster than Oakley and scooped up a ball before he'd covered three quarters of his side. I aimed, threw, and popped him right on the knee. "One–zip!" I heard Gilchrest shout. The ball bounced off his knee and shot right back into my hands. I hurried my throw and missed. Oakley bent down, clutched the two remaining balls. I remember being amazed that he could palm each ball, run full out, and throw left-handed or right-handed without a shade of awkwardness. I spun, ran, but one of Oakley's throws glanced off the back of my head. "One–one!" hollered Gilchrest. I fell and spun on my ass as the other ball came sailing at me. I caught it. "He's out!" I yelled. Gilchrest's voice boomed, "No catch outs. Three hits. Three hits." I leapt to my feet as Oakley scrambled across the floor for another ball. I chased him down, leapt, and heaved the ball hard as he drew himself erect. The ball hit him dead in the face, and he went down flat. He rolled around, cupping his hands over his nose. Gilchrest sped to his side, helped him to his feet, asked him whether he was OK. Blood flowed from Oakley's nose, dripped in startlingly bright spots on the floor, his shoes, Gilchrest's shirt. The coach removed Oakley's T-shirt and pressed it against the big kid's nose to stanch the bleeding. As they walked past me toward the office I mumbled an apology to Oakley, but couldn't catch his reply. "You watch your filthy mouth, boy," said Gilchrest to Oakley.

The locker room was unnaturally quiet as I stepped into its steamy atmosphere. Eyes clicked in my direction, looked away. After I was out of my shorts, had my towel wrapped around me, my shower kit in hand, Jack Preston and Brian Nailor approached me. Preston's hair was combed slick and plastic looking. Nailor's stood up like frozen flames. Nailor smiled at me with his big teeth and pale eyes. He poked my arm with a finger. "You fucked up," he said.

"I tried to apologize."

"Won't do you no good," said Preston.

"I swanee," said Nailor.

"It's part of the game," I said. "It was an accident. Wasn't my idea to use volleyballs."

"Don't matter," Preston said. "He's jest lookin for an excuse to fight you."

"I never done nothing to him."

"Don't matter," said Nailor. "He don't like you."

"Brian's right, Clint. He'd jest as soon kill you as look at you."

"I never done nothing to him."

"Look," said Preston, "I know him pretty good. And jest between you and me, it's 'cause you're a city boy—"

"Whadda you mean? I've never—"

"He don't like your clothes—"

"And he don't like the fancy way you talk in class."

"What fancy—"

"I'm tellin him, if you don't mind, Brian."

"Tell him then."

"He don't like the way you say 'tennis shoes' instead of sneakers. He don't like coloreds. A whole bunch a things, really."

"I never done nothing to him. He's got no reason—"

"*And,*" said Nailor, grinning, "*and,* he says you're a stuck-up rich kid." Nailor's eyes had crow's-feet, bags beneath them. They were a man's eyes.

"My dad's a sergeant," I said.

"You chicken to fight him?" said Nailor.

"Yeah, Clint, don't be chicken. Jest go on and git it over with. He's whupped pert near ever'body else in the class. It ain't so bad."

"Might as well, Oates."

"Yeah, yer pretty skinny, but yer jest about his height. Jest git 'im in a headlock and don't let go."

"Goddamn," I said, "he's got no reason to—"

Their eyes shot right and I looked over my shoulder. Oakley stood at his locker, turning its tumblers. From where I stood I could see that a piece of cotton was wedged up one of his nostrils, and he already had the makings of a good shiner. His acne burned red like a fresh abrasion. He snapped the locker open and kicked his shoes off without sitting. Then he pulled off his shorts, revealing two paddle stripes on his ass. They were fresh red bars speckled with white, the white speckles being the reverse impression of the paddle's suction holes. He must not have watched his filthy mouth while in Gilchrest's presence. Behind me, I heard Preston and Nailor pad to their lockers.

Oakley spoke without turning around. "Somebody's gonna git his skinny black ass kicked, right today, right after school." He said it softly. He slipped his jock off, turned around. I looked away. Out the corner of my eye I saw him stride off, his hairy nakedness a weapon clearing the younger boys from his path. Just before he rounded the corner of the shower stalls, I threw my toilet kit to the floor and stammered, "I—I never did nothing to you,

Oakley." He stopped, turned, stepped closer to me, wrapping his towel around himself. Sweat streamed down my rib cage. It felt like ice water. "You wanna go at it right now, boy?"

"I never did nothing to you." I felt tears in my eyes. I couldn't stop them even though I was blinking like mad. "Never."

He laughed. "You busted my nose, asshole."

"What about before? What'd I ever do to you?"

"See you after school, Coonie." Then he turned away, flashing his acne-spotted back like a semaphore. "Why?" I shouted. "Why you wanna fight me?" Oakley stopped and turned, folded his arms, leaned against a toilet stall. "Why you wanna fight *me,* Oakley?" I stepped over the bench. "What'd I do? Why me?" And then unconsciously, as if scratching, as if breathing, I walked toward Marvin, who stood a few feet from Oakley, combing his hair at the mirror. "Why not him?" I said. "How come you're after *me* and not *him?*" The room froze. Froze for a moment that was both evanescent and eternal, somewhere between an eye blink and a week in hell. No one moved, nothing happened; there was no sound at all. And then it was as if all of us at the same moment looked at Marvin. He just stood there, combing away, the only body in motion, I think. He combed his hair and combed it, as if seeing only his image, hearing only his comb scraping his scalp. I knew he'd heard me. There's no way he could not have heard me. But all he did was slide the comb into his pocket and walk out the door.

"I got no quarrel with Marvin," I heard Oakley say. I turned toward his voice, but he was already in the shower.

I was able to avoid Oakley at the end of the school day. I made my escape by asking Mrs. Wickham if I could go to the rest room.

" 'Rest room,' " Oakley mumbled. "It's a damn toilet, sissy."

"Clinton," said Mrs. Wickham. "Can you *not* wait till the bell rings? It's almost three o'clock."

"No ma'am," I said. "I won't make it."

"Well I should make you wait just to teach you to be more mindful about . . . hygiene . . . uh things." She sucked in her cheeks, squinted. "But I'm feeling charitable today. You may go." I immediately left the building, and got on the bus. "Ain't you a little early?" said the bus driver, swinging the door shut. "Just left the office," I said. The driver nodded, apparently not giving me a second thought. I had no idea why I'd told her I'd come from the office, or why she found it a satisfactory answer. Two minutes later the bus filled, rolled, and shook its way to Connolly Air Base. When I got home, my mother was sitting in the living room, smoking her Slims, watching her soap opera. She absently asked me how my day had gone and I told her fine. "Hear from Dad?" I said.

"No, but I'm sure he's fine." She always said that when we hadn't heard from him in a while. I suppose she thought I was worried about him, or that I felt vulnerable without him. It was neither. I just wanted to discuss something with my mother that we both cared about. If I spoke with her about things that happened at school, or on my weekends, she'd listen with half an ear, say something like, "Is that so?" or "You don't say?" I couldn't stand that sort of thing. But when I mentioned my father, she treated me a bit more like an adult, or at least someone who was worth listening to. I didn't want to feel like a boy that afternoon. As I turned from my mother and walked down the hall I thought about the day my father left for Viet Nam. Sharp in his uniform, sure behind his aviator specs, he slipped a cigar from his pocket and stuck it in mine. "Not till I get back," he said. "We'll have us one when we go fishing. Just you and me, out on the lake all day, smoking and casting and sitting. Don't let Mama see it. Put it in y'back pocket." He hugged me, shook my hand, and told me I was the man of the house now. He told me he was depending on me to take good care of my mother and sister. "Don't you let me down, now, hear?" And he tapped his thick finger on my chest. "You almost as big as me. Boy, you something else." I believed him when he told me those things. My heart swelled big enough to swallow my father, my mother, Claire. I loved, feared, and respected myself, my manhood. That day I could have put all of Waco, Texas, in my heart. And it wasn't till about three months later that I discovered I really wasn't the man of the house, that my mother and sister, as they always had, were taking care of me.

For a brief moment I considered telling my mother about what had happened at school that day, but for one thing, she was deep down in the halls of *General Hospital,* and never paid you much mind till it was over. For another thing, I just wasn't the kind of person—I'm still not, really—to discuss my problems with anyone. Like my father I kept things to myself, talked about my problems only in retrospect. Since my father wasn't around I consciously wanted to be like him, doubly like him, I could say. I wanted to be the man of the house in some respect, even if it had to be in an inward way. I went to my room, changed my clothes, and laid out my homework. I couldn't focus on it. I thought about Marvin, what I'd said about him or done to him—I couldn't tell which. I'd done something to him, said something about him; said something about and done something to myself. *How come you're after* me *and not* him? I kept trying to tell myself I hadn't meant it that way. *That* way. I thought about approaching Marvin, telling him what I really meant was that he was more Oakley's age and weight than I. I would tell him I meant I was no match for Oakley. *See, Marvin, what I meant was that he wants to fight a colored guy, but is afraid to fight you 'cause you could beat him.* But try as I did, I couldn't for a moment convince myself that Marvin would believe me. I meant it *that* way and no other. Everybody heard. Everybody knew. That afternoon I forced myself to confront the notion that tomorrow I would probably have to fight both Oakley and Marvin. I'd have to be two men.

I rose from my desk and walked to the window. The light made my skin look orange, and I started thinking about what Wickham had told us once about light. She said that oranges and apples, leaves and flowers, the whole multicolored world, was not what it appeared to be. The colors we see, she said, look like they do only because of the light or ray that shines on them. "The color of the thing isn't what you see, but the light that's reflected off it." Then she shut out the lights and shone a white light lamp on a prism. We watched the pale splay of colors on the projector screen; some people oohed and aahed. Suddenly, she switched on a black light and the color of everything changed. The prism colors vanished, Wickham's arms were purple, the buttons of her dress were as orange as hot coals, rather than the blue they had been only seconds before. We were all very quiet. "Nothing," she said, after a while, "is really what it appears to be." I didn't really understand then. But as I stood at the window, gazing at my orange skin, I wondered what kind of light I could shine on Marvin, Oakley, and me that would reveal us as the same.

I sat down and stared at my arms. They were dark brown again. I worked up a bit of saliva under my tongue and spat on my left arm. I spat again, then rubbed the spittle into it, polishing, working till my arm grew warm. As I spat, and rubbed, I wondered why Marvin did this weird, nasty thing to himself, day after day. Was he trying to rub away the black, or deepen it, doll it up? And if he did this weird nasty thing for a hundred years, would he spit-shine himself invisible, rolling away the eggplant skin, revealing the scarlet muscle, blue vein, pink and yellow tendon, white bone? Then disappear? Seen through, all colors, no colors. Spitting and rubbing. Is this the way you do it? I leaned forward, sniffed the arm. It smelled vaguely of mayonnaise. After an hour or so, I fell asleep.

I saw Oakley the second I stepped off the bus the next morning. He stood outside the gym in his usual black penny loafers, white socks, high-water jeans, T-shirt, and black jacket. Nailor stood with him, his big teeth spread across his bottom lip like playing cards. If there was anyone I felt like fighting, that day, it was Nailor. But I wanted to put off fighting for as long as I could. I stepped toward the gymnasium, thinking that I shouldn't run, but if I hurried I could beat Oakley to the door and secure myself near Gilchrest's office. But the moment I stepped into the gym, I felt Oakley's broad palm clap down on my shoulder. "Might as well stay out here, Coonie," he said. "I need me a little target practice." I turned to face him and he slapped me, one-two, with the back, then the palm of his hand, as I'd seen Bogart do to Peter Lorre in

The Maltese Falcon. My heart went wild. I could scarcely breathe. I couldn't swallow.

"Call me a nigger," I said. I have no idea what made me say this. All I know is that it kept me from crying. "Call me a nigger, Oakley."

"Fuck you, ya black-ass slope." He slapped me again, scratching my eye. "I don't do what coonies tell me."

"Call me a nigger."

"Outside, Coonie."

"Call me one. Go ahead!"

He lifted his hand to slap me again, but before his arm could swing my way, Marvin Pruitt came from behind me and calmly pushed me aside. "Git out my way, boy," he said. And he slugged Oakley on the side of his head. Oakley stumbled back, stiff-legged. His eyes were big. Marvin hit him twice more, once again to the side of the head, once to the nose. Oakley went down and stayed down. Though blood was drawn, whistles blowing, fingers pointing, kids hollering, Marvin just stood there, staring at me with cool eyes. He spat on the ground, licked his lips, and just stared at me, till Coach Gilchrest and Mr. Calderon tackled him and violently carried him away. He never struggled, never took his eyes off me.

Nailor and Mrs. Wickham helped Oakley to his feet. His already fattened nose bled and swelled so that I had to look away. He looked around, bemused, walleyed, maybe scared. It was apparent he had no idea how bad he was hurt. He didn't blink. He didn't even touch his nose. He didn't look like he knew much of anything. He looked at me, looked me dead in the eye, in fact, but didn't seem to recognize me.

That morning, like all other mornings, we said the Pledge of Allegiance, sang "The Yellow Rose of Texas," "The Eyes of Texas Are upon You," and "Mistress Shady." The room stood strangely empty without Oakley, and without Marvin, but at the same time you could feel their presence more intensely somehow. I felt like I did when I'd walk into my mother's room and could smell my father's cigars or cologne. He was more palpable, in certain respects, than when there in actual flesh. For some reason, I turned to look at Ah-so, and just this once I let my eyes linger on her face. She had a very gentle-looking face, really. That surprised me. She must have felt my eyes on her because she glanced up at me for a second and smiled, white teeth, downcast eyes. Such a pretty smile. That surprised me too. She held it for a few seconds, then let it fade. She looked down at her desk, and sat still as a photograph.

LORRIE MOORE

You're Ugly, Too

LORRIE MOORE (1957–) is a professor of English at the University of Wisconsin–Madison. Her work has appeared in *The New Yorker,* The Best American Short Stories, and Prize Stories: The O. Henry Awards. She is the author of two novels and three short-story collections, including *Birds of America.*

You had to get out of them occasionally, those Illinois towns with the funny names: Paris, Oblong, Normal. Once, when the Dow-Jones dipped two hundred points, the Paris paper boasted a banner headline: NORMAL MAN MARRIES OBLONG WOMAN. They knew what was important. They did! But you had to get out once in a while, even if it was just across the border to Terre Haute, for a movie.

Outside of Paris, in the middle of a large field, was a scatter of brick buildings, a small liberal arts college with the improbable name of Hilldale-Versailles. Zoë Hendricks had been teaching American History there for three years. She taught "The Revolution and Beyond" to freshmen and sophomores, and every third semester she had the Senior Seminar for Majors, and although her student evaluations had been slipping in the last year and a half—*Professor Hendricks is often late for class and usually arrives with a cup of hot chocolate, which she offers the class sips of*—generally, the department of nine men was pleased to have her. They felt she added some needed feminine touch to the corridors—that faint trace of Obsession and sweat, the light, fast clicking of heels. Plus they had had a sex-discrimination suit, and the dean had said, well, it was time.

The situation was not easy for her, they knew. Once, at the start of last semester, she had skipped into her lecture hall singing "Getting to Know You"—both verses. At the request of the dean, the chairman had called her into his office, but did not ask her for an explanation, not really. He asked her how she was and then smiled in an avuncular way. She said, "Fine," and he studied the way she said it, her front teeth catching on the inside of her lower lip. She was almost pretty, but her face showed the strain and ambition of always having been close but not quite. There was too much effort with the eyeliner, and her earrings, worn no doubt for the drama her features lacked, were a little frightening, jutting out from the side of her head like antennae.

"I'm going out of my mind," said Zoë to her younger sister, Evan, in Manhattan. *Professor Hendricks seems to know the entire sound track to* The King and I. *Is this history?* Zoë phoned her every Tuesday.

"You always say that," said Evan, "but then you go on your trips and vacations and then you settle back into things and then you're quiet for a while and then you say you're fine, you're busy, and then after a while you say you're going crazy again, and you start all over." Evan was a part-time food designer for photo shoots. She cooked vegetables in green dye. She propped up beef stew with a bed of marbles and shopped for new kinds of silicone sprays and plastic ice cubes. She thought her life was "OK." She was living with her boyfriend of many years, who was independently wealthy and had an amusing little job in book publishing. They were five years out of college, and they lived in a luxury midtown high-rise with a balcony and access to a pool. "It's not the same as having your own pool," Evan was always sighing, as if to let Zoë know that, as with Zoë, there were still things she, Evan, had to do without.

"Illinois. It makes me sarcastic to be here," said Zoë on the phone. She used to insist it was irony, something gently layered and sophisticated, something alien to the Midwest, but her students kept calling it sarcasm, something they felt qualified to recognize, and now she had to agree. It wasn't irony. *What is your perfume?* a student once asked her. *Room freshener,* she said. She smiled, but he looked at her, unnerved.

Her students were by and large good Midwesterners, spacey with estrogen from large quantities of meat and cheese. They shared their parents' suburban values; their parents had given them things, things, things. They were complacent. They had been purchased. They were armed with a healthy vagueness about anything historical or geographic. They seemed actually to know very little about anything, but they were extremely good-natured about it. "All those states in the East are so tiny and jagged and bunched up," complained one of her undergraduates the week she was lecturing on "The Turning Point of Independence: The Battle at Saratoga." "Professor Hendricks, you're from Delaware originally, right?" the student asked her.

"Maryland," corrected Zoë.

"Aw," he said, waving his hand dismissively. "New England."

Her articles—chapters toward a book called *Hearing the One About: Uses of Humor in the American Presidency*—were generally well received, though they came slowly for her. She liked her pieces to have something from every time of day in them—she didn't trust things written in the morning only—so she reread and rewrote painstakingly. No part of a day, its moods, its light, was allowed to dominate. She hung on to a piece for over a year sometimes, revising at all hours, until the entirety of a day had registered there.

The job she'd had before the one at Hilldale-Versailles had been at a small college in New Geneva, Minnesota, Land of the Dying Shopping Mall. Everyone was so blond there that brunettes were often presumed to be from foreign countries. *Just because Professor Hendricks is from Spain doesn't give her the right to be so negative about our country.* There was a general emphasis on cheerfulness. In New Geneva you weren't supposed to be critical or complain. You weren't supposed to notice that the town had overextended and that its shopping malls were raggedy and going under. You were never to say you weren't fine thank you and yourself. You were supposed to be Heidi. You were supposed to lug goat milk up the hills and not think twice. Heidi did not complain. Heidi did not do things like stand in front of the new IBM photocopier, saying, "If this fucking Xerox machine breaks on me one more time, I'm going to slit my wrists."

But now, in her second job, in her fourth year of teaching in the Midwest, Zoë was discovering something she never suspected she had: a crusty edge, brittle and pointed. Once she had pampered her students, singing them songs, letting them call her at home, even, and ask personal questions. Now she was losing sympathy. They were beginning to seem different. They were beginning to seem demanding and spoiled.

"You act," said one of her Senior Seminar students at a scheduled conference, "like your opinion is worth more than everybody else's in the class."

Zoë's eyes widened. "I *am* the teacher," she said. "I *do* get paid to act like that." She narrowed her gaze at the student, who was wearing a big leather bow in her hair, like a cowgirl in a TV ranch show. "I mean, otherwise *every body* in the class would have little offices and office hours." *Sometimes Professor Hendricks will take up the class's time just talking about movies she's seen.* She stared at the student some more, then added, "I bet you'd like that."

"Maybe I sound whiny to you," said the girl, "but I simply want my history major to mean something."

"Well, there's your problem," said Zoë, and with a smile, she showed the student to the door. "I like your bow," she added.

Zoë lived for the mail, for the postman, that handsome blue jay, and when she got a real letter, with a real full-price stamp, from someplace else, she took it to bed with her and read it over and over. She also watched television until all hours and had her set in the bedroom, a bad sign. *Professor Hendricks has said critical things about Fawn Hall, the Catholic religion, and the whole state of*

Illinois. It is unbelievable. At Christmastime she gave twenty-dollar tips to the mailman and to Jerry, the only cabbie in town, whom she had gotten to know from all her rides to and from the Terre Haute airport, and who, since he realized such rides were an extravagance, often gave her cut rates.

"I'm flying in to visit you this weekend," announced Zoë.

"I was hoping you would," said Evan. "Charlie and I are having a party for Halloween. It'll be fun."

"I have a costume already. It's a bonehead. It's this thing that looks like a giant bone going through your head."

"Great," said Evan.

"It is, it's great."

"Alls I have is my moon mask from last year and the year before. I'll probably end up getting married in it."

"Are you and Charlie getting *married?*" Foreboding filled her voice.

"Hmmmmmmnnno, not immediately."

"Don't get married."

"Why?"

"Just not yet. You're too young."

"You're only saying that because you're five years older than I am and *you're* not married."

"*I'm* not married? Oh, my God," said Zoë. "I forgot to get married."

Zoë had been out with three men since she'd come to Hilldale-Versailles. One of them was a man in the Paris municipal bureaucracy who had fixed a parking ticket she'd brought in to protest and who then asked her to coffee. At first she thought he was amazing—at last, someone who did not want Heidi! But soon she came to realize that all men, deep down, wanted Heidi. Heidi with cleavage. Heidi with outfits. The parking ticket bureaucrat soon became tired and intermittent. One cool fall day, in his snazzy, impractical convertible, when she asked him what was wrong, he said, "You would not be ill-served by new clothes, you know." She wore a lot of gray-green corduroy. She had been under the impression that it brought out her eyes, those shy stars. She flicked an ant from her sleeve.

"Did you have to brush that off in the car?" he said, driving. He glanced down at his own pectorals, giving first the left, then the right, a quick survey. He was wearing a tight shirt.

"Excuse me?"

He slowed down at a yellow light and frowned. "Couldn't you have picked it up and thrown it outside?"

"The ant? It might have bitten me. I mean, what difference does it make?"

"It might have bitten you! Ha! How ridiculous! Now it's going to lay eggs in my car!"

The second guy was sweeter, lunkier, though not insensitive to certain paintings and songs, but too often, too, things he'd do or say would startle her. Once, in a restaurant, he stole the garnishes off her dinner plate and waited for her to notice. When she didn't, he finally thrust his fist across the table and said, "Look," and when he opened it, there was her parsley sprig and her orange slice, crumpled to a wad. Another time he described to her his recent trip to the Louvre. "And there I was in front of Géricault's *Raft of the Medusa,* and everyone else had wandered off, so I had my own private audience with it, all those painted, drowning bodies splayed in every direction, and there's this motion in that painting that starts at the bottom left, swirling and building, and building, and building, and going up to the right-hand corner, where there's this guy waving a flag, and on the horizon in the distance you could see this teeny tiny boat. . . ." He was breathless in the telling. She found this touching and smiled in encouragement. "A painting like that," he said, shaking his head. "It just makes you shit."

"I have to ask you something," said Evan. "I know every woman complains about not meeting men, but really, on my shoots, I meet a lot of men. And they're not all gay, either." She paused. "Not anymore."

"What are you asking?"

The third guy was a political science professor named Murray Peterson, who liked to go out on double dates with colleagues whose wives he was attracted to. Usually the wives would consent to flirt with him. Under the table sometimes there was footsie, and once there was even kneesie. Zoë and the husband would be left to their food, staring into their water glasses, chewing like goats. "Oh, Murray," said one wife, who had never finished her master's in physical therapy and wore great clothes. "You know, I know everything about you: your birthday, your license plate number. I have everything memorized. But then that's the kind of mind I have. Once at a dinner party I amazed the host by getting up and saying good-bye to every single person there, first *and* last names."

"I knew a dog who could do that," said Zoë, with her mouth full. Murray and the wife looked at her with vexed and rebuking expressions, but the husband seemed suddenly twinkling and amused. Zoë swallowed. "It was a Talking Lab, and after about ten minutes of listening to the dinner conversation this dog knew everyone's name. You could say, 'Bring this knife to Murray Peterson,' and it would."

"Really," said the wife, frowning, and Murray Peterson never called again.

"Are you seeing anyone?" said Evan. "I'm asking for a particular reason, I'm not just being like mom."

"I'm seeing my house. I'm tending to it when it wets, when it cries, when it throws up." Zoë had bought a mint-green ranch house near campus, though now she was thinking that maybe she shouldn't have. It was hard to live in a house. She kept wandering in and out of the rooms, wondering where she had put things. She went downstairs into the basement for no reason at all except that it amused her to own a basement. It also amused her to own a tree. The day she moved in, she had tacked to her tree a small paper sign that said *Zoë's Tree.*

Her parents, in Maryland, had been very pleased that one of their children had at last been able to afford real estate, and when she closed on the house they sent her flowers with a Congratulations card. Her mother had even UPS'd a box of old decorating magazines saved over the years, photographs of beautiful rooms her mother used to moon over, since there never had been any money to redecorate. It was like getting her mother's pornography, that box, inheriting her drooled-upon fantasies, the endless wish and tease that had been her life. But to her mother it was a rite of passage that pleased her. "Maybe you will get some ideas from these," she had written. And when Zoë looked at the photographs, at the bold and beautiful living rooms, she was filled with longing. Ideas and ideas of longing.

Right now Zoë's house was rather empty. The previous owner had wallpapered around the furniture, leaving strange gaps and silhouettes on the walls, and Zoë hadn't done much about that yet. She had bought furniture, then taken it back, furnishing and unfurnishing, preparing and shedding, like a womb. She had bought several plain pine chests to use as love seats or boot boxes, but they came to look to her more and more like children's coffins, so she returned them. And she had recently bought an Oriental rug for the living room, with Chinese symbols on it she didn't understand. The salesgirl had kept saying she was sure they meant *Peace* and *Eternal Life,* but when Zoë got the rug home, she worried. What if they didn't mean *Peace* and *Eternal Life*? What if they meant, say, *Bruce Springsteen.* And the more she thought about it, the more she became convinced she had a rug that said *Bruce Springsteen,* and so she returned that, too.

She had also bought a little baroque mirror for the front entryway, which she had been told, by Murray Peterson, would keep away evil spirits. The mirror, however, tended to frighten *her,* startling her with an image of a woman she never recognized. Sometimes she looked puffier and plainer than she remembered. Sometimes shifty and dark. Most times she just looked vague. *You look like someone I know,* she had been told twice in the last year by strangers in restaurants in Terre Haute. In fact, sometimes she seemed not to have a look of her own, or any look whatsoever, and it began to amaze her that her students and colleagues were able to recognize her at all. How did they know? When she walked into a room, how did she look so that they knew it was her? Like this? Did she look like this? And so she returned the mirror.

"The reason I'm asking is that I know a man I think you should meet," said Evan. "He's fun. He's straight. He's single. That's all I'm going to say."

"I think I'm too old for fun," said Zoë. She had a dark bristly hair in her chin, and she could feel it now with her finger. Perhaps when you had been without the opposite sex for too long, you began to resemble them. In an act of desperate invention, you began to grow your own. "I just want to come, wear my bonehead, visit with Charlie's tropical fish, ask you about your food shoots."

She thought about all the papers on "Our Constitution: How It Affects Us" she was going to have to correct. She thought about how she was going in for ultrasound tests on Friday, because, according to her doctor and her doctor's assistant, she had a large, mysterious growth in her abdomen. Gallbladder, they kept saying. Or ovaries or colon. "You guys practice medicine?" asked Zoë, aloud, after they had left the room. Once, as a girl, she brought her dog to a vet, who had told her, "Well, either your dog has worms or cancer or else it was hit by a car."

She was looking forward to New York.

"Well, whatever. We'll just play it cool. I can't wait to see you, hon. Don't forget your bonehead," said Evan.

"A bonehead you don't forget," said Zoë.

"I suppose," said Evan.

The ultrasound Zoë was keeping a secret, even from Evan. "I feel like I'm dying," Zoë had hinted just once on the phone.

"You're not dying," said Evan. "You're just annoyed."

"Ultrasound," Zoë now said jokingly to the technician who put the cold jelly on her bare stomach. "Does that sound like a really great stereo system, or what?" She had not had anyone make this much fuss over her bare stomach since her boyfriend in graduate school, who had hovered over her whenever she felt ill, waved his arms, pressed his hands upon her navel, and drawled evangelically, "Heal! Heal for thy Baby Jesus' sake!" Zoë would laugh and they would make love, both secretly hoping she would get pregnant. Later they would worry together, and he would sink a cheek to her belly and ask whether she was late, was she late, was she sure, she might be late, and when after two years she had not gotten pregnant, they took to quarreling and drifted apart.

"OK," said the technician absently.

The monitor was in place, and Zoë's insides came on the screen in all their gray and ribbony hollowness. They were marbled in the finest gradations of black and white, like stone in an old church or a picture of the moon. "Do you suppose," she babbled at the technician, "that the rise in infertility among so many couples in this country is due to completely different species trying to reproduce?" The technician moved the scanner around and took more pictures. On one view in particular, on Zoë's right side, the technician became suddenly alert, the machine he was operating clicking away.

Zoë stared at the screen. "That must be the growth you found there," suggested Zoë.

"I can't tell you anything," said the technician rigidly. "Your doctor will get the radiologist's report this afternoon and will phone you then."

"I'll be out of town," said Zoë.

"I'm sorry," said the technician.

Driving home, Zoë looked in the rearview mirror and decided she looked—well, how would one describe it? A little wan. She thought of the joke about the guy who visits his doctor and the doctor says, "Well, I'm sorry to say you've got six weeks to live."

"I want a second opinion," says the guy. *You act like your opinion is worth more than everyone else's in the class.*

"You want a second opinion? OK," says the doctor. "You're ugly, too." She liked that joke. She thought it was terribly, terribly funny.

She took a cab to the airport, Jerry the cabbie happy to see her.

"Have fun in New York," he said, getting her bag out of the trunk. He liked her, or at least he always acted as if he did. She called him "Jare."

"Thanks, Jare."

"You know, I'll tell you a secret: I've never been to New York. I'll tell you two secrets: I've never been on a plane." And he waved at her sadly as she pushed her way in through the terminal door. "Or an escalator!" he shouted.

The trick to flying safe, Zoë always said, was never to buy a discount ticket and to tell yourself you had nothing to live for anyway, so that when the plane crashed it was no big deal. Then, when it didn't crash, when you had succeeded in keeping it aloft with your own worthlessness, all you had to do was stagger off, locate your luggage, and, by the time a cab arrived, come up with a persuasive reason to go on living.

"You're here!" shrieked Evan over the doorbell, before she even opened the door. Then she opened it wide. Zoë set her bags on the hall floor and hugged Evan hard. When she was little, Evan had always been affectionate and devoted. Zoë had always taken care of her, advising, reassuring, until recently, when it seemed Evan had started advising and reassuring *her.* It startled Zoë. She suspected it had something to do with Zoë's being alone. It made people uncomfortable. "How *are* you?"

"I threw up on the plane. Besides that, I'm OK."

"Can I get you something? Here, let me take your suitcase. Sick on the plane. Eeeyew."

"It was into one of those sickness bags," said Zoë, just in case Evan thought she'd lost it in the aisle. "I was very quiet."

The apartment was spacious and bright, with a view all the way downtown along the East Side. There was a balcony and sliding glass doors. "I keep forgetting how nice this apartment is. Twentieth floor, doorman . . ." Zoë could work her whole life and never have an apartment like this. So could Evan. It was Charlie's apartment. He and Evan lived in it like two kids in a dorm, beer cans and clothes strewn around. Evan put Zoë's bag away from the mess, over by the fish tank. "I'm so glad you're here," she said. "Now what can I get you?"

Evan made them a snack—soup from a can, and saltines.

"I don't know about Charlie," she said, after they had finished. "I feel like we've gone all sexless and middle-aged already."

"Hmmm," said Zoë. She leaned back into Evan's sofa and stared out the window at the dark tops of the buildings. It seemed a little unnatural to live up in the sky like this, like birds that out of some wrongheaded derring-do had nested too high. She nodded toward the lighted fish tanks and giggled. "I feel like a bird," she said, "with my own personal supply of fish."

Evan sighed. "He comes home and just sacks out on the sofa, watching fuzzy football. He's wearing the psychic cold cream and curlers, if you know what I mean."

Zoë sat up, readjusted the sofa cushions. "What's fuzzy football?"

"We haven't gotten cable yet. Everything comes in fuzzy. Charlie just watches it that way."

"Hmmm, yeah, that's a little depressing," Zoë said. She looked at her hands. "Especially the part about not having cable."

"This is how he gets into bed at night." Evan stood up to demonstrate. "He whips all his clothes off, and when he gets to his underwear, he lets it drop to one ankle. Then he kicks up his leg and flips the underwear in the air and catches it. I, of course, watch from the bed. There's nothing else. There's just that."

"Maybe you should just get it over with and get married."

"Really?"

"Yeah. I mean, you guys probably think living together like this is the best of both worlds, but . . ." Zoë tried to sound like an older sister; an older sister was supposed to be the parent you could never have, the hip, cool mom. ". . . I've always found that as soon as you think you've got the best of both worlds"—she thought now of herself, alone in her house; of the toad-faced cicadas that flew around like little caped men at night, landing on her screens, staring; of the size fourteen shoes she placed at the doorstep, to scare off intruders; of the ridiculous inflatable blow-up doll someone had told her to keep propped up at the breakfast table—"it can suddenly twist and become the worst of both worlds."

"Really?" Evan was beaming. "Oh, Zoë. I have something to tell you. Charlie and I *are* getting married."

"Really." Zoë felt confused.

"I didn't know how to tell you."

"Yes, well, I guess the part about fuzzy football misled me a little."

"I was hoping you'd be my maid of honor," said Evan, waiting. "Aren't you happy for me?"

"Yes," said Zoë, and she began to tell Evan a story about an award-winning violinist at Hilldale-Versailles, how the violinist had come home from a competition in Europe and taken up with a local man, who made her go to all his summer softball games, made her cheer for him from the stands, with the wives, until she later killed herself. But when she got halfway through, to the part about cheering at the softball games, Zoë stopped.

"What?" said Evan. "So what happened?"

"Actually, nothing," said Zoë lightly. "She just really got into softball. I mean, really. You should have seen her."

Zoë decided to go to a late-afternoon movie, leaving Evan to chores she needed to do before the party—*I have to do them alone,* she'd said, a little tense after the violinist story. Zoë thought about going to an art museum, but women alone in art museums had to look good. They always did. Chic and serious, moving languidly, with a great handbag. Instead, she walked over and down through Kips Bay, past an earring boutique called Stick It in Your Ear, past a beauty salon called Dorian Gray's. That was the funny thing about *beauty,* thought Zoë. Look it up in the yellow pages, and you found a hundred entries, hostile with wit, cutesy with warning. But look up *truth*—ha! There was nothing at all.

Zoë thought about Evan getting married. Would Evan turn into Peter Pumpkin Eater's wife? Mrs. Eater? At the wedding would she make Zoë wear some flouncy lavender dress, identical with the other maids'? Zoë hated uniforms, had even, in the first grade, refused to join Elf Girls, because she didn't want to wear the same dress as everyone else. Now she might have to. But maybe she could distinguish it. Hitch it up on one side with a clothespin. Wear surgical gauze at the waist. Clip to her bodice one of those pins that said in loud letters, SHIT HAPPENS.

At the movie—*Death by Number*—she bought strands of red licorice to tug and chew. She took a seat off to one side in the theater. She felt strangely self-conscious sitting alone and hoped for the place to darken fast. When it did, and the coming attractions came on, she reached inside her purse for her glasses. They were in a Baggie. Her Kleenex was also in a Baggie. So were her pen and her aspirin and her mints. Everything was in Baggies. This was what she'd become: *a woman alone at the movies with everything in a Baggie.*

* * *

At the Halloween party, there were about two dozen people. There were people with ape heads and large hairy hands. There was someone dressed as a leprechaun. There was someone dressed as a frozen dinner. Some man had brought his two small daughters: a ballerina and a ballerina's sister, also dressed as a ballerina. There was a gaggle of sexy witches—women dressed entirely in black, beautifully made up and jeweled. "I hate those sexy witches. It's not in the spirit of Halloween," said Evan. Evan had abandoned the moon mask and dolled herself up as a hausfrau, in curlers and an apron, a decision she now regretted. Charlie, because he liked fish, because he owned fish, collected fish, had decided to go as a fish. He had fins and eyes on the side of his head. "Zoë! How are you! I'm sorry I wasn't here when you first arrived!" He spent the rest of his time chatting up the sexy witches.

"Isn't there something I can help you with here?" Zoë asked her sister. "You've been running yourself ragged." She rubbed her sister's arm, gently, as if she wished they were alone.

"Oh, God, not at all," said Evan, arranging stuffed mushrooms on a plate. The timer went off, and she pulled another sheetful out of the oven. "Actually, you know what you can do?"

"What?" Zoë put on her bonehead.

"Meet Earl. He's the guy I had in mind for you. When he gets here, just talk to him a little. He's nice. He's fun. He's going through a divorce."

"I'll try." Zoë groaned. "OK? I'll try." She looked at her watch.

When Earl arrived, he was dressed as a naked woman, steel wool glued strategically to a body stocking, and large rubber breasts protruding like hams.

"Zoë, this is Earl," said Evan.

"Good to meet you," said Earl, circling Evan to shake Zoë's hand. He stared at the top of Zoë's head. "Great bone."

Zoë nodded. "Great tits," she said. She looked past him, out the window at the city thrown glitteringly up against the sky; people were saying the usual things: how it looked like jewels, like bracelets and necklaces unstrung. You could see Grand Central station, the clock of the Con Ed building, the red-and-gold-capped Empire State, the Chrysler like a rocket ship dreamed up in a depression. Far west you could glimpse the Astor Plaza, its flying white roof like a nun's habit. "There's beer out on the balcony, Earl—can I get you one?" Zoë asked.

"Sure, uh, I'll come along. Hey, Charlie, how's it going?"

Charlie grinned and whistled. People turned to look. "Hey, Earl," someone called, from across the room. "Va-va-va-voom."

They squeezed their way past the other guests, past the apes and the sexy witches. The suction of the sliding door gave way in a whoosh, and Zoë and Earl stepped out onto the balcony, a bonehead and a naked woman, the night air roaring and smoky cool. Another couple was out here, too, murmuring privately. They were not wearing costumes. They smiled at Zoë and Earl. "Hi," said Zoë. She found the plastic-foam cooler, dug into it, and retrieved two beers.

"Thanks," said Earl. His rubber breasts folded inward, dimpled and dented, as he twisted open the bottle.

"Well," sighed Zoë anxiously. She had to learn not to be afraid of a man, the way, in your childhood, you learned not to be afraid of an earthworm or a bug. Often, when she spoke to men at parties, she rushed things in her mind. As the man politely blathered on, she would fall in love, marry, then find herself in a bitter custody battle with him for the kids and hoping for a reconciliation, so that despite all his betrayals she might no longer despise him, and in the few minutes remaining, learn, perhaps, what his last name was and what he did for a living, though probably there was already too much history between them. She would nod, blush, turn away.

"Evan tells me you're a professor. Where do you teach?"

"Just over the Indiana border into Illinois."

He looked a little shocked. "I guess Evan didn't tell me that part."

"She didn't?"

"No."

"Well, that's Evan for you. When we were kids we both had speech impediments."

"That can be tough," said Earl. One of his breasts was hidden behind his drinking arm, but the other shone low and pink, full as a strawberry moon.

"Yes, well, it wasn't a total loss. We used to go to what we called peach pearapy. For about ten years of my life I had to map out every sentence in my mind, way ahead, before I said it. That was the only way I could get a coherent sentence out."

Earl drank from his beer. "How did you do that? I mean, how did you get through?"

"I told a lot of jokes. Jokes you know the lines to already—you can just say them. I love jokes. Jokes and songs."

Earl smiled. He had on lipstick, a deep shade of red, but it was wearing off from the beer. "What's your favorite joke?"

"Uh, my favorite joke is probably . . . OK, all right. This guy goes into a doctor's office and—"

"I think I know this one," interrupted Earl, eagerly. He wanted to tell it himself. "A guy goes into a doctor's office, and the doctor tells him he's got some good news and some bad news—that one, right?"

"I'm not sure," said Zoë. "This might be a different version."

"So the guy says, 'Give me the bad news first,' and the doctor says, 'OK. You've got three weeks to live.' And the guy cries, 'Three weeks to live! Doctor, what is the good news?' And the doctor says, 'Did you see that secretary out front? I finally fucked her.' "

Zoë frowned.

"That's not the one you were thinking of?"

"No." There was accusation in her voice. "Mine was different."

"Oh," said Earl. He looked away and then back again. "You teach history, right? What kind of history do you teach?"

"I teach American, mostly—eighteenth and nineteenth century." In graduate school, at bars, the pickup line was always: "So what's your century?"

"Occasionally I teach a special theme course," she added, "say, 'Humor and Personality in the White House.' That's what my book's on." She thought of something someone once told her about bowerbirds, how they build elaborate structures before mating.

"Your book's on *humor?*"

"Yeah, and, well, when I teach a theme course like that, I do all the centuries." *So what's your century?*

"All three of them."

"Pardon?" The breeze glistened her eyes. Traffic revved beneath them. She felt high and puny, like someone lifted into heaven by mistake and then spurned.

"Three. There's only three."

"Well, four, really." She was thinking of Jamestown, and of the Pilgrims coming here with buckles and witch hats to say their prayers.

"I'm a photographer," said Earl. His face was starting to gleam, his rouge smearing in a sunset beneath his eyes.

"Do you like that?"

"Well, actually I'm starting to feel it's a little dangerous."

"Really?"

"Spending all your time in a darkroom with that red light and all those chemicals. There's links with Parkinson's, you know."

"No, I didn't."

"I suppose I should wear rubber gloves, but I don't like to. Unless I'm touching it directly, I don't think of it as real."

"Hmmm," said Zoë. Alarm buzzed through her, mildly, like a tea.

"Sometimes, when I have a cut or something, I feel the sting and think, *Shit.* I wash constantly and just hope. I don't like rubber over the skin like that."

"Really."

"I mean, the physical contact. That's what you want, or why bother?"

"I guess," said Zoë. She wished she could think of a joke, something slow and deliberate, with the end in sight. She thought of gorillas, how when they had been kept too long alone in cages, they would smack each other in the head instead of mating.

"Are you . . . in a relationship?" Earl suddenly blurted.

"Now? As we speak?"

"Well, I mean, I'm sure you have a relationship to your *work.*" A smile, a weird one, nestled in his mouth like an egg. She thought of zoos in parks, how when cities were under siege, during world wars, people are the animals. "But I mean, with a *man.*"

"No, I'm not in a relationship with a *man.*" She rubbed her chin with her hand and could feel the one bristly hair there. "But my last relationship was with a very sweet man," she said. She made something up. "From Switzerland. He was a botanist—a weed expert. His name was Jerry. I called him 'Jare.' He was so funny. You'd go to the movies with him and all he would notice were the plants. He would never pay attention to the plot. Once, in a jungle movie, he started rattling off all these Latin names, out loud. It was very exciting for him." She paused, caught her breath. "Eventually he went back to Europe to, uh, study the edelweiss." She looked at Earl. "Are you involved in a relationship? With a *woman?*"

Earl shifted his weight, and the creases in his body stocking changed, splintering outward like something broken. His pubic hair slid over to one hip, like a corsage on a saloon girl. "No," he said, clearing his throat. The steel wool in his underarms was inching toward his biceps. "I've just gotten out of a marriage that was full of bad dialogue, like 'You want more *space?* I'll give you more space!' *Clonk.* Your basic Three Stooges."

Zoë looked at him sympathetically. "I suppose it's hard for love to recover after that."

His eyes lit up. He wanted to talk about love. "But *I* keep thinking love should be like a tree. You look at trees and they've got bumps and scars from tumors, infestations, what have you, but they're still growing. Despite the bumps and bruises, they're . . . straight."

"Yeah, well," said Zoë, "where I'm from, they're all married or gay. Did you see that movie *Death by Number*?"

Earl looked at her, a little lost. She was getting away from him. "No," he said.

One of his breasts had slipped under his arm, tucked there like a baguette. She kept thinking of trees, of gorillas and parks, of people in wartime eating the zebras. She felt a stabbing pain in her abdomen.

"Want some hors d'oeuvres?" Evan came pushing through the sliding door. She was smiling, though her curlers were coming out, hanging bedraggled at the ends of her hair like Christmas decorations, like food put out for the birds. She thrust forward a plate of stuffed mushrooms.

"Are you asking for donations or giving them away," said Earl, wittily. He liked Evan, and he put his arm around her.

"You know, I'll be right back," said Zoë.

"Oh," said Evan, looking concerned.

"Right back. I promise."

Zoë hurried inside, across the living room, into the bedroom, to the adjoining bath. It was empty; most of the guests were using the half bath near the kitchen. She flicked on the light and closed the door. The pain had stopped and she didn't really have to go to the bathroom, but she stayed there anyway, resting. In the mirror above the sink she looked haggard beneath her bonehead, violet grays showing under the skin like a plucked and pocky bird. She leaned closer, raising her chin a little to find the bristly hair. It was there, at the end of the jaw, sharp and dark as a wire. She opened the medicine cabinet, pawed through it until she found some tweezers. She lifted her head again and poked at her face with the metal tips, grasping and pinching and missing. Outside the door she could hear two people talking low. They had come into the bedroom and were discussing something. They were sitting on the bed. One of them giggled in a false way. She stabbed again at her chin, and it started to bleed a little. She pulled the skin tight along the jawbone, gripped the tweezers hard around what she hoped was the hair, and tugged. A tiny square of skin came away with it, but the hair remained, blood bright at the root of it. Zoë clenched her teeth. "Come on," she whispered. The couple outside in the bedroom were now telling stories, softly, and laughing. There was a bounce and squeak of mattress, and the sound of a chair being moved out of the way. Zoë aimed the tweezers carefully, pinched, then pulled gently away, and this time the hair came, too, with a slight twinge of pain and then a great flood of relief. "Yeah!" breathed Zoë. She grabbed some toilet paper and dabbed at her chin. It came away spotted with blood, and so she tore off some more and pressed hard until it stopped. Then she turned off the light and opened the door, to return to the party. "Excuse me," she said to the couple in the bedroom. They were the couple from the balcony, and they looked at her, a bit surprised. They had their arms around each other, and they were eating candy bars.

Earl was still out on the balcony, alone, and Zoë rejoined him there.

"Hi," she said. He turned around and smiled. He had straightened his costume out a bit, though all the secondary sex characteristics seemed slightly doomed, destined to shift and flip and zip around again any moment.

"Are you OK?" he asked. He had opened another beer and was chugging.

"Oh, yeah. I just had to go to the bathroom." She paused. "Actually I have been going to a lot of doctors recently."

"What's wrong?" asked Earl.

"Oh, probably nothing. But they're putting me through tests." She sighed. "I've had sonograms. I've had mammograms. Next week I'm going in for a candygram." He looked at her worriedly. "I've had too many gram words," she said.

"Here, I saved you these." He held out a napkin with two stuffed mushroom caps. They were cold and leaving oil marks on the napkin.

"Thanks," said Zoë, and pushed them both in her mouth. "Watch," she said, with her mouth full. "With my luck, it'll be a gallbladder operation."

Earl made a face. "So your sister's getting married," he said, changing the subject. "Tell me, really, what you think about love."

"*Love?*" Hadn't they done this already? "I don't know." She chewed thoughtfully and swallowed. "All right. I'll tell you what I think about love. Here is a love story. This friend of mine—"

"You've got something on your chin," said Earl, and he reached over to touch it.

"*What?*" said Zoë, stepping back. She turned her face away and grabbed at her chin. A piece of toilet paper peeled off it, like tape. "It's nothing," she said. "It's just—it's nothing."

Earl stared at her.

"At any rate," she continued, "this friend of mine was this award-winning violinist. She traveled all over Europe and won competitions; she made records, she gave concerts, she got famous. But she had no social life. So one day she threw herself at the feet of this conductor she had a terrible crush on. He picked her up, scolded her gently, and sent her back to her hotel room. After that she came home from Europe. She went back to her old hometown, stopped playing the violin, and took up with a local boy. This was in Illinois. He took her to some Big Ten bar every night to drink with his buddies from the team. He used to say things like 'Katrina here likes to play the violin,' and then he'd pinch her cheek. When she once suggested that they go home, he said, 'What, you think you're too famous for a place like this? Well, let me tell you something. You may think you're famous, but you're not *famous* famous.' Two famouses. 'No one here's ever heard of you.' Then he went up and bought a round of drinks for everyone but her. She got her coat, went home, and shot a gun through her head."

Earl was silent.

"That's the end of my love story," said Zoë.

"You're not at all like your sister," said Earl.

"Ho, really," said Zoë. The air had gotten colder, the wind singing minor and thick as a dirge.

"No." He didn't want to talk about love anymore. "You know, you should wear a lot of blue—blue and white—around your face. It would bring out your coloring." He reached an arm out to show her how the blue bracelet he was wearing might look against her skin, but she swatted it away.

"Tell me, Earl. Does the word *fag* mean anything to you?"

He stepped back, away from her. He shook his head in disbelief. "You know, I just shouldn't try to go out with career women. You're all stricken. A guy can really tell what life has done to you. I do better with women who have part-time jobs."

"Oh, yes?" said Zoë. She had once read an article entitled "Professional Women and the Demographics of Grief." Or no, it was a poem: *If there were a lake, the moonlight would dance across it in conniptions.* She remembered that line. But perhaps the title was "The Empty House: Aesthetics of Barrenness." Or maybe "Space Gypsies: Girls in Academe." She had forgotten.

Earl turned and leaned on the railing of the balcony. It was getting late. Inside, the party guests were beginning to leave. The sexy witches were already gone. "Live and learn," Earl murmured.

"Live and get dumb," replied Zoë. Beneath them on Lexington there were no cars, just the gold rush of an occasional cab. He leaned hard on his elbows, brooding.

"Look at those few people down there," he said. "They look like bugs. You know how bugs are kept under control? They're sprayed with bug hormones, female bug hormones. The male bugs get so crazy in the presence of this hormone, they're screwing everything in sight: trees, rocks—everything but female bugs. Population control. That's what's happening in this country," he said drunkenly. "Hormones sprayed around, and now men are screwing rocks. Rocks!"

In the back the Magic Marker line of his buttocks spread wide, a sketchy black on pink like a funnies page. Zoë came up, slow, from behind and gave him a shove. His arms slipped forward, off the railing, out over the street. Beer spilled out of his bottle, raining twenty stories down to the street.

"Hey, what are you doing?!" he said, whipping around. He stood straight and readied and moved away from the railing, sidestepping Zoë. "What the *hell* are you doing?"

"Just kidding," she said. "I was just kidding." But he gazed at her, appalled and frightened, his Magic Marker buttocks turned away now toward all of downtown, a naked pseudowoman with a blue bracelet at the wrist, trapped out on a balcony with—with *what? "Really, I was just kidding!"* Zoë shouted. The wind lifted the hair up off her head, skyward in spines behind the bone. If there were a lake, the moonlight would dance across it in conniptions. She smiled at him, and wondered how she looked.

BHARATI MUKHERJEE

The Management of Grief

BHARATI MUKHERJEE (1940–) is the author of the novels *Leave It to Me, The Holder of the World, Jasmine, Wife,* and *The Tiger's Daughter;* the short-story collections *Darkness* and *The Middleman and Other Stories;* and the nonfiction books *Days and Nights in Calcutta* and *The Sorrow and the Terror* (both coauthored with Clark Blaise). She has been awarded many grants and honors, including the National Book Critics Circle Award for Best Fiction (for *The Middleman and Other Stories*), a Guggenheim Fellowship, an NEA grant, and a Canada Council Senior Arts Fellowship. She is currently Professor of English at the University of California, Berkeley.

A woman I don't know is boiling tea the Indian way in my kitchen. There are a lot of women I don't know in my kitchen, whispering and moving tactfully. They open doors, rummage through the pantry, and try not to ask me where things are kept. They remind me of when my sons were small, on Mother's Day or when Vikram and I were tired, and they would make big, sloppy omelets. I would lie in bed pretending I didn't hear them.

Dr. Sharma, the treasurer of the Indo-Canada Society, pulls me into the hallway. He wants to know if I am worried about money. His wife, who has just come up from the basement with a tray of empty cups and glasses, scolds him. "Don't bother Mrs. Bhave with mundane details." She looks so monstrously pregnant her baby must be days overdue. I tell her she shouldn't be carrying heavy things. "Shaila," she says, smiling, "this is the fifth." Then she grabs a teenager by his shirttails. He slips his Walkman off his head. He has to be one of her four children; they have the same domed and dented foreheads. "What's the official word now?" she demands. The boy slips the headphones back on. "They're acting evasive, Ma. They're saying it could be an accident or a terrorist bomb."

All morning, the boys have been muttering, Sikh bomb, Sikh bomb. The men, not using the word, bow their heads in agreement. Mrs. Sharma touches her forehead at such a word. At least they've stopped talking about space debris and Russian lasers.

Two radios are going in the dining room. They are tuned to different stations. Someone must have brought the radios down from my boys' bedrooms. I haven't gone into their rooms since Kusum came running across the front lawn in her bathrobe. She looked so funny, I was laughing when I opened the door.

The big TV in the den is being whizzed through American networks and cable channels.

"Damn!" some man swears bitterly. "How can these preachers carry on like nothing's happened?" I want to tell him we're not that important. You look at the audience, and at the preacher in his blue robe with his beautiful white hair, the potted palm trees under a blue sky, and you know they care about nothing.

The phone rings and rings. Dr. Sharma's taken charge. "We're with her," he keeps saying. "Yes, yes, the doctor has given calming pills. Yes, yes, pills are having necessary effect." I wonder if pills alone explain this calm. Not peace, just a deadening quiet. I was always controlled, but never repressed. Sound can reach me, but my body is tensed, ready to scream. I hear their voices all around me. I hear my boys and Vikram cry, "Mommy, Shaila!" and their screams insulate me, like headphones.

The woman boiling water tells her story again and again. "I got the news first. My cousin called from Halifax before six A.M., can you imagine? He'd gotten up for prayers and his son was studying for medical exams and he heard on a rock channel that something had happened to a plane. They said first it had disappeared from the radar, like a giant eraser just reached out. His father called me, so I said to him, what do you mean, 'something bad'? You mean a hijacking? And he said, *Behn,* there is no confirmation of anything yet, but check with your neighbors because a lot of them must be on that plane. So I called poor Kusum straight-away. I knew Kusum's husband and daughter were booked to go yesterday."

Kusum lives across the street from me. She and Satish had moved in less than a month ago. They said they needed a bigger place. All these people, the Sharmas and friends from the Indo-Canada Society, had been there for the housewarming. Satish and Kusum made tandoori on their big gas grill and even the white neighbors piled their plates high with that luridly red, charred, juicy chicken. Their younger daughter had danced, and even our boys had broken away from the Stanley Cup telecast to put in a reluctant appearance. Everyone took pictures for their albums and for the community newspapers—another of our families had made it big in Toronto—and now I wonder how many of those happy faces are gone. "Why does God give us so much if all along He intends to take it away?" Kusum asks me.

I nod. We sit on carpeted stairs, holding hands like children. "I never once told him that I loved him," I say. I was too much the well-brought-up woman. I was so well brought up I never felt comfortable calling my husband by his first name.

"It's all right," Kusum says. "He knew. My husband knew. They felt it. Modern young girls have to say it because what they feel is fake."

Kusum's daughter Pam runs in with an overnight case. Pam's in her McDonald's uniform. "Mummy! You have to get dressed!" Panic makes her cranky. "A reporter's on his way here."

"Why?"

"You want to talk to him in your bathrobe?" She starts to brush her mother's long hair. She's the daughter who's always in trouble. She dates Canadian boys and hangs out in the mall, shopping for tight sweaters. The younger one, the goody-goody one according to Pam, the one with a voice so sweet that when she sang *bhajans* for Ethiopian relief even a frugal man like my husband wrote out a hundred-dollar check, *she* was on that plane. *She* was going to spend July and August with grandparents because Pam wouldn't go. Pam said she'd rather waitress at McDonald's. "If it's a choice between Bombay and Wonderland, I'm picking Wonderland," she'd said.

"Leave me alone," Kusum yells. "You know what I want to do? If I didn't have to look after you now, I'd hang myself."

Pam's young face goes blotchy with pain. "Thanks," she says, "don't let me stop you."

"Hush," pregnant Mrs. Sharma scolds Pam. "Leave your mother alone. Mr. Sharma will tackle the reporters and fill out the forms. He'll say what has to be said."

Pam stands her ground. "You think I don't know what Mummy's thinking? *Why her?* That's what. That's sick! Mummy wishes my little sister were alive and I were dead."

Kusum's hand in mine is trembly hot. We continue to sit on the stairs.

She calls before she arrives, wondering if there's anything I need. Her name is Judith Templeton and she's an appointee of the provincial government. "Multiculturalism?" I ask, and she says "partially," but that her mandate is bigger. "I've been told you knew many of the people on the flight," she says. "Perhaps if you'd agree to help us reach the others . . . ?"

She gives me time at least to put on tea water and pick up the mess in the front room. I have a few *samosas* from Kusum's housewarming that I could fry up, but then I think, why prolong this visit?

Judith Templeton is much younger than she sounded. She wears a blue suit with a white blouse and a polka-dot tie. Her blond hair is cut short, her only jewelry is pearl-drop earrings. Her briefcase is new and expensive looking, a gleaming cordovan leather. She sits with it across her lap. When she looks out the front windows onto the street, her contact lenses seem to float in front of her light blue eyes.

"What sort of help do you want from me?" I ask. She has refused the tea, out of politeness, but I insist, along with some slightly stale biscuits.

"I have no experience," she admits. "That is, I have an M.S.W. and I've worked in liaison with accident victims, but I mean I have no experience with a tragedy of this scale—"

"Who could?" I ask.

"—and with the complications of culture, language, and customs. Someone mentioned that Mrs. Bhave is a pillar—because you've taken it more calmly."

At this, perhaps, I frown, for she reaches forward, almost to take my hand. "I hope you understand my meaning, Mrs. Bhave. There are hundreds of people in Metro directly affected, like you, and some of them speak no English. There are some widows who've never handled money or gone on a bus, and there are old parents who still haven't eaten or gone outside their bedrooms. Some houses and apartments have been looted. Some wives are still hysterical. Some husbands are in shock and profound depression. We want to help, but our hands are tied in so many ways. We have to distribute money to some people, and there are legal documents—these things can be done. We have interpreters, but we don't always have the human touch, or maybe the right human touch. We don't want to make mistakes, Mrs. Bhave, and that's why we'd like to ask you to help us."

"More mistakes, you mean," I say.

"Police matters are not in my hands," she answers.

"Nothing I can do will make any difference," I say. "We must all grieve in our own way."

"But you are coping very well. All the people said, Mrs. Bhave is the strongest person of all. Perhaps if the others could see you, talk with you, it would help them."

"By the standards of the people you call hysterical, I am behaving very oddly and very badly, Miss Templeton." I want to say to her, *I wish I could scream, starve, walk into Lake Ontario, jump from a bridge.* "They would not see me as a model. I do not see myself as a model."

I am a freak. No one who has ever known me would think of me reacting this way. This terrible calm will not go away.

She asks me if she may call again, after I get back from a long trip that we all must make. "Of course," I say. "Feel free to call, anytime."

* * *

Four days later, I find Kusum squatting on a rock overlooking a bay in Ireland. It isn't a big rock, but it juts sharply out over water. This is as close as we'll ever get to them. June breezes balloon out her sari and unpin her knee-length hair. She has the bewildered look of a sea creature whom the tides have stranded.

It's been one hundred hours since Kusum came stumbling and screaming across my lawn. Waiting around the hospital, we've heard many stories. The police, the diplomats, they tell us things thinking that we're strong, that knowledge is helpful to the grieving, and maybe it is. Some, I know, prefer ignorance, or their own versions. The plane broke into two, they say. Unconsciousness was instantaneous. No one suffered. My boys must have just finished their breakfasts. They loved eating on planes, they loved the smallness of plates, knives, and forks. Last year they saved the airline salt and pepper shakers. Half an hour more and they would have made it to Heathrow.

Kusum says that we can't escape our fate. She says that all those people—our husbands, my boys, her girl with the nightingale voice, all those Hindus, Christians, Sikhs, Muslims, Parsis, and atheists on that plane—were fated to die together off this beautiful bay. She learned this from a swami in Toronto.

I have my Valium.

Six of us "relatives"—two widows and four widowers—chose to spend the day today by the waters instead of sitting in a hospital room and scanning photographs of the dead. That's what they call us now: relatives. I've looked through twenty-seven photos in two days. They're very kind to us, the Irish are very understanding. Sometimes understanding means freeing a tourist bus for this trip to the bay, so we can pretend to spy our loved ones through the glassiness of waves or in sun-speckled cloud shapes.

I could die here, too, and be content.

"What is that, out there?" She's standing and flapping her hands, and for a moment I see a head shape bobbing in the waves. She's standing in the water, I on the boulder. The tide is low, and a round, black, head-sized rock has just risen from the waves. She returns, her sari end dripping and ruined, and her face is a twisted remnant of hope, the way mine was a hundred hours ago, still laughing but inwardly knowing that nothing but the ultimate tragedy could bring two women together at six o'clock on a Sunday morning. I watch her face sag into blankness.

"That water felt warm, Shaila," she says at length.

"You can't," I say. "We have to wait for our turn to come."

I haven't eaten in four days, haven't brushed my teeth.

"I know," she says. "I tell myself I have no right to grieve. They are in a better place than we are. My swami says depression is a sign of our selfishness."

Maybe I'm selfish. Selfishly I break away from Kusum and run, sandals slapping against stones, to the water's edge. What if my boys aren't lying pinned under the debris? What if they aren't stuck a mile below that innocent blue chop? What if, given the strong currents . . .

Now I've ruined my sari, one of my best. Kusum has joined me, knee deep in water that feels to me like a swimming pool. I could settle in the water, and my husband would take my hand and the boys would slap water in my face just to see me scream.

"Do you remember what good swimmers my boys were, Kusum?"

"I saw the medals," she says.

One of the widowers, Dr. Ranganathan from Montreal, walks out to us, carrying his shoes in one hand. He's an electrical engineer. Someone at the hotel mentioned his work is famous around the world, something about the place where physics and electricity come together. He has lost a huge family, something indescribable. "With some luck," Dr. Ranganathan suggests to me, "a good swimmer could make it safely to some island. It is quite possible that there may be many, many microscopic islets scattered around."

"You're not just saying that?" I tell Dr. Ranganathan about Vinod, my elder son. Last year he took diving as well.

"It's a parent's duty to hope," he says. "It is foolish to rule out possibilities that have not been tested. I myself have not surrendered hope."

Kusum is sobbing once again. "Dear lady," he says, laying his free hand on her arm, and she calms down.

"Vinod is how old?" he asks me. He's very careful, as we all are. *Is,* not was.

"Fourteen. Yesterday he was fourteen. His father and uncle were going to take him down to the Taj and give him a big birthday party. I couldn't go with them because I couldn't get two weeks off from my stupid job in June." I process bills for a travel agent. June is a big travel month.

Dr. Ranganathan whips the pockets of his suit jacket inside out. Squashed roses, in darkening shades of pink, float on the water. He tore the roses off creepers in somebody's garden. He didn't ask anyone if he could pluck the roses, but now there's been an article about it in the local papers. When you see an Indian person, it says, please give them flowers.

"A strong youth of fourteen," he says, "can very likely pull to safety a younger one."

My sons, though four years apart, were very close. Vinod wouldn't let Mithun drown. *Electrical engineering,* I think, foolishly perhaps: this man knows important secrets of the universe, things closed to me. Relief spins me lightheaded. No wonder my boys' photographs haven't turned up in the gallery of photos of the recovered dead. "Such pretty roses," I say.

"My wife loved pink roses. Every Friday I had to bring a bunch home. I used to say, Why? After twenty-odd years of marriage you're still needing proof positive of my love?" He has identified his wife and three of his children. Then others from Montreal, the lucky ones, intact families with no survivors. He chuckles as he wades back to shore. Then he swings around to ask me a question. "Mrs. Bhave, you are wanting to throw in some roses for your loved ones? I have two big ones left."

But I have other things to float: Vinod's pocket calculator; a half-painted model B-52 for my Mithun. They'd want them on their island. And for my husband? For him I let fall into the calm, glassy waters a poem I wrote in the hospital yesterday. Finally he'll know my feelings for him.

"Don't tumble, the rocks are slippery," Dr. Ranganathan cautions. He holds out a hand for me to grab.

Then it's time to get back on the bus, time to rush back to our waiting posts on hospital benches.

Kusum is one of the lucky ones. The lucky ones flew here, identified in multiplicate their loved ones, then will fly to India with the bodies for proper ceremonies. Satish is one of the few males who surfaced. The photos of faces we saw on the walls in an office at Heathrow and here in the hospital are mostly of women. Women have more body fat, a nun said to me matter-of-factly. They float better.

Today I was stopped by a young sailor on the street. He had loaded bodies, he'd gone into the water when—he checks my face for signs of strength—when the sharks were first spotted. I don't blush, and he breaks down. "It's all right," I say. "Thank you." I heard about the sharks from Dr. Ranganathan. In his orderly mind, science brings understanding, it holds no terror. It is the shark's duty. For every deer there is a hunter, for every fish a fisherman.

The Irish are not shy; they rush to me and give me hugs and some are crying. I cannot imagine reactions like that on the streets of Toronto. Just strangers, and I am touched. Some carry flowers with them and give them to any Indian they see.

After lunch, a policeman I have gotten to know quite well catches hold of me. He says he thinks he has a match for Vinod. I explain what a good swimmer Vinod is.

"You want me with you when you look at photos?" Dr. Ranganathan walks ahead of me into the picture gallery. In these matters, he is a scientist, and I am grateful. It is a new perspective. "They have performed miracles," he says. "We are indebted to them."

The first day or two the policemen showed us relatives only one picture at a time; now they're in a hurry, they're eager to lay out the possibles, and even the probables.

The face on the photo is of a boy much like Vinod; the same intelligent eyes, the same thick brows dipping into a V. But this boy's features, even his cheeks, are puffier, wider, mushier.

"No." My gaze is pulled by other pictures. There are five other boys who look like Vinod.

The nun assigned to console me rubs the first picture with a fingertip. "When they've been in the water for a while, love, they look a little heavier." The bones under the skin are broken, they said on the first day—try to adjust your memories. It's important.

"It's not him. I'm his mother. I'd know."

"I know this one!" Dr. Ranganathan cries out, and suddenly, from the back of the gallery, "And this one!" I think he senses that I don't want to find my boys. "They are the Kutty brothers. They were also from Montreal." I don't mean to be crying. On the contrary, I am ecstatic. My suitcase in the hotel is packed heavy with dry clothes for my boys.

The policeman starts to cry. "I am so sorry, I am so sorry, ma'am. I really thought we had a match."

With the nun ahead of us and the policeman behind, we, the unlucky ones without our children's bodies, file out of the makeshift gallery.

From Ireland most of us go on to India. Kusum and I take the same direct flight to Bombay, so I can help her clear customs quickly. But we have to argue with a man in uniform. He has large boils on his face. The boils swell and glow with sweat as we argue with him. He wants Kusum to wait in line and he refuses to take authority because his boss is on a tea break. But Kusum won't let her coffins out of sight, and I shan't desert her though I know that my parents, elderly and diabetic, must be waiting in a stuffy car in a scorching lot.

"You bastard!" I scream at the man with the popping boils. Other passengers press closer. "You think we're smuggling contraband in those coffins!"

Once upon a time we were well-brought-up women; we were dutiful wives who kept our heads veiled, our voices shy and sweet.

In India, I become, once again, an only child of rich, ailing parents. Old friends of the family come to pay their respects. Some are Sikh, and inwardly, involuntarily, I cringe. My parents are progressive people; they do not blame communities for a few individuals.

In Canada it is a different story now.

"Stay longer," my mother pleads. "Canada is a cold place. Why would you want to be by yourself?" I stay.

Three months pass. Then another.

"Vikram wouldn't have wanted you to give up things!" they protest. They call my husband by the name he was born with. In Toronto he'd changed to Vik so the men he worked with at his office would find his name as easy as Rod or Chris. "You know, the dead aren't cut off from us!"

My grandmother, the spoiled daughter of a rich zamindar, shaved her head with rusty razor blades when she was widowed at sixteen. My grandfather died of childhood diabetes when he was nineteen, and she saw herself as the harbinger of bad luck. My mother grew up without parents, raised indifferently by an uncle, while her true mother slept in a hut behind the main estate house and took her food with the servants. She grew up a rationalist. My parents abhor mindless mortification.

The zamindar's daughter kept stubborn faith in Vedic rituals; my parents rebelled. I am trapped between two modes of knowledge. At thirty-six, I am too old to start over and too young to give up. Like my husband's spirit, I flutter between worlds.

Courting aphasia, we travel. We travel with our phalanx of servants and poor relatives. To hill stations and to beach resorts. We play contract bridge in dusty gymkhana clubs. We ride stubby ponies up crumbly mountain trails. At tea dances, we let ourselves be twirled twice round the ballroom. We hit the holy spots we hadn't made time for before. In Varanasi, Kalighat, Rishikesh, Hardwar, astrologers and palmists seek me out and for a fee offer me cosmic consolations.

Already the widowers among us are being shown new bride candidates. They cannot resist the call of custom, the authority of their parents and older brothers. They must marry; it is the duty of a man to look after a wife. The new wives will be young widows with children, destitute but of good family. They will make loving wives, but the men will shun them. I've had calls from the men over crackling Indian telephone lines. "Save me," they say, these substantial, educated, successful men of forty. "My parents are arranging a marriage for me." In a month they will have buried one family and returned to Canada with a new bride and partial family.

I am comparatively lucky. No one here thinks of arranging a husband for an unlucky widow.

Then, on the third day of the sixth month into this odyssey, in an abandoned temple in a tiny Himalayan village, as I make my offering of flowers and sweetmeats to the god of a tribe of animists, my husband descends to me. He is squatting next to a scrawny sadhu in moth-eaten robes. Vikram wears the vanilla suit he wore the last time I hugged him. The sadhu tosses petals on a butter-fed flame, reciting Sanskrit mantras, and sweeps his face of flies. My husband takes my hands in his.

You're beautiful, he starts. Then, *What are you doing here?*

Shall I stay? I ask. He only smiles, but already the image is fading. *You must finish alone what we started together.* No seaweed wreathes his mouth. He speaks too fast, just as he used to when we were an envied family in our pink split-level. He is gone.

In the windowless altar room, smoky with joss sticks and clarified butter lamps, a sweaty hand gropes for my blouse. I do not shriek. The sadhu arranges his robe. The lamps hiss and sputter out.

When we come out of the temple, my mother says, "Did you feel something weird in there?"

My mother has no patience with ghosts, prophetic dreams, holy men, and cults.

"No," I lie. "Nothing."

But she knows that she's lost me. She knows that in days I shall be leaving.

Kusum's put up her house for sale. She wants to live in an ashram in Hardwar. Moving to Hardwar was her swami's idea. Her swami runs two ashrams, the one in Hardwar and another here in Toronto.

"Don't run away," I tell her.

"I'm not running away," she says. "I'm pursuing inner peace. You think you or that Ranganathan fellow are better off?"

Pam's left for California. She wants to do some modeling, she says. She says when she comes into her share of the insurance money she'll open a yoga-cum-aerobics studio in Hollywood. She sends me postcards so naughty I daren't leave them on the coffee table. Her mother has withdrawn from her and the world.

The rest of us don't lose touch, that's the point. Talk is all we have, says Dr. Ranganathan, who has also resisted his relatives and returned to Montreal and to his job, alone. He says, Whom better to talk with than other relatives? We've been melted down and recast as a new tribe.

He calls me twice a week from Montreal. Every Wednesday night and every Saturday afternoon. He is changing jobs, going to Ottawa. But Ottawa is over a hundred miles away, and he is forced to drive two hundred and twenty miles a day from his home in Montreal. He can't bring himself to sell his house. The house is a temple, he says; the king-sized bed in the master bedroom is a shrine. He sleeps on a folding cot. A devotee.

There are still some hysterical relatives. Judith Templeton's list of those needing help and those who've "accepted" is in nearly perfect balance. Acceptance means you speak of your family in the past tense and you make active plans for moving ahead with your life. There are courses at Seneca and Ryerson we could be taking. Her gleaming leather briefcase is full of college catalogues and lists of cultural societies that need our help. She has done impressive work, I tell her.

"In the textbooks on grief management," she replies—I am her confidante, I realize, one of the few whose grief has not sprung bizarre obsessions—"there are stages to pass through: rejection, depression, acceptance, reconstruction." She has compiled a chart and finds that six months after the tragedy, none of us still rejects reality, but only a handful are reconstructing. "Depressed acceptance" is the plateau we've reached. Remarriage is a major step in reconstruction (though she's a little surprised, even shocked, over *how* quickly some of the men have taken on new families). Selling one's house and changing jobs and cities is healthy.

How to tell Judith Templeton that my family surrounds me, and that like creatures in epics, they've changed shapes? She sees me as calm and accepting but worries that I have no job, no career. My closest friends are worse off than I. I cannot tell her my days, even my nights, are thrilling.

She asks me to help with families she can't reach at all. An elderly couple in Agincourt whose sons were killed just weeks after they had brought their parents over from a village in Punjab. From their names, I know they are Sikh. Judith Templeton and a translator have visited them twice with offers of money for airfare to Ireland, with bank forms, power-of-attorney forms, but they have refused to sign, or to leave their tiny apartment. Their sons' money is frozen in the bank. Their sons' investment apartments have been trashed by tenants, the furnishings sold off. The parents fear that anything they sign or any money they receive will end the company's or the country's obligations to them. They fear they are selling their sons for two airline tickets to a place they've never seen.

The high-rise apartment is a tower of Indians and West Indians, with a sprinkling of Orientals. The nearest bus-stop kiosk is lined with women in saris. Boys practice cricket in the parking lot. Inside the building, even I wince a bit from the ferocity of onion fumes, the distinctive and immediate Indianness of frying ghee, but Judith Templeton maintains a steady flow of information. These poor old people are in imminent danger of losing their place and all their services.

I say to her, "They are Sikh. They will not open up to a Hindu woman." And what I want to add is, as much as I try not to, I stiffen now at the sight of beards and turbans. I remember a time when we all trusted each other in this new country, it was only the new country we worried about.

The two rooms are dark and stuffy. The lights are off, and an oil lamp sputters on the coffee table. The bent old lady has let us in, and her husband is wrapping a white turban over his oiled, hip-length hair. She immediately goes to the kitchen, and I hear the most familiar sound of an Indian home, tap water hitting and filling a teapot.

They have not paid their utility bills, out of fear and inability to write a check. The telephone is gone; electricity and gas and water are soon to follow. They have told Judith their sons will provide. They are good boys, and they have always earned and looked after their parents.

We converse a bit in Hindi. They do not ask about the crash and I wonder if I should bring it up. If they think I am here merely as a translator, then they may feel insulted. There are thousands of Punjabi speakers, Sikhs, in Toronto to do a better job. And so I say to the old lady, "I too have lost my sons, and my husband, in the crash."

Her eyes immediately fill with tears. The man mutters a few words which sound like a blessing. "God provides and God takes away," he says.

I want to say, But only men destroy and give back nothing. "My boys and my husband are not coming back," I say. "We have to understand that."

Now the old woman responds. "But who is to say? Man alone does not decide these things." To this her husband adds his agreement.

Judith asks about the bank papers, the release forms. With a stroke of the pen, they will have a provincial trustee to pay their bills, invest their money, send them a monthly pension.

"Do you know this woman?" I ask them.

The man raises his hand from the table, turns it over, and seems to regard each finger separately before he answers. "This young lady is always coming here, we make tea for her, and she leaves papers for us to sign." His eyes scan a pile of papers in the corner of the room. "Soon we will be out of tea, then will she go away?"

The old lady adds, "I have asked my neighbors and no one else gets *angrezi* visitors. What have we done?"

"It's her job," I try to explain. "The government is worried. Soon you will have no place to stay, no lights, no gas, no water."

"Government will get its money. Tell her not to worry, we are honorable people."

I try to explain the government wishes to give money, not take. He raises his hand. "Let them take," he says. "We are accustomed to that. That is no problem."

"We are strong people," says the wife. "Tell her that."

"Who needs all this machinery?" demands the husband. "It is unhealthy, the bright lights, the cold air on a hot day, the cold food, the four gas rings. God will provide, not government."

"When our boys return," the mother says.

Her husband sucks his teeth. "Enough talk," he says.

Judith breaks in. "Have you convinced them?" The snaps on her cordovan briefcase go off like firecrackers in that quiet apartment. She lays the sheaf of legal papers on the coffee table. "If they can't write their names, an X will do—I've told them that."

Now the old lady has shuffled to the kitchen and soon emerges with a pot of tea and two cups. "I think my bladder will go first on a job like this," Judith says to me, smiling. "If only there was some way of reaching them. Please thank her for the tea. Tell her she's very kind."

I nod in Judith's direction and tell them in Hindi, "She thanks you for the tea. She thinks you are being very hospitable but she doesn't have the slightest idea what it means."

I want to say, Humor her. I want to say, My boys and my husband are with me too, more than ever. I look in the old man's eyes and I can read his stubborn, peasant's message: *I have protected this woman as best I can. She is the only person I have left. Give to me or take from me what you will, but I will not sign for it. I will not pretend that I accept.*

In the car, Judith says, "You see what I'm up against? I'm sure they're lovely people, but their stubbornness and ignorance are driving me crazy. They think signing a paper is signing their sons' death warrants, don't they?"

I am looking out the window. I want to say, *In our culture, it is a parent's duty to hope.*

"Now Shaila, this next woman is a real mess. She cries day and night, and she refuses all medical help. We may have to—"

"Let me out at the subway," I say.

"I beg your pardon?" I can feel those blue eyes staring at me.

It would not be like her to disobey. She merely disapproves, and slows at a corner to let me out. Her voice is plaintive. "Is there anything I said? Anything I did?"

I could answer her suddenly in a dozen ways, but I choose not to. "Shaila? Let's talk about it," I hear, then slam the door.

A wife and mother begins her new life in a new country, and that life is cut short. Yet her husband tells her, Complete what we have started. We, who stayed out of politics and came halfway around the world to avoid religious and political feuding, have been the first in the New World to die from it. I no longer know what we started, nor how to complete it. I write letters to the editors of local papers and to members of Parliament. Now at least they admit it was a bomb. One MP answers back, with sympathy, but with a challenge. You want to make a difference? Work on a campaign. Work on mine. Politicize the Indian voter.

My husband's old lawyer helps me set up a trust. Vikram was a saver and a careful investor. He had saved the boys' boarding school and college fees. I sell the pink house at four times what we paid for it and take a small apartment downtown. I am looking for a charity to support.

We are deep in the Toronto winter, gray skies, icy pavements. I stay indoors, watching television. I have tried to assess my situation, how best to live my life, to complete what we began so many years ago. Kusum has written me from Hardwar that her life is now serene. She has seen Satish and has heard her daughter sing again. Kusum was on a pilgrimage, passing through a village, when she heard a young girl's voice, singing one of her daughter's favorite *bhajans.* She followed the music through the squalor of a Himalayan village, to a hut where a young girl, an exact replica of her daughter, was fanning coals under the kitchen fire. When she appeared, the girl cried out, "Ma!" and ran away. What did I think of that?

I think I can only envy her.

Pam didn't make it to California, but writes me from Vancouver. She works in a department store, giving makeup hints to Indian and Oriental girls. Dr. Ranganathan has given up his commute, given up his house and job, and accepted an academic position in Texas, where no one knows his story and he has vowed not to tell it. He calls me now once a week.

I wait, I listen and I pray, but Vikram has not returned to me. The voices and the shapes and the nights filled with visions ended abruptly several weeks ago.

I take it as a sign.

One rare, beautiful, sunny day last week, returning from a small errand on Yonge Street, I was walking through the park from the subway to my apartment. I live equidistant from the Ontario Houses of Parliament and the University of Toronto. The day was not cold, but something in the bare trees caught my attention. I looked up from the gravel, into the branches and the clear blue sky beyond. I thought I heard the rustling of larger forms, and I waited a moment for voices. Nothing.

"What?" I asked.

Then as I stood in the path looking north to Queen's Park and west to the university, I heard the voices of my family one last time. *Your time has come,* they said. *Go, be brave.*

I do not know where this voyage I have begun will end. I do not know which direction I will take. I dropped the package on a park bench and started walking.

ALICE MUNRO

Meneseteung

ALICE MUNRO (1931–) grew up in Wingham, Ontario. She has published many collections of stories, including *Dance of the Happy Shades, Something I've Been Meaning to Tell You, The Beggar Maid, The Moons of Jupiter, The Progress of Love, Friend of My Youth, Open Secrets,* and *Selected Stories,* as well as a novel, *Lives of Girls and Women.* She has received many awards, including three Governor General's Literary Awards, the Lannan Literary Award, and the W. H. Smith Award. Munro and her husband divide their time between Clinton, Ontario, near Lake Huron, and Comox, British Columbia.

I

Columbine, bloodroot,
And wild bergamot,
Gathering armfuls,
Giddily we go.

Offerings, the book is called. Gold lettering on a dull-blue cover. The author's full name underneath: Almeda Joynt Roth. The local paper, the *Vidette,* referred to her as "our poetess." There seems to be a mixture of respect and contempt, both for her calling and for her sex—or for their predictable conjuncture. In the front of the book is a photograph, with the photographer's name in one corner, and the date: 1865. The book was published later, in 1873.

The poetess has a long face; a rather long nose; full, somber dark eyes, which seem ready to roll down her cheeks like giant tears; a lot of dark hair gathered around her face in droopy rolls and curtains. A streak of gray hair plain to see, although she is, in this picture, only twenty-five. Not a pretty girl but the sort of woman who may age well, who probably won't get fat. She wears a tucked and braid-trimmed dark dress or jacket, with a lacy, floppy arrangement of white material—frills or a bow—filling the deep V at the neck. She also wears a hat, which might be made of velvet, in a dark color to match the dress. It's the untrimmed, shapeless hat, something like a soft beret, that makes me see artistic intentions, or at least a shy and stubborn eccentricity, in this young woman, whose long neck and forward-inclining head indicate as well that she is tall and slender and somewhat awkward. From the waist up, she looks like a young nobleman of another century. But perhaps it was the fashion.

"In 1854," she writes in the preface to her book, "my father brought us—my mother, my sister Catherine, my brother William, and me—to the wilds of Canada West (as it then was). My father was a harness-maker by trade, but a cultivated man who could quote by heart from the Bible, Shakespeare, and the writings of Edmund Burke. He prospered in this newly opened land and was able to set up a harness and leather-goods store, and after a year to build the comfortable house in which I live (alone) today. I was fourteen years old, the eldest of the children, when we came into this country from Kingston, a town whose handsome streets I have not seen again but often remember. My sister was eleven and my brother nine. The third summer that we lived here, my brother and sister were taken ill of a prevalent fever and died within a few days of each other. My dear mother did not regain her spirits after this blow to our family. Her health declined, and after another three years she died. I then became housekeeper to my father and was happy to make his home for twelve years, until he died suddenly one morning at his shop.

"From my earliest years I have delighted in verse and I have occupied myself—and sometimes allayed my griefs, which have been no more, I know, than any sojourner on earth must encounter—with many floundering efforts at its composition. My fingers, indeed, were always too clumsy for crochetwork, and those dazzling productions of embroidery which one sees often today—the overflowing fruit and flower baskets, the little Dutch boys, the bonneted maidens with their watering cans—have likewise proved to be beyond my skill. So I offer instead, as the product of my leisure hours, these rude posies, these ballads, couplets, reflections."

Titles of some of the poems: "Children at Their Games," "The Gypsy Fair," "A Visit to My Family," "Angels in the Snow," "Champlain at the Mouth of the Meneseteung," "The Passing of the Old Forest," and "A Garden Medley." There are some other, shorter poems, about birds and wildflowers and snowstorms. There is some comically intentioned doggerel about what people are thinking about as they listen to the sermon in church.

"Children at Their Games": The writer, a child, is playing with her brother and sister—one of those games in which children on different sides try to entice and catch each other. She plays on in the deepening twilight, until she realizes that she is alone, and much older. Still she hears the (ghostly) voices of her brother and sister calling. *Come over, come over, let Meda come over.* (Perhaps Almeda was called Meda in the family, or perhaps she shortened her name to fit the poem.)

"The Gypsy Fair": The Gypsies have an encampment near the town, a "fair," where they sell cloth and trinkets, and the writer as a child is afraid that she may be stolen by them, taken away from her family. Instead, her family has been taken away from her, stolen by Gypsies she can't locate or bargain with.

"A Visit to My Family": A visit to the cemetery, a one-sided conversation.

"Angels in the Snow": The writer once taught her brother and sister to make "angels" by lying down in the snow and moving their arms to create wing shapes. Her brother always jumped up carelessly, leaving an angel with a crippled wing. Will this be made perfect in Heaven, or will he be flying with his own makeshift, in circles?

"Champlain at the Mouth of the Meneseteung": This poem celebrates the popular, untrue belief that the explorer sailed down the eastern shore of Lake Huron and landed at the mouth of the major river.

"The Passing of the Old Forest": A list of all the trees—their names, appearance, and uses—that were cut down in the original forest, with a general description of the bears, wolves, eagles, deer, waterfowl.

"A Garden Medley": Perhaps planned as a companion to the forest poem. Catalogue of plants brought from European countries, with bits of history and legend attached, and final Canadianness resulting from this mixture.

The poems are written in quatrains or couplets. There are a couple of attempts at sonnets, but mostly the rhyme scheme is simple—*abab* or *abcb.* The rhyme used is what was once called "masculine" ("shore"/"before"), though once in a while it is "feminine" ("quiver"/"river"). Are those terms familiar anymore? No poem is unrhymed.

II

White roses cold as snow
Bloom where those "angels" lie.
Do they but rest below
Or, in God's wonder, fly?

In 1879, Almeda Roth was still living in the house at the corner of Pearl and Dufferin streets, the house her father had built for his family. The house is there today: the manager of the liquor store lives in it. It's covered with aluminum siding; a closed-in porch has replaced the veranda. The woodshed, the fence, the gates, the privy, the barn—all these are gone. A photograph taken in the eighteen-eighties shows them all in place. The house and fence look a little shabby, in need of paint, but perhaps that is just because of the bleached-out look of the brownish photograph. The lace-curtained windows look like white eyes. No big shade tree is in sight, and, in fact, the tall elms that overshadowed the town until the nineteen-fifties, as well as the maples that shade it now, are skinny young trees with rough fences around them to protect them from the cows. Without the shelter of those trees, there is a great exposure—back yards, clotheslines, woodpiles, patchy sheds and barns and privies—all bare, exposed, provisional looking. Few houses would have anything like a lawn, just a patch of plantains and anthills and raked dirt. Perhaps petunias growing on top of a stump, in a round box. Only the main street is graveled; the other streets are dirt roads, muddy or dusty according to season. Yards must be fenced to keep animals out. Cows are tethered in vacant lots or pastured in back yards, but sometimes they get loose. Pigs get loose, too, and dogs roam free or nap in a lordly way on the boardwalks. The town has taken root, it's not going to vanish, yet it still has some of the look of an encampment. And, like an encampment, it's busy all the time—full of people, who, within the town, usually walk wherever they're going; full of animals, which leave horse buns, cowpats, dog turds, that ladies have to hitch up their skirts for; full of the noise of building and of drivers shouting at their horses and of the trains that come in several times a day.

I read about that life in the *Vidette.*

The population is younger than it is now, than it will ever be again. People past fifty usually don't come to a raw, new place. There are quite a few people in the cemetery already, but most of them died young, in accidents or childbirth or epidemics. It's youth that's in evidence in town. Children—boys—rove through the streets in gangs. School is compulsory for only four months a year, and there are lots of occasional jobs that even a child of eight or nine can do—pulling flax, holding horses, delivering groceries, sweeping the boardwalk in front of stores. A good deal of time they spend looking for adventures. One day they follow an old woman, a drunk nicknamed Queen Aggie. They get her into a wheelbarrow and trundle her all over town, then dump her into a ditch to sober her up. They also spend a lot of time around the railway station. They jump on shunting cars and dart between them and dare each other to take chances, which once in a while result in their getting maimed or killed. And they keep an eye out for any strangers coming into town. They follow them, offer to carry their bags, and direct them (for a five-cent piece) to a hotel. Strangers who don't look so prosperous are taunted and tormented. Speculation surrounds all of them—it's like a cloud of flies. Are they coming to town to start up a new business, to persuade people to invest in some scheme, to sell cures or gimmicks, to preach on the street corners? All these things are possible any day of the week. Be on your guard, the *Vidette* tells people. These are times of opportunity and danger. Tramps, confidence men, hucksters, shysters, plain thieves, are traveling the roads, and particularly the railroads. Thefts are announced: money invested and never seen again, a pair of trousers taken from the clothesline, wood from the woodpile, eggs from the henhouse. Such incidents increase in the hot weather.

Hot weather brings accidents, too. More horses run wild then, upsetting buggies. Hands caught in the wringer while doing the washing, a man lopped in two at the sawmill, a leaping boy killed in a fall of lumber at the lumberyard. Nobody sleeps well. Babies wither with summer complaint, and fat people can't catch their breath. Bodies must be buried in a hurry. One day a man goes through the streets ringing a cowbell and calling "Repent! Repent!" It's not a stranger this time, it's a young man who works at the butcher shop. Take him home, wrap him in cold wet cloths, give him some nerve medicine, keep him in bed, pray for his wits. If he doesn't recover, he must go to the asylum.

Almeda Roth's house faces on Dufferin Street, which is a street of considerable respectability. On this street merchants, a mill owner, an operator of salt wells, have their houses. But Pearl Street, which her back windows overlook and her back gate opens onto, is another story. Workmen's houses are adjacent to hers. Small but decent row houses—that is all right. Things deteriorate toward the end of the block, and the next, last one becomes dismal. Nobody but the poorest people, the unrespectable and undeserving poor, would live there at the edge of a boghole (drained since then), called the Pearl Street Swamp. Bushy and luxuriant weeds grow there, makeshift shacks have been put up, there are piles of refuse and debris and crowds of runty children, slops are flung from doorways. The town tries to compel these people to build privies, but they would just as soon go in the bushes. If a gang of boys goes down there in search of adventure, it's likely they'll get more than they bargained for. It is said that even the town constable won't go down Pearl Street on a Saturday night. Almeda Roth has never walked past the row housing. In one of those houses lives the young girl Annie, who helps her with her housecleaning. That young girl herself, being a decent girl, has never walked down to the last block or the swamp. No decent woman ever would.

But that same swamp, lying to the east of Almeda Roth's house, presents a fine sight at dawn. Almeda sleeps at the back of the house. She keeps to the same bedroom she once shared with her sister Catherine—she would not think of moving to the larger front bedroom, where her mother used to lie in bed all day, and which was later the solitary domain of her father. From her window she can see the sun rising, the swamp mist filling with light, the bulky, nearest trees floating against that mist and the trees behind turning transparent. Swamp oaks, soft maples, tamarack, bitternut.

III

Here where the river meets the inland sea,
Spreading her blue skirts from the solemn wood,
I think of birds and beasts and vanished men,
Whose pointed dwellings on these pale sands stood.

One of the strangers who arrived at the railway station a few years ago was Jarvis Poulter, who now occupies the house next to Almeda Roth's—separated from hers by a vacant lot, which he has bought, on Dufferin Street. The house is plainer than the Roth house and has no fruit trees or flowers planted around it. It is understood that this is a natural result of Jarvis Poulter's being a widower and living alone. A man may keep his house decent, but he will never—if he is a proper man—do much to decorate it. Marriage forces him to live with more ornament as well as sentiment, and it protects him, also, from the extremities of his own nature—from a frigid parsimony or a luxuriant sloth, from squalor, and from excessive sleeping, drinking, smoking, or freethinking.

> In the interests of economy, it is believed, a certain estimable gentleman of our town persists in fetching water from the public tap and supplementing his fuel supply by picking up the loose coal along the railway track. Does he think to repay the town or the railway company with a supply of free salt?

This is the *Vidette,* full of shy jokes, innuendo, plain accusation, that no newspaper would get away with today. It's Jarvis Poulter they're talking about—though in other passages he is spoken of with great respect, as a civil magistrate, an employer, a churchman. He is close, that's all. An eccentric, to a degree. All of which may be a result of his single condition, his widower's life. Even carrying his water from the town tap and filling his coal pail along the railway track. This is a decent citizen, prosperous: a tall—slightly paunchy?—man in a dark suit with polished boots. A beard? Black hair streaked with gray. A severe and self-possessed air, and a large pale wart among the bushy hairs of one eyebrow? People talk about a young, pretty, beloved wife, dead in childbirth or some horrible accident, like a house fire or a railway disaster. There is no ground for this, but it adds interest. All he has told them is that his wife is dead.

He came to this part of the country looking for oil. The first oil well in the world was sunk in Lambton County, south of here, in the eighteen-fifties.

Drilling for oil, Jarvis Poulter discovered salt. He set to work to make the most of that. When he walks home from church with Almeda Roth, he tells her about his salt wells. They are twelve hundred feet deep. Heated water is pumped down into them, and that dissolves the salt. Then the brine is pumped to the surface. It is poured into great evaporator pans over slow, steady fires, so that the water is steamed off and the pure, excellent salt remains. A commodity for which the demand will never fail.

"The salt of the earth," Almeda says.

"Yes," he says, frowning. He may think this disrespectful. She did not intend it so. He speaks of competitors in other towns who are following his lead and trying to hog the market. Fortunately, their wells are not drilled so deep, or their evaporating is not done so efficiently. There is salt everywhere under this land, but it is not so easy to come by as some people think.

Does that not mean, Almeda says, that there was once a great sea?

Very likely, Jarvis Poulter says. Very likely. He goes on to tell her about other enterprises of his—a brickyard, a lime kiln. And he explains to her how this operates, and where the good clay is found. He also owns two farms, whose woodlots supply the fuel for his operations.

> Among the couples strolling home from church on a recent, sunny Sabbath morning we noted a certain salty gentleman and literary lady, not perhaps in their first youth but by no means blighted by the frosts of age. May we surmise?

This kind of thing pops up in the *Vidette* all the time.

May they surmise, and is this courting? Almeda Roth has a bit of money, which her father left her, and she has her house. She is not too old to have a couple of children. She is a good enough housekeeper, with the tendency toward fancy iced cakes and decorated tarts which is seen fairly often in old maids. (Honorable mention at the Fall Fair.) There is nothing wrong with her looks, and naturally she is in better shape than most married women of her age, not having been loaded down with work and children. But why was she passed over in her earlier, more marriageable years, in a place that needs women to be partnered and fruitful? She was a rather gloomy girl—that may have been the trouble. The deaths of her brother and sister and then of her mother, who lost her reason, in fact, a year before she died, and lay in her bed talking nonsense—those weighed on her, so she was not lively company. And all that reading and poetry—it seemed more of a drawback, a barrier, an obsession, in the young girl than in the middle-aged woman, who needed something, after all, to fill her time. Anyway, it's five years since her book was published, so perhaps she has got over that. Perhaps it was the proud, bookish father, encouraging her?

Everyone takes it for granted that Almeda Roth is thinking of Jarvis Poulter as a husband and would say yes if he asked her. And she is thinking of him.

She doesn't want to get her hopes up too much, she doesn't want to make a fool of herself. She would like a signal. If he attended church on Sunday evenings, there would be a chance, during some months of the year, to walk home after dark. He would carry a lantern. (There is as yet no street lighting in town.) He would swing the lantern to light the way in front of the lady's feet and observe their narrow and delicate shape. He might catch her arm as they step off the boardwalk. But he does not go to church at night.

Nor does he call for her, and walk with her *to* church on Sunday mornings. That would be a declaration. He walks her home, past his gate as far as hers; he lifts his hat then and leaves her. She does not invite him to come in—a woman living alone could never do such a thing. As soon as a man and woman of almost any age are alone together within four walls, it is assumed that anything may happen. Spontaneous combustion, instant fornication, an attack of passion. Brute instinct, triumph of the senses. What possibilities men and women must see in each other to infer such dangers. Or, believing in the dangers, how often they must think about the possibilities.

When they walk side by side she can smell his shaving soap, the barber's oil, his pipe tobacco, the wool and linen and leather smell of his manly clothes. The correct, orderly, heavy clothes are like those she used to brush and starch and iron for her father. She misses that job—her father's appreciation, his dark, kind authority. Jarvis Poulter's garments, his smell, his movement, all cause the skin on the side of her body next to him to tingle hopefully, and a meek shiver raises the hairs on her arms. Is this to be taken as a sign of love? She thinks of him coming into her—*their*—bedroom in his long underwear and his hat. She knows this outfit is ridiculous, but in her mind he does not look so; he has the solemn effrontery of a figure in a dream. He comes into the room and lies down on the bed beside her, preparing to take her in his arms. Surely he removes his hat? She doesn't know, for at this point a fit of welcome and submission overtakes her, a buried gasp. He would be her husband.

One thing she has noticed about married women, and that is how many of them have to go about creating their husbands. They have to start ascribing preferences, opinions, dictatorial ways. Oh, yes, they say, my husband is very particular. He won't touch turnips. He won't eat fried meat. (Or he will only eat fried meat.) He likes me to wear blue (brown) all the time. He can't stand organ music. He hates to see a woman go out bareheaded. He would kill me if I took one puff of tobacco. This way, bewildered, sidelong-looking men are made over, made into husbands, heads of households. Almeda Roth cannot imagine herself doing that. She wants a man who doesn't have to be made, who is firm already and determined and mysterious to her. She does not look for companionship. Men—except for her father—seem to her deprived in some way, incurious. No doubt that is necessary, so that they will do what they have to do. Would she herself, knowing that there was salt in the earth, discover how to get it out and sell it? Not likely. She would be thinking about the ancient sea. That kind of speculation is what Jarvis Poulter has, quite properly, no time for.

Instead of calling for her and walking her to church, Jarvis Poulter might make another, more venturesome declaration. He could hire a horse and take her for a drive out to the country. If he did this, she would be both glad and sorry. Glad to be beside him, driven by him, receiving this attention from him in front of the world. And sorry to have the countryside removed for her—filmed over, in a way, by his talk and preoccupations. The countryside that she has written about in her poems actually takes diligence and determination to see. Some things must be disregarded. Manure piles, of course, and boggy fields full of high, charred stumps, and great heaps of brush waiting for a good day for burning. The meandering creeks have been straightened, turned into ditches with high, muddy banks. Some of the crop fields and pasture fields are fenced with big, clumsy uprooted stumps, others are held in a crude stitchery of rail fences. The trees have all been cleared back to the woodlots. And the woodlots are all second growth. No trees along the roads or lanes or around the farmhouses, except a few that are newly planted, young and weedy looking. Clusters of log barns—the grand barns that are to dominate the countryside for the next hundred years are just beginning to be built—and mean-looking log houses, and every four or five miles a ragged little settlement with a church and school and store and a blacksmith shop. A raw countryside just wrenched from the forest, but swarming with people. Every hundred acres is a farm, every farm has a family, most families have ten or twelve children. (This is the country that will send out wave after wave of settlers—it's already starting to send them—to northern Ontario and the West.) It's true that you can gather wildflowers in spring in the woodlots, but you'd have to walk through herds of horned cows to get to them.

IV

The Gypsies have departed.
Their camping-ground is bare.
Oh, boldly would I bargain now
At the Gypsy Fair.

Almeda suffers a good deal from sleeplessness, and the doctor has given her bromides and nerve medicine. She takes the bromides, but the drops gave her dreams that were too vivid and disturbing, so she has put the bottle by for an emergency. She told the doctor her eyeballs felt dry, like hot glass, and her joints ached. Don't read so much, he said, don't study; get yourself good and tired out with housework, take exercise. He believes that her troubles would clear up if she got married. He believes this in spite of the fact that most of his nerve medicine is prescribed for married women.

So Almeda cleans house and helps clean the church, she lends a hand to friends who are wallpapering or getting ready for a wedding, she bakes one of her famous cakes for the Sunday-school picnic. On a hot Saturday in August she decides to make some grape jelly. Little jars of grape jelly will make fine Christmas presents, or offerings to the sick. But she started late in the day and the jelly is not made by nightfall. In fact, the hot pulp has just been dumped into the cheesecloth bag, to strain out the juice. Almeda drinks some tea and eats a slice of cake with butter (a childish indulgence of hers), and that's all she wants for supper. She washes her hair at the sink and sponges off her body, to be clean for Sunday. She doesn't light a lamp. She lies down on the bed with the window wide open and a sheet just up to her waist, and she does feel wonderfully tired. She can even feel a little breeze.

When she wakes up, the night seems fiery hot and full of threats. She lies sweating on her bed, and she has the impression that the noises she hears are knives and saws and axes—all angry implements chopping and jabbing and boring within her head. But it isn't true. As she comes further awake she recognizes the sounds that she has heard sometimes before—the fracas of a summer Saturday night on Pearl Street. Usually the noise centers on a fight. People are drunk, there is a lot of protest and encouragement concerning the fight, somebody will scream "Murder!" Once, there was a murder. But it didn't happen in a fight. An old man was stabbed to death in his shack, perhaps for a few dollars he kept in the mattress.

She gets out of bed and goes to the window. The night sky is clear, with no moon and with bright stars. Pegasus hangs straight ahead, over the swamp. Her father taught her that constellation—automatically, she counts its stars. Now she can make out distinct voices, individual contributions to the row. Some people, like herself, have evidently been wakened from sleep. "Shut up!" they are yelling. "Shut up that caterwauling or I'm going to come down and tan the arse off yez!"

But nobody shuts up. It's as if there were a ball of fire rolling up Pearl Street, shooting off sparks—only the fire is noise, it's yells and laughter and shrieks and curses, and the sparks are voices that shoot off alone. Two voices gradually distinguish themselves—a rising and falling howling cry and a steady throbbing, low-pitched stream of abuse that contains all those words which Almeda associates with danger and depravity and foul smells and disgusting sights. Someone—the person crying out, "Kill me! Kill me now!"—is being beaten. A woman is being beaten. She keeps crying, "Kill me! Kill me!" and sometimes her mouth seems choked with blood. Yet there is something taunting and triumphant about her cry. There is something theatrical about it. And the people around are calling out, "Stop it! Stop that!" or "Kill her! Kill her!" in a frenzy, as if at the theater or a sporting match or a prizefight. Yes, thinks Almeda, she has noticed that before—it is always partly a charade with these people; there is a clumsy sort of parody, an exaggeration, a missed connection. As if anything they did—even a murder—might be something they didn't quite believe but were powerless to stop.

Now there is the sound of something thrown—a chair, a plank?—and of a woodpile or part of a fence giving way. A lot of newly surprised cries, the sound of running, people getting out of the way, and the commotion has come much closer. Almeda can see a figure in a light dress, bent over and running. That will be the woman. She has got hold of something like a stick of wood or a shingle, and she turns and flings it at the darker figure running after her.

"Ah, go get her!" the voices cry. "Go baste her one!"

Many fall back now; just the two figures come on and grapple, and break loose again, and finally fall down against Almeda's fence. The sound they make becomes very confused—gagging, vomiting, grunting, pounding. Then a long, vibrating, choking sound of pain and self-abasement, self-abandonment, which could come from either or both of them.

Almeda has backed away from the window and sat down on the bed. Is that the sound of murder she has heard? What is to be done, what is she to do? She must light a lantern, she must go downstairs and light a lantern—she must go out into the yard, she must go downstairs. Into the yard. The lantern. She falls over on her bed and pulls the pillow to her face. In a minute. The stairs, the lantern. She sees herself already down there, in the back hall, drawing the bolt of the back door. She falls asleep.

She wakes, startled, in the early light. She thinks there is a big crow sitting on her windowsill, talking in a disapproving but unsurprised way about the events of the night before. "Wake up and move the wheelbarrow!" it says to her, scolding, and she understands that it means something else by "wheelbarrow"—something foul and sorrowful. Then she is awake and sees that there is no such bird. She gets up at once and looks out the window.

Down against her fence there is a pale lump pressed—a body.

Wheelbarrow.

She puts a wrapper over her nightdress and goes downstairs. The front rooms are still shadowy, the blinds down in the kitchen. Something goes *plop, plup,* in a leisurely, censorious way, reminding her of the conversation of the crow. It's just the grape juice, straining overnight. She pulls the bolt and goes out the back door. Spiders have draped their webs over the doorway in the night, and the hollyhocks are drooping, heavy with dew. By the fence, she parts the sticky hollyhocks and looks down and she can see.

A woman's body heaped up there, turned on her side with her face squashed down into the earth. Almeda can't see her face. But there is a bare breast let loose, brown nipple pulled long like a cow's teat, and a bare haunch and leg, the haunch bearing a bruise as big as a sunflower. The unbruised skin is grayish, like a plucked, raw drumstick. Some kind of nightgown or all-purpose dress she has on. Smelling of vomit. Urine, drink, vomit.

Barefoot, in her nightgown and flimsy wrapper, Almeda runs away. She runs around the side of her house between the apple trees and the veranda; she opens the front gate and flees down Dufferin Street to Jarvis Poulter's house, which is the nearest to hers. She slaps the flat of her hand many times against the door.

"There is the body of a woman," she says when Jarvis Poulter appears at last. He is in his dark trousers, held up with braces, and his shirt is half unbuttoned, his face unshaven, his hair standing up on his head. "Mr. Poulter, excuse me. A body of a woman. At my back gate."

He looks at her fiercely. "Is she dead?"

His breath is dank, his face creased, his eyes bloodshot.

"Yes. I think murdered," says Almeda. She can see a little of his cheerless front hall. His hat on a chair. "In the night I woke up. I heard a racket down on Pearl Street," she says, struggling to keep her voice low and sensible. "I could hear this—pair. I could hear a man and a woman fighting."

He picks up his hat and puts it on his head. He closes and locks the front door, and puts the key in his pocket. They walk along the boardwalk and she sees that she is in her bare feet. She holds back what she feels a need to say next—that she is responsible, she could have run out with a lantern, she could have screamed (but who needed more screams?), she could have beat the man off. She could have run for help then, not now.

They turn down Pearl Street, instead of entering the Roth yard. Of course the body is still there. Hunched up, half bare, the same as before.

Jarvis Poulter doesn't hurry or halt. He walks straight over to the body and looks down at it, nudges the leg with the toe of his boot, just as you'd nudge a dog or a sow.

"You," he says, not too loudly but firmly, and nudges again.

Almeda tastes bile at the back of her throat.

"Alive," says Jarvis Poulter, and the woman confirms this. She stirs, she grunts weakly.

Almeda says, "I will get the doctor." If she had touched the woman, if she had forced herself to touch her, she would not have made such a mistake.

"Wait," says Jarvis Poulter. "Wait. Let's see if she can get up."

"Get up, now," he says to the woman. "Come on. Up, now. Up."

Now a startling thing happens. The body heaves itself onto all fours, the head is lifted—the hair all matted with blood and vomit—and the woman begins to bang this head, hard and rhythmically, against Almeda Roth's picket fence. As she bangs her head she finds her voice, and lets out an open-mouthed yowl, full of strength and what sounds like an anguished pleasure.

"Far from dead," says Jarvis Poulter. "And I wouldn't bother the doctor."

"There's blood," says Almeda as the woman turns her smeared face.

"From her nose," he says. "Not fresh." He bends down and catches the horrid hair close to the scalp to stop the head banging.

"You stop that now," he says. "Stop it. Gwan home now. Gwan home, where you belong." The sound coming out of the woman's mouth has stopped. He shakes her head slightly, warning her, before he lets go of her hair. "Gwan home!"

Released, the woman lunges forward, pulls herself to her feet. She can walk. She weaves and stumbles down the street, making intermittent, cautious noises of protest. Jarvis Poulter watches her for a moment to make sure that she's on her way. Then he finds a large burdock leaf, on which he wipes his hand. He says, "There goes your dead body!"

The back gate being locked, they walk around to the front. The front gate stands open. Almeda still feels sick. Her abdomen is bloated; she is hot and dizzy.

"The front door is locked," she says faintly. "I came out by the kitchen." If only he would leave her, she could go straight to the privy. But he follows. He follows her as far as the back door and into the back hall. He speaks to her in a tone of harsh joviality that she has never before heard from him. "No need for alarm," he says. "It's only the consequences of drink. A lady oughtn't to be living alone so close to a bad neighborhood." He takes hold of her arm just above the elbow. She can't open her mouth to speak to him, to say thank you. If she opened her mouth she would retch.

What Jarvis Poulter feels for Almeda Roth at this moment is just what he has not felt during all those circumspect walks and all his own solitary calculations of her probable worth, undoubted respectability, adequate comeliness. He has not been able to imagine her as a wife. Now that is possible. He is sufficiently stirred by her loosened hair—prematurely gray but thick and soft—her flushed face, her light clothing, which nobody but a husband should see. And by her indiscretion, her agitation, her foolishness, her need?

"I will call on you later," he says to her. "I will walk with you to church."

> At the corner of Pearl and Dufferin streets last Sunday morning there was discovered, by a lady resident there, the body of a certain woman of Pearl Street, thought to be dead but only, as it turned out, dead drunk. She was roused from her heavenly—or otherwise—stupor by the firm persuasion of Mr. Poulter, a neighbour and a Civil Magistrate, who had been summoned by the lady resident. Incidents of this sort, unseemly, troublesome, and disgraceful to our town, have of late become all too common.

V

I sit at the bottom of sleep,
As on the floor of the sea.
And fanciful Citizens of the Deep
Are graciously greeting me.

As soon as Jarvis Poulter has gone and she has heard her front gate close, Almeda rushes to the privy. Her relief is not complete, however, and she realizes that the pain and fullness in her lower body come from an accumulation of menstrual blood that has not yet started to flow. She closes and locks the back door. Then, remembering Jarvis Poulter's words about church, she writes on a piece of paper, "I am not well, and wish to rest today." She sticks this firmly into the outside frame of the little window in the front door. She locks that door, too. She is trembling, as if from a great shock or danger. But she builds a fire, so that she can make tea. She boils water, measures the tea leaves, makes a large pot of tea, whose steam and smell sicken her further. She pours out a cup while the tea is still quite weak and adds to it several dark drops of nerve medicine. She sits to drink it without raising the kitchen blind. There, in the middle of the floor, is the cheesecloth bag hanging on its broom handle between the two chair backs. The grape pulp and juice has stained the swollen cloth a dark purple. *Plop, plup* into the basin beneath. She can't sit and look at such a thing. She takes her cup, the teapot, and the bottle of medicine into the dining room.

She is still sitting there when the horses start to go by on the way to church, stirring up clouds of dust. The roads will be getting hot as ashes. She is there when the gate is opened and a man's confident steps sound on her veranda. Her hearing is so sharp she seems to hear the paper taken out of the frame and unfolded—she can almost hear him reading it, hear the words in his mind. Then the footsteps go the other way, down the steps. The gate closes. An image comes to her of tombstones—it makes her laugh. Tombstones are marching down the street on their little booted feet, their long bodies inclined forward, their expressions preoccupied and severe. The church bells are ringing.

Then the clock in the hall strikes twelve and an hour has passed.

The house is getting hot. She drinks more tea and adds more medicine. She knows that the medicine is affecting her. It is responsible for her extraordinary languor, her perfect immobility, her unresisting surrender to her surroundings. That is all right. It seems necessary.

Her surroundings—some of her surroundings—in the dining room are these: walls covered with dark green garlanded wallpaper, lace curtains and mulberry velvet curtains on the windows, a table with a crocheted cloth and a bowl of wax fruit, a pinkish-gray carpet with nosegays of blue and pink roses, a sideboard spread with embroidered runners and holding various patterned plates and jugs and the silver tea things. A lot of things to watch. For every one of these patterns, decorations, seems charged with life, ready to move and flow and alter. Or possibly to explode. Almeda Roth's occupation throughout the day is to keep an eye on them. Not to prevent their alteration so much as to catch them at it—to understand it, to be a part of it. So much is going on in this room that there is no need to leave it. There is not even the thought of leaving it.

Of course, Almeda in her observations cannot escape words. She may think she can, but she can't. Soon this glowing and swelling begins to suggest words—not specific words but a flow of words somewhere, just about ready to make themselves known to her. Poems, even. Yes, again, poems. Or one poem. Isn't that the idea—one very great poem that will contain everything and, oh, that will make all the other poems, the poems she has written, inconsequential, mere trial and error, mere rags? Stars and flowers and birds and trees and angels in the snow and dead children at twilight—that is not the half of it. You have to get in the obscene racket on Pearl Street and the polished toe of Jarvis Poulter's boot and the plucked-chicken haunch with its blue-black flower. Almeda is a long way now from human sympathies or fears or cozy household considerations. She doesn't think about what could be done for that woman or about keeping Jarvis Poulter's dinner warm and hanging his long underwear on the line. The basin of grape juice has overflowed and is running over her kitchen floor, staining the boards of the floor, and the stain will never come out.

She has to think of so many things at once—Champlain and the naked Indians and the salt deep in the earth but as well as the salt the money, the money-making intent brewing forever in heads like Jarvis Poulter's. Also, the brutal storms of winter and the clumsy and benighted deeds on Pearl Street. The changes of climate are often violent, and if you think about it there is no peace even in the stars. All this can be borne only if it is channeled into a poem, and the word "channeled" is appropriate, because the name of the poem will be—it *is*—"The Meneseteung." The name of the poem is the name of the river. No, in fact it is the river, the Meneseteung, that is the poem—with its deep holes and rapids and blissful pools under the summer trees and its grinding blocks of ice thrown up at the end of winter and its desolating spring floods. Almeda looks deep, deep into the river of her mind and into the tablecloth, and she sees the crocheted roses floating. They look bunchy and foolish, her mother's crocheted roses—they don't look much like real flowers. But their effort, their floating independence, their pleasure in their silly selves, does seem to her so admirable. A hopeful sign. *Meneseteung.*

She doesn't leave the room until dusk, when she goes out to the privy again and discovers that she is bleeding, her flow has started. She will have to get a towel, strap it on, bandage herself up. Never before, in health, has she passed a whole day in her nightdress. She doesn't feel any particular anxiety about this. On her way through the kitchen she walks through the pool of grape juice. She knows that she will have to mop it up, but not yet, and she walks upstairs leaving purple footprints and smelling her escaping blood and the sweat of her body that has sat all day in the closed hot room.

No need for alarm.

For she hasn't thought that crocheted roses could float away or that tombstones could hurry down the street. She doesn't mistake that for reality, and neither does she mistake anything else for reality, and that is how she knows that she is sane.

VI

I dream of you by night,
I visit you by day.
Father, Mother,
Sister, Brother,
Have you no word to say?

April 22, 1903. At her residence, on Tuesday last, between three and four o'clock in the afternoon, there passed away a lady of talent and refinement whose pen, in days gone by, enriched our local literature with a volume of sensitive, eloquent verse. It is a sad misfortune that in later years the mind of this fine person had become somewhat clouded and her behaviour, in consequence, somewhat rash and unusual. Her attention to decorum and to the care and adornment of her person had suffered, to the degree that she had become, in the eyes of those unmindful of her former pride and daintiness, a familiar eccentric, or even, sadly, a figure of fun. But now all such lapses pass from memory and what is recalled is her excellent published verse, her labours in former days in the Sunday school, her dutiful care of her parents, her noble womanly nature, charitable concerns, and unfailing religious faith. Her last illness was of mercifully short duration. She caught cold, after having become thoroughly wet from a ramble in the Pearl Street bog. (It has been said that some urchins chased her into the water, and such is the boldness and cruelty of some of our youth, and their observed persecution of this lady, that the tale cannot be entirely discounted.) The cold developed into pneumonia, and she died, attended at the last by a former neighbour, Mrs. Bert (Annie) Friels, who witnessed her calm and faithful end.

January, 1904. One of the founders of our community, an early maker and shaker of this town, was abruptly removed from our midst on Monday morning last, whilst attending to his correspondence in the office of his company. Mr. Jarvis Poulter possessed a keen and lively commercial spirit, which was instrumental in the creation of not one but several local enterprises, bringing the benefits of industry, productivity, and employment to our town.

I looked for Almeda Roth in the graveyard. I found the family stone. There was just one name on it—Roth. Then I noticed two flat stones in the ground, a distance of a few feet—six feet?—from the upright stone. One of these said "Papa," the other "Mama." Farther out from these I found two other flat stones, with the names William and Catherine on them. I had to clear away some overgrowing grass and dirt to see the full name of Catherine. No birth or death dates for anybody, nothing about being dearly beloved. It was a private sort of memorializing, not for the world. There were no roses, either—no sign of a rosebush. But perhaps it was taken out. The grounds keeper doesn't like such things, they are a nuisance to the lawnmower, and if there is nobody left to object he will pull them out.

I thought that Almeda must have been buried somewhere else. When this plot was bought—at the time of the two children's deaths—she would still have been expected to marry, and to lie finally beside her husband. They might not have left room for her here. Then I saw that the stones in the ground fanned out from the upright stone. First the two for the parents, then the two for the children, but these were placed in such a way that there was room for a third, to complete the fan. I paced out from "Catherine" the same number of steps that it took to get from "Catherine" to "William," and at this spot I began pulling grass and scrabbling in the dirt with my bare hands. Soon I felt the stone and knew that I was right. I worked away and got the whole stone clear and I read the name "Meda." There it was with the others, staring at the sky.

I made sure I had got to the edge of the stone. That was all the name there was—Meda. So it was true that she was called by that name in the family. Not just in the poem. Or perhaps she chose her name from the poem, to be written on her stone.

I thought that there wasn't anybody alive in the world but me who would know this, who would make the connection. And I would be the last person to do so. But perhaps this isn't so. People are curious. A few people are. They will be driven to find things out, even trivial things. They will put things together, knowing all along that they may be mistaken. You see them going around with notebooks, scraping the dirt off gravestones, reading microfilm, just in the hope of seeing this trickle in time, making a connection, rescuing one thing from the rubbish.

JOYCE CAROL OATES

Ghost Girls

JOYCE CAROL OATES (1938–) is the author of a number of novels—including most recently *My Heart Laid Bare, We Were the Mulvaneys, Zombie, Man Crazy,* and *What I Lived For,* a finalist for the 1995 PEN/Faulkner Award and a Pulitzer Prize—and collections of stories, poetry, and plays. The recipient of the 1996 PEN/Malamud Award for Achievement in the Short Story, she is the Roger S. Berlind Distinguished Professor of Humanities at Princeton University.

This story I want to tell began in upstate New York, in the Chautauqua Mountains, in August 1972.

It was a time when Momma had to take us—her and me—into hiding. The first time I saw what isn't there to be seen.

Arrangements had been made for Daddy's friend Vaughn Brownlee he'd known in Vietnam to fly us from Marsena where we'd been living to Wolf's Head Lake in the Chautauqua Mountains where we'd stay at somebody's camp. How long? Momma wanted to know, and Brownlee shrugged saying, As long as required.

I was five years old and sharp for my age, Smartass they called me but I didn't know if Momma and me had to go into hiding because Daddy had enemies who wanted to hurt us or if it was Daddy himself who was the danger.

Some things you know without asking. Other things, you can't ask. And you never know.

That airstrip at Marsena!—just a single unpainted hangar outside town, rusty corrugated tin roof and rotted wind sock slapping listless in the breeze, a single dirt runway between cornfields you'd swear wouldn't be long enough for even the smallest plane to rise from. On the far side of one of the cornfields, out of sight from the airport, was the Chautauqua River, narrow as a creek above Marsena, rocky white-water rapids. There were airports Daddy used in those years at Mt. Ephraim, Tintern Falls, South Lebanon and each one of them is clear in my memory but Marsena is the most vivid because of what happened afterward. Also, the biggest plane you could rent at Marsena was an ex–Air Force trainer with a canopied open cockpit, a two-seater that flew at an altitude of twelve thousand feet, higher than any of the other planes, that was Daddy's favorite. It was a Vultee basic trainer—VULTEE in fading black letters on the fuselage—Daddy said of another era, World War II, not his war but his own father's now gone. That past spring he'd taken Momma up in the Vultee and they flew to Lake Ontario and back, gone for almost an hour and I kept having to go to the bathroom to pee in the concrete-stinking stall where the hard dry shells of beetles lay underfoot, at last returning to the airport and buzzing the hangar so Gus Speer the owner ran out shaking his fist, and the others hanging around watching and drinking beer on a Sunday afternoon and Daddy in the Vultee was circling the field, landing in a deafening blurred roar like a dream you can't wake from, Fucking-O perfect landing they said. And taxiing back to the hangar, and the sun glaring like knife blades off the wings. And the terrible wind of the twin propellers dying. And Momma emerged from the cockpit shaken and white-faced and not so pretty, dazed pulling off her helmet and goggles and trying to smile squinting at me and the others, and climbing down half-falling into Daddy's arms, groping as if she couldn't see him clearly, nor the ground which must have seemed strange to her, so solid, but still Momma was smiling, her happy smile, her mouth bright red like something shiny pressed into soft white bread dough. And there was the promise Daddy would take me up in the Vultee some Sunday afternoon, too.

One of these days, Birdie, Daddy would say. Smiling the way he did. Like there was some secret understanding between him and me, even Momma couldn't guess.

Birdie wasn't my name!—my name is Ingrid.

Momma pulled me by the hand murmuring under her breath Oh God, oh Jesus, and there was Brownlee waiting for us on the other side of the hangar, with a look of a man who isn't happy with waiting. His big sunburnt face like a red cabbage, and his mouth working—he was always chewing something, a big wad of gum, or a plug of tobacco. Brownlee was heavier than Daddy in those days, in his flying clothes a sky blue nylon zip-up jacket and oil-spotted khakis, brown helmet and goggles that made him look like a big beetle on its hind legs. Brownlee waved at us and Momma pulled me along. The plane he'd be flying was one of the small ones, a two-seater Cessna silvery yellow across the wings, with fading black trim. One propeller. Seeing it, hearing the motor, I pulled back on Momma's arm and she didn't like that. She was half-carrying half-pushing me. "Honey, stop crying!" she said. "Crying never did anybody any Goddamned good."

I didn't know I'd been crying. Momma's eyes were wet, too. Shining like tarnished-coppery pennies.

I knew not to cross Momma in certain of her moods. However scared I was. Just let myself go limp, a rag doll, boneless.

Brownlee stared at Momma like it hurt him to see her, the way men stared at Momma in those days. Saying, "O.K., Chloe, let's go. We need to land up there before dark."

Brownlee and Daddy had been Navy pilots in the War, Airman First Class they called each other, saluting, sneering like kids. Like the words tasted bad in their mouths. But the War was over for them now. That's some of the trouble, Momma said.

Brownlee helped Momma into the Cessna stooping beneath the wing, then I climbed inside onto her lap. It was unlawful for Brownlee to take us like this, no belt for me, the space cramped smaller than a motorcycle sidecar. But Gus Speer who owned the airport was a friend of Daddy's and Brownlee's and no friend of the law.

Brownlee shut Momma's door. She latched it from the inside. We watched as Brownlee spat into the dirt and hitched up his khaki trousers slung low on his hips and went to start the propeller, that way of squinting that was Daddy's way, too, starting a propeller by hand. Slow at first like a ceiling fan you can follow the turning of the blade with your eyes then faster and faster until you can't make out the blade any longer only the blurred circular motion it would hurt you to set your hand inside.

"Now sit still, Ingrid," Momma said. "And be brave, O.K.?"

Brownlee spat out the rest of what was in his mouth and climbed into the cockpit behind us with a grunt. The plane creaked beneath his weight. Momma was holding me tight murmuring under her breath Oh God, oh Jesus, her quick warm breath, her beery-sour breath in my face. She'd been drinking beer in the car, her and the man who'd driven us to the airport whose name I didn't know, a six-pack she'd taken from the refrigerator on our way out the door. No time for Momma to throw together more than a few things of ours in her zebra-stripe tote bag. We'd only been living in the farmhouse off a dirt road outside Marsena for about two weeks, there were other people living there too and trouble of some kind and Daddy drove away in the night and next day men came by to ask about him, yesterday morning two Eden County sheriff's deputies. The first thing you hear when a police car turns up the drive is radio voices, ratchety and loud. Looking for Lucas Boone, they said. The German shepherd was barking like crazy straining at his leash, neck hairs bristling and ears laid back and one of the deputies had his pistol drawn ready to fire but Happy was tied to a clothesline post and Momma was screaming, Don't shoot him please!—he's no harm to you! and the deputy didn't shoot Happy.

Brownlee was asking Momma was she belted in? O.K.?

Momma said, "O.K." Hugging me tight.

Brownlee started the Cessna in motion, taxiing out the runway. Slow at first. The wheels bumping. Gus Speer in his overalls lifted a hand as we passed, a worried look on his face. We passed the row of parked planes, the Vultee at the end. The sun was beginning to set like fire melting into the sky atop the cliff above the river. Momma whispered to me gripping me tight saying it was a short flight, we'd be there before we knew it, just stay still. I understood that if there was any danger Momma would be holding me like that, Momma would never give me up. Daddy had said these little shithead civilian planes were the dangerous ones not the bomber jets he'd flown in Nam but I was thinking even if we crashed and died I would be safe in Momma's arms.

The plane was rushing along the runway and the wheels began to skip. With Brownlee behind us it was like no one was the pilot, no one in control just Momma and me staring past the plane's nose and the spinning blades. There was a sickening lurch into the air, straight into the wind. The hard-packed dirt rushing beneath like a torrent. Weeds coated with dust, and a stack of scrap lumber and corrugated tin in a field, and beyond the cornstalks in almost-uniform rows dun-colored and bleached in the heat of August looking like paper cutouts. We were in the air now, and banking right. Headed north where the sky was dense with clouds. We saw telephone poles and wires above the highway, and the asphalt highway too, and a lone pickup truck moving on it, everything falling suddenly away as if sucked down. And now the Chautauqua River was visible, the color of tin, rippling red streaks from the sunset, a long snaky stretch of it out of sight. The plane was shuddering so in the wind, the engine was so loud, you would think it would break into pieces, it would never hold.

"Here we go," Momma said, raising her voice so I could hear her over the propeller, "—we're having *fun*, aren't we?"

She knows I love her, I'm crazy about her, doesn't she? It's just a hard time right now.

Of course she knows, Luke.

And you, too?

Momma's voice dipped so I almost couldn't hear lying still not breathing my eyes shut tight so I was seeing flashes of light like fireflies against my eyelids. *That's what I've been saying, darling. Me, too.*

Because I wouldn't want any further misunderstanding. Not at this crucial time.

Luke, no! There's no misunderstanding on my part.

That's how people get hurt. They cause their own sorrow. If things get confused.

That can't happen with us, we've been together too long. You know that.
I know it, and I want you to know it, too. And her.
Ingrid's too young to understand, darling.
Well, you explain to her, then. You're her mother for Christ's sake.

North of Marsena, in the mountains, everything was changed. The wind was stronger and Brownlee seemed to be having trouble keeping on course. I'd been asleep on Momma's lap, the wind was so loud shaking the plane, voices shouting past, I couldn't stay awake. My drooling mouth against Momma's soft breast so finally it hurt her and she woke me up.

Outside the sky was darkening in the direction we were headed. Clouds roiling up at the horizon thick with storms, heat lightning flashing in the distance like eyes blinking. Below were thick expanses of woods, foothills and mountains and curving streams and pockets of low-lying clouds. The sun was just a narrow funnel of rapidly diminishing pale red light and it scared and excited me seeing it from such a height like we were above the sun, we could see it sinking over. *The edge of the world that's always there whether you see it or not or know of it or not. So close you could be sucked over easy as sleep.*

Momma pointed out Wolf's Head Lake, or what she thought was the lake, below us. The valley was a deep ditch of shadow smudged with mist. A mirrorlike patch of water inside. We were starting to descend, not smoothly but in lurches, like going down steps in the dark. I wasn't afraid, with Momma holding me so tight. I stared at the light skimming the mountaintops, the pines beginning to become distinct, individual. And there was a road!—curving alongside one of the mountains, suddenly visible. And another road, crossing a strip of water. Narrow lakes like fingers, so many of them, and closer in farmland and pastures in neat rectangles, I could see cattle grazing, the tin-glaring roof of a barn, a truck moving along a highway. We were coming in to land—where? A narrow airstrip ahead. The plane's shadow wasn't visible skimming the ground below, the sun was too far gone.

Momma said worried in my ear, "Hold on, darling. It might be a little—" but already the runway was coming up fast, our little plane swerved in a gust of wind and Brownlee cursed behind us and there was a split second when he might've raised the nose and risen again to circle for another try but instead he brought us down clumsily hitting the ground so Momma and I screamed and the plane went bouncing and skipping and finally rolled dazed along the runway the right wing tilted almost skimming the ground. We came to a skidding stop at the end of the runway, a field beyond, as the first fat hissing raindrops began to fall.

Momma was half-sobbing screaming at Brownlee, "You asshole! All of you! You want to kill us don't you!"

* * *

A woman friend of Brownlee's named Maude was waiting for us at the airport and by the time we drove out to Wolf's Head Lake to the hunting camp it was dark and raining hard. The mountain road curved, the car's yellow headlights flew ahead. Where we'd all be staying wasn't a house exactly, they called it a lodge, single-story with missing shingles and a crumbling stone chimney and a rotted porch across the width of the front. Wild bushes pushing up close. Scrap lumber, an old auto chassis in the yard. Inside it smelled of kerosene. There were few pieces of furniture—a battered sofa, some chairs—and no carpet on the loose-fitting floorboards. Above the fireplace stuffed with debris was a deer's handsome mounted head and antlers. From Daddy I knew to count the points: there were ten. I stood staring at the deer on the wall seeing his fur was faded to the color of sand and mangy with time, his dark-glassy eyes were coated with dust.

Brownlee said, like he was playing Daddy, in that way Daddy would with me, "He can't see you, Birdie: he's blind."

I said, "I know that."

Brownlee said, smiling, and winking at Momma and the woman named Maude, "I mean he's blinder than blind, poor fucker. His eyes are glass."

Momma said, "Did you shoot him, Vaughn?—he's your trophy?"

"Hell, no. I'm not a hunter. I don't give a shit about hunting animals."

Brownlee said this and there was a silence and the woman named Maude laughed like she was clearing her throat, and Momma said nothing just took my hand and pulled me along into one of the back rooms where we'd be sleeping. When she switched on the light the first thing we saw was something dead on the floor beneath a window—"Jesus!" Momma said. She thought it was a bat, kept me from getting too close. I stared seeing two long columns of black ants leading to it from the wall.

Not Death only but what follows, you don't want to know.

The things I saw, in Nam, Daddy said, *oh sweet fucking Christ you don't want to know.*

Momma was breathing hard. Ran her hands through her hair in that way of hers, angry, but like she's about to cry, too. Instead lighting a cigarette from out of her tote bag. She laughed, her eyes shining so you'd swear she was happy. "What the hell, honey, right? We're alive, and we're here."

"Is Daddy going to be with us?"

Momma was stamping the ants to death. Both feet. These tinsel-looking flat sandals, and her feet delicate, narrow, bluish-pale, red polish on the toenails chipped. Momma was wearing her white rayon slacks fitted close to her body, her shiny white plastic belt that made her waist so tiny, red jersey top that pulled across her breasts. A thin gold chain with a green cross on it Daddy said was jade, bought in Saigon. Momma was so young, only twenty-three. She was just a girl, wasn't she. And so beautiful, it hurt you to look but you had to look. Silky white-blond hair, her brown eyes set deep, her mouth that seemed always pouting, even when she smiled. Momma was smoking her cigarette at the same time pushing the dead thing away with her foot, toward the door, the door was open and in the front room Brownlee and the woman named Maude were talking. Sometimes when Momma spoke up her voice was so loud and laughing-angry you'd be surprised, and it was like that now.

"Say, Vaughn—Airman First Class Brownlee—get your ass in here, will you? There's something nasty scaring my little girl I want taken care of *now.*"

I was disappointed, Wolf's Head Lake wasn't close by the damn old "lodge" at all. A mile away, at least, down a bumpy dirt lane. You couldn't hear any waves, and you couldn't smell any water. Outside everywhere you looked, no moon, no stars and nothing but pitch-black night.

Maude had brought some food in grocery bags that ripped and spilled on the counter and she and Momma made supper finally though it took a long while, always it seemed to take a long while to make meals in those days because people got interrupted, there was drinking to be done, cigarettes lit and relit, pots and pans missing or nonexistent and often there was a problem locating cutlery—what was called "silverware." And there were arguments, discussions. But finally a meal would be prepared like this late-night supper which was hamburger patties grilled in the fireplace, big doughy-soft buns the size of a man's hand, and ketchup, and relish sugary-tasting as candy, and Frito-Lay potato chips the kind that came in the cardboard box and smelled of the cardboard—we were all starving, especially Brownlee who as he ate blinked like his eyes were welling tears. And there was beer for them, just water for me that Momma wasn't too happy about—rust-streaked trickling out of the kitchen faucet.

It started then, my way of eating. If it's ground meat like hamburger pink or runny-red in the center I'll eat just the edges shutting my eyes, if it's muscle-meat like steak or cutlets where you can see the texture of the flesh I can't eat it at all unless I'm drunk or stoned and somebody can talk me out of seeing what it is.

It was around midnight when we were eating and headlights flashed up the drive and I ran to see if it was Daddy but it wasn't—two men I'd never seen before, one of them with spidery tattoos up and down his arms. They'd brought more six-packs of beer, and a bottle of Four Roses, and a little plastic Baggie of what Momma called "dope"—which she said scared her for the weird thoughts it made her think but she couldn't say no to trying it most of the time. Later on they played cards, Momma and Maude and Brownlee who got happy and loud when he drank and the man with the tattooed arms whose name was Skaggs and the other man, a little younger, with a mustache, moist yellowish-dark eyes like Happy's eyes, whose name was McCarry. McCarry's hair was greased back in quills and his skin was pimply but he was sweet-boy-looking sitting close beside Momma offering to help her with her cards but Momma laughed saying no thanks, friend, she didn't need anybody's help she'd been playing gin rummy since the age of ten.

"And winning my fair share, too."

"*That,* Miz Boone, I don't doubt."

It was one of those times that any minute Daddy would drive up and come through the door except he didn't and I started to cry and Momma said I was tired and it's time for bed and I said no I didn't want to go to bed not in that nasty bed I was scared I said and everybody was looking at me holding their cards, Momma's voice was soft and pleading and guilty-sounding and she was stroking my face she said was feverish, my skin was sunburnt, my hair all tangles and I kicked at her and she grabbed my ankles to stop me and a little table fell over with some empty beer cans on it and a styrofoam cup used as an ashtray and Maude helped Momma and I squirmed away from them but Momma caught me harder, carried me into our room, I went limp and boneless and too tired to cry or protest, Momma shined a flashlight into the corners of the room and under the bed to see there wasn't anything waiting to hurt me, Momma pulled off my T-shirt and slacks and laid me atop the lumpy bed that creaked and pulled a spread over me, it was a thin chenille spread with a smell of damp and mildew, a familiar smell like the smell of Black Flag insecticide that was an undercurrent in the air, you could never escape. Momma said, "Things are going to be O.K., Ingrid," kissing me on the cheek, her kiss tasting of beer and cigarette smoke, "—we'll make it up to you, honey, we promise." I grabbed her hair to pull her down next to me but she slapped my hand away and then she was gone back out to the card game and I'd wake up hearing low murmurous voices like water rushing past, the noise of the water churning white and frothy below the dam at Marsena, Daddy lifting me on his shoulder to see it better, except Daddy wasn't here, I was somewhere hearing men's voices I didn't know, now and then they'd laugh loud, and women's voices too, that rising-wailing sound of women's voices late at night. *Oh you bastard! You Goddamned motherfucker-bastard!*—a woman's voice loud in teasing.

Waking then when Momma came tiptoeing into the room carrying her sandals. Trying to be quiet but colliding with a chair and cursing under her breath and climbing onto the bed and the springs creaking beneath her and she was too exhausted even to draw the cover partway over her, just fell asleep. A wet gurgling click in her throat. "Momma," I whispered. "Momma, I hate you."

She didn't hear, she was starting to snore, not like Daddy snored but softer and discontinuous like asking questions? each little breathy snore a question? and I smelled Momma's special smell when she was tired and hadn't washed in a while, I tried to nudge into her arms so she might hold me like she used to all the time when I was little, "Momma, I love you," I said. Big Mommy Cat she'd called herself and I was Baby Kitten and we'd nap together during the day sometimes, sometimes in the backseat of the car if Daddy was late getting back but Momma was deep asleep now and didn't give a damn about me. I was wide awake. Those shrill insect noises outside in the night like tiny chain saws and there were Goddamned mosquitoes in the room that'd come through the broken screen drawn by the smell of our blood. Bites on my face that swelled and itched, I scratched at them hard and mean to spite Momma, it was Momma's fault I was so bit up, in the morning she'd be sorry.

Now this happened. I'd been hearing these voices thinking it was Maude and somebody else, but after a while I decided it was not, it was girls' voices, *little girls somewhere outside.* I climbed down from the bed where Momma was sleeping so hard and I went to the window to look out and the sky surprised me, it was lighter than the trees, a hard-glaring blue like ink. The insects were singing like crazy but over on top of them were these girls' voices, *—eena?* one of them was saying, *—eena?* like it was part of a name. I couldn't make out any words, I pressed my face against the dirty screen and at first I couldn't see anybody but then I saw them, I'd been looking at them not recognizing what it was, these figures toward the front of the lodge by the porch. The girls were a little older than me I estimated, and they were sisters. I knew that. They were sisters crouched and hiding, the taller one hugging the other who was crying trying to make her hush, *—eena? —eena?* I wondered if they'd just crawled out from under the porch? or were they about to crawl under the porch? Was somebody after them, was that why they were so scared? Out there in the dark, in the dripping bushes. If they were Maude's children where'd they been earlier, why hadn't they eaten with us, I wanted to wake Momma to ask but didn't dare, I knew that kind of hard panting sleep of Momma's, skin clammy with sweat.

The girls made me feel sad. And scared something was going to happen that couldn't be stopped.

How long I listened to them not hearing any actual words but only their voices, I don't know. Pressing my face against the screen until finally the voices went away, the little girls were gone without my noticing and there was just the night insects like before, crazy and loud. And Momma's breathless little pants and snores in the bed behind me.

"Momma?—hey!"

It was early morning. I tried to wake Momma but she groaned and shoved me away. She was still sleeping hard, her mouth open, eyelids fluttering and twitching like she was arguing with somebody in a dream. I laughed seeing Momma's face swollen with mosquito bites, her upper lip was swollen twice its normal size. Her red jersey top was pulled off one shoulder and her bra strap, which was white, but a kind of yellow-white, was twisted. Momma'd kicked the chenille cover onto the floor, I saw her white rayon slacks were stained, she wasn't going to like that. I touched her in stealth like I'd do sometimes when she didn't know, when she was flat on her back asleep I'd touch her stomach, that's where I'd come from Momma had told me, I'd stare and stare wondering was it so, how could I be so little, wouldn't I suffocate, it scared me to think of it and so I did not think of it except at such times and even then I didn't think of it, I said, "Momma damn you!"—gave up trying to wake her and went into the front room barefoot quiet as I could hoping nobody would see me, I hoped Skaggs and McCarry were gone, the room was empty except for the buck's head above the mantel, those glassy-dusty eyes watching me.

Always, there's been somebody watching me. Holding me in His vision, so I can't escape even if I wished to escape.

This was a room like so many rooms where there'd been a party and the smells of such a room in the morning, the stale smoke, the beer spillage, potato chips—these were smells I knew. Scattered over the table they'd been using which was a wooden table with scars and burns in it were beer cans and bottles and styrofoam cups and ashes and butts, a flattened Frito-Lay box, playing cards. I always liked playing cards, watching Daddy and Momma and their friends at their games, the cards were precious things because adults handled them with such importance, you didn't ever interrupt them at a serious moment, especially you didn't interrupt any man. There was the queen of hearts on the floor I picked up to look at, also the ace of clubs, the cards were sticky and the reverse side disappointing—no picture just a design of black and mustard-yellow stripes.

Outside in the puddled-dirt drive Maude's car was the only car, Skaggs and McCarry were gone. There'd been times when people who showed up late at night were not gone in the morning nor would be gone for days, a friend of Daddy's once only a few months ago before Marsena in a back bedroom shouting and crying and Daddy had to watch over him, try to talk to him Momma said, he'd had a shotgun with him and some grievance to make right and Daddy and Brownlee had finally talked him out of it but it was a long time before he went away.

I went outside. Barefoot onto the splintery porch. Some of the planks too were rotted, you had to be careful where you walked.

I was shivering looking to where the little girls had been hiding—but I couldn't see anything. Tall grasses gone to seed, a straggly bush speckled with aphids. Momma wouldn't like me going barefoot out here, but I crawled under the railing and jumped down to the ground and it was strange how still my mind got, and how empty like I was waiting for something to fill it. "Hey? Are you here? Where are you?—I saw you," I said, like calling out but not raising my voice much, too scared to raise my voice. I squatted down to look under the porch but couldn't see much—it was a nasty dark cobwebby place, smelling of damp. That was when I started shivering hard and jumped up and backed away.

Walked around the yard, in the high grass that was wet from the night, and some of it sharp against my feet, and cold. My eyes swung up seeing how clear the sky was this morning, no clouds, everything washed clean, a sharp whitish light so you couldn't tell where the sun was, and everywhere, excited, calling out to one another, were birds in the pine trees.

There was an old rotted doghouse or rabbit hutch I looked into behind the lodge but nobody was there, nor any sign of anybody.

When Momma was up finally and her face mottled and swollen with mosquito bites, her lip still swollen so she looked like somebody'd punched her with his fist, I told her about the little girls, I was talking fast and excited and Momma said, squinting at me like the morning light was hurtful to her eyes, "Honey, you were just dreaming, there aren't any other children here. Only you." I said, "Yes there are, Momma. I heard them, and I saw them." Momma went out into the kitchen where she tried to get the gas stove to light up so she could make coffee and I followed her repeating what I'd said, the girls were here somewhere hiding I said, but Momma didn't pay too much attention to me. She was cursing under her breath looking for something then she found a box of wooden matches and with a shaky hand tried to light one, scraping it against a stove burner but the match must've been damp, the stick broke in her hand, she let the pieces fall to the floor and went to get her silver lighter Daddy'd given her out of her tote bag and that did work, a bluish flame flaring up at one of the burners with a hissing noise. I repeated what I said about the little girls, I'd seen them right outside by the front porch and they were sisters and they were crying because somebody was after them, it wasn't any Goddamn dream I told Momma it was *not.* Bringing my bare heels down hard on the worn-out linoleum floor so the floorboards wobbled. Not minding how I was hurting myself till Momma slapped at me to quiet me.

I was like the gas burner flaring up, the blue flame going to orange if the gas's turned too high.

The others came in, Maude and Brownlee, and after a while we ate breakfast, some stale sweet rolls out of a package, and some mealy bananas, and the adults had coffee and smoked their cigarettes and I was telling them about the little girls I knew were somewhere at the camp, Momma kept trying to shush me but I wouldn't be shushed and there came a look into Maude's face and her eyes moved onto me for the first time like she hadn't seen me before. "What little girls are you talking about, Ingrid?" she asked. I said I didn't know their names, how would I know their names. I'd seen them in the middle of the night when everybody was asleep, out by the front porch they'd been, hiding in the grass, and crying. They were scared of something, I said. Like somebody was after them.

"What's this?" Maude asked, looking from me to Momma, and back again. "When was this?"

Maude was older than Momma by five or six years, heavier, with streaked brown hair tied up in a kerchief, eyebrows plucked thin and arching like she was in perpetual surprise, and her bloodshot eyes too she was always widening to show surprise or interest or mockery. She was good-looking I guess but I didn't like her and for sure I knew she didn't like me. Earlier that morning I'd heard her and Brownlee curse each other because Brownlee was flying back to Marsena instead of staying with her the way she wanted. Now she was staring at me asking what did the little girls look like? and I tried to say but there weren't the right words, I was getting excited and picking at my mosquito bites and Momma took both my hands to calm me saying, "Ingrid, that's enough. Jesus, you had one of your dreams, that's all." But Maude was exhaling smoke in that slow watchful way of grown women, and she was looking at Brownlee, and Brownlee who hadn't been listening said, "What?" like he was pissed and Maude said, "Vaughn, she's talking about Earl Meltzer's little girls—that's who she's talking about. My God." Brownlee said, "She isn't talking about anything, she's just a kid making things up," and Maude said, shaking her head, her voice quick and scared, "She's talking about Earl Meltzer's little girls, there's nobody else she's talking about."

Now Momma set her coffee cup down. "Who's Earl Meltzer?—what is this?"

Brownlee was telling Maude, "She couldn't know about them, it was two-three years ago at least. So drop it. You're wasted from last night." But Maude was making these soft sighing scared-sounding noises to herself, fluttering her eyes, "Oh God, oh Jesus. She's seen them. Those poor little girls," and Momma said, "Maude? Vaughn? What the hell is this?" and Brownlee was telling Maude, "Look, somebody must've told her, that's all. She had a dream, that's all." Momma said, "Tell her what, for Christ's sake?" Momma's eyes were sore-looking and her lip so swollen she hadn't even tried to put on lipstick like she always did, her skin looked dry as ashes in the morning light. Maude said, "Meltzer's little girls Cheryl and Doreen—*I* knew them! Meltzer and Lena his wife weren't living together, Lena was living with this other guy, in Watertown, and one night Meltzer went with a gun to get the girls from Lena's mother where they were staying, and he brought them out to the camp here, and—" and Brownlee cut her off saying, "Maude, shut the fuck up, you'll scare the kid," and Maude said, "*You* shut the fuck up, God damn you—you were a buddy of Meltzer's weren't you—thank God the prick put a bullet through his own brains too—"

Brownlee brought his opened hand around and hit the side of Maude's face, she screamed spilling hot coffee, and Momma screamed, and already I was running, out of the kitchen and through the back door where the screen was rusted and torn and I forgot I was barefoot running in the high grass around the side of the lodge, I wasn't crying because it wasn't me he'd hit, but I was scared, I crawled under the porch near where the girls had been and jays were screaming at me out of the pine trees and I pushed my way head-on through a rotted lattice covered in poison ivy and cobwebs till I was inside in this dark place smelling of something sharp crawling on my hands and knees and stones were stabbing me, pieces of glass, I was panting like a dog crawling halfway under the porch hearing how back in the kitchen they were still arguing.

Then it was quiet. It was still. Under the porch where the sun came through cracks in the floorboards in cobwebbed rays and there was this smell so sharp my nostrils pinched like something had died there, and old soft decayed leaves sticking to my skin, gnats buzzing in my face. And a mosquito whining, close by my ear. I knew to make myself as small as I could hugging my knees to my chest, hunched over so nobody could see if they came looking peering through the lattice. My right knee stung where it was bleeding but I wasn't crying. My hands were bleeding, too, but I paid them no mind. Momma's footsteps came quick overhead, I knew they were Momma's, so light and fast and then she was on the porch calling, "Ingrid? Honey, where are you?"

I waited like I knew to wait. I was used to hiding and some times I'd hidden nobody had even known I was gone, that was the safest kind of hiding and a principle to take to heart all your life.

So Momma didn't know where I was and she came down the porch steps talking to herself, muttering and cursing and I could see her legs, her legs in the white slacks, not clear but like I was seeing them through greenish water. Momma calling my name in that tight-scared way of hers so I knew if I revealed myself she'd be angry so I stayed where I was not making a sound.

I saw them then. At the farthest corner where it was darkest. The sisters crouched together in each other's arms. I saw their faces that were pale but smeared with something—dirt? blood? and I saw they were crying and they saw me, for a long time we looked at each other. "I'm an alive girl," I whispered. "I'm an alive girl not like you."

TIM O'BRIEN

The Things They Carried

TIM O'BRIEN (1946–) is the winner of the 1979 National Book Award for Fiction for his novel *Going After Cacciato.* He is also the author of *In the Lake in the Woods,* named Best Work of Fiction in 1994 by *Time* magazine; *The Things They Carried,* a finalist for the Pulitzer Prize and the National Book Critics Circle Award; and two other novels, as well as *If I Die in a Combat Zone,* a Vietnam memoir.

First Lieutenant Jimmy Cross carried letters from a girl named Martha, a junior at Mount Sebastian College in New Jersey. They were not love letters, but Lieutenant Cross was hoping, so he kept them folded in plastic at the bottom of his rucksack. In the late afternoon, after a day's march, he would dig his foxhole, wash his hands under a canteen, unwrap the letters, hold them with the tips of his fingers, and spend the last hour of light pretending. He would imagine romantic camping trips into the White Mountains in New Hampshire. He would sometimes taste the envelope flaps, knowing her tongue had been there. More than anything, he wanted Martha to love him as he loved her, but the letters were mostly chatty, elusive on the matter of love. She was a virgin, he was almost sure. She was an English major at Mount Sebastian, and she wrote beautifully about her professors and roommates and midterm exams, about her respect for Chaucer and her great affection for Virginia Woolf. She often quoted lines of poetry; she never mentioned the war, except to say, Jimmy, take care of yourself. The letters weighed 10 ounces. They were signed Love, Martha, but Lieutenant Cross understood that Love was only a way of signing and did not mean what he sometimes pretended it meant. At dusk, he would carefully return the letters to his rucksack. Slowly, a bit distracted, he would get up and move among his men, checking the perimeter, then at full dark he would return to his hole and watch the night and wonder if Martha was a virgin.

* * *

The things they carried were largely determined by necessity. Among the necessities or near-necessities were P-38 can openers, pocket knives, heat tabs, wristwatches, dog tags, mosquito repellent, chewing gum, candy, cigarettes, salt tablets, packets of Kool-Aid, lighters, matches, sewing kits, Military Payment Certificates, C rations, and two or three canteens of water. Together, these items weighed between 15 and 20 pounds, depending upon a man's habits or rate of metabolism. Henry Dobbins, who was a big man, carried extra rations; he was especially fond of canned peaches in heavy syrup over pound cake. Dave Jensen, who practiced field hygiene, carried a toothbrush, dental floss, and several hotel-sized bars of soap he'd stolen on R&R in Sydney, Australia. Ted Lavender, who was scared, carried tranquilizers until he was shot in the head outside the village of Than Khe in mid-April. By necessity, and because it was SOP, they all carried steel helmets that weighed 5 pounds including the liner and camouflage cover. They carried the standard fatigue jackets and trousers. Very few carried underwear. On their feet they carried jungle boots—2.1 pounds—and Dave Jensen carried three pairs of socks and a can of Dr. Scholl's foot powder as a precaution against trench foot. Until he was shot, Ted Lavender carried six or seven ounces of premium dope, which for him was a necessity. Mitchell Sanders, the RTO, carried condoms. Norman Bowker carried a diary. Rat Kiley carried comic books. Kiowa, a devout Baptist, carried an illustrated New Testament that had been presented to him by his father, who taught Sunday school in Oklahoma City, Oklahoma. As a hedge against bad times, however, Kiowa also carried his grandmother's distrust of the white man, his grandfather's old hunting hatchet. Necessity dictated. Because the land was mined and booby-trapped, it was SOP for each man to carry a steel-centered, nylon-covered flak jacket, which weighed 6.7 pounds, but which on hot days seemed much heavier. Because you could die so quickly, each man carried at least one large compress bandage, usually in the helmet band for easy access. Because the nights were cold, and because the monsoons were wet, each carried a green plastic poncho that could be used as a raincoat or groundsheet or makeshift tent. With its quilted liner, the poncho weighed almost two pounds, but it was worth every ounce. In April, for instance, when Ted Lavender was shot, they used his poncho to wrap him up, then to carry him across the paddy, then to lift him into the chopper that took him away.

They were called legs or grunts.

To carry something was to hump it, as when Lieutenant Jimmy Cross humped his love for Martha up the hills and through the swamps. In its intransitive form, to hump meant to walk, or to march, but it implied burdens far beyond the intransitive.

Almost everyone humped photographs. In his wallet, Lieutenant Cross carried two photographs of Martha. The first was a Kodacolor snapshot signed Love, though he knew better. She stood against a brick wall. Her eyes were gray and neutral, her lips slightly open as she stared straight-on at the camera. At night, sometimes, Lieutenant Cross wondered who had taken the picture, because he knew she had boyfriends, because he loved her so much, and because he could see the shadow of the picture-taker spreading out against the brick wall. The second photograph had been clipped from the 1968 Mount Sebastian yearbook. It was an action shot—women's volleyball—and Martha was bent horizontal to the floor, reaching, the palms of her hands in sharp focus, the tongue taut, the expression frank and competitive. There was no visible sweat. She wore white gym shorts. Her legs, he thought, were almost certainly the legs of a virgin, dry and without hair, the left knee cocked and carrying her entire weight, which was just over one hundred pounds. Lieutenant Cross remembered touching that left knee. A dark theater, he remembered, and the movie was *Bonnie and Clyde,* and Martha wore a tweed skirt, and during the final scene, when he touched her knee, she turned and looked at him in a sad, sober way that made him pull his hand back, but he would always remember the feel of the tweed skirt and the knee beneath it and the sound of the gunfire that killed Bonnie and Clyde, how embarrassing it was, how slow and oppressive. He remembered kissing her good night at the dorm door. Right then, he thought, he should've done something brave. He should've carried her up the stairs to her room and tied her to the bed and touched that left knee all night long. He should've risked it. Whenever he looked at the photographs, he thought of new things he should've done.

What they carried was partly a function of rank, partly of field specialty.

As a first lieutenant and platoon leader, Jimmy Cross carried a compass, maps, code books, binoculars, and a .45-caliber pistol that weighed 2.9 pounds fully loaded. He carried a strobe light and the responsibility for the lives of his men.

As an RTO, Mitchell Sanders carried the PRC-25 radio, a killer, 26 pounds with its battery.

As a medic, Rat Kiley carried a canvas satchel filled with morphine and plasma and malaria tablets and surgical tape and comic books and all the things a medic must carry, including M&M's for especially bad wounds, for a total weight of nearly 20 pounds.

As a big man, therefore a machine gunner, Henry Dobbins carried the M-60, which weighed 23 pounds unloaded, but which was almost always loaded. In addition, Dobbins carried between 10 and 15 pounds of ammunition draped in belts across his chest and shoulders.

As PFCs or Spec 4s, most of them were common grunts and carried the standard M-16 gas-operated assault rifle. The weapon weighed 7.5 pounds unloaded, 8.2 pounds with its full 20-round magazine. Depending on numerous factors, such as topography and psychology, the riflemen carried anywhere from 12 to 20 magazines, usually in cloth bandoliers, adding on another 8.4 pounds at minimum, 14 pounds at maximum. When it was available, they also carried M-16 maintenance gear—rods and steel brushes and swabs and tubes of LSA oil—all of which weighed about a pound. Among the grunts, some carried the M-79 grenade launcher, 5.9 pounds unloaded, a reasonably light weapon except for the ammunition, which was heavy. A single round weighed 10 ounces. The typical load was 25 rounds. But Ted Lavender, who was scared, carried 34 rounds when he was shot and killed outside Than Khe, and he went down under an exceptional burden, more than 20 pounds of ammunition, plus the flak jacket and helmet and rations and water and toilet paper and tranquilizers and all the rest, plus the unweighed fear. He was dead weight. There was no twitching or flopping. Kiowa, who saw it happen, said it was like watching a rock fall, or a big sandbag or something—just boom, then down—not like the movies where the dead guy rolls around and does fancy spins and goes ass over teakettle—not like that, Kiowa said, the poor bastard just flat-fuck fell. Boom. Down. Nothing else. It was a bright morning in mid-April. Lieutenant Cross felt the pain. He blamed himself. They stripped off Lavender's canteens and ammo, all the heavy things, and Rat Kiley said the obvious, the guy's dead, and Mitchell Sanders used his radio to report one U.S. KIA and to request a chopper. Then they wrapped Lavender in his poncho. They carried him out to a dry paddy, established security, and sat smoking the dead man's dope until the chopper came. Lieutenant Cross kept to himself. He pictured Martha's smooth young face, thinking he loved her more than anything, more than his men, and now Ted Lavender was dead because he loved her so much and could not stop thinking about her. When the dustoff arrived, they carried Lavender aboard. Afterward they burned Than Khe. They marched until dusk, then dug their holes, and that night Kiowa kept explaining how you had to be there, how fast it was, how the poor guy just dropped like so much concrete. Boom-down, he said. Like cement.

In addition to the three standard weapons—the M-60, M-16, and M-79—they carried whatever presented itself, or whatever seemed appropriate as a means of killing or staying alive. They carried catch-as-catch-can. At various times, in various situations, they carried M-14s and CAR-15s and Swedish Ks and grease guns and captured AK-47s and Chi-Coms and RPGs and Simonov carbines and black market Uzis and .38-caliber Smith & Wesson handguns and 66 mm LAWs and shotguns and silencers and blackjacks and bayonets and C-4 plastic explosives. Lee Strunk carried a slingshot; a weapon of last resort, he called it. Mitchell Sanders carried brass knuckles. Kiowa carried his grandfather's feathered hatchet. Every third or fourth man carried a Claymore antipersonnel mine—3.5 pounds with its firing device. They all carried fragmentation grenades—14 ounces each. They all carried at least one M-18 colored smoke grenade—24 ounces. Some carried CS or tear gas grenades. Some carried white phosphorus grenades. They carried all they could bear, and then some, including a silent awe for the terrible power of the things they carried.

In the first week of April, before Lavender died, Lieutenant Jimmy Cross received a good-luck charm from Martha. It was a simple pebble, an ounce at most. Smooth to the touch, it was a milky white color with flecks of orange and violet, oval-shaped, like a miniature egg. In the accompanying letter, Martha wrote that she had found the pebble on the Jersey shoreline, precisely where the land touched water at high tide, where things came together but also separated. It was this separate-but-together quality, she wrote, that had inspired her to pick up the pebble and to carry it in her breast pocket for several days, where it seemed weightless, and then to send it through the mail, by air, as a token of her truest feelings for him. Lieutenant Cross found this romantic. But he wondered what her truest feelings were, exactly, and what she meant by separate-but-together. He wondered how the tides and waves had come into play on that afternoon along the Jersey shoreline when Martha saw the pebble and bent down to rescue it from geology. He imagined bare feet. Martha was a poet, with the poet's sensibilities, and her feet would be brown and bare, the toenails unpainted, the eyes chilly and somber like the ocean in March, and though it was painful, he wondered who had been with her that afternoon. He imagined a pair of shadows moving along the strip of sand where things came together but also separated. It was phantom jealousy, he knew, but he couldn't help himself. He loved her so much. On the march, through the hot days of early April, he carried the pebble in his mouth, turning it with his tongue, tasting sea salt and moisture. His mind wandered. He had difficulty keeping his attention on the war. On occasion he would yell at his men to spread out the column, to keep their eyes open, but then he would slip away into daydreams, just pretending, walking barefoot along the Jersey shore, with Martha, carrying nothing. He would feel himself rising. Sun and waves and gentle winds, all love and lightness.

What they carried varied by mission.

When a mission took them to the mountains, they carried mosquito netting, machetes, canvas tarps, and extra bug juice.

If a mission seemed especially hazardous, or if it involved a place they knew to be bad, they carried everything they could. In certain heavily mined AOs, where the land was dense with Toe Poppers and Bouncing Betties, they took turns humping a 28-pound mine detector. With its headphones and big sensing plate, the equipment was a stress on the lower back and shoulders, awkward to handle, often useless because of the shrapnel in the earth, but they carried it anyway, partly for safety, partly for the illusion of safety.

On ambush, or other night missions, they carried peculiar little odds and ends. Kiowa always took along his New Testament and a pair of moccasins for silence. Dave Jensen carried night-sight vitamins high in carotene. Lee Strunk carried his slingshot; ammo, he claimed, would never be a problem. Rat Kiley carried brandy and M&M's candy. Until he was shot, Ted Lavender carried the starlight scope, which weighed 6.3 pounds with its aluminum carrying case. Henry Dobbins carried his girlfriend's pantyhose wrapped around his neck as a comforter. They all carried ghosts. When dark came, they would move out single file across the meadows and paddies to their ambush coordinates, where they would quietly set up the Claymores and lie down and spend the night waiting.

Other missions were more complicated and required special equipment. In mid-April, it was their mission to search out and destroy the elaborate tunnel complexes in the Than Khe area south of Chu Lai. To blow the tunnels, they carried one-pound blocks of pentrite high explosives, four blocks to a man, 68 pounds in all. They carried wiring, detonators, and battery-powered clackers. Dave Jensen carried earplugs. Most often, before blowing the tunnels, they were ordered by higher command to search them, which was considered bad news, but by and large they just shrugged and carried out orders. Because he was a big man, Henry Dobbins was excused from tunnel duty. The others would draw numbers. Before Lavender died there were 17 men in the platoon, and whoever drew the number 17 would strip off his gear and crawl in head-first with a flashlight and Lieutenant Cross's .45-caliber pistol. The rest of them would fan out as security. They would sit down or kneel, not facing the hole, listening to the ground beneath them, imagining cobwebs and ghosts, whatever was down there—the tunnel walls squeezing in—how the flashlight seemed impossibly heavy in the hand and how it was tunnel vision in the very strictest sense, compression in all ways, even time, and how you had to wiggle in—ass and elbows—a swallowed-up feeling—and how you found yourself worrying about odd things: Will your flashlight go dead? Do rats carry rabies? If you screamed, how far would the sound carry? Would your buddies hear it? Would they have the courage to drag you out? In some respects, though not many, the waiting was worse than the tunnel itself. Imagination was a killer.

On April 16, when Lee Strunk drew the number 17, he laughed and muttered something and went down quickly. The morning was hot and very still.

Not good, Kiowa said. He looked at the tunnel opening, then out across a dry paddy toward the village of Than Khe. Nothing moved. No clouds or birds or people. As they waited, the men smoked and drank Kool-Aid, not talking much, feeling sympathy for Lee Strunk but also feeling the luck of the draw. You win some, you lose some, said Mitchell Sanders, and sometimes you settle for a rain check. It was a tired line and no one laughed.

Henry Dobbins ate a tropical chocolate bar. Ted Lavender popped a tranquilizer and went off to pee.

After five minutes, Lieutenant Jimmy Cross moved to the tunnel, leaned down, and examined the darkness. Trouble, he thought—a cave-in maybe. And then suddenly, without willing it, he was thinking about Martha. The stresses and fractures, the quick collapse, the two of them buried alive under all that weight. Dense, crushing love. Kneeling, watching the hole, he tried to concentrate on Lee Strunk and the war, all the dangers, but his love was too much for him, he felt paralyzed, he wanted to sleep inside her lungs and breathe her blood and be smothered. He wanted her to be a virgin and not a virgin, all at once. He wanted to know her. Intimate secrets: Why poetry? Why so sad? Why that grayness in her eyes? Why so alone? Not lonely, just alone—riding her bike across campus or sitting off by herself in the cafeteria—even dancing, she danced alone—and it was the aloneness that filled him with love. He remembered telling her that one evening. How she nodded and looked away. And how, later, when he kissed her, she received the kiss without returning it, her eyes wide open, not afraid, not a virgin's eyes, just flat and uninvolved.

Lieutenant Cross gazed at the tunnel. But he was not there. He was buried with Martha under the white sand at the Jersey shore. They were pressed together, and the pebble in his mouth was her tongue. He was smiling. Vaguely, he was aware of how quiet the day was, the sullen paddies, yet he could not bring himself to worry about matters of security. He was beyond that. He was just a kid at war, in love. He was twenty-four years old. He couldn't help it.

A few moments later Lee Strunk crawled out of the tunnel. He came up grinning, filthy but alive. Lieutenant Cross nodded and closed his eyes while the others clapped Strunk on the back and made jokes about rising from the dead.

Worms, Rat Kiley said. Right out of the grave. Fuckin' zombie.

The men laughed. They all felt great relief.

Spook city, said Mitchell Sanders.

Lee Strunk made a funny ghost sound, a kind of moaning, yet very happy, and right then, when Strunk made that high happy moaning sound, when he went *Ahhooooo,* right then Ted Lavender was shot in the head on his way back from peeing. He lay with his mouth open. The teeth were broken. There was a swollen black bruise under his left eye. The cheekbone was gone. Oh shit, Rat Kiley said, the guy's dead. The guy's dead, he kept saying, which seemed profound—the guy's dead. I mean really.

The things they carried were determined to some extent by superstition. Lieutenant Cross carried his good-luck pebble. Dave Jensen carried a rabbit's foot. Norman Bowker, otherwise a very gentle person, carried a thumb that had been presented to him as a gift by Mitchell Sanders. The thumb was dark brown, rubbery to the touch, and weighed four ounces at most. It had been cut from a VC corpse, a boy of fifteen or sixteen. They'd found him at the bottom of an irrigation ditch, badly burned, flies in his mouth and eyes. The boy wore black shorts and sandals. At the time of his death he had been carrying a pouch of rice, a rifle, and three magazines of ammunition.

You want my opinion, Mitchell Sanders said, there's a definite moral here.

He put his hand on the dead boy's wrist. He was quiet for a time, as if counting a pulse, then he patted the stomach, almost affectionately, and used Kiowa's hunting hatchet to remove the thumb.

Henry Dobbins asked what the moral was.

Moral?

You know. *Moral.*

Sanders wrapped the thumb in toilet paper and handed it across to Norman Bowker. There was no blood. Smiling, he kicked the boy's head, watched the flies scatter, and said, It's like with that old TV show—Paladin. Have gun, will travel.

Henry Dobbins thought about it.

Yeah, well, he finally said. I don't see no moral.

There it *is,* man.

Fuck off.

They carried USO stationery and pencils and pens. They carried Sterno, safety pins, trip flares, signal flares, spools of wire, razor blades, chewing tobacco, liberated joss sticks and statuettes of the smiling Buddha, candles, grease pencils, *The Stars and Stripes,* fingernail clippers, Psy Ops leaflets, bush hats, bolos, and much more. Twice a week, when the resupply choppers came in, they carried hot chow in green mermite cans and large canvas bags filled with iced beer and soda pop. They carried plastic water containers, each with a two-gallon capacity. Mitchell Sanders carried a set of starched tiger fatigues for special occasions. Henry Dobbins carried Black Flag insecticide. Dave Jensen carried empty sandbags that could be filled at night for added protection. Lee Strunk carried tanning lotion. Some things they carried in common. Taking turns, they carried the big PRC-77 scrambler radio, which weighed 30 pounds with its battery. They shared the weight of memory. They took up what others could no longer bear. Often, they carried each other, the wounded or weak. They carried infections. They carried chess sets, basketballs, Vietnamese-English dictionaries, insignia of rank, Bronze Stars and Purple Hearts, plastic cards imprinted with the Code of Conduct. They carried diseases, among them malaria and dysentery. They carried lice and ringworm and leeches and paddy algae and various rots and molds. They carried the land itself—Vietnam, the place, the soil—a powdery orange-red dust that covered their boots and fatigues and faces. They carried the sky. The whole atmosphere, they carried it, the humidity, the monsoons, the stink of fungus and decay, all of it, they carried gravity. They moved like mules. By daylight they took sniper fire, at night they were mortared, but it was not battle, it was just the endless march, village to village, without purpose, nothing won or lost. They marched for the sake of the march. They plodded along slowly, dumbly, leaning forward against the heat, unthinking, all blood and bone, simple grunts, soldiering with their legs, toiling up the hills and down into the paddies and across the rivers and up again and down, just humping, one step and then the next and then another, but no volition, no will, because it was automatic, it was anatomy, and the war was entirely a matter of posture and carriage, the hump was everything, a kind of inertia, a kind of emptiness, a dullness of desire and intellect and conscience and hope and human sensibility. Their principles were in their feet. Their calculations were biological. They had no sense of strategy or mission. They searched the villages without knowing what to look for, not caring, kicking over jars of rice, frisking children and old men, blowing tunnels, sometimes setting fires and sometimes not, then forming up and moving on to the next village, then other villages, where it would always be the same. They carried their own lives. The pressures were enormous. In the heat of early afternoon, they would remove their helmets and flak jackets, walking bare, which was dangerous but which helped ease the strain. They would often discard things along the route of march. Purely for comfort, they would throw away rations, blow their Claymores and grenades, no matter, because by nightfall the resupply choppers would arrive with more of the same, then a day or two later still more, fresh watermelons and crates of ammunition and sunglasses and woolen sweaters—the resources were stunning—sparklers for the Fourth of July, colored eggs for Easter—it was the great American war chest—the fruits of science, the smokestacks, the canneries, the arsenals at Hartford, the Minnesota forests, the machine shops, the vast fields of corn and wheat—they carried like freight trains; they carried it on their backs and shoulders—and for all the ambiguities of Vietnam, all the mysteries and unknowns, there was at least the single abiding certainty that they would never be at a loss for things to carry.

After the chopper took Lavender away, Lieutenant Jimmy Cross led his men into the village of Than Khe. They burned everything. They shot chickens and dogs, they trashed the village well, they called in artillery and watched the wreckage, then they marched for several hours through the hot afternoon, and then at dusk, while Kiowa explained how Lavender died, Lieutenant Cross found himself trembling.

He tried not to cry. With his entrenching tool, which weighed five pounds, he began digging a hole in the earth.

He felt shame. He hated himself. He had loved Martha more than his men, and as a consequence Lavender was now dead, and this was something he would have to carry like a stone in his stomach for the rest of the war.

All he could do was dig. He used his entrenching tool like an ax, slashing, feeling both love and hate, and then later, when it was full dark, he sat at the bottom of his foxhole and wept. It went on for a long while. In part, he was grieving for Ted Lavender, but mostly it was for Martha, and for himself, because she belonged to another world, which was not quite real, and because she was a junior at Mount Sebastian College in New Jersey, a poet and a virgin and uninvolved, and because he realized she did not love him and never would.

Like cement, Kiowa whispered in the dark. I swear to God—boom, down. Not a word.

I've heard this, said Norman Bowker.

A pisser, you know? Still zipping himself up. Zapped while zipping.

All right, fine. That's enough.

Yeah, but you had to see it, the guy just—

I *heard,* man. Cement. So why not shut the fuck *up?*

Kiowa shook his head sadly and glanced over at the hole where Lieutenant Jimmy Cross sat watching the night. The air was thick and wet. A warm dense fog had settled over the paddies and there was the stillness that precedes rain.

After a time Kiowa sighed.

One thing for sure, he said. The lieutenant's in some deep hurt. I mean that crying jag—the way he was carrying on—it wasn't fake or anything, it was real heavy-duty hurt. The man cares.

Sure, Norman Bowker said.

Say what you want, the man does care.

We all got problems.

Not Lavender.

No, I guess not, Bowker said. Do me a favor, though.

Shut up?

That's a smart Indian. Shut up.

Shrugging, Kiowa pulled off his boots. He wanted to say more, just to lighten up his sleep, but instead he opened his New Testament and arranged it beneath his head as a pillow. The fog made things seem hollow and unattached. He tried not to think about Ted Lavender, but then he was thinking how fast it was, no drama, down and dead, and how it was hard to feel anything except surprise. It seemed unchristian. He wished he could find some great sadness, or even anger, but the emotion wasn't there and he couldn't make it happen. Mostly he felt pleased to be alive. He liked the smell of the New Testament under his cheek, the leather and ink and paper and glue, whatever the chemicals were. He liked hearing the sounds of night. Even his fatigue, it felt fine, the stiff muscles and the prickly awareness of his own body, a floating feeling. He enjoyed not being dead. Lying there, Kiowa admired Lieutenant Jimmy Cross's capacity for grief. He wanted to share the man's pain, he wanted to care as Jimmy Cross cared. And yet when he closed his eyes, all he could think was Boom-down, and all he could feel was the pleasure of having his boots off and the fog curling in around him and the damp soil and the Bible smells and the plush comfort of night.

After a moment Norman Bowker sat up in the dark.

What the hell, he said. You want to talk, *talk*. Tell it to me.

Forget it.

No, man, go on. One thing I hate, it's a silent Indian.

For the most part they carried themselves with poise, a kind of dignity. Now and then, however, there were times of panic, when they squealed or wanted to squeal but couldn't, when they twitched and made moaning sounds and covered their heads and said Dear Jesus and flopped around on the earth and fired their weapons blindly and cringed and sobbed and begged for the noise to stop and went wild and made stupid promises to themselves and to God and to their mothers and fathers, hoping not to die. In different ways, it happened to all of them. Afterward, when the firing ended, they would blink and peek up. They would touch their bodies, feeling shame, then quickly hiding it. They would force themselves to stand. As if in slow motion, frame by frame, the world would take on the old logic—absolute silence, then the wind, then sunlight, then voices. It was the burden of being alive. Awkwardly, the men would reassemble themselves, first in private, then in groups, becoming soldiers again. They would repair the leaks in their eyes. They would check for casualties, call in dustoffs, light cigarettes, try to smile, clear their throats and spit and begin cleaning their weapons. After a time someone would shake his head and say, No lie, I almost shit my pants, and someone else would laugh, which meant it was bad, yes, but the guy had obviously not shit his pants, it wasn't that bad, and in any case nobody would ever do such a thing and then go ahead and talk about it. They would squint into the dense, oppressive sunlight. For a few moments, perhaps, they would fall silent, lighting a joint and tracking its passage from man to man, inhaling, holding in the humiliation. Scary stuff, one of them might say. But then someone else would grin or flick his eyebrows and say, Roger-dodger, almost cut me a new asshole, *almost.*

There were numerous such poses. Some carried themselves with a sort of wistful resignation, others with pride or stiff soldierly discipline or good humor or macho zeal. They were afraid of dying but they were even more afraid to show it.

They found jokes to tell.

They used a hard vocabulary to contain the terrible softness. *Greased* they'd say. *Offed, lit up, zapped while zipping.* It wasn't cruelty, just stage presence. They were actors. When someone died, it wasn't quite dying, because in a curious way it seemed scripted, and because they had their lines mostly memorized, irony mixed with tragedy, and because they called it by other names, as if to encyst and destroy the reality of death itself. They kicked corpses. They cut off thumbs. They talked grunt lingo. They told stories about Ted Lavender's supply of tranquilizers, how the poor guy didn't feel a thing, how incredibly tranquil he was.

There's a moral here, said Mitchell Sanders.

They were waiting for Lavender's chopper, smoking the dead man's dope.

The moral's pretty obvious, Sanders said, and winked. Stay away from drugs. No joke, they'll ruin your day every time.

Cute, said Henry Dobbins.

Mind blower, get it? Talk about wiggy. Nothing left, just blood and brains.

They made themselves laugh.

There it is, they'd say. Over and over—there it is, my friend, there it is—as if the repetition itself were an act of poise, a balance between crazy and almost crazy, knowing without going, there it is, which meant be cool, let it ride, because Oh yeah, man, you can't change what can't be changed, there it is, there it absolutely and positively and fucking well *is.*

They were tough.

They carried all the emotional baggage of men who might die. Grief, terror, love, longing—these were intangibles, but the intangibles had their own mass and specific gravity, they had tangible weight. They carried shameful memories. They carried the common secret of cowardice barely restrained, the instinct to run or freeze or hide, and in many respects this was the heaviest burden of all, for it could never be put down, it required perfect balance and perfect posture. They carried their reputations. They carried the soldier's greatest fear, which was the fear of blushing. Men killed, and died, because they were embarrassed not to. It was what had brought them to the war in the first place, nothing positive, no dreams of glory or honor, just to avoid the blush of dishonor. They died so as not to die of embarrassment. They crawled into tunnels and walked point and advanced under fire. Each morning, despite the unknowns, they made their legs move. They endured. They kept humping. They did not submit to the obvious alternative, which was simply to close the eyes and fall. So easy, really. Go limp and tumble to the ground and let the muscles unwind and not speak and not budge until your buddies picked you up and lifted you into the chopper that would roar and dip its nose and carry you off to the world. A mere matter of falling, yet no one ever fell. It was not courage, exactly; the object was not valor. Rather, they were too frightened to be cowards.

By and large they carried these things inside, maintaining the masks of composure. They sneered at sick call. They spoke bitterly about guys who had found release by shooting off their own toes or fingers. Pussies, they'd say. Candy-asses. It was fierce, mocking talk, with only a trace of envy or awe, but even so the image played itself out behind their eyes.

They imagined the muzzle against flesh. So easy: squeeze the trigger and blow away a toe. They imagined it. They imagined the quick, sweet pain, then the evacuation to Japan, then a hospital with warm beds and cute geisha nurses.

And they dreamed of freedom birds.

At night, on guard, staring into the dark, they were carried away by jumbo jets. They felt the rush of takeoff. *Gone!* they yelled. And then velocity—wings and engines—a smiling stewardess—but it was more than a plane, it was a real bird, a big sleek silver bird with feathers and talons and high screeching. They were flying. The weights fell off; there was nothing to bear. They laughed and held on tight, feeling the cold slap of wind and altitude, soaring, thinking *It's over, I'm gone!*—they were naked, they were light and free—it was all lightness, bright and fast and buoyant, light as light, a helium buzz in the brain, a giddy bubbling in the lungs as they were taken up over the clouds and the war, beyond duty, beyond gravity and mortification and global entanglements—*Sin loi!* they yelled. *I'm sorry, motherfuckers, but I'm out of it, I'm goofed, I'm on a space cruise, I'm gone!*—and it was a restful, unencumbered sensation, just riding the light waves, sailing that big silver freedom bird over the mountains and oceans, over America, over the farms and great sleeping cities and cemeteries and highways and the golden arches of McDonald's, it was flight, a kind of fleeing, a kind of falling, falling higher and higher, spinning off the edge of the earth and beyond the sun and through the vast, silent vacuum where there were no burdens and where everything weighed exactly nothing—*Gone!* they screamed. *I'm sorry but I'm gone!*—and so at night, not quite dreaming, they gave themselves over to lightness, they were carried, they were purely borne.

On the morning after Ted Lavender died, First Lieutenant Jimmy Cross crouched at the bottom of his foxhole and burned Martha's letters. Then he burned the two photographs. There was a steady rain falling, which made it difficult, but he used heat tabs and Sterno to build a small fire, screening it with his body, holding the photographs over the tight blue flame with the tips of his fingers.

He realized it was only a gesture. Stupid, he thought. Sentimental, too, but mostly just stupid.

Lavender was dead. You couldn't burn the blame.

Besides, the letters were in his head. And even now, without photographs, Lieutenant Cross could see Martha playing volleyball in her white gym shorts and yellow T-shirt. He could see her moving in the rain.

When the fire died out, Lieutenant Cross pulled his poncho over his shoulders and ate breakfast from a can.

There was no great mystery, he decided.

In those burned letters Martha had never mentioned the war, except to say, Jimmy, take care of yourself. She wasn't involved. She signed the letters Love, but it wasn't love, and all the fine lines and technicalities did not matter. Virginity was no longer an issue. He hated her. Yes, he did. He hated her. Love, too, but it was a hard, hating kind of love.

The morning came up wet and blurry. Everything seemed part of everything else, the fog and Martha and the deepening rain.

He was a soldier, after all.

Half smiling, Lieutenant Jimmy Cross took out his maps. He shook his head hard, as if to clear it, then bent forward and began planning the day's march. In ten minutes, or maybe twenty, he would rouse the men and they would pack up and head west, where the maps showed the country to be green and inviting. They would do what they had always done. The rain might add some weight, but otherwise it would be one more day layered upon all the other days.

He was realistic about it. There was that new hardness in his stomach. He loved her but he hated her.

No more fantasies, he told himself.

Henceforth, when he thought about Martha, it would be only to think that she belonged elsewhere. He would shut down the daydreams. This was not Mount Sebastian, it was another world, where there were no pretty poems or midterm exams, a place where men died because of carelessness and gross stupidity. Kiowa was right. Boom-down, and you were dead, never partly dead.

Briefly, in the rain, Lieutenant Cross saw Martha's gray eyes gazing back at him.

He understood.

It was very sad, he thought. The things men carried inside. The things men did or felt they had to do.

He almost nodded at her, but didn't.

Instead he went back to his maps. He was now determined to perform his duties firmly and without negligence. It wouldn't help Lavender, he knew that, but from this point on he would comport himself as an officer. He would dispose of his good-luck pebble. Swallow it, maybe, or use Lee Strunk's slingshot, or just drop it along the trail. On the march he would impose strict field discipline. He would be careful to send out flank security, to prevent straggling or bunching up, to keep his troops moving at the proper pace and at the proper interval. He would insist on clean weapons. He would confiscate the remainder of Lavender's dope. Later in the day, perhaps, he would call the men together and speak to them plainly. He would accept the blame for what had happened to Ted Lavender. He would be a man about it. He would look them in the eyes, keeping his chin level, and he would issue the new SOPs in a calm, impersonal tone of voice, a lieutenant's voice, leaving no room for argument or discussion. Commencing immediately, he'd tell them, they would no longer abandon equipment along the route of march. They would police up their acts. They would get their shit together, and keep it together, and maintain it neatly and in good working order.

He would not tolerate laxity. He would show strength, distancing himself.

Among the men there would be grumbling, of course, and maybe worse, because their days would seem longer and their loads heavier, but Lieutenant Jimmy Cross reminded himself that his obligation was not to be loved but to lead. He would dispense with love; it was not now a factor. And if anyone quarreled or complained, he would simply tighten his lips and arrange his shoulders in the correct command posture. He might give a curt little nod. Or he might not. He might just shrug and say, Carry on, then they would saddle up and form into a column and move out toward the villages west of Than Khe.

CYNTHIA OZICK

The Shawl

CYNTHIA OZICK (1928–) has won many awards for her essays, novels, and short stories, including the American Academy of Arts and Letters Strauss Living Award, four O. Henry First Prizes, the Rea Award for the Short Story, and a Guggenheim Fellowship. She lives near New York City.

Stella, cold, cold, the coldness of hell. How they walked on the roads together, Rosa with Magda curled up between sore breasts, Magda wound up in the shawl. Sometimes Stella carried Magda. But she was jealous of Magda. A thin girl of fourteen, too small, with thin breasts of her own, Stella wanted to be wrapped in a shawl, hidden away, asleep, rocked by the march, a baby, a round infant in arms. Magda took Rosa's nipple, and Rosa never stopped walking, a walking cradle. There was not enough milk; sometimes Magda sucked air; then she screamed. Stella was ravenous. Her knees were tumors on sticks, her elbows chicken bones.

Rosa did not feel hunger; she felt light, not like someone walking but like someone in a faint, in trance, arrested in a fit, someone who is already a floating angel, alert and seeing everything, but in the air, not there, not touching the road. As if teetering on the tips of her fingernails. She looked into Magda's face through a gap in the shawl: a squirrel in a nest, safe, no one could reach her inside the little house of the shawl's windings. The face, very round, a pocket mirror of a face: but it was not Rosa's bleak complexion, dark like cholera, it was another kind of face altogether, eyes blue as air, smooth feathers of hair nearly as yellow as the Star sewn into Rosa's coat. You could think she was one of *their* babies.

Rosa, floating, dreamed of giving Magda away in one of the villages. She could leave the line for a minute and push Magda into the hands of any woman on the side of the road. But if she moved out of line they might shoot. And even if she fled the line for half a second and pushed the shawl-bundle at a stranger, would the woman take it? She might be surprised, or afraid; she might drop the shawl, and Magda would fall out and strike her head and die. The little round head. Such a good child, she gave up screaming, and sucked now only for the taste of the drying nipple itself. The neat grip of the tiny gums. One mite of a tooth tip sticking up in the bottom gum, how shining, an elfin tombstone of white marble gleaming there. Without complaining, Magda relinquished Rosa's teats, first the left, then the right; both were cracked, not a sniff of milk. The duct-crevice extinct, a dead volcano, blind eye, chill hole, so Magda took the corner of the shawl and milked it instead. She sucked and sucked, flooding the threads with wetness. The shawl's good flavor, milk of linen.

It was a magic shawl, it could nourish an infant for three days and three nights. Magda did not die, she stayed alive, although very quiet. A peculiar smell, of cinnamon and almonds, lifted out of her mouth. She held her eyes open every moment, forgetting how to blink or nap, and Rosa and sometimes Stella studied their blueness. On the road they raised one burden of a leg after another and studied Magda's face. "Aryan," Stella said, in a voice grown as thin as a string; and Rosa thought how Stella gazed at Magda like a young cannibal. And the time that Stella said "Aryan," it sounded to Rosa as if Stella had really said "Let us devour her."

But Magda lived to walk. She lived that long, but she did not walk very well, partly because she was only fifteen months old, and partly because the spindles of her legs could not hold up her fat belly. It was fat with air, full and round. Rosa gave almost all her food to Magda, Stella gave nothing; Stella was ravenous, a growing child herself, but not growing much. Stella did not menstruate. Rosa did not menstruate. Rosa was ravenous, but also not; she learned from Magda how to drink the taste of a finger in one's mouth. They were in a place without pity, all pity was annihilated in Rosa, she looked at Stella's bones without pity. She was sure that Stella was waiting for Magda to die so she could put her teeth into the little thighs.

Rosa knew Magda was going to die very soon; she should have been dead already, but she had been buried away deep inside the magic shawl, mistaken there for the shivering mound of Rosa's breasts; Rosa clung to the shawl as if it covered only herself. No one took it away from her. Magda was mute. She never cried. Rosa hid her in the barracks, under the shawl, but she knew that one day someone would inform; or one day someone, not even Stella, would steal Magda to eat her. When Magda began to walk Rosa knew that Magda was going to die very soon, something would happen. She was afraid to fall asleep; she slept with the weight of her thigh on Magda's body; she was afraid she would smother Magda under her thigh. The weight of Rosa was becoming less and less; Rosa and Stella were slowly turning into air.

Magda was quiet, but her eyes were horribly alive, like blue tigers. She watched. Sometimes she laughed—it seemed a laugh, but how could it be? Magda had never seen anyone laugh. Still, Magda laughed at her shawl when the wind blew its corners, the bad wind with pieces of black in it, that made Stella's and Rosa's eyes tear. Magda's eyes were always clear and tearless. She watched like a tiger. She guarded her shawl. No one could touch it; only Rosa could touch it. Stella was not allowed. The shawl was Magda's own baby, her pet, her little sister. She tangled herself up in it and sucked on one of the corners when she wanted to be very still.

Then Stella took the shawl away and made Magda die.

Afterward Stella said: "I was cold."

And afterward she was always cold, always. The cold went into her heart: Rosa saw that Stella's heart was cold. Magda flopped onward with her little pencil legs scribbling this way and that, in search of the shawl; the pencils faltered at the barracks opening, where the light began. Rosa saw and pursued. But already Magda was in the square outside the barracks, in the jolly light. It was the roll-call arena. Every morning Rosa had to conceal Magda under the shawl against a wall of the barracks and go out and stand in the arena with Stella and hundreds of others, sometimes for hours, and Magda, deserted, was quiet under the shawl, sucking on her corner. Every day Magda was silent, and so she did not die. Rosa saw that today Magda was going to die, and at the same time a fearful joy ran in Rosa's two palms, her fingers were on fire, she was astonished, febrile: Magda, in the sunlight, swaying on her pencil legs, was howling. Ever since the drying up of Rosa's nipples, ever since Magda's last scream on the road, Magda had been devoid of any syllable; Magda was a mute. Rosa believed that something had gone wrong with her vocal cords, with her windpipe, with the cave of her larynx; Magda was defective, without a voice; perhaps she was deaf; there might be something amiss with her intelligence; Magda was dumb. Even the laugh that came when the ash-stippled wind made a clown out of Magda's shawl was only the air-blown showing of her teeth. Even when the lice, head lice and body lice, crazed her so that she became as wild as one of the big rats that plundered the barracks at daybreak looking for carrion, she rubbed and scratched and kicked and bit and rolled without a whimper. But now Magda's mouth was spilling a long viscous rope of clamor.

"Maaaa—"

It was the first noise Magda had ever sent out from her throat since the drying up of Rosa's nipples.

"Maaaa . . . aaa!"

Again! Magda was wavering in the perilous sunlight of the arena, scribbling on such pitiful little bent shins. Rosa saw. She saw that Magda was grieving for the loss of her shawl, she saw that Magda was going to die. A tide of commands hammered in Rosa's nipples: Fetch, get, bring! But she did not know which to go after first, Magda or the shawl. If she jumped out into the arena to snatch Magda up, the howling would not stop, because Magda would still not have the shawl; but if she ran back into the barracks to find the shawl, and if she found it, and if she came after Magda holding it and shaking it, then she would get Magda back, Magda would put the shawl in her mouth and turn dumb again.

Rosa entered the dark. It was easy to discover the shawl. Stella was heaped under it, asleep in her thin bones. Rosa tore the shawl free and flew—she could fly, she was only air—into the arena. The sunheat murmured of another life, of butterflies in summer. The light was placid, mellow. On the other side of the steel fence, far away, there were green meadows speckled with dandelions and deep-colored violets; beyond them, even farther, innocent tiger lilies, tall, lifting their orange bonnets. In the barracks they spoke of "flowers," of "rain": excrement, thick turd-braids, and the slow stinking maroon waterfall that slunk down from the upper bunks, the stink mixed with a bitter fatty floating smoke that greased Rosa's skin. She stood for an instant at the margin of the arena. Sometimes the electricity inside the fence would seem to hum; even Stella said it was only an imagining, but Rosa heard real sounds in the wire: grainy sad voices. The farther she was from the fence, the more clearly the voices crowded at her. The lamenting voices strummed so convincingly, so passionately, it was impossible to suspect them of being phantoms. The voices told her to hold up the shawl, high; the voices told her to shake it, to whip with it, to unfurl it like a flag. Rosa lifted, shook, whipped, unfurled. Far off, very far, Magda leaned across her air-fed belly, reaching out with the rods of her arms. She was high up, elevated, riding someone's shoulder. But the shoulder that carried Magda was not coming toward Rosa and the shawl, it was drifting away, the speck of Magda was moving more and more into the smoky distance. Above the shoulder a helmet glinted. The light tapped the helmet and sparkled it into a goblet. Below the helmet a black body like a domino and a pair of black boots hurled themselves in the direction of the electrified fence. The electric voices began to chatter wildly. "Maamaa, maaamaaa," they all hummed together. How far Magda was from Rosa now, across the whole square, past a dozen barracks, all the way on the other side! She was no bigger than a moth.

All at once Magda was swimming through the air. The whole of Magda traveled through loftiness. She looked like a butterfly touching a silver vine. And the moment Magda's feathered round head and her pencil legs and balloonish belly and zigzag arms splashed against the fence, the steel voices went mad in their growling, urging Rosa to run and run to the spot where Magda had fallen from her flight against the electrified fence; but of course Rosa did not obey them. She only stood, because if she ran they would shoot, and if she tried to pick up the sticks of Magda's body they would shoot, and if she let the wolf's screech ascending now through the ladder of her skeleton break out, they would shoot; so she took Magda's shawl and filled her own mouth with it, stuffed it in and stuffed it in, until she was swallowing up the wolf's screech and tasting the cinnamon and almond depth of Magda's saliva; and Rosa drank Magda's shawl until it dried.

ANNIE PROULX

Brokeback Mountain

ANNIE PROULX (1935–) is the author of two short-story collections, *Heart Songs and Other Stories* and *Close Range.* She has also written three novels: *Postcards, The Shipping News,* and *Accordion Crimes.* Her books have been translated into twenty languages. Winner of the Pulitzer Prize, a National Book Award, the *Irish Times* International Fiction Prize, and a PEN/Faulkner Award, she lives and writes in Wyoming.

Ennis del Mar wakes before five, wind rocking the trailer, hissing in around the aluminum door and window frames. The shirts hanging on a nail shudder slightly in the draft. He gets up, scratching the grey wedge of belly and pubic hair, shuffles to the gas burner, pours leftover coffee in a chipped enamel pan; the flame swathes it in blue. He turns on the tap and urinates in the sink, pulls on his shirt and jeans, his worn boots, stamping the heels against the floor to get them full on. The wind booms down the curved length of the trailer and under its roaring passage he can hear the scratching of fine gravel and sand. It could be bad on the highway with the horse trailer. He has to be packed and away from the place that morning. Again the ranch is on the market and they've shipped out the last of the horses, paid everybody off the day before, the owner saying, "Give em to the real estate shark, I'm out a here," dropping the keys in Ennis's hand. He might have to stay with his married daughter until he picks up another job, yet he is suffused with a sense of pleasure because Jack Twist was in his dream.

The stale coffee is boiling up but he catches it before it goes over the side, pours it into a stained cup and blows on the black liquid, lets a panel of the dream slide forward. If he does not force his attention on it, it might stoke the day, rewarm that old, cold time on the mountain when they owned the world and nothing seemed wrong. The wind strikes the trailer like a load of dirt coming off a dump truck, eases, dies, leaves a temporary silence.

*   *   *

They were raised on small, poor ranches in opposite corners of the state, Jack Twist in Lightning Flat up on the Montana border, Ennis del Mar from around Sage, near the Utah line, both high school dropout country boys with no prospects, brought up to hard work and privation, both rough-mannered, rough-spoken, inured to the stoic life. Ennis, reared by his older brother and sister after their parents drove off the only curve on Dead Horse Road leaving them twenty-four dollars in cash and a two-mortgage ranch, applied at age fourteen for a hardship license that let him make the hour-long trip from the ranch to the high school. The pickup was old, no heater, one windshield wiper and bad tires; when the transmission went there was no money to fix it. He had wanted to be a sophomore, felt the word carried a kind of distinction, but the truck broke down short of it, pitching him directly into ranch work.

In 1963 when he met Jack Twist, Ennis was engaged to Alma Beers. Both Jack and Ennis claimed to be saving money for a small spread; in Ennis's case that meant a tobacco can with two five-dollar bills inside. That spring, hungry for any job, each had signed up with Farm and Ranch Employment—they came together on paper as herder and camp tender for the same sheep operation north of Signal. The summer range lay above the tree line on Forest Service land on Brokeback Mountain. It would be Jack Twist's second summer on the mountain, Ennis's first. Neither of them was twenty.

They shook hands in the choky little trailer office in front of a table littered with scribbled papers, a Bakelite ashtray brimming with stubs. The venetian blinds hung askew and admitted a triangle of white light, the shadow of the foreman's hand moving into it. Joe Aguirre, wavy hair the color of cigarette ash and parted down the middle, gave them his point of view.

"Forest Service got designated campsites on the allotments. Them camps can be a couple a miles from where we pasture the sheep. Bad predator loss, nobody near lookin after em at night. What I want, camp tender in the main camp where the Forest Service says, but the HERDER"—pointing at Jack with a chop of his hand—"pitch a pup tent on the q.t. with the sheep, out a sight, and he's goin a SLEEP there. Eat supper, breakfast in camp, but SLEEP WITH THE SHEEP, hundred percent, NO FIRE, don't leave NO SIGN. Roll up that tent every mornin case Forest Service snoops around. Got the dogs, your .30-.30, sleep there. Last summer had goddamn near twenty-five percent loss. I don't want that again. YOU," he said to Ennis, taking in the ragged hair, the big nicked hands, the jeans torn, button-gaping shirt, "Fridays twelve noon be down at the bridge with your next week list and mules. Somebody with supplies'll be there in a pickup." He didn't ask if Ennis had a watch but took a cheap round ticker on a braided cord from a box on a high shelf, wound and set it, tossed it to him as if he weren't worth the reach. "TOMORROW MORNIN we'll truck you up the jump-off." Pair of deuces going nowhere.

They found a bar and drank beer through the afternoon, Jack telling Ennis about a lightning storm on the mountain the year before that killed forty-two sheep, the peculiar stink of them and the way they bloated, the need for plenty of whiskey up there. He had shot an eagle, he said, turned his head to show the tail feather in his hatband. At first glance Jack seemed fair enough with his curly hair and quick laugh, but for a small man he carried some weight in the haunch and his smile disclosed buckteeth, not pronounced enough to let him eat popcorn out of the neck of a jug, but noticeable. He was infatuated with the rodeo life and fastened his belt with a minor bull-riding buckle, but his boots were worn to the quick, holed beyond repair and he was crazy to be somewhere, anywhere else than Lightning Flat.

Ennis, high-arched nose and narrow face, was scruffy and a little cave-chested, balanced a small torso on long, caliper legs, possessed a muscular and supple body made for the horse and for fighting. His reflexes were uncommonly quick and he was farsighted enough to dislike reading anything except Hamley's saddle catalog.

The sheep trucks and horse trailers unloaded at the trailhead and a bandy-legged Basque showed Ennis how to pack the mules, two packs and a riding load on each animal ring-lashed with double diamonds and secured with half hitches, telling him, "Don't never order soup. Them boxes a soup are real bad to pack." Three puppies belonging to one of the blue heelers went in a pack basket, the runt inside Jack's coat, for he loved a little dog. Ennis picked out a big chestnut called Cigar Butt to ride, Jack a bay mare who turned out to have a low startle point. The string of spare horses included a mouse-colored grullo whose looks Ennis liked. Ennis and Jack, the dogs, horses and mules, a thousand ewes and their lambs flowed up the trail like dirty water through the timber and out above the tree line into the great flowery meadows and the coursing, endless wind.

They got the big tent up on the Forest Service's platform, the kitchen and grub boxes secured. Both slept in camp that first night, Jack already bitching about Joe Aguirre's sleep-with-the-sheep-and-no-fire order, though he saddled the bay mare in the dark morning without saying much. Dawn came glassy orange, stained from below by a gelatinous band of pale green. The sooty bulk of the mountain paled slowly until it was the same color as the smoke from Ennis's breakfast fire. The cold air sweetened, banded pebbles and crumbs of soil cast sudden pencil-long shadows and the rearing lodgepole pines below them massed in slabs of somber malachite.

During the day Ennis looked across a great gulf and sometimes saw Jack, a small dot moving across a high meadow as an insect moves across a tablecloth; Jack, in his dark camp, saw Ennis as night fire, a red spark on the huge black mass of mountain.

* * *

Jack came lagging in late one afternoon, drank his two bottles of beer cooled in a wet sack on the shady side of the tent, ate two bowls of stew, four of Ennis's stone biscuits, a can of peaches, rolled a smoke, watched the sun drop.

"I'm commutin four hours a day," he said morosely. "Come in for breakfast, go back to the sheep, evenin get em bedded down, come in for supper, go back to the sheep, spend half the night jumpin up and checkin for coyotes. By rights I should be spendin the night here. Aguirre got no right a make me do this."

"You want a switch?" said Ennis. "I wouldn't mind herdin. I wouldn't mind sleepin out there."

"That ain't the point. Point is, we both should be in this camp. And that goddamn pup tent smells like cat piss or worse."

"Wouldn't mind bein out there."

"Tell you what, you got a get up a dozen times in the night out there over them coyotes. Happy to switch but give you warnin I can't cook worth a shit. Pretty good with a can opener."

"Can't be no worse than me, then. Sure, I wouldn't mind a do it."

They fended off the night for an hour with the yellow kerosene lamp and around ten Ennis rode Cigar Butt, a good night horse, through the glimmering frost back to the sheep, carrying leftover biscuits, a jar of jam and a jar of coffee with him for the next day saying he'd save a trip, stay out until supper.

"Shot a coyote just first light," he told Jack the next evening, sloshing his face with hot water, lathering up soap and hoping his razor had some cut left in it, while Jack peeled potatoes. "Big son of a bitch. Balls on him size a apples. I bet he'd took a few lambs. Looked like he could a eat a camel. You want some a this hot water? There's plenty."

"It's all yours."

"Well, I'm goin a warsh everthing I can reach," he said, pulling off his boots and jeans (no drawers, no socks, Jack noticed), slopping the green washcloth around until the fire spat.

They had a high-time supper by the fire, a can of beans each, fried potatoes and a quart of whiskey on shares, sat with their backs against a log, boot soles and copper jeans rivets hot, swapping the bottle while the lavender sky emptied of color and the chill air drained down, drinking, smoking cigarettes, getting up every now and then to piss, firelight throwing a sparkle in the arched stream, tossing sticks on the fire to keep the talk going, talking horses and rodeo, roughstock events, wrecks and injuries sustained, the submarine *Thresher* lost two months earlier with all hands and how it must have been in the last doomed minutes, dogs each had owned and known, the draft, Jack's home ranch where his father and mother held on, Ennis's family place folded years ago after his folks died, the older brother in Signal and a married sister in Casper. Jack said his father had been a pretty well known bullrider years back but kept his secrets to himself, never gave Jack a word of advice, never came once to see Jack ride, though he had put him on the woolies when he was a little kid. Ennis said the kind of riding that interested him lasted longer than eight seconds and had some point to it. Money's a good point, said Jack, and Ennis had to agree. They were respectful of each other's opinions, each glad to have a companion where none had been expected. Ennis, riding against the wind back to the sheep in the treacherous, drunken light, thought he'd never had such a good time, felt he could paw the white out of the moon.

The summer went on and they moved the herd to new pasture, shifted the camp; the distance between the sheep and the new camp was greater and the night ride longer. Ennis rode easy, sleeping with his eyes open, but the hours he was away from the sheep stretched out and out. Jack pulled a squalling burr out of the harmonica, flattened a little from a fall off the skittish bay mare, and Ennis had a good raspy voice; a few nights they mangled their way through some songs. Ennis knew the salty words to "Strawberry Roan." Jack tried a Carl Perkins song, bawling "what I say-ay-ay," but he favored a sad hymn, "Water-Walking Jesus," learned from his mother who believed in the Pentecost, that he sang at dirge slowness, setting off distant coyote yips.

"Too late to go out to them damn sheep," said Ennis, dizzy drunk on all fours one cold hour when the moon had notched past two. The meadow stones glowed white-green and a flinty wind worked over the meadow, scraped the fire low, then ruffled it into yellow silk sashes. "Got you a extra blanket I'll roll up out here and grab forty winks, ride out at first light."

"Freeze your ass off when that fire dies down. Better off sleepin in the tent."

"Doubt I'll feel nothin." But he staggered under canvas, pulled his boots off, snored on the ground cloth for a while, woke Jack with the clacking of his jaw.

"Jesus Christ, quit hammerin and get over here. Bedroll's big enough," said Jack in an irritable sleep-clogged voice. It was big enough, warm enough, and in a little while they deepened their intimacy considerably. Ennis ran full-throttle on all roads whether fence mending or money spending, and he wanted none of it when Jack seized his left hand and brought it to his erect cock. Ennis jerked his hand away as though he'd touched fire, got to his knees, unbuckled his belt, shoved his pants down, hauled Jack onto all fours and, with the help of the clear slick and a little spit, entered him, nothing he'd done before but no instruction manual needed. They went at it in silence except for a few sharp intakes of breath and Jack's choked "gun's goin *off*," then out, down, and asleep.

Ennis woke in red dawn with his pants around his knees, a top-grade headache, and Jack butted against him; without saying anything about it both knew how it would go for the rest of the summer, sheep be damned.

As it did go. They never talked about the sex, let it happen, at first only in the tent at night, then in the full daylight with the hot sun striking down, and at evening in the fire glow, quick, rough, laughing and snorting, no lack of noises, but saying not a goddamn word except once Ennis said, "I'm not no queer," and Jack jumped in with "Me neither. A one-shot thing. Nobody's business but ours." There were only the two of them on the mountain flying in the euphoric, bitter air, looking down on the hawk's back and the crawling lights of vehicles on the plain below, suspended above ordinary affairs and distant from tame ranch dogs barking in the dark hours. They believed themselves invisible, not knowing Joe Aguirre had watched them through his 10 x 42 binoculars for ten minutes one day, waiting until they'd buttoned up their jeans, waiting until Ennis rode back to the sheep, before bringing up the message that Jack's people had sent word that his uncle Harold was in the hospital with pneumonia and expected not to make it. Though he did, and Aguirre came up again to say so, fixing Jack with his bold stare, not bothering to dismount.

In August Ennis spent the whole night with Jack in the main camp and in a blowy hailstorm the sheep took off west and got among a herd in another allotment. There was a damn miserable time for five days, Ennis and a Chilean herder with no English trying to sort them out, the task almost impossible as the paint brands were worn and faint at this late season. Even when the numbers were right Ennis knew the sheep were mixed. In a disquieting way everything seemed mixed.

The first snow came early, on August thirteenth, piling up a foot, but was followed by a quick melt. The next week Joe Aguirre sent word to bring them down—another, bigger storm was moving in from the Pacific—and they packed in the game and moved off the mountain with the sheep, stones rolling at their heels, purple cloud crowding in from the west and the metal smell of coming snow pressing them on. The mountain boiled with demonic energy, glazed with flickering broken-cloud light, the wind combed the grass and drew from the damaged krummholz and slit rock a bestial drone. As they descended the slope Ennis felt he was in a slow-motion, but headlong, irreversible fall.

Joe Aguirre paid them, said little. He had looked at the milling sheep with a sour expression, said, "Some a these never went up there with you." The count was not what he'd hoped for either. Ranch stiffs never did much of a job.

"You goin a do this next summer?" said Jack to Ennis in the street, one leg already up in his green pickup. The wind was gusting hard and cold.

"Maybe not." A dust plume rose and hazed the air with fine grit and he squinted against it. "Like I said, Alma and me's gettin married in December.

Try to get somethin on a ranch. You?" He looked away from Jack's jaw, bruised blue from the hard punch Ennis had thrown him on the last day.

"If nothin better comes along. Thought some about going back up to my daddy's place, give him a hand over the winter, then maybe head out for Texas in the spring. If the draft don't get me."

"Well, see you around, I guess." The wind tumbled an empty feed bag down the street until it fetched up under his truck.

"Right," said Jack, and they shook hands, hit each other on the shoulder, then there was forty feet of distance between them and nothing to do but drive away in opposite directions. Within a mile Ennis felt like someone was pulling his guts out hand over hand a yard at a time. He stopped at the side of the road and, in the whirling new snow, tried to puke but nothing came up. He felt about as bad as he ever had and it took a long time for the feeling to wear off.

In December Ennis married Alma Beers and had her pregnant by mid-January. He picked up a few short-lived ranch jobs, then settled in as a wrangler on the old Elwood Hi-Top place north of Lost Cabin in Washakie County. He was still working there in September when Alma Jr., as he called his daughter, was born and their bedroom was full of the smell of old blood and milk and baby shit, and the sounds were of squalling and sucking and Alma's sleepy groans, all reassuring of fecundity and life's continuance to one who worked with livestock.

When the Hi-Top folded they moved to a small apartment in Riverton up over a laundry. Ennis got on the highway crew, tolerating it but working weekends at the Rafter B in exchange for keeping his horses out there. The second girl was born and Alma wanted to stay in town near the clinic because the child had an asthmatic wheeze.

"Ennis, please, no more damn lonesome ranches for us," she said, sitting on his lap, wrapping her thin, freckled arms around him. "Let's get a place here in town?"

"I guess," said Ennis, slipping his hand up her blouse sleeve and stirring the silky armpit hair, then easing her down, fingers moving up her ribs to the jelly breast, over the round belly and knee and up into the wet gap all the way to the north pole or the equator depending which way you thought you were sailing, working at it until she shuddered and bucked against his hand and he rolled her over, did quickly what she hated. They stayed in the little apartment which he favored because it could be left at any time.

The fourth summer since Brokeback Mountain came on and in June Ennis had a general delivery letter from Jack Twist, the first sign of life in all that time.

Friend this letter is a long time over due. Hope you get it. Heard you was in Riverton. Im coming thru on the 24th, thought Id stop and buy you a beer. Drop me a line if you can, say if your there.

The return address was Childress, Texas. Ennis wrote back, *you bet,* gave the Riverton address.

The day was hot and clear in the morning, but by noon the clouds had pushed up out of the west rolling a little sultry air before them. Ennis, wearing his best shirt, white with wide black stripes, didn't know what time Jack would get there and so had taken the day off, paced back and forth, looking down into a street pale with dust. Alma was saying something about taking his friend to the Knife & Fork for supper instead of cooking it was so hot, if they could get a baby-sitter, but Ennis said more likely he'd just go out with Jack and get drunk. Jack was not a restaurant type, he said, thinking of the dirty spoons sticking out of the cans of cold beans balanced on the log.

Late in the afternoon, thunder growling, that same old green pickup rolled in and he saw Jack get out of the truck, beat-up Resistol tilted back. A hot jolt scalded Ennis and he was out on the landing pulling the door closed behind him. Jack took the stairs two and two. They seized each other by the shoulders, hugged mightily, squeezing the breath out of each other, saying, son of a bitch, son of a bitch, then, and easily as the right key turns the lock tumblers, their mouths came together, and hard, Jack's big teeth bringing blood, his hat falling to the floor, stubble rasping, wet saliva welling, and the door opening and Alma looking out for a few seconds at Ennis's straining shoulders and shutting the door again and still they clinched, pressing chest and groin and thigh and leg together, treading on each other's toes until they pulled apart to breathe and Ennis, not big on endearments, said what he said to his horses and daughters, little darlin.

The door opened again a few inches and Alma stood in the narrow light.

What could he say? "Alma, this is Jack Twist, Jack, my wife Alma." His chest was heaving. He could smell Jack—the intensely familiar odor of cigarettes, musky sweat and a faint sweetness like grass, and with it the rushing cold of the mountain. "Alma," he said, "Jack and me ain't seen each other in four years." As if it were a reason. He was glad the light was dim on the landing but did not turn away from her.

"Sure enough," said Alma in a low voice. She had seen what she had seen. Behind her in the room lightning lit the window like a white sheet waving and the baby cried.

"You got a kid?" said Jack. His shaking hand grazed Ennis's hand, electrical current snapped between them.

"Two little girls," Ennis said. "Alma Jr. and Francine. Love them to pieces." Alma's mouth twitched.

"I got a boy," said Jack. "Eight months old. Tell you what, I married a cute little old Texas girl down in Childress—Lureen." From the vibration of the floorboard on which they both stood Ennis could feel how hard Jack was shaking.

"Alma," he said. "Jack and me is goin out and get a drink. Might not get back tonight, we get drinkin and talkin."

"Sure enough," Alma said, taking a dollar bill from her pocket. Ennis guessed she was going to ask him to get her a pack of cigarettes, bring him back sooner.

"Please to meet you," said Jack, trembling like a run-out horse.

"Ennis—" said Alma in her misery voice, but that didn't slow him down on the stairs and he called back, "Alma, you want smokes there's some in the pocket a my blue shirt in the bedroom."

They went off in Jack's truck, bought a bottle of whiskey and within twenty minutes were in the Motel Siesta jouncing a bed. A few handfuls of hail rattled against the window followed by rain and slippery wind banging the unsecured door of the next room then and through the night.

The room stank of semen and smoke and sweat and whiskey, of old carpet and sour hay, saddle leather, shit and cheap soap. Ennis lay spread-eagled, spent and wet, breathing deep, still half tumescent, Jack blowing forceful cigarette clouds like whale spouts, and Jack said, "Christ, it got a be all that time a yours ahorseback makes it so goddamn good. We got to talk about this. Swear to god I didn't know we was goin a get into this again—yeah, I did. Why I'm here. I fuckin knew it. Redlined all the way, couldn't get here fast enough."

"I didn't know where in the *hell* you was," said Ennis. "Four years. I about give up on you. I figured you was sore about that punch."

"Friend," said Jack, "I was in Texas rodeoin. How I met Lureen. Look over on that chair."

On the back of the soiled orange chair he saw the shine of a buckle. "Bull-ridin?"

"Yeah. I made three fuckin thousand dollars that year. Fuckin starved. Had to borrow everthing but a toothbrush from other guys. Drove grooves across Texas. Half the time under that cunt truck fixin it. Anyway, I didn't never think about losin. Lureen? There's some serious money there. Her old man's got it. Got this farm machinery business. Course he don't let her have none a the money, and he hates my fuckin guts, so it's a hard go now but one a these days—"

"Well, you're goin a go where you look. Army didn't get you?" The thunder sounded far to the east, moving from them in its red wreaths of light.

"They can't get no use out a me. Got some crushed vertebrates. And a stress fracture, the arm bone here, you know how bullridin you're always leverin it off your thigh?—she gives a little ever time you do it. Even if you tape it good you break it a little goddamn bit at a time. Tell you what, hurts like a bitch afterwards. Had a busted leg. Busted in three places. Come off the bull and it was a big bull with a lot a drop, he got rid a me in about three flat and he come after me and he was sure faster. Lucky enough. Friend a mine got his oil checked with a horn dipstick and that was all she wrote. Bunch a other things, fuckin busted ribs, sprains and pains, torn ligaments. See, it ain't like it was in my daddy's time. It's guys with money go to college, trained athaletes. You got a have some money to rodeo now. Lureen's old man wouldn't give me a dime if I dropped it, except one way. And I know enough about the game now so I see that I ain't never goin a be on the bubble. Other reasons. I'm gettin out while I still can walk."

Ennis pulled Jack's hand to his mouth, took a hit from the cigarette, exhaled. "Sure as hell seem in one piece to me. You know, I was sittin up here all that time tryin to figure out if I was—? I know I ain't. I mean here we both got wives and kids, right? I like doin it with women, yeah, but Jesus H., ain't nothin like this. I never had no thoughts a doin it with another guy except I sure wrang it out a hunderd times thinkin about you. You do it with other guys? Jack?"

"Shit no," said Jack, who had been riding more than bulls, not rolling his own. "You know that. Old Brokeback got us good and it sure ain't over. We got a work out what the fuck we're goin a do now."

"That summer," said Ennis. "When we split up after we got paid out I had gut cramps so bad I pulled over and tried to puke, thought I ate somethin bad at that place in Dubois. Took me about a year a figure out it was that I shouldn't a let you out a my sights. Too late then by a long, long while."

"Friend," said Jack. "We got us a fuckin situation here. Got a figure out what to do."

"I doubt there's nothin now we can do," said Ennis. "What I'm sayin, Jack, I built a life up in them years. Love my little girls. Alma? It ain't her fault. You got your baby and wife, that place in Texas. You and me can't hardly be decent together if what happened back there"—he jerked his head in the direction of the apartment—"grabs on us like that. We do that in the wrong place we'll be dead. There's no reins on this one. It scares the piss out a me."

"Got to tell you, friend, maybe somebody seen us that summer. I was back there the next June, thinkin about goin back—I didn't, lit out for Texas instead—and Joe Aguirre's in the office and he says to me, he says, 'You boys found a way to make the time pass up there, didn't you,' and I give him a look but when I went out I seen he had a big-ass pair a binoculars hangin off his rearview." He neglected to add that the foreman had leaned back in his squeaky wooden tilt chair, said, Twist, you guys wasn't gettin paid to leave the dogs baby-sit the sheep while you stemmed the rose, and declined to rehire him. He went on, "Yeah, that little punch a yours surprised me. I never figured you to throw a dirty punch."

"I come up under my brother K.E., three years older'n me, slugged me silly ever day. Dad got tired a me come bawlin in the house and when I was about six he set me down and says, Ennis, you got a problem and you got a fix it or it's gonna be with you until you're ninety and K.E.'s ninety-three. Well, I says, he's bigger'n me. Dad says, you got a take him unawares, don't say nothin to him, make him feel some pain, get out fast and keep doin it until he takes the message. Nothin like hurtin somebody to make him hear good. So I did. I got him in the outhouse, jumped him on the stairs, come over to his pillow in the night while he was sleepin and pasted him damn good. Took about two days. Never had trouble with K.E. since. The lesson was, don't say nothin and get it over with quick." A telephone rang in the next room, rang on and on, stopped abruptly in mid-peal.

"You won't catch me again," said Jack. "Listen. I'm thinkin, tell you what, if you and me had a little ranch together, little cow and calf operation, your horses, it'd be some sweet life. Like I said, I'm gettin out a rodeo. I ain't no broke-dick rider but I don't got the bucks a ride out this slump I'm in and I don't got the bones a keep gettin wrecked. I got it figured, got this plan, Ennis, how we can do it, you and me. Lureen's old man, you bet he'd give me a bunch if I'd get lost. Already more or less said it—"

"Whoa, whoa, whoa. It ain't goin a be that way. We can't. I'm stuck with what I got, caught in my own loop. Can't get out of it. Jack, I don't want a be like them guys you see around sometimes. And I don't want a be dead. There was these two old guys ranched together down home, Earl and Rich—Dad would pass a remark when he seen them. They was a joke even though they was pretty tough old birds. I was what, nine years old and they found Earl dead in a irrigation ditch. They'd took a tire iron to him, spurred him up, drug him around by his dick until it pulled off, just bloody pulp. What the tire iron done looked like pieces a burned tomatoes all over him, nose tore down from skiddin on gravel."

"You seen that?"

"Dad made sure I seen it. Took me to see it. Me and K.E. Dad laughed about it. Hell, for all I know he done the job. If he was alive and was to put his head in that door right now you bet he'd go get his tire iron. Two guys livin together? No. All I can see is we get together once in a while way the hell out in the back a nowhere—"

"How much is once in a while?" said Jack. "Once in a while ever four fuckin years?"

"No," said Ennis, forbearing to ask whose fault that was. "I goddamn hate it that you're goin a drive away in the mornin and I'm goin back to work. But if you can't fix it you got a stand it," he said. "Shit. I been lookin at people on the street. This happen a other people? What the hell do they do?"

"It don't happen in Wyomin and if it does I don't know what they do, maybe go to Denver," said Jack, sitting up, turning away from him, "and I don't give a flyin fuck. Son of a bitch, Ennis, take a couple days off. Right now. Get us out a here. Throw your stuff in the back a my truck and let's get up in the mountains. Couple a days. Call Alma up and tell her you're goin. Come on, Ennis, you just shot my airplane out a the sky—give me somethin a go on. This ain't no little thing that's happenin here."

The hollow ringing began again in the next room, and as if he were answering it, Ennis picked up the phone on the bedside table, dialed his own number.

A slow corrosion worked between Ennis and Alma, no real trouble, just widening water. She was working at a grocery store clerk job, saw she'd always have to work to keep ahead of the bills on what Ennis made. Alma asked Ennis to use rubbers because she dreaded another pregnancy. He said no to that, said he would be happy to leave her alone if she didn't want any more of his kids. Under her breath she said, "I'd have em if you'd support em." And under that, thought, anyway, what you like to do don't make too many babies.

Her resentment opened out a little every year: the embrace she had glimpsed, Ennis's fishing trips once or twice a year with Jack Twist and never a vacation with her and the girls, his disinclination to step out and have any fun, his yearning for low-paid, long-houred ranch work, his propensity to roll to the wall and sleep as soon as he hit the bed, his failure to look for a decent permanent job with the county or the power company, put her in a long, slow dive and when Alma Jr. was nine and Francine seven she said, what am I doin hangin around with him, divorced Ennis and married the Riverton grocer.

Ennis went back to ranch work, hired on here and there, not getting much ahead but glad enough to be around stock again, free to drop things, quit if he had to, and go into the mountains at short notice. He had no serious hard feelings, just a vague sense of getting shortchanged, and showed it was all right by taking Thanksgiving dinner with Alma and her grocer and the kids, sitting between his girls and talking horses to them, telling jokes, trying not to be a sad daddy. After the pie Alma got him off in the kitchen, scraped the plates and said she worried about him and he ought to get married again. He saw she was pregnant, about four, five months, he guessed.

"Once burned," he said, leaning against the counter, feeling too big for the room.

"You still go fishin with that Jack Twist?"

"Some." He thought she'd take the pattern off the plate with the scraping.

"You know," she said, and from her tone he knew something was coming, "I used to wonder how come you never brought any trouts home. Always said you caught plenty. So one time I got your creel case open the night before you went on one a your little trips—price tag still on it after five years—and I tied a note on the end of the line. It said, hello Ennis, bring some fish home, love, Alma. And then you come back and said you'd caught a bunch a browns and ate them up. Remember? I looked in the case when I got a chance and there was my note still tied there and that line hadn't touched water in its life." As though the word "water" had called out its domestic cousin she twisted the faucet, sluiced the plates.

"That don't mean nothin."

"Don't lie, don't try to fool me, Ennis. I know what it means. Jack Twist? Jack Nasty. You and him—"

She'd overstepped his line. He seized her wrist; tears sprang and rolled, a dish clattered.

"Shut up," he said. "Mind your own business. You don't know nothin about it."

"I'm goin a yell for Bill."

"You fuckin go right ahead. Go on and fuckin yell. I'll make him eat the fuckin floor and you too." He gave another wrench that left her with a burning bracelet, shoved his hat on backwards and slammed out. He went to the Black and Blue Eagle bar that night, got drunk, had a short dirty fight and left. He didn't try to see his girls for a long time, figuring they would look him up when they got the sense and years to move out from Alma.

They were no longer young men with all of it before them. Jack had filled out through the shoulders and hams, Ennis stayed as lean as a clothes-pole, stepped around in worn boots, jeans and shirts summer and winter, added a canvas coat in cold weather. A benign growth appeared on his eyelid and gave it a drooping appearance, a broken nose healed crooked.

Years on years they worked their way through the high meadows and mountain drainages, horse-packing into the Big Horns, Medicine Bows, south end of the Gallatins, Absarokas, Granites, Owl Creeks, the Bridger-Teton Range, the Freezeouts and the Shirleys, Ferrises and the Rattlesnakes, Salt River Range, into the Wind Rivers over and again, the Sierra Madres, Gros Ventres, the Washakies, Laramies, but never returning to Brokeback.

Down in Texas Jack's father-in-law died and Lureen, who inherited the farm equipment business, showed a skill for management and hard deals. Jack found himself with a vague managerial title, traveling to stock and agricultural machinery shows. He had some money now and found ways to spend it on his buying trips. A little Texas accent flavored his sentences, "cow" twisted into "kyow" and "wife" coming out as "waf." He'd had his front teeth filed down and capped, said he'd felt no pain, and to finish the job grew a heavy mustache.

In May of 1983 they spent a few cold days at a series of little icebound, no-name high lakes, then worked across into the Hail Strew River drainage.

Going up, the day was fine but the trail deep-drifted and slopping wet at the margins. They left it to wind through a slashy cut, leading the horses through brittle branchwood, Jack, the same eagle feather in his old hat, lifting his head in the heated noon to take the air scented with resinous lodgepole, the dry needle duff and hot rock, bitter juniper crushed beneath the horses' hooves. Ennis, weather-eyed, looked west for the heated cumulus that might come up on such a day but the boneless blue was so deep, said Jack, that he might drown looking up.

Around three they swung through a narrow pass to a southeast slope where the strong spring sun had had a chance to work, dropped down to the trail again which lay snowless below them. They could hear the river muttering and making a distant train sound a long way off. Twenty minutes on they surprised a black bear on the bank above them rolling a log over for grubs and Jack's horse shied and reared, Jack saying "Wo! Wo!" and Ennis's bay dancing and snorting but holding. Jack reached for the .30-.06 but there was no need; the startled bear galloped into the trees with the lumpish gait that made it seem it was falling apart.

The tea-colored river ran fast with snowmelt, a scarf of bubbles at every high rock, pools and setbacks streaming. The ochre-branched willows swayed stiffly, pollened catkins like yellow thumbprints. The horses drank and Jack dismounted, scooped icy water up in his hand, crystalline drops falling from his fingers, his mouth and chin glistening with wet.

"Get beaver fever doin that," said Ennis, then, "Good enough place," looking at the level bench above the river, two or three fire-rings from old hunting camps. A sloping meadow rose behind the bench, protected by a stand of lodgepole. There was plenty of dry wood. They set up camp without saying much, picketed the horses in the meadow. Jack broke the seal on a bottle of whiskey, took a long, hot swallow, exhaled forcefully, said, "That's one a the two things I need right now," capped and tossed it to Ennis.

On the third morning there were the clouds Ennis had expected, a grey racer out of the west, a bar of darkness driving wind before it and small flakes. It faded after an hour into tender spring snow that heaped wet and heavy. By nightfall it turned colder. Jack and Ennis passed a joint back and forth, the fire burning late, Jack restless and bitching about the cold, poking the flames with a stick, twisting the dial of the transistor radio until the batteries died.

Ennis said he'd been putting the blocks to a woman who worked part-time at the Wolf Ears bar in Signal where he was working now for Stoutamire's cow and calf outfit, but it wasn't going anywhere and she had some problems he didn't want. Jack said he'd had a thing going with the wife of a rancher down the road in Childress and for the last few months he'd slank around expecting to get shot by Lureen or the husband, one. Ennis laughed a little and said he probably deserved it. Jack said he was doing all right but he missed Ennis bad enough sometimes to make him whip babies.

The horses nickered in the darkness beyond the fire's circle of light. Ennis put his arm around Jack, pulled him close, said he saw his girls about once a month, Alma Jr. a shy seventeen-year-old with his beanpole length, Francine a little live wire. Jack slid his cold hand between Ennis's legs, said he was worried about his boy who was, no doubt about it, dyslexic or something, couldn't get anything right, fifteen years old and couldn't hardly read, *he* could see it though goddamn Lureen wouldn't admit to it and pretended the kid was o.k., refused to get any bitchin kind a help about it. He didn't know what the fuck the answer was. Lureen had the money and called the shots.

"I used a want a boy for a kid," said Ennis, undoing buttons, "but just got little girls."

"I didn't want none a either kind," said Jack. "But fuck-all has worked the way I wanted. Nothin never come to my hand the right way." Without getting up he threw deadwood on the fire, the sparks flying up with their truths and lies, a few hot points of fire landing on their hands and faces, not for the first time, and they rolled down into the dirt. One thing never changed: the brilliant charge of their infrequent couplings was darkened by the sense of time flying, never enough time, never enough.

A day or two later in the trailhead parking lot, horses loaded into the trailer, Ennis was ready to head back to Signal, Jack up to Lightning Flat to see the old man. Ennis leaned into Jack's window, said what he'd been putting off the whole week, that likely he couldn't get away again until November after they'd shipped stock and before winter feeding started.

"November. What in hell happened a August? Tell you what, we said August, nine, ten days. Christ, Ennis! Whyn't you tell me this before? You had a fuckin week to say some little word about it. And why's it we're always in the friggin cold weather? We ought a do somethin. We ought a go south. We ought a go to Mexico one day."

"Mexico? Jack, you know me. All the travelin I ever done is goin around the coffeepot lookin for the handle. And I'll be runnin the baler all August, that's what's the matter with August. Lighten up, Jack. We can hunt in

November, kill a nice elk. Try if I can get Don Wroe's cabin again. We had a good time that year."

"You know, friend, this is a goddamn bitch of a unsatisfactory situation. You used a come away easy. It's like seein the pope now."

"Jack, I got a work. Them earlier days I used a quit the jobs. You got a wife with money, a good job. You forget how it is bein broke all the time. You ever hear a child support? I been payin out for years and got more to go. Let me tell you, I can't quit this one. And I can't get the time off. It was tough gettin this time—some a them late heifers is still calvin. You don't leave then. You don't. Stoutamire is a hell-raiser and he raised hell about me takin the week. I don't blame him. He probly ain't got a night's sleep since I left. The trade-off was August. You got a better idea?"

"I did once." The tone was bitter and accusatory.

Ennis said nothing, straightened up slowly, rubbed at his forehead; a horse stamped inside the trailer. He walked to his truck, put his hand on the trailer, said something that only the horses could hear, turned and walked back at a deliberate pace.

"You been a Mexico, Jack?" Mexico was the place. He'd heard. He was cutting fence now, trespassing in the shoot-em zone.

"Hell yes, I been. Where's the fuckin problem?" Braced for it all these years and here it came, late and unexpected.

"I got a say this to you one time, Jack, and I ain't foolin. What I don't know," said Ennis, "all them things I don't know could get you killed if I should come to know them."

"Try this one," said Jack, "and *I'll* say it just one time. Tell you what, we could a had a good life together, a fuckin real good life. You wouldn't do it, Ennis, so what we got now is Brokeback Mountain. Everthing built on that. It's all we got, boy, fuckin all, so I hope you know that if you don't never know the rest. Count the damn few times we been together in twenty years. Measure the fuckin short leash you keep me on, then ask me about Mexico and then tell me you'll kill me for needin it and not hardly never gettin it. You got no fuckin idea how bad it gets. I'm not you. I can't make it on a couple a high-altitude fucks once or twice a year. You're too much for me, Ennis, you son of a whoreson bitch. I wish I knew how to quit you."

Like vast clouds of steam from thermal springs in winter the years of things unsaid and now unsayable—admissions, declarations, shames, guilts, fears—rose around them. Ennis stood as if heart-shot, face grey and deep-lined, grimacing, eyes screwed shut, fists clenched, legs caving, hit the ground on his knees.

"Jesus," said Jack. "Ennis?" But before he was out of the truck, trying to guess if it was heart attack or the overflow of an incendiary rage, Ennis was back on his feet and somehow, as a coat hanger is straightened to open a locked car and then bent again to its original shape, they torqued things almost to where they had been, for what they'd said was no news. Nothing ended, nothing begun, nothing resolved.

What Jack remembered and craved in a way he could neither help nor understand was the time that distant summer on Brokeback when Ennis had come up behind him and pulled him close, the silent embrace satisfying some shared and sexless hunger.

They had stood that way for a long time in front of the fire, its burning tossing ruddy chunks of light, the shadow of their bodies a single column against the rock. The minutes ticked by from the round watch in Ennis's pocket, from the sticks in the fire settling into coals. Stars bit through the wavy heat layers above the fire. Ennis's breath came slow and quiet, he hummed, rocked a little in the sparklight and Jack leaned against the steady heartbeat, the vibrations of the humming like faint electricity and, standing, he fell into sleep that was not sleep but something else drowsy and tranced until Ennis, dredging up a rusty but still useable phrase from the childhood time before his mother died, said, "Time to hit the hay, cowboy. I got a go. Come on, you're sleepin on your feet like a horse," and gave Jack a shake, a push, and went off in the darkness. Jack heard his spurs tremble as he mounted, the words "see you tomorrow," and the horse's shuddering snort, grind of hoof on stone.

Later, that dozy embrace solidified in his memory as the single moment of artless, charmed happiness in their separate and difficult lives. Nothing marred it, even the knowledge that Ennis would not then embrace him face to face because he did not want to see nor feel that it was Jack he held. And maybe, he thought, they'd never got much farther than that. Let be, let be.

Ennis didn't know about the accident for months until his postcard to Jack saying that November still looked like the first chance came back stamped DECEASED. He called Jack's number in Childress, something he had done only once before when Alma divorced him and Jack had misunderstood the reason for the call, had driven twelve hundred miles north for nothing. This would be all right, Jack would answer, had to answer. But he did not. It was Lureen and she said who? who is this? and when he told her again she said in a level voice yes, Jack was pumping up a flat on the truck out on a back road when the tire blew up. The bead was damaged somehow and the force of the explosion slammed the rim into his face, broke his nose and jaw and knocked him unconscious on his back. By the time someone came along he had drowned in his own blood.

No, he thought, they got him with the tire iron.

"Jack used to mention you," she said. "You're the fishing buddy or the hunting buddy, I know that. Would have let you know," she said, "but I wasn't sure about your name and address. Jack kept most a his friends' addresses in his head. It was a terrible thing. He was only thirty-nine years old."

The huge sadness of the northern plains rolled down on him. He didn't know which way it was, the tire iron or a real accident, blood choking down Jack's throat and nobody to turn him over. Under the wind drone he heard steel slamming off bone, the hollow chatter of a settling tire rim.

"He buried down there?" He wanted to curse her for letting Jack die on the dirt road.

The little Texas voice came slip-sliding down the wire. "We put a stone up. He use to say he wanted to be cremated, ashes scattered on Brokeback Mountain. I didn't know where that was. So he was cremated, like he wanted, and like I say, half his ashes was interred here, and the rest I sent up to his folks. I thought Brokeback Mountain was around where he grew up. But knowing Jack, it might be some pretend place where the bluebirds sing and there's a whiskey spring."

"We herded sheep on Brokeback one summer," said Ennis. He could hardly speak.

"Well, he said it was his place. I thought he meant to get drunk. Drink whiskey up there. He drank a lot."

"His folks still up in Lightnin Flat?"

"Oh yeah. They'll be there until they die. I never met them. They didn't come down for the funeral. You get in touch with them. I suppose they'd appreciate it if his wishes was carried out."

No doubt about it, she was polite but the little voice was cold as snow.

The road to Lightning Flat went through desolate country past a dozen abandoned ranches distributed over the plain at eight- and ten-mile intervals, houses sitting blank-eyed in the weeds, corral fences down. The mailbox read John C. Twist. The ranch was a meagre little place, leafy spurge taking over. The stock was too far distant for him to see their condition, only that they were black baldies. A porch stretched across the front of the tiny brown stucco house, four rooms, two down, two up.

Ennis sat at the kitchen table with Jack's father. Jack's mother, stout and careful in her movements as though recovering from an operation, said, "Want some coffee, don't you? Piece a cherry cake?"

"Thank you, ma'am, I'll take a cup a coffee but I can't eat no cake just now."

The old man sat silent, his hands folded on the plastic tablecloth, staring at

Ennis with an angry, knowing expression. Ennis recognized in him a not uncommon type with the hard need to be the stud duck in the pond. He couldn't see much of Jack in either one of them, took a breath.

"I feel awful bad about Jack. Can't begin to say how bad I feel. I knew him a long time. I come by to tell you that if you want me to take his ashes up there on Brokeback like his wife says he wanted I'd be proud to."

There was a silence. Ennis cleared his throat but said nothing more.

The old man said, "Tell you what, I know where Brokeback Mountain is. He thought he was too goddamn special to be buried in the family plot."

Jack's mother ignored this, said, "He used a come home every year, even after he was married and down in Texas, and help his daddy on the ranch for a week, fix the gates and mow and all. I kept his room like it was when he was a boy and I think he appreciated that. You are welcome to go up in his room if you want."

The old man spoke angrily. "I can't get no help out here. Jack used a say, 'Ennis del Mar,' he used a say, 'I'm goin a bring him up here one a these days and we'll lick this damn ranch into shape.' He had some half-baked idea the two a you was goin a move up here, build a log cabin and help me run this ranch and bring it up. Then, this spring he's got another one's goin a come up here with him and build a place and help run the ranch, some ranch neighbor a his from down in Texas. He's goin a split up with his wife and come back here. So he says. But like most a Jack's ideas it never come to pass."

So now he knew it had been the tire iron. He stood up, said, you bet he'd like to see Jack's room, recalled one of Jack's stories about this old man. Jack was dick-clipped and the old man was not; it bothered the son who had discovered the anatomical disconformity during a hard scene. He had been about three or four, he said, always late getting to the toilet, struggling with buttons, the seat, the height of the thing and often as not left the surroundings sprinkled down. The old man blew up about it and this one time worked into a crazy rage. "Christ, he licked the stuffin out a me, knocked me down on the bathroom floor, whipped me with his belt. I thought he was killin me. Then he says, 'You want a know what it's like with piss all over the place? I'll learn you,' and he pulls it out and lets go all over me, soaked me, then he throws a towel at me and makes me mop up the floor, take my clothes off and warsh them in the bathtub, warsh out the towel, I'm bawlin and blubberin. But while he was hosin me down I seen he had some extra material that I was missin. I seen they'd cut me different like you'd crop a ear or scorch a brand. No way to get it right with him after that."

The bedroom, at the top of a steep stair that had its own climbing rhythm, was tiny and hot, afternoon sun pounding through the west window, hitting the narrow boy's bed against the wall, an ink-stained desk and wooden chair, a b.b. gun in a hand-whittled rack over the bed. The window looked down on the gravel road stretching south and it occurred to him that for his growing-up years that was the only road Jack knew. An ancient magazine photograph of some dark-haired movie star was taped to the wall beside the bed, the skin tone gone magenta. He could hear Jack's mother downstairs running water, filling the kettle and setting it back on the stove, asking the old man a muffled question.

The closet was a shallow cavity with a wooden rod braced across, a faded cretonne curtain on a string closing it off from the rest of the room. In the closet hung two pairs of jeans crease-ironed and folded neatly over wire hangers, on the floor a pair of worn packer boots he thought he remembered. At the north end of the closet a tiny jog in the wall made a slight hiding place and here, stiff with long suspension from a nail, hung a shirt. He lifted it off the nail. Jack's old shirt from Brokeback days. The dried blood on the sleeve was his own blood, a gushing nosebleed on the last afternoon on the mountain when Jack, in their contortionistic grappling and wrestling, had slammed Ennis's nose hard with his knee. He had staunched the blood which was everywhere, all over both of them, with his shirtsleeve, but the staunching hadn't held because Ennis had suddenly swung from the deck and laid the ministering angel out in the wild columbine, wings folded.

The shirt seemed heavy until he saw there was another shirt inside it, the sleeves carefully worked down inside Jack's sleeves. It was his own plaid shirt, lost, he'd thought, long ago in some damn laundry, his dirty shirt, the pocket ripped, buttons missing, stolen by Jack and hidden here inside Jack's own shirt, the pair like two skins, one inside the other, two in one. He pressed his face into the fabric and breathed in slowly through his mouth and nose, hoping for the faintest smoke and mountain sage and salty sweet stink of Jack but there was no real scent, only the memory of it, the imagined power of Brokeback Mountain of which nothing was left but what he held in his hands.

In the end the stud duck refused to let Jack's ashes go. "Tell you what, we got a family plot and he's goin in it." Jack's mother stood at the table coring apples with a sharp, serrated instrument. "You come again," she said.

Bumping down the washboard road Ennis passed the country cemetery fenced with sagging sheep wire, a tiny fenced square on the welling prairie, a few graves bright with plastic flowers, and didn't want to know Jack was going in there, to be buried on the grieving plain.

A few weeks later on the Saturday he threw all Stoutamire's dirty horse blankets into the back of his pickup and took them down to the Quik Stop Car Wash to turn the high-pressure spray on them. When the wet clean blankets were stowed in the truck bed he stepped into Higgins's gift shop and busied himself with the postcard rack.

"Ennis, what are you lookin for rootin through them postcards?" said Linda Higgins, throwing a sopping brown coffee filter into the garbage can.

"Scene a Brokeback Mountain."

"Over in Fremont County?"

"No, north a here."

"I didn't order none a them. Let me get the order list. They got it I can get you a hunderd. I got a order some more cards anyway."

"One's enough," said Ennis.

When it came—thirty cents—he pinned it up in his trailer, brass-headed tack in each corner. Below it he drove a nail and on the nail he hung the wire hanger and the two old shirts suspended from it. He stepped back and looked at the ensemble through a few stinging tears.

"Jack, I swear—" he said, though Jack had never asked him to swear anything and was himself not the swearing kind.

Around that time Jack began to appear in his dreams, Jack as he had first seen him, curly-headed and smiling and bucktoothed, talking about getting up off his pockets and into the control zone, but the can of beans with the spoon handle jutting out and balanced on the log was there as well, in a cartoon shape and lurid colors that gave the dreams a flavor of comic obscenity. The spoon handle was the kind that could be used as a tire iron. And he would wake sometimes in grief, sometimes with the old sense of joy and release; the pillow sometimes wet, sometimes the sheets.

There was some open space between what he knew and what he tried to believe, but nothing could be done about it, and if you can't fix it you've got to stand it.

MARK RICHARD

Strays

MARK RICHARD (1955–) is the author of the novels *Charity* (Nan Talese/Doubleday, 1998) and *Fishboy* (Nan Talese/Doubleday, 1996). His debut collection of stories, *The Ice at the Bottom of the World* (Knopf, 1989), won the PEN/Hemingway Award for Best First Fiction. His short fiction has appeared in *The New Yorker, Esquire,* and *The Paris Review,* among other places. Richard lives in Los Angeles, where he is currently a story editor on the television program *Party of Five.*

At night stray dogs come up underneath our house to lick our leaking pipes. Beneath my brother and my's room we hear them coughing and growling, scratching their ratted backs against the boards beneath our beds. We lie awake listening, my brother thinking of names to name the one he is setting out to catch. Salute and Topboy are high on his list.

I tell my brother these dogs are wild and cowering. A bare-heeled stomp on the floor off our beds sends them scuttling spine-bowed out the crawl space beneath our open window. Sometimes when my brother is quick he leans out and touches one slipping away.

Our father has meant to put the screens back on the windows for spring. He has even hauled them out of the storage shed and stacked them in the drive. He lays them one by one over sawhorses to tack in the frames tighter and weave patches against mosquitoes. This is what he means to do, but our mother that morning pulls all the preserves off the shelves onto the floor, sticks my brother and my's Easter Sunday drawings in her mouth, and leaves the house on through the fields cleared the week before for corn.

Uncle Trash is our nearest relative with a car, and our mother has a good half-day head start on our father when Uncle Trash arrives. Uncle Trash runs his car up the drive in a big speed splitting all the screens stacked there from their frames. There is an exploded chicken in the grill of Uncle Trash's car.

They don't even turn it off as Uncle Trash slides out and our father gets behind the wheel, backing back over the screens, setting out in search of our mother.

Uncle Trash finds out that he has left his bottle under the seat of his car. He goes in our kitchen pulling out all the shelves our mother missed. Then he is in the towel box in the hall, looking, pulling out stuff in stacks. He is in our parents' room opening short doors. He is in the storage shed opening and sniffing a Mason jar of gasoline for the power mower. Uncle Trash comes up and asks, Which way is it to town for a drink? I point up the road and he sets off saying, Don't y'all burn the house down.

My brother and I hang out in the side yard doing handstands until dark. We catch handfuls of lightning bugs and smear bright yellow on our shirts. It is late. I wash our feet and put us to bed. We wait for somebody to come back home but nobody ever does. Lucky for me when my brother begins to whine for our mother the stray dogs show up under the house and he starts making up lists of new names for them, soothing himself to sleep.

Hungry, we wake up to something sounding in the kitchen not like our mother fixing us anything to eat. It is Uncle Trash throwing up and spitting blood into the pump-handled sink. I ask him did he have an accident and he sends my brother upstairs for Merthiolate and Q-Tips. His face is angled out from his head on one side, so that sided eye is shut. His good eye waters wiggling loose teeth with cut-up fingers. Uncle Trash says he had an accident all right. He says he was up in a card game and then he was real up in a card game, so up he bet his car, accidentally forgetting that our father had driven off with it in search of our mother. Uncle Trash said the man who won the card game went ahead and beat up Uncle Trash on purpose anyway.

All day Uncle Trash sleeps in our parents' room. We can hear him snoring from the front yard where my brother and I dig in the dirt with spoons making roadbeds and highways for my tin-metal trucks. In the evening Uncle Trash comes down in one of our father's shirts, dirty, but cleaner than the one he had gotten beat up in. We then have banana sandwiches for supper and Uncle Trash asks do we have a deck of cards in the house. He says he wants to see do his tooth-cut fingers still flex enough to work. I have to tell him how our mother disallows all card playing in the house but that my brother has a pack of Old Maid somewhere in the toy box. While my brother goes out to look I brag at how I always beat him out, leaving him the Old Maid, and Uncle Trash says, Oh yeah? and digs around in his pocket for a nickel he puts on the table. He says we'll play a nickel a game and I go into my brother and my's room to get the Band-Aid box of nickels and dimes I sometimes short from the collection plate on Sunday.

Uncle Trash is making painful faces, flexing his red-painted fingers around the Old Maid deck of circus-star cards, but he still shuffles, cuts, and deals a three-way hand one-handed, and not much longer I lose my Band-Aid box of money and all the tin-metal trucks of mine out in the front yard. He makes me go out and get them and put them on his side of the table. My brother loses a set of bowling pins and a stuffed beagle. In two more hands we stack up our winter boots and coats with hoods on Uncle Trash's side of the table. In the last hand my brother and I step out of our shorts and underdrawers while Uncle Trash smiles and says, And now, gentlemen, if you please, the shirts off y'all's backs.

Uncle Trash rakes everything my brother and I own into the pillowcases off our beds and says let that be a lesson to me. He is off through the front porch leaving us buck naked across the table, his last words as he goes up the road shoulder-slinging his loot, Don't y'all burn the house down.

I am burning hot at Uncle Trash, then I am burning hot at our father for leaving us with him to look for our mother, and then I am burning hot at my mother for running off through the fields leaving me with my brother, and then I am burning hot at my brother who is starting to cry. There is only one thing left to do and that is to take all we still have left that we own and throw it at my brother, and I do, and Old Maid cards explode on his face setting him off on a really good red-face howl.

I tell my brother that making so much noise will keep the stray dogs away and he believes it, and then I start to believe it when it gets later than usual, past the crickets and into a long moon over the trees, but they finally do come after my brother finally falls asleep, so I just wait until I know there are several beneath the bed boards scratching their rat-matted backs and growling, and I stomp on the floor, what is my favorite part about the dogs, watching them scatter in a hundred directions and then seeing them one by one collect in a pack at the edge of the field near the trees.

In the morning right off I recognize the bicycle coming wobble-wheeling into the front yard. It's the one the boy outside Cuts uses to run lunches and ice water to the pulpwood truck Mr. Cuts has working cut-over timber on the edge of town. The colored boy that usually drives it snaps bottle caps off his fingers at my brother and I when we go to Cuts with our mother to make groceries. We have to wait outside by the kerosene pump, out by the papered-over lean-to shed, the pop-crate place where the men sit around and Uncle Trash does his card work now. White people generally don't go into Cuts unless they have to buy on credit.

We at school know Mr. and Mrs. Cuts come from a family that eats children. There is a red metal tree with plastic wrapped toys in the window and a long candy counter case inside to lure you in. Mr. and Mrs. Cuts have no children of their own. They ate them during a hard winter and salted the rest down for sandwiches the colored boy runs out to the pulpwood crew at noon. I count colored children going in to buy some candy to see how many make it back out, but generally our mother is ready to go home way before I can tell. Our credit at Cuts is short.

The front tire catches in one of our tin-metal truck's underground tunnel tracks and Uncle Trash takes a spill. The cut crate bolted to the bicycle handlebars spills out brown paper packages sealed with electrical tape into the yard along with a case of Champale and a box of cigars. Uncle Trash is down where he falls. He lays asleep all day under the tree in the yard moving just to crawl back into the wandering shade.

We have for supper sirloins, Champale, and cigars. Uncle Trash teaches how to cross our legs up on the table after dinner but says he'll go ahead and leave my brother and my's cigars unlit. There is no outlook for our toys and my Band-Aid can of nickels and dimes, checking all the packages, even checking twice again the cut crate bolted on the front of the bicycle. Uncle Trash shows us a headstand on the table drinking a bottle of Champale, then he stands in the sink and sings "Gather My Far-flung Thoughts Together." My brother and I chomp our cigars and clap, but in our hearts we are low and lonesome.

Don't y'all burn down the house, says Uncle Trash pedaling out the yard to Cuts. My brother leans out our window with a rope coil and scraps strung on strings. He is in a greasy-finger sleep when the strings slither like white snakes off our bed and over the sill into the fields out back.

There's July corn and no word from our parents. Uncle Trash doesn't remember the Fourth of July or the Fourth of July parade. Uncle Trash bunches cattails in the fenders of his bicycle and clips our Old Maid cards in the spokes and follows the fire engine through town with my brother and I in the front cut-out crate throwing penny candy to the crowds. What are you trying to be, the colored men at Cuts ask us when we end up there. I spot a tin-metal truck of mine broken by the Cuts' front step. Foolish, says Uncle Trash.

Uncle Trash doesn't remember winning Mrs. Cuts in a game for a day to come out and clean the house and us in the bargain. She pushes the furniture around with a broom and calls us abominations. There's a bucket of soap to wash our heads and a jar of sour-smelling cream for our infected bites. Fleas from under the house and mosquitoes through the windows. The screens are rusty squares in the driveway dirt. Uncle Trash leaves her his razor opened as long as my arm. She comes after my brother and I with it to cut our hair, she says. We know better. My brother dives under the house and I am up a tree.

Uncle Trash doesn't remember July, but when we tell him about it he says he thinks July was probably a good idea at the time.

It is August with the brown twisted corn in the fields next to the house. There is word from our parents. They are in the state capital. One of them has been in jail. I try to decide which. Uncle Trash is still promising screens. We get from Cuts bug spray instead.

I wake up in the middle of a night. My brother floats through the window. Out in the yard he and a stray have each other on the end of a rope. He reels her in and I make the tackle. Already I feel the fleas leave her rag-matted coat and crawl over my arms and up my neck. We spray her down with a whole can of bug spray until her coat lathers like soap. My brother gets some matches to burn a tick like a grape out of her ear. The touch of the match covers her like a blue-flame sweater. She's a fireball shooting beneath the house. By the time Uncle Trash and the rest of town get there the fire warden says the house is Fully Involved.

In the morning our parents drive past where our house used to be. They go by again until they recognize the yard. Uncle Trash is trying to bring my brother out of the trance he is in by showing him how some card tricks work on the left-standing steps of the stoop. Uncle Trash shows Jack-Away, Queen in the Whorehouse, and No Money Down. Our father says for Uncle Trash to stand up so he can knock him down. Uncle Trash says he deserves that one. Our father knocks him down again and tells him not to get up. If you get up I'll kill you, our father says.

Uncle Trash crawls on all fours across our yard out to the road. Goodbye, Uncle Trash, I say. Goodbye, men, Uncle Trash says. Don't y'all burn the house down, he says and I say, We won't.

During the knocking down nobody notices our mother. She is a flat-footed running rustle through the corn all burned up by the summer sun.

LEE SMITH

Intensive Care

LEE SMITH (1944–) grew up an only child in Grundy, Virginia (population 2,000), an isolated mountain community in the western part of the state. She attended Hollins College in Roanoke, Virginia, where she graduated with a bachelor's degree. She has been the recipient of many awards and honors, including the Robert Penn Warren Prize for Fiction (1991), the Sir Walter Raleigh Award (1989), the John Dos Passos Award for Literature (1987), and the North Carolina Award for Fiction (1984). She also won the 1994 Lila Wallace–Reader's Digest Writers' Award and the fifth annual John William Corrington Award for Literary Excellence. Smith is the author of eight novels, *The Last Day the Dogbushes Bloomed, Something in the Wind, Fancy Strut, Black Mountain Breakdown, Oral History, Family Linen, Fair and Tender Ladies,* and *The Devil's Dream;* and three story collections, *Me and My Baby View the Eclipse, Cakewalk,* and *News of the Spirit.* Lee Smith lives in North Carolina.

Cherry Oxendine is dying now, and everybody knows it. Everybody in town except maybe her new husband, Harold Stikes, although Lord knows he ought to, it's as plain as the nose on your face. And it's not like he hasn't been *told* either, by both Dr. Thacker and Dr. Pinckney and also that hotshot young Jew doctor from Memphis, Dr. Shapiro, who comes over here once a week. "Harold just can't take it in," is what the head nurse in Intensive Care, Lois Hickey, said in the Beauty Nook last week. Lois ought to know. She's been right there during the past six weeks while Cherry Oxendine has been in Intensive Care, writing down Cherry's blood pressure every hour on the hour, changing bags on the IV, checking the stomach tube, moving the bed up and down to prevent bedsores, monitoring the respirator—and calling in Rodney Broadbent, the respiratory therapist, more and more frequently. "Her blood gases is not but twenty-eight," Lois said in the Beauty Nook. "If we was to unhook that respirator, she'd die in a day."

"I would go on and do it then, if I was Harold," said Mrs. Hooker, the Presbyterian minister's wife, who was getting a permanent. "It is the Christian thing."

"You wouldn't either," Lois said, "because she *still knows him.* That's the awful part. She still knows him. In fact she peps right up ever time he comes in, like they are going on a date or something. It's the saddest thing. And ever time we open the doors, here comes Harold, regular as clockwork. Eight o'clock, one o'clock, six o'clock, eight o'clock, why shoot, he'd stay in there all day and all night if we'd let him. Well, she opens her mouth and says *Hi honey,* you can tell what she's saying even if she can't make a sound. And her eyes get real bright and her face looks pretty good too, that's because of the Lasix, only Harold don't know that. He just can't take it all in," Lois said.

"Oh, I feel so sorry for him," said Mrs. Hooker. Her face is as round and flat as a dime.

"Well, I don't." Dot Mains, owner of the Beauty Nook, started cutting Lois Hickey's hair. Lois wears it too short, in Dot's opinion. "I certainly don't feel sorry for Harold Stikes, after what he did." Dot snipped decisively at Lois Hickey's frosted hair. Mrs. Hooker made a sad little sound, half sigh, half words, as Janice stuck her under the dryer, while Miss Berry, the old-maid home demonstration agent waiting for her appointment, snapped the pages of *Cosmopolitan* magazine one by one, blindly, filled with somewhat gratuitous rage against the behavior of Harold Stikes. Miss Berry is Harold Stikes's ex-wife's cousin. So she does not pity him, not one bit. He got what's coming to him, that's all, in Miss Berry's opinion. Most people don't. It's a pleasure to see it, but Miss Berry would never say this out loud since Cherry Oxendine is of course dying. Cherry Oxendine! Like it was yesterday, Miss Berry remembers how Cherry Oxendine acted in high school, wearing her skirts too tight, popping her gum.

"The doctors can't do a thing," said Lois Hickey.

Silence settled like fog then on the Beauty Nook, on Miss Berry and her magazine, on Dot Mains cutting Lois Hickey's hair, on little Janice thinking about her boyfriend Bruce, and on Mrs. Hooker crying gently under the dryer. Suddenly, Dot remembered something her old granny used to say about such moments of sudden absolute quiet: "An angel is passing over."

After a while, Mrs. Hooker said, "It's all in the hands of God, then." She spread out her fingers one by one on the tray, for Janice to give her a manicure.

And as for Harold Stikes, he's not even considering God. Oh, he doesn't interfere when Mr. Hooker comes by the hospital once a day to check on him—

Harold was a Presbyterian in his former life—or even when the Baptist preacher from Cherry's mama's church shows up and insists that everybody in the whole waiting room join hands and bow heads in prayer while he raises his big red face and curly gray head straight up to heaven and prays in a loud voice that God will heal these loved ones who walk through the Valley of Death, and comfort these others who watch, through their hour of need. This includes Mrs. Eunice Sprayberry, whose mother has had a stroke, John and Paula Ripman, whose infant son is dying of encephalitis, and different others who drift in and out of Intensive Care following surgery or wrecks. Harold is losing track. He closes his eyes and bows his head, figuring it can't hurt, like taking out insurance. But deep down inside, he knows that if God is worth His salt, He is not impressed by the prayer of Harold Stikes, who knowingly gave up all hope of peace on earth and heaven hereafter for the love of Cherry Oxendine.

Not to mention his family.

He gave them up too.

But this morning when he leaves the hospital after his eight-o'clock visit to Cherry, Harold finds himself turning left out of the lot instead of right toward Food Lion, his store. Harold finds himself taking 15-501 just south of town and then driving through those ornate marble gates that mark the entrance to Camelot Hills, his old neighborhood. Some lucky instinct makes him pull into the little park and stop there, beside the pond. Here comes his ex-wife, Joan, driving the Honda Accord he paid for last year. Joan looks straight ahead. She's still wearing her shiny blond hair in the pageboy she's worn ever since Harold met her at Mercer College so many years ago. Harold is sure she's wearing low heels and a shirtwaist dress. He knows her briefcase is in the backseat, containing lesson plans for today, yogurt, and a banana. Potassium is important. Harold has heard this a million times. Behind her, the beds are all made, the breakfast dishes stacked in the sink. As a home ec teacher, Joan believes that breakfast is the most important meal of the day. The two younger children, Brenda and Harold Jr., are already on the bus to the Academy. James rides to the high school with his mother, hair wet, face blank, staring straight ahead. They don't see Harold. Joan brakes at the stop sign before entering 15-501. She always comes to a complete stop, even if nothing's coming. Always. She looks both ways. Then she's gone.

Harold drives past well-kept lawn after well-kept lawn and lovely house after lovely house, many of them houses where Harold has attended Cub Scout meetings, eaten barbecue, watched bowl games. Now these houses have a blank, closed look to them, like mean faces. Harold turns left on Oxford, then right on Shrewsbury. He comes to a stop beside the curb at 1105 Cambridge and just sits there with the motor running, looking at the house. His house. The Queen Anne house he and Joan planned so carefully, down to the last detail, the fish-scale siding. The house he is still paying for and will be until his dying day, if Joan has her way about it.

Which she will, of course. Everybody is on her side: *desertion.* Harold Stikes deserted his lovely wife and three children for a redheaded waitress. For a fallen woman with a checkered past. Harold can hear her now. "I fail to see why I and the children should lower our standards of living, Harold, and go to the dogs just because you have chosen to become insane in mid-life." Joan's voice is slow and amiable. It has a down-to-earth quality which used to appeal to Harold but now drives him wild. Harold sits at the curb with the motor running and looks at his house good. It looks fine. It looks just like it did when they picked it out of the pages of *Southern Living* and wrote off for the plans. The only difference is, that house was in Stone Mountain, Georgia, and this house is in Greenwood, Mississippi. Big deal.

Joan's response to Harold's desertion has been a surprise to him. He expected tears, recriminations, fireworks. He did not expect her calm, reasonable manner, treating Harold the way she treats the Mormon missionaries who come to the door in their black suits, for instance, that very calm sweet careful voice. Joan acts like Harold's desertion is nothing much. And nothing much appears to have changed for her except the loss of Harold's actual presence, and this cannot be a very big deal since everything else has remained exactly the same.

What the hell. After a while Harold turns off the motor and walks up the flagstone walk to the front door. His key still fits. All the furniture is arranged exactly the way it was arranged four years ago. The only thing that ever changes here is the display of magazines on the glass coffee table before the fireplace, Joan keeps them up to date. *Newsweek, National Geographic, Good Housekeeping, Gourmet.* It's a mostly educational grouping, unlike what Cherry reads—*Parade, Coronet, National Enquirer.* Now these magazines litter the floor at the side of the bed like little souvenirs of Cherry. Harold can't stand to pick them up.

He sits down heavily on the white sofa and stares at the coffee table. He remembers the quiz and the day he found it, four years ago now although it feels like only yesterday, funny thing though that he can't remember which magazine it was in. Maybe *Reader's Digest.* The quiz was titled "How Good Is Your Marriage?" and Harold noticed that Joan had filled it in carefully. This did not surprise him. Joan was so law-abiding, such a *good girl,* that she always filled in such quizzes when she came across them, as if she *had to,* before she could go ahead and finish the magazine. Usually Harold didn't pay much attention.

This time, he picked the magazine up and started reading. One of the questions said: "What is your idea of the perfect vacation? (a) a romantic getaway for you and your spouse alone; (b) a family trip to the beach; (c) a business convention; (d) an organized tour of a foreign land." Joan had wavered on this one. She had marked and then erased "an organized tour of a foreign land." Finally she had settled on "a family trip to the beach." Harold skimmed along. The final question was: "When you think of the love between yourself and your spouse, do you think of (a) a great passion; (b) a warm, meaningful companionship; (c) an average love; (d) an unsatisfying habit." Joan had marked "(c) an average love." Harold stared at these words, knowing they were true. An average love, nothing great, an average marriage between an average man and woman. Suddenly, strangely, Harold was filled with rage.

"It is not enough!" He thought he actually said these words out loud. Perhaps he *did* say them out loud, into the clean hushed air-conditioned air of his average home. Harold's rage was followed by a brief period, maybe five minutes, of unbearable longing, after which he simply closed the magazine and put it back on the table and got up and poured himself a stiff shot of bourbon. He stood for a while before the picture window in the living room, looking out at his even green grass, his clipped hedge, and the impatiens blooming in its bed, the clematis climbing the mailbox. The colors of the world fairly leaped at him—the sky so blue, the grass so green. A passing jogger's shorts glowed unbearably red. He felt that he had never seen any of these things before. Yet in another way it all seemed so familiar as to be an actual part of his body—his throat, his heart, his breath. Harold took another drink. Then he went out and played nine holes of golf at the country club with Bubba Fields, something he did every Wednesday afternoon. He shot 82.

By the time he came home for dinner he was okay again. He was very tired and a little lightheaded, all his muscles tingling. His face was hot. Yet Harold felt vaguely pleased with himself, as if he had been through something and come out the other side of it, as if he had done a creditable job on a difficult assignment. But right then, during dinner, Harold could not have told you exactly what had happened to him that day, or why he felt this way. Because the mind will forget what it can't stand to remember, and anyway the Stikeses had beef Stroganoff that night, a new recipe that Joan was testing for the Junior League cookbook, and Harold Jr. had written them a funny letter from camp, and for once Brenda did not whine. James, who was twelve that year, actually condescended to talk to his father, with some degree of interest, about baseball, and after supper was over he and Harold went out and pitched to each other until it grew dark and lightning bugs emerged. This is how it's supposed to be, Harold thought, father and son playing catch in the twilight.

Then he went upstairs and joined Joan in bed to watch TV, after which they turned out the light and made love. But Joan had greased herself all over with Oil of Olay, earlier, and right in the middle of doing it, Harold got a crazy terrified feeling that he was losing her, that Joan was slipping, slipping away.

But time passed, as it does, and Harold forgot that whole weird day, forgot it until *right now,* in fact, as he sits on the white sofa in his old house again and stares at the magazines on the coffee table, those magazines so familiar except for the date, which is four years later. Now Harold wonders: If he hadn't picked up that quiz and read it, would he have even *noticed* when Cherry Oxendine spooned out that potato salad for him six months later, in his own Food Lion deli? Would the sight of redheaded Cherry Oxendine, the Food Lion smock mostly obscuring her dynamite figure, have hit him like a bolt out of the blue the way it did?

Cherry herself does not believe there is any such thing as coincidence. Cherry thinks there is a master plan for the universe, and what is *meant* to happen will. She thinks it's all set in the stars. For the first time, Harold thinks maybe she's right. He sees part of a pattern in the works, but dimly, as if he is looking at a constellation hidden by clouds. Mainly, he sees her face.

Harold gets up from the sofa and goes into the kitchen, suddenly aware that he isn't supposed to be here. He could be arrested, probably! He looks back at the living room but there's not a trace of him left, not even an imprint on the soft white cushions of the sofa. Absentmindedly, Harold opens and shuts the refrigerator door. There's no beer, he notices. He can't have a Coke. On the kitchen calendar, he reads:

Harold Jr to dentist, 3:30 p.m. Tues
Change furnace filter 2/18/88 (James)

So James is changing the furnace filters now, James is the man of the house. Why not? It's good for him. He's been given too much, kids these days grow up so fast, no responsibilities, they get on drugs, you read about it all the time. But deep down inside, Harold knows that James is not on drugs and he feels something awful, feels the way he felt growing up, that sick little flutter in his stomach that took years to go away.

Harold's dad died of walking pneumonia when he was only three, so his mother raised him alone. She called him her "little man." This made Harold feel proud but also wild, like a boy growing up in a cage. Does James feel this way now? Harold suddenly decides to get James a car for his birthday, and take him hunting.

Hunting is something Harold never did as a boy, but it means a lot to him now. In fact Harold never owned a gun until he was thirty-one, when he bought a shotgun in order to accept the invitation of his regional manager, "Little Jimmy" Fletcher, to go quail hunting in Georgia. He had a great time. Now he's invited back every year, and Little Jimmy is in charge of the company's whole eastern division. Harold has a great future with Food Lion too. He owns three stores, one in downtown Greenwood, one out at the mall, and one over in Indianola. He owned two of them when his mother died, and he's pleased to think that she died proud—proud of the good little boy he'd always been, and the good man he'd become.

Of course she'd wanted him to make a preacher, but Harold never got the call, and she gave that up finally when he was twenty. Harold was not going to pretend to get the call if he never got it, and he held strong to this principle. He *wanted* to see a burning bush, but if this was not vouchsafed to him, he wasn't going to lie about it. He would just major in math instead, which he was good at anyway. Majoring in math at Mercer College, the small Baptist school his mother had chosen for him, Harold came upon Joan Berry, a home ec major from his own hometown who set out single-mindedly to marry him, which wasn't hard. After graduation, Harold got a job as management trainee in the Food Lion store where he had started as a bagboy at fourteen. Joan produced their three children, spaced three years apart, and got her tubes tied. Harold got one promotion, then another. Joan and Harold prospered. They built this house.

Harold looks around and now this house, his house, strikes him as creepy, a wax museum. He lets himself out the back door and walks quickly, almost runs, to his car. It's real cold out, a gray day in February, but Harold's sweating. He starts his car and roars off toward the hospital, driving—as Cherry would say—like a bat out of hell.

They're letting Harold stay with her longer now. He knows it, they know it, but nobody says a word. Lois Hickey just looks the other way when the announcement "Visiting hours are over" crackles across the PA. Is this a good sign or a bad sign? Harold can't tell. He feels slow and confused, like a man underwater. "I think she looks better, don't you?" he said last night to Cherry's son Stan, the TV weatherman, who had driven down from Memphis for the day. Eyes slick and bright with tears, Stan went over to Harold and hugged him tight. This scared Harold to death, he has practically never touched his own sons, and he doesn't even *know* Stan, who's been grown and gone for years. Harold is not used to hugging anybody, especially men. Harold breathed in Stan's strong go-get-'em cologne, he buried his face in Stan's long curly hair. He thinks it is possible that Stan has a permanent. They'll do anything up in Memphis. Then Stan stepped back and put one hand on each of Harold's shoulders, holding him out at arm's length. Stan has his mother's wide, mobile mouth. The bright white light of Intensive Care glinted off the gold chain and the crystal that he wore around his neck. "I'm afraid we're going to lose her, Pop," he said.

But Harold doesn't think so. Today he thinks Cherry looks the best she's looked in weeks, with a bright spot of color in each cheek to match her flaming hair. She's moving around a lot too, she keeps kicking the sheet off.

"She's getting back some of that old energy now," he tells Cherry's daughter, Tammy Lynn Palladino, when she comes by after school. Tammy Lynn and Harold's son James are both members of the senior class, but they aren't friends. Tammy Lynn says James is a "stuck-up jock," a "preppie," and a "country-clubber." Harold can't say a word to defend his own son against these charges, he doesn't even *know* James anymore. It might be true, anyway. Tammy Lynn is real smart, a teenage egghead. She's got a full scholarship to Millsaps College for next year. She applied for it all by herself. As Cherry used to say, Tammy Lynn came into this world with a full deck of cards and an ace or two up her sleeve. Also she looks out for Number One.

In this regard Tammy Lynn is as different from her mama as night from day, because Cherry would give you the shirt off her back and frequently has. That's gotten her into lots of trouble. With Ed Palladino, for instance, her second husband and Tammy Lynn's dad. Just about everybody in this town got took by Ed Palladino, who came in here wearing a seersucker suit and talking big about putting in an outlet mall across the river. A lot of people got burned on that outlet mall deal. But Ed Palladino had a way about him that made you want to cast your lot with his, it is true. You wanted to give Ed Palladino your savings, your time-sharing condo, your cousin, your ticket to the Super Bowl. Cherry gave it all.

She married him and turned over what little inheritance she had from her daddy's death—and that's the only time in her life she ever had *any* money, mind you—and then she just shrugged and smiled her big crooked smile when he left town under cover of night. "*C'est la vie,*" Cherry said. She donated the rest of his clothes to the Salvation Army. "*Que será, será,*" Cherry said, quoting a song that was popular when she was in junior high.

Tammy Lynn sits by her mama's bed and holds Cherry's thin dry hand. "I brought you a Chick-Fil-A," she says to Harold. "It's over there in that bag." She points to the shelf by the door. Harold nods. Tammy Lynn works at Chick-Fil-A. Cherry's eyes are wide and blue and full of meaning as she stares at her daughter. Her mouth moves, both Harold and Tammy Lynn lean forward, but then her mouth falls slack and her eyelids flutter shut. Tammy sits back.

"I think she looks some better today, don't you?" Harold asks.

"No," Tammy Lynn says. She has a flat little redneck voice. She sounds just the way she did last summer when she told Cherry that what she saw in the field was a cotton picker working at night, and not a UFO after all. "I wish I did but I don't, Harold. I'm going to go on home now and heat up some Beanee Weenee for Mamaw. You come on as soon as you can."

"Well," Harold says. He feels like things have gotten all turned around here some way, he feels like he's the kid and Tammy Lynn has turned into a freaky little grown-up. He says, "I'll be along directly."

But they both know he won't leave until Lois Hickey throws him out. And speaking of Lois, as soon as Tammy Lynn takes off, here she comes again, checking something on the respirator, making a little clucking sound with her mouth, then whirling to leave. When Lois walks, her panty girdle goes *swish, swish, swish* at the top of her legs. She comes right back with the young black man named Rodney Broadbent, Respiratory Therapist. It says so on his badge. Rodney wheels a complicated-looking cart ahead of himself. He's all built up, like a weightlifter.

"How you doing tonight, Mr. Stipe?" Rodney says.

"I think she's some better," Harold says.

Lois Hickey and Rodney look at him.

"Well, lessee here," Rodney says. He unhooks the respirator tube at Cherry's throat, sticks the tube from his own machine down the opening, and switches on the machine. It makes a whirring sound. It looks like an electric ice cream mixer. Rodney Broadbent looks at Lois Hickey in a significant way as she turns to leave the room.

They don't have to tell him, Harold knows. Cherry is worse, not better. Harold gets the Chick-Fil-A, unwraps it, eats it, and then goes over to stand by the window. It's already getting dark. The big mercury arc light glows in the hospital parking lot. A little wind blows some trash around on the concrete. He has had Cherry for three years, that's all. One trip to Disney World, two vacations at Gulf Shores, Alabama, hundreds of nights in the old metal bed out at the farm with Cherry sleeping naked beside him, her arm thrown over his stomach. They had a million laughs.

"Alrightee," Rodney Broadbent nearly sings, unhooking his machine. Harold turns to look at him. Rodney Broadbent certainly looks more like a middle linebacker than a respiratory therapist. But Harold likes him.

"Well, Rodney?" Harold says.

Rodney starts shadow-boxing in the middle of the room. "Tough times," he says finally. "These is tough times, Mr. Stipe." Harold stares at him. Rodney is light on his feet as can be.

Harold sits down in the chair by the respirator. "What do you mean?" he asks.

"I mean she is drowning, Mr. Stipe," Rodney says. He throws a punch which lands real close to Harold's left ear. "What I'm doing here, see, is suctioning. I'm pulling all the fluid up out of her lungs. But now looka here, Mr. Stipe, they is just too damn much of it. See this little doohickey here I'm measuring it with? This here is the danger zone, man. Now Mrs. Stipe, she has been in the danger zone for some time. They is just too much damn fluid in there. What she got, anyway? Cancer and pneumonia both, am I right? What can I tell you, man? She is *drowning.*" Rodney gives Harold a short affectionate punch in the ribs, then wheels his cart away. From the door, apparently struck by some misgivings, he says, "Well, man, if it was me, I'd want to know what the story is, you follow me, man? If it was me, what I'm saying." Harold can't see Rodney anymore, only hear his voice from the open door.

"Thank you, Rodney," Harold says. He sits in the chair. In a way he has known this already, for quite some time. In a way, Rodney's news is no news, to Harold. He just hopes he will be man enough to bear it, to do what will have to be done. Harold has always been scared that he is not man enough for Cherry Oxendine, anyway. This is his worst secret fear. He looks around the little Intensive Care room, searching for a sign, some sign, anything, that he will be man enough. Nothing happens. Cherry lies strapped to the bed, flanked by so many machines that it looks like she's in the cockpit of a jet. Her eyes are closed, eyelids fluttering, red spots on her freckled cheeks. Her chest rises and falls as the respirator pushes air in and out through the tube in her neck. He doesn't see how she can sleep in the bright white light of Intensive Care, where it is always noon. And does she dream? Cherry used to tell him her dreams, which were wild, long Technicolor dreams, like movies. Cherry played different parts in them. If you dream in color, it means you're intelligent, Cherry said. She used to tease him all the time. She thought Harold's own dreams were a stitch, dreams more boring than his life, dreams in which he'd drive to Jackson, say, or be washing his car.

"Harold?" It's Ray Muncey, manager of the Food Lion at the mall.

"Why, what are you doing over here, Ray?" Harold asks, and then in a flash he *knows,* Lois Hickey must have called him, to make Harold go on home.

"I was just driving by and I thought, Hey, maybe Harold and me might run by the Holiday Inn, get a bite to eat." Ray shifts from foot to foot in the doorway. He doesn't come inside, he's not supposed to, nobody but immediate family is allowed in Intensive Care, and Harold's glad—Cherry would just die if people she barely knows, like Ray Muncey, got to see her looking so bad.

"No, Ray, you go on and eat," Harold says. "I already ate. I'm leaving right now, anyway."

"Well, how's the missus doing?" Ray is a big man, afflicted with big, heavy manners.

"She's drowning," Harold says abruptly. Suddenly he remembers Cherry in a water ballet at the town pool, it must have been the summer of junior year, Fourth of July, Cherry and the other girls floating in a circle on their backs to form a giant flower—legs high, toes pointed. Harold doesn't know it when Ray Muncey leaves. Out the window, the parking lot light glows like a big full moon. Lois Hickey comes in. "You've got to go home now, Harold," she says. "I'll call if there's any change." He remembers Cherry at Glass Lake, on the senior class picnic. Cherry's getting real agitated now, she tosses her head back and forth, moves her arms. She'd pull out the tubes if she could. She kicks off the sheet. Her legs are still good, great legs in fact, the legs of a beautiful young woman.

Harold at seventeen was tall and skinny, brown hair in a soft flat crew cut, glasses with heavy black frames. His jeans were too short. He carried a pen-and-pencil set in a clear plastic case in his breast pocket. Harold and his best friend, Ben Hill, looked so much alike that people had trouble telling them apart. They did everything together. They built model rockets, they read every science fiction book they could get their hands on, they collected Lionel train parts and Marvel comics. They loved superheroes with special powers, enormous beings who leaped across rivers and oceans. Harold's friendship with Ben Hill kept the awful loneliness of the only child at bay, and it also kept him from having to talk to girls. You couldn't talk to those two, not seriously. They were giggling and bumping into each other all the time. They were immature.

So it was in Ben's company that Harold experienced the most private, the most *personal* memory he has of Cherry Oxendine in high school. Oh, he also has those other memories you'd expect, the big public memories of Cherry being crowned Miss Greenwood High (for her talent; she surprised everybody by reciting "Abou Ben Adhem" in such a stirring way that there wasn't a dry eye in the whole auditorium when she got through), or running out onto the field ahead of the team with the other cheerleaders, red curls flying, green and white skirt whirling out around her hips like a beach umbrella when she turned a cartwheel. Harold noticed her then, of course. He noticed her when she moved through the crowded halls of the high school with her walk that was almost a prance, she put a little something extra into it, all right. Harold noticed Cherry Oxendine then in the way that he noticed Sandra Dee on the cover of a magazine, or Annette Funicello on *American Bandstand.*

But such girls were not for the likes of Harold, and Harold knew it. Girls like Cherry always had boyfriends like Lamar Peebles, who was hers—a doctor's son with a baby-blue convertible and plenty of money. They used to drive around town in his car, smoking cigarettes. Harold saw them, as he carried out grocery bags. He did not envy Lamar Peebles, or wish he had a girl like Cherry Oxendine. Only something about them made him stand where he was in the Food Lion lot, watching, until they had passed from sight.

So Harold's close-up encounter with Cherry was unexpected. It took place at the senior class picnic, where Harold and Ben had been drinking beer all afternoon. No alcohol was allowed at the senior class picnic, but some of the more enterprising boys had brought out kegs the night before and hidden them in the woods. Anybody could go back there and pay some money and get some beer. The chaperones didn't know, or appeared not to know. In any case, the chaperones all left at six o'clock, when the picnic was officially over. Some of the class members left then too. Then some of them came back with more beer, more blankets. It was a free lake. Nobody could *make* you go home. Normally, Harold and Ben would have been among the first to leave, but because they had had four beers apiece, and because this was the first time they had ever had *any* beer ever, at all, they were still down by the water, skipping rocks and waiting to sober up so that they would not wreck Harold's mother's green Gremlin on the way home. All the cool kids were on the other side of the lake, listening to transistor radios. The sun went down. Bullfrogs started up. A mist came out all around the sides of the lake. It was a cloudy, humid day anyway, not a great day for a picnic.

"If God is really God, how come He let Himself get crucified, is what I want to know," Ben said. Ben's daddy was a Holiness preacher, out in the county.

But Harold heard something. "Hush, Ben," he said.

"If I was God I would go around and really kick some ass," Ben said.

Harold heard it again. It was almost too dark to see.

"Damn." It was a girl's voice, followed by a splash.

All of a sudden, Harold felt sober. "Who's there?" he asked. He stepped forward, right up to the water's edge. Somebody was in the water. Harold was wearing his swim trunks under his jeans, but he had not gone in the water himself. He couldn't stand to show himself in front of people. He thought he was too skinny.

"Well, *do something.*" It was the voice of Cherry Oxendine, almost wailing. She stumbled up the bank. Harold reached out and grabbed her arm. Close up, she was a mess, wet and muddy, with her hair all over her head. But the thing that got Harold, of course, was that she didn't have any top on. She didn't even try to cover them up either, just stomped her little foot on the bank and said, "I am going to *kill* Lamar Peebles when I get ahold of him." Harold had never even imagined so much skin.

"What's going on?" asked Ben, from up the bank.

Harold took off his own shirt as fast as he could and handed it over to Cherry Oxendine. "Cover yourself," he said.

"Why, thank you." Cherry didn't bat an eye. She took his shirt and put it on, tying it stylishly at the waist. Harold couldn't believe it. Close up, Cherry was a lot smaller than she looked on the stage or the football field. She looked up at Harold through her dripping hair and gave him her crooked grin.

"Thanks, hey?" she said.

And then she was gone, vanished into the mist and trees before Harold could say another word. He opened his mouth and closed it. Mist obscured his view. From the other side of the lake he could hear "Ramblin' Rose" playing on somebody's radio. He heard a girl's high-pitched giggle, a boy's whooping laugh.

"What's going on?" asked Ben.

"Nothing," Harold said. It was the first time he had ever lied to Ben. Harold never told anybody what had happened that night, not ever. He felt that it was up to him to protect Cherry Oxendine's honor. Later, much later, when he and Cherry were lovers, he was astonished to learn that she couldn't remember any of this, not who she was with or what had happened or what she was doing in the lake like that with her top off, or Harold giving her his shirt. "I think that was sweet, though," Cherry told him.

When Harold and Ben finally got home that night at nine or ten o'clock, Harold's mother was frantic. "You've been drinking," she shrilled at him under the hanging porch light. "And where's your shirt?" It was a new madras shirt which Harold had gotten for graduation. Now Harold's mother is out at the Hillandale Rest Home. Ben died in Vietnam, and Cherry is drowning. This time, and Harold knows it now, he can't help her.

Oh, Cherry! Would she have been so wild if she hadn't been so cute? And what if her parents had been younger when she was born—normal-age parents—couldn't they have controlled her better? As it was, the Oxendines were sober, solid people living in a farmhouse out near the county line, and Cherry lit up their lives like a rocket. Her dad, Martin "Buddy" Oxendine, went to sleep in his chair every night right after supper, woke back up for the eleven-o'clock news, and then went to bed for good. Buddy was an elder in the Baptist church. Cherry's mom, Gladys Oxendine, made drapes for people. She assumed she would never have children at all because of her spastic colitis. Gladys and Buddy had started raising cockapoos when they gave up on children. Imagine Gladys's surprise, then, to find herself pregnant at thirty-eight, when she was already old! They say she didn't even know it when she went to the doctor. She thought she had a tumor.

But then she got so excited, that old farm woman, when Dr. Grimwood told her what was what, and she wouldn't even consider an abortion when he mentioned the chances of a mongoloid. People didn't use to have babies so old then as they do now, so Gladys Oxendine's pregnancy was the talk of the county. Neighbors crocheted little jackets and made receiving blankets. Buddy built a baby room onto the house and made a cradle by hand. During the last two months of the pregnancy, when Gladys had to stay in bed because of toxemia, people brought over casseroles and boiled custard, everything good. Gladys's pregnancy was the only time in her whole life that she was ever pretty, and she loved it, and she loved the attention, neighbors in and out of the house. When the baby was finally born on November 1, 1944, no parents were ever more ready than Gladys and Buddy Oxendine. And the baby was everything they hoped for too, which is not usually the case—the prettiest baby in the world, a baby like a little flower.

They named her Doris Christine which is who she was until eighth grade, when she made junior varsity cheerleader and announced that she was changing her name to Cherry. Cherry! Even her parents had to admit it suited her better than Doris Christine. As a little girl, Doris Christine was redheaded, bouncy, and busy—she was always into something, usually something you'd never thought to tell her not to do. She started talking early and never shut up. Her old dad, old Buddy Oxendine, was so crazy about Doris Christine that he took her everywhere with him in his red pickup truck. You got used to seeing the two of them, Buddy and his curly-headed little daughter, riding the country roads together, going to the seed-and-feed together, sharing a shake at the Dairy Queen. Gladys made all of Doris Christine's clothes, the most beautiful little dresses in the world, with hand-smocking and French seams. They gave Doris Christine everything they could think of—what she asked for, what she didn't. "That child is going to get spoiled," people started to say. And of course she did get spoiled, she couldn't have helped *that,* but she was never spoiled rotten as so many are. She stayed sweet in spite of it all.

Then along about ninth grade, soon after she changed her name to Cherry and got interested in boys, things changed between Cherry and the old Oxendines. Stuff happened. Instead of being the light of their lives, Cherry became the bane of their existence, the curse of their old age. She wanted to wear makeup, she wanted to have car dates. You can't blame her—she was old enough, sixteen. Everybody else did it. But you can't blame Gladys and Buddy either—they were old people by then, all worn out. They were not up to such a daughter. Cherry sneaked out. She wrecked a car. She ran away to Pensacola with a soldier. Finally, Gladys and Buddy just gave up. When Cherry eloped with the disc jockey, Don Westall, right after graduation, they threw up their hands. They did not do a thing about it. They had done the best they could, and everybody knew it. They went back to raising cockapoos.

Cherry, living up in Nashville, Tennessee, had a baby, Stan, the one that's in his twenties now. Cherry sent baby pictures back to Gladys and Buddy, and wrote that she was going to be a singer. Six years later, she came home. She said nothing against Don Westall, who was still a disc jockey on WKIX, Nashville. You could hear him on the radio every night after ten P.M. Cherry said the breakup was all her fault. She said she had made some mistakes, but she didn't say what they were. She was thin and noble. Her kid was cute. She did not go back out to the farm then. She rented an apartment over the hardware store, down by the river, and got a job downtown working in Ginger's Boutique. After a year or so, she started acting more like herself again, although not *quite* like herself, she had grown up somehow in Nashville, and quit being spoiled. She put Stan, her kid, first. And if she did run around a little bit, or if she was the life of the party sometimes out at the country club, so what? Stan didn't want for a thing. By then the Oxendines were failing and she had to take care of them too, she had to drive her daddy up to Grenada for dialysis twice a week. It was not an easy life for Cherry, but if it ever got her down, you couldn't tell it. She was still cute. When her daddy finally died and left her a little money, everybody was real glad. Oh *now,* they said, Cherry Oxendine can quit working so hard and put her mama in a home or something and have a decent life. She can go on a cruise. But then along came Ed Palladino, and the rest is history.

Cherry Oxendine was left with no husband, no money, a little girl, and a mean old mama to take care of. At least by this time Stan was in the Navy. Cherry never complained, though. She moved back out to the farm. When Ginger retired from business and closed her boutique, Cherry got another job, as a receptionist at Wallace, Wallace and Peebles. This was her undoing. Because Lamar Peebles had just moved back to town with his family, to join his father's firm. Lamar had two little girls. He had been married to a tobacco heiress since college. All this time he had run around on her. He was not on the up-and-up. And when he encountered redheaded Cherry Oxendine again after the passage of so many years, all those old fireworks went off again. They got to be a scandal, then a disgrace. Lamar said he was going to marry her, and Cherry believed him. After six months of it, Mrs. Lamar Peebles checked herself into a mental hospital in Silver Hill, Connecticut. First, she called her lawyers.

And then it was all over, not even a year after it began. Mr. and Mrs. Lamar Peebles were reconciled and moved to Winston-Salem, North Carolina, her hometown. Cherry Oxendine lost her job at Wallace, Wallace and Peebles, and was reduced to working in the deli at Food Lion. Why did she do it? Why did she lose all the goodwill she'd built up in this community over so many years? It is because she doesn't know how to look out for Number One. Her own daughter, Tammy Lynn Palladino, is aware of this.

"You have got a fatal flaw, Mama," Tammy said after learning about fatal flaws in English class. "You believe everything everybody tells you."

Still, Tammy loves her mother. Sometimes she writes her mother's whole name, Cherry Oxendine Westall Palladino Stikes, over and over in her Blue Horse notebook. Tammy Lynn will never be half the woman her mother is, and she's so smart she knows it. She gets a kick out of her mother's wild ideas.

"When you get too old to be cute, honey, you get to be eccentric," Cherry told Tammy one time. It's the truest thing she ever said.

It seems to Tammy that the main thing about her mother is, Cherry always has to have *something* going on. If it isn't a man it's something else, such as having her palm read by that woman over in French Camp, or astrology, or the grapefruit diet. Cherry believes in the Bermuda Triangle, Bigfoot, Atlantis, and ghosts. It kills her that she's not psychic. The UFO Club was just the latest in a long string of interests although it has lasted the longest, starting back before Cherry's marriage to Harold Stikes. And then Cherry got cancer, and she kind of forgot about it. But Tammy still remembers the night her mama first got so turned on to UFOs.

Rhonda Ramey, Cherry's best friend, joined the UFO Club first. Rhonda and Cherry are a lot alike, although it's hard to see this at first. While Cherry is short and peppy, Rhonda is tall, thin, and listless. She looks like Cher. Rhonda doesn't have any children. She's crazy about her husband, Bill, but he's a workaholic who runs a string of video rental stores all over northern Mississippi, so he's gone a lot, and Rhonda gets bored. She works out at the spa, but it isn't enough. Maybe this is why she got so interested when the UFO landed at a farm outside her mother's hometown of Como. It was first spotted by sixteen-year-old Donnie Johnson just at sunset, as he was finishing his chores on his parents' farm. He heard a loud rumbling sound "in the direction of the hog house," it said in the paper. Looking up, he suddenly saw a "brilliantly lit mushroom-shaped object" hovering about two feet above the ground, with a shaft of white light below and glowing all over with an intensely bright multicolored light, "like the light of a welder's arc."

Donnie said it sounded like a jet. He was temporarily blinded and paralyzed. He fell down on the ground. When he came back to his senses again, it was gone. Donnie staggered into the kitchen where his parents, Durel, fifty-four, and Erma, forty-nine, were eating supper, and told them what had happened. They all ran back outside to the field, where they found four large imprints and four small imprints in the muddy ground, and a nearby clump of sage grass on fire. The hogs were acting funny, bunching up, looking dazed. Immediately, Durel jumped in his truck and went to get the sheriff, who came right back with two deputies. All in all, six people viewed the site while the bush continued to burn, and who knows how many people—half of Como—saw the imprints the next day. Rhonda saw them too. She drove out to the Johnson farm with her mother, as soon as she heard about it.

It was a close encounter of the second kind, according to Civil Air Patrol head Glenn Raines, who appeared on TV to discuss it, because the UFO "interacted with its surroundings in a significant way." A close encounter of the first kind is simply a close-range sighting, while a close encounter of the third kind is something like the most famous example, of Betty and Barney Hill of Exeter, New Hampshire, who were actually kidnapped by a UFO while they were driving along on a trip. Betty and Barney Hill were taken aboard the alien ship and given physical exams by intelligent humanoid beings. Two hours and thirty-five minutes were missing from their trip, and afterward, Betty had to be treated for acute anxiety. Glenn Raines, wearing his brown Civil Air Patrol uniform, said all this on TV.

His appearance, plus what had happened at the Johnson farm, sparked a rash of sightings all across Mississippi, Louisiana, and Texas for the next two years. Metal disk-like objects were seen, and luminous objects appearing as lights at night. In Levelland, Texas, fifteen people called the police to report an egg-shaped UFO appearing over State Road 1173. Overall, the UFOs seemed to show a preference for soybean fields and teenage girl viewers. But a pretty good photograph of a UFO flying over the Gulf was taken by a retired man from Pascagoula, so you can't generalize. Clubs sprang up all over the place. The one that Rhonda and Cherry went to had seventeen members and met once a month at the junior high school.

Tammy recalls exactly how her mama and Rhonda acted the night they came home from Cherry's first meeting. Cherry's eyes sparkled in her face like Brenda Starr's eyes in the comics. She started right in telling Tammy all about it, beginning with the Johnsons from Como and Betty and Barney Hill.

Tammy was not impressed. "I don't believe it," she said. She was president of the Science Club at the junior high school.

"You are the most irritating child!" Cherry said. "*What* don't you believe?"

"Well, any of it," Tammy said then. "All of it," and this has remained her attitude ever since.

"Listen, honey, *Jimmy Carter* saw one," Cherry said triumphantly. "In nineteen seventy-one, at the Executive Mansion in Georgia. He turned in an official report on it."

"How come nobody knows about it, then?" Tammy asked. She was a tough customer.

"Because the government covered it up!" said Rhonda, just dying to tell this part. "People see UFOs all the time, it's common knowledge, they are trying to make contact with us right now, honey, but the government doesn't want the average citizen to know about it. There's a big cover-up going on."

"It's just like Watergate." Cherry opened a beer and handed it over to Rhonda.

"That's right," Rhonda said, "and every time there's a major incident, you know what happens? These men from the government show up at your front door dressed all in black. After they get through with you, you'll wish you never heard the word 'saucer.' You turn pale and get real sick. You can't get anything to stay on your stomach."

Tammy cracked up. But Rhonda and Cherry went on and on. They had official-looking gray notebooks to log their sightings in. At their meetings, they reported these sightings to each other, and studied up on the subject in general. Somebody in the club was responsible for the educational part of each meeting, and somebody else brought the refreshments.

Tammy Lynn learned to keep her mouth shut. It was less embarrassing than belly dancing; she had a friend whose mother took belly dancing at the YMCA. Tammy did not tell her mama about all the rational explanations for UFOs that she found in the school library. They included: (1) hoaxes; (2) natural phenomena, such as fungus causing the so-called fairy rings sometimes found after a landing; (3) real airplanes flying off course; and Tammy's favorite, (4) the Fata Morgana, described as a "rare and beautiful type of mirage, constantly changing, the result of unstable layers of warm and cold air. The Fata Morgana takes its name from fairy lore and is said to evoke in the viewer a profound sense of longing," the book went on to say. Tammy's biology teacher, Mr. Owens, said he thought that the weather patterns in Mississippi might be especially conducive to this phenomenon. But Tammy kept her mouth shut. And after a while, when nobody in the UFO Club saw anything, its membership declined sharply. Then her mama met Harold Stikes, then Harold Stikes left his wife and children and moved out to the farm with them, and sometimes Cherry forgot to attend the meetings, she was so happy with Harold Stikes.

Tammy couldn't see *why,* initially. In her opinion, Harold Stikes was about as interesting as a telephone pole. "But he's so *nice!*" Cherry tried to explain it to Tammy Lynn. Finally Tammy decided that there is nothing in the world that makes somebody as attractive as if they really love you. And Harold Stikes really did love her mama, there was no question. That old man—what a crazy old Romeo! Why, he proposed to Cherry when she was still in the hospital after she had her breast removed (this was back when they thought that was *it,* that the doctors had gotten it all).

"Listen, Cherry," he said solemnly, gripping a dozen red roses. "I want you to marry me."

"What?" Cherry said. She was still groggy.

"I want you to marry me," Harold said. He knelt down heavily beside her bed.

"Harold! Get up from there!" Cherry said. "Somebody will see you."

"Say yes," said Harold.

"I just had my breast removed."

"Say yes," he said again.

"*Yes, yes, yes!*" Cherry said.

And as soon as she got out of the hospital, they were married out in the orchard, on a beautiful April day, by Lew Uggams, a JP from out of town. They couldn't find a local preacher to do it. The sky was bright blue, not a cloud in sight. Nobody was invited except Stan, Tammy, Rhonda and Bill, and Cherry's mother, who wore her dress inside out. Cherry wore a new pink lace dress, the color of cherry blossoms. Tough little Tammy cried and cried. It's the most beautiful wedding she's ever seen, and now she's completely devoted to Harold Stikes.

So Tammy leaves the lights on for Harold when she finally goes to bed that night. She tried to wait up for him, but she has to go to school in the morning, she's got a chemistry test. Her mamaw is sound asleep in the little added-on baby room that Buddy Oxendine built for Cherry. Gladys acts like a baby now, a spoiled baby at that. The only thing she'll drink is Sprite out of a can. She talks mean. She doesn't like anything in the world except George and Tammy, the two remaining cockapoos.

They bark up a storm when Harold finally gets back out to the farm, at one-thirty. The cockapoos are barking, Cherry's mom is snoring like a chain saw. Harold doesn't see how Tammy Lynn can sleep through all of this, but she always does. Teenagers can sleep through anything. Harold himself has started waking up several times a night, his heart pounding. He wonders if he's going to have a heart attack. He almost mentioned his symptoms to Lois Hickey last week, in fact, but then thought, What the hell. His heart is broken. Of course it's going to act up some. And everything, not only his heart, is out of whack. Sometimes he'll break into a sweat for no reason. Often he forgets really crucial things, such as filing his estimated income tax on January 15. Harold is not the kind to forget something this important. He has strange aches that float from joint to joint. He has headaches. He's lost twelve pounds. Sometimes he has no appetite at all. Other times, like right now, he's just starving.

Harold goes in the kitchen and finds a flat rectangular casserole, carefully wrapped in tinfoil, on the counter, along with a Tupperware cake carrier. He lifts off the top of the cake carrier and finds a piña colada cake, his favorite. Then he pulls back the tinfoil on the casserole. Lasagna! Plenty is left over. Harold sticks it in the microwave. He knows that the cake and the lasagna were left here by his ex-wife. Ever since Cherry has been in Intensive Care, Joan has been bringing food out to the farm. She comes when Harold's at work or at the hospital, and leaves it with Gladys or Tammy. She probably figures that Harold would refuse it, if she caught him at home, which he would. She's a great cook, though. Harold takes the lasagna out of the microwave, opens a beer, and sits down at the kitchen table. He loves Joan's lasagna.

Cherry's idea of a terrific meal is one she doesn't have to cook. Harold remembers eating in bed with Cherry, tacos from Taco Bell, sour-cream-and-onion chips, beer. He gets some more lasagna and a big wedge of piña colada cake.

Now it's two-thirty, but for some reason Harold is not a bit sleepy. His mind whirls with thoughts of Cherry. He snaps off all the lights and stands in the darkened house. His heart is racing. Moonlight comes in the windows, it falls on the old patterned rug. Outside, it's as bright as day. He puts his coat on and goes out, with the cockapoos scampering along beside him. They are not even surprised. They think it's a fine time for a walk. Harold goes past the mailbox, down the dirt road between the fields. Out here in the country, the sky is both bigger and closer than it is in town. Harold feels like he's in a huge bowl turned upside down, with tiny little pinpoints of light shining through. And everything is silvered by the moonlight—the old fenceposts, the corn stubble in the flat long fields, a distant barn, the highway at the end of the dirt road, his own strange hand when he holds it out to look at it.

He remembers when she waited on him in the Food Lion deli, three years ago. He had asked for a roast beef sandwich, which come prepackaged. Cherry put it on his plate. Then she paused, and cocked her hip, and looked at him. "Can I give you some potato salad to go with that?" she asked. "Some slaw?"

Harold looked at her. Some red curls had escaped the required net. "Nothing else," he said.

But Cherry spooned a generous helping of potato salad onto his plate. "Thank you so much," he said. They looked at each other.

"I know I know you," Cherry said.

It came to him then. "Cherry Oxendine," said Harold. "I remember you from high school."

"Lord, you've got a great memory, then!" Cherry had an easy laugh. "That was a hundred years ago."

"Doesn't seem like it." Harold knew he was holding up the line.

"Depends on who you're talking to," Cherry said.

Later that day, Harold found an excuse to go back over to the deli for coffee and apple pie, then he found an excuse to look through the personnel files. He started eating lunch at the deli every day, without making any conscious decision to do so. In the afternoons, when he went back for coffee, Cherry would take her break and sit at a table with him.

Harold and Cherry talked and talked. They talked about their families, their kids, high school. Cherry told him everything that had happended to her. She was tough and funny, not bitter or self-pitying. They talked and talked. In his whole life, Harold had never had so much to say. During this period, which lasted for several weeks, his whole life took on a heightened aspect. Everything that happened to him seemed significant, a little incident to tell Cherry about. Every song he liked on the radio he remembered, so he could ask Cherry if she liked it too. Then there came the day when they were having coffee and she mentioned she'd left her car at Al's Garage that morning to get a new clutch.

"I'll give you a ride over there to pick it up," said Harold instantly. In his mind he immediately canceled the sales meeting he had scheduled for four o'clock.

"Oh, that's too much trouble," Cherry said.

"But I insist." In his conversations with Cherry, Harold had developed a brand-new gallant manner he had never had before.

"Well, if you're sure it's not any trouble . . ." Cherry grinned at him like she knew he really wanted to do it, and that afternoon when he grabbed her hand suddenly before letting her out at Al's Garage, she did not pull it away.

The next weekend Harold took her up to Memphis and they stayed at the Peabody Hotel, where Cherry got the biggest kick out of the ducks in the lobby, and ordering from room service.

"You're a fool," Harold's friends told him later, when the shit hit the fan.

But Harold didn't think so. He doesn't think so now, walking the old dirt road on the Oxendine farm in the moonlight. He loves his wife. He feels that he has been ennobled and enlarged, by knowing Cherry Oxendine. He feels like he has been specially selected among men, to receive a precious gift. He stepped out of his average life for her, he gave up being a good man, but the rewards have been extraordinary. He's glad he did it. He'd do it all over again.

Still walking, Harold suddenly knows that something is going to happen. But he doesn't stop walking. Only, the whole world around him seems to waver a bit, and intensify. The moonlight shines whiter than ever. A little wind whips up out of nowhere. The stars are twinkling so brightly that they seem to dance, actually dance, in the sky. And then, while Harold watches, one of them detaches itself from the rest of the sky and grows larger, moves closer, until it's clear that it is actually moving across the sky, at an angle to the earth. A falling star, perhaps? A comet?

Harold stops walking. The star moves faster and faster, with an erratic pattern. It's getting real close now. It's no star. Harold hears a high whining noise, like a blender. The cockapoos huddle against his ankles. They don't bark. Now he can see the blinking red lights on the top of it, and the beam of white light shooting out the bottom. His coat is blown straight out behind him by the wind. He feels like he's going blind. He shields his eyes. At first it's as big as a barn, then a tobacco warehouse. It covers the field. Although Harold can't say exactly how it communicates to him or even if it does, suddenly his soul is filled to bursting. The ineffable occurs. And then, more quickly than it came, it's gone, off toward Carrollton, rising into the night, leaving the field, the farm, the road. Harold turns back.

It will take Cherry Oxendine two more weeks to die. She's tough. And even when there's nothing left of her but heart, she will fight all the way. She will go out furious, squeezing Harold's hand at the very moment of death, clinging fast to every minute of this bright, hard life. And although at first he won't want to, Harold will go on living. He will buy another store. Gladys will die. Tammy Lynn will make Phi Beta Kappa. Harold will start attending the Presbyterian church again. Eventually Harold may even go back to his family, but he will love Cherry Oxendine until the day he dies, and he will never, ever, tell anybody what he saw.

SUSAN SONTAG

The Way We Live Now

SUSAN SONTAG (1933–) is the author of the recent book *In America,* a novel (Farrar Straus & Giroux, 1999). Among her other books are *The Volcano Lover,* a novel; *Alice in Bed,* a play; and *I, etcetera,* a collection of stories. Ms. Sontag is working on another collection of short fiction.

At first he was just losing weight, he felt only a little ill, Max said to Ellen, and he didn't call for an appointment with his doctor, according to Greg, because he was managing to keep on working at more or less the same rhythm, but he did stop smoking, Tanya pointed out, which suggests he was frightened, but also that he wanted, even more than he knew, to be healthy, or healthier, or maybe just to gain back a few pounds, said Orson, for he told her, Tanya went on, that he expected to be climbing the walls (isn't that what people say?) and found, to his surprise, that he didn't miss cigarettes at all and revelled in the sensation of his lungs being ache-free for the first time in years. But did he have a good doctor, Stephen wanted to know, since it would have been crazy not to go for a checkup after the pressure was off and he was back from the conference in Helsinki, even if by then he was feeling better. And he said, to Frank, that he would go, even though he was indeed frightened, as he admitted to Jan, but who wouldn't be frightened now, though, odd as that might seem, he hadn't been worrying until recently, he avowed to Quentin, it was only in the last six months that he had the metallic taste of panic in his mouth, because becoming seriously ill was something that happened to other people, a normal delusion, he observed to Paolo, if one was thirty-eight and had never had a serious illness; he wasn't, as Jan confirmed, a hypochondriac. Of course, it was hard not to worry, everyone was worried, but it wouldn't do to panic, because, as Max pointed out to Quentin, there wasn't anything one could do except wait and hope, wait and start being careful, be careful, and hope. And even if one did prove to be ill, one shouldn't give up, they had new treatments that promised an arrest of the disease's inexorable course, research was progressing. It seemed that everyone was in touch with everyone else several times a week, checking in, I've never spent so many hours at a time on the phone, Stephen said to Kate, and when I'm exhausted after the two or three calls made to me, giving me the latest, instead of switching off the phone to give myself a respite I tap out the number of another friend or acquaintance, to pass on the news. I'm not sure I can afford to think so much about it, Ellen said, and I suspect my own motives, there's something morbid I'm getting used to, getting excited by, this must be like what people felt in London during the Blitz. As far as I know, I'm not at risk, but you never know, said Aileen. This thing is totally unprecedented, said Frank. But don't you think he ought to see a doctor, Stephen insisted. Listen, said Orson, you can't force people to take care of themselves, and what makes you think the worst, he could be just run down, people still do get ordinary illnesses, awful ones, why are you assuming it has to be *that.* But all I want to be sure, said Stephen, is that he understands the options, because most people don't, that's why they won't see a doctor or have the test, they think there's nothing one can do. But is there anything one can do, he said to Tanya (according to Greg), I mean what do I gain if I go to the doctor; if I'm really ill, he's reported to have said, I'll find out soon enough.

And when he was in the hospital, his spirits seemed to lighten, according to Donny. He seemed more cheerful than he had been in the last months, Ursula said, and the bad news seemed to come almost as a relief, according to Ira, as a truly unexpected blow, according to Quentin, but you'd hardly expect him to have said the same thing to all his friends, because his relation to Ira was so different from his relation to Quentin (this according to Quentin, who was proud of their friendship), and perhaps he thought Quentin wouldn't be undone by seeing him weep, but Ira insisted that couldn't be the reason he behaved so differently with each, and that maybe he was feeling less shocked, mobilizing his strength to fight for his life, at the moment he saw Ira but overcome by feelings of hopelessness when Quentin arrived with flowers, because anyway the flowers threw him into a bad mood, as Quentin told Kate, since the hospital room was choked with flowers, you couldn't have crammed another flower into that room, but surely you're exaggerating, Kate said, smiling, everybody likes flowers. Well, who wouldn't exaggerate at a time like this, Quentin said sharply. Don't you think *this* is an exaggeration. Of course I do, said Kate gently, I was only teasing, I mean I didn't mean to tease. I know that, Quentin said, with tears in his eyes, and Kate hugged him and said well, when I go this evening I guess I won't bring flowers, what does he want, and Quentin said, according to Max, what he likes best is chocolate. Is there anything else, asked Kate, I mean like chocolate but not chocolate. Licorice, said Quentin, blowing his nose. And besides that. Aren't *you* exaggerating now, Quentin said, smiling. Right, said Kate, so if I want to bring him a whole raft of stuff, besides chocolate and licorice, what else. Jelly beans, Quentin said.

He didn't want to be alone, according to Paolo, and lots of people came in the first week, and the Jamaican nurse said there were other patients on the floor who would be glad to have the surplus flowers, and people weren't afraid to visit, it wasn't like the old days, as Kate pointed out to Aileen, they're not even segregated in the hospital any more, as Hilda observed, there's nothing on the door of his room warning visitors of the possibility of contagion, as there was a few years ago; in fact, he's in a double room and, as he told Orson, the old guy on the far side of the curtain (who's clearly on the way out, said Stephen) doesn't even have the disease, so, as Kate went on, you really should go and see him, he'd be happy to see you, he likes having people visit, you aren't not going because you're afraid, are you. Of course not, Aileen said, but I don't know what to say, I think I'll feel awkward, which he's bound to notice, and that will make him feel worse, so I won't be doing him any good, will I. But he won't notice anything, Kate said, patting Aileen's hand, it's not like that, it's not the way you imagine, he's not judging people or wondering about their motives, he's just happy to see his friends. But I never was really a friend of his, Aileen said, you're a friend, he's always liked you, you told me he talks about Nora with you, I know he likes me, he's even attracted to me, but he respects you. But, according to Wesley, the reason Aileen was so stingy with her visits was that she could never have him to herself, there were always others there already and by the time they left still others had arrived, she'd been in love with him for years, and I can understand, said Donny, that Aileen should feel bitter that if there could have been a woman friend he did more than occasionally bed, a woman he really loved, and my God, Victor said, who had known him in those years, he was crazy about Nora, what a heartrending couple they were, two surly angels, then it couldn't have been she.

And when some of the friends, the ones who came every day, waylaid the doctor in the corridor, Stephen was the one who asked the most informed questions, who'd been keeping up not just with the stories that appeared several times a week in the *Times* (which Greg confessed to have stopped reading, unable to stand it any more) but with articles in the medical journals published here and in England and France, and who knew socially one of the principal doctors in Paris who was doing some much-publicized research on the disease, but his doctor said little more than that the pneumonia was not life-threatening, the fever was subsiding, of course he was still weak but he was responding well to the antibiotics, that he'd have to complete his stay in the hospital, which entailed a minimum of twenty-one days on the I.V., before she could start him on the new drug, for she was optimistic about the possibility of getting him into the protocol; and when Victor said that if he had so much trouble eating (he'd say to everyone, when they coaxed him to eat some of the hospital meals, that food didn't taste right, that he had a funny metallic taste in his mouth) it couldn't be good that friends were bringing him all that chocolate, the doctor just smiled and said that in these cases the patient's morale was also an important factor, and if chocolate made him feel better she saw no harm in it, which worried Stephen, as Stephen said later to Donny, because they wanted to believe in the promises and taboos of today's high-tech medicine but here this reassuringly curt and silver-haired specialist in the disease, someone quoted frequently in the papers, was talking like some oldfangled country G.P. who tells the family that tea with honey or chicken soup may do as much for the patient as penicillin, which might mean, as Max said, that they were just going through the motions of treating him, that they were not sure about what to do, or rather, as Xavier interjected, that they didn't know what the hell they were doing, that the truth, the real truth, as Hilda said, upping the ante, was that they didn't, the doctors, really have any hope.

Oh, no, said Lewis, I can't stand it, wait a minute, I can't believe it, are you sure, I mean are they sure, have they done all the tests, it's getting so when the phone rings I'm scared to answer because I think it will be someone telling me someone else is ill; but did Lewis really not know until yesterday, Robert said testily, I find that hard to believe, everybody is talking about it, it seems impossible that someone wouldn't have called Lewis; and perhaps Lewis did know, was for some reason pretending not to know already, because, Jan recalled, didn't Lewis say something months ago to Greg, and not only to Greg, about his not looking well, losing weight, and being worried about him and wishing he'd see a doctor, so it couldn't come as a total surprise. Well, everybody is worried about everybody now, said Betsy, that seems to be the way we live, the way we live now. And, after all, they were once very close, doesn't Lewis still have the keys to his apartment, you know the way you let someone keep the keys after you've broken up, only a little because you hope the person might just saunter in, drunk or high, late some evening, but mainly because it's wise to have a few sets of keys strewn around town, if you live alone, at the top of a former commercial building that, pretentious as it is, will never acquire a doorman or even a resident superintendent, someone whom you can call on for the keys late one night if you find you've lost yours or have locked yourself out. Who else has keys, Tanya inquired, I was thinking somebody might drop by tomorrow before coming to the hospital and bring some treasures, because the other day, Ira said, he was complaining about how dreary the hospital room was, and how it was like being locked up in a motel room, which got everybody started telling funny stories about motel rooms they'd known, and at Ursula's story, about the Luxury Budget Inn in Schenectady, there was an uproar of laughter around his bed, while he watched them in silence, eyes bright with fever, all the while, as Victor recalled, gobbling that damned chocolate. But, according to Jan, whom Lewis's keys enabled to tour the swank of his bachelor lair with an eye to bringing over some art consolation to brighten up the hospital room, the Byzantine icon wasn't on the wall over his bed, and that was a puzzle until Orson remembered that he'd recounted without seeming upset (this disputed by Greg) that the boy he'd recently gotten rid of had stolen it, along with four of the *maki-e* lacquer boxes, as if these were objects as easy to sell on the street as a TV or a stereo. But he's always been very generous, Kate said quietly, and though he loves beautiful things isn't really attached to them, to things, as Orson said, which is unusual in a collector, as Frank commented, and when Kate shuddered and tears sprang to her eyes and Orson inquired anxiously if he, Orson, had said something wrong, she pointed out that they'd begun talking about him in a retrospective mode, summing up what he was like, what made them fond of him, as if he were finished, completed, already a part of the past.

Perhaps he was getting tired of having so many visitors, said Robert, who was, as Ellen couldn't help mentioning, someone who had come only twice and was probably looking for a reason not to be in regular attendance, but there could be no doubt, according to Ursula, that his spirits had dipped, not that there was any discouraging news from the doctors, and he seemed now to prefer being alone a few hours of the day; and he told Donny that he'd begun keeping a diary for the first time in his life, because he wanted to record the course of his mental reactions to this astonishing turn of events, to do something parallel to what the doctors were doing, who came every morning and conferred at his bedside about his body, and that perhaps it wasn't so important what he wrote in it, which amounted, as he said wryly to Quentin, to little more than the usual banalities about terror and amazement that this was happening to him, to him also, plus the usual remorseful assessments of his past life, his pardonable superficialities, capped by resolves to live better, more deeply, more in touch with his work and his friends, and not to care so passionately about what people thought of him, interspersed with admonitions to himself that in this situation his will to live counted more than anything else and that if he really wanted to live, and trusted life, and liked himself well enough (down, ol' debbil Thanatos!), he *would* live, he would be an exception; but perhaps all this, as Quentin ruminated, talking on the phone to Kate, wasn't the point, the point was that by the very keeping of the diary he was accumulating something to reread one day, slyly staking out his claim to a future time, in which the diary would be an object, a relic, in which he might not actually reread it, because he would want to have put this ordeal behind him, but the diary would be there in the drawer of his stupendous Majorelle desk, and he could already, he did actually say to Quentin one late sunny afternoon, propped up in the hospital bed, with the stain of chocolate framing one corner of a heartbreaking smile, see himself in the penthouse, the October sun streaming through those clear windows instead of this streaked one, and the diary, the pathetic diary, safe inside the drawer.

It doesn't matter about the treatment's side effects, Stephen said (when talking to Max), I don't know why you're so worried about that, every strong treatment has some dangerous side effects, it's inevitable, you mean otherwise the treatment wouldn't be effective, Hilda interjected, and anyway, Stephen went on doggedly, just because there *are* side effects it doesn't mean he has to get them, or all of them, each one, or even some of them. That's just a list of all the possible things that could go wrong, because the doctors have to cover themselves, so they make up a worst-case scenario, but isn't what's happening to him, and to so many other people, Tanya interrupted, a worst-case scenario, a catastrophe no one could have imagined, it's too cruel, and isn't everything a side effect, quipped Ira, even *we* are all side effects, but we're not bad side effects, Frank said, he likes having his friends around, and we're helping each other, too; because his illness sticks us all in the same glue, mused Xavier, and, whatever the jealousies and grievances from the past that have made us wary and cranky with each other, when something like this happens (the sky is falling, the sky is falling!) you understand what's really important. I agree, Chicken Little, he is reported to have said. But don't you think, Quentin observed to Max, that being as close to him as we are, making time to drop by the hospital every day, is a way of our trying to define ourselves more firmly and irrevocably as the well, those who aren't ill, who aren't going to fall ill, as if what's happened to him couldn't happen to us, when in fact the chances are that before long one of us will end up where he is, which is probably what he felt when he was one of the cohort visiting Zack in the spring (you never knew Zack, did you?), and, according to Clarice, Zack's widow, he didn't come very often, he said he hated hospitals, and didn't feel he was doing Zack any good, that Zack would see on his face how uncomfortable he was. Oh, he was one of those, Aileen said. A coward. Like me.

And after he was sent home from the hospital, and Quentin had volunteered to move in and was cooking meals and taking telephone messages and keeping the mother in Mississippi informed, well, mainly keeping her from flying to New York and heaping her grief on her son and confusing the household routine with her oppressive ministrations, he was able to work an hour or two in his study, on days he didn't insist on going out, for a meal or a movie, which tired him. He seemed optimistic, Kate thought, his appetite was good, and what he said, Orson reported, was that he agreed when Stephen advised him that the main thing was to keep in shape, he was a fighter, right, he wouldn't be who he was if he weren't, and was he ready for the big fight, Stephen asked rhetorically (as Max told it to Donny), and he said you bet, and Stephen added it could be a lot worse, you could have gotten the disease two years ago, but now so many scientists are working on it, the American team and the French team, everyone bucking for that Nobel Prize a few years down the road, that all you have to do is stay healthy for another year or two and then there will be good treatment, real treatment. Yes, he said, Stephen said, my timing is good. And Betsy, who had been climbing on and rolling off macrobiotic diets for a decade, came up with a Japanese specialist she wanted him to see but thank God, Donny reported, he'd had the sense to refuse, but he did agree to see Victor's visualization therapist, although what could one possibly visualize, said Hilda, when the point of visualizing disease was to see it as an entity with contours, borders, here rather than there, something limited, something you were the host of, in the sense that you could disinvite the disease, while this was so total; or would be, Max said. But the main thing, said Greg, was to see that he didn't go the macrobiotic route, which might be harmless for plump Betsy but could only be devastating for him, lean as he'd always been, with all the cigarettes and other appetite-suppressing chemicals he'd been welcoming into his body for years; and now was hardly the time, as Stephen pointed out, to be worried about cleaning up his act, and eliminating the chemical additives and other pollutants that we're all blithely or not so blithely feasting on, blithely since we're healthy, healthy as we can be; so far, Ira said. Meat and potatoes is what I'd be happy to see him eating, Ursula said wistfully. And spaghetti and clam sauce, Greg added. And thick cholesterol-rich omelettes with smoked mozzarella, suggested Yvonne, who had flown from London for the weekend to see him. Chocolate cake, said Frank. Maybe not chocolate cake, Ursula said, he's already eating so much chocolate.

And when, not right away but still only three weeks later, he was accepted into the protocol for the new drug, which took considerable behind-the-scenes lobbying with the doctors, he talked less about being ill, according to Donny, which seemed like a good sign, Kate felt, a sign that he was not feeling like a victim, feeling not that he *had* a disease but, rather, was living *with* a disease (that was the right cliché, wasn't it?), a more hospitable arrangement, said Jan, a kind of cohabitation which implied that it was something temporary, that it could be terminated, but terminated how, said Hilda, and when you say hospitable, Jan, I hear hospital. And it was encouraging, Stephen insisted, that from the start, at least from the time he was finally persuaded to make the telephone call to his doctor, he was willing to say the name of the disease, pronounce it often and easily, as if it were just another word, like boy or gallery or cigarette or money or deal, as in no big deal, Paolo interjected, because, as Stephen continued, to utter the name is a sign of health, a sign that one has accepted being who one is, mortal, vulnerable, not exempt, not an exception after all, it's a sign that one is willing, truly willing, to fight for one's life. And we must say the name, too, and often, Tanya added, we mustn't lag behind him in honesty, or let him feel that, the effort of honesty having been made, it's something done with and he can go on to other things. One is so much better prepared to help him, Wesley replied. In a way he's fortunate, said Yvonne, who had taken care of a problem at the New York store and was flying back to London this evening, sure, fortunate, said Wesley, no one is shunning him, Yvonne went on, no one's afraid to hug him or kiss him lightly on the mouth, in London we are, as usual, a few years behind you, people I know, people who would seem to be not even remotely at risk, are just terrified, but I'm impressed by how cool and rational you all are; you find us cool, asked Quentin. But I have to say, he's reported to have said, I'm terrified, I find it very hard to read (and you know how he loves to read, said Greg; yes, reading is his television, said Paolo) or to think, but I don't feel hysterical. I feel quite hysterical, Lewis said to Yvonne. But you're able to *do* something for him, that's wonderful, how I wish I could stay longer, Yvonne answered, it's rather beautiful, I can't help thinking, this utopia of friendship you've assembled around him (this pathetic utopia, said Kate), so that the disease, Yvonne concluded, is not, any more, out there. Yes, don't you think we're more at home here, with him, with the disease, said Tanya, because the imagined disease is so much worse than the reality of him, whom we all love, each in our fashion, having it. I know for me his getting it has quite demystified the disease, said Jan, I don't feel afraid, spooked, as I did before he became ill, when it was only news about remote acquaintances, whom I never saw again after they became ill. But you know you're not going to come down with the disease, Quentin said, to which Ellen replied, on her behalf, that's not the point, and possibly untrue, my gynaecologist says that everyone is at risk, everyone who has a sexual life, because sexuality is a chain that links each of us to many others, unknown others, and now the great chain of being has become a chain of death as well. It's not the same for you, Quentin insisted, it's not the same for you as it is for me or Lewis or Frank or Paolo or Max, I'm more and more frightened, and I have every reason to be. I don't think about whether I'm at risk or not, said Hilda, I know that I was afraid to know someone with the disease, afraid of what I'd see, what I'd feel, and after the first day I came to the hospital I felt so relieved. I'll never feel that way, that fear, again; he doesn't seem different from me. He's not, Quentin said.

According to Lewis, he talked more often about those who visited more often, which is natural, said Betsy, I think he's even keeping a tally. And among those who came or checked in by phone every day, the inner circle as it were, those who were getting more points, there was still a further competition, which was what was getting on Betsy's nerves, she confessed to Jan; there's always that vulgar jockeying for position around the bedside of the gravely ill, and though we all feel suffused with virtue at our loyalty to him (speak for yourself, said Jan), to the extent that we're carving time out of every day, or almost every day, though some of us are dropping out, as Xavier pointed out, aren't we getting at least as much out of this as he is. Are we, said Jan. We're rivals for a sign from him of special pleasure over a visit, each stretching for the brass ring of his favour, wanting to feel the most wanted, the true nearest and dearest, which is inevitable with someone who doesn't have a spouse and children or an official in-house lover, hierarchies that no one would dare contest, Betsy went on, so we are the family he's founded, without meaning to, without official titles and ranks (we, we, snarled Quentin); and is it so clear, though some of us, Lewis and Quentin and Tanya and Paolo, among others, are ex-lovers and all of us more or less than friends, which one of us he prefers, Victor said (now it's us, raged Quentin), because sometimes I think he looks forward more to seeing Aileen, who has visited only three times, twice at the hospital and once since he's been home, than he does you or me; but, according to Tanya, after being very disappointed that Aileen hadn't come, now he was angry, while, according to Xavier, he was not really hurt but touchingly passive, accepting Aileen's absence as something he somehow deserved. But he's happy to have people around, said Lewis; he says when he doesn't have company he gets very sleepy, he sleeps (according to Quentin), and then perks up when someone arrives, it's important that he not feel ever alone. But, said Victor, there's one person he hasn't heard from, whom he'd probably like to hear from more than most of us; but she didn't just vanish, even right after she broke away from him, and he knows exactly where she lives now, said Kate, he told me he put in a call to her last Christmas Eve, and she said it's nice to hear from you and Merry Christmas, and he was shattered, according to Orson, and furious and disdainful, according to Ellen (what do you expect of her, said Wesley, she was burned out), but Kate wondered if maybe he hadn't phoned Nora in the middle of a sleepless night, what's the time difference, and Quentin said no, I don't think so, I think he wouldn't want her to know.

* * *

And when he was feeling even better and had regained the pounds he'd shed right away in the hospital, though the refrigerator started to fill up with organic wheat germ and grapefruit and skimmed milk (he's worried about his cholesterol count, Stephen lamented), and told Quentin he could manage by himself now, and did, he started asking everyone who visited how he looked, and everyone said he looked great, so much better than a few weeks ago, which didn't jibe with what anyone had told him at that time; but then it was getting harder and harder to know how he looked, to answer such a question honestly when among themselves they wanted to be honest, both for honesty's sake and (as Donny thought) to prepare for the worst, because he'd been looking like *this* for so long, at least it seemed so long, that it was as if he'd always been like this, how did he look before, but it was only a few months, and those words, pale and wan-looking and fragile, hadn't they always applied? And one Thursday Ellen, meeting Lewis at the door of the building, said, as they rode up together in the elevator, how is he *really?* But you see how he is, Lewis said tartly, he's fine, he's perfectly healthy, and Ellen understood that of course Lewis didn't think he was perfectly healthy but that he wasn't worse, and that was true, but wasn't it, well, almost heartless to talk like that. Seems inoffensive to me, Quentin said, but I know what you mean, I remember once talking to Frank, somebody, after all, who has volunteered to do five hours a week of office work at the Crisis Center (I know, said Ellen), and Frank was going on about this guy, diagnosed almost a year ago, and so much further along, who'd been complaining to Frank on the phone about the indifference of some doctor, and had gotten quite abusive about the doctor, and Frank was saying there was no reason to be so upset, the implication being that *he,* Frank, wouldn't behave so irrationally, and I said, barely able to control my scorn, but Frank, Frank, he has every reason to be upset, he's dying, and Frank said, said according to Quentin, oh, I don't like to think about it that way.

And it was while he was still home, recuperating, getting his weekly treatment, still not able to do much work, he complained, but, according to Quentin, up and about most of the time and turning up at the office several days a week, that bad news came about two remote acquaintances, one in Houston and one in Paris, news that was intercepted by Quentin on the ground that it could only depress him, but Stephen contended that it was wrong to lie to him, it was so important for him to live in the truth; that had been one of his first victories, that he was candid, that he was even willing to crack jokes about the disease, but Ellen said it wasn't good to give him this end-of-the-world feeling, too many people were getting ill, it was becoming such a common destiny that maybe some of the will to fight for his life would be drained out of him if it seemed to be as natural as, well, death. Oh, Hilda said, who didn't know personally either the one in Houston or the one in Paris, but knew *of* the one in Paris, a pianist who specialized in twentieth-century Czech and Polish music, I have his records, he's such a valuable person, and, when Kate glared at her, continued defensively, I know every life is equally sacred, but that *is* a thought, another thought, I mean, all these valuable people who aren't going to have their normal four score as it is now, these people aren't going to be replaced, and it's such a loss to the culture. But this isn't going to go on for ever, Wesley said, it can't, they're bound to come up with something (they, they, muttered Stephen), but did you ever think, Greg said, that if some people don't die, I mean even if they can keep them alive (they, they, muttered Kate), they continue to be carriers, and that means, if you have a conscience, that you can never make love, make love fully, as you'd been wont—wantonly, Ira said—to do. But it's better than dying, said Frank. And in all his talk about the future, when he allowed himself to be hopeful, according to Quentin, he never mentioned the prospect that even if he didn't die, if he were so fortunate as to be among the first generation of the disease's survivors, never mentioned, Kate confirmed, that whatever happened it was over, the way he had lived until now, but, according to Ira, he did think about it, the end of bravado, the end of folly, the end of trusting life, the end of taking life for granted, and of treating life as something that, samurai-like, he thought himself ready to throw away lightly, impudently; and Kate recalled, sighing, a brief exchange she'd insisted on having as long as two years ago, huddling on a banquette covered with steel-grey industrial carpet on an upper level of The Prophet and toking up for their next foray on to the dance floor: she'd said hesitantly, for it felt foolish asking a prince of debauchery to, well, take it easy, and she wasn't keen on playing big sister, a role, as Hilda confirmed, he inspired in many women, are you being careful, honey, you know what I mean. And he replied, Kate went on, no, I'm not, listen, I can't, I just can't, sex is too important to me, always has been (he started talking like that, according to Victor, after Nora left him), and if I get it, well, I get it. But he wouldn't talk like that now, would he, said Greg; he must feel awfully foolish now, said Betsy, like someone who went on smoking, saying I can't give up cigarettes, but when the bad X-ray is taken even the most besotted nicotine addict can stop on a dime. But sex isn't like cigarettes, is it, said Frank, and, besides, what good does it do to remember that he was reckless, said Lewis angrily, the appalling thing is that you just have to be unlucky once, and wouldn't he feel even worse if he'd stopped three years ago and had come down with it anyway, since one of the most terrifying features of the disease is that you don't know when you contracted it, it could have been ten years ago, because surely this disease has existed for years and years, long before it was recognized; that is, named. Who knows how long (I think a lot about that, said Max) and who knows (I know what you're going to say, Stephen interrupted) how many are going to get it.

I'm feeling fine, he's reported to have said whenever someone asked him how he was, which was almost always the first question anyone asked. Or: I'm feeling better, how are you? But he said other things, too. I'm playing leapfrog with myself, he is reported to have said, according to Victor. And: There must be a way to get something positive out of this situation, he's reported to have said to Kate. How American of him, said Paolo. Well, said Betsy, you know the old American adage: When you've got a lemon, make lemonade. The one thing I'm sure I couldn't take, Jan said he said to her, is becoming disfigured, but Stephen hastened to point out the disease doesn't take that form very often any more, its profile is mutating, and, in conversation with Ellen, wheeled up words like blood-brain barrier; I never thought there was a barrier *there,* said Jan. But he mustn't know about Max, Ellen said, that would really depress him, please don't tell him, he'll have to know, Quentin said grimly, and he'll be furious not to have been told. But there's time for that, when they take Max off the respirator, said Ellen; but isn't it incredible, Frank said, Max was fine, not feeling ill at all, and then to wake up with a fever of a hundred and five, unable to breathe, but that's the way it often starts, with absolutely no warning, Stephen said, the disease has so many forms. And when, after another week had gone by, he asked Quentin where Max was, he didn't question Quentin's account of a spree in the Bahamas, but then the number of people who visited regularly was thinning out, partly because the old feuds that had been put aside through the first hospitalization and the return home had resurfaced, and the flickering enmity between Lewis and Frank exploded, even though Kate did her best to mediate between them, and also because he himself had done something to loosen the bonds of love that united the friends around him, by seeming to take them all for granted, as if it were perfectly normal for so many people to carve out so much time and attention for him, visit him every few days, talk about him incessantly on the phone with each other; but, according to Paolo, it wasn't that he was less grateful, it was just something he was getting used to, the visits. It had become, with time, a more ordinary kind of situation, a kind of ongoing party, first at the hospital and now since he was home, barely on his feet again, it being clear, said Robert, that I'm on the B list; but Kate said, that's absurd, there's no list; and Victor said, but there is, only it's not he, it's Quentin who's drawing it up. He wants to see us, we're helping him, we have to do it the way he wants, he fell down yesterday on the way to the bathroom, he mustn't be told about Max (but he already knew, according to Donny), it's getting worse.

* * *

When I was home, he is reported to have said, I was afraid to sleep, as I was dropping off each night it felt like just that, as if I were falling down a black hole, to sleep felt like giving in to death, I slept every night with the light on; but here, in the hospital, I'm less afraid. And to Quentin he said, one morning, the fear rips through me, it tears me open; and, to Ira, it presses me together, squeezes me toward myself. Fear gives everything its hue, its high. I feel so, I don't know how to say it, exalted, he said to Quentin. Calamity is an amazing high, too. Sometimes I feel *so* well, so powerful, it's as if I could jump out of my skin. Am I going crazy, or what? Is it all this attention and coddling I'm getting from everybody, like a child's dream of being loved? Is it the drugs? I know it sounds crazy but sometimes I think this is a *fantastic* experience, he said shyly; but there was also the bad taste in the mouth, the pressure in the head and at the back of the neck, the red, bleeding gums, the painful, if pink-lobed, breathing, and his ivory pallor, colour of white chocolate. Among those who wept when told over the phone that he was back in the hospital were Kate and Stephen (who'd been called by Quentin), and Ellen, Victor, Aileen, and Lewis (who were called by Kate), and Xavier and Ursula (who were called by Stephen). Among those who didn't weep were Hilda, who said that she'd just learned that her seventy-five-year-old aunt was dying of the disease, which she'd contracted from a transfusion given during her successful double bypass of five years ago, and Frank and Donny and Betsy, but this didn't mean, according to Tanya, that they weren't moved and appalled, and Quentin thought they might not be coming soon to the hospital but would send presents; the room, he was in a private room this time, was filling up with flowers, and plants, and books, and tapes. The high tide of barely suppressed acrimony of the last weeks at home subsided into the routines of hospital visiting, though more than a few resented Quentin's having charge of the visiting book (but it was Quentin who had the idea, Lewis pointed out); now, to insure a steady stream of visitors, preferably no more than two at a time (this, the rule in all hospitals, wasn't enforced here, at least on his floor; whether out of kindness or inefficiency, no one could decide), Quentin had to be called first, to get one's time slot, there was no more casual dropping by. And his mother could no longer be prevented from taking a plane and installing herself in a hotel near the hospital; but he seemed to mind her daily presence less than expected, Quentin said; said Ellen it's we who mind, do you suppose she'll stay long. It was easier to be generous with each other visiting him here in the hospital, as Donny pointed out, than at home, where one minded never being alone with him; coming here, in our twos and twos, there's no doubt about what our role is, how we should be, collective, funny, distracting, undemanding, light, it's important to be light, for in all this dread there is gaiety, too, as the poet said, said Kate. (His eyes, his glittering eyes, said Lewis.) His eyes looked dull, extinguished, Wesley said to Xavier, but Betsy said his face, not just his eyes, looked soulful, warm; whatever is there, said Kate, I've never been so aware of his eyes; and Stephen said, I'm afraid of what my eyes show, the way I watch him, with too much intensity, or a phony kind of casualness, said Victor. And, unlike at home, he was clean-shaven each morning, at whatever hour they visited him; his curly hair was always combed; but he complained that the nurses had changed since he was here the last time, and that he didn't like the change, he wanted everyone to be the same. The room was furnished now with some of his personal effects (odd word for one's things, said Ellen), and Tanya brought drawings and a letter from her nine-year-old dyslexic son, who was writing now, since she'd purchased a computer; and Donny brought champagne and some helium balloons, which were anchored to the foot of his bed; tell me about something that's going on, he said, waking up from a nap to find Donny and Kate at the side of his bed, beaming at him; tell me a story, he said wistfully, said Donny, who couldn't think of anything to say; *you're* the story, Kate said. And Xavier brought an eighteenth-century Guatemalan wooden statue of St. Sebastian with upcast eyes and open mouth, and when Tanya said what's that, a tribute to eros past, Xavier said where I come from Sebastian is venerated as a protector against pestilence. Pestilence symbolized by arrows? Symbolized by arrows. All people remember is the body of a beautiful youth bound to a tree, pierced by arrows (of which he always seems oblivious, Tanya interjected), people forget that the story continues, Xavier continued, that when the Christian women came to bury the martyr they found him still alive and nursed him back to health. And he said, according to Stephen, I didn't know St. Sebastian didn't die. It's undeniable, isn't it, said Kate on the phone to Stephen, the fascination of the dying. It makes me ashamed. We're learning how to die, said Hilda, I'm not ready to learn, said Aileen; and Lewis, who was coming straight from the other hospital, the hospital where Max was still being kept in I.C.U., met Tanya getting out of the elevator on the tenth floor, and as they walked together down the shiny corridor past the open doors, averting their eyes from the other patients sunk in their beds, with tubes in their noses, irradiated by the bluish light from the television sets, the thing I can't bear to think about, Tanya said to Lewis, is someone dying with the TV on.

He has that strange, unnerving detachment now, said Ellen, that's what upsets me, even though it makes it easier to be with him. Sometimes he was querulous. I can't stand them coming in here taking my blood every morning, what are they doing with all that blood, he is reported to have said; but where was his anger, Jan wondered. Mostly he was lovely to be with, always saying how are *you,* how are you feeling. He's so sweet now, said Aileen. He's so nice, said Tanya. (Nice, nice, groaned Paolo.) At first he was very ill, but he was rallying, according to Stephen's best information, there was no fear of his not recovering this time, and the doctor spoke of his being discharged from the hospital in another ten days if all went well, and the mother was persuaded to fly back to Mississippi, and Quentin was readying the penthouse for his return. And he was still writing his diary, not showing it to anyone, though Tanya, first to arrive one late-winter morning, and finding him dozing, peeked, and was horrified, according to Greg, not by anything she read but by a progressive change in his handwriting: in the recent pages, it was becoming spidery, less legible, and some lines of script wandered and tilted about the page. I was thinking, Ursula said to Quentin, that the difference between a story and a painting or photograph is that in a story you can write, He's still alive. But in a painting or a photo you can't show 'still'. You can just show him being alive. He's still alive, Stephen said.

AMY TAN

Two Kinds

AMY TAN (1952–) was born in Oakland, California, after her mother and father emigrated from China, and was raised in the San Francisco Bay Area. Tan attended Linfield College in McMinnville, Oregon; San Jose City College; San Jose State University, where she received a B.A. in English and linguistics and an M.A. in Linguistics; then enrolled as a doctoral student in linguistics at the University of California, Berkeley.

Following the murder of one of her closest friends, Tan left her doctoral program before completing her degree, and for the next five years worked as a language-development consultant and project director for programs serving disabled children. She then became a freelance writer specializing in corporate communications.

She attended her first writers' workshop, the Squaw Valley Community of Writers, where she met the writer Molly Giles, who later led a small workshop that often met in Tan's house. In 1989, *The Joy Luck Club* was published and stayed more than forty weeks on the *New York Times* best-seller list. Though Tan wrote the book as a collection of linked short stories, reviewers enthusiastically and erroneously referred to the book as an intricately woven "novel." The label stuck. *The Joy Luck Club* was nominated for the National Book Award and the National Book Critics Award. It received the Commonwealth Gold Award and the Bay Area Book Reviewers Award. It was also adapted into a feature film made for Hollywood Pictures in 1994, for which Tan was a co-screenwriter with Ron Bass and a coproducer with Bass and Wayne Wang.

Tan's second book, *The Kitchen God's Wife,* was published in 1991, followed by *The Hundred Secret Senses* in 1995. Her short stories and essays have appeared in *The Atlantic Monthly, Grand Street, Harper's, The New Yorker, Threepenny Review,* and others. Her essay "Mother Tongue" was chosen for *The Best American Essays 1991,* and she is the guest editor for *The Best American Short Stories 1999.* Tan has also written two children's books, *The Moon Lady* (1992) and *The Chinese Siamese Cat* (1994).

Along with novelist Stephen King and columnist Dave Barry, Tan is a member of the literary garage band the Rock Bottom Remainders. She lives in San Francisco and New York with her husband, Lou DeMattei, and their two Yorkshire terriers, Bubba Zo and Lilliput.

My mother believed you could be anything you wanted to be in America. You could open a restaurant. You could work for the government and get good retirement. You could buy a house with almost no money down. You could become rich. You could become instantly famous.

"Of course you can be prodigy, too," my mother told me when I was nine. "You can be best anything. What does Auntie Lindo know? Her daughter, she is only best tricky."

America was where all my mother's hopes lay. She had come here in 1949 after losing everything in China: her mother and father, her family home, her first husband, and two daughters, twin baby girls. But she never looked back with regret. There were so many ways for things to get better.

We didn't immediately pick the right kind of prodigy. At first my mother thought I could be a Chinese Shirley Temple. We'd watch Shirley's old movies on TV as though they were training films. My mother would poke my arm and say, *"Ni kan"*—You watch. And I would see Shirley tapping her feet, or singing a sailor song, or pursing her lips into a very round O while saying, "Oh my goodness."

"Ni kan," said my mother as Shirley's eyes flooded with tears. "You already know how. Don't need talent for crying!"

Soon after my mother got this idea about Shirley Temple, she took me to a beauty training school in the Mission district and put me in the hands of a student who could barely hold the scissors without shaking. Instead of getting big fat curls, I emerged with an uneven mass of crinkly black fuzz. My mother dragged me off to the bathroom and tried to wet down my hair.

"You look like Negro Chinese," she lamented, as if I had done this on purpose.

The instructor of the beauty training school had to lop off these soggy clumps to make my hair even again. "Peter Pan is very popular these days," the instructor assured my mother. I now had hair the length of a boy's, with straight-across bangs that hung at a slant two inches above my eyebrows. I liked the haircut and it made me actually look forward to my future fame.

In fact, in the beginning, I was just as excited as my mother, maybe even more so. I pictured this prodigy part of me as many different images, trying each one on for size. I was a dainty ballerina girl standing by the curtains, waiting to hear the right music that would send me floating on my tiptoes. I was like the Christ child lifted out of the straw manger, crying with holy indignity. I was Cinderella stepping from her pumpkin carriage with sparkly cartoon music filling the air.

In all of my imaginings, I was filled with a sense that I would soon become *perfect.* My mother and father would adore me. I would be beyond reproach. I would never feel the need to sulk for anything.

But sometimes the prodigy in me became impatient. "If you don't hurry up and get me out of here, I'm disappearing for good," it warned. "And then you'll always be nothing."

Every night after dinner, my mother and I would sit at the Formica kitchen table. She would present new tests, taking her examples from stories of amazing children she had read in *Ripley's Believe It or Not,* or *Good Housekeeping, Reader's Digest,* and a dozen other magazines she kept in a pile in our bathroom. My mother got these magazines from people whose houses she cleaned. And since she cleaned many houses each week, we had a great assortment. She would look through them all, searching for stories about remarkable children.

The first night she brought out a story about a three-year-old boy who knew the capitals of all the states and even most of the European countries. A teacher was quoted as saying the little boy could also pronounce the names of the foreign cities correctly.

"What's the capital of Finland?" my mother asked me, looking at the magazine story.

All I knew was the capital of California, because Sacramento was the name of the street we lived on in Chinatown. "Nairobi!" I guessed, saying the most foreign word I could think of. She checked to see if that was possibly one way to pronounce "Helsinki" before showing me the answer.

The tests got harder—multiplying numbers in my head, finding the queen of hearts in a deck of cards, trying to stand on my head without using my hands, predicting the daily temperatures in Los Angeles, New York, and London.

One night I had to look at a page from the Bible for three minutes and then report everything I could remember. "Now Jehoshaphat had riches and honor in abundance and . . . that's all I remember, Ma," I said.

And after seeing my mother's disappointed face once again, something inside of me began to die. I hated the tests, the raised hopes and failed expectations. Before going to bed that night, I looked in the mirror above the bathroom sink and when I saw only my face staring back—and that it would always be this ordinary face—I began to cry. Such a sad, ugly girl! I made high-pitched noises like a crazed animal, trying to scratch out the face in the mirror.

And then I saw what seemed to be the prodigy side of me—because I had never seen that face before. I looked at my reflection, blinking so I could see more clearly. The girl staring back at me was angry, powerful. This girl and I were the same. I had new thoughts, willful thoughts, or rather thoughts filled with lots of won'ts. I won't let her change me, I promised myself. I won't be what I'm not.

So now on nights when my mother presented her tests, I performed listlessly, my head propped on one arm. I pretended to be bored. And I was. I got so bored I started counting the bellows of the foghorns out on the bay while my mother drilled me in other areas. The sound was comforting and reminded me of the cow jumping over the moon. And the next day, I played a game with myself, seeing if my mother would give up on me before eight bellows. After a while I usually counted only one, maybe two bellows at most. At last she was beginning to give up hope.

Two or three months had gone by without any mention of my being a prodigy again. And then one day my mother was watching *The Ed Sullivan Show* on TV. The TV was old and the sound kept shorting out. Every time my mother got halfway up from the sofa to adjust the set, the sound would go back on and Ed would be talking. As soon as she sat down, Ed would go silent again. She got up, the TV broke into loud piano music. She sat down. Silence. Up and down, back and forth, quiet and loud. It was like a stiff embraceless dance between her and the TV set. Finally she stood by the set with her hand on the sound dial.

She seemed entranced by the music, a little frenzied piano piece with this mesmerizing quality, sort of quick passages and then teasing lilting ones before it returned to the quick playful parts.

"Ni kan," my mother said, calling me over with hurried hand gestures. "Look here."

I could see why my mother was fascinated by the music. It was being pounded out by a little Chinese girl, about nine years old, with a Peter Pan haircut. The girl had the sauciness of a Shirley Temple. She was proudly modest like a proper Chinese child. And she also did this fancy sweep of a curtsy, so that the fluffy skirt of her white dress cascaded slowly to the floor like the petals of a large carnation.

In spite of these warning signs, I wasn't worried. Our family had no piano and we couldn't afford to buy one, let alone reams of sheet music and piano lessons. So I could be generous in my comments when my mother badmouthed the little girl on TV.

"Play note right, but doesn't sound good! No singing sound," complained my mother.

"What are you picking on her for?" I said carelessly. "She's pretty good. Maybe she's not the best, but she's trying hard." I knew almost immediately I would be sorry I said that.

"Just like you," she said. "Not the best. Because you not trying." She gave a little huff as she let go of the sound dial and sat down on the sofa.

The little Chinese girl sat down also to play an encore of "Anitra's Dance" by Grieg. I remember the song, because later on I had to learn how to play it.

Three days after watching *The Ed Sullivan Show,* my mother told me what my schedule would be for piano lessons and piano practice. She had talked to Mr. Chong, who lived on the first floor of our apartment building. Mr. Chong was a retired piano teacher and my mother had traded housecleaning services for weekly lessons and a piano for me to practice on every day, two hours a day, from four until six.

When my mother told me this, I felt as though I had been sent to hell. I whined and then kicked my foot a little when I couldn't stand it anymore.

"Why don't you like me the way I am? I'm *not* a genius! I can't play the piano. And even if I could, I wouldn't go on TV if you paid me a million dollars!" I cried.

My mother slapped me. "Who ask you be genius?" she shouted. "Only ask you be your best. For you sake. You think I want you be genius? Hnnh! What for! Who ask you!"

"So ungrateful," I heard her mutter in Chinese. "If she had as much talent as she has temper, she would be famous now."

Mr. Chong, whom I secretly nicknamed Old Chong, was very strange, always tapping his fingers to the silent music of an invisible orchestra. He looked ancient in my eyes. He had lost most of the hair on top of his head and he wore thick glasses and had eyes that always looked tired and sleepy. But he must have been younger than I thought, since he lived with his mother and was not yet married.

I met Old Lady Chong once and that was enough. She had this peculiar smell like a baby that had done something in its pants. And her fingers felt like a dead person's, like an old peach I once found in the back of the refrigerator; the skin just slid off the meat when I picked it up.

I soon found out why Old Chong had retired from teaching piano. He was deaf. "Like Beethoven!" he shouted to me. "We're both listening only in our head!" And he would start to conduct his frantic silent sonatas.

Our lessons went like this. He would open the book and point to different things, explaining their purpose: "Key! Treble! Bass! No sharps or flats! So this is C major! Listen now and play after me!"

And then he would play the C scale a few times, a simple chord, and then, as if inspired by an old, unreachable itch, he gradually added more notes and running trills and a pounding bass until the music was really something quite grand.

I would play after him, the simple scale, the simple chord, and then I just played some nonsense that sounded like a cat running up and down on top of garbage cans. Old Chong smiled and applauded and then said, "Very good! But now you must learn to keep time!"

So that's how I discovered that Old Chong's eyes were too slow to keep up with the wrong notes I was playing. He went through the motions in half-time. To help me keep rhythm, he stood behind me, pushing down on my right shoulder for every beat. He balanced pennies on top of my wrists so I would keep them still as I slowly played scales and arpeggios. He had me curve my hand around an apple and keep that shape when playing chords. He marched stiffly to show me how to make each finger dance up and down, staccato like an obedient little soldier.

He taught me all these things, and that was how I also learned I could be lazy and get away with mistakes, lots of mistakes. If I hit the wrong notes because I hadn't practiced enough, I never corrected myself. I just kept playing in rhythm. And Old Chong kept conducting his own private reverie.

So maybe I never really gave myself a fair chance. I did pick up the basics pretty quickly, and I might have become a good pianist at that young age. But I was so determined not to try, not to be anybody different that I learned to play only the most ear-splitting preludes, the most discordant hymns.

Over the next year, I practiced like this, dutifully in my own way. And then one day I heard my mother and her friend Lindo Jong both talking in a loud bragging tone of voice so others could hear. It was after church, and I was leaning against the brick wall wearing a dress with stiff white petticoats. Auntie Lindo's daughter, Waverly, who was about my age, was standing farther down the wall about five feet away. We had grown up together and shared all the closeness of two sisters squabbling over crayons and dolls. In other words, for the most part, we hated each other. I thought she was snotty. Waverly Jong had gained a certain amount of fame as "Chinatown's Littlest Chinese Chess Champion."

"She bring home too many trophy," lamented Auntie Lindo that Sunday. "All day she play chess. All day I have no time do nothing but dust off her winnings." She threw a scolding look at Waverly, who pretended not to see her.

"You lucky you don't have this problem," said Auntie Lindo with a sigh to my mother.

And my mother squared her shoulders and bragged: "Our problem worser than yours. If we ask Jing-mei wash dish, she hear nothing but music. It's like you can't stop this natural talent."

And right then, I was determined to put a stop to her foolish pride.

A few weeks later, Old Chong and my mother conspired to have me play in a talent show which would be held in the church hall. By then, my parents had saved up enough to buy me a secondhand piano, a black Wurlitzer spinet with a scarred bench. It was the showpiece of our living room.

For the talent show, I was to play a piece called "Pleading Child" from Schumann's *Scenes from Childhood.* It was a simple, moody piece that sounded more difficult than it was. I was supposed to memorize the whole thing, playing the repeat parts twice to make the piece sound longer. But I dawdled over it, playing a few bars and then cheating, looking up to see what notes followed. I never really listened to what I was playing. I daydreamed about being somewhere else, about being someone else.

The part I liked to practice best was the fancy curtsy: right foot out, touch the rose on the carpet with a pointed foot, sweep to the side, left leg bends, look up and smile.

My parents invited all the couples from the Joy Luck Club to witness my debut. Auntie Lindo and Uncle Tin were there. Waverly and her two older brothers had also come. The first two rows were filled with children both younger and older than I was. The littlest ones got to go first. They recited simple nursery rhymes, squawked out tunes on miniature violins, twirled Hula Hoops, pranced in pink ballet tutus, and when they bowed or curtsied, the audience would sigh in unison, "Awww," and then clap enthusiastically.

When my turn came, I was very confident. I remember my childish excitement. It was as if I knew, without a doubt, that the prodigy side of me really did exist. I had no fear whatsoever, no nervousness. I remember thinking to myself, This is it! This is it! I looked out over the audience, at my mother's blank face, my father's yawn, Auntie Lindo's stiff-lipped smile, Waverly's sulky expression. I had on a white dress layered with sheets of lace, and a pink bow in my Peter Pan haircut. As I sat down I envisioned people jumping to their feet and Ed Sullivan rushing up to introduce me to everyone on TV.

And I started to play. It was so beautiful. I was so caught up in how lovely I looked that at first I didn't worry how I would sound. So it was a surprise to me when I hit the first wrong note and I realized something didn't sound quite right. And then I hit another and another followed that. A chill started at the top of my head and began to trickle down. Yet I couldn't stop playing, as though my hands were bewitched. I kept thinking my fingers would adjust themselves back, like a train switching to the right track. I played this strange jumble through two repeats, the sour notes staying with me all the way to the end.

When I stood up, I discovered my legs were shaking. Maybe I had just been nervous and the audience, like Old Chong, had seen me go through the right motions and had not heard anything wrong at all. I swept my right foot out, went down on my knee, looked up and smiled. The room was quiet, except for Old Chong, who was beaming and shouting, "Bravo! Bravo! Well done!" But then I saw my mother's face, her stricken face. The audience clapped weakly, and as I walked back to my chair, with my whole face quivering as I tried not to cry, I heard a little boy whisper loudly to his mother, "That was awful," and the mother whispered back, "Well, she certainly tried."

And now I realized how many people were in the audience, the whole world it seemed. I was aware of eyes burning into my back. I felt the shame of my mother and father as they sat stiffly throughout the rest of the show.

We could have escaped during intermission. Pride and some strange sense of honor must have anchored my parents to their chairs. And so we watched it all: the eighteen-year-old boy with a fake mustache who did a magic show and juggled flaming hoops while riding a unicycle. The breasted girl with white makeup who sang from *Madama Butterfly* and got honorable mention. And the eleven-year-old boy who won first prize playing a tricky violin song that sounded like a busy bee.

After the show, the Hsus, the Jongs, and the St. Clairs from the Joy Luck Club came up to my mother and father.

"Lots of talented kids," Auntie Lindo said vaguely, smiling broadly.

"That was somethin' else," said my father, and I wondered if he was referring to me in a humorous way, or whether he even remembered what I had done.

Waverly looked at me and shrugged her shoulders. "You aren't a genius like me," she said matter-of-factly. And if I hadn't felt so bad, I would have pulled her braids and punched her stomach.

But my mother's expression was what devastated me: a quiet, blank look that said she had lost everything. I felt the same way, and it seemed as if everybody were now coming up, like gawkers at the scene of an accident, to see what parts were actually missing. When we got on the bus to go home, my father was humming the busy-bee tune and my mother was silent. I kept thinking she wanted to wait until we got home before shouting at me. But when my father unlocked the door to our apartment, my mother walked in and then went to the back, into the bedroom. No accusations. No blame.

And in a way, I felt disappointed. I had been waiting for her to start shouting, so I could shout back and cry and blame her for all my misery.

I assumed my talent-show fiasco meant I never had to play the piano again. But two days later, after school, my mother came out of the kitchen and saw me watching TV.

"Four clock," she reminded me as if it were any other day. I was stunned, as though she were asking me to go through the talent-show torture again. I wedged myself more tightly in front of the TV.

"Turn off TV," she called from the kitchen five minutes later.

I didn't budge. And then I decided. I didn't have to do what my mother said anymore. I wasn't her slave. This wasn't China. I had listened to her before and look what happened. She was the stupid one.

She came out from the kitchen and stood in the arched entryway of the living room. "Four clock," she said once again, louder.

"I'm not going to play anymore," I said nonchalantly. "Why should I? I'm not a genius."

She walked over and stood in front of the TV. I saw her chest was heaving up and down in an angry way.

"No!" I said, and I now felt stronger, as if my true self had finally emerged. So this was what had been inside me all along.

"No! I won't!" I screamed.

She yanked me by the arm, pulled me off the floor, snapped off the TV. She was frighteningly strong, half pulling, half carrying me toward the piano as I kicked the throw rugs under my feet. She lifted me up and onto the hard bench. I was sobbing by now, looking at her bitterly. Her chest was heaving even more and her mouth was open, smiling crazily as if she were pleased I was crying.

"You want me to be someone that I'm not!" I sobbed. "I'll never be the kind of daughter you want me to be!"

"Only two kinds of daughters," she shouted in Chinese. "Those who are obedient and those who follow their own mind! Only one kind of daughter can live in this house. Obedient daughter!"

"Then I wish I wasn't your daughter. I wish you weren't my mother," I shouted. As I said these things I got scared. I felt like worms and toads and slimy things were crawling out of my chest, but it also felt good, as if this awful side of me had surfaced, at last.

"Too late change this," said my mother shrilly.

And I could sense her anger rising to its breaking point. I wanted to see it spill over. And that's when I remembered the babies she had lost in China, the ones we never talked about. "Then I wish I'd never been born!" I shouted. "I wish I were dead! Like them."

It was as if I had said the magic words, Alakazam!—and her face went blank, her mouth closed, her arms went slack, and she backed out of the room, stunned, as if she were blowing away like a small brown leaf, thin, brittle, lifeless.

It was not the only disappointment my mother felt in me. In the years that followed, I failed her so many times, each time asserting my own will, my right to fall short of expectations. I didn't get straight As. I didn't become class president. I didn't get into Stanford. I dropped out of college.

For unlike my mother, I did not believe I could be anything I wanted to be. I could only be me.

And for all those years, we never talked about the disaster at the recital or my terrible accusations afterward at the piano bench. All that remained unchecked, like a betrayal that was now unspeakable. So I never found a way to ask her why she had hoped for something so large that failure was inevitable.

And even worse, I never asked her what frightened me the most: Why had she given up hope?

For after our struggle at the piano, she never mentioned my playing again. The lessons stopped, the lid to the piano was closed, shutting out the dust, my misery, and her dreams.

So she surprised me. A few years ago, she offered to give me the piano, for my thirtieth birthday. I had not played in all those years. I saw the offer as a sign of forgiveness, a tremendous burden removed.

"Are you sure?" I asked shyly. "I mean, won't you and Dad miss it?"

"No, this your piano," she said firmly. "Always your piano. You only one can play."

"Well, I probably can't play anymore," I said. "It's been years."

"You pick up fast," said my mother, as if she knew this was certain. "You have natural talent. You could been genius if you want to."

"No I couldn't."

"You just not trying," said my mother. And she was neither angry nor sad. She said it as if to announce a fact that could never be disproved. "Take it," she said.

But I didn't at first. It was enough that she had offered it to me. And after that, every time I saw it in my parents' living room, standing in front of the bay windows, it made me feel proud, as if it were a shiny trophy I had won back.

Last week I sent a tuner over to my parents' apartment and had the piano reconditioned, for purely sentimental reasons. My mother had died a few months before and I had been getting things in order for my father, a little bit at a time. I put the jewelry in special silk pouches. The sweaters she had knitted in yellow, pink, bright orange—all the colors I hated—I put those in moth-proof boxes. I found some old Chinese silk dresses, the kind with little slits up the sides. I rubbed the old silk against my skin, then wrapped them in tissue and decided to take them home with me.

After I had the piano tuned, I opened the lid and touched the keys. It sounded even richer than I remembered. Really, it was a very good piano. Inside the bench were the same exercise notes with handwritten scales, the same secondhand music books with their covers held together with yellow tape.

I opened up the Schumann book to the dark little piece I had played at the recital. It was on the left-hand side of the page, "Pleading Child." It looked more difficult than I remembered. I played a few bars, surprised at how easily the notes came back to me.

And for the first time, or so it seemed, I noticed the piece on the right-hand side. It was called "Perfectly Contented." I tried to play this one as well. It had a lighter melody but the same flowing rhythm and turned out to be quite easy. "Pleading Child" was shorter but slower; "Perfectly Contented" was longer but faster. And after I played them both a few times, I realized they were two halves of the same song.

MELANIE RAE THON

First, Body

MELANIE RAE THON (1957–) is the author of two collections of stories, *First, Body* and *Girls in the Grass,* and two novels, *Meteors in August* and *Iona Moon.* Her fiction has been included in *The Best American Short Stories 1995* and *1996*; she has received grants from the National Endowment for the Arts, the Massachusetts Artists Foundation, and the New York Foundation for the Arts; and she is a recipient of the Whiting Writers' Award. In 1996 the literary journal *Granta* included Ms. Thon on its list of twenty Best Young American Novelists. Originally from Montana, she now teaches at Ohio State University.

Two nurses with scissors could make a man naked in eleven seconds. Sid Elliott had been working Emergency eight months and it amazed him every time. Slicing through denim and leather, they peeled men open faster than Sid's father flayed rabbits.

Roxanne said it would take her longer than eleven seconds to make him naked. "But not that much longer." It was Sunday. They'd met in the park on Tuesday, and she hadn't left Sid's place since Friday night. She was skinny, very dark-skinned. She had fifteen teeth of her own and two bridges to fill the spaces. "Rotted out on smack and sugar. But I don't do that shit anymore." It was one of the first things she told him. He looked at her arms. She had scars, hard places where the skin was raised. He traced her veins with his fingertips, feeling for bruises. She was never pretty. She said this too. "So don't go thinking you missed out on something."

He took her home that night, to the loft in the warehouse overlooking the canal, one room with a high ceiling, a mattress on the floor beneath the window, a toilet behind a screen, one huge chair, one sink, a hot plate with two burners, and a miniature refrigerator for the beer he couldn't drink anymore.

"It's perfect," she said.

Now they'd known each other six days. She said, "What do you see in me?"

"Two arms, two ears. Someone who doesn't leave the room when I eat chicken."

"Nowhere to go," she said.

"You know what I mean."

He told her about the last boy on the table in Emergency. He'd fallen thirty feet. When he woke, numb from the waist, he said, *Are those my legs?* She lay down beside him, and he felt the stringy ligaments of her thighs, the rippled bone of her sternum; he touched her whole body the way he'd touched her veins that night in the park, by the water.

He sat at his mother's kitchen table. "What is it you do?" she said.

"I clean up."

"Like a janitor?"

Up to our booties in blood all night, Dr. Enos said.

"Something like that."

She didn't want to know, not exactly, not any more than she'd wanted to know what his father was going to do with the rabbits.

She nodded. "Well, it's respectable work."

She meant she could tell her friends Sid had a hospital job.

He waited.

"Your father would be proud."

He remembered a man slipping rabbits out of their fur coats. His father had been laid off a month before he thought of this.

Tonight his mother had made meatloaf, which was safe—so long as he remembered to take small bites and chew slowly. Even so, she couldn't help watching, and he kept covering his mouth with his napkin. Finally he couldn't chew at all and had to wash each bite down with milk. When she asked, "Are you happy there?" he wanted to tell her about the men with holes in their skulls, wanted to bring them, trembling, into this room. Some had been wounded three or four times. They had beards, broken teeth, scraped heads. The nurses made jokes about burning their clothes.

But the wounds weren't bullet holes. Before the scanners, every drunk who hit the pavement got his head drilled. "A precautionary measure," Dr. Enos explained. "In case of hemorrhage."

"Did the patient have a choice?"

"Unconscious men don't make choices."

Sid wanted to tell his mother that. *Unconscious men don't make choices.* He wanted her to understand the rules of Emergency: first, body, then brain—stop the blood, get the heart beating. No fine tuning. Don't worry about a man's head till his guts are back in his belly.

Dr. Enos made bets with the nurses on Saturday nights. By stars and fair weather they guessed how many motorcyclists would run out of luck cruising from Seattle to Marysville without their helmets, how many times the choppers would land on the roof of the hospital, how many men would be stripped and pumped but not saved.

Enos collected the pot week after week. "If you've bet on five and only have three by midnight, do you wish for accidents?" Dr. Roseland asked. Roseland never played. She was beyond it, a grown woman. She had two children and was pregnant with the third.

"Do you?" Enos said.

"Do I what?"

Enos stared at Roseland's swollen belly. "Wish for accidents," he said.

Skulls crushed, hearts beating, the ones lifted from the roads arrived all night. Enos moved stiffly, like a man just out of the saddle. He had watery eyes—bloodshot, blue. Sid thought he was into the pharmaceuticals. But when he had a body on the table, Enos was absolutely focused.

Sid wanted to describe the ones who flew from their motorcycles and fell to earth, who offered themselves this way. *Like Jesus.* His mother wouldn't let him say that. *With such grace.* He wished he could make her see how beautiful it was, how ordinary, the men who didn't live, whose parts were packed in plastic picnic coolers and rushed back to the choppers on the roof, whose organs and eyes were delivered to Portland or Spokane. He was stunned by it, the miracle of hearts in ice, corneas in milk. These exchanges became the sacrament, transubstantiated in the bodies of startled men and weary children. Sometimes the innocent died and the faithless lived. Sometimes the blind began to see. Enos said, "We save bodies, not souls."

Sid tasted every part of Roxanne's body: sweet, fleshy lobe of the ear, sinewy neck, sour pit of the arm, scarred hollow of the elbow. He sucked each finger, licked her salty palm. He could have spent weeks kissing her, hours with his tongue inside her. Sometimes he forgot to breathe and came up gasping. She said, "Aren't you afraid of me?"

And he said, "You think you can kill me?"

"Yes," she said, "anybody can."

She had narrow hips, a flat chest. He weighed more than twice what she did. He was too big for himself, always—born too big, grown too fast. Too big to cry. Too big to spill his milk. At four he looked six; at six, ten. Clumsy, big-footed ten. Slow, stupid ten. *Like living with a bear,* his mother said, something broken every day, her precious blown-glass ballerina crumbling in his hand, though he held her so gently, lifting her to the window to let the light pass through her. He had thick wrists, enormous thumbs. Even his eyebrows were bushy. *My monster,* Roxanne said the second night, *who made you this way?*

"How would you kill me?" he said. He put one heavy leg over her skinny legs, pinning her to the bed.

"You know, with my body."

"Yes, but how?"

"You know what I'm saying."

"I want you to explain."

She didn't. He held his hand over her belly, not quite touching, the thinnest veil of air between them. "I can't think when you do that," she said.

"I haven't laid a finger on you."

"But you will," she said.

He'd been sober twenty-seven days when she found him. Now it was forty-two. Not by choice. He'd had a sudden intolerance for alcohol. Two shots and he was on the floor, puking his guts out. He suspected Enos had slipped him some Antabuse and had a vague memory: his coffee at the edge of the counter, Enos drifting past it. Did he linger? Did he know whose it was? But it kept happening. Sid tried whiskey instead of rum, vodka instead of whiskey. After the third experiment he talked to Roseland. "Count your blessings," she said. "Maybe you'll have a liver when you're sixty." She looked at him in her serious, sad way, felt his neck with her tiny hands, thumped his back and chest, shined her flashlight into his eyes. When he was sitting down, she was his height. He wanted to lay his broad hand on her bulging stomach.

No one was inclined to offer a cure. He started smoking pot instead, which was what he was doing that night in the park when Roxanne appeared. *Materialized,* he said afterward, *out of smoke and air.*

But she was no ghost. She laughed loudly. She even breathed loudly—through her mouth. They lay naked on the bed under the open window. The curtains fluttered and the air moved over them.

"Why do you like me?" she said.

"Because you snore."

"I don't."

"How would you know?"

"It's my body."

"It does what it wants when you're sleeping."

"You like women who snore?"

"I like to know where you are."

He thought of his sister's three daughters. They were slim and quick, moving through trees, through dusk, those tiny bodies—disappearing, reassembling—those children's bodies years ago. Yes, it was true. His sister was right.

Better that he stayed away. Sometimes when he'd chased them in the woods, their bodies had frightened him—the narrowness of them, the way they hid behind trees, the way they stepped in the river, turned clear and shapeless, flowed away. When they climbed out downstream, they were whole and hard but cold as water. They sneaked up behind him to grab his knees and pull him to the ground. They touched him with their icy hands, laughing like water over stones. He never knew where they might be, or what.

He always knew exactly where Roxanne was: behind the screen, squatting on the toilet; standing at the sink, splashing water under her arms. Right now she was shaving her legs, singing nonsense words, *Sha-na-na-na-na,* like the backup singer she said she was once. "The Benders—you probably heard of them." He nodded but he hadn't. He tried to picture her twenty-four years younger, slim but not scrawny. Roxanne with big hair and white sequins. Two other girls just like her, one in silver, one in black, all of them shimmering under the lights. "But it got too hard, dragging the kid around—so I gave it up." She'd been with Sid twenty-nine days and this was the first he'd heard of any kid. He asked her. "Oh yeah," she said, "of course." She gave him a look like, *What d'you think—I was a virgin?* "But I got smart after the first one." She was onto the second leg, humming again. "Pretty kid. Kids of her own now. I got pictures." He asked to see them, and she said, "Not *with* me."

"Where?" he said.

She whirled, waving the razor. "You the police?"

She'd been sober five days. That's when the singing started. "If you can do it, so can I," she'd said.

He reminded her he'd had no choice.

"Neither do I," she said, "if I want to stay."

He didn't agree. He wasn't even sure it was a good idea. She told him she'd started drinking at nine: stole her father's bottle and sat in the closet, passed out and no one found her for two days. Sid knew it was wrong, but he was almost proud of her for that, forty years of drinking—he didn't know anyone else who'd started so young. She had conviction, a vision of her life, like Roseland, who said she'd wanted to be a doctor since fifth grade.

Sid was out of Emergency. Not a demotion. A lateral transfer. That's what Mrs. Mendelson in personnel said. Her eyes and half her face were shrunken behind her glasses.

"How can it be lateral if I'm in the basement?"

"I'm not speaking literally, Sid."

He knew he was being punished for trying to stop the girl from banging her head on the wall.

Inappropriate interference with a patient. There was a language for everything. *Sterilized equipment contaminated.*

Dropped—he'd dropped the tray to help the girl.

"I had to," he told Roxanne.

"Shush, it's okay—you did the right thing."

There was no reward for doing the right thing. When he got the girl to the floor, she bit his arm.

Unnecessary risk. "She won't submit to a test," Enos said after Sid's arm was washed and bandaged. Sid knew she wasn't going to submit to anything—why should she? She was upstairs in four-point restraint, doped but still raving; she was a strong girl with a shaved head, six pierced holes in one ear, a single chain looped through them all. Sid wanted Enos to define *unnecessary.*

Now he was out of harm's way. Down in Postmortem. The dead don't bite. *Unconscious men don't make choices.* Everyone pretended it was for his own sake.

Sid moved the woman from the gurney to the steel table. He was not supposed to think of her as a woman, he knew this. She was a body, female. He was not supposed to touch her thin blue hair or wrinkled eyelids—for his own sake. He was not supposed to look at her scars and imagine his mother's body—three deep puckers in one breast, a raised seam across the belly—was not supposed to see the ghost there, imprint of a son too big, taken this way, and later another scar, something else stolen while she slept. He was not to ask what they had hoped to find, opening her again.

Roxanne smoked more and more to keep from drinking. She didn't stash her cartons of cigarettes in the freezer anymore. No need. She did two packs a day, soon it would be three. Sid thought of her body, inside: her starved, black lungs shriveled in her chest, her old, swollen liver.

He knew exactly when she started again, their sixty-third day together, the thirty-ninth and final day of her sobriety.

He drew a line down her body, throat to belly, with his tongue. She didn't want to make love. She wanted to lie here, beneath the window, absolutely still. She was hot. He moved his hands along the wet, dark line he'd left on her ashy skin, as if to open her.

"Forget it," she said. The fan beat at the air, the blade of a chopper, hovering. He smelled of formaldehyde, but she didn't complain about that. It covered other smells: the garbage in the corner, her own body.

They hadn't made love for nineteen days. He had to go to his mother's tonight but was afraid to leave Roxanne naked on the bed, lighting each cigarette from the butt of the last one. He touched her hip, the sharp bone. He wanted her to know it didn't matter to him if they made love or not. If she drank or not. He didn't mind cigarette burns on the sheets, bills missing from his wallet. As long as she stayed.

The pictures of his three nieces in his mother's living room undid him. He didn't know them now, but he remembered their thin fingers, their scabbed knees, the way Lena kissed him one night—as a woman, not a child, as if she saw already how their lives would be—a solemn kiss, on the mouth, but not a lover's kiss. Twelve years old, and she must have heard her mother say, *Look, Sid, maybe it would be better if you didn't come around—just for a while—know what I mean?* When he saw her again she was fifteen and fat, seven months pregnant. Christina said, *Say hello to your uncle Sid,* and the girl stared at him, unforgiving, as if he were to blame for this too.

These were the things that broke his heart: his nieces on the piano and the piano forever out of tune; dinner served promptly at six, despite the heat; the smell of leather in the closet, a pile of rabbit skin and soft fur; the crisp white sheets of his old bed and the image of his mother bending, pulling the corners tight, tucking them down safe, a clean bed for her brave boy who was coming home.

Those sheets made him remember everything, the night sweats, the yellow stain of him on his mother's clean sheets. He washed them but she knew, and nothing was the way they expected it to be, the tossing in the too-small bed, the rust-colored blotches in his underwear, tiny slivers of shrapnel working their way to the surface, wounding him again. *How is it a man gets shot in the ass?* It was a question they never asked, and he couldn't have told them without answering other questions, questions about what had happened to the men who stepped inside the hut, who didn't have time to turn and hit the ground, who blew sky-high and fell down in pieces.

He touched his mother too often and in the wrong way. He leaned too close, tapping her arm to be sure she was listening. He tore chicken from the bone with his teeth, left his face greasy. Everything meant something it hadn't meant before.

She couldn't stand it, his big hands on her. He realized now how rarely she'd touched him. He remembered her cool palm on his forehead, pushing the hair off his face. Did he have a temperature? He couldn't remember. He felt an old slap across his mouth for a word he'd spit out once and forgotten. He remembered his mother licking her thumb and rubbing his cheek, wiping a dark smudge.

He thought of the body he couldn't touch, then or now—her velvety, loose skin over loose flesh, soft crepe folding into loose wrinkles.

His father was the one to tell him. They were outside after dinner, more than twenty years ago, but Sid could see them still, his father and himself standing at the edge of the yard by the empty hutches. Next door, Ollie Kern spoke softly to his roses in the dark. Sid could see it killed his father to do it. He cleared his throat three times before he said, "You need to find your own place to live, son." Sid nodded. He wanted to tell his father it was okay, he understood, he was ready. He wanted to say he forgave him—not just for this, but for everything, for not driving him across the border one day, to Vancouver, for not suggesting he stay there a few days, alone, for not saying, "It's okay, son, if you don't want to go."

Sid wanted to say no one should come between a husband and a wife, not even a child, but he only nodded, like a man, and his father patted his back, like a man. He said, "I guess I should turn on the sprinkler." And Sid said, "I'll do it, Dad."

They must have talked after that, many times. But in Sid's mind this was always the last time. He remembered forever crawling under the prickly juniper bushes to turn on the spigot as the last thing he did for his father. Remembered forever how they stood, silent in the dark, listening to water hitting leaves and grass.

He was in the living room now with his mother, after all these years, drinking instant coffee made from a little packet—it was all she had. It was still so hot. She said it. *It's still so hot.* It was almost dark, but they hadn't turned on the lights because of the heat, so it was easy for Sid to imagine the shadow of his father's shape in the chair, easy to believe that now might have been the time his father said at last, *Tell me, son, how it was, the truth, tell me.* It was like this. Think of the meanest boy you knew in sixth grade, the one who caught cats to cut off their tails. It's like that. But not all the time. Keep remembering your eleven-year-old self, your unbearable boy energy, how you sat in the classroom hour after hour, day after day, looking out the window at light, at rain. Remember the quivering leaves, how you felt them moving in your own body when you were a boy—it's like that, the waiting, the terrible boredom, the longing for something to happen, *anything,* so you hate the boy with the cat but you're thrilled too, and then you hate yourself, and then you hate the cat for its ridiculous howling and you're glad when it runs into the street crazy with pain—you're glad when the car hits it, smashes it flat. Then the bell rings, recess is over, and you're in the room again—you're taking your pencils out of your little wooden desk. The girl in front of you has long, shiny braids you know you'll never touch, not now, not after what you've seen, and then you imagine the braids in your hands, limp as cats' tails, and Mrs. Richards is saying the words *stifle, release, mourn,* and you're supposed to spell them, print them on the blank page, pass the paper forward, and later you're supposed to think the red marks—her sharp corrections, her grade—matter.

He could be more specific. If his father wanted to know. At night, you dig a hole in red clay and sleep in the ground. Then there's rain. Sheets and rivers and days of rain. The country turns to mud and smells of shit. A tiny cut on your toe festers and swells, opens wider and wider, oozes and stinks, an ulcer, a hole. You think about your foot all the time, more than you think about your mother, your father, minute after minute, the pain there, you care about your foot more than your life—you could lose it, your right big toe, leave it here, in this mud, your foot, your leg, and you wonder, how many pieces of yourself can you leave behind and still be called yourself? Mother, father, sister—heart, hand, leg. One mosquito's trapped under your net. You've used repellent—you're sticky with it, poisoned by it—but she finds the places you've missed: behind your ear, between your fingers. There's a sweet place up your sleeve, under your arm. And you think, *This is the wound that will kill me.* She's threading a parasite into your veins. These are the enemies: mud, rain, rot, mosquito. She's graceful. She's not malicious. She has no brain, no intentions. She wants to live, that's all. If she finds you, she'll have you. She buzzes at your head, but when she slips inside there's no sound.

It's still so hot. He wants to bang the keys of the out-of-tune piano. He wants a racket here, in his mother's house. He longs for all the dark noise of Roxanne, his plates with their tiny roses smashing to the floor two nights ago, his blue glasses flying out of the drainer. She wanted a drink, and he said she could have one, and she told him to fuck himself, and then the dishes exploded. He thinks of her walking through the broken glass, barefoot but not cutting her feet, brilliant Roxanne. *Roxanne Roxanne.* He has to say her name here, now, bring her into this room where the silent television flickers like a small fire in the corner. He wants to walk her up the stairs to that boy's room, wants her to run her fingers through the silky fur of rabbit pelts in the closet, wants to explain how fast his father was with the knife but too old, too slow, to collect tolls for the ferry. He wants to show her the tight corners of the white sheets, wants her to touch him, here, in this room, to bring him back together, who he was then, who he is now.

So he is saying it, her name. He is telling his mother, *I've been seeing someone,* and his mother is saying, *That's nice, Sid—you should bring her to dinner,* and he understands she means sometime, in some future she can't yet imagine, but he says, *Next week?*

She sips at her too-hot coffee, burns her pursed lips, says, *Fine, that would be fine.*

Roxanne will never agree to it. He knows this. He sees the glow of her cigarette moving in the dark, hand to mouth. He knows he won't ask because he can't bear the bark of her laughter. He doesn't turn on the light, doesn't speak. He sees what's happening, what will happen—this room in winter, the gray light leaking across the floor, the windows closed, the rain streaming down the glass.

He lies down beside her. She stubs out her cigarette, doesn't light another, says nothing but moves closer, so the hair of her arm brushes the hair of his.

He knows she hasn't eaten tonight, hasn't moved all day, living on cigarettes and air, a glass of orange juice he brought her hours ago. Roxanne. But she must have stood at the windows once while he was gone, he sees that now: the blinds are down; the darkness is complete, final, the heat close. There's only sound: a ship's horn on the canal; a man in the distance who wails and stops, wails and stops, turning himself into a siren. She rolls toward him, touches his lips with her tongue, presses her frail, naked body against him. He feels the bones of her back with his fingers, each disk of the spine. He knows he can't say anything—now or forever—such tender kisses, but he's afraid she'll stop, that she'll break him here, on this bed, so he holds back, in case she says she's tired or hungry, too hot, though he's shaking already, weeks of wanting her pulled into this moment. He touches her as if for the first time, each finger forming a question: *Here and here, and this way, can I?* He's trembling against his own skin, inside. If she says no, he'll shatter, break through himself, explode. She's unbuttoning his shirt, unzipping his pants, peeling him open. She's tugging his trousers down toward his feet but not off—they shackle him. And he knows if they make love this way, without talking, it will be the last time. He wants to grab her wrists and speak, but he can't—the silence is everything, hope and the lack of it. He wants the dark to come inside him, to be him, and there are no words even now, no sounds of pleasure, no soft murmurs, no names, no gods, only their skin—hot, blurred—their damp skin and the place where his becomes hers no longer clear, only her hair in his mouth, her eyes, her nose, her mouth in his mouth, her nipple, her fingers, her tongue in his mouth, brittle Roxanne going soft now, skinny Roxanne huge in the heat of them, swollen around him, her body big enough for all of him and he's down in her, all the way down in the dark and she has no edges, no outline, no place where her dark becomes the other dark, the thinning, separate air, and he doesn't know his own arms, his own legs, and still he keeps moving into her, deeper and deeper, feeling too late what she is, what she's become, softer and softer under him, the ground, the black mud, the swamp swallowing him—he's there, in that place, trying to pull himself out of it, but his boots are full of mud—he's thigh-deep, falling face down in the swamp, and then he feels fingernails digging into his back, a bony hand clutching his balls. He tries to grab her wrist but she's let go—she's slipped away from him, and he knows he never had a chance—this swamp takes everyone. He's gasping, mouth full of mud, and then there's a word, a name, a plea: *Stop, Sid, please,* and then there's a body beneath him, and then there's his body: heavy, slick with sweat, and then there's a man sitting on the edge of a mattress, his head in his hands, and then there's the air, surprising and cool, the fan beating and beating.

He opens the shades and rolls a joint, sits in the big chair, smoking. She's fallen asleep—to escape him, he thinks, and he doesn't blame her. If his father moved out of these shadows, Sid would say, Look at her. It was like this, exactly like this. After the rain, after the toe heals, after you don't die of malaria. The sniper's bullet whizzes past your ear, and you're almost relieved. You think this is an enemy you'll know. Bouncing Bettys and Toe Poppers jump out of the ground all day. Two wounded, two dead. The choppers come and take them all. You expect it to happen and it does, just after dark: one shot, and then all of you are shooting—you tear the trees apart. In the morning, you find them, two dead boys and a girl in the river. Her blood flowers around her in the muddy water. Her hands float. Her long black hair streams out around her head and moves like the river. She's the one who strung the wire, the one who made the booby trap with your grenade and a tin can. She tried to trip you up, yesterday and the day before. She's the sniper who chose you above all others. Her shot buzzed so close you thought she had you. She looks at the M-16 slung over your shoulder. She looks at your hands. She murmurs in her language which you will never understand. Then she speaks in your language. She says, Your bullet's in my liver. She tells you. Your bullet ripped my bowel. She says, Look for yourself if you don't believe me. You try to pull her from the water. You slip in the mud. The water here knows her. The mud filling your boots is her mud. Slight as she is, she could throw you down and hold you under.

How would you kill me?

You know, with my body.

But you get her to the bank. You pull her from the river. Then the medic's there and he tells you she's dead, a waste of time, *unnecessary risk*, and you tell him she wasn't dead when you got there, she wasn't, and you look at her lying on the bank, and she's not your enemy now, she's not anyone's enemy—she's just a dead girl in the grass, and you leave her there, by the river.

Sid thinks of the doctors at the hospital, their skills, how they use them, their endless exchanges—merciful, futile, extravagant—hearts and lungs, kidneys and marrow. What would they have given her, what would they have taken?

If his mother had looked out the window soon enough, if Sid had been there to carry him to the car, his father could have been saved by a valve; but the man was alone, absolutely, and the blood fluttering in his heart couldn't flow in the right direction. So he lay there in his own back yard, the hose in his hand, the water running and running in the half-dark.

* * *

Sid no longer knows when Roxanne will be lying on his bed and when she won't. She's got her own life, she tells him, and suddenly she does: friends who call at midnight, business she won't describe. One night she doesn't come home at all, but the next morning she's there, downstairs, hunched in the entryway, one eye swollen shut. *Mugged,* she says. *Son of a bitch.* And he knows what's happened. Even her cigarettes stolen. She forages for butts, checking the ashtray, the garbage. There aren't many. She's smoked them down to the filters almost every time, but she finds enough to get by while he runs to the store for a carton, for juice and bread, a jar of raspberry jam. He wants her to eat, but she won't. She doesn't give a shit about that. She doesn't give a shit about him. One line leads to the next. He nods, he knows this. She says she loves whiskey more than she loves him—the park, the tracks, the ground more than a mattress on the floor. She says the bottle's always there and sometimes he's not and who the fuck does he think he is, Jesus? And he says no, he never saved anyone. And then she's crying, beating his chest with her fists, falling limp against him, sobbing so hard he thinks her skinny body will break and he holds her until she stops and he carries her to the bed. He brings her orange juice, the jar of jam, ice in a rag for her swollen eye. She eats jam by the spoonful but no bread. He combs her tangled hair. He lays her down and she wants to make love but they don't, he can't, and he doesn't go to work that day but he does the next and then she's gone.

Days become weeks become winter, the one he imagined, the rain on the window. She's here but not here. She's left the smell of her hair on the pillow, her underpants twisted in the sheet at the foot of the bed, the butts of her cigarettes in the ashtray. He sees her everywhere. She's the boy in the hooded sweatshirt huddled on the stoop, whispering *I got what you need,* trying to sell crack or his own thin body. She's the bloated woman asleep on a bench in the park, the newspaper over her face coming apart in the rain. She's the bearded man at Pike's Market who pulls fishbones from the trash to eat the raw flesh. She's the dark man cuffed and shoved into the cruiser. She turns to stare out the back window, blaming him. She's the girl on Broadway with blond hair shaved to stubble. She's fifteen. She wears fishnets under ripped jeans, black boots, a leather jacket with studded spikes along the shoulders. She smacks gum, smokes, says *Fuck you* when he looks too long. He wants to stop, wants to warn her of the risks, wants to say, *Just go home.* But she can't, he knows; at least it's strangers on the street, not someone you know. *And anyway, what about you?* she'd say. She'd drop her cigarette, grind it out. She'd whisper, *I saw Roxanne—she's not doing too good, she's sick—so don't be giving me any shit about risk.*

She's the scarred man on the table with his twice-cleaved chest and gouged belly. When they open him, they'll find things missing. She's the woman without a name, another body from the river. He knows her. She rises, floating in the dirty water.

Dr. Juste says, "Shove her up there on the slab any way you can."

This one's fat. That's the first thing Sid notices. Later there will be other things: the downy hair on her cheeks, the long black hairs sprouting from her blotched legs, the unbelievable white expanse of her breasts. And she's dead, of course, like the others.

But she's not exactly like them, not dead so long, not so cold or stiff. He'd thought he could no longer be surprised, but she surprises him, Gloria Luby, the fattest dead person he has ever seen.

She weighs three hundred and twenty-six pounds. That gives her eighty-three on Sid and the gravity of death.

Dr. Juste turns at the door. He's lean and hard, not too tall, bald; he has a white beard, the impatience of a thin man. He says, "You'll have to roll this one." He says, "She won't mind."

Now they're alone, Gloria and Sid. She was a person a few hours ago, until the intern blasted her eyes with light and the pupils stayed frozen. Sid can't grasp it, the transformation. If she was a person in the room upstairs, she's a person still. He imagines her upstairs, alive in her bed, a mountain of a woman in white, her frizz of red hair matted and wild, no one to comb it. Blind, unblinking as a queen, she sat while the interns clustered around her and the head resident told them about her body and its defeats, the ravages of alcohol and the side effects of untreated diabetes: her engorged cirrhotic liver, the extreme edema of her abdomen, fluid accumulating from her liver disease, which accounted for her pain—were they listening to her moan?—which put pressure on her lungs till she could barely breathe—did they see her writhing under the sheets? It was the gastrointestinal bleeding that couldn't be stopped, even after the fluid was drained from the belly.

She pissed people off, getting fatter every day, filling with fluids and gases, seventeen days in all. If she'd lived two more, they would have taken her legs, which Dr. Juste says would have been a waste because it wouldn't have saved her but might have prolonged this. Sid wanted to ask what he meant, exactly, when he said *this.*

She's valuable now, at last: she's given herself up, her body in exchange for care. In an hour, Dr. Juste will begin his demonstration and Gloria Luby will be exposed, her massive mistakes revealed.

Sid thinks they owe her something, a lift instead of a shove, some trace of respect. He won't prod. He isn't going to call another orderly for help, isn't going to subject Gloria Luby to one more joke. *How many men does it take to change a light bulb for a fat lady?*

Later, he may think it isn't so important. Later, he may realize no one was watching, not even Gloria Luby. But just now this is his only duty: clear, specific. It presented itself.

None, she has to turn herself on. He knew what Juste would say when the interns gathered: *Shall we cut or blast?*

A first-timer might be sick behind his mask when they opened her abdomen and the pools of toxins began to drain into the grooves of the metal table, when the whole room filled with the smell of Gloria Luby's failures. But everyone would keep laughing, making cracks about women big enough for a man to live inside. He knew how scared they'd be, really, looking at her, the vastness of her opened body, because she *was* big enough for a man to crawl inside, like a cow, like a cave. Hollowed out, she could hide him forever. Some of them might think of this later, might dream themselves into the soft swamp of her body, might feel themselves waking in the warm, sweet, rotten smell of it, in the dark, in the slick, glistening fat with the loose bowels tangled around them. They might hear the jokes and wish to speak. Why didn't anyone notice? There's a man inside this woman, and he's alive. But he can't speak—she can't speak—the face is peeled back, the skull empty, and now the cap of bone is being plastered back in place, and now the skin is being stitched shut. The autopsy is over—she's closed, she's done—and he's still in there, with her, in another country, with the smell of shit and blood that's never going to go away, and he's not himself at all, he's her, he's Gloria Luby—bloated, full of gas, fat and white and dead forever.

It could happen to anyone. Anytime. Sid thinks, The body you hate might be your own; your worst fear might close around you, might be stitched tight by quick, clever hands. You might find yourself on this table. You might find yourself sprawled on a road or submerged in a swamp; you might find yourself in a bed upstairs, your red hair blazing, your useless legs swelling. Shadows come and go and speak, describing the deterioration of your retinas, the inefficiency of your kidneys, the necessity of amputation due to decreasing circulation in the lower extremities. *Extremities.* Your legs. They mean your legs. You might find yourself face down in your own sweet back yard, the hose still in your hand.

He doesn't think about God or ask himself what he believes—he knows: he believes in her, in Gloria Luby, in the three-hundred-and-twenty-six-pound fact of her body. He is the last person alive who will touch her with tenderness.

The others will have rubber gloves, and masks, and knives.

So he is going to lift her, gently, her whole body, not her shoulders, then her torso, then her terrible bruised thighs. She's not in pieces, not yet—she's a woman, and he is going to lift her as a woman. He is going to move her from the gurney to the table with the strength of his love.

He knows how to use his whole body, to lift from the thighs, to use the power of the back without depending on it. He crouches. It's a short lift, but he's made it harder for himself, standing between the gurney and the table. If he pressed them together, they'd almost touch—a man alone could roll her.

He squats. He works his arms under her, surprised by the coolness of her flesh, surprised, already, by her unbelievable weight.

For half a second, his faith is unwavering, and he is turning with her in his arms; they're almost there, and then something shifts—her immense left breast slaps against his chest, and something else follows; her right arm slips from his grasp—and he knows, close as they are, they'll never make it: an inch, a centimeter, a whole lifetime, lost. He feels the right knee give and twist, his own knee; he feels something deep inside tear, muscle wrenching, his knee springing out from under him, from under them. And still he holds her, trying to take the weight on the left leg, but there's no way. They hit the gurney going down, send it spinning across the room. The pain in his knee is an explosion, a booby trap, a wire across a path and hot metal ripping cartilage from bone, blasting his kneecap out his pants leg.

When they hit the floor, his leg twists behind him, and he's howling. All three hundred and twenty-six pounds of Gloria Luby pin him to the cold concrete.

She amazes him. She's rolled in his arms so his face is pressed into her soft belly. The knee is wrecked. He knows that already, doesn't need to wait for a doctor to tell him. *Destroyed.* He keeps wailing, though there's no point, no one in that room but the woman on top of him, insisting she will not hear, not ever. There's no one in the hallway, no one in the basement. There are three closed doors between Sidney Elliott and all the living.

He has to crawl out from under her, has to prod and shove at her thick flesh, has to claw at her belly to get a breath. Inch by inch he moves, dragging himself, his shattered leg, across the smooth floor. He leaves her there, just as she is, face down, the lumpy mound of her rump rising in the air.

Dr. Enos is trying not to smile while Sid explains, again, how it happened. Everyone smiles, thinking of it, Sid Elliott on the floor underneath Gloria Luby. They're sorry about his leg, truly. It's not going to be okay. There'll be a wheelchair, and then a walker. In the end, he'll get by with a cane. If he's lucky. It's a shame, Dr. Roseland tells him, to lose a leg that way, and Sid wonders if she thinks there are good ways to lose a leg. He remembers the boy on the table. He remembers all the boys. *Are those my legs?*

He's drifting in and out. He hears Roxanne laughing in the hallway. Then he sees her at the window, her mouth tight and grim as she sucks smoke.

She wants to know if it's worth it, the risk, the exchange: Gloria Luby's dignity for his leg. The *idea* of her dignity. She laughs, but it's bitter. She tells him he's a failure; she tells him how they found Gloria Luby. It took six orderlies to get her on the slab. They grunted, mocking her, cursing him.

He sleeps and wakes. Roxanne's gone. Even her smoke is gone. He asks the nurse, a thin, dark-skinned man, *Where is she?* And the nurse says, *Where's who, baby? Nobody been here but you and me.*

His father stands in the corner, shaking his head. He can't believe Sid's come back from the jungle, nothing worse than shrapnel in his ass, only to get it from a three-hundred-pound dead woman in a hospital in Seattle. *Three hundred and twenty-six,* Sid says. *What? Three hundred and twenty-six pounds.* His father looks as if he wants to weep, and Sid's sorry—not for himself, he'd do it again. He's sorry for his father, who's disappointed, and not just in him. He's been standing in the closet in Sid's old room all these years, sobbing in the musty dark, pressing his face into the soft rabbit fur. He's been in the other room, in the summer heat, listening to Sid plead with Roxanne, *Just let me lick you.* He's been in the kitchen, watching Sid's mother fry pork chops, chop onions, mash potatoes. He's tried to tell her something and failed. He's stood there, silent in the doorway, while she and Sid sat at the table chewing and chewing. Now, at last, when he speaks to his son, he has nothing to tell him, no wisdom to impart, only a phrase to mutter to himself, *What a waste, what a waste,* and Sid knows that when he says it he's not thinking of the leg. He wants to forgive his father for something, but the old man's turned down his hearing aid. He looks befuddled. He says, *What is it, Sid?*

The nurse shows him the button to press when the pain comes back. *Straight into the vein, babe. No need to suffer. Just give yourself a little pop. Some people think they got to be strong, lie there sweating till I remind them. Not me, honey—you give me one of those, I'd be fine all the time.* He grins. He has a wide mouth, bright teeth; he says, *You need me tonight, honey, you just buzz.*

Gloria Luby lies down beside him. She tells him, *I was exactly what they expected me to be. My brain was light, my liver heavy; the walls of my heart were thick. But there were other things they never found.* She rolls toward him, presses herself against him. Her soft body has warmth but no weight. She envelops him. She says, *I'll tell you now, if you want to know.*

* * *

The blond girl with the spikes on her jacket leans in the doorway. Outside, the rain. Behind her, the yellow light of the hall. She's wearing her black combat boots, those ripped fishnets, a sheer black dress, a black slip. She says, *Roxanne's dead. So don't give me any of that shit about risk.* He turns to the wall. He doesn't have to listen to this. *All right then,* she says, *maybe she's not dead. But I saw her—she don't look too good.*

She comes into the room, slumps in the chair by the bed. She says, *I heard all about you and that fat lady.*

She's waiting. She thinks he'll have something to say. She lights a cigarette, says, *Wanna drag?* And he does, so they smoke, passing the cigarette back and forth. She says, *Roxanne thinks you're an idiot, but who knows.* She grinds the cigarette out on the floor, then stuffs the filter back in the pack, between the plastic and the paper. She says, *Don't tell anybody I was here.*

The nurse brings Sid a wet cloth, washes his face, says, *You been talking yourself silly, babe.*

You know what I did?

The nurse touches Sid's arm, strokes him from elbow to wrist. *You're famous here, Mr. Elliott—everybody knows what you did.*

Roxanne sits on the windowsill. She says, *Looks like you found yourself another sweetheart.*

Sid's forehead beads with sweat. The pain centers in his teeth, not his knee; it throbs through his head. He's forgotten the button on his IV, forgotten the buzzer that calls the nurse. Roxanne drifts toward the bed like smoke. She says, *Does it hurt, Sid?* He doesn't know if she's trying to be mean or trying to be kind. She says, *This is only the beginning.* But she presses the button, releases the Demerol into the tube. She stoops as if to kiss him but doesn't kiss. She whispers, *I'm gone now.*

Sidney Elliott stands in a white room at the end of a long hallway. He's alone with a woman. He looks at her. He thinks, Nobody loved you enough or in the right way.

In some part of his mind, he knows exactly what will happen if he lifts her, if he takes her home, but it's years too late to stop.

He tries to be tender.

He prays to be strong.

STEPHANIE VAUGHN

Able, Baker, Charlie, Dog

STEPHANIE VAUGHN (1944–) was born in Millersburg, Ohio, and she grew up in Ohio, New York, Oklahoma, Texas, the Philippine Islands, and Italy. She was educated at Ohio State University, the University of Iowa, and Stanford University, and her stories have appeared in the O. Henry Award and Pushcart Prize series anthologies. *Sweet Talk* is her first book. Stephanie Vaughn now teaches English at Cornell University.

When I was twelve years old, my father was tall and awesome. I can see him walking across the parade ground behind our quarters. The wind blew snow into the folds of his coat and made the hem swoop around his legs. He did not lower his head, he did not jam his hands into the pockets. He was coming home along a diagonal that would cut the parade ground into perfect triangles, and he was not going to be stopped by any snowstorm. I stood at the kitchen door and watched him through a hole I had rubbed in the steamy glass.

My grandmother and mother fidgeted with pans of food that had been kept warm too long. It was one o'clock on Saturday and he had been expected home at noon.

"You want to know what this chicken looks like?" said my grandmother. "It looks like it died last year."

My mother looked into the pan but didn't say anything.

My grandmother believed my mother should have married a minister, not an Army officer. Once my mother had gone out with a minister, and now he was on the radio every Sunday in Ohio. My grandmother thought my father had misrepresented himself as a religious man. There was a story my mother told about their first date. They went to a restaurant and my father told her that he was going to have twelve sons and name them Peter, James, John, et cetera. "And I thought, Twelve sons!" said my mother. "Boy, do I pity your poor wife." My mother had two miscarriages and then she had me. My father named me Gemma, which my grandmother believed was not even a Christian name.

"You want to know what this squash looks like?" said my grandmother.

"It'll be fine," said my mother.

Just then the wind gusted on the parade ground, and my father veered to the left. He stopped and looked up. How is it possible you have caught me off guard, he seemed to ask. Exactly where have I miscalculated the velocities, how have I misjudged the vectors?

"It looks like somebody peed in it," my grandmother said.

"Keep your voice low," my father told me that day as we ate the ruined squash and chicken. "Keep your voice low and you can win any point."

We were living in Fort Niagara, a little Army post at the juncture of the Niagara River and Lake Ontario. We had been there through the fall and into the winter, as my father, who was second in command, waited for his next promotion. It began to snow in October. The arctic winds swept across the lake from Canada and shook the windows of our house. Snow drifted across the parade ground, and floes of ice piled up against each other in the river, so that if a person were courageous enough, or foolhardy enough, and also lucky, he could walk the mile across the river to Canada.

"And always speak in sentences," he told me. "You have developed a junior-high habit of speaking in fragments. Learn to come to a full stop when you complete an idea. Use semicolons and periods in your speech."

My mother put down her fork and knife. Her hands were so thin and light they seemed to pass through the table as she dropped them in her lap. "Zachary, perhaps we could save some of the lecture for dessert?" she said.

My grandmother leaned back into her own heaviness. "The poor kid never gets to eat a hot meal," she said. She was referring to the rule that said I could not cut my food or eat while I was speaking or being spoken to. My father used mealtimes to lecture on the mechanics of life, the how-tos of a civilized world. Normally I was receptive to his advice, but that day I was angry with him.

"You know, Dad," I said, "I don't think my friends are going to notice a missing semicolon."

I thought he would give me a fierce look, but instead he winked. "And don't say 'you know,' " he said.

He never said "you know," never spoke in fragments, never slurred his speech, even years later when he had just put away a fifth of scotch and was trying to describe the Eskimo custom of chewing up the meat before it was given to the elders, who had no teeth. He spoke with such calculation and precision that his sentences hung over us like high vaulted ceilings, or rolled across the table like ornaments sculptured from stone. It was a huge cathedral of a voice, full of volume and complexity.

He taught me the alphabet. Able, Baker, Charlie, Dog. It was the alphabet the military used to keep *b*'s separate from *v*'s and i's separate from *y*'s. He liked the music of it, the way it sounded on his fine voice. I was four years old and my grandmother had not come to live with us yet. We were stationed in Manila, and living in a house the Army had built on squat stilts to protect us from the insects. There was a typhoon sweeping inland, and we could hear the hoarse sound of metal scraping across the Army's paved street. It was the corrugated roof of the house next door.

"Don't you think it's time we went under the house?" my mother said. She was sitting on a duffel bag that contained our tarps and food rations. The house had a loose plank in the living-room floor, so that if the roof blew away, or the walls caved in, we could escape through the opening and sit in the low space between the reinforced floor and the ground until the military rescue bus came.

My father looked at me and said, "Able, Baker, Charlie, Dog. Can you say it, Gemma?"

I looked up at the dark slope of our own metal roof.

"Can you say it?"

"Able, Baker, Charlie, Dog," I said.

The metal rumbled on the road outside. My mother lifted the plank.

"We will be all right," he said. "Easy, Fox, George, How."

"Anybody want to join me?" said my mother.

"Easy."

"Rachel, please put that plank back."

"Easy, Fox, George, How," I said.

My mother replaced the plank and sat on the floor beside me. The storm grew louder, the rain fell against the roof like handfuls of gravel.

"Item, Jig, King." My father's voice grew lower, fuller. We sat under the sound of it and felt safe. "Love, Mike, Nan."

But then we heard another sound—something that went *whap-whap*, softly, between the gusts of rain. We tilted our heads toward the shuttered windows.

"Well," said my father, standing up to stretch. "I think we are losing a board or two off the side of the house."

"Where are you going?" said my mother. "Just where do you think you're going?"

He put on his rain slicker and went into the next room. When he returned, he was carrying a bucket of nails and a hammer. "Obviously," he said, "I am going fishing."

* * *

We moved back to the States when I was six, and he taught me how to play Parcheesi, checkers, chess, cribbage, dominoes, and twenty questions. "When you lose," he told me, "don't cry. When you win, don't gloat."

He taught me how to plant tomatoes and load a shotgun shell. He showed me how to gut a dove, turning it inside out as the Europeans do, using the flexible breastbone for a pivot. He read a great many books and never forgot a fact or a technical description. He explained the principles of crop rotation and the flying buttress. He discussed the Defenestration of Prague.

When I was in elementary school, he was sent abroad twice on year-long tours—once to Turkey and once to Greenland, both strategic outposts for America's Early Warning System. I wanted to, but I could not write him letters. His came to me every week, but without the rhythms of his voice the words seemed pale and flat, like the transparent shapes of cells under a microscope. He did not write about his work, because his work was secret. He did not send advice, because that he left to my mother and grandmother in his absence. He wrote about small things—the smooth white rocks he found on a mountainside in Turkey, the first fresh egg he ate in Greenland. When I reread the letters after he died, I was struck by their grace and invention. But when I read them as a child, I looked through the words—"eggs . . . shipment . . . frozen"—and there was nothing on the other side but the great vacuum of his missing voice.

"I can't think of anything to say," I told my mother the first time she urged me to write to him. He had already been in Turkey for three months. She stood behind me at the heavy library table and smoothed my hair, touched my shoulders. "Tell him about your tap lessons," she said. "Tell him about ballet."

"Dear Dad," I wrote. "I am taking tap lessons. I am also taking ballet." I tried to imagine what he looked like. I tried to put a face before my face, but it was gray and featureless, like the face of a statue worn flat by wind and rain. "And I hope you have a Happy Birthday next month," I concluded, hoping to evade the necessity of writing him again in three weeks.

The autumn I turned twelve, we moved to Fort Niagara, which was the administrative base for the missile sites strung along the Canadian border between Lake Erie and Lake Ontario. It was a handsome post, full of oak trees, brick buildings, and history. The French had taken the land from the Indians and built the original fort. The British took the fort from the French, and the Americans took it from the British. My father recounted the battles for us as we drove there along the wide sweep of the Niagara River, past apple orchards and thick pastures. My grandmother sat in the back seat and made a note of each red convertible that passed. I was supposed to be counting the white ones. When we drove through the gate and saw the post for the first time—the expanses of clipped grass, the tall trees, the row of Colonial houses overlooking the river—my grandmother put down her tablet and said, "This is some post." She looked at my father admiringly, the first indication she had ever given that he might be a good match for my mother after all. She asked to be taken to the far end of the post, where the Old Fort was. It sat on a point of land at the juncture of the lake and river, and looked appropriately warlike, with its moat and tiny gun windows, but it was surprisingly small—a simple square of yellow stone, a modest French château. "Is this all there is?" I said as my grandmother and I posed for pictures on the drawbridge near two soldiers dressed in Revolutionary War costumes. It was hard to imagine that chunks of a vast continent had been won and lost within the confines of a fortress hardly bigger than Sleeping Beauty's castle at Disneyland. Later, as we drove back along the river, my father said in his aphoristic way, "Sometimes the biggest battles are the smallest ones."

The week after we settled in our quarters, we made the obligatory trip to the Falls. It was a sultry day—Indian summer—and our eyes began to water as we neared the chemical factories that surrounded the city of Niagara Falls. We stopped for iced tea and my father explained how the glaciers had formed the escarpment through which the Falls had cut a deep gorge. *Escarpment*—that was the term he used, instead of *cliff*. It skidded along the roof of his mouth and entered the conversation with a soft explosion.

We went to the Niagara Falls Museum and examined the containers people had used successfully to go over the Falls early in the century, when there was a thousand-dollar prize given to survivors. Two were wooden barrels strapped with metal bands. One was a giant rubber ball reinforced with a steel cage. A fourth was a long steel capsule. On the walls were photographs of each survivor and plaques explaining who had been injured and how. The steel capsule was used by a man who had broken every bone in his body. The plaque said that he was in the hospital for twenty-three weeks and then took his capsule around the world on a speaking tour. One day when he was in New Zealand, he slipped on an orange peel, broke his leg, and died of complications.

We went next to Goat Island and stood on the open bank to watch the leap and dive of the white water. My mother held her handbag close to her breasts. She had a habit of always holding things this way—a stack of dinner plates, the dish towel, some mail she had brought in from the porch; she hunched over slightly, so that her body seemed at once to be protective and protected. "I don't like the river," she said. "I think it wants to hypnotize you." My father put his hands in his pockets to show how at ease he was, and my grandmother went off to buy an ice-cream cone.

At the observation point, we stood at a metal fence and looked into the frothing water at the bottom of the gorge. We watched bits and pieces of rainbows appear and vanish in the sunlight that was refracted off the water through the mist. My father pointed to a black shape in the rapids above the Horseshoe Falls. "That's a river barge," he said. He lowered his voice so that he could be heard under the roar of the water. "A long time ago, there were two men standing on that barge waiting to see whether in the next moment of their lives they would go over."

He told us the story of the barge then—how it had broken loose from a tug near Buffalo and floated downriver, gathering speed. The two men tore at the air, waved and shouted to people on shore, but the barge entered the rapids. They bumped around over the rocks, and the white water rose in the air. One man—"He was the thinking man," said my father—thought they might be able to wedge the barge among the rocks if they allowed the hull to fill with water. They came closer to the Falls—four hundred yards, three hundred—before the barge jerked broadside and stopped. They were there all afternoon and night, listening to the sound of the water pounding into the boulders at the bottom of the gorge. The next morning they were rescued, and one of the men, the thinking man, told the newspapers that he had spent the night playing poker in his head. He played all the hands, and he bluffed himself. He drew to inside straights. If the barge had torn loose from the rocks in the night, he was going to go over the Falls saying, "Five-card draw, jacks or better to open." The other man sat on the barge, his arms clasped around his knees, and watched the mist blow back from the edge of the Falls in the moonlight. He could not speak.

"The scream of the water entered his body," said my father. He paused to let us think about that.

"Well, what does that mean?" my grandmother said at last.

My father rested his arms on the fence and gazed pleasantly at the Falls. "He went insane."

The river fascinated me. I often stood between the yellow curtains of my bedroom and looked down upon it and thought about how deep and swift it was, how black under the glittering surface. The newspaper carried stories about people who jumped over the Falls, fourteen miles upriver from our house. I thought of their bodies pushed along the soft silt of the bottom, tumbling silently, huddled in upon themselves like fetuses—jilted brides, unemployed factory workers, old people who did not want to go to rest homes, teenagers who got bad grades, young women who fell in love with married men. They floated invisibly past my bedroom window, out into the lake.

That winter, I thought I was going to die. I thought I had cancer of the breasts. My mother had explained to me about menstruation, she had given me a book about the reproductive systems of men and women, but she had not told me about breasts and how they begin as invisible lumps that become tender and sore.

I thought the soreness had begun in a phys. ed. class one day in December when I was hit in the chest with a basketball. I didn't worry about it, and it went away by New Year's. In January, I found a pamphlet at the bus stop. I was stamping my feet in the cold, looking down at my boots, when I saw the headline—CANCER: SEVEN WARNING SIGNALS. When I got home, I went into the bathroom and undressed. I examined myself for enlarged moles and small wounds that wouldn't heal. I was systematic. I sat on the edge of the tub with the pamphlet by my side and began with my toenails, looking under the tips of them. I felt my soles, arches, ankles. I worked my way up my body and then I felt the soreness again, around both nipples. At dinner that night I didn't say anything all through the meal. In bed I slept on my back, with my arms stiff against my sides.

The next Saturday was the day my father came home late for lunch. The squash sat on the back of the stove and turned to ocher soup. The chicken fell away from the bones. After lunch he went into the living room and drank scotch and read a book. When I came down for supper, he was still sitting there, and he told my mother he would eat later. My grandmother, my mother, and I ate silently at the kitchen table. I took a long bath. I scrubbed my chest hard.

I went straight to my bedroom, and after a while my mother came upstairs and said, "What's wrong?"

I didn't say anything.

She stood in front of me with her hands clasped in front of her. She seemed to lean toward her own hands. "But you've been acting, you know"—and here she laughed self-consciously, as she used the forbidden phrase—"you know, you've been acting different. You were so quiet today."

I went to my chest of drawers and took the pamphlet out from under a stack of folded underpants and gave it to her.

"What's this?" she said.

"I think I have Number Four," I said.

She must have known immediately what the problem was, but she didn't smile. She asked me to raise my nightgown and she examined my chest, pressing firmly, as if she were a doctor. I told her about the soreness. "Here?" she said. "And here? What about here, too?" She told me I was beginning to "develop." I knew what she meant, but I wanted her to be precise.

"You're getting breasts," she said.

"But I don't *see* anything."

"You will."

"You never told me it would hurt."

"Oh, dear. I just forgot. When you're grown up you just forget what it was like."

I asked her whether, just to be safe, I could see a doctor. She said that of course I could, and I felt better, as if I had had a disease and already been cured. As she was leaving the room, I said, "Do you think I need a bra?" She smiled. I went to sleep watching the snow fall past the window. I had my hands cupped over my new breasts.

When I awoke, I did not recognize the window. The snow had stopped and moonlight slanted through the glass. I could not make out the words, but I heard my father's voice filling up the house. I tiptoed down the back staircase that led to the kitchen and stood in the slice of shadow near the doorjamb. My grandmother was telling my mother to pack her bags. He was a degenerate, she said—she had always seen that in him. My mother said, "Why, Zachary, why are you doing this?"

"Just go pack your bags," my grandmother said. "I'll get the child."

My father said conversationally, tensely, "Do I have to break your arms?"

I leaned into the light. He was holding on to a bottle of scotch with one hand, and my mother was trying to pull it away with both of hers. He jerked his arm back and forth, so that she was drawn into a little dance, back and forth across the linoleum in front of him.

"The Lord knows the way of righteousness," said my grandmother.

"Please," said my mother. "Please, please."

"And the way of the ungodly shall perish," said my grandmother.

"Whose house is this?" said my father. His voice exploded. He snapped his arm back, trying to take the bottle from my mother in one powerful gesture. It smashed against the wall, and I stepped into the kitchen. The white light from the ceiling fixture burned across the smooth surfaces of the refrigerator, the stove, the white Formica countertops. It was as if an atom had been smashed somewhere and a wave of radiation was rolling through the kitchen. I looked him in the eye and waited for him to speak. I sensed my mother and grandmother on either side of me, in petrified postures. At last, he said, "Well." His voice cracked. The word split in two. "Wel-el." He said it again. His face took on a flatness.

"I am going back to bed," I said. I went up the narrow steps, and he followed me. My mother and grandmother came along behind, whispering. He tucked in the covers, and sat on the edge of the bed, watching me. My mother and grandmother stood stiff against the door. "I am sorry I woke you up," he said finally, and his voice was deep and soothing. The two women watched him go down the hall, and when I heard his steps on the front staircase I rolled over and put my face in the pillow. I heard them turn off the lights and say good-night to me. I heard them go to their bedrooms. I lay there for a long time, listening for a sound downstairs, and then it came—the sound of the front door closing.

I went downstairs and put on my hat, coat, boots. I followed his footsteps in the snow, down the front walk, and across the road to the riverbank. He did not seem surprised to see me next to him. We stood side by side, hands in our pockets, breathing frost into the air. The river was filled from shore to shore with white heaps of ice, which cast blue shadows in the moonlight.

"This is the edge of America," he said, in a tone that seemed to answer a question I had just asked. There was a creak and crunch of ice as two floes below us scraped each other and jammed against the bank.

"You knew all week, didn't you? Your mother and your grandmother didn't know, but I knew that you could be counted on to know."

I hadn't known until just then, but I guessed the unspeakable thing—that his career was falling apart—and I knew. I nodded. Years later, my mother told me what she had learned about the incident, not from him but from another Army wife. He had called a general a son of a bitch. That was all. I never knew what the issue was or whether he had been right or wrong. Whether the defense of the United States of America had been at stake, or merely the pot in a card game. I didn't even know whether he had called the general a son of a bitch to his face or simply been overheard in an unguarded moment. I only knew that he had been given a 7 instead of a 9 on his Efficiency Report and then passed over for promotion. But that night I nodded, not knowing the cause but knowing the consequences, as we stood on the riverbank above the moonlit ice. "I am looking at that thin beautiful line of Canada," he said. "I think I will go for a walk."

"No," I said. I said it again. "No." I wanted to remember later that I had told him not to go.

"How long do you think it would take to go over and back?" he said.

"Two hours."

He rocked back and forth in his boots, looked up at the moon, then down at the river. I did not say anything.

He started down the bank, sideways, taking long, graceful sliding steps, which threw little puffs of snow in the air. He took his hands from his pockets and hopped from the bank to the ice. He tested his weight against the weight of the ice, flexing his knees. I watched him walk a few yards from the shore and then I saw him rise in the air, his long legs scissoring the moonlight, as he crossed from the edge of one floe to the next. He turned and waved to me, one hand making a slow arc.

I could have said anything. I could have said "Come back" or "I love you."

Instead, I called after him, "Be sure and write!" The last thing I heard, long after I had lost sight of him far out on the river, was the sound of his laugh splitting the cold air.

In the spring he resigned his commission and we went back to Ohio. He used his savings to invest in a chain of hardware stores with my uncle. My uncle arranged the contracts with builders and plumbers, and supervised the employees. My father controlled the inventory and handled the books. He had been a logistics officer, and all the skills he might have used in supervising the movement of land, air, and sea cargoes, or in calculating the disposition of several billion dollars' worth of military supplies, were instead brought to bear on the deployment of nuts and bolts, plumbers' joints and nipples, No. 2 pine, Con-Tact paper, acrylic paint, caulking guns, and rubber dishpans. He learned a new vocabulary—traffic builders, margins, end-cap displays, perfboard merchandisers, seasonal impulse items—and spoke it with the ostentation and faint amusement of a man who has just mastered a foreign language.

"But what I really want to know, Mr. Jenkins," I heard him tell a man on the telephone one day, "is why you think the Triple Gripper Vegetable Ripper would make a good loss-leader item in mid-winter." He had been in the hardlines industry, as it was called, for six months, and I was making my first visit to his office, and then only because my mother had sent me there on the pretext of taking him a midmorning snack during a busy Saturday. I was reluctant to confront him in his civilian role, afraid I would find him somehow diminished. In fact, although he looked incongruous among the reds, yellows, and blues that the previous owner had used to decorate the office, he sounded much like the man who had taught me to speak in complete sentences.

"Mr. Jenkins, I am not asking for a discourse on coleslaw."

When he hung up, he winked at me and said, "Your father is about to become the emperor of the building-and-housewares trade in Killbuck, Ohio."

I nodded and took a seat in a red-and-blue chair.

Then he looked at his hands spread upon the spotless ink blotter and said, "Of course, you know that I do not give a damn about the Triple Gripper Vegetable Ripper."

I had skipped a grade and entered high school. I saw less and less of him, because I ate dinner early so that I could go to play rehearsals, basketball games, dances. In the evenings he sat in a green chair and smoked cigarettes, drank scotch, read books—the same kinds of books, year after year. They were all about Eskimos and Arctic explorations—an interest he had developed during his tour in Greenland. Sometimes, when I came in late and was in the kitchen making a snack, I watched him through the doorway. Often he looked away from the book and gazed toward the window. He would strike a match and let it burn to his thumb and fingertip, then wave it out. He would raise the glass but not drink from it. I think he must have imagined himself to be in the Arctic during those moments, a warrior tracking across the ice for bear or seal. Sometimes he was waiting for me to join him. He wanted to tell me about the techniques the Eskimos had developed for survival, the way they stitched up skins to make them watertight vessels. He became obsessive on the subject of meat. The Eskimo diet was nearly all protein. "Eat meat," he said. Two professors at Columbia had tested the value of the Eskimo diet by eating nothing but caribou for a year and claimed they were healthier at the end of the experiment than they had been before.

Later, when I went to college, he developed the habit of calling me long distance when my mother and grandmother had gone to bed and he was alone downstairs with a drink. "Are you getting enough protein?" he asked me once at three in the morning. It was against dorm rules to put through calls after midnight except in cases of emergency, but his deep, commanding voice was so authoritative ("This is Gemma Jackson's father, and I must speak with her immediately") that it was for some time believed on my corridor that the people in my family were either accident-prone or suffering from long terminal illnesses.

He died the summer I received my master's degree. I had accepted a teaching position at a high school in Chicago, and I went home for a month before school began. He was overweight and short of breath. He drank too much, smoked too many cigarettes. The doctor told him to stop, my mother told him, my grandmother told him.

My grandmother was upstairs watching television and my mother and I were sitting on the front porch. He was asleep in the green chair, with a book in his lap. I left the porch to go to the kitchen to make a sandwich, and as I passed by the chair I heard him say, "Ahhhh. Ahhhhh." I saw his fist rise to his chest. I saw his eyes open and dilate in the lamplight. I knelt beside him.

"Are you okay?" I said. "Are you dreaming?"

We buried him in a small cemetery near the farm where he was born. In the eulogy he was remembered for having survived the first wave of the invasion of Normandy. He was admired for having been the proprietor of a chain of excellent hardware stores.

"He didn't have to do this," my mother said after the funeral. "He did this to himself."

"He was a good man," said my grandmother. "He put a nice roof over our heads. He sent us to Europe twice."

Afterward I went alone to the cemetery. I knelt beside the heaps of wilting flowers—mostly roses and gladiolus, and one wreath of red, white, and blue carnations. Above me, the maple pods spun through the sunlight like wings, and in the distance the corn trumpeted green across the hillsides. I touched the loose black soil at the edge of the flowers. Able, Baker, Charlie, Dog. I could remember the beginning of the alphabet, up through Mike and Nan. I could remember the end. X-ray, Yoke, Zebra. I was his eldest child, and he taught me what he knew. I wept then, but not because he had gone back to Ohio to read about the Eskimos and sell the artifacts of civilized life to homeowners and builders. I wept because when I was twelve years old I had stood on a snowy riverbank as he became a shadow on the ice, and waited to see whether he would slip between the cracking floes into the water.

ALICE WALKER

Nineteen Fifty-five

ALICE WALKER (1944–) is the author of the novels *The Third Life of Grange Copeland; Meridian; The Color Purple,* which won an American Book Award and the Pulitzer Prize; *The Temple of My Familiar; Possessing the Secret of Joy;* and *By the Light of My Father's Smile.* She is also the author of two short-story collections, *In Love & Trouble* and *You Can't Keep a Good Woman Down;* five volumes of poetry: *Once; Revolutionary Petunias; Good Night, Willie Lee, I'll See You in the Morning; Horses Make a Landscape More Beautiful;* and *Her Blue Body Everything We Know;* and two volumes of essays, *In Search of Our Mothers' Gardens* and *Living by the Word.* She has edited a Zora Neale Hurston reader, and her short story "To Hell with Dying" has been published as an illustrated children's book. Born in Eatonton, Georgia, she now lives in northern California.

1955

The car is a brandnew red Thunderbird convertible, and it's passed the house more than once. It slows down real slow now, and stops at the curb. An older gentleman dressed like a Baptist deacon gets out on the side near the house, and a young fellow who looks about sixteen gets out on the driver's side. They are white, and I wonder what in the world they doing in this neighborhood.

Well, I say to J. T., put your shirt on, anyway, and let me clean these glasses offa the table.

We had been watching the ballgame on TV. I wasn't actually watching, I was sort of daydreaming, with my foots up in J. T.'s lap.

I seen 'em coming on up the walk, brisk, like they coming to sell something, and then they rung the bell, and J. T. declined to put on a shirt but instead disappeared into the bedroom where the other television is. I turned down the one in the living room; I figured I'd be rid of these two double quick and J. T. could come back out again.

Are you Gracie Mae Still? asked the old guy, when I opened the door and put my hand on the lock inside the screen.

And I don't need to buy a thing, said I.

What makes you think we're sellin'? he asks, in that hearty Southern way that makes my eyeballs ache.

Well, one way or another and they're inside the house and the first thing the young fellow does is raise the TV a couple of decibels. He's about five feet nine, sort of womanish looking, with real dark white skin and a red pouting mouth. His hair is black and curly and he looks like a Loosianna creole.

About one of your songs, says the deacon. He is maybe sixty, with white hair and beard, white silk shirt, black linen suit, black tie and black shoes. His cold gray eyes look like they're sweating.

One of my songs?

Traynor here just *loves* your songs. Don't you, Traynor? He nudges Traynor with his elbow. Traynor blinks, says something I can't catch in a pitch I don't register.

The boy learned to sing and dance livin' round you people out in the country. Practically cut his teeth on you.

Traynor looks up at me and bites his thumbnail.

I laugh.

Well, one way or another they leave with my agreement that they can record one of my songs. The deacon writes me a check for five hundred dollars, the boy grunts his awareness of the transaction, and I am laughing all over myself by the time I rejoin J. T.

Just as I am snuggling down beside him though I hear the front door bell going off again.

Forgit his hat? asks J. T.

I hope not, I say.

The deacon stands there leaning on the door frame and once again I'm thinking of those sweaty-looking eyeballs of his. I wonder if sweat makes your eyeballs pink because his are sure pink. Pink and gray and it strikes me that nobody I'd care to know is behind them.

I forgot one little thing, he says pleasantly. I forgot to tell you Traynor and I would like to buy up all of those records you made of the song. I tell you we sure do love it.

Well, love it or not, I'm not so stupid as to let them do that without making 'em pay. So I says, Well, that's gonna cost you. Because, really, that song never did sell all that good, so I was glad they was going to buy it up. But on the other hand, them two listening to my song by themselves, and nobody else getting to hear me sing it, give me a pause.

Well, one way or another the deacon showed me where I would come out ahead on any deal he had proposed so far. Didn't I give you five hundred dollars? he asked. What white man—and don't even need to mention colored—would give you more? We buy up all your records of that particular song: first, you git royalties. Let me ask you, how much you sell that song for in the first place? Fifty dollars? A hundred, I say. And no royalties from it yet, right? Right. Well, when we buy up all of them records you gonna git royalties. And that's gonna make all them race record shops sit up and take notice of Gracie Mae Still. And they gonna push all them other records of yourn they got. And you no doubt will become one of the big name colored recording artists. And then we can offer you another five hundred dollars for letting us do all this for you. And by God you'll be sittin' pretty! You can go out and buy you the kind of outfit a star should have. Plenty sequins and yards of red satin.

I had done unlocked the screen when I saw I could get some more money out of him. Now I held it wide open while he squeezed through the opening between me and the door. He whipped out another piece of paper and I signed it.

He sort of trotted out to the car and slid in beside Traynor, whose head was back against the seat. They swung around in a u-turn in front of the house and then they was gone.

J. T. was putting his shirt on when I got back to the bedroom. Yankees beat the Orioles 10–6, he said. I believe I'll drive out to Paschal's pond and go fishing. Wanta go?

While I was putting on my pants J. T. was holding the two checks.

I'm real proud of a woman that can make cash money without leavin' home, he said. And I said *Umph.* Because we met on the road with me singing in first one little low-life jook after another, making ten dollars a night for myself if I was lucky, and sometimes bringin' home nothing but my life. And J. T. just loved them times. The way I was fast and flashy and always on the go from one town to another. He loved the way my singin' made the dirt farmers cry like babies and the womens shout Honey, hush! But that's mens. They loves any style to which you can get 'em accustomed.

1956

My little grandbaby called me one night on the phone: Little Mama, Little Mama, there's a white man on the television singing one of your songs! Turn on channel 5.

Lord, if it wasn't Traynor. Still looking half asleep from the neck up, but kind of awake in a nasty way from the waist down. He wasn't doing too bad with my song either, but it wasn't just the song the people in the audience was screeching and screaming over, it was that nasty little jerk he was doing from the waist down.

Well, Lord have mercy, I said, listening to him. If I'da closed my eyes, it could have been me. He had followed every turning of my voice, side streets, avenues, red lights, train crossings and all. It give me a chill.

Everywhere I went I heard Traynor singing my song, and all the little white girls just eating it up. I never had so many ponytails switched across my line of vision in my life. They was so *proud.* He was a *genius.*

Well, all that year I was trying to lose weight anyway and that and high blood pressure and sugar kept me pretty well occupied. Traynor had made a smash from a song of mine, I still had seven hundred dollars of the original one thousand dollars in the bank, and I felt if I could just bring my weight down, life would be sweet.

1957

I lost ten pounds in 1956. That's what I give myself for Christmas. And J. T. and me and the children and their friends and grandkids of all description had just finished dinner—over which I had put on nine and a half of my lost ten—when who should appear at the front door but Traynor. Little Mama, Little Mama! It's that white man who sings —— —— ——. The children didn't call it my song anymore. Nobody did. It was funny how that happened. Traynor and the deacon had bought up all my records, true, but on his record he had put "written by Gracie Mae Still." But that was just another name on the label, like "produced by Apex Records."

On the TV he was inclined to dress like the deacon told him. But now he looked presentable.

Merry Christmas, said he.

And same to you, Son.

I don't know why I called him Son. Well, one way or another they're all our sons. The only requirement is that they be younger than us. But then again, Traynor seemed to be aging by the minute.

You looks tired, I said. Come on in and have a glass of Christmas cheer.

J. T. ain't never in his life been able to act decent to a white man he wasn't working for, but he poured Traynor a glass of bourbon and water, then he took all the children and grandkids and friends and whatnot out to the den. After while I heard Traynor's voice singing the song, coming from the stereo console. It was just the kind of Christmas present my kids would consider cute.

I looked at Traynor, complicit. But he looked like it was the last thing in the world he wanted to hear. His head was pitched forward over his lap, his hands holding his glass and his elbows on his knees.

I done sung that song seem like a million times this year, he said. I sung it on the Grand Ole Opry, I sung it on the Ed Sullivan show. I sung it on Mike Douglas, I sung it at the Cotton Bowl, the Orange Bowl. I sung it at Festivals. I sung it at Fairs. I sung it overseas in Rome, Italy, and once in a submarine *underseas.* I've sung it and sung it, and I'm making forty thousand dollars a day offa it, and you know what, I don't have the faintest notion what that song means.

Whatchumean, what do it mean? It mean what it says. All I could think was: These suckers is making forty thousand a *day* offa my song and now they gonna come back and try to swindle me out of the original thousand.

It's just a song, I said. Cagey. When you fool around with a lot of no count mens you sing a bunch of 'em. I shrugged.

Oh, he said. Well. He started brightening up. I just come by to tell you I think you are a great singer.

He didn't blush, saying that. Just said it straight out.

And I brought you a little Christmas present too. Now you take this little box and you hold it until I drive off. Then you take it outside under that first streetlight back up the street aways in front of that green house. Then you open the box and see . . . Well, just *see.*

What had come over this boy, I wondered, holding the box. I looked out the window in time to see another white man come up and get in the car with him and then two more cars full of white mens start out behind him. They was all in long black cars that looked like a funeral procession.

Little Mama, Little Mama, what it is? One of my grandkids come running up and started pulling at the box. It was wrapped in gay Christmas paper—the thick, rich kind that it's hard to picture folks making just to throw away.

J. T. and the rest of the crowd followed me out the house, up the street to the streetlight and in front of the green house. Nothing was there but somebody's gold-grilled white Cadillac. Brandnew and most distracting. We got to looking at it so till I almost forgot the little box in my hand. While the others were busy making 'miration I carefully took off the paper and ribbon and folded them up and put them in my pants pocket. What should I see but a pair of genuine solid gold caddy keys.

Dangling the keys in front of everybody's nose, I unlocked the caddy, motioned for J. T. to git in on the other side, and us didn't come back home for two days.

1960

Well, the boy was sure nuff famous by now. He was still a mite shy of twenty but already they was calling him the Emperor of Rock and Roll.

Then what should happen but the draft.

Well, says J. T. There goes all this Emperor of Rock and Roll business.

But even in the army the womens was on him like white on rice. We watched it on the News.

Dear Gracie Mae [he wrote from Germany],

How you? Fine I hope as this leaves me doing real well. Before I come in the army I was gaining a lot of weight and gitting jittery from making all them dumb movies. But now I exercise and eat right and get plenty of rest. I'm more awake than I been in ten years.

I wonder if you are writing any more songs?

Sincerely,
Traynor

I wrote him back:

Dear Son,

We is all fine in the Lord's good grace and hope this finds you the same. J. T. and me be out all times of the day and night in that car you give me—which you know you didn't have to do. Oh, and I do appreciate the mink and the new self-cleaning oven. But if you send anymore stuff to eat from Germany I'm going to have to open up a store in the neighborhood just to get rid of it. Really, we have more than enough of everything. The Lord is good to us and we don't know Want.

Glad to here you is well and gitting your right rest. There ain't nothing like exercising to help that along. J. T. and me work some part of every day that we don't go fishing in the garden.

Well, so long Soldier.

Sincerely,
Gracie Mae

He wrote:

Dear Gracie Mae,

I hope you and J. T. like that automatic power tiller I had one of the stores back home send you. I went through a mountain of catalogs looking for it—I wanted something that even a woman could use.

I've been thinking about writing some songs of my own but every time I finish one it don't seem to be about nothing I've actually lived myself. My agent keeps sending me other people's songs but they just sound mooney. I can hardly git through 'em without gagging.

Everybody still loves that song of yours. They ask me all the time what do I think it means, really. I mean, they want to know just what *I* want to know. Where out of your life did it come from?

Sincerely,
Traynor

1968

I didn't see the boy for seven years. No. Eight. Because just about everybody was dead when I saw him again. Malcolm X, King, the president and his brother, and even J. T. J. T. died of a head cold. It just settled in his head like a block of ice, he said, and nothing we did moved it until one day he just leaned out the bed and died.

His good friend Horace helped me put him away, and then about a year later Horace and me started going together. We was sitting out on the front porch swing one summer night, dusk-dark, and I saw this great procession of lights winding to a stop.

Holy Toledo! said Horace. (He's got a real sexy voice like Ray Charles.) Look *at* it. He meant the long line of flashy cars and the white men in white summer suits jumping out on the drivers' sides and standing at attention. With wings they could pass for angels, with hoods they could be the Klan.

Traynor comes waddling up the walk.

And suddenly I know what it is he could pass for. An Arab like the ones you see in storybooks. Plump and soft and with never a care about weight. Because with so much money, who cares? Traynor is almost dressed like someone from a storybook too. He has on, I swear, about ten necklaces. Two sets of bracelets on his arms, at least one ring on every finger, and some kind of shining buckles on his shoes, so that when he walks you get quite a few twinkling lights.

Gracie Mae, he says, coming up to give me a hug. J. T.

I explain that J. T. passed. That this is Horace.

Horace, he says, puzzled but polite, sort of rocking back on his heels, Horace.

That's it for Horace. He goes in the house and don't come back.

Looks like you and me is gained a few, I say.

He laughs. The first time I ever heard him laugh. It don't sound much like a laugh and I can't swear that it's better than no laugh a'tall.

He's gitting fat for sure, but he's still slim compared to me. I'll never see three hundred pounds again and I've just about said (excuse me) fuck it. I got to thinking about it one day an' I thought: aside from the fact that they say it's unhealthy, my fat ain't never been no trouble. Mens always have loved me. My kids ain't never complained. Plus they's fat. And fat like I is I looks distinguished. You see me coming and know somebody's *there.*

Gracie Mae, he says, I've come with a personal invitation to you to my house tomorrow for dinner. He laughed. What did it sound like? I couldn't place it. See them men out there? he asked me. I'm sick and tired of eating with them. They don't never have nothing to talk about. That's why I eat so much. But if you come to dinner tomorrow we can talk about the old days. You can tell me about that farm I bought you.

I sold it, I said.

You did?

Yeah, I said, I did. Just cause I said I liked to exercise by working in a garden didn't mean I wanted five hundred acres! Anyhow, I'm a city girl now. Raised in the country it's true. Dirt poor—the whole bit—but that's all behind me now.

Oh well, he said, I didn't mean to offend you.

We sat a few minutes listening to the crickets.

Then he said: You wrote that song while you was still on the farm, didn't you, or was it right after you left?

You had somebody spying on me? I asked.

You and Bessie Smith got into a fight over it once, he said.

You *is* been spying on me!

But I don't know what the fight was about, he said. Just like I don't know what happened to your second husband. Your first one died in the Texas electric chair. Did you know that? Your third one beat you up, stole your touring costumes and your car and retired with a chorine to Tuskegee. He laughed. He's still there.

I had been mad, but suddenly I calmed down. Traynor was talking very dreamily. It was dark but seems like I could tell his eyes weren't right. It was like some*thing* was sitting there talking to me but not necessarily with a person behind it.

You gave up on marrying and seem happier for it. He laughed again. I married but it never went like it was supposed to. I never could squeeze any of my own life either into it or out of it. It was like singing somebody else's record. I copied the way it was sposed to be *exactly* but I never had a clue what marriage meant.

I bought her a diamond ring big as your fist. I bought her clothes. I built her a mansion. But right away she didn't want the boys to stay there. Said they smoked up the bottom floor. Hell, there were *five* floors.

No need to grieve, I said. No need to. Plenty more where she come from.

He perked up. That's part of what that song means, ain't it? No need to grieve. Whatever it is, there's plenty more down the line.

I never really believed that way back when I wrote that song, I said. It was all bluffing then. The trick is to live long enough to put your young bluffs to use. Now if I was to sing that song today I'd tear it up. 'Cause I done lived long enough to know it's *true.* Them words could hold me up.

I ain't lived that long, he said.

Look like you on your way, I said. I don't know why, but the boy seemed to need some encouraging. And I don't know, seem like one way or another you talk to rich white folks and you end up reassuring *them.* But what the hell, by now I feel something for the boy. I wouldn't be in his bed all alone in the middle of the night for nothing. Couldn't be nothing worse than being famous the world over for something you don't even understand. That's what I tried to tell Bessie. She wanted that same song. Overheard me practicing it one day, said, with her hands on her hips: Gracie Mae, I'ma sing your song tonight. I *likes* it.

Your lips be too swole to sing, I said. She was mean and she was strong, but I trounced her.

Ain't you famous enough with your own stuff? I said. Leave mine alone. Later on, she thanked me. By then she was Miss Bessie Smith to the World, and I was still Miss Gracie Mae Nobody from Notasulga.

The next day all these limousines arrived to pick me up. Five cars and twelve bodyguards. Horace picked that morning to start painting the kitchen.

Don't paint the kitchen, fool, I said. The only reason that dumb boy of ours is going to show me his mansion is because he intends to present us with a new house.

What you gonna do with it? he asked me, standing there in his shirtsleeves stirring the paint.

Sell it. Give it to the children. Live in it on weekends. It don't matter what I do. He sure don't care.

Horace just stood there shaking his head. Mama you sure looks *good,* he says. Wake me up when you git back.

Fool, I say, and pat my wig in front of the mirror.

The boy's house is something else. First you come to this mountain, and then you commence to drive and drive up this road that's lined with magnolias. Do magnolias grow on mountains? I was wondering. And you come to lakes and you come to ponds and you come to deer and you come up on some sheep. And I figure these two is sposed to represent England and Wales. Or something out of Europe. And you just keep on coming to stuff. And it's all pretty. Only the man driving my car don't look at nothing but the road. Fool. And then *finally,* after all this time, you begin to go up the driveway. And there's more magnolias—only they're not in such good shape. It's sort of cool up this high and I don't think they're gonna make it. And then I see this building that looks like if it had a name it would be The Tara Hotel. Columns and steps and outdoor chandeliers and rocking chairs. Rocking chairs? Well, and there's the boy on the steps dressed in a dark green satin jacket like you see folks wearing on TV late at night, and he looks sort of like a fat dracula with all that house rising behind him, and standing beside him there's this little white vision of loveliness that he introduces as his wife.

He's nervous when he introduces us and he says to her: This is Gracie Mae Still, I want you to know me. I mean . . . and she gives him a look that would fry meat.

Won't you come in, Gracie Mae, she says, and that's the last I see of her.

He fishes around for something to say or do and decides to escort me to the kitchen. We go through the entry and the parlor and the breakfast room and the dining room and the servants' passage and finally get there. The first thing I notice is that, altogether, there are five stoves. He looks about to introduce me to one.

Wait a minute, I say. Kitchens don't do nothing for me. Let's go sit on the front porch.

Well, we hike back and we sit in the rocking chairs rocking until dinner.

Gracie Mae, he says down the table, taking a piece of fried chicken from the woman standing over him, I got a little surprise for you.

It's a house, ain't it? I ask, spearing a chitlin.

You're getting *spoiled,* he says. And the way he says *spoiled* sounds funny. He slurs it. It sounds like his tongue is too thick for his mouth. Just that quick he's finished the chicken and is now eating chitlins *and* a pork chop. *Me* spoiled, I'm thinking.

I already got a house. Horace is right this minute painting the kitchen. I bought that house. My kids feel comfortable in that house.

But this one I bought you is just like mine. Only a little smaller.

I still don't need no house. And anyway who would clean it?

He looks surprised.

Really, I think, some peoples advance *so* slowly.

I hadn't thought of that. But what the hell, I'll get you somebody to live in.

I don't want other folks living 'round me. Makes me nervous.

You *don't?* It *do?*

What I want to wake up and see folks I don't even know for?

He just sits there downtable staring at me. Some of that feeling is in the song, ain't it? Not the words, the *feeling*. What I want to wake up and see folks I don't even know for? But I see twenty folks a day I don't even know, including my wife.

This food wouldn't be bad to wake up to though, I said. The boy had found the genius of corn bread.

He looked at me real hard. He laughed. Short. They want what you got but they don't want you. They want what I got only it ain't mine. That's what makes 'em so hungry for me when I sing. They getting the flavor of something but they ain't getting the thing itself. They like a pack of hound dogs trying to gobble up a scent.

You talking 'bout your fans?

Right. Right. He says.

Don't worry 'bout your fans, I say. They don't know their asses from a hole in the ground. I doubt there's a honest one in the bunch.

That's the point. Dammit, that's the point! He hits the table with his fist. It's so solid it don't even quiver. You need a honest audience! You can't have folks that's just gonna lie right back to you.

Yeah, I say, it was small compared to yours, but I had one. It would have been worth my life to try to sing 'em somebody else's stuff that I didn't know nothing about.

He must have pressed a buzzer under the table. One of his flunkies zombies up.

Git Johnny Carson, he says.

On the phone? asks the zombie.

On the phone, says Traynor, what you think I mean, git him offa the front porch? Move your ass.

So two weeks later we's on the Johnny Carson show.

Traynor is all corseted down nice and looks a little bit fat but mostly good. And all the women that grew up on him and my song squeal and squeal. Traynor says: The lady who wrote my first hit record is here with us tonight, and she's agreed to sing it for all of us, just like she sung it forty-five years ago. Ladies and Gentlemen, the great Gracie Mae Still!

Well, I had tried to lose a couple of pounds my own self, but failing that I had me a very big dress made. So I sort of rolls over next to Traynor, who is dwarfted by me, so that when he puts his arm around back of me to try to hug me it looks funny to the audience and they laugh.

I can see this pisses him off. But I smile out there at 'em. Imagine squealing for twenty years and not knowing why you're squealing? No more sense of endings and beginnings than hogs.

It don't matter, Son, I say. Don't fret none over me.

I commence to sing. And I sound —— wonderful. Being able to sing good ain't all about having a good singing voice a'tall. A good singing voice helps. But when you come up in the Hard Shell Baptist church like I did you understand early that the fellow that sings is the singer. Them that waits for programs and arrangements and letters from home is just good voices occupying body space.

So there I am singing my own song, my own way. And I give it all I got and enjoy every minute of it. When I finish Traynor is standing up clapping and clapping and beaming at first me and then the audience like I'm his mama for true. The audience claps politely for about two seconds.

Traynor looks disgusted.

He comes over and tries to hug me again. The audience laughs.

Johnny Carson looks at us like we both weird.

Traynor is mad as hell. He's supposed to sing something called a love ballad. But instead he takes the mike, turns to me and says: Now see if my imitation still holds up. He goes into the same song, *our* song, I think, looking out at his flaky audience. And he sings it just the way he always did. My voice, my tone, my inflection, everything. But he forgets a couple of lines. Even before he's finished the matronly squeals begin.

He sits down next to me looking whipped.

It don't matter, Son, I say, patting his hand. You don't even know those people. Try to make the people you know happy.

Is that in the song? he asks.

Maybe, I say.

1977

For a few years I hear from him, then nothing. But trying to lose weight takes all the attention I got to spare. I finally faced up to the fact that my fat is the hurt I don't admit, not even to myself, and that I been trying to bury it from the day I was born. But also when you git real old, to tell the truth, it ain't as pleasant. It gits lumpy and slack. Yuck. So one day I said to Horace, I'ma git this shit offa me.

And he fell in with the program like he always try to do and Lord such a procession of salads and cottage cheese and fruit juice!

One night I dreamed Traynor had split up with his fifteenth wife. He said: *You meet 'em for no reason. You date 'em for no reason. You marry 'em for no reason. I do it all but I swear it's just like somebody else doing it. I feel like I can't remember Life.*

The boy's in trouble, I said to Horace.

You've always said that, he said.

I have?

Yeah. You always said he looked asleep. You can't sleep through life if you wants to live it.

You not such a fool after all, I said, pushing myself up with my cane and hobbling over to where he was. Let me sit down on your lap, I said, while this salad I ate takes effect.

In the morning we heard Traynor was dead. Some said fat, some said heart, some said alcohol, some said drugs. One of the children called from Detroit. Them dumb fans of his is on a crying rampage, she said. You just ought to turn on the t.v.

But I didn't want to see 'em. They was crying and crying and didn't even know what they was crying for. One day this is going to be a pitiful country, I thought.

JOHN EDGAR WIDEMAN

Fever

JOHN EDGAR WIDEMAN (1941–) is the first writer to win the PEN/Faulkner Award twice—in 1984 for *Sent for You Yesterday* and in 1990 for *Philadelphia Fire.* His nonfiction book, *Brothers and Keepers,* received a National Book Critics Circle nomination, and his memoir, *Fatheralong,* was a finalist for the National Book Award. In 1998 he won the Rea Award for the Short Story. His most recent novel is *The Cattle Killing.* He teaches at the University of Massachusetts at Amherst.

> To Matthew Carey, Esq., who fled Philadelphia in its hour of need and upon his return published a libelous account of the behavior of black nurses and undertakers, thereby injuring all people of my race and especially those without whose unselfish, courageous labours the city could not have survived the late calamity.

> *Consider Philadelphia from its centrical situation, the extent of its commerce, the number of its artificers, manufacturers and other circumstances, to be to the United States what the heart is to the human body in circulating the blood.*
>
> *Robert Morris, 1777.*

He stood staring through a tall window at the last days of November. The trees were barren women starved for love and they'd stripped off all their clothes, but nobody cared. And not one of them gave a fuck about him, sifting among them, weightless and naked, knowing just as well as they did, no hands would come to touch them, warm them, pick leaves off the frozen ground and stick them back in place. Before he'd gone to bed a flutter of insects had stirred in the dark outside his study. Motion worrying the corner of his eye till he turned and focused where light pooled on the deck, a cone in which he could trap slants of snow so they materialized into wet, gray feathers that blotted against the glass, the planks of the deck. If he stood seven hours, dark would come again. At some point his reflection would hang in the glass, a ship from the other side of the world, docked in the ether. Days were shorter now. A whole one spent wondering what goes wrong would fly away, fly in the blink of an eye.

Perhaps, *perhaps it may be acceptable to the reader to know how we found the sick affected by the sickness; our opportunities of hearing and seeing them have been very great. They were taken with a chill, a headache, a sick stomach, with pains in their limbs and back, this was the way the sickness in general began, but all were not affected alike, some appeared but slightly affected with some of these symptoms, what confirmed us in the opinion of a person being smitten was the colour of their eyes.*

Victims in this low-lying city perished every year, and some years were worse than others, but the worst by far was the long hot dry summer of '93, when the dead and dying wrested control of the city from the living. Most who were able, fled. The rich to their rural retreats, others to relatives and friends in the countryside or neighboring towns. Some simply left, with no fixed destination, the prospect of privation or starvation on the road preferable to cowering in their homes awaiting the fever's fatal scratching at their door. Busy streets deserted, commerce halted, members of families shunning one another, the sick abandoned to suffer and die alone. Fear ruled. From August when the first cases of fever appeared below Water Street, to November when merciful frosts ended the infestation, the city slowly deteriorated, as if it, too, could suffer the terrible progress of the disease: fever, enfeeblement, violent vomiting and diarrhea, helplessness, delirium, settled dejection when patients *concluded they must go (so the phrase for dying was), and therefore in a kind of fixed determined state of mind went off.*

In some it raged more furiously than in others—some have languished for seven and ten days, and appeared to get better the day, or some hours before they died, while others were cut off in one, two or three days, but their complaints were similar. Some lost their reason and raged with all the fury madness could produce, and died in strong convulsions. Others retained their reason to the last, and seemed rather to fall asleep than die.

Yellow fever: an acute infectious disease of subtropical and tropical New World areas, caused by a filterable virus transmitted by a mosquito of the genus *Aëdes* and characterized by jaundice and dark colored vomit resulting from hemorrhages. Also called *yellow jack.*

Dengue: an infectious, virulent tropical and subtropical disease transmitted by mosquitos and characterized by fever, rash and severe pains in the joints. Also called *breakbone fever, dandy.* [Spanish, of African origin, akin to Swahili *kindinga.*]

Curled in the black hold of the ship he wonders why his life on solid green earth had to end, why the gods had chosen this new habitation for him, floating, chained to other captives, no air, no light, the wooden walls shuddering, battered, as if some madman is determined to destroy even this last pitiful refuge where he skids in foul puddles of waste, bumping other bodies, skinning himself on splintery beams and planks, always moving, shaken and spilled like palm nuts in the diviner's fist, and Esu casts his fate, constant motion, tethered to an iron ring.

In the darkness he can't see her, barely feels her light touch on his fevered skin. Sweat thick as oil but she doesn't mind, straddles him, settles down to do her work. She enters him and draws his blood up into her belly. When she's full, she pauses, dreamy, heavy. He could kill her then; she wouldn't care. But he doesn't. Listens to the whine of her wings lifting till the whimper is lost in the roar and crash of waves, creaking wood, prisoners groaning. If she returns tomorrow and carries away another drop of him, and the next day and the next, a drop each day, enough days, he'll be gone. Shrink to nothing, slip out of this iron noose and disappear.

Aëdes aegypti: a mosquito of the family *Culicidae,* genus *Aëdes* in which the female is distinguished by a long proboscis for sucking blood. This winged insect is a vector (an organism that carries pathogens from one host to another) of yellow fever and dengue. [New Latin *Aëdes,* from Greek *aedes,* unpleasant: *a* -, not + *edos,* pleasant . . .]

All things arrive in the waters and waters carry all things away. So there is no beginning or end, only the waters' flow, ebb, flood, trickle, tides emptying and returning, salt seas and rivers and rain and mist and blood, the sun drowning in an ocean of night, wet sheen of dawn washing darkness from our eyes. This city is held in the water's palm. A captive as surely as I am captive. Long fingers of river, Schuylkill, Delaware, the rest of the hand invisible; underground streams and channels feed the soggy flesh of marsh, clay pit, sink, gutter, stagnant pool. What's not seen is heard in the suck of footsteps through spring mud of unpaved streets. Noxious vapors that sting your eyes, cause you to gag, spit and wince are evidence of a presence, the dead hand cupping this city, the poisons that circulate through it, the sweat on its rotting flesh.

No one has asked my opinion. No one will. Yet I have seen this fever before, and though I can prescribe no cure, I could tell stories of other visitations, how it came and stayed and left us, the progress of disaster, its several stages, its horrors and mitigations. My words would not save one life, but those mortally affrighted by the fever, by the prospect of universal doom, might find solace in knowing there are limits to the power of this scourge that has befallen us, that some, yea, most will survive, that this condition is temporary, a season, that the fever must disappear with the first deep frosts and its disappearance is as certain as the fact it will come again.

They say the rat's-nest ships from Santo Domingo brought the fever. Frenchmen and their black slaves fleeing black insurrection. Those who've seen Barbados's distemper say our fever is its twin born in the tropical climate of the hellish Indies. I know better. I hear the drum, the forest's heartbeat, pulse of the sea that chains the moon's wandering, the spirit's journey. Its throb is source and promise of all things being connected, a mirror storing everything, forgetting nothing. To explain the fever we need no boatloads of refugees, ragged and wracked with killing fevers, bringing death to our shores. We have bred the affliction within our breasts. Each solitary heart contains all the world's tribes, and its precarious dance echoes the drum's thunder. We are our ancestors and our children, neighbors and strangers to ourselves. Fever descends when the waters that connect us are clogged with filth. When our seas are garbage. The waters cannot come and go when we are shut off one from the other, each in his frock coat, wig, bonnet, apron, shop, shoes, skin, behind locks, doors, sealed faces, our blood grows thick and sluggish. Our bodies void infected fluids. Then we are dry and cracked as a desert country, vital parts wither, all dust and dry bones inside. Fever is a drought consuming us from within. Discolored skin caves in upon itself, we burn, expire.

I regret there is so little comfort in this explanation. It takes into account neither climatists nor contagionists, flies in the face of logic and reason, the good doctors of the College of Physicians who would bleed us, purge us, quarantine, plunge us in icy baths, starve us, feed us elixirs of bark and wine, sprinkle us with gunpowder, drown us in vinegar according to the dictates of their various healing sciences. Who, then, is this foolish, old man who receives his wisdom from pagan drums in pagan forests? Are these the delusions of one whose brain the fever has already begun to gnaw? Not quite. True, I have survived other visitations of the fever, but while it prowls this city, I'm in jeopardy again as you are, because I claim no immunity, no magic. The messenger who bears the news of my death will reach me precisely at the stroke determined when it was determined I should tumble from the void and taste air the first time. Nothing is an accident. Fever grows in the secret places of our hearts, planted there when one of us decided to sell one of us to another. The drum must pound ten thousand thousand years to drive that evil away.

Fires burn on street corners. Gunshots explode inside wooden houses. Behind him a carter's breath expelled in low, labored pants warns him to edge closer to housefronts forming one wall of a dark, narrow, twisting lane. Thick wheels furrow the unpaved street. In the fire glow the cart stirs a shimmer of dust, faint as a halo, a breath smear on a mirror. Had the man locked in the traces of the cart cursed him or was it just a wheeze of exertion, a complaint addressed to the unforgiving weight of his burden? Creaking wheels, groaning wood, plodding footsteps, the cough of dust, bulky silhouette blackened as it lurches into brightness at the block's end. All gone in a moment. Sounds, motion, sight extinguished. What remained, as if trapped by a lid clamped over the lane, was the stench of dead bodies. A stench cutting through the ubiquitous pall of vinegar and gunpowder. Two, three, four corpses being hauled to Potter's Field, trailed by the unmistakable wake of decaying flesh. He'd heard they raced their carts to the burial ground. Two or three entering Potter's Field from different directions would acknowledge one another with challenges, raised fists, gather their strength for a last dash to the open trenches where they tip their cargoes. Their brethren would wager, cheer, toast the victor with tots of rum. He could hear the rumble of coffins crashing into a common grave, see the comical chariots bouncing, the men's legs pumping, faces contorted by fires that blazed all night at the burial ground. Shouting and curses would hang in the torpid night air, one more nightmare troubling the city's sleep.

He knew this warren of streets as well as anyone. Night or day he could negotiate the twists and turnings, avoid cul-de-sacs, find the river even if his vision was obscured in tunnel-like alleys. He anticipated when to duck a jutting signpost, knew how to find doorways where he was welcome, wooden steps down to a cobbled terrace overlooking the water where his shod foot must never trespass. Once beyond the grand houses lining one end of Water Street, in this quarter of hovels, beneath these wooden sheds leaning shoulder to shoulder were cellars and caves dug into the earth, poorer men's dwellings under these houses of the poor, an invisible region where his people burrow, pull earth like blanket and quilt round themselves to shut out cold and dampness, sleeping multitudes to a room, stacked and crosshatched and spoon fashion, themselves the only fuel, heat of one body passed to others and passed back from all to one. Can he blame the lucky ones who are strong enough to pull the death carts, who celebrate and leap and roar all night around the bonfires? Why should they return here? Where living and dead, sick and well must lie face to face, shivering or sweltering on the same dank floor.

Below Water Street the alleys proliferate. Named and nameless. He knows where he's going but fever has transformed even the familiar. He'd been waiting in Dr. Rush's entrance hall. An English mirror, oval framed in scalloped brass, drew him. He watched himself glide closer, a shadow, a blur, then the shape of his face materialized from silken depths. A mask he did not recognize. He took the thing he saw and murmured to it. Had he once been in control? Could he tame it again? Like a garden ruined overnight, pillaged, overgrown, trampled by marauding beasts. He stares at the chaos until he can recall familiar contours of earth, seasons of planting, harvesting, green shoots, nodding blossoms, scraping, digging, watering. Once upon a time he'd cultivated this thing, this plot of flesh and blood and bone, but what had it become? Who owned it now? He'd stepped away. His eyes constructed another face and set it there, between him and the wizened old man in the glass. He'd aged twenty years in a glance and the fever possessed the same power to alter suddenly what it touched. This city had grown ancient and fallen into ruin in two months since early August, when the first cases of fever appeared. Something in the bricks, mortar, beams and stones had gone soft, had lost its permanence. When he entered sickrooms, walls fluttered, floors buckled. He could feel roofs pressing down. Putrid heat expanding. In the bodies of victims. In rooms, buildings, streets, neighborhoods. Membranes that preserved the integrity of substances and shapes, kept each in its proper place, were worn thin. He could poke his finger through yellowed skin. A stone wall. The eggshell of his skull. What should be separated was running together. Threatened to burst. Nothing contained the way it was supposed to be. No clear lines of demarcation. A mongrel city. Traffic where there shouldn't be traffic. An awful void opening around him, preparing itself to hold explosions of bile, vomit, gushing bowels, ooze, sludge, seepage.

Earlier in the summer, on a July afternoon, he'd tried to escape the heat by walking along the Delaware. The water was unnaturally calm, isolated into stagnant pools by outcroppings of wharf and jetty. A shelf of rotting matter paralleled the river edge. As if someone had attempted to sweep what was unclean and dead from the water. Bones, skins, entrails, torn carcasses, unrecognizable tatters and remnants broomed into a neat ridge. No sigh of the breeze he'd sought, yet fumes from the rim of garbage battered him in nauseating waves, a palpable medium intimate as wind. Beyond the tidal line of refuge, a pale margin lapped clean by receding waters. Then the iron river itself, flat, dark, speckled by sores of foam that puckered and swirled, worrying the stillness with a life of their own.

Spilled. Spoiled. Those words repeated themselves endlessly as he made his rounds. Dr. Rush had written out his portion, his day's share from the list of dead and dying. He'd purged, bled, comforted and buried victims of the fever. In and out of homes that had become tombs, prisons, charnel houses. Dazed children wandering the streets, searching for their parents. How can he explain to a girl, barely more than an infant, that the father and mother she sobs for are gone from this earth? Departed. Expired. They are resting, child. Asleep forever. In a far, far better place, my sweet, dear, suffering one. In God's bosom. Wrapped in His incorruptible arms. A dead mother with a dead baby at her breast. Piteous cries of the helpless offering all they own for a drink of water. How does he console the delirious boy who pummels him, fastens himself on his leg because he's put the boy's mother in a box and now must nail shut the lid?

Though light-headed from exhaustion, he's determined to spend a few hours here, among his own people. But were these lost ones really his people? The doors of his church were open to them, yet these were the ones who stayed away, wasting their lives in vicious pastimes of the idle, the unsaved, the ignorant. His benighted brethren who'd struggled to reach this city of refuge and then, once inside the gates, had fallen, prisoners again, trapped by chains of dissolute living as they'd formerly been snared in the bonds of slavery. He'd come here and preached to them. Thieves, beggars, loose women, debtors, fugitives, drunkards, gamblers, the weak, crippled and outcast with nowhere else to go. They spurned his church so he'd brought church to them, preaching in gin mills, whoring dens, on street corners. He'd been jeered and hooted, spat upon, clods of unnameable filth had spattered his coat. But a love for them, as deep and unfathomable as his sorrow, his pity, brought him back again and again, exhorting them, setting the gospel before them so they might partake of its bounty, the infinite goodness, blessed sustenance therein. Jesus had toiled among the wretched, the outcast, that flotsam and jetsam deposited like a ledge of filth on the banks of the city. He understood what had brought the dark faces of his brethren north, to the Quaker promise of this town, this cradle and capital of a New World, knew the misery they were fleeing, the bright star in the Gourd's handle that guided them, the joy leaping in their hearts when at last, at last the opportunity to be viewed as men instead of things was theirs. He's dreamed such dreams himself, oh yes, and prayed that the light of hope would never be extinguished. He'd been praying for deliverance, for peace and understanding when God had granted him a vision, hordes of sable bondsmen throwing off their chains, marching, singing, a path opening in the sea, the sea shaking its shaggy shoulders, resplendent with light and power. A radiance sparkling in this walkway through the water, pearls, diamonds, spears of light. This was the glistening way home. Waters parting, glory blinking and winking. Too intense to stare at, a promise shimmering, a rainbow arching over the end of the path. A hand tapped him. He'd waited for it to blend into the vision, for its meaning to shine forth in the language neither word nor thought, God was speaking in His visitation. Tapping became a grip. Someone was shoving him. He was being pushed off his knees, hauled to his feet. Someone was snatching him from the honeyed dream of salvation. When his eyes popped open he knew the name of each church elder man-handling him. Pale faces above a wall of black cloth belonged to his fellow communicants. He knew without looking the names of the men whose hands touched him gently, steering, coaxing, and those whose hands dug into his flesh, the impatient, imperious, rough hands that shunned any contact with him except as overseer or master.

Allen, Allen. Do you hear me? You and your people must not kneel at the front of the gallery. On your feet. Come. Come. Now. On your feet.

Behind the last row of pews. There ye may fall down on your knees and give praise.

And so we built our African house of worship. But its walls could not imprison the Lord's word. Go forth. Go forth. And he did so. To this sinful quarter. Tunnels, cellars and caves. Where no sunlight penetrates. Where wind off the river cuts like a knife. Chill of icy spray channeled here from the ocean's wintry depths. Where each summer the brackish sea that is mouth and maw and bowel deposits its waste in puddles stinking to high heaven.

Water Street becomes what it's named, rises round his ankles, soaks his boots, threatens to drag him down. Patrolling these murky depths he's predator, scavenger, the prey of some dagger-toothed creature whose shadow closes over him like a net.

When the first settlers arrived here they'd scratched caves into the soft earth of the riverbank. Like ants. Rats. Gradually they'd pushed inland, laying out a geometrical grid of streets, perpendicular, true angled and straight edged, the mirror of their rectitude. Black Quaker coats and dour visages were remembrances of mud, darkness, the place of their lying in, cocooned like worms, propagating dreams of a holy city. The latest comers must always start here, on this dotted line, in this riot of alleys, lanes, tunnels. Wave after wave of immigrants unloaded here, winnowed here, dying in these shanties, grieving in strange languages. But white faces move on, bury their dead, bear their children, negotiate the invisible reef between this broken place and the foursquare town. Learn enough of their new tongue to say to the blacks they've left behind, *thou shalt not pass.*

I watched him bring the scalding liquid to his lips and thought to myself that's where his color comes from. The black brew he drinks every morning. Coloring him, changing him. A hue I had not considered until that instant as other than absence, something nonwhite and therefore its opposite, what light would be if extinguished, sky or sea drained of the color blue when the sun disappears, the blackness of cinders. As he sips, steam rises. I peer into the cup that's become mine, at the moon in its center, waxing, waning. A light burning in another part of the room caught there, as my face would be if I leaned over the cup's hot mouth. But I have no wish to see my face. His is what I study as I stare into my cup and see not absence, but the presence of wood darkly stained, wet plowed earth, a boulder rising from a lake, blackly glistening as it sheds crowns and beards and necklaces of water. His color neither neglect nor abstention, nor mystery, but a swelling tide in his skin of this bitter morning beverage it is my habit to imbibe.

We were losing, clearly losing the fight. One day in mid-September fifty-seven were buried before noon.

He'd begun with no preamble. Our conversation taken up again directly as if the months since our last meeting were no more than a cobweb his first words lightly brush away. I say conversation but a better word would be soliloquy because I was only a listener, a witness learning his story, a story buried so deeply he couldn't recall it, but dreamed pieces, a conversation with himself, a reverie with the power to sink us both into its unreality. So his first words did not begin the story where I remembered him ending it in our last session, but picked up midstream the ceaseless play of voices only he heard, always, summoning him, possessing him, enabling him to speak, to be.

Despair was in my heart. The fiction of our immunity had been exposed for the vicious lie it was, a not so subtle device for wresting us from our homes, our loved ones, the afflicted among us, and sending us to aid strangers. First they blamed us, called the sickness Barbados fever, a contagion from those blood-soaked islands, brought to these shores by refugees from the fighting in Santo Domingo. We were not welcome anywhere. A dark skin was seen not only as a badge of shame for its wearer. Now we were evil incarnate, the mask of long agony and violent death. Black servants were discharged. The draymen, carters, barbers, caterers, oyster sellers, street vendors could find no custom. It mattered not that some of us were born here and spoke no language but the English language, second-, even third-generation African Americans who knew no other country, who laughed at the antics of newly landed immigrants, Dutchmen, Welshmen, Scots, Irish, Frenchmen who had turned our marketplaces into Babel, stomping along in their clodhopper shoes, strange costumes, haughty airs, Lowlander gibberish that sounded like men coughing or dogs barking. My fellow countrymen searching everywhere but in their own hearts, the foulness upon which this city is erected, to lay blame on others for the killing fever, pointed their fingers at foreigners and called it Palatine fever, a pestilence imported from those low countries in Europe where, I have been told, war for control of the sea-lanes, the human cargoes transported thereupon, has raged for a hundred years.

But I am losing the thread, the ironical knot I wished to untangle for you. How the knife was plunged in our hearts, then cruelly twisted. We were proclaimed carriers of the fever and treated as pariahs, but when it became expedient to command our services to nurse the sick and bury the dead, the previous allegations were no longer mentioned. Urged on by desperate counselors, the mayor granted us a blessed immunity. We were ordered to save the city.

I swear to you, and the bills of mortality, published by the otherwise unreliable Mr. Carey, support my contention, that the fever dealt with us severely. Among the city's poor and destitute the fever's ravages were most deadly and we are always the poorest of the poor. If an ordinance forbidding ringing of bells to mourn the dead had not been passed, that awful tolling would have marked our days, the watches of the night in our African American community, as it did in those environs of the city we were forbidden to inhabit. Every morning before I commenced my labors for the sick and dying, I would hear moaning, screams of pain, fearful cries and supplications, a chorus of lamentations scarring daybreak, my people awakening to a nightmare that was devouring their will to live.

The small strength I was able to muster each morning was sorely tried the moment my eyes and ears opened upon the sufferings of my people, the reality that gave the lie to the fiction of our immunity. When my duties among the whites were concluded, how many nights did I return and struggle till dawn with victims here, my friends, parishioners, wandering sons of Africa whose faces I could not look upon without seeing my own. I was commandeered to rise and go forth to the general task of saving the city, forced to leave this neighborhood where my skills were sorely needed. I nursed those who hated me, deserted the ones I loved, who loved me.

I recite the story many, many times to myself, let many voices speak to me till one begins to sound like the sea or rain or my feet those mornings shuffling through thick dust.

We arrived at Bush Hill early. To spare ourselves a long trek in the oppressive heat of day. Yellow haze hung over the city. Plumes of smoke from blazes in Potter's Field, from fires on street corners curled above the rooftops, lending the dismal aspect of a town sacked and burned. I've listened to the Santo Domingans tell of the burning of Cap François. How the capital city was engulfed by fires set in cane fields by the rebelling slaves. Horizon in flames all night as they huddled offshore in ships, terrified, wondering where next they'd go, if any port would permit them to land, empty-handed slaves, masters whose only wealth now was naked black bodies locked in the hold, wide-eyed witnesses of an empire's downfall, chanting, moaning, uncertain as the sea rocked them, whether or not anything on earth could survive the fearful conflagration consuming the great city of Cap François.

Dawn breaking on a smoldering landscape, writhing columns of smoke, a general cloud of haze the color of a fever victim's eyes. I turn and stare at it a moment, then fall in again with my brother's footsteps trudging through untended fields girding Bush Hill.

From a prisoner-of-war ship in New York harbor where the British had interned him he'd seen that city shed its grave-clothes of fog. Morning after morning it would paint itself damp and gray, a flat sketch on the canvas of sky, a tentative, shivering screen of housefronts, sheds, sprawling warehouses floating above the river. Then shadows and hollows darkened. A jumble of masts, spars, sails began to sway, little boats plied lanes between ships, tiny figures inched along wharves and docks, doors opened, windows slid up or down, lending an illusion of depth and animation to the portrait. This city infinitely beyond his reach, this charade other men staged to mock him, to mark the distance he could not travel, the shore he'd never reach, the city, so to speak, came to life and with its birth each morning dropped the palpable weight of his despair. His loneliness and exile. Moored in pewter water, on an island that never stopped moving but never arrived anywhere. The city a mirage of light and air, chimera of paint, brush and paper, mattered naught except that it was denied him. It shimmered. Tolled. Unsettled the watery place where he was sentenced to dwell. Conveyed to him each morning the same doleful tidings: *The dead are legion, the living a froth on dark, layered depths. But you are neither, and less than both.* Each night he dreamed it burning, razed the city till nothing remained but a dry, black crust, crackling, crunching under his boots as he strides, king of the nothing he surveys.

We passed holes dug into the earth where the sick are interred. Some died in these shallow pits, awash in their own vomited and voided filth, before a bed in the hospital could be made ready for them. Others believed they were being buried alive, and unable to crawl out, howled till reason or strength deserted them. A few, past caring, slept soundly in these ditches, resisted the attendants sent to rouse them and transport them inside, once they realized they were being resurrected to do battle again with the fever. I'd watched the red-bearded French doctor from Santo Domingo with his charts and assistants inspecting this zone, his *salle d'attente* he called it, greeting and reassuring new arrivals, interrogating them, nodding and bowing, hurrying from pit to pit, peering down at his invisible patients like a gardener tending seeds.

An introduction to the grave, a way into the hospital that prefigured the way most would leave it. That's what this bizarre rite of admission had seemed at first. But through this and other peculiar stratagems, Deveze, with his French practice, had transformed Bush Hill from lazarium to a clinic where victims of the fever, if not too weak upon arrival, stood a chance of surviving.

The cartman employed by Bush Hill had suddenly fallen sick. Faithful Wilcox had never missed a day, ferrying back and forth from town to hospital, hospital to Potter's Field. Bush Hill had its own cemetery now. Daily rations of dead could be disposed of less conspicuously in a plot on the grounds of the estate, screened from the horror-struck eyes of the city. No one had trusted the hospital. Tales of bloody chaos reigning there had filtered back to the city. Citizens believed it was a place where the doomed were stored until they died. Fever victims would have to be dragged from their beds into Bush Hill's cart. They'd struggle and scream, pitch themselves from the rolling cart, beg for help when the cart passed a rare pedestrian daring or foolish enough to be abroad in the deadly streets.

I wondered for the thousandth time why some were stricken, some not. Dr. Rush and this Deveze dipped their hands into the entrails of corpses, stirred the black, corrupted blood, breathed infected vapors exhaled from mortified remains. I'd observed both men steeped in noxious fluids expelled by their patients, yet neither had fallen prey to the fever. Stolid, dim Wilcox maintained daily concourse with the sick and buried the dead for two months before he was infected. They say a woman, undiscovered until boiling stench drove her neighbors into the street crying for aid, was the cause of Wilcox's downfall. A large woman, bloated into an even more cumbersome package by gases and liquids seething inside her body, had slipped from his grasp as he and another had hoisted her up into the cart. Catching against a rail, her body had slammed down and burst, spraying Wilcox like a fountain. Wilcox did not pride himself on being the tidiest of men, nor did his job demand one who was overfastidious, but the reeking stench from that accident was too much even for him and he departed in a huff to change his polluted garments. He never returned. So there I was at Bush Hill, where Rush had assigned me with my brother, to bury the flow of dead that did not ebb just because the Charon who was their familiar could no longer attend them.

The doctors believe they can find the secret of the fever in the victims' dead bodies. They cut, saw, extract, weigh, measure. The dead are carved into smaller and smaller bits and the butchered parts studied but they do not speak. What I know of the fever I've learned from the words of those I've treated, from stories of the living that are ignored by the good doctors. When lancet and fleam bleed the victims, they offer up stories like prayers.

* * *

It was a jaunty day. We served our white guests and after they'd eaten, they served us at the long, linen-draped tables. A sumptuous feast in the oak grove prepared by many and willing hands. All the world's eyes seemed to be watching us. The city's leading men, black and white, were in attendance to celebrate laying the cornerstone of St. Thomas Episcopal African Church. In spite of the heat and clouds of mettlesome insects, spirits were high. A gathering of whites and blacks in good Christian fellowship to commemorate the fruit of shared labor. Perhaps a new day was dawning. The picnic occurred in July. In less than a month the fever burst upon us.

When you open the dead, black or white, you find: the dura mater covering the brain is white and fibrous in appearance. The leptomeninges covering the brain are clear and without opacifications. The brain weighs 1450 grams and is formed symmetrically. Cut sections of the cerebral hemispheres reveal normal-appearing gray matter throughout. The white matter of the corpus callosum is intact and bears no lesions. The basal ganglia are in their normal locations and grossly appear to be without lesions. The ventricles are symmetrical and filled with crystal-clear cerebrospinal fluid.

The cerebellum is formed symmetrically. The nuclei of the cerebellum are unremarkable. Multiple sections through the pons, medulla oblongata and upper brain stem reveal normal gross anatomy. The cranial nerves are in their normal locations and unremarkable.

The muscles of the neck are in their normal locations. The cartilages of the larynx and the hyoid bone are intact. The thyroid and parathyroid glands are normal on their external surface. The mucosa of the larynx is shiny, smooth and without lesions. The vocal cords are unremarkable. A small amount of bloody material is present in the upper trachea.

The heart weighs 380 grams. The epicardial surface is smooth, glistening and without lesions. The myocardium of the left ventricle and septum are of a uniform meaty-red, firm appearance. The endocardial surfaces are smooth, glistening and without lesions. The auricular appendages are free from thrombi. The valve leaflets are thin and delicate, and show no evidence of vegetation.

The right lung weighs 400 grams. The left lung 510 grams. The pleural surfaces of the lungs are smooth and glistening.

The esophageal mucosa is glistening, white and folded. The stomach contains a large amount of black, noxious bile. A veriform appendix is present. The ascending, transverse and descending colon reveal hemorrhaging, striations, disturbance of normal mucosa patterns throughout. A small amount of bloody, liquid feces is present in the ano-rectal canal.

The liver weighs 1720 grams. The spleen weighs 150 grams. The right kidney weighs 190 grams. The left kidney weighs 180 grams. The testes show a glistening white tunica albuginea. Sections are unremarkable.

Dr. Rush and his assistants examined as many corpses as possible in spite of the hurry and tumult of never-ending attendance on the sick. Rush hoped to prove his remedy, his analysis of the cause and course of the fever correct. Attacked on all sides by his medical brethren for purging and bleeding patients already in a drastically weakened state, Rush lashed back at his detractors, wrote pamphlets, broadsides, brandished the stinking evidence of his postmortems to demonstrate conclusively how the sick drowned in their own poisoned fluids. The putrefaction, the black excess, he proclaimed, must be drained away, else the victim inevitably succumbs.

Dearest:

I shall not return home again until this business of the fever is terminated. I fear bringing the dread contagion into our home. My life is in the hands of God and as long as He sees fit to spare me I will persist in my labors on behalf of the sick, dying and dead. We are losing the battle. Eighty-eight were buried this past Thursday. I tremble for your safety. Wish the lie of immunity were true. Please let me know by way of a note sent to the residence of Dr. Rush that you and our dear Martha are well. I pray every hour that God will preserve you both. As difficult as it is to rise each morning and go with Thomas to perform our duties, the task would be unbearable if I did not hold in my heart a vision of these horrors ending, a blessed shining day when I return to you and drop this weary head upon your sweet bosom.

Allen, Allen, he called to me. Observe how even after death, the body rejects this bloody matter from nose and bowel and mouth. Verily, the patient who had expired at least an hour before, continued to stain the cloth I'd wrapped round him. We'd searched the rooms of a regal mansion, discovering six members of a family, patriarch, son, son's wife and three children, either dead or in the last frightful stages of the disease. Upon the advice of one of Dr. Rush's most outspoken critics, they had refused mercury purges and bleeding until now, when it was too late for any earthly remedy to preserve them. In the rich furnishings of this opulent mansion, attended by one remaining servant whom fear had not driven away, three generations had withered simultaneously, this proud family's link to past and future cut off absolutely, the great circle broken. In the first bedroom we'd entered we'd found William Spurgeon, merchant, son and father, present manager of the family fortune, so weak he could not speak, except with pained blinks of his terrible golden eyes.

Did he welcome us? Was he apologizing to good Dr. Rush for doubting his cure? Did he fear the dark faces of my brother and myself? Quick, too quickly, he was gone. Answering no questions. Revealing nothing of his state of mind. A savaged face frozen above the blanket. Ancient beyond years. Jaundiced eyes not fooled by our busy ministrations, but staring through us, fixed on the eternal stillness soon to come. And I believe I learned in that yellow cast of his eyes, the exact hue of the sky, if sky it should be called, hanging over the next world where we abide.

Allen, Allen. He lasted only moments and then I wrapped him in a sheet from the chest at the foot of his canopied bed. We lifted him into a humbler litter, crudely nailed together, the lumber still green. Allen, look. Stench from the coffin cut through the oppressive odors permeating this doomed household. See. Like an infant the master of the house had soiled his swaddling clothes. Seepage formed a dark river and dripped between roughly jointed boards. We found his wife where she'd fallen, naked, yellow above the waist, black below. As always the smell presaged what we'd discover behind a closed door. This woman had possessed closets of finery, slaves who dressed, fed, bathed and painted her, and yet here she lay, no one to cover her modesty, to lift her from the floor. Dr. Rush guessed from the discoloration she'd been dead two days, a guess confirmed by the loyal black maid, sick herself, who'd elected to stay when all others had deserted her masters. The demands of the living too much for her. She'd simply shut the door on her dead mistress. No breath, no heartbeat, Sir. I could not rouse her, Sir. I intended to return, Sir, but I was too weak to move her, too exhausted by my labors, Sir. Tears rolled down her creased black face and I wondered in my heart how this abused and despised old creature in her filthy apron and turban, this frail, worn woman, had survived the general calamity while the strong and pampered toppled round her.

I wanted to demand of her why she did not fly out the door now, finally freed of her burden, her lifelong enslavement to the whims of white people. Yet I asked her nothing. Considered instead myself, a man who'd worked years to purchase his wife's freedom, then his own, a so-called freeman, and here I was following in the train of Rush and his assistants, a functionary, a lackey, insulted daily by those I risked my life to heal.

Why did I not fly? Why was I not dancing in the streets, celebrating God's judgment on this wicked city? Fever made me freer than I'd ever been. Municipal government had collapsed. Anarchy ruled. As long as fever did not strike me I could come and go anywhere I pleased. Fortunes could be amassed in the streets. I could sell myself to the highest bidder, as nurse or undertaker, as surgeon trained by the famous Dr. Rush to apply his lifesaving cure. Anyone who would enter houses where fever was abroad could demand outrageous sums for negligible services. To be spared the fever was a chance for anyone, black or white, to be a king.

So why do you follow him like a loyal puppy, you confounded black fool? He wagged his finger. *You* . . . His finger a gaunt, swollen-jointed, cracked-bone, chewed thing. Like the nose on his face. The nose I'd thought looked more like finger than nose. *Fool. Fool.* Finger wagging, then the cackle. The barnyard braying. Berserk chickens cackling in his skinny, goiter-knobbed throat. You are a fool, you black son of Ham. You slack-witted, Nubian ape. You progeny of Peeping Toms and orangutans. Who forces you to accompany that madman Rush on his murderous tours? He kills a hundred for every one he helps with his lamebrain, nonsensical, unnatural, Sangrado cures. Why do you tuck your monkey tail between your legs and skip after that butcher? Are you his shadow, a mindless, spineless black puddle of slime with no will of its own?

You are a good man, Allen. You worry about the souls of your people in this soulless wilderness. You love your family and your God. You are a beacon and steadfast. Your fatal flaw is narrowness of vision. You cannot see beyond these shores. The river, that stinking gutter into which the city shovels its shit and extracts its drinking water, that long-suffering string of spittle winds to an ocean. A hundred miles downstream the foamy mouth of the land sucks on the Atlantic's teat, trade winds saunter and a whole wide world awaits the voyager. I know, Allen. I've been everywhere. Buying and selling everywhere.

If you would dare be Moses to your people and lead them out of this land, you'd find fair fields for your talent. Not lapdogging or doggy-trotting behind or fetch doggy or lie doggy or doggy open your legs or doggy stay still while I beat you. Follow the wound that is a river back to the sea. Be gone, be gone. While there's still time. If there is time, *mon frère.* If the pestilence has not settled in you already, breathed from my foul guts into yours, even as we speak.

Here's a master for you. A real master, Allen. The fever that's supping on my innards. I am more slave than you've ever been. I do its bidding absolutely. Cough up my lungs. Shit hunks of my bowel. When I die, they say my skin will turn as black as yours, Allen.

Return to your family. Do not leave them again. Whatever the Rushes promise, whatever they threaten.

Once, ten thousand years ago I had a wife and children. I was like you, Allen, proud, innocent, forward looking, well-spoken, well-mannered, a beacon and steadfast. I began to believe the whispered promise that I could have more. More of what, I didn't ask. Didn't know, but I took my eyes off what I loved in order to obtain this more. Left my wife and children and when I returned they were gone. Forever lost to me. The details are not significant. Suffice to say the circumstances of my leaving were much like yours. Very much like yours, Allen. And I lost everything. Became a wanderer among men. Bad news people see coming from miles away. A pariah. A joke. I'm not black like you, Allen. But I will be soon. Sooner than you'll be white. And if you're ever white, you'll be as dead as I'll be when I'm black.

Why do you desert your loved ones? What impels you to do what you find so painful, so unjust? Are you not a man? And free?

Her sleepy eyes, your lips on her warm cheek, each time may be the last meeting on this earth. The circumstances are similar, my brother. My shadow. My dirty face.

The dead are legion, the living a froth on dark, layered depths.

Master Abraham. There's a gentleman to see you, Sir. The golden-haired lad bound to me for seven years was carted across the seas, like you, Allen, in the bowels of a leaky tub. A son to replace my son his fathers had clubbed to death when they razed the ghetto of Antwerp. But I could not tame the inveterate hate, his aversion and contempt for me. From my aerie, at my desk secluded among barrels, bolts, crates and trunks of the shop's attic, I watched him steal, drink, fornicate. I overheard him denounce me to a delegate sent round to collect a tithe during the emergency. 'Tis well known in the old country that Jews bring the fever. Palatine fever that slays whole cities. They carry it under dirty fingernails, in the wimples of lizardy private parts. Pass it on with the evil eye. That's why we hound them from our towns, exterminate them. Beware of Master Abraham's glare. And the black-coated vulture listened intently. I could see him toting up the account in his small brain. Kill the Jew. Gain a shop and sturdy prentice, too. But I survived till fever laid me low and the cart brought me here to Bush Hill. For years he robbed and betrayed me and all my revenge was to treat him better. Allow him to pilfer, lie, embezzle. Let him grow fat and careless as I knew he would. With a father's boundless kindness I destroyed him. The last sorry laugh coming when I learned he died in agony, fever shriven, following by a day his Water Street French whore my indulgence allowed him to keep.

In Amsterdam I sold diamonds, Allen. In Barcelona they plucked hairs from my beard to fashion charms that brought ill fortune to their enemies. There were nights in dungeons when the mantle of my suffering was all I possessed to wrap round me and keep off mortal cold. I cursed God for choosing me, choosing my people to cuckold and slaughter. Have you heard of the Lamed-Vov, the Thirty Just Men set apart to suffer the reality humankind cannot bear? Saviors. But not Gods like your Christ. Not magicians, not sorcerers with bags of tricks, Allen. No divine immunities. Flesh and blood saviors. Men like we are, Allen. If man you are beneath your sable hide. Men who cough and scratch their sores and bleed and stink. Whose teeth rot. Whose wives and children are torn from them. Who wander the earth unable to die, but men always, men till God plucks them up and returns them to His side where they must thaw ten centuries to melt the crust of earthly grief and misery they've taken upon themselves. Ice men. Snowmen. I thought for many years I might be one of them. In my vanity. My self-pity. My foolishness. But no. One lifetime of sorrows enough for me. I'm just another customer. One more in the crowd lined up at his stall to purchase his wares.

You do know, don't you, Allen, that God is a bookseller? He publishes one book—the text of suffering—over and over again. He disguises it between new boards, in different shapes and sizes, prints on varying papers, in many fonts, adds prefaces and postscripts to deceive the buyer, but it's always the same book.

You say you do not return to your family because you don't want to infect them. Perhaps your fear is well-founded. But perhaps it also masks a greater fear. Can you imagine yourself, Allen, as other than you are? A free man with no charlatan Rush to blame. The weight of your life in your hands.

You've told me tales of citizens paralyzed by fear, of slaves on shipboard who turn to stone in their chains, their eyes boiled in the sun. Is it not possible that you suffer the converse of this immobility? You, sir, unable to stop an endless round of duty and obligation. Turning pages as if the next one or the next will let you finish the story and return to your life.

Your life, man. Tell me what sacred destiny, what nigger errand keeps you standing here at my filthy pallet? Fly, fly, fly away home. Your house is on fire, your children burning.

I have lived to see the slaves free. My people frolic in the streets. Black and white. The ones who believe they are either or both or neither. I am too old for dancing. Too old for foolishness. But this full moon makes me wish for two good legs. For three. Straddled a broomstick when I was a boy. Giddy-up, Giddy-up. Galloping m'lord, m'lady, around the yard I should be sweeping. Dust in my wake. Chickens squawking. My eyes everywhere at once so I would not be caught out by mistress or master in the sin of idleness. Of dreaming. Of following a child's inclination. My broom steed snatched away. Become a rod across my back. Ever cautious. Dreaming with one eye open. The eye I am now, old and gimpy limbed, watching while my people celebrate the rumor of Old Pharaoh's capitulation.

I've shed this city like a skin, wiggling out of it tenscore and more years, by miles and els, fretting, twisting. Many days I did not know whether I'd wrenched freer or crawled deeper into the sinuous pit. Somewhere a child stood, someplace green, keeping track, waiting for me. Hoping I'd meet him again, hoping my struggle was not in vain. I search that child's face for clues to my blurred features. Flesh drifted and banked, eroded by wind and water, the landscape of this city fitting me like a skin. Pray for me, child. For my unborn parents I carry in this orphan's potbelly. For this ancient face that slips like water through my fingers.

Night now. Bitter cold night. Fires in the hearths of lucky ones. Many of us still abide in dark cellars, caves dug into the earth below poor men's houses. For we are poorer still, burrow there, pull earth like blanket and quilt round us to shut out cold, sleep multitudes to a room, stacked and crosshatched and spoon fashion, ourselves the fuel, heat of one body passed to others and passed back from all to one. No wonder then the celebration does not end as a blazing chill sweeps off the Delaware. Those who leap and roar round the bonfires are better off where they are. They have no place else to go.

Given the derivation of the words, you could call the deadly, winged visitors an *unpleasantness from Egypt.*

Putrid stink rattles in his nostrils. He must stoop to enter the cellar. No answer as he shouts his name, his mission of mercy. Earthen floor, ceiling and walls buttressed by occasional beams, slabs of wood. Faint bobbing glow from his lantern. He sees himself looming and shivering on the walls, a shadowy presence with more substance than he feels he possesses at this late hour. After a long day of visits, this hovel his last stop before returning to his brother's house for a few hours of rest. He has learned that exhaustion is a swamp he can wade through and on the far side another region where a thin trembling version of himself toils while he observes, bemused, slipping in and out of sleep, amazed at the likeness, the skill with which that other mounts and sustains him. Mimicry. Puppetry. Whatever controls this other, he allows the impostor to continue, depends upon it to work when he no longer can. After days in the city proper with Rush, he returns to these twisting streets beside the river that are infected veins and arteries he must bleed.

At the rear of the cave, so deep in shadow he stumbles against it before he sees it, is a mound of rags. When he leans over it, speaking down into the darkness, he knows instantly this is the source of the terrible smell, that something once alive is rotting under the rags. He thinks of autumn leaves blown into mountainous, crisp heaps, the north wind cleansing itself and the city of summer. He thinks of anything, any image that will rescue him momentarily from the nauseating stench, postpone what he must do next. He screams no, no to himself as he blinks away his wife's face, the face of his daughter. His neighbors had promised to check on them, he hears news almost daily. There is no rhyme or reason in whom the fever takes, whom it spares, but he's in the city every day, exposed to its victims, breathing fetid air, touching corrupted flesh. Surely if someone in his family must die, it will be him. His clothes are drenched in vinegar, he sniffs the nostrum of gunpowder, bark and asafetida in a bag pinned to his coat. He's prepared to purge and bleed himself, he's also ready and quite willing to forgo these precautions and cures if he thought surrendering his life might save theirs. He thinks and unthinks a picture of her hair, soft against his check, the wet warmth of his daughter's backside in the crook of his arm as he carries her to her mother's side where she'll be changed and fed. No. Like a choking mist, the smell of decaying flesh stifles him, forces him to turn away, once, twice, before he watches himself bend down into the brunt of it and uncover the sleepers.

Two Santo Domingan refugees, slave or free, no one knew for sure, inhabited this cellar. They had moved in less than a week before, the mother huge with child, man and woman both wracked by fever. No one knows how long the couple's been unattended. There was shame in the eyes and voices of the few from whom he'd gleaned bits and pieces of the Santo Domingans' history. Since no one really knew them and few nearby spoke their language, no one was willing to risk, et cetera. Except for screams one night, no one had seen or heard signs of life. If he'd been told nothing about them, his nose would have led him here.

He winces when he sees the dead man and woman, husband and wife, not entwined as in some ballad of love eternal, but turned back to back, distance between them, as if the horror were too visible, too great to bear, doubled in the other's eyes. What had they seen before they flung away from each other? If he could, he would rearrange them, spare the undertakers this vision.

Rat feet and rat squeak in the shadows. He'd stomped his feet, shooed them before he entered, hollered as he threw back the covers, but already they were accustomed to his presence, back at work. They'd bite indiscriminately, dead flesh, his flesh. He curses and flails his staff against the rags, strikes the earthen floor to keep the scavengers at bay. Those sounds are what precipitate the high-pitched cries that first frighten him, then shame him, then propel him to a tall packing crate turned on its end, atop which another crate is balanced. Inside the second wicker container, which had imported some item from some distant place into this land, twin brown babies hoot and wail.

We are passing over the Dismal Swamp. On the right is the Appalachian range, some of the oldest mountains on earth. Once there were steep ridges and valleys all through here but erosion off the mountains created landfill several miles deep in places. This accounts for the rich loamy soil of the region. Over the centuries several southern states were formed from this gradual erosion. The cash crops of cotton and tobacco so vital to southern prosperity were ideally suited to the fertile soil.

Yeah, I nurse these old funky motherfuckers, all right. White people, specially old white people, lemme tell you, boy, them peckerwoods stink. Stone dead fishy wet stink. Talking all the time bout niggers got BO. Well, white folks got the stink and gone, man. Don't be putting my hands on them, neither. Never. Huh uh. If I touch them, be wit gloves. They some nasty people, boy. And they don't be paying me enough to take no chances wit my health. Matter of fact they ain't paying me enough to really be expecting me to work. Yeah. Starvation wages. So I ain't hardly touching them. Or doing much else either. Got to smoke a cigarette to get close to some of them. Piss and shit theyselves like babies. They don't need much taking care anyway. Most of them three-quarters dead already. Ones that ain't is crazy. Nobody don't want them round, that's why they here. Talking to theyselves. Acting like they speaking to a roomful of people and not one soul in the ward paying attention. There's one old black dude, must be a hundred, he be muttering away to hisself non-stop everyday. Pitiful, man. Hope I don't never get that old. Shoot me, bro, if I start to getting old and fucked up in body and mind like them. Don't want no fools like me hanging over me when I can't do nothing no more for my ownself. Shit. They ain't paying me nothing so that's what I do. Nothing. Least I don't punch em or tease em or steal they shit like some the staff. And I don't pretend I'm God like these so-called professionals and doctors flittin round here drawing down that long bread. Naw. I just mind my own business, do my time. Cop a little TV, sneak me a joint when nobody's around. It ain't all that bad, really. Long as I ain't got no ole lady and crumb crushers. Don't know how the married cats make it on the little bit of chump change they pay us. But me, I'm free. It ain't that bad, really.

By the time his brother brought him the news of their deaths . . .

Almost an afterthought. The worst, he believed, had been overcome. Only a handful of deaths the last weeks of November. The city was recovering. Commerce thriving. Philadelphia must be revictualed, refueled, rebuilt, reconnected to the countryside, to markets foreign and domestic, to products, pleasures and appetites denied during the quarantine months of the fever. A new century would soon be dawning. We must forget the horrors. The Mayor proclaims a new day. Says let's put the past behind us. Of the eleven who died in the fire he said extreme measures were necessary as we cleansed ourselves of disruptive influences. The cost could have been much greater, he said I regret the loss of life, especially the half dozen kids, but I commend all city officials, all volunteers who helped return the city to the arc of glory that is its proper destiny.

When they cut him open, the one who decided to stay, to be a beacon and steadfast, they will find: liver (1720 grams), spleen (150 grams), right kidney (190 grams), left kidney (180 grams), brain (1450 grams), heart (380 grams) and right next to his heart, the miniature hand of a child, frozen in a grasping gesture, fingers like hard tongues of flame, still reaching for the marvel of the beating heart, fascinated still, though the heart is cold, beats not, the hand as curious about this infinite stillness as it was about thump and heat and quickness.

JOY WILLIAMS

Taking Care

JOY WILLIAMS (1944–) has written three novels, one of which, *State of Grace,* was a finalist for the National Book Award; two collections of stories, *Taking Care* and *Escapes;* and a history and guide to the Florida Keys, praised by *Condé Nast Traveler* as "a magnificent tragicomic guide, one of the best guidebooks ever written." She has also written numerous essays, many included in The Best American Essays. She has received a Guggenheim Fellowship, and a Strauss Living Award from the American Academy and Institute of Arts and Letters. She lives in Key West and Tucson.

Jones, the preacher, has been in love all his life. He is baffled by this because as far as he can see, it has never helped anyone, even when they have acknowledged it, which is not often. Jones's love is much too apparent and arouses neglect. He is like an animal in a traveling show who, through some aberration, wears a vital organ outside the skin, awkward and unfortunate, something that shouldn't be seen, certainly something that shouldn't be watched working. Now he sits on a bed beside his wife in the self-care unit of a hospital fifteen miles from their home. She has been committed here for tests. She is so weak, so tired. There is something wrong with her blood. Her arms are covered with bruises where they have gone into the veins. Her hip, too, is blue and swollen where they have drawn out samples of bone marrow. All of this is frightening. The doctors are severe and wise, answering Jones's questions in a way that makes him feel hopelessly deaf. They have told him that there really is no such thing as a disease of the blood, for the blood is not a living tissue but a passive vehicle for the transportation of food, oxygen and waste. They have told him that abnormalities in the blood corpuscles, which his wife seems to have, must be regarded as symptoms of disease elsewhere in the body. They have shown him, upon request, slides and charts of normal and pathological blood cells which look to Jones like canapés. They speak (for he insists) of leukocytosis, myelocytes and megaloblasts. None of this takes into account the love he has for his wife! Jones sits beside her in this dim pleasant room, wearing a grey suit and his clerical collar, for when he leaves her he must visit other parishioners who are patients here. This part of the hospital is like a motel. One may wear one's regular clothes. The rooms have ice-buckets, rugs and colorful bedspreads. How he wishes that they were traveling and staying overnight, this night, in a motel. A nurse comes in with a tiny paper cup full of pills. There are three pills, or rather, capsules, and they are not for his wife but for her blood. The cup is the smallest of its type that Jones has ever seen. All perspective, all sense of time and scale seem abandoned in this hospital. For example, when Jones turns to kiss his wife's hair, he nicks the air instead.

Jones and his wife have one child, a daughter, who, in turn, has a single child, a girl, born one-half year ago. Jones's daughter has fallen in with the stars and is using the heavens, as Jones would be the first to admit, more than he ever has. It has, however, brought her only grief and confusion. She has left her husband and brought the baby to Jones. She has also given him her dog. She is going to Mexico where soon, in the mountains, she will have a nervous breakdown. Jones does not know this, but his daughter has seen it in the stars and is going out to meet it. Jones quickly agrees to care for both the baby and the dog, as this seems to be the only thing his daughter needs from him. The day of the baby's birth is secondary to the position of the planets and the terms of houses, quadrants and gradients. Her symbol is a bareback rider. To Jones, this is a graceful thought. It signifies audacity. It also means luck. Jones slips a twenty dollar bill in the pocket of his daughter's suitcase and drives her to the airport. The plane taxis down the runway and Jones waves, holding all their luck in his arms.

One afternoon, Jones had come home and found his wife sitting in the garden, weeping. She had been transplanting flowers, putting them in pots before the first frost came. There was dirt on her forehead and around her mouth. Her light clothes felt so heavy. Their weight made her body ache. Each breath was a stone she had to swallow. She cried and cried in the weak autumn sunshine. Jones could see the veins throbbing in her neck. "I'm dying," she said. "It's taking me months to die." But after he had brought her inside, she insisted that she felt better and made them both a cup of tea while Jones potted the rest of the plants and carried them down cellar. She lay on the sofa and Jones sat beside her. They talked quietly with one another. Indeed, they were almost whispering, as though they were in a public place surrounded by strangers instead of in their own house with no one present but themselves. "It's the season," Jones said. "In fall everything slows down, retreats. I'm feeling tired myself. We need iron. I'll go to the druggist right now and buy some iron tablets." His wife agreed. She wanted to go with him, for the ride. Together they ride, through the towns, for miles and miles, even into the next state. She does not want to stop driving. They buy sandwiches and milkshakes and eat in the car. Jones drives. They have to buy more gasoline. His wife sits close to him, her eyes closed, her head tipped back against the seat. He can see the veins beating on in her neck. Somewhere there is a dreadful sound, almost audible. "First I thought it was my imagination," his wife said. "I couldn't sleep. All night I would stay awake, dreaming. But it's not in my head. It's in my ears, my eyes. They ache. Everything. My tongue. My hair. The tips of my fingers are dead." Jones pressed her cold hand to his lips. He thinks of something mad and loving better than he—running out of control, deeply in the darkness of his wife. "Just don't make me go to the hospital," she pleaded. Of course she will go there. The moment has already occurred.

Jones is writing to his daughter. He received a brief letter from her this morning, telling him where she could be reached. The foreign postmark was so large that it almost obliterated Jones's address. She did not mention either her mother or the baby, which makes Jones feel peculiar. His life seems increate as his God's life, perhaps even imaginary. His daughter tells him about the town in which she lives. She does not plan to stay there long. She wants to travel. She will find out exactly what she wants to do and then she will come home again. The town is poor but interesting and there are many Americans there her own age. There is a zoo right on the beach. Almost all the towns, no matter how small, have little zoos. There are primarily eagles and hawks in the cages. And what can Jones reply to that? He writes *Every thing is fine here. We are burning wood from the old apple tree in the fire place and it smells wonderful. Has the baby had her full series of polio shots? Take care.* Jones uses this expression constantly, usually in totally unwarranted situations, as when he purchases pipe cleaners or drives through toll booths. Distracted, Jones writes off the edge of the paper and onto the blotter. He must begin again. He will mail this on the way to the hospital. They have been taking X-rays for three days now but the pictures are cloudy. They cannot read them. His wife is now in a real sickbed with high metal sides. He sits with her while she eats her dinner. She asks him to take her good nightgown home and wash it with a bar of Ivory. They won't let her do anything now, not even wash out a few things. *You must take care.*

Jones is driving down a country road. It is the first snowfall of the season and he wants to show it to the baby who rides beside him in a small cushioned car seat all her own. Her head is almost on a level with his and she looks earnestly at the landscape, sometimes smiling. They follow the road that winds tightly between fields and deep pine woods. Everything is white and clean. It has been snowing all afternoon and is doing so still, but very very lightly. Fat snowflakes fall solitary against the windshield. Sometimes the baby reaches out for them. Sometimes she gives a brief kick and cry of joy. They have done their errands. Jones has bought milk and groceries and two yellow roses which lie wrapped in tissue and newspaper in the trunk, in the cold. He must buy two on Saturday as the florist is closed on Sunday. He does not like to do this but there is no alternative. The roses do not keep well. Tonight he will give one to his wife. The other he will pack in sugar water and store in the refrigerator. He can only hope that the bud will remain tight until Sunday when he brings it into the terrible heat of the hospital. The baby rocks against the straps of her small carrier. Her lips are pursed as she watches intently the fields, the grey stalks of crops growing out of the snow, the trees. She is warmly dressed and she wears a knitted orange cap. The cap is twenty-three years old, the age of her mother. Jones found it just the other day. It has faded almost to pink on one side. At one time, it must have been stored in the sun. Jones, driving, feels almost gay. The snow is so beautiful. Everything is white. Jones is an educated man. He has read Melville, who says that white is the colorless all-color of atheism from which we shrink. Jones does not believe this. He sees a holiness in snow, a promise. He hopes that his wife will know that it is snowing even though she is separated from the window by a curtain. Jones sees something moving across the snow, a part of the snow itself, running. Although he is going slowly, he takes his foot completely off the accelerator. "Look, darling, a snowshoe rabbit." At the sound of his voice, the baby stretches open her mouth and narrows her eyes in soundless glee. The hare is splendid. So fast! It flows around invisible obstructions, something out of a kind dream. It flies across the ditch, its paws like paddles, faintly yellow, the color of raw wood. "Look, sweet," cries Jones, "how big he is!" But suddenly the hare is curved and falling, round as a ball, its feet and head tucked closely against its body. It strikes the road and skids upside down for several yards. The car passes around it, avoids it. Jones brakes and stops, amazed. He opens the door and trots back to the animal. The baby twists about in her seat as well as she can and peers after him. It is as though the animal had never been alive at all. Its head is broken in several places. Jones bends to touch its fur, but straightens again, not doing so. A man emerges from the woods, swinging a shotgun. He nods at Jones and picks the hare up by the ears. As he walks away, the hare's legs rub across the ground. There are small crystal stains on the snow. Jones returns to the car. He wants to apologize but he does not know to whom or for what. His life has been devoted to apologetics. It is his profession. He is concerned with both justification and remorse. He has always acted rightly, but nothing has ever come of it. He gets in the car, starts the engine. "Oh, sweet," he says to the baby. She smiles at him, exposing her tooth. At home that night, after the baby's supper, Jones reads a story to her. She is asleep, panting in her sleep, but Jones tells her the story of al-Boraq, the milk-white steed of Mohammed, who could stride out of the sight of mankind with a single step.

Jones sorts through a collection of records, none of which have been opened. They are still wrapped in cellophane. The jacket designs are subdued, epic. Names, instruments and orchestras are mentioned confidently. He would like to agree with their importance, for he knows that they have worth, but he is not familiar with the references. His daughter brought these records with her. They had been given to her by an older man, a professor she had been having an affair with. Naturally, this pains Jones. His daughter speaks about the men she has been involved with but no longer cares about. Where did these men come from? Where were they waiting and why have they gone? Jones remembers his daughter when she was a little girl, helping him rake leaves. What can he say? For years on April Fool's Day, she would take tobacco out of his humidor and fill it with corn flakes. Jones is full of remorse and astonishment. When he saw his daughter only a few weeks ago, she was thin and nervous. She had torn out almost all her eyebrows with her fingers from this nervousness. And her lashes. The roots of her eyes were white, like the bulbs of flowers. Her fingernails were crudely bitten, some bleeding below the quick. She was tough and remote, wanting only to go on a trip for which she had a ticket. What can he do? He seeks her in the face of the baby but she is not there. All is being both continued and resumed, but the dream is different. The dream cannot be revived. Jones breaks into one of the albums, blows the dust from the needle, plays a record. Outside it is dark. The parsonage is remote and the only buildings nearby are barns. The river cannot be seen. The music is Bruckner's *Te Deum.* Very nice. Dedicated to God. He plays the other side. A woman, Kathleen Ferrier, is singing in German. Jones cannot understand the words but the music stuns him. *Kindertotenlieder.* It is devastating. In college he had studied only scientific German, the vocabulary of submarines, dirigibles and steam engines. Jones plays the record again and again, searching for his old grammar. At last he finds it. The wings of insects are between some of the pages. There are notes in pencil, written in his own young hand.

RENDER:

A. WAS THE TEACHER SATISFIED WITH YOU TODAY?

B. NO, HE WAS NOT. MY ESSAY WAS GOOD BUT IT WAS NOT COPIED WELL.

C. I AM SORRY YOU WERE NOT INDUSTRIOUS THIS TIME FOR YOU GENERALLY ARE.

These lessons are neither of life or death. Why was he instructed in them? In the hospital, his wife waits to be translated, no longer a woman, the woman whom he loves, but a situation. Her blood moves mysteriously as constellations. She is under scrutiny and attack and she has abandoned Jones. She is a swimmer waiting to get on with the drowning. Jones is on the shore. In Mexico, his daughter walks along the beach with two men. She is acting out a play that has become her life. Jones is on the mountaintop. The baby cries and Jones takes her from the crib to change her. The dog paws the door. Jones lets him out. He settles down with the baby and listens to the record. He still cannot make out many of the words. The baby wiggles restlessly on his lap. Her eyes are a foal's eyes, navy-blue. She has grown in a few weeks to expect everything from Jones. He props her on one edge of the couch and goes to her small toy box where he keeps a bear, a few rattles and balls. On the way, he opens the door and the dog immediately enters. His heavy coat is cold, fragrant with ice. He noses the baby and she squeals.

Oft denk'ich, sie sind nur ausgegangen
Bald werden sie wieder nach Hause gelangen

Jones selects a bright ball and pushes it gently in her direction.

It is Sunday morning and Jones is in the pulpit. The church is very old but the walls of the sanctuary have recently been painted a pale blue. In the cemetery adjoining, some of the graves are three hundred years old. It has become a historical landmark and no one has been buried there since World War I. There is a new place, not far away, which the families now use. Plots are marked not with stones but with small tablets, and immediately after any burial, workmen roll grassed sod over the new graves so that there is no blemish on the grounds, not even for a little while. Present for today's service are seventy-eight adults, eleven children and the junior choir. Jones counts them as the offertory is received. The church rolls say that there are three hundred fifty members but as far as Jones can see, everyone is here today. This is the day he baptizes the baby. He has made arrangements with one of the ladies to hold her and bring her up to the font at the end of the first hymn. The baby looks charming in a lacy white dress. Jones has combed her fine hair carefully, slicking it in a curl with water, but now it has dried and it sticks up awkwardly like the crest of a kingfisher. Jones bought the dress in Mammoth Mart, an enormous store which has a large metal elephant dressed in overalls dancing on the roof. He feels foolish at buying it there but he had gone to several stores and that is where he saw the prettiest dress. He blesses the baby with water from the silver bowl. He says, *We are saved not because we are worthy. We are saved because we are loved.* It is a brief ceremony. The baby, looking curiously at Jones, is taken out to the nursery. Jones begins his sermon. He can't remember when he wrote it, but here it is, typed, in front of him. *There is nothing wrong in what one does but there is something wrong in what one becomes.* He finds this questionable but goes on speaking. He has been preaching for thirty-four years. He is gaunt with belief. But his wife has a red cell count of only 2.3 million. It is not enough! She is not getting enough oxygen! Jones is giving his sermon. Somewhere he has lost what he was looking for. He must have known once, surely. The congregation sways, like the wings of a ray in water. It is Sunday and for patients it is a holiday. The doctors don't visit. There are no tests or diagnoses. Jones would like to leave, to walk down the aisle and out into the winter, where he would read his words into the ground. Why can't he remember his life! He finishes, sits down, stands up to present communion. Tiny cubes of bread lie in a slumped pyramid. They are offered and received. Jones takes his morsel, hacked earlier from a sliced enriched loaf with his own hand. It is so dry, almost wicked. The very thought now sickens him. He chews it over and over again, but it lies unconsumed, like a muscle in his mouth.

Jones is waiting in the lobby for the results of his wife's operation. Has there ever been a time before dread? He would be grateful even to have dread back, but it has been lost, for a long time, in rapid possibility, probability and fact. The baby sits on his knees and plays with his tie. She woke very early this morning for her orange juice and then gravely, immediately, spit it all up. She seems fine now, however, her fingers exploring Jones's tie. Whenever he looks at her, she gives him a dazzling smile. He has spent most of the day fiercely cleaning the house, changing the bed-sheets and the pages of the many calendars that hang in the rooms, things he should have done a week ago. He has dusted and vacuumed and pressed all his shirts. He has laundered all the baby's clothes, soft small sacks and gowns and sleepers which froze in his hands the moment he stepped outside. And now he is waiting and watching his wristwatch. The tumor is precisely this size, they tell him, the size of his clock's face.

Jones has the baby on his lap and he is feeding her. The evening meal is lengthy and complex. First he must give her vitamins, then, because she has a cold, a dropper of liquid aspirin. This is followed by a bottle of milk, eight ounces, and a portion of strained vegetables. He gives her a rest now so that the food can settle. On his hip, she rides through the rooms of the huge house as Jones turns lights off and on. He comes back to the table and gives her a little more milk, a half jar of strained chicken and a few spoonfuls of dessert, usually cobbler, buckle or pudding. The baby enjoys all equally. She is good.

She eats rapidly and neatly. Sometimes she grasps the spoon, turns it around and thrusts the wrong end into her mouth. Of course there is nothing that cannot be done incorrectly. Jones adores the baby. He sniffs her warm head. Her birth is a deep error, an abstraction. Born in wedlock but out of love. He puts her in the playpen and tends to the dog. He fills one dish with water and one with horsemeat. He rinses out the empty can before putting it in the wastebasket. The dog eats with great civility. He eats a little meat and then takes some water, then meat, then water. When the dog has finished, the dishes are as clean as though they'd been washed. Jones now thinks about his own dinner. He opens the refrigerator. The ladies of the church have brought brownies, venison, cheese and apple sauce. There are turkey pies, pork chops, steak, haddock and sausage patties. A brilliant light exposes all this food. There is so much of it. It must be used. A crust has formed around the punctures in a can of Pet. There is a clear bag of chicken livers stapled shut. There are large brown eggs in a bowl. Jones stares unhappily at the beads of moisture on cartons and bottles, at the pearls of fat on the cold cooked stew. He sits down. The room is full of lamps and cords. He thinks of his wife, her breathing body deranged in tubes, and begins to shake. All objects here are perplexed by such grief.

Now it is almost Christmas and Jones is walking down by the river, around an abandoned house. The dog wades heavily through the snow, biting it. There are petals of ice on the tree limbs and when Jones lingers under them, the baby puts out her hand and her mouth starts working because she would like to have it, the ice, the branch, everything. His wife will be coming home in a few days, in time for Christmas. Jones has already put up the tree and brought the ornaments down from the attic. He will not trim it until she comes home. He wants very much to make a fine occasion out of opening the boxes of old decorations. The two of them have always enjoyed this greatly in the past. Jones will doubtlessly drop and smash a bauble, for he does every year. He tramps through the snow with his small voyager. She dangles in a shoulder sling, her legs wedged around his hip. They regard the rotting house seriously. Once it was a doctor's home and offices but long before Jones's time, the doctor, who was very respected, had been driven away because a town girl accused him of fathering her child. The story goes that all the doctor said was, "Is that so?" This incensed the town and the girl's parents, who insisted that he take the child as soon as it was born. He did and he cared for the child very well even though his practice was ruined and no one had anything to do with him. A year later the girl told the truth—that the actual father was a young college boy whom she was now going to marry. They wanted the child back, and the doctor willingly returned the infant to them. Of course it is a very old, important story. Jones has always appreciated it, but now he is annoyed at the man's passivity. His wife's sickness has changed everything for Jones. He will continue to accept but he will no longer surrender. Surely things are different for Jones now.

For insurance purposes, Jones's wife is brought out to the car in a wheelchair. She is thin and beautiful. Jones is grateful and confused. He has a mad wish to tip the orderly. Have so many years really passed? Is this not his wife, his love, fresh from giving birth? Isn't everything about to begin? In Mexico, his daughter wanders disinterestedly through a jewelry shop where she picks up a small silver egg. It opens on a hinge and inside are two figures, a bride and groom. Jones puts the baby in his wife's arms. At first the baby is alarmed because she cannot remember this person very well and she reaches for Jones, whimpering. But soon she is soothed by his wife's soft voice and she falls asleep in her arms as they drive. Jones has readied everything carefully for his wife's homecoming. The house is clean and orderly. For days he has restricted himself to only one part of the house so that his clutter will be minimal. Jones helps his wife up the steps to the door. Together they enter the shining rooms.

Grateful acknowledgment is made to the publications from which the stories in this volume were chosen. Unless specifically noted otherwise, copyright of the stories is held by the individual writers.

"This Is What It Means to Say Phoenix, Arizona," from *The Lone Ranger and Tonto Fistfight in Heaven.* Copyright © 1993 by Sherman Alexie. Used by permission of Grove/Atlantic, Inc.

"Death by Landscape," from *Wilderness Tips* by Margaret Atwood. Copyright © 1991 by O. W. Toad Limited. Used by permission of Doubleday, a division of Random House, and McClelland & Stewart, Inc., the Canadian publishers.

"Raymond's Run," from *Gorilla, My Love* by Toni Cade Bambara. Copyright © 1971 by Toni Cade Bambara. Reprinted by permission of Random House, Inc.

All pages from "Sarah Cole: A Type of Love Story" from *Success Stories* by Russell Banks. Copyright © 1985 by Russell Banks. Reprinted by permission of HarperCollins Publishers, Inc. This story originally appeared in the *Missouri Review.*

"Click," copyright © 1997 by John Barth. Used by permission of the author. This story originally appeared in *The Atlantic Monthly.*

"The School," from *Amateurs* by Donald Barthelme. Copyright © 1974 by Donald Barthelme; first published in *The New Yorker.* No changes shall be made to the text of the above work without the express written consent of The Wylie Agency, Inc.

"Wild Horses," from *The Watch* by Rick Bass. Copyright © 1989 by Rick Bass. Reprinted by permission of W. W. Norton & Company, Inc.

"The Man Who Knew Belle Starr," from *Spirits and Other Stories* by Richard Bausch. Copyright © 1987 by Richard Bausch. Used by permission of the author. This story originally appeared in *The Atlantic Monthly.*

"Gryphon," from *Through the Safety Net* by Charles Baxter. Copyright © 1985 by Charles Baxter. Used by permission of Vintage Books, a division of Random House, Inc.

"Customs of the Country," from *Barking Man* by Madison Smartt Bell. Copyright © 1990 by Madison Smartt Bell. Used by permission of the author. This story originally appeared in *Harper's.*

"Silver Water," from *Come to Me,* by Amy Bloom. Copyright © 1993 by Amy Bloom. Reprinted by permission of HarperCollins.

"Tall Tales from the Mekong Delta," from *Squandering the Blue* by Kate Braverman. Copyright © 1990 by Kate Braverman. Used by permission of the author. This story originally appeared in *Story.*

"A Good Scent from a Strange Mountain," from *A Good Scent from a Strange Mountain.* Copyright © 1991 by Robert Olen Butler. Used by permission of the author. This story originally appeared in the *New England Review.*

"The Year of Getting to Know Us," from *Emperor of the Air* by Ethan Canin. Copyright © 1988 by Ethan Canin. Reprinted by permission of Houghton Mifflin Company. All rights reserved.

"Errand," from *Where I'm Calling From* by Raymond Carver. Copyright © 1988 by Raymond Carver. Reprinted by permission of International Creative Management, Inc.

"Woman Hollering Creek," from *Woman Hollering Creek and Other Stories* by Sandra Cisneros. Copyright © 1991 by Sandra Cisneros. Published by Vintage Books, a division of Random House, Inc., New York, and originally in hardcover by Random House, Inc. Reprinted by permission of Susan Bergholz Literary Services, New York. All rights reserved.

"White Angel," originally published as "Bobby," from *A Home at the End of the World* by Michael Cunningham. Copyright © 1990 by Michael Cunningham. Reprinted by permission of Farrar, Straus & Giroux, Inc.

"Fiesta 1980," from *Drown* by Junot Diaz. Copyright © 1996 by Junot Diaz. Used by permission of Putnam Berkley, a division of Penguin Putnam, Inc.

"Pet Milk," from *The Coast of Chicago* by Stuart Dybek. Copyright © 1981 by Stuart Dybek. Reprinted by permission of International Creative Management, Inc.

"The Prophet from Jupiter," from *Here We Are in Paradise* by Tony Earley. Copyright © 1993 by Tony Earley. Reprinted by permission of the author. This story originally appeared in *Harper's* and was reprinted in *The Best American Short Stories 1994* and *New Stories from the South: The Year's Best 1994.*

"Saint Marie," from *Love Medicine* by Louise Erdrich. Copyright © 1984 by Louise Erdrich. Reprinted by permission of the author. This story originally appeared in *The Atlantic Monthly.*

"Rock Springs," from *Rock Springs* by Richard Ford. Copyright © 1987 by Richard Ford. Used by permission of Grove/Atlantic, Inc.

"The Mail Lady," from *The Wonders of the Invisible World* by David Gates. Copyright © 1999 by David Gates. Reprinted by permission of Alfred A. Knopf, Inc.

"Same Place, Same Things," from *Same Place, Same Things* by Tim Gautreaux. Copyright © 1996 by Tim Gautreaux. Used by permission of the author.

"Nebraska," from *Nebraska* by Ron Hansen. Copyright © 1989 by Ron Hansen. Used by permission of Darhonsoff & Verrill.

"In the Cemetery Where Al Jolson Is Buried," from *Reasons to Live* by Amy Hempel. Copyright © 1985 by Amy Hempel. Used by permission of the author.

"Emergency," from *Jesus' Son* by Denis Johnson. Copyright © 1992 by Denis Johnson. Reprinted by permission of Farrar, Straus & Giroux, Inc.

"Marie," from *Lost in the City* by Edward P. Jones. Copyright © 1992 by Edward P. Jones. Used by permission of the author.

"Cold Snap," from *Cold Snap* by Thom Jones. Copyright © 1995 by Thom Jones. This story first appeared in *The New Yorker.* Used by permission of Little, Brown and Company.

"Doe Season," from *Comfort* by David Michael Kaplan. Copyright © 1985 by David Michael Kaplan. Used by permission of the author.

"Patriotic," from *Places in the World a Woman Could Walk* by Janet Kauffman. Copyright © 1983 by Janet Kauffman. Used by permission of the author.

"Girl," from *At the Bottom of the River* by Jamaica Kincaid. Copyright © 1983 by Jamaica Kincaid. Reprinted by permission of Farrar, Straus & Giroux, Inc.

"Territory," from *Family Dancing* by David Leavitt. Copyright © 1983, 1984 by David Leavitt. Reprinted by permission of Alfred A. Knopf, Inc.

"The Kind of Light That Shines on Texas," from *The Kind of Light That Shines on Texas* by Reginald McKnight. Copyright © 1992 by Reginald McKnight. Reprinted by permission of the author.

"You're Ugly, Too," from *Like Life* by Lorrie Moore. Copyright © 1988, 1989, 1990 by Lorrie Moore. Reprinted by permission of Alfred A. Knopf, Inc.

"The Management of Grief," from *The Middleman and Other Stories* by Bharati Mukherjee. Copyright © 1988 by Bharati Mukherjee. Published by Grove Press. Reprinted by permission of the author and Janklow Nesbit Associates.

"Meneseteung," from *Friend of My Youth* by Alice Munro. Copyright © 1990 by Alice Munro. Reprinted by permission of Alfred A. Knopf, Inc., and McClelland & Stewart, Inc., the Canadian publishers.

"Ghost Girls," from *Man Crazy* by Joyce Carol Oates. Copyright © 1995 by The Ontario Review, Inc. Used by permission of Dutton, a division of Penguin Putnam, Inc.

"The Things They Carried," from *The Things They Carried* by Tim O'Brien. Copyright © 1990 by Tim O'Brien. Reprinted by permission of Houghton Mifflin Company. All rights reserved.

"The Shawl," from *The Shawl* by Cynthia Ozick. Copyright © 1990, 1983 by Cynthia Ozick. Reprinted by permission of Alfred A. Knopf, Inc.

"Brokeback Mountain," from *Close Range* by Annie Proulx. Copyright © 1999 by E. Annie Proulx. Reprinted with the permission of Scribner, a division of Simon & Schuster.

"Strays," from *The Ice at the Bottom of the World* by Mark Richard. Copyright © 1989 by Mark Richard. Reprinted by permission of Alfred A. Knopf, Inc.

"Intensive Care," from *Me and My Baby View the Eclipse* by Lee Smith. Copyright © 1988, 1990 by Lee Smith. Used by permission of G. P. Putnam's Sons, a division of Penguin Putnam, Inc.

"The Way We Live Now," from *The Way We Live Now* by Susan Sontag. Copyright © 1986 by Susan Sontag. Reprinted by permission of the author.

"Two Kinds," from *The Joy Luck Club* by Amy Tan. Copyright © 1989 by Amy Tan. Reprinted by permission of Putnam Berkley, a division of Penguin Putnam, Inc.

"First, Body," from *First, Body* by Melanie Rae Thon. Copyright © 1997 by Melanie Rae Thon. Reprinted by permission of Houghton Mifflin Company. All rights reserved.

"Able, Baker, Charlie, Dog," from *Sweet Talk* by Stephanie Vaughn. Copyright © 1978, 1979, 1980, 1990 by Stephanie Vaughn. Reprinted by permission of Georges Borchardt, Inc. for the author.

"Nineteen Fifty-five," from *You Can't Keep a Good Woman Down* by Alice Walker. Copyright © 1981 by Alice Walker. Reprinted by permission of Harcourt Brace & Co.

"Fever," from *Fever: Twelve Stories* by John Edgar Wideman. Copyright © 1989 by John Edgar Wideman. Reprinted by permission of Henry Holt and Company, Inc.

"Taking Care," from *Taking Care* by Joy Williams. Copyright © 1972, 1973, 1974, 1976, 1977, 1980, 1981 and 1982 by Joy Williams. Reprinted by permission of Random House, Inc.